To Dad,

'Merry Christmas'
1986

lots of Love

Helen & Hayley

xxx

ROALD DAHL

ROALD DAHL

KISS, KISS
OVER TO YOU
SWITCH BITCH
SOMEONE LIKE YOU
FOUR TALES OF THE UNEXPECTED
MY UNCLE OSWALD

Heinemann/Octopus

Kiss, Kiss first published in Great Britain in 1960
by Michael Joseph Limited
Over to You first published in Great Britain in 1946
by Hamish Hamilton, Limited
Switch Bitch first published in Great Britain in 1974
by Michael Joseph Limited
Someone Like You first published in Great Britain in 1954
by Martin Secker and Warburg. This revised and expanded
edition published in 1961 by Michael Joseph Limited
More Tales of the Unexpected first published in Great Britain
in 1980 by Michael Joseph Limited
My Uncle Oswald first published in Great Britain in 1979
by Michael Joseph Limited

This edition first published in Great Britain in 1986
jointly by

William Heinemann Limited
10 Upper Grosvenor Street
London W1

Martin Secker and Warburg Limited
54 Poland Street
London W1

and
Octopus Books Limited
59 Grosvenor Street
London W1

ISBN 0 905712 92 7

Printed and Bound in Great Britain by Collins, Glasgow

CONTENTS

KISS, KISS

THE LANDLADY

Billy Weaver had travelled down from London on the slow afternoon train, with a change at Swindon on the way, and by the time he got to Bath it was about nine o'clock in the evening and the moon was coming up out of a clear starry sky over the houses opposite the station entrance. But the air was deadly cold and the wind was like a flat blade of ice on his cheeks.

'Excuse me,' he said, 'but is there a fairly cheap hotel not too far away from here?'

'Try The Bell and Dragon,' the porter answered, pointing down the road. 'They might take you in. It's about a quarter of a mile along on the other side.'

Billy thanked him and picked up his suitcase and set out to walk the quarter-mile to The Bell and Dragon. He had never been to Bath before. He didn't know anyone who lived there. But Mr Greenslade at the Head Office in London had told him it was a splendid city. 'Find your own lodgings,' he had said, 'and then go along and report to the Branch Manager as soon as you've got yourself settled.'

Billy was seventeen years old. He was wearing a new navy-blue overcoat, a new brown trilby hat, and a new brown suit, and he was feeling fine. He walked briskly down the street. He was trying to do everything briskly these days. Briskness, he had decided, was *the* one common characteristic of all successful businessmen. The big shots up at Head Office were absolutely fantastically brisk all the time. They were amazing.

There were no shops on this wide street that he was walking along, only a line of tall houses on each side, all of them identical. They had porches and pillars and four or five steps going up to their front doors, and it was obvious that once upon a time they had been very swanky residences. But now, even in the darkness, he could see that the paint was peeling from the woodwork on their doors and windows, and that the handsome white façades were cracked and blotchy from neglect.

Suddenly, in a downstairs window that was brilliantly illuminated by a street-lamp not six yards away, Billy caught sight of a printed notice propped up against the glass in one of the upper panes. It said BED AND BREAKFAST. There was a vase of pussy-willows, tall and beautiful, standing just underneath the notice.

He stopped walking. He moved a bit closer. Green curtains (some sort of velvety material) were hanging down on either side of the window. The pussy-willows looked wonderful beside them. He went right up and peered through the glass into the room, and the first thing he saw was a bright fire burning in the hearth. On the carpet in front of the fire, a pretty little dachshund was curled up asleep with its nose tucked into its belly. The room itself, so far as he could see in the half-darkness, was filled with pleasant furniture. There was a baby-grand piano and a big sofa and several plump armchairs; and in one corner he spotted a large parrot in a cage. Animals were usually a good sign in a place like this, Billy told himself; and all in all, it looked to him as though it would be a pretty decent house to stay in. Certainly it would be more comfortable than The Bell and Dragon.

On the other hand, a pub would be more congenial than a boarding-house. There would be beer and darts in the evenings, and lots of people to talk to, and it would probably be a good bit cheaper, too. He had stayed a couple of nights in a pub once before and he had liked it. He had never stayed in any boarding-houses, and, to be perfectly honest, he was a tiny bit frightened of them. The name itself conjured up images of watery cabbage, rapacious landladies, and a powerful smell of kippers in the living-room.

After dithering about like this in the cold for two or three minutes, Billy decided that he would walk on and take a look at The Bell and Dragon before making up his mind. He turned to go.

And now a queer thing happened to him. He was in the act of stepping back and turning away from the window when all at once his eye was caught and held in the most peculiar manner by the small notice that was there. BED AND BREAKFAST, it said. BED AND BREAKFAST, BED AND BREAKFAST, BED AND BREAKFAST. Each word was like a large black eye staring at him through the glass, holding him, compelling him, forcing him to stay where he was and not to walk away from that house, and the next thing he knew, he was actually moving across from the window to the front door of the house, climbing the steps that led up to it, and reaching for the bell.

He pressed the bell. Far away in a back room he heard it ringing, and then *at once* – it must have been at once because he hadn't even had time to take his finger from the bell-button – the door swung open and a woman was standing there.

Normally you ring the bell and you have at least a half-minute's wait before the door opens. But this dame was like a jack-in-the-box. He pressed the bell – and out she popped! It made him jump.

She was about forty-five or fifty years old, and the moment she saw him, she gave him a warm welcoming smile.

'*Please* come in,' she said pleasantly. She stepped aside, holding the door wide open, and Billy found himself automatically starting forward into the house. The compulsion or, more accurately, the desire to follow after her into that house was extraordinarily strong.

'I saw the notice in the window,' he said, holding himself back.

'Yes, I know.'

'I was wondering about a room.'

'It's *all* ready for you, my dear,' she said. She had a round pink face and very gentle blue eyes.

'I was on my way to The Bell and Dragon,' Billy told her. 'But the notice in your window just happened to catch my eye.'

'My dear boy,' she said, 'why don't you come in out of the cold?'

'How much do you charge?'

'Five and sixpence a night, including breakfast.'

It was fantastically cheap. It was less than half of what he had been willing to pay.

'If that is too much,' she added, 'then perhaps I can reduce it just a tiny bit. Do you desire an egg for breakfast? Eggs are expensive at the moment. It would be sixpence less without the egg.'

'Five and sixpence is fine,' he answered. 'I should like very much to stay here.'

'I knew you would. Do come in.'

She seemed terribly nice. She looked exactly like the mother of one's best school-friend welcoming one into the house to stay for the Christmas holidays. Billy took off his hat, and stepped over the threshold.

'Just hang it there,' she said, 'and let me help you with your coat.'

There were no other hats or coats in the hall. There were no umbrellas, no walking-sticks – nothing.

'We have it *all* to ourselves,' she said, smiling at him over her shoulder as she led the way upstairs. 'You see, it isn't very often I have the pleasure of taking a visitor into my little nest.'

The old girl is slightly dotty, Billy told himself. But at five and sixpence a night, who gives a damn about that? 'I should've thought you'd be simply swamped with applicants,' he said politely.

'Oh, I am, my dear, I am, of course I am. But the trouble is that I'm inclined to be just a teeny weeny bit choosey and particular – if you see what I mean.'

'Ah, yes.'

'But I'm always ready. Everything is always ready day and night in this house just on the off-chance that an acceptable young gentleman will come along. And it is such a pleasure, my dear, such a very great pleasure when now and again I open the door and I see someone standing there who is just *exactly* right.' She was half-way up the stairs, and she paused with one hand on the stair-rail, turning her head and smiling down at him with pale lips. 'Like you,' she added, and her blue eyes travelled slowly all the way down the length of Billy's body, to his feet, and then up again.

On the first-floor landing she said to him, 'This floor is mine.'

They climbed up a second flight. 'And this one is *all* yours,' she said. 'Here's your room. I do hope you'll like it.' She took him into a small but charming front bedroom, switching on the light as she went in.

'The morning sun comes right in the window, Mr Perkins. It *is* Mr Perkins, isn't it?'

'No,' he said. 'It's Weaver.'

'Mr Weaver. How nice. I've put a water-bottle between the sheets to air them out, Mr Weaver. It's such a comfort to have a hot water-bottle in a strange bed with clean sheets, don't you agree? And you may light the gas fire at any time if you feel chilly.'

'Thank you,' Billy said. 'Thank you ever so much.' He noticed that the bedspread had been taken off the bed, and that the bedclothes had been neatly turned back on one side, all ready for someone to get in.

'I'm so glad you appeared,' she said, looking earnestly into his face. 'I was beginning to get worried.'

'That's all right,' Billy answered brightly. 'You mustn't worry about me.' He put his suitcase on the chair and started to open it.

'And what about supper, my dear? Did you manage to get anything to eat before you came here?'

'I'm not a bit hungry, thank you,' he said. 'I think I'll just go to bed as soon as possible because tomorrow I've got to get up rather early and report to the office.'

'Very well, then. I'll leave you now so that you can unpack. But before you go to bed, would you be kind enough to pop into the sitting-room on the ground floor and sign the book? Everyone has to do that because it's the law of the land, and we don't want to go breaking any laws at *this* stage in the proceedings, do we?' She gave him a little wave of the hand and went quickly out of the room and closed the door.

Now, the fact that his landlady appeared to be slightly off her rocker didn't worry Billy in the least. After all, she was not only harmless – there was no question about that – but she was also quite obviously a kind and generous soul. He guessed that she had probably lost a son in the war, or something like that, and had never got over it.

So a few minutes later, after unpacking his suitcase and washing his hands, he trotted downstairs to the ground floor and entered the living-room. His landlady wasn't there, but the fire was glowing in the hearth, and the little dachshund was still sleeping in front of it. The room was wonderfully warm and cosy. I'm a lucky fellow, he thought, rubbing his hands. This is a bit of all right.

He found the guest-book lying open on the piano, so he took out his pen and wrote down his name and address. There were only two other entries above his on the page, and, as one always does with guest-books, he started to read them. One was a Christopher Mulholland from Cardiff. The other was Gregory W. Temple from Bristol.

That's funny, he thought suddenly. Christopher Mulholland. It rings a bell.

Now where on earth had he heard that rather unusual name before?

Was he a boy at school? No. Was it one of his sister's numerous young men, perhaps, or a friend of his father's? No, no, it wasn't any of those. He glanced down again at the book.

Christopher Mulholland   *231 Cathedral Road, Cardiff*

Gregory W. Temple   *27 Sycamore Drive, Bristol*

As a matter of fact, now he came to think of it, he wasn't at all sure that the second name didn't have almost as much of a familiar ring about it as the first.

'Gregory Temple?' he said aloud, searching his memory. 'Christopher Mulholland? . . .'

'Such charming boys,' a voice behind him answered, and he turned and saw his landlady sailing into the room with a large silver tea-tray in her hands. She was holding it well out in front of her, and rather high up, as though the tray were a pair of reins on a frisky horse.

'They sound somehow familiar,' he said.

'They do? How interesting.'

'I'm almost positive I've heard those names before somewhere. Isn't that queer? Maybe it was in the newspapers. They weren't famous in any way, were they? I mean famous cricketers or footballers or something like that?'

'Famous,' she said, setting the tea-tray down on the low table in front of the sofa. 'Oh no, I don't think they were famous. But they were extraordinarily handsome, both of them, I can promise you that. They were tall and young and handsome, my dear, just exactly like you.'

Once more, Billy glanced down at the book. 'Look here,' he said, noticing the dates. 'This last entry is over two years old.'

'It is?'

'Yes, indeed. And Christopher Mulholland's is nearly a year before that – more than *three years* ago.'

'Dear me,' she said, shaking her head and heaving a dainty little sigh. 'I would never have thought it. How time does fly away from us all, doesn't it, Mr Wilkins?'

'It's Weaver,' Billy said. 'W-e-a-v-e-r.'

'Oh, of course it is!' she cried, sitting down on the sofa. 'How silly of me. I do apologize. In one ear and out the other, that's me, Mr Weaver.'

'You know something?' Billy said. 'Something that's really quite extraordinary about all this?'

'No, dear, I don't.'

'Well, you see – both of these names, Mulholland and Temple, I not only seem to remember each one of them separately, so to speak, but somehow or other, in some peculiar way, they both appear to be sort of connected together as well. As though they were both famous for the same sort of thing, if you see what I mean – like ... like Dempsey and Tunney, for example, or Churchill and Roosevelt.'

'How amusing,' she said. 'But come over here now, dear, and sit down beside me on the sofa and I'll give you a nice cup of tea and a ginger biscuit before you go to bed.'

'You really shouldn't bother,' Billy said. 'I didn't mean you to do anything like that.' He stood by the piano, watching her as she fussed about with the cups and saucers. He noticed that she had small, white, quickly moving hands, and red finger-nails.

'I'm almost positive it was in the newspapers I saw them,' Billy said. 'I'll think of it in a second. I'm sure I will.'

There is nothing more tantalizing than a thing like this which lingers just outside the borders of one's memory. He hated to give up.

'Now wait a minute,' he said. 'Wait just a minute. Mulholland ... Christopher Mulholland ... wasn't *that* the name of the Eton schoolboy who was on a walking-tour through the West Country, and then all of a sudden ...'

'Milk?' she said. 'And sugar?'

'Yes, please. And then all of a sudden ...'

'Eton schoolboy?' she said. 'Oh no, my dear, that can't possibly be right because *my* Mr Mulholland was certainly not an Eton schoolboy when he came to me. He was a Cambridge undergraduate. Come over here now and sit next to me and warm yourself in front of this lovely fire. Come on. Your tea's all ready for you.' She patted the empty place beside her on the sofa, and she sat there smiling at Billy and waiting for him to come over.

He crossed the room slowly, and sat down on the edge of the sofa. She placed his teacup on the table in front of him.

'*There* we are,' she said. 'How nice and cosy this is, isn't it?'

Billy started sipping his tea. She did the same. For half a minute or so, neither of them spoke. But Billy knew that she was looking at him. Her body was half-turned towards him, and he could feel her eyes resting on his face, watching him over the rim of her teacup. Now and again, he caught a whiff of a peculiar smell that seemed to emanate directly from her person. It was not in the least unpleasant, and it reminded him – well, he wasn't quite sure what it reminded him of. Pickled walnuts? New leather? Or was it the corridors of a hospital?

'Mr Mulholland was a great one for his tea,' she said at length. 'Never in my life have I seen anyone drink as much tea as dear, sweet Mr Mulholland.'

'I suppose he left fairly recently,' Billy said. He was still puzzling his head about the two names. He was positive now that he had seen them in the newspapers – in the headlines.

'Left?' she said, arching her brows. 'But my dear boy, he never left. He's still here. Mr Temple is also here. They're on the third floor, both of them together.'

Billy set down his cup slowly on the table, and stared at his landlady. She smiled back at him, and then she put out one of her white hands and patted him comfortingly on the knee. 'How old are you, my dear?' she asked.

'Seventeen.'

'Seventeen!' she cried. 'Oh, it's the perfect age! Mr Mulholland was also seventeen. But I think he was a trifle shorter than you are, in fact I'm sure he was, and his teeth weren't *quite* so white. You have the most beautiful teeth, Mr Weaver, did you know that?'

'They're not as good as they look,' Billy said. 'They've got simply masses of fillings in them at the back.'

'Mr Temple, of course, was a little older,' she said, ignoring his remark. 'He was actually twenty-eight. And yet I never would have guessed it if he hadn't told me, never in my whole life. There wasn't a *blemish* on his body.'

'A what?' Billy said.

'His skin was *just* like a baby's.'

There was a pause. Billy picked up his teacup and took another sip of his tea, then he set it down again gently in its saucer. He waited for her to say something else, but she seemed to have lapsed into another of her silences. He sat there staring straight ahead of him into the far corner of the room, biting his lower lip.

'That parrot,' he said at last. 'You know something? It had me completely fooled when I first saw it through the window from the street. I could have sworn it was alive.'

'Alas, no longer.'

'It's most terribly clever the way it's been done,' he said. 'It doesn't look in the least bit dead. Who did it?'

'I did.'

'*You* did?'

'Of course,' she said. 'And have you met my little Basil as well?' She nodded towards the dachshund curled up so comfortably in front of the fire. Billy looked at it. And suddenly, he realized that this animal had all the time been just as silent and motionless as the parrot. He put out a hand and touched it gently on the top of its back. The back was hard and cold, and when he pushed the hair to one side with his fingers, he could see the skin underneath, greyish-black and dry and perfectly preserved.

'Good gracious me,' he said. 'How absolutely fascinating.' He turned away from the dog and stared with deep admiration at the little woman beside him on the sofa. 'It must be most awfully difficult to do a thing like that.'

'Not in the least,' she said. 'I stuff *all* my little pets myself when they pass away. Will you have another cup of tea?'

'No, thank you,' Billy said. The tea tasted faintly of bitter almonds, and he didn't much care for it.

'You did sign the book, didn't you?'

'Oh, yes.'

'That's good. Because later on, if I happen to forget what you were. called, then I can always come down here and look it up. I still do that almost every day with Mr Mulholland and Mr ... Mr ...'

'Temple,' Billy said. 'Gregory Temple. Excuse my asking, but haven't there been *any* other guests here except them in the last two or three years?'

Holding her teacup high in one hand, inclining her head slightly to the left, she looked up at him out of the corners of her eyes and gave him another gentle little smile.

'No, my dear,' she said. 'Only you.'

WILLIAM AND MARY

William Pearl did not leave a great deal of money when he died, and his will was a simple one. With the exception of a few small bequests to relatives, he left all his property to his wife.

The solicitor and Mrs Pearl went over it together in the solicitor's office, and when the business was completed, the widow got up to leave. At that point, the solicitor took a sealed envelope from the folder on his desk and held it out to his client.

'I have been instructed to give you this,' he said. 'Your husband sent it to us shortly before he passed away.' The solicitor was pale and prim, and out of respect for a widow he kept his head on one side as he spoke, looking downward. 'It appears that it might be something personal, Mrs Pearl. No doubt you'd like to take it home with you and read it in privacy.'

Mrs Pearl accepted the envelope and went out into the street. She paused on the pavement, feeling the thing with her fingers. A letter of farewell from William? Probably, yes. A formal letter. It was bound to be formal – stiff and formal. The man was incapable of acting otherwise. He had never done anything informal in his life.

My dear Mary, I trust that you will not permit my departure from this world to upset you too much, but that you will continue to observe those precepts which have guided you so well during our partnership together. Be diligent and dignified in all things. Be thrifty with your money. Be very careful that you do not ... et cetera, et cetera.

A typical William letter.

Or was it possible that he might have broken down at the last moment and written her something beautiful? Maybe this was a beautiful tender message, a sort of love letter, a lovely warm note of thanks to her for giving him thirty years of her life and for ironing a million shirts and cooking a million meals and making a million beds, something that she could read over and over again, once a day at least, and she would keep it for ever in the box on the dressing-table together with her brooches.

There is no knowing what people will do when they are about to die, Mrs Pearl told herself, and she tucked the envelope under her arm and hurried home.

She let herself in the front door and went straight to the living-room and sat down on the sofa without removing her hat or coat. Then she opened the envelope and drew out the contents. These consisted, she saw, of some fifteen or twenty sheets of lined white paper, folded over once and held together at the top left-hand corner by a clip. Each sheet was covered with the small, neat, forward-sloping writing that she knew so well, but when she noticed now much of it there was, and in what a neat businesslike manner it was written, and how the first page didn't even begin in the nice way a letter should, she began to get suspicious.

She looked away. She lit herself a cigarette. She took one puff and laid the cigarette in the ash-tray.

If this is about what I am beginning to suspect it is about, she told herself, then I don't want to read it.

Can one refuse to read a letter from the dead?

Yes.

Well . . .

She glanced over at William's empty chair on the other side of the fireplace. It was a big brown leather armchair, and there was a depression on the seat of it, made by his buttocks over the years. Higher up, on the backrest, there was a dark oval stain on the leather where his head had rested. He used to sit reading in that chair and she would be opposite him on the sofa, sewing on buttons or mending socks or putting a patch on the elbow of one of his jackets, and every now and then a pair of eyes would glance up from the book and settle on her, watchful, but strangely impersonal, as if calculating something. She had never liked those eyes. They were ice blue, cold, small, and rather close together, with two deep vertical lines of disapproval dividing them. All her life they had been watching her. And even now, after a week alone in the house, she sometimes had an uneasy feeling that they were still there, following her around, staring at her from doorways, from empty chairs, through a window at night.

Slowly she reached into her handbag and took out her spectacles and put them on. Then, holding the pages up high in front of her so that they caught the late afternoon light from the window behind, she started to read:

This note, my dear Mary, is entirely for you, and will be given you shortly after I am gone.

Do not be alarmed by the sight of all this writing. It is nothing but an attempt on my part to explain to you precisely what Landy is going to do to me, and why I have agreed that he should do it, and what are his theories and his hopes. You are my wife and you have a right to know these things. In fact you *must* know them. During the past few days I have tried very hard to speak with you about Landy, but you have steadfastly refused to give me a hearing. This, as I have already told you, is a very foolish attitude to take, and I find it not entirely an unselfish one either. It stems mostly from ignorance, and I am absolutely convinced that if only you were made aware of all the facts, you would immediately change your view. That is why I am hoping that when I am no longer with you, and your mind is less distracted, you will consent to listen to me more carefully through these pages. I swear to you that when you have read my story, your sense of antipathy will vanish, and enthusiasm will take its place. I even dare to hope that you will become a little proud of what I have done.

As you read on, you must forgive me, if you will, for the coolness of my style, but this is the only way I know of getting my message over to you clearly. You see, as my time draws near, it is natural that I begin to brim with every kind of sentimentality under the sun. Each day I grow more extravagantly wistful, especially in the evenings, and unless I watch myself closely my emotions will be overflowing on to these pages.

I have a wish, for example, to write something about you and what a satisfactory wife you have been to me through the years, and I am promising myself that if there is time, and I still have the strength, I shall do that next.

I have a yearning also to speak about this Oxford of mine where I have been living and teaching for the past seventeen years, to tell something about the glory of the place and to explain, if I can, a little of what it has meant to have been allowed to work in its midst. All the things and places that I loved so well keep crowding in on me now in this gloomy bedroom. They are bright and beautiful as they always were, and today, for some reason, I can see them more clearly than ever. The path around the lake in the gardens of Worcester College, where Lovelace used to walk. The gateway at Pembroke. The view westward over the town from Magdalen Tower. The great hall at Christchurch. The little rockery at St John's where I have counted more than a dozen varieties of campanula, including the rare and dainty C. Waldsteiniana. But there, you see! I haven't even begun and already I'm falling into the trap. So let me get started now; and let you read it slowly, my dear, without any of that sense of sorrow or disapproval that might otherwise embarrass your understanding. Promise me now that you will read it slowly, and that you will put yourself in a cool and patient frame of mind before you begin.

The details of the illness that struck me down so suddenly in my middle life are known to you. I need not waste time upon them – except to admit at once how foolish I was not to have gone earlier to my doctor. Cancer is one of the few remaining diseases that these modern drugs cannot cure. A surgeon can operate if it has not spread too far; but with me, not only did I leave it too late, but the thing had the effrontery to attack me in the pancreas, making both surgery and survival equally impossible.

So here I was with somewhere between one and six months left to live, growing more melancholy every hour – and then, all of a sudden, in comes Landy.

That was six weeks ago, on a Tuesday morning, very early, long before your visiting time, and the moment he entered I knew there was some sort of madness in the wind. He didn't creep in on his toes, sheepish and embarrassed, not knowing what to say, like all my other visitors. He came in strong and smiling, and he strode up to the bed and stood there looking down at me with a wild bright glimmer in his eyes, and he said, 'William, my boy, this is perfect. You're just the one I want!'

Perhaps I should explain to you here that although John Landy has never been to our house, and you have seldom if ever met him, I myself have been friendly with him for at least nine years. I am, of course, primarily a teacher of philosophy, but as you know I've lately been dabbling a good deal in psychology as well. Landy's interests and mine have therefore slightly overlapped. He is a magnificent neuro-surgeon, one of the finest, and recently he has been kind enough to let me study the results of some of his work, especially the varying effects of prefrontal lobotomies upon different types of psychopath. So you can see that when he suddenly burst in on me that Tuesday morning, we were by no means strangers to one another.

'Look,' he said, pulling up a chair beside the bed. 'In a few weeks you're going to be dead. Correct?'

Coming from Landy, the question didn't seem especially unkind. In a way it was refreshing to have a visitor brave enough to touch upon the forbidden subject.

'You're going to expire right here in this room, and then they'll take you out and cremate you.'

'Bury me,' I said.

'That's even worse. And then what? Do you believe you'll go to heaven?'

'I doubt it,' I said, 'though it would be comforting to think so.'

'Or hell, perhaps?'

'I don't really see why they should send me there.'

'You never know, my dear William.'

'What's all this about?' I asked.

'Well,' he said, and I could see him watching me carefully, 'personally, I don't believe that after you're dead you'll ever hear of yourself again – unless . . .' and here he paused and smiled and leaned closer '. . . unless, of course, you have the sense to put yourself into my hands. Would you care to consider a proposition?'

The way he was staring at me, and studying me, and appraising me with a queer kind of hungriness, I might have been a piece of prime beef on the counter and he had bought it and was waiting for them to wrap it up.

'I'm really serious about it, William. Would you care to consider a proposition?'

'I don't know what you're talking about.'

'Then listen and I'll tell you. Will you listen to me?'

'Go on then, if you like. I doubt I've got very much to lose by hearing it.'

'On the contrary, you have a great deal to gain – especially *after you're dead.*'

I am sure he was expecting me to jump when he said this, but for some reason I was ready for it. I lay quite still, watching his face and that slow white smile of his that always revealed the gold clasp of an upper denture curled around the canine on the left side of his mouth.

'This is a thing, William, that I've been working on quietly for some years. One or two others here at the hospital have been helping me, especially Morrison, and we've completed a number of fairly successful trials with laboratory animals. I'm at the stage now where I'm ready to have a go with a man. It's a big idea, and it may sound a bit far-fetched at first, but from a surgical point of view there doesn't seem to be any reason why it shouldn't be more or less practicable.'

Landy leaned forward and placed both hands on the edge of my bed. He has a good face, handsome in a bony sort of way, with none of the usual doctor's look about it. You know that look, most of them have it. It glimmers at you out of their eyeballs like a dull electric sign and it reads *Only I can save you.* But John Landy's eyes were wide and bright and little sparks of excitement were dancing in the centres of them.

'Quite a long time ago,' he said, 'I saw a short medical film that had been brought over from Russia. It was a rather gruesome thing, but interesting. It showed a dog's head completely severed from the body, but with the normal blood supply being maintained through the arteries and veins by means of an artificial heart. Now the thing is this: that dog's head, sitting there all alone on a sort of tray, was *alive*. The brain was functioning. They proved it by several tests. For example, when food was smeared on the dog's lips, the tongue would come out and lick it away: and the eyes would follow a person moving across the room.

'It seemed reasonable to conclude from this that the head and the brain did not need to be attached to the rest of the body in order to remain alive – provided, of course, that a supply of properly oxygenated blood could be maintained.

'Now then. My own thought, which grew out of seeing this film, was to remove the brain from the skull of a human and keep it alive and functioning as an independent unit for an unlimited period after he is dead. *Your* brain, for example, after *you* are dead.'

'I don't like that,' I said.

'Don't interrupt, William. Let me finish. So far as I can tell from subsequent experiments, the brain is a peculiarly self-supporting object. It manufactures its own cerebrospinal fluid. The magic processes of thought and memory which go on inside it are manifestly not impaired by the absence of limbs or trunk or even of skull, provided, as I say, that you keep pumping in the right kind of oxygenated blood under the proper conditions.

'My dear William, just think for a moment of your own brain. It is in perfect shape. It is crammed full of a lifetime of learning. It has taken you years of work to make it what it is. It is just beginning to give out some first-rate original ideas. Yet soon it is going to have to die along with the rest of your body simply because your silly little pancreas is riddled with cancer.'

'No thank you,' I said to him. 'You can stop there. It's a repulsive idea, and even if you could do it, which I doubt, it would be quite pointless. What possible use is there is keeping my brain alive if I couldn't talk or see or hear or feel? Personally, I can think of nothing more unpleasant.'

'I believe that you *would* be able to communicate with us,' Landy said. 'And we might even succeed in giving you a certain amount of vision. But let's take this slowly. I'll come to all that later on. The fact remains that you're going to die fairly soon whatever happens; and my plans would not involve touching you at all until *after* you are dead. Come now, William. No true philosopher could object to lending his dead body to the cause of science.'

'That's not putting it quite straight,' I answered. 'It seems to me there'd be some doubts as to whether I were dead or alive by the time you'd finished with me.'

'Well,' he said, smiling a little, 'I suppose you're right about that. But I don't think you ought to turn me down quite so quickly, before you know a bit more about it.'

'I said I don't want to hear it.'

'Have a cigarette,' he said, holding out his case.

'I don't smoke, you know that.'

He took one himself and lit it with a tiny silver lighter that was no bigger than a shilling piece. 'A present from the people who make my instruments,' he said. 'Ingenious, isn't it?'

I examined the lighter, then handed it back.

'May I go on?' he asked.

'I'd rather you didn't.'

'Just lie still and listen. I think you'll find it quite interesting.'

There were some blue grapes on a plate beside my bed. I put the plate on my chest and began eating the grapes.

'At the very moment of death,' Landy said, 'I should have to be standing by so that I could step in immediately and try to keep your brain alive.'

'You mean leaving it in the head?'

'To start with, yes. I'd have to.'

'And where would you put it after that?'

'If you want to know, in a sort of basin.'

'Are you really serious about this?'

'Certainly I'm serious.'

'All right. Go on.'

'I suppose you know that when the heart stops and the brain is deprived of fresh blood and oxygen, its tissues die very rapidly. Anything from four to six minutes and the whole thing's dead. Even after three minutes you may get a certain amount of damage. So I should have to work rapidly to prevent this from happening. But with the help of the machine, it should all be quite simple.'

'What machine?'

'The artificial heart. We've got a nice adaptation here of the one originally devised by Alexis Carrel and Lindbergh. It oxygenates the blood, keeps it at the right temperature, pumps it in at the right pressure, and does a number of other little necessary things. It's really not at all complicated.'

'Tell me what you would do at the moment of death,' I said. 'What is the first thing you would do?'

'Do you know anything about the vascular and venous arrangement of the brain?'

'No.'

'Then listen. It's not difficult. The blood supply to the brain is derived from two main sources, the internal carotid arteries and the vertebral arteries. There are two of each, making four arteries in all. Got that?'

'Yes.'

'And the return system is even simpler. The blood is drained away by only two large veins, the internal jugulars. So you have four arteries going up – they go up the neck of course – and two veins coming down. Around the brain itself they naturally branch out into other channels, but those don't concern us. We never touch them.'

'All right,' I said. 'Imagine that I've just died. Now what would you do?'

'I should immediately open your neck and locate the four arteries, the carotids and the vertebrals. I should then perfuse them, which means that I'd stick a large hollow needle into each. These four needles would be connected by tubes to the artificial heart.

'Then, working quickly, I would dissect out both the left and right jugular veins and hitch these also to the heart machine to complete the circuit. Now switch on the machine, which is already primed with the right type of blood, and there you are. The circulation through your brain would be restored.'

'I'd be like that Russian dog.'

'I don't think you would. For one thing, you'd certainly lose consciousness when you died, and I very much doubt whether you would come to again for quite a long time – if indeed you came to at all. But, conscious or not, you'd be in a rather interesting position, wouldn't you? You'd have a cold dead body and a living brain.'

Landy paused to savour this delightful prospect. The man was so entranced and bemused by the whole idea that he evidently found it impossible to believe I might not be feeling the same way.

'We could now afford to take our time,' he said. 'And believe me, we'd need it. The first thing we'd do would be to wheel you to the operating-room, accompanied of course by the machine, which must never stop pumping. The next problem ...'

'All right,' I said. 'That's enough. I don't have to hear the details.'

'Oh but you must,' he said. 'It is important that you should know precisely what is going to happen to you all the way through. You see, afterwards, when you regain consciousness, it will be much more satisfactory from your point of view if you are able to remember exactly *where* you are and *how* you came to be there. If only for your own peace of mind you should know that. You agree?'

I lay still on the bed, watching him.

'So the next problem would be to remove your brain, intact

and undamaged, from your dead body. The body is useless. In fact it has already started to decay. The skull and the face are also useless. They are both encumbrances and I don't want them around. All I want is the brain, the clean beautiful brain, alive and perfect. So when I get you on the table I will take a saw, a small oscillating saw, and with this I shall proceed to remove the whole vault of your skull. You'd still be unconscious at that point so I wouldn't have to bother with anaesthetic.'

'Like hell you wouldn't,' I said.

'You'd be out cold, I promise you that, William. Don't forget you *died* just a few minutes before.'

'Nobody's sawing off the top of my skull without an anaesthetic,' I said.

Landy shrugged his shoulders. 'It makes no difference to me,' he said. 'I'll be glad to give you a little procaine if you want it. If it will make you any happier I'll infiltrate the whole scalp with procaine, the whole head, from the neck up.'

'Thanks very much,' I said.

'You know,' he went on, 'it's extraordinary what sometimes happens. Only last week a man was brought in unconscious, and I opened his head without any anaesthetic at all and removed a small blood clot. I was still working inside the skull when he woke up and began talking.

' "Where am I?" he asked.

' "You're in hospital."

' "Well," he said. "Fancy that."

' "Tell me," I asked him, "is this bothering you, what I'm doing?"

' "No," he answered. "Not at all. What *are* you doing?"

' "I'm just removing a blood clot from your brain."

' "You *are*?"

' "Just lie still. Don't move. I'm nearly finished."

' "So that's the bastard who's been giving me all those headaches," the man said.'

Landy paused and smiled, remembering the occasion. 'That's word for word what the man said,' he went on, 'although the next day he couldn't even recollect the incident. It's a funny thing, the brain.'

'I'll have the procaine,' I said.

'As you wish, William. And now, as I say, I'd take a small oscillating saw and carefully remove your complete calvarium – the whole vault of the skull. This would expose the top half of the brain, or rather the outer covering in which it is wrapped. You may or may not know that there are three separate coverings around the brain itself – the outer one called the dura mater or dura, the middle one called the arachnoid, and the inner one called the pia mater or pia. Most laymen seem to have the idea that the brain is a naked thing floating around in fluid in your head. But it isn't. It's wrapped up neatly in these three strong coverings, and the cerebrospinal fluid actually flows within the little gap between the two coverings, known as the subarachnoid space. As I told you before, this fluid is manufactured by the brain and it drains off into the venous system by osmosis.

'I myself would leave all three coverings – don't they have lovely names, the dura, the arachnoid, and the pia? – I'd leave them all intact. There are many reasons for this, not least among them being the fact that within the dura run the venous channels that drain the blood from the brain into the jugular.

'Now,' he went on, 'we've got the upper half of your skull off so that the top of the brain, wrapped in its outer covering, is exposed. The next step is the really tricky one: to release the whole package so that it can be lifted cleanly away, leaving the stubs of the four supply arteries and the two veins hanging underneath ready to be re-connected to the machine. This is an immensely lengthy and complicated business involving the delicate chipping away of much bone, the severing of many nerves, and the cutting and tying of numerous blood vessels. The only way I could do it with any hope of success would be by taking a rongeur and slowly biting off the rest of your skull, peeling it off downward like an orange until the sides and underneath of the brain covering are fully exposed. The problems involved are highly technical and I won't go into them, but I feel fairly sure that the work can be done. It's simply a question of surgical skill and patience. And don't forget that I'd have plenty of time, as much as I wanted, because the artificial heart would be continually pumping away alongside the operating-table, keeping the brain alive.

'Now, let's assume that I've succeeded in peeling off your skull and removing everthing else that surrounds the sides of the brain. That leaves it connected to the body only at the base, mainly by the spinal column and by the two large veins and the four arteries that are supplying it with blood. So what next?

'I would sever the spinal column just above the first cervical vertebra, taking great care not to harm the two vertebral arteries which are in that area. But you must remember that the dura or outer covering is open at this place to receive the spinal column, so I'd have to close this opening by sewing the edges of the dura together. There'd be no problem there.

'At this point, I would be ready for the final move. To one side, on a table, I'd have a basin of a special shape, and this would be filled with what we call Ringer's Solution. That is a special kind of fluid we use for irrigation in neurosurgery. I would now cut the brain completely loose by severing the supply arteries and the veins. Then I would simply pick it up in my hands and transfer it to the basin. This would be the only other time during the whole proceeding when the blood flow would be cut off; but once it was in the basin, it wouldn't take a moment to re-connect the stubs of the arteries and veins to the artificial heart.

'So there you are,' Landy said. 'Your brain is now in the basin, and still alive, and there isn't any reason why it shouldn't stay alive for a very long time, years and years perhaps, provided we looked after the blood and the machine.'

'But would it *function*?'

'My dear William, how should I know? I can't even tell you whether it would regain consciousness.'

'And if it did?'

'There now! That would be fascinating!'

'Would it?' I said, and I must admit I had my doubts.

'Of course it would! Lying there with all your thinking processes working beautifully, and your memory as well ...'

'And not being able to see or feel or smell or hear or talk,' I said.

'Ah!' he cried. 'I knew I'd forgotten something! I never told you about the eye. Listen. I am going to try to leave one of your optic nerves intact, as well as the eye itself. The optic nerve is a little thing about the thickness of a clinical thermometer and about two inches in length as it stretches between the brain and the eye. The beauty of it is that it's not really a nerve at all. It's an outpouching of the brain itself, and the dura or brain covering extends along it and is attached to the eyeball. The back of the eye is therefore in very close contact with the brain, and cerebrospinal fluid flows right up to it.

'All this suits my purpose very well, and makes it reasonable to suppose that I could succeed in preserving one of your eyes. I've already constructed a small plastic case to contain the eyeball, instead of your own socket, and when the brain is in the basin, submerged in Ringer's Solution, the eyeball in its case will float on the surface of the liquid.'

'Staring at the ceiling,' I said.

'I suppose so, yes. I'm afraid there wouldn't be any muscles there to move it around. But it might be sort of fun to lie there so quietly and comfortably peering out at the world from your basin.'

'Hilarious,' I said. 'How about leaving me an ear as well?'

'I'd rather not try an ear this time.'

'I want an ear,' I said. 'I insist upon an ear.'

'No.'

'I want to listen to Bach.'

'You don't understand how difficult it would be,' Landy said gently. 'The hearing apparatus – the cochlea, as it's called – is a far more delicate mechanism than the eye. What's more, it is encased in bone. So is a part of the auditory nerve that connects it with the brain. I couldn't possibly chisel the whole thing out intact.'

'Couldn't you leave it encased in the bone and bring the bone to the basin?'

'No,' he said firmly. 'This thing is complicated enough already. And anyway, if the eye works, it doesn't matter all that much about your hearing. We can always hold up messages for you to read. You really must leave me to decide what is possible and what isn't.'

'I haven't yet said that I'm going to do it.'

'I know, William, I know.'

'I'm not sure I fancy the idea very much.'

'Would you rather be dead, altogether?'

'Perhaps I would. I don't know yet. I wouldn't be able to talk, would I?'

'Of course not.'

'Then how would I communicate with you? How would you know that I'm conscious?'

'It would be easy for us to know whether or not you regain consciousness,' Landy said. 'The ordinary electro-encephalograph could tell us that. We'd attach the electrodes directly to the frontal lobes of your brain, there in the basin.'

'And you could actually tell?'

'Oh, definitely. Any hospital could do that part of it.'

'But *I* couldn't communicate with *you*.'

'As a matter of fact,' Landy said, 'I believe you could. There's a man up in London called Wertheimer who's doing some interesting work on the subject of thought communication, and I've been in touch with him. You know, don't you, that the thinking brain throws off electrical and chemical discharges? And that these discharges go out in the form of waves, rather like radio waves?'

'I know a bit about it,' I said.

'Well, Wertheimer has constructed an apparatus somewhat similar to the encephalograph, though far more sensitive, and he maintains that within certain narrow limits it can help him to interpret the actual things that a brain is thinking. It produces a kind of graph which is apparently decipherable into words or thoughts. Would you like me to ask Wertheimer to come and see you?'

'No,' I said. Landy was already taking it for granted that I was going to go through with this business, and I resented his attitude. 'Go away now and leave me alone,' I told him. 'You won't get anywhere by trying to rush me.'

He stood up at once and crossed to the door.

'One question,' I said.

He paused with a hand on the doorknob. 'Yes, William?'

'Simply this. Do you yourself honestly believe that when my brain is in that basin, my mind will be able to function exactly as it is doing at present? Do you believe that I will be able to think and reason as I can now? And will the power of memory remain?'

'I don't see why not,' he answered. 'It's the same brain. It's alive. It's undamaged. In fact, it's completely untouched. We haven't even opened the dura. The big difference, of course, would be that we've severed every single nerve that leads into it – except for the one optic nerve – and this means that your thinking would no longer be influenced by your senses. You'd be living in an extraordinary pure and detached world. Nothing to bother you at all, not even pain. You couldn't possibly feel pain because there wouldn't be any nerves to feel it with. In a way, it would be an almost perfect situation. No worries or fears or pains or hunger or thirst. Not even any desires. Just your memories and your thoughts, and if the remaining eye happened to function, then you could read books as well. It all sounds rather pleasant to me.'

'It does, does it?'

'Yes, William, it does. And particularly for a Doctor of Philosophy. It would be a tremendous experience. You'd be able to reflect upon the ways of the world with a detachment and a serenity that no man had ever attained before. And who knows what might not happen then! Great thoughts and solutions might come to you, great ideas that could revolutionize our way of life! Try to imagine, if you can, the degree of concentration that you'd be able to achieve!'

'And the frustration,' I said.

'Nonsense. There couldn't be any frustration. You can't have frustration without desire, and you couldn't possibly have any desire. Not physical desire, anyway.'

'I should certainly be capable of remembering my previous life in the world, and I might desire to return to it.'

'What, to this mess! Out of your comfortable basin and back into this madhouse!'

'Answer one more question,' I said. 'How long do you believe you could keep it alive?'

'The brain? Who knows? Possibly for years and years. The conditions would be ideal. Most of the factors that cause deterioration would be absent, thanks to the artificial heart. The blood-pressure would remain constant at all times, an impossible condition in real life. The temperature would also be constant. The chemical composition of the blood would be near perfect. There would be no impurities in it, or virus, no bacteria, nothing. Of course it's foolish to guess, but I believe that a brain might live for two or three hundred years in circumstances like these. Goodbye for now,' he said. 'I'll drop in and see you tomorrow.' He went out quickly, leaving me, as you might guess, in a fairly disturbed state of mind.

My immediate reaction after he had gone was one of revulsion towards the whole business. Somehow, it wasn't at all nice. There was something basically repulsive about the idea that I myself, with all my mental faculties intact, should be reduced to a small slimy blob lying in a pool of water. It was monstrous, obscene, unholy. Another thing that bothered me was the feeling of helplessness that I was bound to experience once Landy had got me into the basin. There could be no going back after that, no way of protesting or explaining. I would be committed for as long as they could keep me alive.

And what, for example, if I could not stand it? What if it turned out to be terribly painful? What if I became hysterical?

No legs to run away on. No voice to scream with. Nothing. I'd just have to grin and bear it for the next two centuries.

No mouth to grin with either.

At this point, a curious thought struck me, and it was this: Does not a man who has had a leg amputated often suffer from the delusion that the leg is still there? Does he not tell the nurse that the toes he doesn't have any more are itching like mad, and so on and so forth? I seemed to have heard something to that effect quite recently.

Very well. On the same premise, was it not possible that my brain, lying there alone in that basin, might not suffer from a similar delusion in regard to my body? In which case, all my usual aches and pains could come flooding over me and I wouldn't even be able to take an aspirin to relieve them. One moment I might be imagining that I had the most excruciating cramp in my leg, or a violent indigestion, and a few minutes later, I might easily get the feeling that my poor bladder – you know me – was so full that if I didn't get to emptying it soon it would burst.

Heaven forbid.

I lay there for a long time thinking these horrid thoughts. Then quite suddenly, round about midday, my mood began to change. I became less concerned with the unpleasant aspect of the affair and found myself able to examine Landy's proposals in a more reasonable light. Was there not, after all, I asked myself, something a bit comforting in the thought that my brain might not necessarily have to die and disappear in a few weeks' time? There was indeed. I am rather proud of my brain. It is a sensitive, lucid, and uberous organ. It contains a prodigious store of information, and it is still capable of producing imaginative and original theories. As brains go, it is a damn good one, though I say it myself. Whereas my body, my poor old body, the thing that Landy wants to throw away – well, even you, my dear Mary, will have to agree with me that there is really nothing about *that* which is worth preserving any more.

I was lying on my back eating a grape. Delicious it was, and there were three little seeds in it which I took out of my mouth and placed on the edge of the plate.

'I'm going to do it,' I said quietly. 'Yes, by God, I'm going to do it. When Landy comes back to see me tomorrow I shall tell him straight out that I'm going to do it.'

It was as quick as that. And from then on, I began to feel very much better. I surprised everyone by gobbling an enormous lunch, and shortly after that you came in to visit me as usual.

But how well I looked, you told me. How bright and well and chirpy. Had anything happened? Was there some good news?

Yes, I said there was. And then, if you remember, I bade you sit down and make yourself comfortable, and I began immediately to explain to you as gently as I could what was in the wind.

Alas, you would have none of it. I had hardly begun telling you the barest details when you flew into a fury and said that the thing was revolting, disgusting, horrible, unthinkable, and when I tried to go on, you marched out of the room.

Well, Mary, as you know, I have tried to discuss this subject with you many times since then, but you have consistently refused to give me a hearing. Hence this note, and I can only hope that you will have the good sense to permit yourself to read it. It has taken me a long time to write. Two weeks have gone since I started to scribble the first sentence, and I'm now a good deal weaker than I was then. I doubt whether I have the strength to say much more. Certainly I won't say good-bye, because there's a chance, just a tiny chance, that if Landy succeeds in his work I may actually *see* you again later, that is if you can bring yourself to come and visit me.

I am giving orders that these pages shall not be delivered to you until a week after I am gone. By now, therefore, as you sit reading them, seven days have already elapsed since Landy did the deed. You yourself may even know what the outcome has been. If you don't, if you have purposely kept yourself apart and have refused to have anything to do with it – which I suspect may be the case – please change your mind now and give Landy a call to see how things went with me. That is the least you can do. I have told him that he may expect to hear from you on the seventh day.

Your faithful husband,
William

ps. Be good when I am gone, and always remember that it is harder to be a widow than a wife. Do not drink cocktails. Do not waste money. Do not smoke cigarettes. Do not eat pastry. Do not use lipstick. Do not buy a television apparatus. Keep my rose beds and my rockery well weeded in the summers. And incidentally I suggest that you have the telephone disconnected now that I shall have no further use for it.

W.

Mrs Pearl laid the last page of the manuscript slowly down on the sofa beside her. Her little mouth was pursed up tight and there was a whiteness around her nostrils.

But really! You would think a widow was entitled to a bit of peace after all these years.

The whole thing was just too awful to think about. Beastly and awful. It gave her the shudders.

She reached for her bag and found herself another cigarette. She lit it, inhaling the smoke deeply and blowing it out in clouds all over the room. Through the smoke she could see her lovely television set, brand new, lustrous, huge, crouching defiantly but also a little self-consciously on top of what used to be William's worktable.

What would he say, she wondered, if he could see that now?

She paused, to remember the last time he had caught her smoking a cigarette. That was about a year ago, and she was sitting in the kitchen by the open window having a quick one before he came home from work. She'd had the radio on loud playing dance music and she had turned round to pour herself another cup of coffee and there he was standing in the doorway, huge and grim, staring down at her with those awful eyes, a little black dot of fury blazing in the centre of each.

For four weeks after that, he had paid the housekeeping bills himself and given her no money at all, but of course he wasn't to know that she had over six pounds salted away in a soap-flake carton in the cupboard under the sink.

'What is it?' she had said to him once during supper. 'Are you worried about me getting lung cancer?'

'I am not,' he had answered.

'Then why can't I smoke?'

'Because I disapprove, that's why.'

He had also disapproved of children, and as a result they had never had any of them either.

Where was he now, this William of hers, the great disapprover?

Landy would be expecting her to call up. Did she *have* to call Landy? Well, not really, no.

She finished her cigarette, then lit another one immediately from the old stub. She looked at the telephone that was sitting on the worktable beside the television set. William had asked her to call. He had specifically requested that she telephone Landy as soon as she had read the letter. She hesitated, fighting hard now against that old ingrained sense of duty that she didn't quite yet dare to shake off. Then, slowly, she got to her feet and crossed over to the phone on the worktable. She found a number in the book, dialled it, and waited.

'I want to speak to Mr Landy, please.'

'Who is calling?'

'Mrs Pearl. Mrs William Pearl.'

'One moment, please.'

Almost at once, Landy was on the other end of the wire.

'Mrs Pearl?'

'This is Mrs Pearl.'

There was a slight pause.

'I am so glad you called at last, Mrs Pearl. You are quite well, I hope?' The voice was quiet, unemotional, courteous. 'I wonder if you would care to come over here to the hospital? Then we can have a little chat. I expect you are very eager to know how it all came out.'

She didn't answer.

'I can tell you now that everything went pretty smoothly, one way and another. Far better, in fact, than I was entitled to hope. It is not only alive, Mrs Pearl, it is conscious. It recovered consciousness on the second day. Isn't that interesting?'

She waited for him to go on.

'And the eye is seeing. We are sure of that because we get an immediate change in the deflections on the encephalograph when we hold something up in front of it. And now we're giving it the newspaper to read every day.'

'Which newspaper?' Mrs Pearl asked sharply.

'The *Daily Mirror*. The headlines are larger.'

'He hates the *Mirror*. Give him *The Times*.'

There was a pause, then the doctor said, 'Very well, Mrs Pearl.

We'll give it *The Times*. We naturally want to do all we can to keep it happy.'

'*Him*,' she said. 'Not it. *Him!*'

'Him,' the doctor said. 'Yes, I beg your pardon. To keep him happy. That's one reason why I suggested you should come along here as soon as possible. I think it would be good for him to see you. You could indicate how delighted you were to be with him again – smile at him and blow him a kiss and all that sort of thing. It's bound to be a comfort to him to know that you are standing by.'

There was a long pause.

'Well,' Mrs Pearl said at last, her voice suddenly very meek and tired. 'I suppose I had better come on over and see how he is.'

'Good. I knew you would. I'll wait here for you. Come straight up to my office on the second floor. Good-bye.'

Half an hour later, Mrs Pearl was at the hospital.

'You mustn't be surprised by what he looks like,' Landy said as he walked beside her down a corridor.

'No, I won't.'

'It's bound to be a bit of a shock to you at first. He's not very prepossessing in his present state, I'm afraid.'

'I didn't marry him for his looks, Doctor.'

Landy turned and stared at her. What a queer little woman this was, he thought, with her large eyes and her sullen, resentful air. Her features, which must have been quite pleasant once, had now gone completely. The mouth was slack, the cheeks loose and flabby, and the whole face gave the impression of having slowly but surely sagged to pieces through years and years of joyless married life. They walked on for a while in silence.

'Take your time when you get inside,' Landy said. 'He won't know you're in there until you place your face directly above his eye. The eye is always open, but he can't move it at all, so the field of vision is very narrow. At present we have it looking up at the ceiling. And of course he can't hear anything. We can talk together as much as we like. It's in here.'

Landy opened a door and ushered her into a small square room.

'I wouldn't go too close yet,' he said, putting a hand on her arm. 'Stay back here a moment with me until you get used to it all.'

There was a biggish white enamel bowl about the size of a washbasin standing on a high white table in the centre of the room, and there were half a dozen thin plastic tubes coming out of it. These tubes were connected with a whole lot of glass piping in which you could see the blood flowing to and from the heart machine. The machine itself made a soft rhythmic pulsing sound.

'He's in there,' Landy said, pointing to the basin, which was too high for her to see into. 'Come just a little closer. Not too near.'

He led her two paces forward.

By stretching her neck, Mrs Pearl could now see the surface of the liquid inside the basin. It was clear and still, and on it there floated a small oval capsule, about the size of a pigeon's egg.

'That's the eye in there,' Landy said. 'Can you see it?'

'Yes.'

'So far as we can tell, it is still in perfect condition. It's his right eye, and the plastic container has a lens on it similar to the one he used in his own spectacles. At this moment he's probably seeing quite as well as he did before.'

'The ceiling isn't much to look at,' Mrs Pearl said.

'Don't worry about that. We're in the process of working out a whole programme to keep him amused, but we don't want to go too quickly at first.'

'Give him a good book.'

'We will, we will. Are you feeling all right, Mrs Pearl?'

'Yes.'

'Then we'll go forward a little more, shall we, and you'll be able to see the whole thing.'

He led her forward until they were standing only a couple of yards from the table, and now she could see right down into the basin.

'There you are,' Landy said. 'That's William.'

He was far larger than she had imagined he would be, and darker in colour. With all the ridges and creases running over his surface, he reminded her of nothing so much as an enormous pickled walnut. She could see the stubs of the four big arteries and the two veins coming out from the base of him and the neat way in which they were joined to the plastic tubes; and with each throb of the heart machine, all the tubes gave a little jerk in unison as the blood was pushed through them.

'You'll have to lean over,' Landy said, 'and put your pretty face right above the eye. He'll see you then, and you can smile at him and blow him a kiss. If I were you I'd say a few nice things as well. He won't actually hear them, but I'm sure he'll get the general idea.'

'He hates people blowing kisses at him,' Mrs Pearl said. 'I'll do it my own way if you don't mind.' She stepped up to the edge of the table, leaned forward until her face was directly over the basin, and looked straight down into William's eye.

'Hallo, dear,' she whispered. 'It's me – Mary.'

The eye, bright as ever, stared back at her with a peculiar, fixed intensity.

'How are you, dear?' she said.

The plastic capsule was transparent all the way round so that the whole of the eyeball was visible. The optic nerve connecting the underside of it to the brain looked like a short length of grey spaghetti.

'Are you feeling all right, William?'

It was a queer sensation peering into her husband's eye when there was no face to go with it. All she had to look at was the eye, and she kept staring at it, and gradually it grew bigger and bigger, and in the end it was the only thing that she could see – a sort of face in itself. There was a network of tiny red veins running over the white surface of the eyeball, and in the ice-blue of the iris there were three or four rather pretty darkish streaks radiating from the pupil in the centre. The pupil was large and black, with a little spark of light reflecting from one side of it.

'I got your letter, dear, and came over at once to see how you were. Dr Landy says you are doing wonderfully well. Perhaps if I talk slowly you can understand a little of what I am saying by reading my lips.'

There was no doubt that the eye was watching her.

'They are doing everything possible to take care of you, dear. This marvellous machine thing here is pumping away all the time and I'm sure it's a lot better than those silly old hearts all the rest of us have. Ours are liable to break down at any moment, but yours will go on for ever.'

She was studying the eye closely, trying to discover what there was about it that gave it such an unusual appearance.

'You seem fine, dear, simply fine. Really you do.'

It looked ever so much nicer, this eye, than either of his eyes used to look, she told herself. There was a softness about it somewhere, a calm, kindly quality that she had never seen before. Maybe it had to do with the dot in the very centre, the pupil. William's pupils used always to be tiny black pinheads. They used to glint at you, stabbing into your brain, seeing right through you, and they always knew at once what you were up to and even what you were thinking. But this one she was looking at now was large and soft and gentle, almost cowlike.

'Are you quite sure he's conscious?' she asked, not looking up.

'Oh yes, completely,' Landy said.

'And he *can* see me?'

'Perfectly.'

'Isn't that marvellous? I expect he's wondering what happened.'

'Not at all. He knows perfectly well where he is and why he's there. He can't possibly have forgotten that.'

'You mean he *knows* he's in this basin?'

'Of course. And if only he had the power of speech, he would probably be able to carry on a perfectly normal conversation with you this very minute. So far as I can see, there should be absolutely no difference mentally between this William here and the one you used to know back home.'

'Good *gracious* me,' Mrs Pearl said, and she paused to consider this intriguing aspect.

You know what, she told herself, looking behind the eye now and staring hard at the great grey pulpy walnut that lay so placidly under the water, I'm not at all sure that I don't prefer him as he is at present. In fact, I believe that I could live very comfortably with this kind of a William. I could cope with this one.

'Quiet, isn't he?' she said.

'Naturally he's quiet.'

No arguments and criticisms, she thought, no constant admonitions, no rules to obey, no ban on smoking cigarettes, no pair of cold disapproving eyes watching me over the top of a book in the evenings, no shirts to wash and iron, no meals to cook – nothing but the throb of the heart machine, which was rather a soothing sound anyway and certainly not loud enough to interfere with television.

'Doctor,' she said. 'I do believe I'm suddenly getting to feel the most enormous affection for him. Does that sound queer?'

'I think it's quite understandable.'

'He looks so helpless and silent lying there under the water in his · little basin.'

'Yes, I know.'

'He's like a baby, that's what he's like. He's exactly like a little baby.'

Landy stood still behind her, watching.

'There,' she said softly, peering into the basin. 'From now on Mary's going to look after you *all* by herself and you've nothing to worry about in the world. When can I have him back home, Doctor?'

'I beg your pardon?'

'I said when can I have him back – back in my own house?'

'You're joking,' Landy said.

She turned her head slowly around and looked directly at him. 'Why should I joke?' she asked. Her face was bright, her eyes round and bright as two diamonds.

'He couldn't possibly be moved.'

'I don't see why not.'

'This is an experiment, Mrs Pearl.'

'It's my husband, Dr Landy.'

A funny little nervous half-smile appeared on Landy's mouth. 'Well ...' he said.

'It *is* my husband, you know.' There was no anger in her voice. She spoke quietly, as though merely reminding him of a simple fact.

'That's rather a tricky point,' Landy said, wetting his lips. 'You're a widow now, Mrs Pearl. I think you must resign yourself to that fact.'

She turned away suddenly from the table and crossed over to the window. 'I mean it,' she said, fishing in her bag for a cigarette. 'I want him back.'

Landy watched her as she put the cigarette between her lips and lit it. Unless he were very much mistaken, there was something a bit odd about this woman, he thought. She seemed almost pleased to have her husband over there in the basin.

He tried to imagine what his own feelings would be if it were *his* wife's brain lying there and *her* eye staring up at him out of that capsule.

He wouldn't like it.

'Shall we go back to my room now?' he said.

She was standing by the window, apparently quite calm and relaxed, puffing her cigarette.

'Yes, all right.'

On her way past the table she stopped and leaned over the basin once more. 'Mary's leaving now, sweetheart,' she said. 'And don't you worry about a single thing, you understand? We're going to get you right back home where we can look after you properly just as soon as we possibly can. And listen dear...' At this point she paused and carried the cigarette to her lips, intending to take a puff.

Instantly the eye flashed.

She was looking straight into it at the time, and right in the centre of it she saw a tiny but brilliant flash of light, and the pupil contracted into a minute black pinpoint of absolute fury.

At first she didn't move. She stood bending over the basin, holding the cigarette up to her mouth, watching the eye.

Then very slowly, deliberately, she put the cigarette between her lips and took a long suck. She inhaled deeply, and she held the smoke inside her lungs for three or four seconds; then suddenly, *whoosh*, out it came through her nostrils in two thin jets which struck the water in the basin and billowed out over the surface in a thick blue cloud, enveloping the eye.

Landy was over by the door, with his back to her, waiting. 'Come on, Mrs Pearl,' he called.

'Don't look so cross, William,' she said softly. 'It isn't any good looking cross.'

Landy turned his head to see what she was doing.

'Not any more it isn't,' she whispered. 'Because from now on, my pet, you're going to do just exactly what Mary tells you. Do you understand that?'

'Mrs Pearl,' Landy said, moving towards her.

'So don't be a naughty boy again, will you, my precious,' she said, taking another pull at the cigarette. 'Naughty boys are liable to get punished most severely nowadays, you ought to know that.'

Landy was beside her now, and he took her by the arm and began drawing her firmly but gently away from the table.

'Good-bye, darling,' she called. 'I'll be back soon.'

'That's enough, Mrs Pearl.'

'Isn't he sweet?' she cried, looking up at Landy with big bright eyes. 'Isn't he heaven? I just can't wait to get him home.'

THE WAY UP TO HEAVEN

All her life, Mrs Foster had had an almost pathological fear of missing a train, a plane, a boat, or even a theatre curtain. In other respects, she was not a particularly nervous woman, but the mere thought of being late on occasions like these would throw her into such a state of nerves that she would begin to twitch. It was nothing much – just a tiny vellicating muscle in the corner of the left eye, like a secret wink – but the annoying thing was that it refused to disappear until an hour or so after the train or plane or whatever it was had been safely caught.

It was really extraordinary how in certain people a simple apprehension about a thing like catching a train can grow into a serious obsession. At least half an hour before it was time to leave the house for the station, Mrs Foster would step out of the elevator all ready to go, with hat and coat and gloves, and then, being quite unable to sit down, she would flutter and fidget about from room to room until her husband, who must have been well aware of her state, finally emerged from his privacy and suggested in a cool dry voice that perhaps they had better get going now, had they not?

Mr Foster may possibly have had a right to be irritated by this foolishness of his wife's, but he could have had no excuse for increasing her misery by keeping her waiting unnecessarily. Mind you, it is by no means certain that this is what he did, yet whenever they were to go somewhere, his timing was so accurate – just a minute or two late, you understand – and his manner so bland that it was hard to believe he wasn't purposely inflicting a nasty private little torture of his own on the unhappy lady. And one thing he must have known – that she would never dare to call out and tell him to hurry. He had disciplined her too well for that. He must also have known that if he was prepared to wait even beyond the last moment of safety, he could drive her nearly into hysterics. On one or two special occasions in the later years of their married life, it seemed almost as though he had *wanted* to miss the train simply in order to intensify the poor woman's suffering.

Assuming (though one cannot be sure) that the husband was guilty, what made his attitude doubly unreasonable was the fact that, with the exception of this one small irrepressible foible, Mrs Foster was and always had been a good and loving wife. For over thirty years, she had served him loyally and well. There was no doubt about this. Even she, a very modest woman, was aware of it, and although she had for years refused to let herself believe that Mr Foster would ever consciously torment her, there had been times recently when she had caught herself beginning to wonder.

Mr Eugene Foster, who was nearly seventy years old, lived with his wife in a large six-storey house in New York City, on East Sixty-second Street, and they had four servants. It was a gloomy place, and few people came to visit them. But on this particular morning in January, the house had come alive and there was a great deal of bustling about. One maid was distributing bundles of dust sheets to every room, while another was draping them over the furniture. The butler was bringing down suitcases and putting them in the hall. The cook kept popping up from the kitchen to have a word with the butler, and Mrs Foster herself, in an old-fashioned fur coat and with a black hat on the top of her head, was flying from room to room and pretending to supervise these operations. Actually, she was thinking of nothing at all except that she was going to miss her plane if her husband didn't come out of his study soon and get ready.

'What time is it, Walker?' she said to the butler as she passed him.

'It's ten minutes past nine, Madam.'

'And has the car come?'

'Yes, Madam, it's waiting. I'm just going to put the luggage in now.'

'It takes an hour to get to Idlewild,' she said. 'My plane leaves at eleven. I have to be there half an hour beforehand for the formalities. I shall be late. I just *know* I'm going to be late.'

'I think you have plenty of time, Madam,' the butler said kindly. 'I warned Mr Foster that you must leave at nine-fifteen. There's still another five minutes.'

'Yes, Walker, I know, I know. But get the luggage in quickly, will you please?'

She began walking up and down the hall, and whenever the butler came by, she asked him the time. This, she kept telling herself, was the *one* plane she must not miss. It had taken months to persuade her husband to allow her to go. If she missed it, he might easily decide that she should cancel the whole thing. And the trouble was that he insisted on coming to the airport to see her off.

'Dear God,' she said aloud, 'I'm going to miss it. I know, I know, I *know* I'm going to miss it.' The little muscle beside the left eye was twitching madly now. The eyes themselves were very close to tears.

'What time is it, Walker?'

'It's eighteen minutes past, Madam.'

'Now I really *will* miss it!' she cried. 'Oh, I wish he would come!'

This was an important journey for Mrs Foster. She was going all alone to Paris to visit her daughter, her only child, who was married to a Frenchman. Mrs Foster didn't care much for the Frenchman, but she was fond of her daughter, and, more than that, she had developed a great yearning to set eyes on her three grandchildren. She knew them only from the many photographs that she had received and that she kept putting up all over the house. They were beautiful, these children. She doted on them, and each time a new picture arrived she would carry it away and sit with it for a long time, staring at it lovingly and searching the small faces for signs of that old satisfying blood likeness that meant so much. And now, lately, she had come more and more to feel that she did not really wish to live out her days in a place where she could not be near these children, and have them visit her, and take them for walks, and buy them presents, and watch them grow. She knew, of course, that it was wrong and in a way disloyal to have thoughts like these while her husband was still alive. She knew also that although he was no longer active in his many enterprises, he would never consent to leave New York and live in Paris. It was a miracle that he had ever agreed to let her fly over there alone for six weeks to visit them. But, oh, how she wished she could live there always, and be close to them!

'Walker, what time is it?'

'Twenty-two minutes past, Madam.'

As he spoke, a door opened and Mr Foster came into the hall. He stood for a moment, looking intently at his wife, and she looked back at him – at this diminutive but still quite dapper old man with the huge bearded face that bore such an astonishing resemblance to those old photographs of Andrew Carnegie.

'Well,' he said, 'I suppose perhaps we'd better get going fairly soon if you want to catch that plane.'

'*Yes*, dear – *yes!* Everything's ready. The car's waiting.'

'That's good,' he said. With his head over to one side, he was watching her closely. He had a peculiar way of cocking the head and then moving it in a series of small, rapid jerks. Because of this and because he was clasping his hands up high in front of him, near the chest, he was somehow like a squirrel standing there – a quick clever old squirrel from the Park.

'Here's Walker with your coat, dear. Put it on.'

'I'll be with you in a moment,' he said. 'I'm just going to wash my hands.'

She waited for him, and the tall butler stood beside her, holding the coat and the hat.

'Walker, will I miss it?'

'No, Madam,' the butler said. 'I think you'll make it all right.'

Then Mr Foster appeared again, and the butler helped him on with his coat. Mrs Foster hurried outside and got into the hired Cadillac. Her husband came after her, but he walked down the steps of the house slowly, pausing halfway to observe the sky and to sniff the cold morning air.

'It looks a bit foggy,' he said as he sat down beside her in the car. 'And it's always worse out there at the airport. I shouldn't be surprised if the flight's cancelled already.'

'Don't say that, dear – *please*.'

They didn't speak again until the car had crossed over the river to Long Island.

'I arranged everything with the servants,' Mr Foster said. 'They're all going off today. I gave them half-pay for six weeks and told Walker I'd send him a telegram when we wanted them back.'

'Yes,' she said. 'He told me.'

'I'll move into the club tonight. It'll be a nice change staying at the club.'

'Yes, dear. I'll write to you.'

'I'll call in at the house occasionally to see that everything's all right and to pick up the mail.'

'But don't you really think Walker should stay there all the time to look after things?' she asked meekly.

'Nonsense. It's quite unnecessary. And anyway, I'd have to pay him full wages.'

'Oh yes,' she said. 'Of course.'

'What's more, you never know what people get up to when they're left alone in a house,' Mr Foster announced, and with that he took out a cigar and, after snipping off the end with a silver cutter, lit it with a gold lighter.

She sat still in the car with her hands clasped together tight under the rug.

'Will you write to me?' she asked.

'I'll see,' he said. 'But I doubt it. You know I don't hold with letter-writing unless there's something specific to say.'

'Yes, dear, I know. So don't you bother.'

They drove on, along Queen's Boulevard, and as they approached the flat marshland on which Idlewild is built, the fog began to thicken and the car had to slow down.

'Oh dear!' cried Mrs Foster. 'I'm *sure* I'm going to miss it now! What time is it?'

'Stop fussing,' the old man said. 'It doesn't matter anyway. It's bound to be cancelled now. They never fly in this sort of weather. I don't know why you bothered to come out.'

She couldn't be sure, but it seemed to her that there was suddenly a new note in his voice, and she turned to look at him. It was difficult to observe any change in his expression under all that hair. The mouth was what counted. She wished, as she had so often before, that she could see the mouth clearly. The eyes never showed anything except when he was in a rage.

'Of course,' he went on, 'if by any chance it *does* go, then I agree with you – you'll be certain to miss it now. Why don't you resign yourself to that?'

She turned away and peered through the window at the fog. It seemed to be getting thicker as they went along, and now she could only just make out the edge of the road and the margin of grassland beyond it. She knew that her husband was still looking at her. She glanced at him again, and this time she noticed with a kind of horror that he was staring intently at the little place in the corner of her left eye where she could feel the muscle twitching.

'Won't you?' he said.

'Won't I what?'

'Be sure to miss it now if it goes. We can't drive fast in this muck.'

He didn't speak to her any more after that. The car crawled on and on. The driver had a yellow lamp directed on to the edge of the road, and this helped him to keep going. Other lights, some white and some yellow, kept coming out of the fog towards them, and there was an especially bright one that followed close behind them all the time.

Suddenly, the driver stopped the car.

'There!' Mr Foster cried. 'We're stuck. I knew it.'

'No, sir,' the driver said, turning round. 'We made it. This is the airport.'

Without a word, Mrs Foster jumped out and hurried through the main entrance into the building. There was a mass of people inside, mostly disconsolate passengers standing around the ticket counters. She pushed her way through and spoke to the clerk.

'Yes,' he said. 'Your flight is temporarily postponed. But please don't go away. We're expecting this weather to clear any moment.'

She went back to her husband who was still sitting in the car and told him the news. 'But don't you wait, dear,' she said. 'There's no sense in that.'

'I won't,' he answered. 'So long as the driver can get me back. Can you get me back, driver?'

'I think so,' the man said.

'Is the luggage out?'

'Yes, sir.'

'Good-bye, dear,' Mrs Foster said, leaning into the car and giving her husband a small kiss on the coarse grey fur of his cheek.

'Good-bye,' he answered. 'Have a good trip.'

The car drove off, and Mrs Foster was left alone.

The rest of the day was a sort of nightmare for her. She sat for hour after hour on a bench, as close to the airline counter as possible, and every thirty minutes or so she would get up and ask the clerk if the situation had changed. She always received the same reply – that she must continue to wait, because the fog might blow away at any moment. It wasn't until after six in the evening that the loudspeakers finally announced that the flight had been postponed until eleven o'clock the next morning.

Mrs Foster didn't quite know what to do when she heard this news. She stayed sitting on her bench for at least another half-hour, wondering, in a tired, hazy sort of way, where she might go to spend the night. She hated to leave the airport. She didn't wish to see her husband. She was terrified that in one way or another he would eventually manage to prevent her from getting to France. She would have liked to remain just where she was, sitting on the bench the whole night through. That would be the safest. But she was already exhausted, and it didn't take her long to realize that this was a ridiculous thing for an elderly lady to do. So in the end she went to a phone and called the house.

Her husband, who was on the point of leaving for the club, answered it himself. She told him the news, and asked whether the servants were still there.

'They've all gone,' he said.

'In that case, dear, I'll just get myself a room somewhere for the night. And don't you bother yourself about it at all.'

'That would be foolish,' he said. 'You've got a large house here at your disposal. Use it.'

'But, dear, it's *empty*.'

'Then I'll stay with you myself.'

'There's no food in the house. There's nothing.'

'Then eat before you come in. Don't be so stupid, woman. Everything you do, you seem to want to make a fuss about it.'

'Yes,' she said. 'I'm sorry. I'll get myself a sandwich here, and then I'll come on in.'

Outside, the fog had cleared a little, but it was still a long, slow drive in the taxi, and she didn't arrive back at the house on Sixty-second Street until fairly late.

Her husband emerged from his study when he heard her coming in. 'Well,' he said, standing by the study door, 'how was Paris?'

'We leave at eleven in the morning,' she answered. 'It's definite.'

'You mean if the fog clears.'

'It's clearing now. There's a wind coming up.'

'You look tired,' he said. 'You must have had an anxious day.'

'It wasn't very comfortable. I think I'll go straight to bed.'

'I've ordered a car for the morning,' he said. 'Nine o'clock.'

'Oh, thank you, dear. And I certainly hope you're not going to bother to come all the way out again to see me off.'

'No,' he said slowly. 'I don't think I will. But there's no reason why you shouldn't drop me at the club on your way.'

She looked at him, and at that moment he seemed to be standing a long way off from her, beyond some borderline. He was suddenly so small and far away that she couldn't be sure what he was doing, or what he was thinking, or even what he was.

'The club is downtown,' she said. 'It isn't on the way to the airport.'

'But you'll have plenty of time, my dear. Don't you want to drop me at the club?'

'Oh, yes – of course.'

'That's good. Then I'll see you in the morning at nine.'

She went up to her bedroom on the second floor, and she was so exhausted from her day that she fell asleep soon after she lay down.

Next morning, Mrs Foster was up early, and by eight-thirty she was downstairs and ready to leave.

Shortly after nine, her husband appeared. 'Did you make any coffee?' he asked.

'No, dear. I thought you'd get a nice breakfast at the club. The car is here. It's been waiting. I'm all ready to go.'

They were standing in the hall – they always seemed to be meeting in the hall nowadays – she with her hat and coat and purse, he in a curiously cut Edwardian jacket with high lapels.

'Your luggage?'

'It's at the airport.'

'Ah yes,' he said. 'Of course. And if you're going to take me to the club first, I suppose we'd better get going fairly soon, hadn't we?'

'Yes!' she cried. 'Oh, yes – *please*!'

'I'm just going to get a few cigars. I'll be right with you. You get in the car.'

She turned and went out to where the chauffeur was standing, and he opened the car door for her as she approached.

'What time is it?' she asked him.

'About nine-fifteen.'

Mr Foster came out five minutes later, and watching him as he walked slowly down the steps, she noticed that his legs were like goat's legs in those narrow stovepipe trousers that he wore. As on the day before, he paused halfway down to sniff the air and to examine the sky. The weather was still not quite clear, but there was a wisp of sun coming through the mist.

'Perhaps you'll be lucky this time,' he said as he settled himself beside her in the car.

'Hurry, please,' she said to the chauffeur. 'Don't bother about the rug. I'll arrange the rug. Please get going. I'm late.'

The man went back to his seat behind the wheel and started the engine.

'*Just* a moment!' Mr Foster said suddenly. 'Hold it a moment, chauffeur, will you?'

'What is it, dear?' She saw him searching the pockets of his overcoat.

'I had a little present I wanted you to take to Ellen,' he said. 'Now, where on earth is it? I'm sure I had it in my hand as I came down.'

'I never saw you carrying anything. What sort of present?'

'A little box wrapped up in white paper. I forgot to give it to you yesterday. I don't want to forget it today.'

'A little box!' Mrs Foster cried. 'I never saw any little box!' She began hunting frantically in the back of the car.

Her husband continued searching through the pockets of his coat. Then he unbuttoned the coat and felt around in his jacket. 'Confound it,' he said, 'I must've left it in my bedroom. I won't be a moment.'

'Oh, *please!*' she cried. 'We haven't got time! *Please* leave it! You can mail it. It's only one of those silly combs anyway. You're always giving her combs.'

'And what's wrong with combs, may I ask?' he said, furious that she should have forgotten herself for once.

'Nothing, dear, I'm sure. But ...'

'Stay here!' he commanded. 'I'm going to get it.'

'Be quick, dear! Oh, *please* be quick!'

She sat still, waiting and waiting.

'Chauffeur, what time is it?'

The man had a wristwatch, which he consulted. 'I make it nearly nine-thirty.'

'Can we get to the airport in an hour?'

'Just about.'

At this point, Mrs Foster suddenly spotted a corner of something white wedged down in the crack of the seat on the side where her husband had been sitting. She reached over and pulled out a small paper-wrapped box, and at the same time she couldn't help noticing that it was wedged down firm and deep, as though with the help of a pushing hand.

'Here it is!' she cried. 'I've found it! Oh dear, and now he'll be up there for ever searching for it! Chauffeur, quickly – run in and call him down, will you please?'

The chauffeur, a man with a small rebellious Irish mouth, didn't care very much for any of this, but he climbed out of the car and went up the steps to the front door of the house. Then he turned and came back. 'Door's locked,' he announced. 'You got a key?'

'Yes – wait a minute.' She began hunting madly in her purse. The little face was screwed up tight with anxiety, the lips pushed outward like a spout.

'Here it is! No – I'll go myself. It'll be quicker. I know where he'll be.'

She hurried out of the car and up the steps to the front door, holding the key in one hand. She slid the key into the keyhole and was about to turn it – and then she stopped. Her head came up, and she stood there absolutely motionless, her whole body arrested right in the middle of all this hurry to turn the key and get into the house, and she waited – five, six, seven, eight, nine, ten seconds, she waited. The way she was standing there, with her head in the air and the body so tense, it seemed as though she were listening for the repetition of some sound that she had heard a moment before from a place far away inside the house.

Yes – quite obviously she was listening. Her whole attitude was a *listening* one. She appeared actually to be moving one of her ears closer and closer to the door. Now it was right up against the door, and for still another few seconds she remained in that position, head up, ear to door, hand on key, about to enter but not entering, trying instead, or so it seemed, to hear and to analyse these sounds that were coming faintly from this place deep within the house.

Then, all at once, she sprang to life again. She withdrew the key from the door and came running back down the steps.

'It's too late!' she cried to the chauffeur. 'I can't wait for him, I simply can't. I'll miss the plane. Hurry now, driver, hurry! To the airport!'

The chauffeur, had he been watching her closely, might have noticed that her face had turned absolutely white and that the whole expression had suddenly altered. There was no longer that rather soft and silly look. A peculiar hardness had settled itself upon the features. The little mouth, usually so flabby, was now tight and thin, the eyes were bright, and the voice, when she spoke, carried a new note of authority.

'Hurry, driver, hurry!'

'Isn't your husband travelling with you?' the man asked, astonished.

'Certainly not! I was only going to drop him at the club. It won't matter. He'll understand. He'll get a cab. Don't sit there talking, man. *Get going!* I've got a plane to catch for Paris!'

With Mrs Foster urging him from the back seat, the man drove fast all the way, and she caught her plane with a few minutes to spare. Soon she was high up over the Atlantic, reclining comfortably in her aeroplane chair, listening to the hum of the motors, heading for Paris at last. The new mood was still with her. She felt remarkably strong and, in a queer sort of way, wonderful. She was a trifle breathless with it all, but this was more from pure astonishment at what she had done than anything else, and as the plane flew farther and farther away from New York and East Sixty-second Street, a great sense of calmness began to settle upon her. By the time she reached Paris, she was just as strong and cool and calm as she could wish.

She met her grandchildren, and they were even more beautiful in the flesh than in their photographs. They were like angels, she told herself, so beautiful they were. And every day she took them for walks, and fed them cakes, and bought them presents, and told them charming stories.

Once a week, on Tuesdays, she wrote a letter to her husband – a nice, chatty letter – full of news and gossip, which always ended with the words 'Now be sure to take your meals regularly, dear, although this is something I'm afraid you may not be doing when I'm not with you.'

When the six weeks were up, everybody was sad that she had to return to America, to her husband. Everybody, that is, except her. Surprisingly, she didn't seem to mind as much as one might have expected, and when she kissed them all good-bye, there was something in her manner and in the things she said that appeared to hint at the possibility of a return in the not too distant future.

However, like the faithful wife she was, she did not overstay her time. Exactly six weeks after she had arrived, she sent a cable to her husband and caught the plane back to New York.

Arriving at Idlewild, Mrs Foster was interested to observe that there was no car to meet her. It is possible that she might even have been a little amused. But she was extremely calm and did not overtip the porter who helped her into a taxi with her baggage.

New York was colder than Paris, and there were lumps of dirty snow lying in the gutters of the streets. The taxi drew up before the house on Sixty-second Street, and Mrs Foster persuaded the driver to carry her two large cases to the top of the steps. Then she paid him off and rang the bell. She waited, but there was no answer. Just to make sure, she rang again, and she could hear it tinkling shrilly far away in the pantry, at the back of the house. But still no one came.

So she took out her own key and opened the door herself.

The first thing she saw as she entered was a great pile of mail lying on the floor where it had fallen after being slipped through the letter box. The place was dark and cold. A dust sheet was still draped over the grandfather clock. In spite of the cold, the atmosphere was peculiarly oppressive, and there was a faint and curious odour in the air that she had never smelled before.

She walked quickly across the hall and disappeared for a moment around the corner to the left, at the back. There was something deliberate and purposeful about this action; she had the air of a woman who is off to investigate a rumour or to confirm a suspicion. And when she returned a few seconds later, there was a little glimmer of satisfaction on her face.

She paused in the centre of the hall, as though wondering what to do next. Then, suddenly, she turned and went across into her husband's

study. On the desk she found his address book, and after hunting
through it for a while she picked up the phone and dialled a number.

'Hello,' she said. 'Listen – this is Nine East Sixty-second Street ...
Yes, that's right. Could you send someone round as soon as possible,
do you think? Yes, it seems to be stuck between the second and third
floors. At least, that's where the indicator's pointing ... Right away?
Oh, that's very kind of you. You see, my legs aren't any too good for
walking up a lot of stairs. Thank you so much. Good-bye.'

She replaced the receiver and sat there at her husband's desk,
patiently waiting for the man who would be coming soon to repair
the lift.

PARSON'S PLEASURE

Mr Boggis was driving the car slowly, leaning back comfortably in the seat with one elbow resting on the sill of the open window. How beautiful the countryside, he thought; how pleasant to see a sign or two of summer once again. The primroses especially. And the hawthorn. The hawthorn was exploding white and pink and red along the hedges and the primroses were growing underneath in little clumps, and it was beautiful.

He took one hand off the wheel and lit himself a cigarette. The best thing now, he told himself, would be to make for the top of Brill Hill. He could see it about half a mile ahead. And that must be the village of Brill, that cluster of cottages among the trees right on the very summit. Excellent. Not many of his Sunday sections had a nice elevation like that to work from.

He drove up the hill and stopped the car just short of the summit on the outskirts of the village. Then he got out and looked around. Down below, the countryside was spread out before him like a huge green carpet. He could see for miles. It was perfect. He took a pad and pencil from his pocket, leaned against the back of the car, and allowed his practised eye to travel slowly over the landscape.

He could see one medium farmhouse over on the right, back in the fields, with a track leading to it from the road. There was another larger one beyond it. There was a house surrounded by tall elms that looked as though it might be a Queen Anne, and there were two likely farms away over on the left. Five places in all. That was about the lot in this direction.

Mr Boggis drew a rough sketch on his pad showing the position of each so that he'd be able to find them easily when he was down below, then he got back into the car and drove up through the village to the other side of the hill. From there he spotted six more possibles – five farms and one big white Georgian house. He studied the Georgian house through his binoculars. It had a clean prosperous look, and the garden was well ordered. That was a pity. He ruled it out immediately. There was no point in calling on the prosperous.

In this square then, in this section, there were ten possibles in all. Ten was a nice number, Mr Boggis told himself. Just the right amount for a leisurely afternoon's work. What time was it now? Twelve o'clock.

He would have liked a pint of beer in the pub before he started, but on Sundays they didn't open until one. Very well, he would have it later. He glanced at the notes on his pad. He decided to take the Queen Anne first, the house with the elms. It had looked nicely dilapidated through the binoculars. The people there could probably do with some money. He was always lucky with Queen Annes, anyway. Mr Boggis climbed back into the car, released the handbrake, and began cruising slowly down the hill without the engine.

Apart from the fact that he was at this moment disguised in the uniform of a clergyman, there was nothing very sinister about Mr Cyril Boggis. By trade he was a dealer in antique furniture, with his own shop and showroom in the King's Road, Chelsea. His premises were not large, and generally he didn't do a great deal of business, but because he always bought cheap, very very cheap, and sold very very dear, he managed to make quite a tidy little income every year. He was a talented salesman, and when buying or selling a piece he could slide smoothly into whichever mood suited the client best. He could become grave and charming for the aged, obsequious for the rich, sober for the godly, masterful for the weak, mischievous for the widow, arch and saucy for the spinster. He was well aware of his gift, using it shamelessly on every possible occasion; and often, at the end of an unusually good performance, it was as much as he could do to prevent himself from turning aside and taking a bow or two as the thundering applause of the audience went rolling through the theatre.

In spite of this rather clownish quality of his, Mr Boggis was not a fool. In fact, it was said of him by some that he probably knew as much about French, English, and Italian furniture as anyone else in London. He also had surprisingly good taste, and he was quick to recognize and reject an ungraceful design, however genuine the article might be. His real love, naturally, was for the work of the great eighteenth-century English designers, Ince, Mayhew, Chippendale, Robert Adam, Manwaring, Inigo Jones, Hepplewhite, Kent, Johnson, George Smith, Lock, Sheraton, and the rest of them, but even with these he occasionally drew the line. He refused, for example, to allow a single piece from Chippendale's Chinese or Gothic period to come into his showroom, and the same was true of some of the heavier Italian designs of Robert Adam.

During the past few years, Mr Boggis had achieved considerable fame among his friends in the trade by his ability to produce unusual and often quite rare items with astonishing regularity. Apparently the man had a source of supply that was almost inexhaustible, a sort of private warehouse, and it seemed that all he had to do was to drive out to it once a week and help himself. Whenever they asked him where he got the stuff, he would smile knowingly and wink and murmur something about a little secret.

The idea behind Mr Boggis's little secret was a simple one, and it had come to him as a result of something that had happened on a certain Sunday afternoon nearly nine years before, while he was driving in the country.

He had gone out in the morning to visit his old mother, who lived in Sevenoaks, and on the way back the fanbelt on his car had broken, causing the engine to overheat and the water to boil away. He had got out of the car and walked to the nearest house, a smallish farm building about fifty yards off the road, and had asked the woman who answered the door if he could please have a jug of water.

While he was waiting for her to fetch it, he happened to glance in through the door to the living-room, and there, not five yards from where he was standing, he spotted something that made him so excited the sweat began to come out all over the top of his head. It was a large oak armchair of a type that he had only seen once before in his life. Each arm, as well as the panel at the back, was supported by a row of eight beautifully turned spindles. The back panel itself was decorated by an inlay of the most delicate floral design, and the head of a duck was carved to lie along half the length of either arm. Good God, he thought. This thing is late fifteenth century!

He poked his head in further through the door, and there, by heavens, was another of them on the other side of the fireplace!

He couldn't be sure, but two chairs like that must be worth at least a thousand pounds up in London. And oh, what beauties they were!

When the woman returned, Mr Boggis introduced himself and straight away asked if she would like to sell her chairs.

Dear me, she said. But why on earth should she want to sell her chairs?

No reason at all, except that he might be willing to give her a pretty nice price.

And how much would he give? They were definitely not for sale, but just out of curiosity, just for fun, you know, how much would he give?

Thirty-five pounds.

How much?

Thirty-five pounds.

Dear me, thirty-five pounds. Well, well, that was very interesting. She'd always thought they were valuable. They were very old. They were very comfortable too. She couldn't possibly do without them, not possibly. No, they were not for sale but thank you very much all the same.

They weren't really so very old, Mr Boggis told her, and they wouldn't be at all easy to sell, but it just happened that he had a client who rather liked that sort of thing. Maybe he could go up another two pounds – call it thirty-seven. How about that?

They bargained for half an hour, and of course in the end Mr Boggis got the chairs and agreed to pay her something less than a twentieth of their value.

That evening, driving back to London in his old station-wagon with the two fabulous chairs tucked away snugly in the back, Mr Boggis had suddenly been struck by what seemed to him to be a most remarkable idea.

Look here, he said. If there is good stuff in one farmhouse, then why not in others? Why shouldn't he search for it? Why shouldn't he comb the countryside? He could do it on Sundays. In that way, it wouldn't interfere with his work at all. He never knew what to do with his Sundays.

So Mr Boggis bought maps, large scale maps of all the counties around London, and with a fine pen he divided each of them up into a series of squares. Each of these squares covered an actual area of five miles by five, which was about as much territory, he estimated, as he could cope with on a single Sunday, were he to comb it thoroughly. He didn't want the towns and the villages. It was the comparatively isolated places, the large farmhouses and the rather dilapidated country mansions, that he was looking for; and in this way, if he did one square each Sunday, fifty-two squares a year, he would gradually cover every farm and every country house in the home counties.

But obviously there was a bit more to it than that. Country folk are a suspicious lot. So are the impoverished rich. You can't go about ringing their bells and expecting them to show you around their houses just for the asking, because they won't do it. That way you would never get beyond the front door. How then was he to gain admittance? Perhaps it would be best if he didn't let them know he was a dealer at all. He could be the telephone man, the plumber, the gas inspector. He could even be a clergyman. . . .

From this point on, the whole scheme began to take on a more practical aspect. Mr Boggis ordered a large quantity of superior cards on which the following legend was engraved:

THE REVEREND
CYRIL WINNINGTON BOGGIS

President of the Society　　　　　　　　In association with
for the Preservation of　　　　　　　　The Victoria and
Rare Furniture　　　　　　　　　　　　Albert Museum

From now on, every Sunday, he was going to be a nice old parson spending his holiday travelling around on a labour of love for the 'Society', compiling an inventory of the treasures that lay hidden in the country homes of England. And who in the world was going to kick him out when they heard that one?

Nobody.

And then, once he was inside, if he happened to spot something he really wanted, well – he knew a hundred different ways of dealing with that.

Rather to Mr Boggis's surprise, the scheme worked. In fact, the friendliness with which he was received in one house after another through the countryside was, in the beginning, quite embarrassing, even to him. A slice of cold pie, a glass of port, a cup of tea, a basket of plums, even a full sit-down Sunday dinner with the family, such things were constantly being pressed upon him. Sooner or later, of course, there had been some bad moments and a number of unpleasant incidents, but then nine years is more than four hundred Sundays, and that adds up to a great quantity of houses visited. All in all, it had been an interesting, exciting, and lucrative business.

And now it was another Sunday and Mr Boggis was operating in the country of Buckinghamshire, in one of the most northerly squares on his map, about ten miles from Oxford, and as he drove down the hill and headed for his first house, the dilapidated Queen Anne, he began to get the feeling that this was going to be one of his lucky days.

He parked the car about a hundred yards from the gates and got out to walk the rest of the way. He never liked people to see his car until after a deal was completed. A dear old clergyman and a large station-wagon somehow never seemed quite right together. Also the short walk gave him time to examine the property closely from the outside and to assume the mood most likely to be suitable for the occasion.

Mr Boggis strode briskly up the drive. He was a small fat-legged man with a belly. The face was round and rosy, quite perfect for the part, and the two large brown eyes that bulged out at you from this rosy face gave an impression of gentle imbecility. He was dressed in a black suit with the usual parson's dog-collar round his neck, and on his head a soft black hat. He carried an old oak walking-stick which lent him, in his opinion, a rather rustic easy-going air.

He approached the front door and rang the bell. He heard the sound of footsteps in the hall and the door opened and suddenly there stood before him, or rather above him, a gigantic woman dressed in riding-breeches. Even through the smoke of her cigarette he could smell the powerful odour of stables and horse manure that clung about her.

'Yes?' she asked, looking at him suspiciously. 'What is it you want?'

Mr Boggis, who half expected her to whinny any moment, raised his hat, made a little bow, and handed her his card. 'I do apologize for bothering you,' he said, and then he waited, watching her face as she read the message.

'I don't understand,' she said, handing back the card. 'What is it you want?'

Mr Boggis explained about the Society for the Preservation of Rare Furniture.

'This wouldn't by any chance be something to do with the Socialist Party?' she asked, staring at him fiercely from under a pair of pale bushy brows.

From then on, it was easy. A Tory in riding-breeches, male or female, was always a sitting duck for Mr Boggis. He spent two minutes delivering an impassioned eulogy on the extreme Right Wing of the Conservative Party, then two more denouncing the Socialists. As a clincher, he made particular reference to the Bill that the Socialists had once introduced for the abolition of bloodsports in the country, and went on to inform his listener that his idea of heaven – 'though you better not tell the bishop, my dear' – was a place where one could hunt the fox, the stag, and the hare with large packs of tireless hounds from morn till night every day of the week, including Sundays.

Watching her as he spoke, he could see the magic beginning to do its work. The woman was grinning now, showing Mr Boggis a set of enormous, slightly yellow teeth. 'Madam,' he cried, 'I beg of you, *please* don't get me started on Socialism.' At that point, she let out a great guffaw of laughter, raised an enormous red hand, and slapped him so hard on the shoulder that he nearly went over.

'Come in!' she shouted. 'I don't know what the hell you want, but come on in!'

Unfortunately, and rather surprisingly, there was nothing of any value in the whole house, and Mr Boggis, who never wasted time on barren territory, soon made his excuses and took his leave. The whole visit had taken less than fifteen minutes, and that, he told himself as he climbed back into his car and started off for the next place, was exactly as it should be.

From now on, it was all farmhouses, and the nearest was about half a mile up the road. It was a large half-timbered brick building of considerable age, and there was a magnificent pear tree still in blossom covering almost the whole of the south wall.

Mr Boggis knocked on the door. He waited, but no one came. He knocked again, but still there was no answer, so he wandered around the back to look for the farmer among the cowsheds. There was no one there either. He guessed that they must all still be in church, so he began peering in the windows to see if he could spot anything interesting. There was nothing in the dining-room. Nothing in the library either. He tried the next window, the living-room, and there, right under his nose, in the little alcove that the window made, he saw a beautiful thing, a semicircular card-table in mahogany, richly veneered, and in the style of Hepplewhite, built around 1780.

'Ah-ha,' he said aloud, pressing his face hard against the glass. 'Well done, Boggis.'

But that was not all. There was a chair there as well, a single chair, and if he were not mistaken it was of an even finer quality than the table. Another Hepplewhite, wasn't it? And oh, what a beauty! The lattices on the back were finely carved with the honeysuckle, the husk, and the paterae, the caning on the seat was original, the legs were very gracefully turned and the two back ones had that peculiar outward splay that meant so much. It was an exquisite chair. 'Before this day is done,' Mr Boggis said softly, 'I shall have the pleasure of sitting down upon that lovely seat.' He never bought a chair without doing this. It was a favourite test of his, and it was always an intriguing sight to see him lowering himself delicately into the seat, waiting for the 'give', expertly gauging the precise but infinitesimal degree of shrinkage that the years had caused in the mortice and dovetail joints.

But there was no hurry, he told himself. He would return here later. He had the whole afternoon before him.

The next farm was situated some way back in the fields, and in order to keep his car out of sight, Mr Boggis had to leave it on the road and walk about six hundred yards along a straight track that led directly into the back yard of the farmhouse. This place, he noticed as he approached, was a good deal smaller than the last, and he didn't hold out much hope for it. It looked rambling and dirty, and some of the sheds were clearly in bad repair.

There were three men standing in a close group in a corner of the yard, and one of them had two large black greyhounds with him, on leashes. When the men caught sight of Mr Boggis walking forward in his black suit and parson's collar, they stopped talking and seemed suddenly to stiffen and freeze, becoming absolutely still, motionless, three faces turned towards him, watching him suspiciously as he approached.

The oldest of the three was a stumpy man with a wide frog-mouth and small shifty eyes, and although Mr Boggis didn't know it, his name was Rummins and he was the owner of the farm.

The tall youth beside him, who appeared to have something wrong with one eye, was Bert, the son of Rummins.

The shortish flat-faced man with a narrow corrugated brow and immensely broad shoulders was Claud. Claud had dropped in on Rummins in the hope of getting a piece of pork or ham out of him from the pig that had been killed the day before. Claud knew about the killing – the noise of it had carried far across the fields – and he also knew that a man should have a government permit to do that sort of thing, and that Rummins didn't have one.

'Good afternoon,' Mr Boggis said. 'Isn't it a lovely day?'

None of the three men moved. At that moment they were all thinking precisely the same thing – that somehow or other this clergyman, who was certainly not the local fellow, had been sent to poke his nose into their business and to report what he found to the government.

'What beautiful dogs,' Mr Boggis said. 'I must say I've never been greyhound-racing myself, but they tell me it's a fascinating sport.'

Again the silence, and Mr Boggis glanced quickly from Rummins to Bert, then to Claud, then back again to Rummins, and he noticed that each of them had the same peculiar expression on his face, something between a jeer and a challenge, with a contemptuous curl to the mouth and a sneer around the nose.

'Might I inquire if you are the owner?' Mr Boggis asked, undaunted, addressing himself to Rummins.

'What is it you want?'

'I do apologize for troubling you, especially on a Sunday.'

Mr Boggis offered his card and Rummins took it and held it up close to his face. The other two didn't move, but their eyes swivelled over to one side, trying to see.

'And what exactly might you be wanting?' Rummins asked.

For the second time that morning, Mr Boggis explained at some length the aims and ideals of the Society for the Preservation of Rare Furniture.

'We don't have any,' Rummins told him when it was over. 'You're wasting your time.'

'Now, just a minute, sir,' Mr Boggis said, raising a finger. 'The last man who said that to me was an old farmer down in Sussex, and when he finally let me into his house, d'you know what I found? A dirty-looking old chair in the corner of the kitchen, and it turned out to be worth *four hundred pounds*! I showed him how to sell it, and he bought himself a new tractor with the money.'

'What on earth are you talking about?' Claud said. 'There ain't no chair in the world worth four hundred pound.'

'Excuse me,' Mr Boggis answered primly, 'but there are plenty of chairs in England worth more than twice that figure. And you know where they are? They're tucked away in the farms and cottages all over the country, with the owners using them as steps and ladders and standing on them with hobnailed boots to reach a pot of jam out of the top cupboard or to hang a picture. This is the truth I'm telling you, my friends.'

Rummins shifted uneasily on his feet. 'You mean to say all you want to do is go inside and stand there in the middle of the room and look around?'

'Exactly,' Mr Boggis said. He was at last beginning to sense what the trouble might be. 'I don't want to pry into your cupboards or into your larder. I just want to look at the furniture to see if you happen to have any treasures here, and then I can write about them in our Society magazine.'

'You know what I think?' Rummins said, fixing him with his small wicked eyes. 'I think you're after buying the stuff yourself. Why else would you be going to all this trouble?'

'Oh, dear me. I only wish I had the money. Of course, if I saw something that I took a great fancy to, and it wasn't beyond my means, I might be tempted to make an offer. But alas, that rarely happens.'

'Well,' Rummins said, 'I don't suppose there's any harm in your taking a look around if that's all you want.' He led the way across the yard to the back door of the farmhouse, and Mr Boggis followed him; so did the son Bert, and Claud with his two dogs. They went through the kitchen, where the only furniture was a cheap deal table with a dead chicken lying on it, and they emerged into a fairly large, exceedingly filthy living-room.

And there it was! Mr Boggis saw it at once, and he stopped dead in his tracks and gave a little shrill gasp of shock. Then he stood there for five, ten, fifteen seconds at least, staring like an idiot, unable to believe, not daring to believe what he saw before him. It *couldn't* be true, not possibly! But the longer he stared, the more true it began to seem. After all, there it was standing against the wall right in front of him, as real and as solid as the house itself. And who in the world could possibly make a mistake about a thing like that? Admittedly it was painted white, but that made not the slightest difference. Some idiot had done that. The paint could easily be stripped off. But good God! Just look at it! And in a place like this!

At this point, Mr Boggis became aware of the three men, Rummins, Bert, and Claud, standing together in a group over by the fireplace, watching him intently. They had seen him stop and gasp and stare, and they must have seen his face turning red, or maybe it was white, but in any event they had seen enough to spoil the whole goddamn business if he didn't do something about it quick. In a flash, Mr Boggis clapped one hand over his heart, staggered to the nearest chair, and collapsed into it, breathing heavily.

'What's the matter with you?' Claud asked.

'It's nothing,' he gasped. 'I'll be all right in a minute. Please – a glass of water. It's my heart.'

Bert fetched him the water, handed it to him, and stayed close beside him, staring down at him with a fatuous leer on his face.

'I thought maybe you were looking at something,' Rummins said. The wide frog-mouth widened a fraction further into a crafty grin, showing the stubs of several broken teeth.

'No, no,' Mr Boggis said. 'Oh dear me, no. It's just my heart. I'm so sorry. It happens every now and then. But it goes away quite quickly. I'll be all right in a couple of minutes.'

He *must* have time to think, he told himself. More important still, he must have time to compose himself thoroughly before he said another word. Take it gently, Boggis. And whatever you do, keep calm. These people may be ignorant, but they are not stupid. They are suspicious and wary and sly. And if it is really true – no it *can't* be, it *can't* be true ...

He was holding one hand up over his eyes in a gesture of pain, and now, very carefully, secretly, he made a little crack between two of the fingers and peeked through.

Sure enough, the thing was still there, and on this occasion he took a good long look at it. Yes – he had been right the first time! There wasn't the slightest doubt about it! It was really unbelievable!

What he saw was a piece of furniture that any expert would have given almost anything to acquire. To a layman, it might not have appeared particularly impressive, especially when covered over as it was with dirty white paint, but to Mr Boggis it was a dealer's dream. He knew, as does every other dealer in Europe and America, that among the most celebrated and coveted examples of eighteenth-century English furniture in existence are the three famous pieces known as 'The Chippendale Commodes'. He knew their history backwards – that the first was 'discovered' in 1920, in a house at Moreton-in-Marsh, and was sold at Sotheby's the same year; that the other two turned up in the same auction rooms a year later, both coming out of Raynham Hall, Norfolk. They all fetched enormous prices. He couldn't quite remember the exact figure for the first one, or even the second, but he knew for certain that the last one to be sold had fetched thirty-nine hundred guineas. And that was in 1921! Today the same piece would surely be worth ten thousand pounds. Some man, Mr Boggis couldn't remember his name, had made a study of these commodes fairly recently and had proved that all three must have come from the same workshop, for the veneers were all from the same log, and the same set of templates had been used in the construction of each. No invoices had been found for any of them, but all the experts were agreed that these three commodes could have been executed only by Thomas Chippendale himself, with his own hands, at the most exalted period in his career.

And here, Mr Boggis kept telling himself as he peered cautiously through the crack in his fingers, here was the fourth Chippendale Commode! And *he* had found it! He would be rich! He would also be famous! Each of the other three was known throughout the furniture world by a special name – The Chastleton Commode, The First Raynham Commode, The Second Raynham Commode. This one

would go down in history as The Boggis Commode! Just imagine the
faces of the boys up there in London when they got a look at it
tomorrow morning! And the luscious offers coming in from the big
fellows over in the West End – Frank Partridge, Mallet, Jetley, and
the rest of them! There would be a picture of it in *The Times*, and it
would say, 'The very fine Chippendale Commode which was recently
discovered by Mr Cyril Boggis, a London dealer. . . .' Dear God, what
a stir he was going to make!

This one here, Mr Boggis thought, was almost exactly similar to the
Second Raynham Commode. (All three, the Chastleton and the two
Raynhams, differed from one another in a number of small ways.) It
was a most impressive handsome affair, built in the French rococo
style of Chippendale's Directoire period, a kind of large fat chest-of-
drawers set upon four carved and fluted legs that raised it about a
foot from the ground. There were six drawers in all, two long ones in
the middle and two shorter ones on either side. The serpentine front
was magnificently ornamented along the top and sides and bottom,
and also vertically between each set of drawers, with intricate carvings
of festoons and scrolls and clusters. The brass handles, although partly
obscured by white paint, appeared to be superb. It was, of course, a
rather 'heavy' piece, but the design had been executed with such
elegance and grace that the heaviness was in no way offensive.

'How're you feeling now?' Mr Boggis heard someone saying.

'Thank you, thank you, I'm much better already. It passes quickly.
My doctor says it's nothing to worry about really so long as I rest for
a few minutes whenever it happens. Ah yes,' he said, raising himself
slowly to his feet. 'That's better. I'm all right now.'

A trifle unsteadily, he began to move around the room examining
the furniture, one piece at a time, commenting upon it briefly. He
could see at once that apart from the commode it was a very poor lot.

'Nice oak table,' he said. 'But I'm afraid it's not old enough to be
of any interest. Good comfortable chairs, but quite modern, yes, quite
modern. Now this cupboard, well, it's rather attractive, but again, not
valuable. This chest-of-drawers' – he walked casually past the
Chippendale Commode and gave it a little contemptuous flip with his
fingers – 'worth a few pounds, I dare say, but no more. A rather crude
reproduction, I'm afraid. Probably made in Victorian times. Did you
paint it white?'

'Yes,' Rummins said, 'Bert did it.'

'A very wise move. It's considerably less offensive in white.'

'That's a strong piece of furniture,' Rummins said. 'Some nice
carving on it too.'

'Machine-carved,' Mr Boggis answered superbly, bending down to
examine the exquisite craftsmanship. 'You can tell it a mile off. But
still, I suppose it's quite pretty in its way. It has its points.'

He began to saunter off, then he checked himself and turned slowly back again. He placed the tip of one finger against the point of his chin, laid his head over to one side, and frowned as though deep in thought.

'You know what?' he said, looking at the commode, speaking so casually that his voice kept trailing off. 'I've just remembered ... I've been wanting a set of legs something like that for a long time. I've got a rather curious table in my own little home, one of those low things that people put in front of the sofa, sort of a coffee-table, and last Michaelmas, when I moved house, the foolish movers damaged the legs in the most shocking way. I'm very fond of that table. I always keep my big Bible on it, and all my sermon notes.'

He paused, stroking his chin with the finger. 'Now I was just thinking. These legs on your chest-of-drawers might be very suitable. Yes, they might indeed. They could easily be cut off and fixed on to my table.'

He looked around and saw the three men standing absolutely still, watching him suspiciously, three pairs of eyes, all different but equally mistrusting, small pig-eyes for Rummins, large slow eyes for Claud, and two odd eyes for Bert, one of them very queer and boiled and misty pale, with a little black dot in the centre, like a fish eye on a plate.

Mr Boggis smiled and shook his head. 'Come, come, what on earth am I saying? I'm talking as though I owned the piece myself. I do apologize.'

'What you mean to say is you'd like to buy it,' Rummins said.

'Well ...' Mr Boggis glanced back at the commode, frowning. 'I'm not sure. I might ... and then again ... on second thoughts ... no ... I think it might be a bit too much trouble. It's not worth it. I'd better leave it.'

'How much were you thinking of offering?' Rummins asked.

'Not much, I'm afraid. You see, this is not a genuine antique. It's merely a reproduction.'

'I'm not so sure about that,' Rummins told him. 'It's been in *here* over twenty years, and before that it was up at the Manor House. I bought it there myself at auction when the old Squire died. You can't tell me that thing's new.'

'It's not exactly new, but it's certainly not more than about sixty years old.'

'It's more than that,' Rummins said. 'Bert, where's that bit of paper you once found at the back of one of them drawers? That old bill.'

The boy looked vacantly at his father.

Mr Boggis opened his mouth, then quickly shut it again without uttering a sound. He was beginning literally to shake with excitement, and to calm himself he walked over to the window and stared out at a plump brown hen pecking around for stray grains of corn in the yard.

'It was in the back of that drawer underneath all them rabbit-snares,' Rummins was saying. 'Go on and fetch it out and show it to the parson.'

When Bert went forward to the commode, Mr Boggis turned round again. He couldn't stand not watching him. He saw him pull out one of the big middle drawers, and he noticed the beautiful way in which the drawer slid open. He saw Bert's hand dipping inside and rummaging around among a lot of wires and strings.

'You mean this?' Bert lifted out a piece of folded yellowing paper and carried it over to the father, who unfolded it and held it up close to his face.

'You can't tell me this writing ain't bloody old,' Rummins said, 'and he held the paper out to Mr Boggis, whose whole arm was shaking as he took it. It was brittle and it cracked slightly between his fingers. The writing was in a long sloping copperplate hand:

Edward Montagu, Esq.   Dr
                          To Thos. Chippendale
A large mahogany Commode Table of exceeding fine wood, very rich carvd, set upon fluted legs, two very neat shapd long drawers in the middle part and two ditto on each side, with rich chasd Brass Handles and Ornaments, the whole completely finished in the most exquisite taste.. £87

Mr Boggis was holding on to himself tight and fighting to suppress the excitement that was spinning round inside him and making him dizzy. Oh God, it was wonderful! With the invoice, the value had climbed even higher. What in heaven's name would it fetch now? Twelve thousand pounds? Fourteen? Maybe fifteen or even twenty? Who knows?

Oh, boy!

He tossed the paper contemptuously on to the table and said quietly, 'It's exactly what I told you, a Victorian reproduction. This is simply the invoice that the seller – the man who made it and passed it off as an antique – gave to his client. I've seen lots of them. You'll notice that he doesn't say he made it himself. That would give the game away.'

'Say what you like,' Rummins announced, 'but that's an old piece of paper.'

'Of course it is, my dear friend. It's Victorian, late Victorian. About eighteen ninety. Sixty or seventy years old. I've seen hundreds of them.

That was a time when masses of cabinet-makers did nothing else but apply themselves to faking the fine furniture of the century before.'

'Listen, Parson,' Rummins said, pointing at him with a thick dirty finger, 'I'm not saying as how you may not know a fair bit about this furniture business, but what I *am* saying is this: How on earth can you be so mighty sure it's a fake when you haven't even seen what it looks like underneath all that paint?'

'Come here,' Mr Boggis said. 'Come over here and I'll show you.' He stood beside the commode and waited for them to gather round. 'Now, anyone got a knife?'

Claud produced a horn-handled pocket knife, and Mr Boggis took it and opened the smallest blade. Then, working with apparent casualness but actually with extreme care, he began chipping off the white paint from a small area on the top of the commode. The paint flaked away cleanly from the old hard varnish underneath, and when he had cleared away about three square inches, he stepped back and said, 'Now, take a look at that!'

It was beautiful – a warm little patch of mahogany, glowing like a topaz, rich and dark with the true colour of its two hundred years.

'What's wrong with it?' Rummins asked.

'It's processed! Anyone can see that!'

'How can you see it, Mister? You tell us.'

'Well, I must say that's a trifle difficult to explain. It's chiefly a matter of experience. My experience tells me that without the slightest doubt this wood has been processed with lime. That's what they use for mahogany, to give it that dark aged colour. For oak, they use potash salts, and for walnut it's nitric acid, but for mahogany it's always lime.'

The three men moved a little closer to peer at the wood. There was a slight stirring of interest among them now. It was always intriguing to hear about some new form of crookery or deception.

'Look closely at the grain. You see that touch of orange in among the dark red-brown. That's the sign of lime.'

They leaned forward, their noses close to the wood, first Rummins, then Claud, then Bert.

'And then there's the patina,' Mr Boggis continued.

'The what?'

He explained to them the meaning of this word as applied to furniture.

'My dear friends, you've no idea the trouble these rascals will go to to imitate the hard beautiful bronze-like appearance of genuine patina. It's terrible, really terrible, and it makes me quite sick to speak of it!' He was spitting each word sharply off the tip of the tongue and making a sour mouth to show his extreme distaste. The men waited, hoping for more secrets.

'The time and trouble that some mortals will go to in order to deceive the innocent!' Mr Boggis cried. 'It's perfectly disgusting! D'you know what they did here, my friends? I can recognize it clearly. I can almost *see* them doing it, the long, complicated ritual of rubbing the wood with linseed oil, coating it over with french polish that has been cunningly coloured, brushing it down with pumice-stone and oil, bees-waxing it with a wax that contains dirt and dust, and finally giving it the heat treatment to crack the polish so that it looks like two-hundred-year-old varnish! It really upsets me to contemplate such knavery!'

The three men continued to gaze at the little patch of dark wood.

'Feel it!' Mr Boggis ordered. 'Put your fingers on it! There, how does it feel, warm or cold?'

'Feels cold,' Rummins said.

'Exactly, my friend! It happens to be a fact that faked patina is always cold to the touch. Real patina has a curiously warm feel to it.'

'This feels normal,' Rummins said, ready to argue.

'No, sir, it's cold. But of course it takes an experienced and sensitive finger-tip to pass a positive judgement. You couldn't really be expected to judge this any more than I could be expected to judge the quality of your barley. Everything in life, my dear sir, is experience.'

The men were staring at this queer moon-faced clergyman with the bulging eyes, not quite so suspiciously now because he did seem to know a bit about his subject. But they were still a long way from trusting him.

Mr Boggis bent down and pointed to one of the metal drawer-handles on the commode. 'This is another place where the fakers go to work,' he said. 'Old brass normally has a colour and character all of its own. Did you know that?'

They stared at him, hoping for still more secrets.

'But the trouble is that they've become exceedingly skilled at matching it. In fact it's almost impossible to tell the difference between "genuine old" and "faked old". I don't mind admitting that it has me guessing. So there's not really any point in our scraping the paint off these handles. We wouldn't be any the wiser.'

'How can you possibly make new brass look like old?' Claud said. 'Brass doesn't rust, you know.'

'You are quite right, my friend. But these scoundrels have their own secret methods.'

'Such as what?' Claud asked. Any information of this nature was valuable, in his opinion. One never knew when it might come in handy.

'All they have to do,' Mr Boggis said, 'is to place these handles overnight in a box of mahogany shavings saturated in sal ammoniac. The sal ammoniac turns the metal green, but if you rub off the green, you will find underneath it a fine soft silvery-warm lustre, a lustre identical to that which comes with very old brass. Oh, it is so bestial, the things they do! With iron they have another trick.'

'What do they do with iron?' Claud asked, fascinated.

'Iron's easy,' Mr Boggis said. 'Iron locks and plates and hinges are simply buried in common salt and they come out all rusted and pitted in no time.'

'All right,' Rummins said. 'So you admit you can't tell about the handles. For all you know, they may be hundreds and hundreds of years old. Correct?'

'Ah,' Mr Boggis whispered, fixing Rummins with two big bulging brown eyes. 'That's where you're wrong. Watch this.'

From his jacket pocket, he took out a small screwdriver. At the same time, although none of them saw him do it, he also took out a little brass screw which he kept well hidden in the palm of his hand. Then he selected one of the screws in the commode – there were four to each handle – and began carefully scraping all traces of white paint from its head. When he had done this, he started slowly to unscrew it.

'If this is a genuine old brass screw from the eighteenth century,' he was saying, 'the spiral will be slightly uneven and you'll be able to see quite easily that it has been hand-cut with a file. But if this brasswork is faked from more recent times, Victorian or later, then obviously the screw will be of the same period. It will be a mass-produced, machine-made article. Anyone can recognize a machine-made screw. Well, we shall see.'

It was not difficult, as he put his hands over the old screw and drew it out, for Mr Boggis to substitute the new one hidden in his palm. This was another little trick of his, and through the years it had proved a most rewarding one. The pockets of his clergyman's jacket were always stocked with a quantity of cheap brass screws of various sizes.

'There you are,' he said, handing the modern screw to Rummins. 'Take a look at that. Notice the exact evenness of the spiral? See it? Of course you do. It's just a cheap common little screw you yourself could buy today in any ironmonger's in the country.'

The screw was handed round from the one to the other, each examining it carefully. Even Rummins was impressed now.

Mr Boggis put the screwdriver back in his pocket together with the fine hand-cut screw that he'd taken from the commode, and then he turned and walked slowly past the three men towards the door.

'My dear friends,' he said, pausing at the entrance to the kitchen, 'it was so good of you to let me peep inside your little home – so kind. I do hope I haven't been a terrible old bore.'

Rummins glanced up from examining the screw. 'You didn't tell us what you were going to offer,' he said.

'Ah,' Mr Boggis said. 'That's quite right. I didn't, did I? Well, to tell you the honest truth, I think it's all a bit too much trouble. I think I'll leave it.'

'How much would you give?'

'You mean that you really wish to part with it?'

'I didn't say I wished to part with it. I asked you how much.'

Mr Boggis looked across at the commode, and he laid his head first to one side, then to the other, and he frowned, and pushed out his lips, and shrugged his shoulders, and gave a little scornful wave of the hand as though to say the thing was hardly worth thinking about really, was it?

'Shall we say ... ten pounds. I think that would be fair.'

'Ten pounds!' Rummins cried. 'Don't be so ridiculous, Parson, *please*!'

'It's worth more'n that for firewood!' Claud said, disgusted.

'Look here at the bill!' Rummins went on, stabbing that precious document so fiercely with his dirty fore-finger that Mr Boggis became alarmed. 'It tells you exactly what it cost! Eighty-seven pounds! And that's when it was new. Now it's antique it's worth double!'

'If you'll pardon me, no, sir, it's not. It's a second-hand reproduction. But I'll tell you what, my friend – I'm being rather reckless, I can't help it – I'll go up as high as fifteen pounds. How's that?'

'Make it fifty,' Rummins said.

A delicious little quiver like needles ran all the way down the back of Mr Boggis's legs and then under the soles of his feet. He had it now. It was his. No question about that. But the habit of buying cheap, as cheap as it was humanly possible to buy, acquired by years of necessity and practice, was too strong in him now to permit him to give in so easily.

'My dear man,' he whispered softly, 'I only *want* the legs. Possibly I could find some use for the drawers later on, but the rest of it, the carcass itself, as your friend so rightly said, it's firewood, that's all.'

'Make it thirty-five,' Rummins said.

'I *couldn't* sir, I *couldn't*! It's not worth it. And I simply mustn't allow myself to haggle like this about a price. It's all wrong. I'll make you one final offer, and then I must go. Twenty pounds.'

'I'll take it,' Rummins snapped. 'It's yours.'

'Oh dear,' Mr Boggis said, clasping his hands. 'There I go again. I should never have started this in the first place.'

'You can't back out now, Parson. A deal's a deal.'

'Yes, yes, I know.'

'How're you going to take it?'

'Well, let me see. Perhaps if I were to drive my car up into the yard, you gentlemen would be kind enough to help me load it?'

'In a car? This thing'll never go in a car! You'll need a truck for this!'

'I don't think so. Anyway, we'll see. My car's on the road. I'll be back in a jiffy. We'll manage it somehow, I'm sure.'

Mr Boggis walked out into the yard and through the gate and then down the long track that led across the field towards the road. He found himself giggling quite uncontrollably, and there was a feeling inside him as though hundreds and hundreds of tiny bubbles were rising up from his stomach and bursting merrily in the top of his head, like sparkling-water. All the buttercups in the field were suddenly turning into golden sovereigns, glistening in the sunlight. The ground was littered with them, and he swung off the track on to the grass so that he could walk among them and tread on them and hear the little metallic tinkle they made as he kicked them around with his toes. He was finding it difficult to stop himself from breaking into a run. But clergymen never run; they walk slowly. Walk slowly, Boggis. Keep calm, Boggis. There's no hurry now. The commode is yours! Yours for twenty pounds, and it's worth fifteen or twenty thousand! The Boggis Commode! In ten minutes it'll be loaded into your car – it'll go in easily – and you'll be driving back to London and singing all the way! Mr Boggis driving the Boggis Commode home in the Boggis car. Historic occasion. What *wouldn't* a newspaperman give to get a picture of that! Should he arrange it? Perhaps he should. Wait and see. Oh, glorious day! Oh, lovely sunny summer day! Oh, glory be!

Back in the farmhouse, Rummins was saying, 'Fancy that old bastard giving twenty pound for a load of junk like this.'

'You did very nicely, Mr Rummins,' Claud told him. 'You think he'll pay you?'

'We don't put it in the car till he do.'

'And what if it won't go in the car?' Claud asked. 'You know what I think, Mr Rummins? You want my honest opinion? I think the blody thing's too big to go in the car. And then what happens? Then he's going to say to hell with it and just drive off without it and you'll never see him again. Nor the money either. He didn't seem all that keen on having it, you know.'

Rummins paused to consider this new and rather alarming prospect.

'How can a thing like that possibly go in a car?' Claud went on relentlessly. 'A parson never has a big car anyway. You ever seen a parson with a big car, Mr Rummins?'

'Can't say I have.'

'Exactly! And now listen to me. I've got an idea. He told us, didn't he, that it was only the legs he was wanting. Right? So all we've got to do is to cut 'em off quick right here on the spot before he comes back, then it'll be sure to go in the car. All we're doing is saving him the trouble of cutting them off himself when he gets home. How about it, Mr Rummins?' Claud's flat bovine face glimmered with a mawkish pride.

'It's not such a bad idea at that,' Rummins said, looking at the commode. 'In fact it's a bloody good idea. Come on then, we'll have to hurry. You and Bert carry it out into the yard. I'll get the saw. Take the drawers out first.'

Within a couple of minutes, Claud and Bert had carried the commode outside and had laid it upside down in the yard amidst the chicken droppings and cow dung and mud. In the distance, half-way across the field, they could see a small black figure striding along the path towards the road. They paused to watch. There was something rather comical about the way in which this figure was conducting itself. Every now and again it would break into a trot, then it did a kind of hop, skip, and jump, and once it seemed as though the sound of a cheerful song came rippling faintly to them from across the meadow.

'I reckon he's balmy,' Claud said, and Bert grinned darkly, rolling his misty eye slowly round in its socket.

Rummins came waddling over from the shed, squat and froglike, carrying a long saw. Claud took the saw away from him and went to work.

'Cut 'em close,' Rummins said. 'Don't forget he's going to use 'em on another table.'

The mahogany was hard and very dry, and as Claud worked, a fine red dust sprayed out from the edge of the saw and fell softly to the ground. One by one, the legs came off, and when they were all severed, Bert stopped down and arranged them carefully in a row.

Claud stepped back to survey the results of his labour. There was a longish pause.

'Just let me ask you one question, Mr Rummins,' he said slowly. 'Even now, could *you* put that enormous thing into the back of a car?'

'Not unless it was a van.'

'Correct!' Claud cried. 'And parsons don't have vans, you know. All they've got usually is piddling little Morris Eights or Austin Sevens.'

'The legs is all he wants,' Rummins said. 'If the rest of it won't go in, then he can leave it. He can't complain. He's got the legs.'

'Now you know better'n that, Mr Rummins,' Claud said patiently. 'You know damn well he's going to start knocking the price if he don't get every single bit of this into the car. A parson's just as cunning as the rest of 'em when it comes to money, don't you make any mistake about that. Especially this old boy. So why don't we give him his firewood now and be done with it. Where d'you keep the axe?'

'I reckon that's fair enough,' Rummins said. 'Bert, go fetch the axe.'

Bert went into the shed and fetched a tall woodcutter's axe and gave it to Claud. Claud spat on the palms of his hands and rubbed them together. Then, with a long-armed high-swinging action, he began fiercely attacking the legless carcass of the commode.

It was hard work, and it took several minutes before he had the whole thing more or less smashed to pieces.

'I'll tell you one thing,' he said, straightening up, wiping his brow. 'That was a bloody good carpenter put this job together and I don't care what the parson says.'

'We're just in time!' Rummins called out. 'Here he comes!'

MRS BIXBY
AND THE COLONEL'S COAT

America is the land of opportunities for women. Already they own about eighty-five per cent of the wealth of the nation. Soon they will have it all. Divorce has become a lucrative process, simple to arrange and easy to forget; and ambitious females can repeat it as often as they please and parlay their winnings to astronomical figures. The husband's death also brings satisfactory rewards and some ladies prefer to rely upon this method. They know that the waiting period will not be unduly protracted, for overwork and hypertension are bound to get the poor devil before long, and he will die at his desk with a bottle of benzedrines in one hand and a packet of tranquillizers in the other.

Succeeding generations of youthful American males are not deterred in the slightest by this terrifying pattern of divorce and death. The higher the divorce rate climbs, the more eager they become. Young men marry like mice, almost before they have reached the age of puberty, and a large proportion of them have at least two ex-wives on the payroll by the time they are thirty-six years old. To support these ladies in the manner to which they are accustomed, the men must work like slaves, which is of course precisely what they are. But now at last, as they approach their premature middle age, a sense of disillusionment and fear begins to creep slowly into their hearts, and in the evenings they take to huddling together in little groups, in clubs and bars, drinking their whiskies and swallowing their pills, and trying to comfort one another with stories.

The basic theme of these stories never varies. There are always three main characters – the husband, the wife, and the dirty dog. The husband is a decent clean-living man, working hard at his job. The wife is cunning, deceitful, and lecherous, and she is invariably up to some sort of jiggery-pokery with the dirty dog. The husband is too good a man even to suspect her. Things look black for the husband. Will the poor man ever find out? Must he be a cuckold for the rest of his life? Yes, he must. But wait! Suddenly, by a brilliant manoeuvre, the husband completely turns the tables on his monstrous spouse. The woman is flabbergasted, stupefied, humiliated, defeated. The audience of men around the bar smiles quietly to itself and takes a little comfort from the fantasy.

There are many of these stories going around, these wonderful wishful-thinking dreamworld inventions of the unhappy male, but most of them are too fatuous to be worth repeating, and far too fruity to be put down on paper. There is one, however, that seems to be superior to the rest, particularly as it has the merit of being true. It is extremely popular with twice- or thrice-bitten males in search of solace, and if you are one of them, and if you haven't heard it before, you may enjoy the way it comes out. The story is called 'Mrs Bixby and the Colonel's Coat', and it goes something like this:

Mr and Mrs Bixby lived in a smallish apartment somewhere in New York City. Mr Bixby was a dentist who made an average income. Mrs Bixby was a big vigorous woman with a wet mouth. Once a month, always on Friday afternoons, Mrs Bixby would board the train at Pennsylvania Station and travel to Baltimore to visit her old aunt. She would spend the night with the aunt and return to New York on the following day in time to cook supper for her husband. Mr Bixby accepted this arrangement good-naturedly. He knew that Aunt Maude lived in Baltimore, and that his wife was very fond of the old lady, and certainly it would be unreasonable to deny either of them the pleasure of a monthly meeting.

'Just so long as you don't ever expect me to accompany you,' Mr Bixby had said in the beginning.

'Of course not, darling,' Mrs Bixby had answered. 'After all, she is not *your* aunt. She's mine.'

So far so good.

As it turned out, however, the aunt was little more than a convenient alibi for Mrs Bixby. The dirty dog, in the shape of a gentleman known as the Colonel, was lurking slyly in the background, and our heroine spent the greater part of her Baltimore time in this scoundrel's company. The Colonel was exceedingly wealthy. He lived in a charming house on the outskirts of the town. No wife or family encumbered him, only a few discreet and loyal servants, and in Mrs Bixby's absence he consoled himself by riding his horses and hunting the fox.

Year after year, this pleasant alliance between Mrs Bixby and the Colonel continued without a hitch. They met so seldom – twelve times a year is not much when you come to think of it – that there was little or no chance of their growing bored with one another. On the contrary, the long wait between meetings only made the heart grow fonder, and each separate occasion became an exciting reunion.

'Tally-ho!' the Colonel would cry each time he met her at the station in the big car. 'My dear, I'd almost forgotten how ravishing you looked. Let's go to earth.'

Eight years went by.

It was just before Christmas, and Mrs Bixby was standing on the station in Baltimore waiting for the train to take her back to New York. This particular visit which had just ended had been more than usually agreeable, and she was in a cheerful mood. But then the Colonel's company always did that to her these days. The man had a way of making her feel that she was altogether a rather remarkable woman, a person of subtle and

exotic talents, fascinating beyond measure; and what a very different thing
that was from the dentist husband at home who never succeeded in making
her feel that she was anything but a sort of eternal patient, someone who
dwelt in the waiting-room, silent among the magazines, seldom if ever
nowadays to be called in to suffer the finicky precise ministrations of those
clean pink hands.

'The Colonel asked me to give you this,' a voice beside her said. She
turned and saw Wilkins, the Colonel's groom, a small wizened dwarf with
grey skin, and he was pushing a large flattish cardboard box into her
arms.

'Good gracious me!' she cried, all of a flutter. 'My heavens, what an
enormous box! What is it, Wilkins? Was there a message? Did he send me
a message?'

'No message,' the groom said, and he walked away.

As soon as she was on the train, Mrs Bixby carried the box into the
privacy of the Ladies' Room and locked the door. How exciting this was!
A Christmas present from the Colonel. She started to undo the string. 'I'll
bet it's a dress,' she said aloud. 'It might even be two dresses. Or it might
be a whole lot of beautiful underclothes. I won't look. I'll just feel around
and try to guess what it is. I'll try to guess the colour as well, and exactly
what it looks like. Also how much it cost.'

She shut her eyes tight and slowly lifted off the lid. Then she put one
hand down into the box. There was some tissue paper on top; she could
feel it and hear it rustling. There was also an envelope or a card of some
sort. She ignored this and began burrowing underneath the tissue paper,
the fingers reaching out delicately, like tendrils.

'My God,' she cried suddenly. 'It can't be true!'

She opened her eyes wide and stared at the coat. Then she pounced on
it and lifted it out of the box. Thick layers of fur made a lovely noise
against the tissue paper as they unfolded, and when she held it up and
saw it hanging to its full length, it was so beautiful it took her breath
away.

Never had she seen mink like this before. It *was* mink, wasn't it? Yes,
of course it was. But what a glorious colour! The fur was almost pure
black. At first she thought it *was* black; but when she held it closer to the
window she saw that there was a touch of blue in it as well, a deep rich
blue, like cobalt. Quickly she looked at the label. It said simply, WILD
LABRADOR MINK. There was nothing else, no sign of where it had been
bought or anything. But that, she told herself, was probably the Colonel's
doing. The wily old fox was making darn sure he didn't leave any tracks.
Good for him. But what in the world could it have cost? She hardly dared
to think. Four, five, six thousand dollars? Possibly more.

She just couldn't take her eyes off it. Nor, for that matter, could she
wait to try it on. Quickly she slipped off her own plain red coat. She was
panting a little now, she couldn't help it, and her eyes were stretched very

wide. But oh God, the feel of that fur! And those huge wide sleeves with their thick turned-up cuffs! Who was it had once told her that they always used female skins for the arms and male skins for the rest of the coat? Someone had told her that. Joan Rutfield, probably; though how *Joan* would know anything about *mink* she couldn't imagine.

The great black coat seemed to slide on to her almost of its own accord, like a second skin. Oh boy! It was the queerest feeling! She glanced into the mirror. It was fantastic. Her whole personality had suddenly changed completely. She looked dazzling, radiant, rich, brilliant, voluptuous, all at the same time. And the sense of power that it gave her! In this coat she could walk into any place she wanted and people would come scurrying around her like rabbits. The whole thing was just too wonderful for words!

Mrs Bixby picked up the envelope that was still lying in the box. She opened it and pulled out the Colonel's letter:

> I once heard you saying you were fond of mink so I got you this. I'm told it's a good one. Please accept it with my sincere good wishes as a parting gift. For my own personal reasons I shall not be able to see you any more. Good-bye and good luck.

Well!
Imagine that!
Right out of the blue, just when she was feeling so happy.
No more Colonel.
What a dreadful shock.
She would miss him enormously.

Slowly, Mrs Bixby began stroking the lovely soft black fur of the coat.

What you lose on the swings you get back on the roundabouts.

She smiled and folded the letter, meaning to tear it up and throw it out of the window, but in folding it she noticed that there was something written on the other side:

> PS. Just tell them that nice generous aunt of yours gave it to you for Christmas.

Mrs Bixby's mouth, at that moment stretched wide in a silky smile, snapped back like a piece of elastic.

'The man must be mad!' she cried. 'Aunt Maude doesn't have that sort of money. She couldn't possibly give me this.'

But if Aunt Maude didn't give it to her, then who did?

Oh God! In the excitement of finding the coat and trying it on, she had completely overlooked this vital aspect.

In a couple of hours she would be in New York. Ten minutes after that she would be home, and the husband would be there to greet her; and even a man like Cyril, dwelling as he did in a dark phlegmy world of root canals, bicuspids, and caries, would start asking a few questions if his wife suddenly waltzed in from a week-end wearing a six-thousand-dollar mink coat.

You know what I think, she told herself. I think that goddamn Colonel has done this on purpose just to torture me. He knew perfectly well Aunt Maude didn't have enough money to buy this. He knew I wouldn't be able to keep it.

But the thought of parting with it now was more than Mrs Bixby could bear.

'I've *got* to have this coat!' she said aloud. 'I've got to have this coat! I've got to have this coat!'

Very well, my dear. You shall have the coat. But don't panic. Sit still and keep calm and start thinking. You're a clever girl, aren't you? You've fooled him before. The man never has been able to see much further than the end of his own probe, you know that. So just sit absolutely still and *think*. There's lots of time.

Two and a half hours later, Mrs Bixby stepped off the train at Pennsylvania Station and walked quietly to the exit. She was wearing her old red coat again now and carrying the cardboard box in her arms. She signalled for a taxi.

'Driver,' she said, 'would you know of a pawnbroker that's still open around here?'

The man behind the wheel raised his brows and looked back at her, amused.

'Plenty along Sixth Avenue,' he answered.

'Stop at the first one you see, then, will you please?' She got in and was driven away.

Soon the taxi pulled up outside a shop that had three brass balls hanging over the entrance.

'Wait for me, please,' Mrs Bixby said to the driver, and she got out of the taxi and entered the shop.

There was an enormous cat crouching on the counter eating fishheads out of a white saucer. The animal looked up at Mrs Bixby with bright yellow eyes, then looked away again and went on eating. Mrs Bixby stood by the counter, as far away from the cat as possible, waiting for someone to come, staring at the watches, the shoe buckles, the enamel brooches, the old binoculars, the broken spectacles, the false teeth. Why did they always pawn their teeth, she wondered.

'Yes?' the proprietor said, emerging from a dark place in the back of the shop.

'Oh, good evening,' Mrs Bixby said. She began to untie the string around the box. The man went up to the cat and started stroking it along the top of its back, and the cat went on eating the fishheads.

'Isn't it silly of me?' Mrs Bixby said. 'I've gone and lost my pocketbook, and this being Saturday, the banks are all closed until Monday and I've simply got to have some money for the week-end. This is quite a valuable coat, but I'm not asking much. I only want to borrow enough on it to tide me over till Monday. Then I'll come back and redeem it.'

The man waited, and said nothing. But when she pulled out the mink and allowed the beautiful thick fur to fall over the counter, his eyebrows went up and he drew his hand away from the cat and came over to look at it. He picked it up and held it out in front of him.

'If only I had a watch on me or a ring,' Mrs Bixby said, 'I'd give you that instead. But the fact is I don't have a thing with me other than this coat.' She spread out her fingers for him to see.

'It looks new,' the man said, fondling the soft fur.

'Oh yes, it is. But, as I said, I only want to borrow enough to tide me over till Monday. How about fifty dollars?'

'I'll loan you fifty dollars.'

'It's worth a hundred times more than that, but I know you'll take good care of it until I return.'

The man went over to a drawer and fetched a ticket and placed it on the counter. The ticket looked like one of those labels you tie on to the handle of your suitcase, the same shape and size exactly, and the same stiff brownish paper. But it was perforated across the middle so that you could tear it in two, and both halves were identical.

'Name?' he asked.

'Leave that out. And the address.'

She saw the man pause, and she saw the nib of the pen hovering over the dotted line, waiting.

'You don't *have* to put the name and address, do you?'

The man shrugged and shook his head and the pen-nib moved on down to the next line.

'It's just that I'd rather not,' Mrs Bixby said. 'It's purely personal.'

'You'd better not lose this ticket, then.'

'I won't lose it.'

'You realize that anyone who gets hold of it can come in and claim the article?'

'Yes, I know that.'

'Simply on the number.'

'Yes, I know.'

'What do you want me to put for a description.'

'No description either, thank you. It's not necessary. Just put the amount I'm borrowing.'

The pen-nib hesitated again, hovering over the dotted line beside the word ARTICLE.

'I think you ought to put a description. A description is always a help if you want to sell the ticket. You never know, you might want to sell it sometime.'

'I don't want to sell it.'

'You might have to. Lots of people do.'

'Look,' Mrs Bixby said. 'I'm not broke, if that's what you mean. I simply lost my purse. Don't you understand?'

'You have it your own way then,' the man said. 'It's your coat.'

At this point an unpleasant thought struck Mrs Bixby. 'Tell me something,' she said. 'If I don't have a description on my ticket, how can I be sure you'll give me back the coat and not something else when I return?'

'It goes in the books.'

'But all I've got is a number. So actually you could hand me any old thing you wanted, isn't that so?'

'Do you want a description or don't you?' the man asked.

'No,' she said. 'I trust you.'

The man wrote 'fifty dollars' opposite the word VALUE on both sections of the ticket, then he tore it in half along the perforations and slid the lower portion across the counter. He took a wallet from the inside pocket of his jacket and extracted five ten-dollar bills. 'The interest is three per cent a month,' he said.

'Yes, all right. And thank you. You'll take good care of it, won't you?'

The man nodded but said nothing.

'Shall I put it back in the box for you?'

'No,' the man said.

Mrs Bixby turned and went out of the shop on to the street where the taxi was waiting. Ten minutes later, she was home.

'Darling,' she said as she bent over and kissed her husband. 'Did you miss me?'

Cyril Bixby laid down the evening paper and glanced at the watch on his wrist. 'It's twelve and a half minutes past six,' he said. 'You're a bit late, aren't you?'

'I know. It's those dreadful trains. Aunt Maude sent you her love as usual. I'm dying for a drink, aren't you?'

The husband folded his newspaper into a neat rectangle and placed it on the arm of his chair. Then he stood up and crossed over to the sideboard. His wife remained in the centre of the room pulling off her gloves, watching him carefully, wondering how long she ought to wait. He had his back to her now, bending forward to measure the gin, putting his face right up close to the measurer and peering into it as though it were a patient's mouth.

It was funny how small he always looked after the Colonel. The Colonel was huge and bristly, and when you were near to him he smelled faintly of horseradish. This one was small and neat and bony and he didn't really smell of anything at all, except peppermint drops, which he sucked to keep his breath nice for the patients.

'See what I've bought for measuring the vermouth,' he said, holding up a calibrated glass beaker. 'I can get it to the nearest milligram with this.'

'Darling, how clever.'

I really must try to make him change the way he dresses, she told herself. His suits are just too ridiculous for words. There had been a time when she thought they were wonderful, those Edwardian jackets with high lapels and six buttons down the front, but now they merely seemed absurd. So did the narrow stovepipe trousers. You had to have a special sort of face to wear things like that, and Cyril just didn't have it. His was a long bony countenance with a narrow nose and a slightly prognathous jaw, and when you saw it coming up out of the top of one of those tightly fitting old-fashioned suits it looked like a caricature of Sam Weller. He probably thought it looked like Beau Brummel. It was a fact that in the office he invariably greeted female patients with his white coat unbuttoned so that they would catch a glimpse of the trappings underneath; and in some obscure way this was obviously meant to convey the impression that he was a bit of a dog. But Mrs Bixby knew better. The plumage was a bluff. It meant nothing. It reminded her of an ageing peacock strutting on the lawn with only half its feathers left. Or one of those fatuous self-fertilizing flowers – like the dandelion. A dandelion never has to get fertilized for the setting of its seed, and all those brilliant yellow petals are just a waste of time, a boast, a masquerade. What's the word the biologists use? Subsexual. A dandelion is subsexual. So, for that matter, are the summer broods of water fleas. It sound a bit like Lewis Carroll, she thought – water fleas and dandelions and dentists.

'Thank you, darling,' she said, taking the martini and seating herself on the sofa with her handbag on her lap. 'And what did *you* do last night?'

'I stayed on in the office and cast a few inlays. I also got my accounts up to date.'

'Now really, Cyril, I think it's high time you let other people do your donkey work for you. You're much too important for that sort of thing. Why don't you give the inlays to the mechanic?'

'I prefer to do them myself. I'm extremely proud of my inlays.'

'I know you are, darling, and I think they're absolutely wonderful. They're the best inlays in the whole world. But I don't want you to burn yourself out. And why doesn't that Pulteney woman do the accounts? That's part of her job, isn't it?'

'She does do them. But I have to price everything up first. She doesn't know who's rich and who isn't.'

'This Martini is perfect,' Mrs Bixby said, setting down her glass on the side table. 'Quite perfect.' She opened her bag and took out a handkerchief as if to blow her nose. 'Oh look!' she cried, seeing the ticket. 'I forgot to show you this! I found it just now on the seat of my taxi. It's got a number on it, and I thought it might be a lottery ticket or something, so I kept it.'

She handed the small piece of stiff brown paper to her husband, who took it in his fingers and began examining it minutely from all angles, as though it were a suspect tooth.

'You know what this is?' he said slowly.

'No dear, I don't.'

'It's a pawn ticket.'

'A what?'

'A ticket from a pawnbroker. Here's the name and address of the shop – somewhere on Sixth Avenue.'

'Oh dear, I *am* disappointed. I was hoping it might be a ticket for the Irish Sweep.'

'There's no reason to be disappointed,' Cyril Bixby said. 'As a matter of fact this could be rather amusing.'

'Why could it be amusing, darling?'

He began explaining to her exactly how a pawn ticket worked, with particular reference to the fact that anyone possessing the ticket was entitled to claim the article. She listened patiently until he had finished his lecture.

'You think it's worth claiming?' she asked.

'I think it's worth finding out what it is. You see this figure of fifty dollars that's written here? You know what that means?'

'No, dear, what does it mean?'

'It means that the item in question is almost certain to be something quite valuable.'

'You mean it'll be worth fifty dollars?'

'More like five hundred.'

'Five hundred!'

'Don't you understand?' he said. 'A pawnbroker never gives you more than about a tenth of the real value.'

'Good gracious! I never knew that.'

'There's a lot of things you don't know, my dear. Now you listen to me. Seeing that there's no name and address of the owner ...'

'But surely there's something to say who it belongs to?'

'Not a thing. People often do that. They don't want anyone to know they've been to a pawnbroker. They're ashamed of it.'

'Then you think we can keep it?'

'Of course we can keep it. This is now *our* ticket.'

'You mean *my* ticket,' Mrs Bixby said firmly. 'I found it.'

'My dear girl, what *does* it matter? The important thing is that we are now in a position to go and redeem it any time we like for only fifty dollars. How about that?'

'Oh, what fun!' she cried. 'I think it's terribly exciting, especially when we don't even know what it is. It could be *anything*, isn't that right, Cyril? Absolutely anything!'

'It could indeed, although it's most likely to be either a ring or a watch.'

'But wouldn't it be marvellous if it was a *real* treasure? I mean something *really* old, like a wonderful old vase or a Roman statue.'

'There's no knowing what it might be, my dear. We shall just have to wait and see.'

'I think it's absolutely fascinating! Give me the ticket and I'll rush over first thing Monday morning and find out!'

'I think I'd better do that.'

'Oh no!' she cried. 'Let *me* do it!'

'I think not. I'll pick it up on my way to work.'

'But it's *my* ticket! *Please* let me do it, Cyril! Why should *you* have all the fun?'

'You don't know these pawnbrokers, my dear. You're liable to get cheated.'

'I wouldn't get cheated, honestly I wouldn't. Give it to me, please.'

'Also you have to have fifty dollars,' he said, smiling. 'You have to pay out fifty dollars in cash before they'll give it to you.'

'I've got that,' she said. 'I think.'

'I'd rather you didn't handle it, if you don't mind.'

'But Cyril, *I found* it. It's mine. Whatever it is, it's mine, isn't that right?'

'Of course it's yours, my dear. There's no need to get so worked up about it.'

'I'm not. I'm just excited, that's all.'

'I suppose it hasn't occurred to you that this might be something entirely masculine – a pocket-watch, for example, or a set of shirt-studs. It isn't only women that go to pawnbrokers, you know.'

'In that case I'll give it to you for Christmas,' Mrs Bixby said magnanimously. 'I'll be delighted. But if it's a woman's thing, I want it myself. Is that agreed?'

'That sounds very fair. Why don't you come with me when I collect it?'

Mrs Bixby was about to say yes to this, but caught herself just in time. She had no wish to be greeted like an old customer by the pawnbroker in her husband's presence.

'No,' she said slowly. 'I don't think I will. You see, it'll be even more thrilling if I stay behind and wait. Oh, I do hope it isn't going to be something that neither of us wants.'

'You've got a point there,' he said. 'If I don't think it's worth fifty dollars, I won't even take it.'

'But you said it would be worth five hundred.'

'I'm quite sure it will. Don't worry.'

'Oh, Cyril, I can hardly wait! Isn't it exciting?'

'It's amusing,' he said, slipping the ticket into his waistcoat pocket. 'There's no doubt about that.'

Monday morning came at last, and after breakfast Mrs Bixby followed her husband to the door and helped him on with his coat.

'Don't work too hard, darling,' she said.

'No, all right.'

'Home at six?'

'I hope so.'

'Are you going to have time to go to that pawnbroker?' she asked.

'My God, I forgot all about it. I'll take a cab and go there now. It's on my way.'

'You haven't lost the ticket, have you?'

'I hope not,' he said, feeling in his waistcoat pocket. 'No, here it is.'

'And you have enough money?'

'Just about.'

'Darling,' she said, standing close to him and straightening his tie, which was perfectly straight. 'If it happens to be something nice, something you think I might like, will you telephone me as soon as you get to the office?'

'If you want me to, yes.'

'You know, I'm sort of hoping it'll be something for you, Cyril. I'd much rather it was for you than for me.'

'That's very generous of you, my dear. Now I must run.'

About an hour later, when the telephone rang, Mrs Bixby was across the room so fast she had the receiver off the hook before the first ring had finished.

'I got it!' he said.

'You did! Oh, Cyril, what was it? Was it something good?'

'Good!' he cried. 'It's fantastic! You wait till you get your eyes on this! You'll swoon!'

'Darling, what is it? Tell me quick!'

'You're a lucky girl, that's what you are.'

'It's for me, then?'

'Of course it's for you. Though how in the world it ever got to be pawned for only fifty dollars I'll be damned if I know. Someone's crazy.'

'Cyril! Stop keeping me in suspense! I can't bear it!'

'You'll go mad when you see it.'

'What is it?'

'Try to guess.'

Mrs Bixby paused. Be careful, she told herself. Be very careful now.

'A necklace,' she said.

'Wrong.'

'A diamond ring.'

'You're not even warm. I'll give you a hint. It's something you can wear.'

'Something I can wear? You mean like a hat?'

'No, it's not a hat,' he said, laughing.

'For goodness sake, Cyril! Why don't you tell me?'

'Because I want it to be a surprise. I'll bring it home with me this evening.'

'You'll do nothing of the sort!' she cried. 'I'm coming right down there to get it now!'

'I'd rather you didn't do that.'

'Don't be silly, darling. Why shouldn't I come?'

'Because I'm too busy. You'll disorganize my whole morning schedule. I'm half an hour behind already.'

'Then I'll come in the lunch hour. All right?'

'I'm not having a lunch hour. Oh well, come at one-thirty then, while I'm having a sandwich. Good-bye.'

At half past one precisely, Mrs Bixby arrived at Mr Bixby's place of business and rang the bell. Her husband, in his white dentist's coat, opened the door himself.

'Oh, Cyril, I'm so excited!'

'So you should be. You're a lucky girl, did you know that?' He led her down the passage and into the surgery.

'Go and have your lunch, Miss Pulteney,' he said to the assistant, who was busy putting instruments into the sterilizer. 'You can finish that when you come back.' He waited until the girl had gone, then he walked over to a closet that he used for hanging up his clothes and stood in front of it, pointing with his finger. 'It's in there,' he said. 'Now – shut your eyes.'

Mrs Bixby did as she was told. Then she took a deep breath and held it, and in the silence that followed she could hear him opening the cupboard door and there was a soft swishing sound as he pulled out a garment from among the other things hanging there.

'All right! You can look!'

'I don't dare to,' she said, laughing.

'Go on. Take a peek.'

Coyly, beginning to giggle, she raised one eyelid a fraction of an inch, just enough to give her a dark blurry view of the man standing there in his white overalls holding something up in the air.

'Mink!' he cried. 'Real mink!'

At the sound of the magic word she opened her eyes quick, and at the same time she actually started forward in order to clasp the coat in her arms.

But there was no coat. There was only a ridiculous little fur neckpiece dangling from her husband's hand.

'Feast your eyes on that!' he said, waving it in front of her face.

Mrs Bixby put a hand up to her mouth and started backing away. I'm going to scream, she told herself. I just know it. I'm going to scream.

'What's the matter, my dear? Don't you like it?' He stopped waving the fur and stood staring at her, waiting for her to say something.

'Why yes,' she stammered. 'I ... I ... think it's ... it's lovely ... really lovely.'

'Quite took your breath away for a moment there, didn't it?'

'Yes, it did.'

'Magnificent quality,' he said. 'Fine colour, too. You know something, my dear? I reckon a piece like this would cost you two or three hundred dollars at least if you had to buy it in a shop.'

'I don't doubt it.'

There were two skins, two narrow mangy-looking skins with their heads still on them and glass beads in their eye sockets and little paws hanging down. One of them had the rear end of the other in its mouth, biting it.

'Here,' he said. 'Try it on.' He leaned forward and draped the thing around her neck, then stepped back to admire. 'It's perfect. It really suits you. It isn't everyone who has mink, my dear.'

'No, it isn't.'

'Better leave it behind when you go shopping or they'll all think we're millionaires and start charging us double.'

'I'll try to remember that, Cyril.'

'I'm afraid you mustn't expect anything else for Christmas. Fifty dollars was rather more than I was going to spend anyway.'

He turned away and went over to the basin and began washing his hands. 'Run along now, my dear, and buy yourself a nice lunch. I'd take you out myself but I've got old man Gorman in the waiting-room with a broken clasp on his denture.'

Mrs Bixby moved towards the door.

I'm going to kill that pawnbroker, she told herself. I'm going right back there to the shop this very minute and I'm going to throw this filthy neckpiece right in his face and if he refuses to give me back my coat I'm going to kill him.

'Did I tell you I was going to be late home tonight?' Cyril Bixby said, still washing his hands.

'No.'

'It'll probably be at least eighty-thirty the way things look at the moment. It may even be nine.'

'Yes, all right. Good-bye.' Mrs Bixby went out, slamming the door behind her.

At that precise moment, Miss Pulteney, the secretary-assistant, came sailing past her down the corridor on her way to lunch.

'Isn't it a gorgeous day?' Miss Pulteney said as she went by, flashing a smile. There was a lilt in her walk, a little whiff of perfume attending her, and she looked like a queen, just exactly like a queen in the beautiful black mink coat that the Colonel had given to Mrs Bixby.

ROYAL JELLY

'It worries me to death, Albert, it really does,' Mrs Taylor said.

She kept her eyes fixed on the baby who was now lying absolutely motionless in the crook of her left arm.

'I just know there's something wrong.'

The skin on the baby's face had a pearly translucent quality and was stretched very tightly over the bones.

'Try again,' Albert Taylor said.

'It won't do any good.'

'You have to keep trying, Mabel,' he said.

She lifted the bottle out of the saucepan of hot water and shook a few drops of milk on to the inside of her wrist, testing for temperature.

'Come on,' she whispered. 'Come on, my baby. Wake up and take a bit more of this.'

There was a small lamp on the table close by that made a soft yellow glow all around her.

'Please,' she said. 'Take just a weeny bit more.'

The husband watched her over the top of his magazine. She was half dead with exhaustion, he could see that, and the pale oval face, usually so grave and serene, had taken on a kind of pinched and desperate look. But even so, the drop of her head as she gazed down at the child was curiously beautiful.

'You see,' she murmured. 'It's no good. She won't have it.'

She held the bottle up to the light, squinting at the calibrations.

'One ounce again. That's all she's taken. No – it isn't even that. It's only three-quarters. It's not enough to keep body and soul together, Albert, it really isn't. It worries me to death.'

'I know,' he said.

'If only they could *find out* what was wrong.'

'There's nothing wrong, Mabel. It's just a matter of time.'

'Of course there's something wrong.'

'Dr Robinson says no.'

'Look,' she said, standing up. 'You can't tell me it's natural for a six-week-old child to weigh less, less by more than *two whole pounds* than she did when she was born! Just look at those legs! They're nothing but skin and bone!'

The tiny baby lay limply on her arm, not moving.

'Dr Robinson said you was to stop worrying, Mabel. So did that other one.'

'Ha!' she said. 'Isn't that wonderful! I'm to stop worrying!'

'Now, Mabel.'

'What does he want me to do? Treat it as some sort of a joke?'

'He didn't say that.'

'I hate doctors! I hate them all!' she cried, and she swung away from him and walked quickly out of the room towards the stairs, carrying the baby with her.

Albert Taylor stayed where he was and let her go.

In a little while he heard her moving about in the bedroom directly over his head, quick nervous footsteps going tap tap tap on the linoleum above. Soon the footsteps would stop, and then he would have to get up and follow her, and when he went into the bedroom he would find her sitting beside the cot as usual, staring at the child and crying softly to herself and refusing to move.

'She's starving, Albert,' she would say.

'Of course she's not starving.'

'She *is* starving. I know she is. And Albert?'

'Yes?'

'I believe you know it too, but you won't admit it. Isn't that right?'

Every night now it was like this.

Last week they had taken the child back to the hospital, and the doctor had examined it carefully and told them that there was nothing the matter.

'It took us nine years to get this baby, Doctor,' Mabel had said. 'I think it would kill me if anything should happen to her.'

That was six days ago and since then it had lost another five ounces.

But worrying about it wasn't going to help anybody, Albert Taylor told himself. One simply had to trust the doctor on a thing like this. He picked up the magazine that was still lying on his lap and glanced idly down the list of contents to see what it had to offer this week:

> *Among the Bees in May*
> *Honey Cookery*
> *The Bee Farmer and the B. Pharm.*
> *Experiences in the Control of Nosema*
> *The Latest on Royal Jelly*
> *This Week in the Apiary*
> *The Healing Power of Propolis*
> *Regurgitations*
> *British Beekeepers Annual Dinner*
> *Association News*

All his life Albert Taylor had been fascinated by anything that had to do with bees. As a small boy he used often to catch them in his bare hands and go running with them into the house to show to his mother, and sometimes he would put them on his face and let them crawl about over his cheeks and neck, and the astonishing thing about it all was that he never got stung. On the contrary, the bees seemed to enjoy being with him. They never tried to fly away, and to get rid of them he would have to brush them off gently with his fingers. Even then they would frequently return and settle again on his arm or hand or knee, any place where the skin was bare.

His father, who was a bricklayer, said there must be some witch's stench about the boy, something noxious that came oozing out through the pores of the skin, and that no good would ever come of it, hypnotizing insects like that. But the mother said it was a gift given him by God, and even went so far as to compare him with St Francis and the birds.

As he grew older, Albert Taylor's fascination with bees developed into an obsession, and by the time he was twelve he had built his first hive. The following summer he had captured his first swarm. Two years later, at the age of fourteen, he had no less than five hives standing neatly in a row against the fence in his father's small back yard, and already – apart from the normal task of producing honey – he was practising the delicate and complicated business of rearing his own queens, grafting larvae into artificial cell cups, and all the rest of it.

He never had to use smoke when there was work to do inside a hive, and he never wore gloves on his hands or a net over his head. Clearly there was some strange sympathy between this boy and the bees, and down in the village, in the shops and pubs, they began to speak about him with a certain kind of respect, and people started coming up to the house to buy his honey.

When he was eighteen, he had rented one acre of rough pasture alongside a cherry orchard down the valley about a mile from the village, and there he had set out to establish his own business. Now, eleven years later, he was still in the same spot, but he had six acres of ground instead of one, two hundred and forty well-stocked hives, and a small house that he'd built mainly with his own hands. He had married at the age of twenty and that, apart from the fact that it had taken them over nine years to get a child, had also been a success. In fact, everything had gone pretty well for Albert until this strange little baby girl came along and started frightening them out of their wits by refusing to eat properly and losing weight every day.

He looked up from the magazine and began thinking about his daughter.

That evening, for instance, when she had opened her eyes at the beginning of the feed, he had gazed into them and seen something that frightened him to death – a kind of misty vacant stare, as though the eyes themselves were not connected to the brain at all but were just lying loose in their sockets like a couple of small grey marbles.

Did those doctors really know what they were talking about?

He reached for an ash-tray and started slowly picking the ashes out from the bowl of his pipe with a matchstick.

One could always take her along to another hospital, somewhere in Oxford perhaps. He might suggest that to Mabel when he went upstairs.

He could still hear her moving around in the bedroom, but she must have taken off her shoes now and put on slippers because the noise was very faint.

He switched his attention back to the magazine and went on with his reading. He finished the article called 'Experiences in the Control of Nosema', then turned over the page and began reading the next one, 'The Latest on Royal Jelly'. He doubted very much whether there would be anything in this that he didn't know already:

What is this wonderful substance called royal jelly?

He reached for the tin of tobacco on the table beside him and began filling his pipe, still reading.

Royal jelly is a glandular secretion produced by the nurse bees to feed the larvae immediately they have hatched from the egg. The pharyngeal glands of bees produce this substance in much the same way as the mammary glands of vertebrates produce milk. The fact is of great biological interest because no other insects in the world are known to have evolved such a process.

All old stuff, he told himself, but for want of anything better to do, he continued to read.

Royal jelly is fed in concentrated form to all bee larvae for the first three days after hatching from the egg; but beyond that point, for all those who are destined to become drones or workers, this precious food is greatly diluted with honey and pollen. On the other hand, the larvae which are destined to become queens are fed throughout the whole of their larval period on a concentrated diet of pure royal jelly. Hence the name.

Above him, up in the bedroom, the noise of the footsteps had stopped altogether. The house was quiet. He struck a match and put it to his pipe.

Royal jelly must be a substance of tremendous nourishing power, for on this diet alone, the honey-bee larvae increases in weight fifteen hundred times in five days.

That was probably about right, he thought, although for some reason it had never occurred to him to consider larval growth in terms of weight before.

This is as if a seven-and-a-half-pound baby should increase in that time to five tons.

Albert Taylor stopped and read that sentence again.
He read it a third time.

This is as if a seven-and-a-half pound baby ...

'Mabel!' he cried, jumping up from his chair. 'Mabel! Come here!'
He went out into the hall and stood at the foot of the stairs calling for her to come down.
There was no answer.
He ran up the stairs and switched on the light on the landing. The bedroom door was closed. He crossed the landing and opened it and stood in the doorway looking into the dark room. 'Mabel,' he said. 'Come downstairs a moment, will you please? I've just had a bit of an idea. It's about the baby.'
The light from the landing behind him cast a faint glow over the bed and he could see her dimly now, lying on her stomach with her face buried in the pillow and her arms up over her head. She was crying again.
'Mabel,' he said, going over to her, touching her shoulder. 'Please come down a moment. This may be important.'
'Go away,' she said. 'Leave me alone.'
'Don't you want to hear about my idea?'
'Oh, Albert, I'm *tired*,' she sobbed. 'I'm so tired I don't know what I'm doing any more. I don't think I can go on. I don't think I can stand it.'
There was a pause. Albert Taylor turned away from her and walked slowly over to the cradle where the baby was lying, and peered in. It was too dark for him to see the child's face, but when he bent down close he could hear the sound of breathing, very faint and quick. 'What time is the next feed?' he asked.
'Two o'clock, I suppose.'
'And the one after that?'
'Six in the morning.'
'I'll do them both,' he said. 'You go to sleep.'

She didn't answer.

'You get properly into bed, Mabel, and go straight to sleep, you understand? And stop worrying. I'm taking over completely for the next twelve hours. You'll give yourself a nervous breakdown going on like this.'

'Yes,' she said. 'I know.'

'I'm taking the nipper and myself *and* the alarm clock into the spare room this very moment, so you just lie down and relax and forget all about us. Right?' Already he was pushing the cradle out through the door.

'Oh, Albert,' she sobbed.

'Don't you worry about a thing. Leave it to me.'

'Albert ...'

'Yes?'

'I love you, Albert.'

'I love you too, Mabel. Now go to sleep.'

Albert Taylor didn't see his wife again until nearly eleven o'clock the next morning.

'Good *gracious* me!' she cried, rushing down the stairs in dressing-gown and slippers. 'Albert! Just look at the time! I must have slept twelve hours at least! Is everything all right? What happened?'

He was sitting quietly in his armchair, smoking a pipe and reading the morning paper. The baby was in a sort of carry-cot on the floor at his feet, sleeping.

'Hullo, dear,' he said, smiling.

She ran over to the cot and looked in. 'Did she take anything, Albert? How many times have you fed her? She was due for another one at ten o'clock, did you know that?'

Albert Taylor folded the newspaper neatly into a square and put it away on the side table. 'I fed her at two in the morning,' he said, 'and she took about half an ounce, no more. I fed her again at six and she did a bit better that time, two ounces ...'

'*Two ounces!* Oh, Albert, that's marvellous!'

'And we just finished the last feed ten minutes ago. There's the bottle on the mantelpiece. Only one ounce left. She drank three. How's that?' He was grinning proudly, delighted with his achievement.

The woman quickly got down on her knees and peered at the baby.

'Don't she look better?' he asked eagerly. 'Don't she look fatter in the face?'

'It may sound silly,' the wife said, 'but I actually think she does. Oh, Albert, you're a marvel! How did you do it?'

'She's turning the corner,' he said. 'That's all it is. Just like the doctor prophesied, she's turning the corner.'

'I pray to God you're right, Albert.'

'Of course I'm right. From now on, you watch her go.'

The woman was gazing lovingly at the baby.

'You look a lot better yourself too, Mabel.'

'I feel wonderful. I'm sorry about last night.'

'Let's keep it this way,' he said. 'I'll do all the night feeds in future. You do the day ones.'

She looked up at him across the cot, frowning. 'No,' she said, 'Oh no, I wouldn't allow you to do that.'

'I don't want you to have a breakdown, Mabel.'

'I won't, not now I've had some sleep.'

'Much better we share it.'

'No, Albert. This is my job and I intend to do it. Last night won't happen again.'

There was a pause. Albert Taylor took the pipe out of his mouth and examined the grain on the bowl. 'All right,' he said. 'In that case I'll just relieve you of the donkey work, I'll do all the sterilizing and the mixing of the food and getting everything ready. That'll help you a bit, anyway.'

She looked at him carefully, wondering what could have come over him all of a sudden.

'You see, Mabel, I've been thinking . . .'

'Yes, dear.'

'I've been thinking that up until last night I've never even raised a finger to help you with this baby.'

'That isn't true.'

'Oh yes it is. So I've decided that from now on I'm going to do *my* share of the work. I'm going to be the feed-mixer and the bottle-sterilizer. Right?'

'It's very sweet of you, dear, but I really don't think it's necessary . . .'

'Come on!' he cried. 'Don't change the luck! I done it the last three times and just *look* what happened! When's the next one? Two o'clock, isn't it?'

'Yes.'

'It's all mixed,' he said. 'Everything's all mixed and ready and all you've got to do when the time comes is to go out there to the larder and take it off the shelf and warm it up. That's *some* help, isn't it?'

The woman got up off her knees and went over to him and kissed him on the cheek. 'You're such a nice man,' she said. 'I love you more and more every day I know you.'

Later, in the middle of the afternoon, when Albert was outside in the sunshine working among the hives, he heard her calling to him from the house.

'Albert!' she shouted. 'Albert, come here!' She was running through the buttercups towards him.

He started forward to meet her, wondering what was wrong.

'Oh, Albert! Guess what!'

'What?'

'I've just finished giving her the two-o'clock feed and she's taken the whole lot!'

'No!'

'Every drop of it! Oh, Albert, I'm so happy! She's going to be all right! She's turned the corner just like you said!' She came up to him and threw her arms around his neck and hugged him, and he clapped her on the back and laughed and said what a marvellous little mother she was.

'Will you come in and watch the next one and see if she does it again, Albert?'

He told her he wouldn't miss it for anything, and she hugged him again, then turned and ran back to the house, skipping over the grass and singing all the way.

Naturally, there was a certain amount of suspense in the air as the time approached for the six-o'clock feed. By five thirty both parents were already seated in the living-room waiting for the moment to arrive. The bottle with the milk formula in it was standing in a saucepan of warm water on the mantelpiece. The baby was asleep in its carry-cot on the sofa.

At twenty minutes to six it woke up and started screaming its head off.

'There you are!' Mrs Taylor cried. 'She's asking for the bottle. Pick her up quick, Albert, and hand her to me here. Give me the bottle first.'

He gave her the bottle, then placed the baby on the woman's lap. Cautiously, she touched the baby's lips with the end of the nipple. The baby seized the nipple between its gums and began to suck ravenously with a rapid powerful action.

'Oh, Albert, isn't it wonderful?' she said, laughing.

'It's terrific, Mabel.'

In seven or eight minutes, the entire contents of the bottle had disappeared down the baby's throat.

'You clever girl,' Mrs Taylor said. 'Four ounces again.'

Albert Taylor was leaning forward in his chair, peering intently into the baby's face. 'You know what?' he said. 'She even seems as though she's put on a touch of weight already. What do you think?'

The mother looked down at the child.

'Don't she seem bigger and fatter to you, Mabel, than she was yesterday?'

'Maybe she does, Albert. I'm not sure. Although actually there couldn't be any *real* gain in such a short time as this. The important thing is that she's eating normally.'

'She's turned the corner,' Albert said. 'I don't think you need worry about her any more.'

'I certainly won't.'

'You want me to go up and fetch the cradle back into our own bedroom, Mabel?'

'Yes, please,' she said.

Albert went upstairs and moved the cradle. The woman followed with the baby, and after changing its nappy, she laid it gently down on its bed. Then she covered it with sheet and blanket.

'Doesn't she look lovely, Albert?' she whispered. 'Isn't that the most beautiful baby you've ever seen in your *entire* life?'

'Leave her be now, Mabel,' he said. 'Come on downstairs and cook us a bit of supper. We both deserve it.'

After they had finished eating, the parents settled themselves in armchairs in the living-room, Albert with his magazine and his pipe, Mrs Taylor with her knitting. But this was a very different scene from the one of the night before. Suddenly, all tensions had vanished. Mrs Taylor's handsome oval face was glowing with pleasure, her cheeks were pink, her eyes were sparkling bright, and her mouth was fixed in a little dreamy smile of pure content. Every now and again she would glance up from her knitting and gaze affectionately at her husband. Occasionally, she would stop the clicking of her needles altogether for a few seconds and sit quite still, looking at the ceiling, listening for a cry or a whimper from upstairs. But all was quiet.

'Albert,' she said after a while.

'Yes, dear?'

'What was it you were going to tell me last night when you came rushing up to the bedroom? You said you had an idea for the baby.'

Albert Taylor lowered the magazine on to his lap and gave her a long sly look.

'Did I?' he said.

'Yes.' She waited for him to go on, but he didn't.

'What's the big joke?' she asked. 'Why are you grinning like that?'

'It's a joke all right,' he said.

'Tell it to me, dear.'

'I'm not sure I ought to,' he said. 'You might call me a liar.'

She had seldom seen him looking so pleased with himself as he was now, and she smiled back at him, egging him on.

'I'd just like to see your face when you hear it, Mabel, that's all.'

'Albert, what *is* all this?'

He paused, refusing to be hurried.

'You do think the baby's better, don't you?' he asked.

'Of course I do.'

'You agree with me that all of a sudden she's feeding marvellously and looking one-hundred-per-cent different?'

'I do, Albert, yes.'

'That's good,' he said, the grin widening. 'You see, it's me that did it.'

'Did what?'

'I cured the baby.'

'Yes, dear, I'm sure you did.' Mrs Taylor went right on with her knitting.

'You don't believe me, do you?'

'Of course I believe you, Albert. I give you all the credit, every bit of it.'

'Then how did I do it?'

'Well,' she said, pausing a moment to think. 'I suppose it's simply that you're a brilliant feed-mixer. Ever since you started mixing the feeds she's got better and better.'

'You mean there's some sort of an art in mixing the feeds?'

'Apparently there is.' She was knitting away and smiling quietly to herself, thinking how funny men were.

'I'll tell you a secret,' he said. 'You're absolutely right. Although, mind you, it isn't so much *how* you mix it that counts. It's what you put in. You realize that, don't you, Mabel?'

Mrs Taylor stopped knitting and looked up sharply at her husband. 'Albert,' she said, 'don't tell me you've been putting things into that child's milk?'

He sat there grinning.

'Well, have you or haven't you?'

'It's possible,' he said.

'I don't believe it.'

He had a strange fierce way of grinning that showed his teeth.

'Albert,' she said. 'Stop playing with me like this.'

'Yes, dear, all right.'

'You haven't *really* put anything into her milk, have you? Answer me properly, Albert. This could be serious with such a tiny baby.'

'The answer is yes, Mabel.'

'*Albert Taylor!* How could you?'

'Now don't get excited,' he said. 'I'll tell you all about it if you really want me to, but for heaven's sake keep your hair on.'

'It was beer!' she cried. 'I just know it was beer!'

'Don't be so daft, Mabel, please.'

'Then what was it?'

Albert laid his pipe down carefully on the table beside him and leaned back in his chair. 'Tell me,' he said, 'did you ever by any chance happen to hear me mentioning something called royal jelly?'

'I did not.'

'It's magic,' he said. 'Pure magic. And last night I suddenly got the idea that if I was to put some of this into the baby's milk ...'

'How *dare* you!'

'Now, Mabel, you don't even know what it is yet.'

'I don't care what it is,' she said. 'You can't go putting foreign bodies like that into a tiny baby's milk. You must be mad.'

'It's perfectly harmless, Mabel, otherwise I wouldn't have done it. It comes from bees.'

'I might have guessed that.'

'And it's so precious that practically no one can afford to take it. When they do, it's only one little drop at a time.'

'And how much did you give to our baby, might I ask?'

'Ah,' he said, 'that's the whole point. That's where the difference lies. I reckon that our baby, just in the last four feeds, has already swallowed about fifty times as much royal jelly as anyone else in the world has ever swallowed before. How about that?'

'Albert, stop pulling my leg.'

'I swear it,' he said proudly.

She sat there staring at him, her brow wrinkled, her mouth slightly open.

'You know what this stuff actually costs, Mabel, if you want to buy it? There's a place in America advertising it for sale at this very moment for something like five hundred dollars a pound jar! *Five hundred dollars!* That's more than gold, you know!'

She hadn't the faintest idea what he was talking about.

'I'll prove it,' he said, and he jumped up and went across to the large bookcase where he kept all his literature about bees. On the top shelf, the back numbers of the *American Bee Journal* were neatly stacked alongside those of the *British Bee Journal, Beecraft,* and other magazines. He took down the last issue of the *American Bee Journal* and turned to a page of small classified advertisements at the back.

'Here you are,' he said. 'Exactly as I told you. "We sell royal jelly – $480 per lb. jar wholesale."'

He handed her the magazine so she could read it herself.

'Now do you believe me? This is an actual shop in New York, Mabel. It says so.'

'It doesn't say you can go stirring it into the milk of a practically new-born baby,' she said. 'I don't know what's come over you, Albert, I really don't.'

'It's curing her, isn't it?'

'I'm not so sure about that, now.'

'Don't be so damn silly, Mabel. You know it is.'

'Then why haven't other people done it with *their* babies?'

'I keep telling you,' he said. 'It's too expensive. Practically nobody in the world can afford to buy royal jelly just for *eating* except maybe one or two multimillionaires. The people who buy it are the big companies that make women's face creams and things like that. They're using it as a stunt. They mix a tiny pinch of it into a big jar of face cream and it's selling like hot cakes for absolutely enormous prices. They claim it takes out the wrinkles.'

'And does it?'

'Now how on earth would I know that, Mabel? Anyway,' he said, returning to his chair, 'that's not the point. The point is this. It's done so much good to our little baby just in the last few hours that I think we ought to go right on giving it to her. Now don't interrupt, Mabel. Let me finish. I've got two hundred and forty hives out there and if I turn over maybe a hundred of them to making royal jelly, we ought to be able to supply her with all she wants.'

'Albert Taylor,' the woman said, stretching her eyes wide and staring at him. 'Have you gone out of your mind?'

'Just hear me through, will you please?'

'I forbid it,' she said, 'absolutely. You're not to give my baby another drop of that horrid jelly, you understand?'

'Now, Mabel ...'

'And quite apart from that, we had a shocking honey crop last year, and if you go fooling around with those hives now, there's no telling what might not happen.'

'There's nothing wrong with my hives, Mabel.'

'You know very well we had only half the normal crop last year.'

'Do me a favour, will you?' he said. 'Let me explain some of the marvellous things this stuff does.'

'You haven't even told me what it is yet.'

'All right, Mabel. I'll do that too. Will you listen? Will you give me a chance to explain it?'

She sighed and picked up her knitting once more. 'I suppose you might as well get it off your chest, Albert. Go on and tell me.'

He paused, a bit uncertain now how to begin. It wasn't going to be easy to explain something like this to a person with no detailed knowledge of apiculture at all.

'You know, don't you,' he said, 'that each colony has only one queen?'

'Yes.'

'And that this queen lays all the eggs?'

'Yes, dear. That much I know.'

'All right. Now the queen can actually lay two different kinds of eggs. You didn't know that, but she can. It's what we call one of the miracles of the hive. She can lay eggs that produce drones, and she can lay eggs that produce workers. Now if that isn't a miracle, Mabel, I don't know what is.'

'Yes, Albert, all right.'

'The drones are the males. We don't have to worry about them. The workers are all females. So is the queen, of course. But the workers are unsexed females, if you see what I mean. Their organs are completely undeveloped, whereas the queen is tremendously sexy. She can actually lay her own weight in eggs in a single day.'

He hesitated, marshalling his thoughts.

'Now what happens is this. The queen crawls around on the comb and lays her eggs in what we call cells. You know all those hundreds of little holes you see in a honeycomb? Well, a brood comb is just about the same except the cells don't have honey in them, they have eggs. She lays one egg to each cell, and in three days each of these eggs hatches out into a tiny grub. We call it a larva.

'Now, as soon as this larva appears, the nurse bees – they're young workers – all crowd round and start feeding it like mad. And you know what they feed it on?'

'Royal jelly,' Mabel answered patiently.

'Right!' he cried. 'That's exactly what they do feed it on. They get this stuff out of a gland in their heads and they start pumping it into the cell to feed the larva. And what happens then?'

He paused dramatically, blinking at her with his small watery-grey eyes. Then he turned slowly in his chair and reached for the magazine that he had been reading the night before.

'You want to know what happens then?' he asked, wetting his lips.

'I can hardly wait.'

'"Royal jelly,"' he read aloud, '"must be a substance of tremendous nourishing power, for on this diet alone, the honeybee larva increases in weight *fifteen hundred times* in five days!"'

'How much?'

'*Fifteen hundred times*, Mabel. And you know what that means if you put it in terms of a human being? It means,' he said, lowering his voice, leaning forward, fixing her with those small pale eyes, 'it means that in five days a baby weighing seven and a half pounds to start off with would increase in weight to *five tons*!'

For the second time, Mrs Taylor stopped knitting.

'Now you mustn't take that too literally, Mabel.'

'Who says I mustn't?'

'It's just a scientific way of putting it, that's all.'

'Very well, Albert. Go on.'

'But that's only half the story,' he said. 'There's more to come. The really amazing thing about royal jelly, I haven't told you yet. I'm going to show you now how it can transform a plain dull-looking little worker bee with practically no sex organs at all into a great big beautiful fertile queen.'

'Are you saying our baby is dull-looking and plain?' she asked sharply.

'Now don't go putting words into my mouth, Mabel, please. Just listen to this. Did you know that the queen bee and the worker bee, although they are completely different when they grow up, are both hatched out of exactly the same kind of egg?'

'I don't believe that,' she said.

'It's true as I'm sitting here, Mabel, honest it is. Any time the bees want a queen to hatch out of the egg instead of a worker, they can do it.'

'How?'

'Ah,' he said, shaking a thick forefinger in her direction. 'That's just what I'm coming to. That's the secret of the whole thing. Now – what do *you* think it is, Mabel, that makes this miracle happen?'

'Royal jelly,' she answered. 'You already told me.'

'Royal jelly it is!' he cried, clapping his hands and bouncing up on his seat. His big round face was glowing with excitement now, and two vivid patches of scarlet had appeared high up on each cheek.

'Here's how it works. I'll put it very simply for you. The bees want a new queen. So they build an extra-large cell, a queen cell we call it, and they get the old queen to lay one of her eggs in there. The other one thousand nine hundred and ninety-nine eggs she lays in ordinary worker cells. Now. As soon as these eggs hatch into larvae, the nurse bees rally round and start pumping in the royal jelly. All of them get it, workers as well as queen. But here's the vital thing, Mabel, so listen carefully. Here's where the difference comes. The worker larvae only receive this special marvellous food for the *first three days* of their larval life. After that they have a complete change of diet. What really happens is they get weaned, except that it's not like an ordinary weaning because it's so sudden. After the third day they're put straight away on to more or less routine bees' food – a mixture of honey and pollen – and then about two weeks later they emerge from the cells as workers.

'But not so the larva in the queen cell! This one gets royal jelly *all the way through its larval life*. The nurse bees simply pour it into the cell, so much so in fact that the little larva is literally floating in it. And that's what makes it into a queen!'

'You can't prove it,' she said.

'Don't talk so damn silly, Mabel, please. Thousands of people have proved it time and time again, famous scientists in every country in the world. All you have to do is take a larva out of a worker cell and put it in a queen cell – that's what we call grafting – and just so long as the nurse bees keep it well supplied with royal jelly, then presto! – it'll grow up into a queen! And what makes it more marvellous still is the absolutely enormous difference between a queen and a worker when they grow up. The abdomen is a different shape. The sting is different. The legs are different. The ...'

'In what way are the legs different?' she asked, testing him.

'The legs? Well, the workers have little pollen baskets on their legs for carrying the pollen. The queen has none. Now here's another thing. The queen has fully developed sex organs. The workers don't. And most amazing of all, Mabel, the queen lives for an average of four to six years. The worker hardly lives that many months. And all this difference simply because one of them got royal jelly and the other didn't!'

'It's pretty hard to believe,' she said, 'that a food can do all that.'

'Of course it's hard to believe. It's another of the miracles of the hive. In fact it's the biggest ruddy miracle of them all. It's such a hell of a big miracle that it's baffled the greatest men of science for hundreds of years. Wait a moment. Stay here. Don't move.'

Again he jumped up and went over to the bookcase and started rummaging among the books and magazines.

'I'm going to find you a few of the reports. Here we are. Here's one of them. Listen to this.' He started reading aloud from a copy of the *American Bee Journal*:

'"Living in Toronto at the head of a fine research laboratory given to him by the people of Canada in recognition of his truly great contribution to humanity in the discovery of insulin, Dr Frederick A. Banting became curious about royal jelly. He requested his staff to do a basic fractional analysis ..."'

He paused.

'Well, there's no need to read it all, but here's what happened. Dr Banting and his people took some royal jelly from queen cells that contained two-day-old larvae, and then they started analysing it. And what d'you think they found?

'They found,' he said, 'that royal jelly contained phenols, sterols, glycerils, dextrose, *and* – now here it comes – and eighty to eighty-five per cent *unidentified* acids!'

He stood beside the bookcase with the magazine in his hand, smiling a funny little furtive smile of triumph, and his wife watched him, bewildered.

He was not a tall man; he had a thick plump pulpy-looking body that was built close to the ground on abbreviated legs. The legs were slighly bowed. The head was huge and round, covered with bristly short-cut hair, and the greater part of the face – now that he had given up shaving altogether – was hidden by a brownish yellow fuzz about an inch long. In one way and another, he was rather grotesque to look at, there was no denying that.

'Eighty to eighty-five per cent,' he said, 'unidentified acids. Isn't that fantastic?' He turned back to the bookshelf and began hunting through the other magazines.

'What does it mean, unidentified acids?'

'That's the whole point! No one knows! Not even Banting could find out. You've heard of Banting?'

'No.'

'He just happens to be about the most famous living doctor in the world today, that's all.'

Looking at him now as he buzzed around in front of the bookcase with his bristly head and his hairy face and his plump pulpy body, she couldn't help thinking that somehow, in some curious way, there was a touch of the bee about this man. She had often seen women grow to look like the horses that they rode, and she had noticed that people who bred birds or bull terriers or pomeranians frequently resembled in some small but startling manner the creature of their choice. But up until now it had never occurred to her that her husband might look like a bee. It shocked her a bit.

'And did Banting ever try to eat it,' she asked, 'this royal jelly?'

'Of course he didn't eat it, Mabel. He didn't have enough for that. It's too precious.'

'You know something?' she said, staring at him but smiling a little all the same. 'You're getting to look just a teeny bit like a bee yourself, did you know that?'

He turned and looked at her.

'I suppose it's the beard mostly,' she said. 'I do wish you'd stop wearing it. Even the colour is sort of bee-ish, don't you think?'

'What the hell are you talking about, Mabel?'

'Albert,' she said. 'Your language.'

'Do you want to hear any more of this or don't you?'

'Yes, dear, I'm sorry. I was only joking. Do go on.'

He turned away again and pulled another magazine out of the bookcase and began leafing through the pages. 'Now just listen to this, Mabel. "In 1939, Heyl experimented with twenty-one-day-old rats, injecting them with royal jelly in varying amounts. As a result, he found a precocious follicular development of the ovaries directly in proportion to the quantity of royal jelly injected."'

'There!' she cried. 'I know it!'

'Knew what?'

'I knew something terrible would happen.'

'Nonsense. There's nothing wrong with that. Now here's another, Mabel. "Still and Burdett found that a male rat which hitherto had been unable to breed, upon receiving a minute daily dose of royal jelly, became a father many times over."'

'Albert,' she cried, 'this stuff is *much* too strong to give to a baby! I don't like it at all.'

'Nonsense, Mabel.'

'Then why do they only try it out on rats, tell me that? Why don't some of these famous scientists take it themselves? They're too clever, that's why. Do you think Dr Banting is going to risk finishing up with precious ovaries? Not him.'

'But they *have* given it to people, Mabel. Here's a whole article about it. Listen.' He turned the page and again began reading from the magazine. '"In Mexico, in 1953, a group of enlightened physicians began prescribing minute doses of royal jelly for such things as cerebral neuritis, arthritis, diabetes, autointoxication from tobacco, impotence in men, asthma, croup, and gout ... There are stacks of signed testimonials ... A celebrated stockbroker in Mexico City contracted a particularly stubborn case of psoriasis. He became physically unattractive. His clients began to forsake him. His business began to suffer. In desperation he turned to royal jelly – one drop with every meal – and presto! – he was cured in a fortnight. A waiter in the Café Jena, also in Mexico City, reported that his father, after taking minute doses of this wonder substance in capsule form, sired a healthy boy child at the age of ninety. A bullfight promoter in Acapulco, finding himself landed with a rather lethargic-looking bull, injected it with one gramme of royal jelly (an excessive dose) just before it entered the arena. Thereupon, the beast became so swift and savage that it promptly dispatched two picadors, three horses, and a matador, and finally ..."'

'Listen!' Mrs Taylor said, interrupting him. 'I think the baby's crying.'

Albert glanced up from his reading. Sure enough, a lusty yelling noise was coming from the bedroom above.

'She must be hungry,' he said.

His wife looked at the clock. 'Good gracious me!' she cried, jumping up. 'It's past her time again already! You mix the feed, Albert, quickly, while I bring her down! But hurry! I don't want to keep her waiting.'

In half a minute, Mrs Taylor was back, carrying the screaming infant in her arms. She was flustered now, still quite unaccustomed to the ghastly nonstop racket that a healthy baby makes when it wants its food. 'Do be quick, Albert!' she called, settling herself in the armchair and arranging the child on her lap. 'Please hurry!'

Albert entered from the kitchen and handed her the bottle of warm milk. 'It's just right,' he said. 'You don't have to test it.'

She hitched the baby's head a little higher in the crook of her arm, then pushed the rubber teat straight into the wide-open yelling mouth. The baby grabbed the teat and began to suck. The yelling stopped. Mrs Taylor relaxed.

'Oh, Albert, isn't she lovely?'

'She's terrific, Mabel – thanks to royal jelly.'

'Now, dear, I don't want to hear another word about that nasty stuff. It frightens me to death.'

'You're making a big mistake,' he said.

'We'll see about that.'

The baby went on sucking the bottle.

'I do believe she's going to finish the whole lot again, Albert.'

'I'm sure she is,' he said.

And a few minutes later, the milk was all gone.

'Oh, what a good girl you are!' Mrs Taylor cried, as very gently she started to withdraw the nipple. The baby sensed what she was doing and sucked harder, trying to hold on. The woman gave a quick little tug, and *plop*, out it came.

'Waa! Waa! Waa! Waa! Waa!' the baby yelled.

'Nasty old wind,' Mrs Taylor said, hoisting the child on to her shoulder and patting its back.

It belched twice in quick succession.

'There you are, my darling, you'll be all right now.'

For a few seconds, the yelling stopped. Then it started again.

'Keep belching her,' Albert said. 'She's drunk it too quick.'

His wife lifted the baby back on to her shoulder. She rubbed its spine. She changed it from one shoulder to the other. She lay it on its stomach on her lap. She sat it up on her knee. But it didn't belch again, and the yelling became louder and more insistent every minute.

'Good for the lungs,' Albert Taylor said, grinning. 'That's the way they exercise their lungs, Mabel, did you know that?'

'There, there, there,' the wife said, kissing it all over the face. 'There, there, there.'

They waited another five minutes, but not for one moment did the screaming stop.

'Change the nappy,' Albert said. 'It's got a wet nappy, that's all it is.' He fetched a clean one from the kitchen, and Mrs Taylor took the old one off and put the new one on.

This made no difference at all.

'Waa! Waa! Waa! Waa! Waa!' the baby yelled.

'You didn't stick the safety pin through the skin, did you, Mabel?'

'Of course I didn't,' she said, feeling under the nappy with her fingers to make sure.

The parents sat opposite one another in their armchairs, smiling nervously, watching the baby on the mother's lap, waiting for it to tire and stop screaming.

'You know what?' Albert Taylor said at last.

'What?'

'I'll bet she's still hungry. I'll bet all she wants is another swig at that bottle. How about me fetching her an extra lot?'

'I don't think we ought to do that, Albert.'

'It'll do her good,' he said, getting up from his chair. 'I'm going to warm her up a second helping.'

He went into the kitchen, and was away several minutes. When he returned he was holding a bottle brimful of milk.

'I made her a double,' he announced. 'Eight ounces. Just in case.'

'Albert! Are you mad? Don't you know it's just as bad to overfeed as it is to underfeed?'

'You don't have to give her the lot, Mabel. You can stop any time you like. Go on,' he said, standing over her. 'Give her a drink.'

Mrs Taylor began to tease the baby's upper lip with the end of the nipple. The tiny mouth closed like a trap over the rubber teat and suddenly there was silence in the room. The baby's whole body relaxed and a look of absolute bliss came over its face as it started to drink.

'There you are, Mabel! What did I tell you?'

The woman didn't answer.

'She's ravenous, that's what she is. Just look at her suck.'

Mrs Taylor was watching the level of the milk in the bottle. It was dropping fast, and before long three or four ounces out of the eight had disappeared.

'There,' she said. 'That'll do.'

'You can't pull it away now, Mabel.'

'Yes, dear. I must.'

'Go on, woman. Give her the rest and stop fussing.'

'But *Albert* . . .'

'She's famished, can't you see that? Go on, my beauty,' he said. 'You finish that bottle.'

'I don't like it, Albert,' the wife said, but she didn't pull the bottle away.

'She's making up for lost time, Mabel, that's all she's doing.'

Five minutes later the bottle was empty. Slowly, Mrs Taylor withdrew the nipple, and this time there was no protest from the baby, no sound at all. It lay peacefully on the mother's lap, the eyes glazed with contentment, the mouth half-open, the lips smeared with milk.

'Twelve whole ounces, Mabel!' Albert Taylor said. 'Three times the normal amount! Isn't that amazing!'

The woman was staring down at the baby. And now the old anxious tight-lipped look of the frightened mother was slowly returning to her face.

'What's the matter with *you*?' Albert asked. 'You're not worried by that, are you? You can't expect her to get back to normal on a lousy four ounces, don't be ridiculous.'

'Come here, Albert,' she said.

'What?'

'I said come here.'

He went over and stood beside her.

'Take a good look and tell me if you see anything different.'

He peered closely at the baby. 'She seems bigger, Mabel, if that's what you mean. Bigger and fatter.'

'Hold her,' she ordered. 'Go on, pick her up.'

He reached out and lifted the baby up off the mother's lap. 'Good
God!' he cried. 'She weighs a ton!'

'Exactly.'

'Now isn't that marvellous!' he cried, beaming. 'I'll bet she must be
back to normal already!'

'It frightens me, Albert. It's too quick.'

'Nonsense, woman.'

'It's that disgusting jelly that's done it,' she said. 'I hate the stuff.'

'There's nothing disgusting about royal jelly,' he answered, indignant.

'Don't be a fool, Albert! You think it's *normal* for a child to start
putting on weight at this speed?'

'You're never satisfied!' he cried. 'You're scared stiff when she's
losing and now you're absolutely terrified because she's gaining! What's
the matter with you, Mabel?'

The woman got up from her chair with the baby in her arms and
started towards the door. 'All I can say is,' she said, 'it's lucky I'm
here to see you don't give her any more of it, that's all I can say.' She
went out, and Albert watched her through the open door as she crossed
the hall to the foot of the stairs and started to ascend, and when she
reached the third or fourth step she suddenly stopped and stood quite
still for several seconds as though remembering something. Then she
turned and came down again rather quickly and re-entered the room.

'Albert,' she said.

'Yes?'

'I assume there wasn't any royal jelly in this last feed we've just
given her?'

'I don't see why you should assume that, Mabel.'

'Albert!'

'What's wrong?' he asked, soft and innocent.

'How *dare* you!' she cried.

Albert Taylor's great bearded face took on a pained and puzzled
look. 'I think you ought to be very glad she's got another big dose of
it inside her,' he said. 'Honest I do. And this *is* a big dose, Mabel,
believe you me.'

The woman was standing just inside the doorway clasping the
sleeping baby in her arms and staring at her husband with huge eyes.
She stood very erect, her body absolutely stiff with fury, her face paler,
more tight-lipped than ever.

'You mark my words,' Albert was saying, 'you're going to have a
nipper there soon that'll win first prize in any baby show in the *entire*
country. Hey, why don't you weigh her now and see what she is? You
want me to get the scales, Mabel, so you can weigh her?'

The woman walked straight over to the large table in the centre of
the room and laid the baby down and quickly started taking off its

clothes. 'Yes!' she snapped. 'Get the scales!' Off came the little nightgown, then the undervest.

Then she unpinned the nappy and she drew it away and the baby lay naked on the table.

'But Mabel!' Albert cried. 'It's a miracle! She's fat as a puppy!'

Indeed, the amount of flesh the child had put on since the day before was astounding. The small sunken chest with the rib bones showing all over it was now plump and round as a barrel, and the belly was bulging high in the air. Curiously, though, the arms and legs did not seem to have grown in proportion. Still short and skinny, they looked like little sticks protruding from a ball of fat.

'Look!' Albert said. 'She's even beginning to get a bit of fuzz on the tummy to keep her warm!' He put out a hand and was about to run the tips of his fingers over the powdering of silky yellowy-brown hairs that had suddenly appeared on the baby's stomach.

'*Don't you touch her!*' the woman cried. She turned and faced him, her eyes blazing, and she looked suddenly like some kind of little fighting bird with her neck arched over towards him as though she were about to fly at his face and peck his eyes out.

'Now wait a minute,' he said, retreating.

'You must be mad!' she cried.

'Now wait just one minute, Mabel, will you please, because if you're still thinking this stuff is dangerous ... That *is* what you're thinking, isn't it? All right, then. Listen carefully. I shall now proceed to *prove* to you once and for all, Mabel, that royal jelly is absolutely harmless to human beings, even in enormous doses. For example – why do you think we had only half the usual honey crop last summer? Tell me that.'

His retreat, walking backwards, had taken him three or four yards away from her, where he seemed to feel more comfortable.

'The reason we had only half the usual crop last summer,' he said slowly, lowering his voice, 'was because I turned one hundred of my hives over to the production of royal jelly.'

'You *what?*'

'Ah,' he whispered. 'I thought that might surprise you a bit. And I've been making it ever since right under your very nose.' His small eyes were glinting at her, and a slow sly smile was creeping around the corners of his mouth.

'You'll never guess the reason, either,' he said. 'I've been afraid to mention it up to now because I thought it might ... well ... sort of embarrass you.'

There was a slight pause. He had his hands clasped high in front of him, level with his chest, and he was rubbing one palm against the other, making a soft scraping noise.

'You remember that bit I read you out of the magazine? That bit about the rat? Let me see now, how does it go? "Still and Burdett found that a male rat which hitherto had been unable to breed ...."' He hesitated, the grin widening, showing his teeth.

'You get the message, Mabel?'

She stood quite still, facing him.

'The very first time I ever read that sentence, Mabel, I jumped straight out of my chair and I said to myself if it'll work with a lousy rat, I said, then there's no reason on earth why it shouldn't work with Albert Taylor.'

He paused again, craning his head forward and turning one ear slightly in his wife's direction, waiting for her to say something. But she didn't.

'And here's another thing,' he went on. 'It made me feel so absolutely marvellous, Mabel, and so sort of completely different to what I was before that I went right on taking it even after you'd announced the joyful tidings. *Buckets* of it I must have swallowed during the last twelve months.'

The big heavy haunted-looking eyes of the woman were moving intently over the man's face and neck. There was no skin showing at all on the neck, not even at the sides below the ears. The whole of it, to a point where it disappeared into the collar of the shirt, was covered all the way around with those shortish silky hairs, yellowy black.

'Mind you,' he said, turning away from her, gazing lovingly now at the baby, 'it's going to work far better on a tiny infant than on a fully developed man like me. You've only got to look at her to see that, don't you agree?'

The woman's eyes travelled slowly downward and settled on the baby. The baby was lying naked on the table, fat and white and comatose, like some gigantic grub that was approaching the end of its larval life and would soon emerge into the world complete with mandibles and wings.

'Why don't you cover her up, Mabel?' he said. 'We don't want our little queen to catch a cold.'

GEORGY PORGY

Without in any way wishing to blow my own trumpet, I think that I can claim to being in most respects a moderately well-matured and rounded individual. I have travelled a good deal. I am adequately read. I speak Greek and Latin. I dabble in science. I can tolerate a mildly liberal attitude in the politics of others. I have compiled a volume of notes upon the evolution of the madrigal in the fifteenth century. I have witnessed the death of a large number of persons in their beds; and in addition, I have influenced, at least I hope I have, the lives of quite a few others by the spoken word delivered from the pulpit.

Yet in spite of all this, I must confess that I have never in any life – well, how shall I put it? – I have never really had anything much to do with women.

To be perfectly honest, up until three weeks ago I had never so much as laid a finger on one of them except perhaps to help her over a stile or something like that when the occasion demanded. And even then I always tried to ensure that I touched only the shoulder or the waist or some other place where the skin was covered, because the one thing I never could stand was actual contact between my skin and theirs. Skin touching skin, my skin, that is, touching the skin of a female, whether it were leg, neck, face, hand, or merely finger, was so repugnant to me that I invariably greeted a lady with my hands clasped firmly behind my back to avoid the inevitable handshake.

I could go further than that and say that any sort of physical contact with them, even when the skin wasn't bare, would disturb me considerably. If a woman stood close to me in a queue so that our bodies touched, or if she squeezed in beside me on a bus seat, hip to hip and thigh to thigh, my cheeks would begin burning like mad and little prickles of sweat would start coming out all over the crown of my head.

This condition is all very well in a schoolboy who has just reached the age of puberty. With him it is simply Dame Nature's way of putting on the brakes and holding the lad back until he is old enough to behave himself like a gentleman. I approve of that.

But there was no reason on God's earth why I, at the ripe old age of thirty-one, should continue to suffer a similar embarrassment. I was well trained to resist temptation, and I was certainly not given to vulgar passions.

Had I been even the slightest bit ashamed of my own personal appearance, then that might possibly have explained the whole thing. But I was not. On the contrary, and though I say it myself, the fates had been rather kind to me in that regard. I stood exactly five and a half feet tall in my stockinged feet, and my shoulders, though they sloped downward a little from the neck, were nicely in balance with my small neat frame. (Personally, I've always thought that a little slope on the shoulder lends a subtle and faintly aesthetic air to a man who is not overly tall, don't you agree?) My features were regular, my teeth were in excellent condition (protruding only a smallish amount from the upper jaw), and my hair, which was an unusually brilliant ginger-red, grew thickly all over my scalp. Good heavens above, I had seen men who were perfect shrimps in comparison with me displaying an astonishing aplomb in their dealings with the fairer sex. And oh, how I envied them! How I longed to do likewise – to be able to share in a few of those pleasant little rituals of contact that I observed continually taking place between men and women – the touching of hands, the peck on the cheek, the linking of arms, the pressure of knee against knee or foot against foot under the dining-table, and most of all, the full-blown violent embrace that comes when two of them join together on the floor – for a dance.

But such things were not for me. Alas, I had to spend my time avoiding them instead. And this, my friends, was easier said than done, even for a humble curate in a small country region far from the fleshpots of the metropolis.

My flock, you understand, contained an inordinate number of ladies. There were scores of them in the parish, and the unfortunate thing about it was that at least sixty per cent of them were spinsters, completely untamed by the benevolent influence of holy matrimony.

I tell you I was jumpy as a squirrel.

One would have thought that with all the careful training my mother had given me as a child, I should have been capable of taking this sort of thing well in my stride; and no doubt I would have done if only she had lived long enough to complete my education. But alas, she was killed when I was still quite young.

She was a wonderful woman, my mother. She used to wear huge bracelets on her wrists, five or six of them at a time, with all sorts of things hanging from them and tinkling against each other as she moved. It didn't matter where she was, you could always find her by listening for the noise of those bracelets. It was better than a cowbell. And in the evenings she used to sit on the sofa in her black trousers with her feet tucked up underneath her, smoking endless cigarettes from a long black holder. And I'd be crouching on the floor, watching her.

'You want to taste my martini, George?' she used to ask.

'Now stop it, Clare,' my father would say. 'If you're not careful you'll stunt the boy's growth.'

'Go on,' she said. 'Don't be frightened of it. Drink it.'

I always did everything my mother told me.

'That's enough,' my father said. 'He only has to know what it tastes like.'

'Please don't interfere, Boris. This is *very* important.'

My mother had a theory that nothing in the world should be kept secret from a child. Show him everything. Make him *experience* it.

'I'm not going to have any boy of mine going around whispering dirty secrets with other children and having to guess about this thing and that simply because no one will tell him.'

Tell him everything. Make him listen.

'Come over here, George, and I'll tell you what there is to know about God.'

She never read stories to me at night before I went to bed; she just 'told' me things instead. And every evening it was something different.

'Come over here, George, because now I'm going to tell you about Mohammed.'

She would be sitting on the sofa in her black trousers with her legs crossed and her feet tucked up underneath her, and she'd beckon to me in a queer languorous manner with the hand that held the long black cigarette-holder, and the bangles would start jingling all the way up her arm.

'If you must have a religion I suppose Mohammedanism is as good as any of them. It's all based on keeping healthy. You have lots of wives, and you mustn't ever smoke or drink.'

'Why mustn't you smoke or drink, Mummy?'

'Because if you've got lots of wives you have to keep healthy and virile.'

'What is virile?'

'I'll go into that tomorrow, my pet. Let's deal with one subject at a time. Another thing about the Mohammedan is that he never never gets constipated.'

'Now, Clare,' my father would say, looking up from his book. 'Stick to the facts.'

'My dear Boris, you don't know anything about it. Now if only *you* would try bending forward and touching the ground with your forehead morning, noon, and night every day, facing Mecca, you might have a bit less trouble in that direction yourself.'

I used to love listening to her, even though I could only understand

about half of what she was saying. She really was telling me secrets,
and there wasn't anything more exciting than that.

'Come over here, George, and I'll tell you precisely how your father
makes his money.'

'Now, Clare, that's quite enough.'

'Nonsense, darling. Why make a *secret* out of it with the child? He'll
only imagine something much much worse.'

I was exactly ten years old when she started giving me detailed
lectures on the subject of sex. This was the biggest secret of them all,
and therefore the most enthralling.

'Come over here, George, because now I'm going to tell you how
you came into this world, right from the very beginning.'

I saw my father glance up quietly, and open his mouth wide the
way he did when he was going to say something vital, but my mother
was already fixing him with those brilliant shining eyes of hers, and
he went slowly back to his book without uttering a sound.

'Your poor father is embarrassed,' she said, and she gave me her
private smile, the one that she gave nobody else, only to me – the one-
sided smile where just one corner of her mouth lifted slowly upward
until it made a lovely long wrinkle that stretched right up to the eye
itself, and became a sort of wink-smile instead.

'Embarrassment, my pet, is the one thing that I want you never to
feel. And don't think for a moment that your father is embarrassed
only because of *you*.'

My father started wriggling about in his chair.

'My God, he's even embarrassed about things like that when he's
alone with me, his own wife.'

'About things like what?' I asked.

At that point my father got up and quietly left the room.

I think it must have been about a week after this that my mother
was killed. It may possibly have been a little later, ten days or a
fortnight, I can't be sure. All I know is that we were getting near the
end of this particular series of 'talks' when it happened; and because
I myself was personally involved in the brief chain of events that led
up to her death, I can still remember every single detail of that curious
night just as clearly as if it were yesterday. I can switch it on in my
memory any time I like and run it through in front of my eyes exactly
as though it were the reel of a cinema film; and it never varies. It
always ends at precisely the same place, no more and no less, and it
always begins in the same peculiarly sudden way, with the screen in
darkness, and my mother's voice somewhere above me, calling my
name:

'George! Wake up, George, wake up!'

And then there is a bright electric light dazzling in my eyes, and right from the very centre of it, but far away, the voice is still calling me:

'George, wake up and get out of bed and put your dressing-gown on! Quickly! You're coming downstairs. There's something I want you to see. Come on, child, come on! Hurry up! And put your slippers on. We're going outside.'

'Outside?'

'Don't argue with me, George. Just do as you're told.' I am so sleepy I can hardly see to walk, but my mother takes me firmly by the hand and leads me downstairs and out through the front door into the night where the cold air is like a sponge of water in my face, and I open my eyes wide and see the lawn all sparkling with frost and the cedar trees with its tremendous arms standing black against a thin small moon. And overhead a great mass of stars is wheeling up into the sky.

We hurry across the lawn, my mother and I, her bracelets all jingling like mad and me having to trot to keep up with her. Each step I take I can feel the crisp frosty grass crunching softly underfoot.

'Josephine has just started having her babies,' my mother says. 'It's a perfect opportunity. You shall watch the whole process.'

There is a light burning in the garage when we get there, and we go inside. My father isn't there, nor is the car, and the place seems huge and bare, and the concrete floor is freezing cold through the soles of my bedroom slippers. Josephine is reclining on a heap of straw inside the low wire cage in one corner of the room – large blue rabbit with small pink eyes that watch us suspiciously as we go towards her. The husband, whose name is Napoleon, is now in a separate cage in the opposite corner, and I notice that he is standing up on his hind legs scratching impatiently at the netting.

'Look!' my mother cries. 'She's just having the first one! It's almost out!'

We both creep closer to Josephine, and I squat down beside the cage with my face right up against the wire. I am fascinated. Here is one rabbit coming out of another. It is magical and rather splendid. It is also very quick.

'Look how it comes out all neatly wrapped up in its own little cellophane bag!' my mother is saying.

'And just look how she's taking care of it now! The poor darling doesn't have a face-flannel, and even if she did she couldn't hold it in her paws, so she's washing it with her tongue instead.'

The mother rabbit rolls her small pink eyes anxiously in our direction, and then I see her shifting position in the straw so that her body is between us and the young one.

'Come round the other side,' my mother says. 'The silly thing has moved. I do believe she's trying to hide her baby from us.'

We go round the other side of the cage. The rabbit follows us with her eyes. A couple of yards away the buck is prancing madly up and down, clawing at the wire.

'Why is Napoleon so excited?' I ask.

'I don't know, dear. Don't you bother about him. Watch Josephine. I expect she'll be having another one soon. Look how carefully she's washing that little baby! She's treating it just like a human mother treats hers! Isn't it funny to think that I did almost exactly the same sort of thing to you once?' The big blue doe is still watching us, and now, again, she pushes the baby away with her nose and rolls slowly over to face the other way. Then she goes on with her licking and cleaning.

'Isn't it wonderful how a mother knows instinctively just what she has to do?' my mother says. 'Now you just imagine, my pet, that the baby is *you*, and Josephine is *me* – wait a minute, come back over here again so you can get a better look.'

We creep back around the cage to keep the baby in view.

'See how she's fondling it and kissing it all over! There! She's *really* kissing it now, isn't she! Exactly like me and you!'

I peer closer. It seems a queer way of kissing to me.

'Look!' I scream. 'She's eating it!'

And sure enough, the head of the baby rabbit is now disappearing swiftly into the mother's mouth.

'Mummy! Quick!'

But almost before the sound of my scream has died away, the whole of that tiny pink body has vanished down the mother's throat.

I swing quickly around, and the next thing I know I'm looking straight into my own mother's face, not six inches above me, and no doubt she is trying to say something or it may be that she is too astonished to say anything, but all I see is the mouth, the huge red mouth opening wider and wider until it is just a great big round gaping hole with a black centre, and I scream again, and this time I can't stop. Then suddenly out come her hands, and I can feel her skin touching mine, the long cold fingers closing tightly over my fists, and I jump back and jerk myself free and rush blindly out into the night. I run down the drive and through the front gates, screaming all the way, and then, above the noise of my own voice I can hear the jingle of bracelets coming up behind me in the dark, getting louder and louder as she keeps gaining on me all the way down the long hill to the bottom of the lane and over the bridge on to the main road where the cars are streaming by at sixty miles an hour with headlights blazing.

Then somewhere behind me I hear a screech of tyres skidding on the road surface, and then there is silence, and I notice suddenly that the bracelets aren't jingling behind me any more.

Poor Mother.

If only she could have lived a little longer.

I admit that she gave me a nasty fright with those rabbits, but it wasn't her fault, and anyway queer things like that were always happening between her and me. I had come to regard them as a sort of toughening process that did me more good than harm. But if only she could have lived long enough to complete my education, I'm sure I should never have had all that trouble I was telling you about a few minutes ago.

I want to get on with that now. I didn't mean to begin talking about my mother. She doesn't have anything to do with what I originally started out to say. I won't mention her again.

I was telling you about the spinsters in my parish. It's an ugly word, isn't it – spinster? It conjures up the vision either of a stringy old hen with a puckered mouth or of a huge ribald monster shouting around the house in riding-breeches. But these were not like that at all. They were a clean, healthy, well-built group of females, the majority of them highly bred and surprisingly wealthy, and I feel sure that the average unmarried man would have been gratified to have them around.

In the beginning, when I first came to the vicarage, I didn't have too bad a time. I enjoyed a measure of protection, of course, by reason of my calling and my cloth. In addition, I myself adopted a cool dignified attitude that was calculated to discourage familiarity. For a few months, therefore, I was able to move freely among my parishioners, and no one took the liberty of linking her arm in mine at a charity bazaar, or of touching my fingers with hers as she passed me the cruet at suppertime. I was very happy. I was feeling better than I had in years. Even that little nervous habit I had of flicking my earlobe with my forefinger when I talked began to disappear.

This was what I call my first period, and it extended over approximately six months. Then came trouble.

I suppose I should have known that a healthy male like myself couldn't hope to evade embroilment indefinitely simply by keeping a fair distance between himself and the ladies. It just doesn't work. If anything it has the opposite effect.

I would see them eyeing me covertly across the room at a whist drive, whispering to one another, nodding, running their tongues over their lips, sucking at their cigarettes, plotting the best approach, but always whispering, and sometimes I overheard snatches of their talk – 'What a shy person ... he's just a trifle nervous, isn't he ... he's much too tense ... he needs companionship ... he wants loosening up ... we must teach him how to relax.' And then slowly as the weeks went by, they began to stalk me. I knew they were doing it. I could feel it happening although at first they did nothing definite to give themselves away.

That was my second period. It lasted for the best part of a year and was very trying indeed. But it was paradise compared with the third and final phase.

For now, instead of sniping at me sporadically from far away, the attackers suddenly came charging out of the wood with bayonets fixed. It was terrible, frightening. Nothing is more calculated to unnerve a man than the swift unexpected assault. Yet I am not a coward. I will stand my ground against any single individual of my own size under any circumstances. But this onslaught, I am now convinced, was conducted by vast numbers operating as one skilfully coordinated unit.

The first offender was Miss Elphinstone, a large woman with moles. I had dropped in on her during the afternoon to solicit a contribution towards a new set of bellows for the organ, and after some pleasant conversation in the library she had graciously handed me a cheque for two guineas. I told her not to bother to see me to the door and I went out into the hall to get my hat. I was about to reach for it when all at once – she must have come tip-toeing up behind me – all at once I felt a bare arm sliding through mine, and one second later her fingers were entwined in my own, and she was squeezing my hand hard, in out, in out, as though it were the bulb of a throat-spray.

'Are you really so Very Reverend as you're always pretending to be?' she whispered.

Well!

All I can tell you is that when that arm of hers came sliding in under mine, it felt exactly as though a cobra was coiling itself around my wrist. I leaped away, pulled open the front door, and fled down the drive without looking back.

The very next day we held a jumble sale in the village hall (again to raise money for the new bellows), and towards the end of it I was standing in a corner quietly drinking a cup of tea and keeping an eye on the villagers crowding round the stalls when all of a sudden I heard a voice beside me saying, 'Dear me, what a hungry look you have in those eyes of yours.' The next instant a long curvaceous body was leaning up against mine and a hand with red fingernails was trying to push a thick slice of coconut cake into my mouth.

'Miss Prattley,' I cried. 'Please!'

But she'd got me up against the wall, and with a teacup in one hand and a saucer in the other I was powerless to resist. I felt the sweat breaking out all over me and if my mouth hadn't quickly become full of the cake she was pushing into it, I honestly believe I would have started to scream.

A nasty incident, that one; but there was worse to come. The next day it was Miss Unwin. Now Miss Unwin happened to be a close friend of Miss Elphinstone's *and* of Miss Prattley's, and this of course should have been enough to make me very cautious. Yet who would have thought that she of all people, Miss Unwin, that quiet gentle little mouse who only a few weeks before had presented me with a new hassock exquisitely worked in needlepoint with her own hands, who would have thought that *she* would ever have taken a liberty with anyone? So when she asked me to accompany her down to the crypt to show her the Saxon murals, it never entered my head that there was devilry afoot. But there was.

I don't propose to describe that encounter; it was too painful. And the ones which followed were no less savage. Nearly every day from then on, some new outrageous incident would take place. I became a nervous wreck. At times I hardly knew what I was doing. I started reading the burial service at young Gladys Pitcher's wedding. I dropped Mrs Harris's new baby into the font during the christening and gave it a nasty ducking. An uncomfortable rash that I hadn't had in over two years reappeared on the side of my neck, and that annoying business with my earlobe came back worse than ever before. Even my hair began coming out in my comb. The faster I retreated, the faster they came after me. Women are like that. Nothing stimulates them quite so much as a display of modesty or shyness in a man. And they become doubly persistent if underneath it all they happen to detect – and here I have a most difficult confession to make – if they happen to detect, as they did in me, a little secret gleam of longing shining in the backs of the eyes.

You see, actually I was mad about women.

Yes, I know. You will find this hard to believe after all that I have said, but it was perfectly true. You must understand that it was only when they touched me with their fingers or pushed up against me with their bodies that I became alarmed. Providing they remained at a safe distance, I could watch them for hours on end with the same peculiar fascination that you yourself might experience in watching a creature you couldn't bear to touch – an octopus, for example, or a long poisonous snake. I loved the smooth white look of a bare arm emerging from a sleeve, curiously naked like a peeled banana. I could get enormously excited just from watching a girl walk across the room in a tight dress; and I particularly enjoyed the back view of a pair of legs when the feet were in rather high heels – the wonderful braced-up look behind the knees, with the legs themselves very taut as though they were made of strong elastic stretched out almost to breaking-point, but not quite. Sometimes, in Lady Birdwell's drawing-room, sitting near the window on a summer's afternoon, I would glance over the rim of my teacup towards the swimming pool and become agitated beyond measure by the sight of a little patch of sunburned stomach bulging between the top and bottom of a two-piece bathing-suit.

There is nothing wrong in having thoughts like these. All men harbour them from time to time. But they did give me a terrible sense of guilt. Is it me, I kept asking myself, who is unwittingly responsible

for the shameless way in which these ladies are now behaving? Is it
the gleam in my eye (which I cannot control) that is constantly rousing
their passions and egging them on? Am I unconsciously giving them
what is sometimes known as the come-hither signal every time I glance
their way? Am I?

Or is this brutal conduct of theirs inherent in the very nature of the
female?

I had a pretty fair idea of the answer to this question, but that was
not good enough for me. I happen to possess a conscience that can
never be consoled by guesswork; it has to have proof. I simply had to
find out who was really the guilty party in this case – me or them,
and with this object in view, I now decided to perform a simple
experiment of my own invention, using Snelling's rats.

A year or so previously I had had some trouble with an objectionable
choirboy named Billy Snelling. On three consecutive Sundays this
youth had brought a pair of white rats into church and had let them
loose on the floor during my sermon. In the end I had confiscated the
animals and carried them home and placed them in a box in the shed
at the bottom of the vicarage garden. Purely for humane reasons I
had then proceeded to feed them, and as a result, but without any
further encouragement from me, the creatures began to multiply very
rapidly. The two became five, and five became twelve.

It was at this point that I decided to use them for research purposes.
There were exactly equal numbers of males and females, six of each,
so that conditions were ideal.

I first isolated the sexes, putting them into two separate cages, and
I left them like that for three whole weeks. Now a rat is a very
lascivious animal, and any zoologist will tell you that for them this is
an inordinately long period of separation. At a guess I would say that
one week of enforced celibacy for a rat is equal to approximately one
year of the same treatment for someone like Miss Elphinstone or Miss
Prattley; so you can see that I was doing a pretty fair job in reproducing
actual conditions.

When the three weeks were up, I took a large box that was divided
across the centre by a little fence, and I placed the females on one
side and the males on the other. The fence consisted of nothing more
than three single strands of naked wire, one inch apart, but there was
a powerful electric current running through the wires.

To add a touch of reality to the proceedings, I gave each female a
name. The largest one, who also had the longest whiskers, was Miss
Elphinstone. The one with a short thick tail was Miss Prattley. The
smallest of them all was Miss Unwin, and so on. The males, all six of
them, were ME.

I now pulled up a chair and sat back to watch the result.

All rats are suspicious by nature, and when I first put the two sexes together in the box with only the wire between them, neither side made a move. The males stared hard at the females through the fence. The females stared back, waiting for the males to come forward. I could see that both sides were tense with yearning. Whiskers quivered and noses twitched and occasionally a long tail would flick sharply against the wall of the box.

After a while, the first male detached himself from his group and advanced gingerly towards the fence, his belly close to the ground. He touched a wire and was immediately electrocuted. The remaining eleven rats froze, motionless.

There followed a period of nine and a half minutes during which neither side moved; but I noticed that while all the males were now staring at the dead body of their colleague, the females had eyes only for the males.

Then suddenly Miss Prattley with the short tail could stand it no longer. She came bounding forward, hit the wire, and dropped dead.

The males pressed their bodies closer to the ground and gazed thoughtfully at the two corpses by the fence. The females also seemed to be quite shaken, and there was another wait, with neither side moving.

Now it was Miss Unwin who began to show signs of impatience. She snorted audibly and twitched a pink mobile nose-end from side to side, then suddenly she started jerking her body quickly up and down as though she were doing pushups. She glanced round at her remaining four companions, raised her tail high in the air as much as to say, 'Here I go, girls,' and with that she advanced briskly to the wire, pushed her head through it, and was killed.

Sixteen minutes later, Miss Foster made her first move. Miss Foster was a woman in the village who bred cats, and recently she had had the effrontery to put up a large sign outside her house in the High Street, saying FOSTER's CATTERY. Through long association with the creatures she herself seemed to have acquired all their most noxious characteristics, and whenever she came near me in a room I could detect, even through the smoke of her Russian cigarette, a faint but pungent aroma of cat. She had never struck me as having much control over her baser instincts, and it was with some satisfaction, therefore, that I watched her now as she foolishly took her own life in a last desperate plunge towards the masculine sex.

A Miss Montgomery-Smith came next, a small determined woman who had once tried to make me believe that she had been engaged to a bishop. She died trying to creep on her belly under the lowest wire, and I must say I thought this a very fair reflection upon the way in which she lived her life.

And still the five remaining males stayed motionless, waiting.

The fifth female to go was Miss Plumley. She was a devious one who was continually slipping little messages addressed to me into the collection bag. Only the Sunday before, I had been in the vestry counting the money after morning service and had come across one of them tucked inside a folded ten-shilling note. *Your poor throat sounded hoarse today during the sermon*, it said. *Let me bring you a bottle of my own cherry pectoral to soothe it down. Most affectionately, Eunice Plumley.*

Miss Plumley ambled slowly up to the wire, sniffed the centre strand with the tip of her nose, came a fraction too close, and received two hundred and forty volts of alternating current through her body.

The five males stayed where they were, watching the slaughter.

And now only Miss Elphinstone remained on the feminine side.

For a full half-hour neither she nor any of the others made a move. Finally one of the males stirred himself slightly, took a step forward, hesitated, thought better of it, and slowly sank back into a crouch on the floor.

This must have frustrated Miss Elphinstone beyond measure, for suddenly, with eyes blazing, she rushed forward and took a flying leap at the wire. It was a spectacular jump and she nearly cleared it; but one of her hind legs grazed the top strand, and thus she also perished with the rest of her sex.

I cannot tell you how much good it did me to watch this simple and, though I say it myself, this rather ingenious experiment. In one stroke I had laid open the incredibly lascivious, stop-at-nothing nature of the female. My own sex was vindicated; my own conscience was cleared. In a trice, all those awkward little flashes of guilt from which I had continually been suffering flew out of the window. I felt suddenly very strong and serene in the knowledge of my own innocence.

For a few moments I toyed with the absurd idea of electrifying the black iron railings that ran around the vicarage garden; or perhaps just the gate would be enough. Then I would sit back comfortably in a chair in the library and watch through the window as the real Misses Elphinstone and Prattley and Unwin came forward one after the other and paid the final penalty for pestering an innocent male.

Such foolish thoughts!

What I must actually do now, I told myself, was to weave around me a sort of invisible electric fence constructed entirely out of my own personal moral fibre. Behind this I would sit in perfect safety while the enemy, one after another, flung themselves against the wire.

I would begin by cultivating a brusque manner. I would speak crisply to all women, and refrain from smiling at them. I would no longer step back a pace when one of them advanced upon me. I would stand my ground and glare at her, and if she said something that I considered suggestive, I would make a sharp retort.

It was in this mood that I set off the very next day to attend Lady Birdwell's tennis party.

I was not a player myself, but her ladyship had graciously invited me to drop in and mingle with the guests when play was over at six o'clock. I believe she thought that it lent a certain tone to a gathering to have a clergyman present, and she was probably hoping to persuade me to repeat the performance I gave the last time I was there, when I sat at the piano for a full hour and a quarter after supper and entertained the guests with a detailed description of the evolution of the madrigal through the centuries.

I arrived at the gates on my cycle promptly at six o'clock and pedalled up the long drive towards the house. This was the first week of June, and the rhododendrons were massed in great banks of pink and purple all the way along on either side. I was feeling unusually blithe and dauntless. The previous day's experiment with rats had made it impossible now for anyone to take me by surprise. I knew exactly what to expect and I was armed accordingly. All around me the little fence was up.

'Ah, good evening, Vicar,' Lady Birdwell cried, advancing upon me with both arms outstretched.

I stood my ground and looked her straight in the eye. 'How's Birdwell?' I said. 'Still up in the city?'

I doubt whether she had ever before in her life heard Lord Birdwell referred to thus by someone who had never even met him. It stopped her dead in her tracks. She looked at me queerly and didn't seem to know how to answer.

'I'll take a seat if I may,' I said, and walked past her towards the terrace where a group of nine or ten guests were settled comfortably in cane chairs, sipping their drinks. They were mostly women, the usual crowd, all of them dressed in white tennis clothes, and as I strode in among them my own sober black suiting seemed to give me, I thought, just the right amount of separateness for the occasion.

The ladies greeted me with smiles. I nodded to them and sat down in a vacant chair, but I didn't smile back.

'I think perhaps I'd better finish my story another time,' Miss Elphinstone was saying. 'I don't believe the vicar would approve.' She giggled and gave me an arch look. I knew she was waiting for me to come out with my usual little nervous laugh and to say my usual little sentence about how broadminded I was; but I did nothing of the sort. I simply raised one side of my upper lip until it shaped itself into a tiny curl of contempt (I had practised in the mirror that morning), and then I said sharply, in a loud voice, '*Mens sana in corpore sano.*'

'What's that?' she cried. 'Come again, Vicar.'

'A clean mind in a healthy body,' I answered. 'It's a family motto.'

There was an odd kind of silence for quite a long time after this. I could see the women exchanging glances with one another, frowning, shaking their heads.

'The vicar's in the dumps,' Miss Foster announced. She was the one who bred cats. 'I think the vicar needs a drink.'

'Thank you,' I said, 'but I never imbibe. You know that.'

'Then do let me fetch you a nice cooling glass of fruit cup?'

This last sentence came softly and rather suddenly from someone just behind me, to my right, and there was a note of such genuine concern in the speaker's voice that I turned round.

I saw a lady of singular beauty whom I had met only once before, about a month ago. Her name was Miss Roach, and I remembered that she had struck me then as being a person far out of the usual run. I had been particularly impressed by her gentle and reticent nature; and the fact that I had felt comfortable in her presence proved beyond doubt that she was not the sort of person who would try to impinge herself upon me in any way.

'I'm sure you must be tired after cycling all that distance,' she was saying now.

I swivelled right round in my chair and looked at her carefully. She was certainly a striking person – unusually muscular for a woman, with broad shoulders and powerful arms and a huge calf bulging on each leg. The flush of the afternoon's exertions was still upon her, and her face glowed with a healthy red sheen.

'Thank you so much, Miss Roach,' I said, 'but I never touch alcohol in any form. Maybe a small glass of lemon squash ...'

'The fruit cup is only made of fruit, Padre.'

How I loved a person who called me 'Padre'. The word has a military ring about it that conjures up visions of stern discipline and officer rank.

'Fruit cup?' Miss Elphinstone said. 'It's harmless.'

'My dear man, it's nothing but vitamin C,' Miss Foster said.

'Much better for you than fizzy lemonade,' Lady Birdwell said. 'Carbon dioxide attacks the lining of the stomach.'

'I'll get you some,' Miss Roach said, smiling at me pleasantly. It was a good open smile, and there wasn't a trace of guile or mischief from one corner of the mouth to the other.

She stood up and walked over to the drink table. I saw her slicing an orange, then an apple, then a cucumber, then a grape, and dropping the pieces into a glass. Then she poured in a large quantity of liquid from a bottle whose label I couldn't quite read without my spectacles, but I fancied that I saw the name JIM on it, or TIM, or PIM, or some such word.

'I hope there's enough left,' Lady Birdwell called out. 'Those greedy children of mine do love it so.'

'Plenty,' Miss Roach answered, and she brought the drink to me and set it on the table.

Even without tasting it I could easily understand why children

adored it. The liquid itself was dark amber-red and there were great
hunks of fruit floating around among the ice cubes; and on top of it
all, Miss Roach had placed a sprig of mint. I guessed that the mint
had been put there specially for me, to take some of the sweetness
away and to lend a touch of grown-upness to a concoction that was
otherwise so obviously for youngsters.

'Too sticky for you, Padre!'

'It's delectable,' I said, sipping it. 'Quite perfect.'

It seemed a pity to gulp it down quickly after all the trouble Miss
Roach had taken to make it, but it was so refreshing I couldn't resist.

'Do let me make you another!'

I liked the way she waited until I had set the glass on the table,
instead of trying to take it out of my hand.

'I wouldn't eat the mint if I were you,' Miss Elphinstone said.

'I'd better get another bottle from the house,' Lady Birdwell called
out. 'You're going to need it, Mildred.'

'Do that,' Miss Roach replied. 'I drink gallons of the stuff myself,'
she went on, speaking to me. 'And I don't think you'd say that I'm
exactly what you might call emaciated.'

'No indeed,' I answered fervently. I was watching her again as she
mixed me another brew, noticing how the muscles rippled under the
skin of the arm that raised the bottle. Her neck also was uncommonly
fine when seen from behind; not thin and stringy like the necks of a
lot of these so-called modern beauties, but thick and strong with a
slight ridge running down either side where the sinews bulged. It
wasn't easy to guess the age of a person like this, but I doubted whether
she could have been more than forty-eight or nine.

I had just finished my second big glass of fruit cup when I began
to experience a most peculiar sensation. I seemed to be floating up
out of my chair, and hundreds of little warm waves came washing in
under me, lifting me higher and higher. I felt as buoyant as a bubble,
and everything around me seemed to be bobbing up and down and
swirling gently from side to side. It was all very pleasant, and I was
overcome by an almost irresistible desire to break into song.

'Feeling happy?' Miss Roach's voice sounded miles and miles away,
and when I turned to look at her, I was astonished to see how near
she really was. She, also, was bobbing up and down.

'Terrific,' I answered. 'I'm feeling absolutely terrific.'

Her face was large and pink, and it was so close to me now that I
could see the pale carpet of fuzz covering both her cheeks, and the
way the sunlight caught each tiny separate hair and made it shine like
gold. All of a sudden I found myself wanting to put out a hand and
stroke those cheeks of hers with my fingers. To tell the truth, I wouldn't
have objected in the least if she had tried to do the same to me.

'Listen,' she said softly. 'How about the two of us taking a little stroll down the garden to see the lupins?'

'Fine,' I answered. 'Lovely. Anything you say.'

There is a small Georgian summer-house alongside the croquet lawn in Lady Birdwell's garden, and the very next thing I knew, I was sitting inside it on a kind of chaise-longue and Miss Roach was beside me. I was still bobbing up and down, and so was she, and so, for that matter, was the summer-house, but I was feeling wonderful. I asked Miss Roach if she would like me to give her a song.

'Not now,' she said, encircling me with her arms and squeezing my chest against hers so hard that it hurt.

'Don't,' I said, melting.

'That's better,' she kept saying. 'That's much better, isn't it?'

Had Miss Roach or any other female tried to do this sort of thing to me an hour before, I don't quite know what would have happened. I think I would probably have fainted. I might even have died. But here I was now, the same old me, actually relishing the contact of those enormous bare arms against my body! Also – and this was the most amazing thing of all – I was beginning to feel the urge to reciprocate.

I took the lobe of her left ear between my thumb and forefinger, and tugged it playfully.

'Naughty boy,' she said.

I tugged harder and squeezed it a bit at the same time. This roused her to such a pitch that she began to grunt and snort like a hog. Her breathing became loud and stertorous.

'Kiss me,' she ordered.

'What?' I said.

'Come on, kiss me.'

At that moment, I saw her mouth. I saw this great mouth of hers coming slowly down on top of me, starting to open, and coming closer and closer, and opening wider and wider; and suddenly my whole stomach began to roll right over inside me and I went stiff with terror.

'No!' I shrieked. 'Don't! Don't, Mummy, don't!'

I can only tell you that I had never in all my life seen anything more terrifying than that mouth. I simply could not *stand* it coming at me like that. Had it been a red-hot iron someone was pushing into my face I wouldn't have been nearly so petrified, I swear I wouldn't. The strong arms were around me, pinning me down so that I couldn't move, and the mouth kept getting larger and larger, and then all at once it was right on top of me, huge and wet and cavernous, and the next second – I was inside it.

I was right inside this enormous mouth, lying on my stomach along the length of the tongue, with my feet somewhere around the back of the throat; and I knew instinctively that unless I got myself out again at once I was going to be swallowed alive – just like that baby rabbit. I could feel my legs being drawn down the throat by some kind of suction, and quickly I threw up my arms and grabbed hold of the lower front teeth and held on for dear life. My head was near the mouth-entrance, and I could actually look right out between the lips and see a little patch of the world outside – sunlight shining on the polished wooden floor of the summer-house, and on the floor itself a gigantic foot in a white tennis shoe.

I had a good grip with my fingers on the edge of the teeth, and in spite of the suction, I was managing to haul myself up slowly towards the daylight when suddenly the upper teeth came down on my knuckles and started chopping away at them so fiercely I had to let go. I went sliding back down the throat, feet first, clutching madly at this and that as I went, but everything was so smooth and slippery I couldn't get a grip. I glimpsed a bright flash of gold on the left as I slid past the last of the molars, and then three inches farther on I saw what must have been the uvula above me, dangling like a thick red stalactite from the roof of the throat. I grabbed at it with both hands but the thing slithered through my fingers and I went on down.

I remember screaming for help, but I could hardly hear the sound of my own voice above the noise of the wind that was caused by the throat-owner's breathing. There seemed to be a gale blowing all the time, a queer erratic gale that blew alternately very cold (as the air came in) and very hot (as it went out again).

I managed to get my elbows hooked over a sharp fleshy ridge – I presume the epiglottis – and for a brief moment I hung there, defying the suction and scrabbling with my feet to find a foothold on the wall of the larynx; but the throat gave a huge swallow that jerked me away, and down I went again.

From then on, there was nothing else for me to catch hold of, and down and down I went until soon my legs were dangling below me in the upper reaches of the stomach, and I could feel the slow powerful pulsing of peristalsis dragging away at my ankles, pulling me down and down and down ...

Far above me, outside in the open air, I could hear the distant babble of women's voices:

'It's not true ...'

'But my dear Mildred, how awful ...'

'The man must be mad ...'

'Your poor mouth, just look at it ... '

'A sex maniac ...'

'A sadist ...'

'Someone ought to write to the bishop ...'

And then Miss Roach's voice, louder than the others, swearing and screeching like a parakeet:

'He's damn lucky I didn't kill him, the little bastard! ... I said to him, listen, I said, if ever I happen to want any of my teeth extracted, I'll go to the dentist, not to a goddam vicar ... It isn't as though I'd given him any encouragement either! ...'

'Where is he now, Mildred?'

'God knows. In the bloody summer-house, I suppose.'

'Hey girls, let's go and root him out!'

Oh dear, oh dear. Looking back on it now, some three weeks later, I don't know how I ever came through the nightmare of that awful afternoon without taking leave of my senses.

A gang of witches like that is a very dangerous thing to fool around with, and had they managed to catch me in the summer-house right then and there when their blood was up, they would as likely as not have torn me limb from limb on the spot.

Either that, or I should have been frog-marched down to the police station with Lady Birdwell and Miss Roach leading the procession through the main street of the village.

But of course they didn't catch me.

They didn't catch me then, and they haven't caught me yet, and if my luck continues to hold, I think I've got a fair chance of evading them altogether – or anyway for a few months, until they forget about the whole affair.

As you might guess, I am having to keep entirely to myself and to take no part in public affairs or social life. I find that writing is a most salutary occupation at a time like this, and I spend many hours each day playing with sentences. I regard each sentence as a little wheel, and my ambition lately has been to gather several hundred of them together at once and to fit them all end to end, with the cogs interlocking, like gears, but each wheel a different size, each turning at a different speed. Now and again I try to put a really big one right next to a very small one in such a way that the big one, turning slowly, will make the small one spin so fast that it hums. Very tricky, that.

I also sing madrigals in the evenings, but I miss my own harpsichord terribly.

All the same, this isn't such a bad place, and I have made myself as comfortable as I possibly can. It is a small chamber situated in what is almost certainly the primary section of the duodenal loop, just before it begins to run vertically downward in front of the right kidney. The floor is quite level – indeed it was the first level place I came to during that horrible descent down Miss Roach's throat – and that's the only reason I managed to stop at all. Above me, I can see a pulpy sort of opening that I take to be the pylorus, where the stomach enters the small intestine (I can still remember some of those diagrams my mother used to show me), and below me, there is a funny little hole in the wall where the pancreatic duct enters the lower section of the duodenum.

It is all a trifle bizarre for a man of conservative tastes like myself. Personally I prefer oak furniture and parquet flooring. But there is anyway one thing here that pleases me greatly, and that is the walls. They are lovely and soft, like a sort of padding, and the advantage of this is that I can bounce up against them as much as I wish without hurting myself.

There are several other people about, which is rather surprising, but thank God they are every one of them males. For some reason or other, they all wear white coats, and they bustle around pretending to be very busy and important. In actual fact, they are an uncommonly ignorant bunch of fellows. They don't even seem to realize where they *are*. I try to tell them, but they refuse to listen. Sometimes I get so angry and frustrated with them that I lose my temper and start to shout; and then a sly mistrustful look comes over the faces and they begin backing slowly away, and saying, 'Now then. Take it easy. Take it easy, Vicar, there's a good boy. Take it easy.'

What sort of talk is that?

But there is one oldish man – he comes in to see me every morning after breakfast – who appears to live slightly closer to reality than the others. He is civil and dignified, and I imagine he is lonely because he likes nothing better than to sit quietly in my room and listen to me talk. The only trouble is that whenever we get on to the subject of our whereabouts, he starts telling me that he's going to help me to escape. He said it again this morning, and we had quite an argument about it.

'But can't you see,' I said patiently, 'I don't *want* to escape.'

'My dear Vicar, why ever not?'

'I keep telling you – because they're all searching for me outside.'

'Who?'

'Miss Elphinstone and Miss Roach and Miss Prattley and all the rest of them.'

'What nonsense.'

'Oh yes they are! And I imagine they're after *you* as well, but you won't admit it.'

'No, my friend, they are not after me.'

'Then may I ask precisely what you are doing down here?'

A bit of a stumper for him, that one. I could see he didn't know how to answer it.

'I'll bet you were fooling around with Miss Roach and got yourself swallowed up just the same as I did. I'll bet that's exactly what happened, only you're ashamed to admit it.'

He looked suddenly so wan and defeated when I said this that I felt sorry for him.

'Would you like me to sing you a song?' I asked.

But he got up without answering and went quietly out into the corridor.

'Cheer up,' I called after him. 'Don't be depressed. There is always some balm in Gilead.'

GENESIS AND CATASTROPHE

A True Story

'Everything is normal,' the doctor was saying. 'Just lie back and relax.'
His voice was miles away in the distance and he seemed to be shouting
at her. 'You have a son.'

'What?'

'You have a fine son. You understand that, don't you? A fine son.
Did you hear him crying?'

'Is he all right, Doctor?'

'Of course he is all right.'

'Please let me see him.'

'You'll see him in a moment.'

'You are certain he is all right?'

'I am quite certain.'

'Is he still crying?'

'Try to rest. There is nothing to worry about.'

'Why has he stopped crying, Doctor? What happened?'

'Don't excite yourself, please. Everything is normal.'

'I want to see him. Please let me see him.'

'Dear lady,' the doctor said, patting her hand. 'You have a fine
strong healthy child. Don't you believe me when I tell you that?'

'What is the woman over there doing to him?'

'Your baby is being made to look pretty for you,' the doctor said.
'We are giving him a little wash, that is all. You must spare us a
moment or two for that.'

'You swear he is all right?'

'I swear it. Now lie back and relax. Close your eyes. Go on, close
your eyes. That's right. That's better. Good girl ...'

'I have prayed and prayed that he will live, Doctor.'

'Of course he will live. What are you talking about?'

'The others didn't.'

'What?'

'None of my other ones lived, Doctor.'

The doctor stood beside the bed looking down at the pale exhausted
face of the young woman. He had never seen her before today. She
and her husband were new people in the town. The innkeeper's wife,

who had come up to assist in the delivery, had told him that the husband worked at the local customs-house on the border and that the two of them had arrived quite suddenly at the inn with one trunk and one suitcase about three months ago. The husband was a drunkard, the innkeeper's wife had said, an arrogant, overbearing, bullying little drunkard, but the young woman was gentle and religious. And she was very sad. She never smiled. In the few weeks that she had been here, the innkeeper's wife had never once seen her smile. Also there was a rumour that this was the husband's third marriage, that one wife had died and that the other had divorced him for unsavoury reasons. But that was only a rumour.

The doctor bent down and pulled the sheet up a little higher over the patient's chest. 'You have nothing to worry about,' he said gently. 'This is a perfectly normal baby.'

'That's exactly what they told me about the others. But I lost them all, Doctor. In the last eighteen months I have lost all three of my children, so you mustn't blame me for being anxious.'

'Three?'

'This is my fourth ... in four years.'

The doctor shifted his feet uneasily on the bare floor.

'I don't think you know what it means, Doctor, to lose them all, all three of them, slowly, separately, one by one. I keep seeing them. I can see Gustav's face now as clearly as if he were lying here beside me in the bed. Gustav was a lovely boy, Doctor. But he was always ill. It is terrible when they are always ill and there is nothing you can do to help them.'

'I know.'

The woman opened her eyes, stared up at the doctor for a few seconds, then closed them again.

'My little girl was called Ida. She died a few days before Christmas. That is only four months ago. I just wish you could have seen Ida, Doctor.'

'You have a new one now.'

'But Ida was so beautiful.'

'Yes,' the doctor said. 'I know.'

'How can you know?' she cried.

'I am sure that she was a lovely child. But this new one is also like that.' The doctor turned away from the bed and walked over to the window and stood there looking out. It was a wet grey April afternoon, and across the street he could see the red roofs of the houses and the huge raindrops splashing on the tiles.

'Ida was two years old, Doctor ... and she was so beautiful I was never able to take my eyes off her from the time I dressed her in the morning until she was safe in bed again at night. I used to live in holy terror of something happening to that child. Gustav had gone and my little Otto had also gone and she was all I had left. Sometimes I used to get up in the night and creep over to the cradle and put my ear close to her mouth just to make sure that she was breathing.'

'Try to rest,' the doctor said, going back to the bed. 'Please try to rest.' The woman's face was white and bloodless, and there was a slight bluish-grey tinge around the nostrils and the mouth. A few strands of damp hair hung down over her forehead, sticking to the skin.

'When she died ... I was already pregnant again when that happened, Doctor. This new one was a good four months on its way when Ida died. "I don't want it!" I shouted after the funeral. "I won't have it! I have buried enough children!" And my husband ... he was strolling among the guests with a big glass of beer in his hand ... he turned around quickly and said, "I have news for you, Klara, I have good news." Can you imagine that, Doctor? We have just buried our third child and he stands there with a glass of beer in his hand and tells me that he has good news. "Today I have been posted to Braunau," he says, "so you can start packing at once. This will be a new start for you, Klara," he says. "It will be a new place and you can have a new doctor ..."'

'Please don't talk any more.'

'You *are* the new doctor, aren't you, Doctor?'

'That's right.'

'And here we are in Braunau.'

'Yes.'

'I am frightened, Doctor.'

'Try not to be frightened.'

'What chance can the fourth one have now?'

'You must stop thinking like that.'

'I can't help it. I am certain there is something inherited that causes my children to die in this way. There must be.'

'That is nonsense.'

'Do you know what my husband said to me when Otto was born, Doctor? He came into the room and he looked into the cradle where Otto was lying and he said, "Why do *all* my children have to be so small and weak?"'

'I am sure he didn't say that.'

'He put his head right into Otto's cradle as though he were examining a tiny insect and he said, "All I am saying is why can't they be better *specimens*? That's all I am saying." And three days after that, Otto was dead. We baptised him quickly on the third day and he died the same evening. And then Gustav died. And then Ida died. All of them died, Doctor ... and suddenly the whole house was empty....'

'Don't think about it now.'

'Is this one so very small?'

'He is a normal child.'

'But small?'

'He is a little small, perhaps. But the small ones are often a lot tougher than the big ones. Just imagine, Frau Hitler, this time next year he will be almost learning how to walk. Isn't that a lovely thought?'

She didn't answer this.

'And two years from now he will probably be talking his head off and driving you crazy with his chatter. Have you settled on a name for him yet?'

'A name?'

'Yes.'

'I don't know. I'm not sure. I think my husband said that if it was a boy we were going to call him Adolfus.'

'That means he would be called Adolf.'

'Yes. My husband likes Adolf because it has a certain similarity to Alois. My husband is called Alois.'

'Excellent.'

'Oh no!' she cried, starting up suddenly from the pillow. 'That's the same question they asked me when Otto was born! It means he is going to die! You are going to baptise him at once!'

'Now, now,' the doctor said, taking her gently by the shoulders. 'You are quite wrong. I promise you you are wrong. I was simply being an inquisitive old man, that is all. I love talking about names. I think Adolphus is a particularly fine name. It is one of my favourites. And look – here he comes now.'

The innkeeper's wife, carrying the baby high up on her enormous bosom, came sailing across the room towards the bed. 'Here is the little beauty!' she cried, beaming. 'Would you like to hold him, my dear? Shall I put him beside you?'

'Is he well wrapped?' the doctor asked. 'It is extremely cold in here.'

'Certainly he is well wrapped.'

The baby was tightly swaddled in a white woollen shawl, and only the tiny pink head protruded. The innkeeper's wife placed him gently on the bed beside the mother. 'There you are,' she said. 'Now you can lie there and look at him to your heart's content.'

'I think you will like him,' the doctor said, smiling. 'He is a fine little baby.'

'He has the most lovely hands!' the innkeeper's wife exclaimed. 'Such long delicate fingers!'

The mother didn't move. She didn't even turn her head to look.

'Go on!' cried the innkeeper's wife. 'He won't bite you!'

'I am frightened to look. I don't care to believe that I have another baby and that he is all right.'

'Don't be so stupid.'

Slowly, the mother turned her head and looked at the small, incredibly serene face that lay on the pillow beside her.

'Is this my baby?'

'Of course.'

'Oh ... oh ... but he is beautiful.'

The doctor turned away and went over to the table and began putting his things into his bag. The mother lay on the bed gazing at the child and smiling and touching him and making little noises of pleasure. 'Hello, Adolfus,' she whispered. 'Hello, my little Adolf ...'

'Ssshh!' said the innkeeper's wife. 'Listen! I think your husband is coming.'

The doctor walked over to the door and opened it and looked out into the corridor.

'Herr Hitler!'

'Yes.'

'Come in, please.'

A small man in a dark-green uniform stepped softly into the room and looked around him.

'Congratulations,' the doctor said. 'You have a son.'

The man had a pair of enormous whiskers meticulously groomed after the manner of the Emperor Franz Josef, and he smelled strongly of beer. 'A son?'

'Yes.'

'How is he?'

'He is fine. So is your wife.'

'Good.' The father turned and walked with a curious little prancing stride over to the bed where his wife was lying. 'Well, Klara,' he said, smiling through his whiskers. 'How did it go?' He bent down to take a look at the baby. Then he bent lower. In a series of quick jerky movements, he bent lower and lower until his face was only about twelve inches from the baby's head. The wife lay sideways on the pillow, staring up at him with a kind of supplicating look.

'He has the most marvellous pair of lungs,' the innkeeper's wife announced. 'You should have heard him screaming just after he came into this world.'

'But my God, Klara ...'

'What is it, dear?'

'This one is even smaller than Otto was!'

The doctor took a couple of quick paces forward. 'There is nothing wrong with that child,' he said.

Slowly, the husband straightened up and turned away from the bed and looked at the doctor. He seemed bewildered and stricken. 'It's no good lying, Doctor,' he said. 'I know what it means. It's going to be the same all over again.'

'Now you listen to me,' the doctor said.

'But do you *know* what happened to the others, Doctor?'

'You must forget about the others, Herr Hitler. Give this one a chance.'

'But so small and weak!'

'My dear sir, he has only just been born.'

'Even so ...'

'What are you trying to do?' cried the innkeeper's wife. 'Talk him into his grave?'

'That's enough!' the doctor said sharply.

The mother was weeping now. Great sobs were shaking her body.

The doctor walked over to the husband and put a hand on his shoulder. 'Be good to her,' he whispered. 'Please. It is very important.' Then he squeezed the husband's shoulder hard and began pushing him forward surreptitiously to the edge of the bed. The husband hesitated. The doctor squeezed harder, signalling him urgently through fingers and thumb. At last, reluctantly, the husband bent down and kissed his wife lightly on the cheek.

'All right, Klara,' he said. 'Now stop crying.'

'I have prayed so hard that he will live, Alois.'

'Yes.'

'Every day for months I have gone to the church and begged on my knees that this one will be allowed to live.'

'Yes, Klara, I know.'

'Three dead children is all that I can stand, don't you realize that?'

'Of course.'

'He *must* live, Alois. He *must*, he *must* ... Oh God, be merciful unto him now ...'

EDWARD THE CONQUEROR

Louisa, holding a dishcloth in her hand, stepped out of the kitchen door at the back of the house into the cool October sunshine.

'Edward!' she called. '*Ed-ward!* Lunch is ready!'

She paused a moment, listening; then she strolled out on to the lawn and continued across it – a little shadow attending her – skirting the rose bed and touching the sundial lightly with one finger as she went by. She moved rather gracefully for a woman who was small and plump, with a lilt in her walk and a gentle swinging of the shoulders and the arms. She passed under the mulberry tree on to the brick path, then went all the way along the path until she came to the place where she could look down into the dip at the end of this large garden.

'*Edward!* Lunch!'

She could see him now, about eighty yards away, down in the dip on the edge of the wood – the tallish narrow figure in khaki slacks and dark-green sweater, working beside a big bonfire with a fork in his hands, pitching brambles on to the top of the fire. It was blazing fiercely, with orange flames and clouds of milky smoke, and the smoke was drifting back over the garden with a wonderful scent of autumn and burning leaves.

Louisa went down the slope towards her husband. Had she wanted, she could easily have called again and made herself heard, but there was something about a first-class bonfire that impelled her towards it, right up close so she could feel the heat and listen to it burn.

'Lunch,' she said, approaching.

'Oh, hello. All right – yes. I'm coming.'

'*What* a good fire.'

'I've decided to clear this place right out,' her husband said. 'I'm sick and tired of all these brambles.' His long face was wet with perspiration. There were small beads of it clinging all over his moustache like dew, and two little rivers were running down his throat on to the turtleneck of the sweater.

'You better be careful you don't overdo it, Edward.'

'Louisa, I do wish you'd stop treating me as though I were eighty. A bit of exercise never did anyone any harm.'

'Yes, dear, I know. Oh, Edward! Look! Look!'

The man turned and looked at Louisa, who was pointing now to the far side of the bonfire.

'Look, Edward! The cat!'

Sitting on the ground, so close to the fire that the flames sometimes seemed actually to be touching it, was a large cat of a most unusual colour. It stayed quite still, with its head on one side and its nose in the air, watching the man and woman with a cool yellow eye.

'It'll get burnt!' Louisa cried, and she dropped the dishcloth and darted swiftly in and grabbed it with both hands, whisking it away and putting it on the grass well clear of the flames.

'You crazy cat,' she said, dusting off her hands. 'What's the matter with you?'

'Cats know what they're doing,' the husband said. 'You'll never find a cat doing something it doesn't want. Not cats.'

'Whose is it? You ever seen it before?'

'No, I never have. Damn peculiar colour.'

The cat had seated itself on the grass and was regarding them with a sidewise look. There was a veiled inward expression about the eyes, something curiously omniscient and pensive, and around the nose a most delicate air of contempt, as though the sight of these two middle-aged persons – the one small, plump, and rosy, the other lean and extremely sweaty – were a matter of some surprise but very little importance. For a cat, it certainly had an unusual colour – a pure silvery grey with no blue in it at all – and the hair was very long and silky.

Louisa bent down and stroked its head. 'You must go home,' she said. 'Be a good cat now and go on home to where you belong.'

The man and wife started to stroll back up the hill towards the house. The cat got up and followed, at a distance first, but edging closer and closer as they went along. Soon it was alongside them, then it was ahead, leading the way across the lawn to the house, walking as though it owned the whole place, holding its tail straight up in the air, like a mast.

'Go home,' the man said. 'Go on home. We don't want you.'

But when they reached the house, it came in with them, and Louisa gave it some milk in the kitchen. During lunch, it hopped up on to the spare chair between them and sat through the meal with its head just above the level of the table watching the proceedings with those dark-yellow eyes which kept moving slowly from the woman to the man and back again.

'I don't like this cat,' Edward said.

'Oh, I think it's a beautiful cat. I do hope it stays a little while.'

'Now, listen to me, Louisa. The creature can't possibly stay here. It belongs to someone else. It's lost. And if it's still trying to hang around this afternoon, you'd better take it to the police. They'll see it gets home.'

After lunch, Edward returned to his gardening. Louisa, as usual, went to the piano. She was a competent pianist and a genuine music-lover, and almost every afternoon she spent an hour or so playing for herself. The cat was now lying on the sofa, and she paused to stroke it as she went by. It opened its eyes, looked at her a moment, then closed them again and went back to sleep.

'You're an awfully nice cat,' she said. 'And such a beautiful colour. I wish I could keep you.' Then her fingers, moving over the fur on the cat's head, came into contact with a small lump, a little growth just above the right eye.

'Poor cat,' she said. 'You've got bumps on your beautiful face. You must be getting old.'

She went over and sat down on the long piano stool but she didn't immediately start to play. One of her special little pleasures was to make every day a kind of concert day, with a carefully arranged programme which she worked out in detail before she began. She never liked to break her enjoyment by having to stop while she wondered what to play next. All she wanted was a brief pause after each piece while the audience clapped enthusiastically and called for more. It was so much nicer to imagine an audience, and now and again while she was playing – on the lucky days, that is – the room would begin to swim and fade and darken, and she would see nothing but row upon row of seats and a sea of white faces upturned towards her, listening with a rapt and adoring concentration.

Sometimes she played from memory, sometimes from music. Today she would play from memory; that was the way she felt. And what should the programme be? She sat before the piano with her small hands clasped on her lap, a plump rosy little person with a round and still quite pretty face, her hair done up in a neat bun at the back of her head. By looking slightly to the right, she could see the cat curled up asleep on the sofa, and its silvery-grey coat was beautiful against the purple of the cushion. How about some Bach to begin with? Or, better still, Vivaldi. The Bach adaptation for organ of the D minor Concerto Grosso. Yes – that first. Then perhaps a little Schumann. *Carnaval?* That would be fun. And after that – well, a touch of Liszt for a change. One of the *Petrarch Sonnets*. The second one – that was the loveliest – the E major. Then another Schumann, another of his gay ones – *Kinderscenen*. And lastly, for the encore, a Brahms waltz, or maybe two of them if she felt like it.

Vivaldi, Schumann, Liszt, Schumann, Brahms. A very nice pro-gramme, one that she could play easily without the music. She moved herself a little closer to the piano and paused a moment while someone in the audience – already she could feel that this was one of the lucky days – while someone in the audience had his last cough; then, with the slow grace that accompanied nearly all her movements, she lifted her hands to the keyboard and began to play.

She wasn't, at that particular moment, watching the cat at all – as a matter of fact she had forgotten its presence – but as the first deep notes of the Vivaldi sounded softly in the room, she became aware, out of the corner of one eye, of a sudden flurry, a flash of movement on the sofa to her right. She stopped playing at once. 'What is it?' she said, turning to the cat. 'What's the matter?'

The animal, who a few seconds before had been sleeping peacefully, was now sitting bolt upright on the sofa, very tense, the whole body aquiver, ears up and eyes wide open, staring at the piano.

'Did I frighten you?' she asked gently. 'Perhaps you've never heard music before.'

No, she told herself. I don't think that's what it is. On second thoughts, it seemed to her that the cat's attitude was not one of fear. There was no shrinking or backing away. If anything, there was a leaning forward, a kind of eagerness about the creature, and the face – well, there was rather an odd expression on the face, something of a mixture between surprise and shock. Of course, the face of a cat is a small and fairly expressionless thing, but if you watch carefully the eyes and ears working together, and particularly that little area of mobile skin below the ears and slightly to one side, you can occasionally see the reflection of very powerful emotions. Louisa was watching the face closely now, and because she was curious to see what would happen a second time, she reached out her hands to the keyboard and began again to play the Vivaldi.

This time the cat was ready for it, and all that happened to begin with was a small extra tensing of the body. But as the music swelled and quickened into that first exciting rhythm of the introduction to the fugue, a strange look that amounted almost to ecstasy began to settle upon the creature's face. The ears, which up to then had been pricked up straight, were gradually drawn back, the eyelids drooped, the head went over to one side, and at that moment Louisa could have sworn that the animal was actually *appreciating* the work.

What she saw (or thought she saw) was something she had noticed many times on the faces of people listening very closely to a piece of music. When the sound takes complete hold of them and drowns them in itself, a peculiar, intensely ecstatic look comes over them that you can recognize as easily as a smile. So far as Louisa could see, the cat was now wearing almost exactly this kind of look.

Louisa finished the fugue, then played the siciliana, and all the way through she kept watching the cat on the sofa. The final proof for her that the animal was listening came at the end, when the music stopped. It blinked, stirred itself a little, stretched a leg, settled into a more comfortable position, took a quick glance round the room, then looked expectantly in her direction. It was precisely the way a concert-goer reacts when the music momentarily releases him in the pause between two movements of a symphony. The behaviour was so throughly human it gave her a queer agitated feeling in the chest.

'You like that?' she asked. 'You like Vivaldi?'

The moment she'd spoken, she felt ridiculous, but not – and this to her was a trifle sinister – not quite so ridiculous as she knew she should have felt.

Well, there was nothing for it now except to go straight ahead with the next number on the programme, which was *Carnaval*. As soon as she began to play, the cat again stiffened and sat up straighter; then, as it became slowly and blissfully saturated with the sound, it relapsed into that queer melting mood of ecstasy that seemed to have something to do with drowning and with dreaming. It was really an extravagant sight – quite a comical one, too – to see this silvery cat sitting on the sofa and being carried away like this. And what made it more screwy than ever, Louisa thought, was the fact that this music, which the animal seemed to be enjoying so much, was manifestly too *difficult*, too *classical*, to be appreciated by the majority of humans in the world.

Maybe, she thought, the creature's not really enjoying it at all. Maybe it's a sort of hypnotic reaction, like with snakes. After all, if you can charm a snake with music, then why not a cat? Except that millions of cats hear the stuff every day of their lives, on radio and gramophone and piano, and, as far as she knew, there'd never yet been a case of one behaving like this. This one was acting as though it were following every single note. It was certainly a fantastic thing.

But was it not also a wonderful thing? Indeed it was. In fact, unless she was much mistaken, it was a kind of miracle, one of those animal miracles that happen about once every hundred years.

'I could see you *loved* that one,' she said when the piece was over. 'Although I'm sorry I didn't play it any too well today. Which did you like best – the Vivaldi or the Schumann?'

The cat made no reply, so Louisa, fearing she might lose the attention of her listener, went straight into the next part of the programme – Liszt's second *Petrarch Sonnet*.

And now an extraordinary thing happened. She hadn't played more than three or four bars when the animal's whiskers began perceptibly to twitch. Slowly it drew itself up to an extra height, laid its head on one side, then on the other, and stared into space with a kind of frowning concentrated look that seemed to say, 'What's this? Don't tell me. I know it so well, but just for the moment I don't seem to be able to place it.' Louisa was fascinated, and with her little mouth half open and half smiling, she continued to play, waiting to see what on earth was going to happen next.

The cat stood up, walked to one end of the sofa, sat down again, listened some more; then all at once it bounded to the floor and leaped up on to the piano stool beside her. There it sat, listening intently to the lovely sonnet, not dreamily this time, but very erect, the large yellow eyes fixed upon Louisa's fingers.

'Well!' she said as she struck the last chord. 'So you came up to sit beside me, did you? You like this better than the sofa? All right, I'll let you stay, but you must keep still and not jump about.' She put out a hand and stroked the cat softly along the back, from head to tail. 'That was Liszt,' she went on. 'Mind you, he can sometimes be quite horribly vulgar, but in things like this he's really charming.'

She was beginning to enjoy this odd animal pantomime, so she went straight on into the next item on the programme, Schumann's *Kinderscenen.*

She hadn't been playing for more than a minute or two when she realized that the cat had again moved, and was now back in its old place on the sofa. She'd been watching her hands at the time, and presumably that was why she hadn't even noticed its going; all the same, it must have been an extremely swift and silent move. The cat was still staring at her, still apparently attending closely to the music, and yet it seemed to Louisa that there was not now the same rapturous enthusiasm there'd been during the previous piece, the Liszt. In addition, the act of leaving the stool and returning to the sofa appeared in itself to be a mild but positive gesture of disappointment.

'What's the matter?' she asked when it was over. 'What's wrong with Schumann? What's so marvellous about Liszt?' The cat looked straight back at her with those yellow eyes that had small jet-black bars lying vertically in their centres.

This, she told herself, is really beginning to get interesting – a trifle spooky, too, when she came to think of it. But one look at the cat sitting there on the sofa, so bright and attentive, so obviously waiting for more music, quickly reassured her.

'All right,' she said. 'I'll tell you what I'm going to do. I'm going to alter my programme specially for you. You seem to like Liszt so much, I'll give you another.'

She hesitated, searching her memory for a good Liszt; then softly she began to play one of the twelve little pieces from *Der Weihnachtsbaum.* She was now watching the cat very closely, and the first thing she noticed was that the whiskers again began to twitch. It jumped down to the carpet, stood still a moment, inclining its head, quivering with excitement, and then, with a slow, silky stride, it walked around the piano, hopped up on the stool, and sat down beside her.

They were in the middle of all this when Edward came in from the garden.

'Edward!' Louisa cried, jumping up. 'Oh, Edward, darling! Listen to this! Listen what's happened!'

'What is it now?' he said. 'I'd like some tea.' He had one of those narrow, sharp-nosed, faintly magenta faces, and the sweat was making it shine as though it were a long wet grape.

'It's the cat!' Louisa cried, pointing to it sitting quietly on the piano stool. 'Just *wait* till you hear what's happened!'

'I thought I told you to take it to the police.'

'But, Edward, *listen* to me. This is *terribly* exciting. This is a *musical* cat.'

'Oh, yes?'

'This cat can appreciate music, and it can understand it too.'

'Now stop this nonsense, Louisa, and for God's sake let's have some tea. I'm hot and tired from cutting brambles and building bonfires.' He sat down in an armchair, took a cigarette from a box beside him, and lit it with an immense patent lighter that stood near the box.

'What you don't understand,' Louisa said, 'is that something extremely exciting has been happening here in our own house while you were out, something that may even be ... well ... almost momentous.'

'I'm quite sure of that.'

'Edward, *please*!'

Louisa was standing by the piano, her little pink face pinker than ever, a scarlet rose high up on each cheek. 'If you want to know,' she said, 'I'll tell you what I think.'

'I'm listening, dear.'

'I think it might be possible that we are at this moment sitting in the presence of –' She stopped, as though suddenly sensing the absurdity of the thought.

'Yes?'

'You may think it silly, Edward, but it's honestly what I think.'

'In the presence of whom, for heaven's sake?'

'Of Franz Liszt himself!'

Her husband took a long slow pull at his cigarette and blew the smoke up at the ceiling. He had the tight-skinned, concave cheeks of a man who has worn a full set of dentures for many years, and every time he sucked at a cigarette, the cheeks went in even more, and the bones of his face stood out like a skeleton's. 'I don't get you,' he said.

'Edward, listen to me. From what I've seen this afternoon with my own eyes, it really looks as though this might be some sort of a reincarnation.'

'You mean this lousy cat?'

'Don't talk like that, dear, please.'

'You're not ill, are you, Louisa?'

'I'm perfectly all right, thank you very much. I'm a bit confused –

I don't mind admitting it, but who wouldn't be after what's just happened? Edward, I swear to you.'

'What *did* happen, if I may ask?'

Louisa told him, and all the while she was speaking, her husband lay sprawled in the chair with his legs stretched out in front of him, sucking at his cigarette and blowing the smoke up at the ceiling. There was a thin cynical smile on his mouth.

'I don't see anything very unusual about that,' he said when it was over. 'All it is – it's a trick cat. It's been taught tricks, that's all.'

'Don't be so silly, Edward. Every time I play Liszt, he gets all excited and comes running over to sit on the stool beside me. But only for Liszt, and nobody can teach a cat the difference between Liszt and Schumann. You don't even know it yourself. But this one can do it every single time. Quite obscure Liszt, too.'

'Twice,' the husband said. 'He's only done it twice.'

'Twice is enough.'

'Let's see him do it again. Come on.'

'No,' Louisa said. 'Definitely not. Because if this *is* Liszt, as I believe it is, or anyway the soul of Liszt or whatever it is that comes back, then it's certainly not right or even very kind to put him through a lot of silly undignified tests.'

'My dear woman! This is a *cat* – a rather stupid grey cat that nearly got its coat singed by the bonfire this morning in the garden. And anyway, what do you know about reincarnation?'

'If the soul is there, that's enough for me,' Louisa said firmly. 'That's all that counts.'

'Come on, then. Let's see him perform. Let's see him tell the difference between his own stuff and someone else's.'

'No, Edward. I've told you before, I refuse to put him through any more silly circus tests. He's had quite enough of that for one day. But I'll tell you what I *will* do. I'll play him a little more of his own music.'

'A fat lot that'll prove.'

'You watch. And one thing is certain – as soon as he recognizes it, he'll refuse to budge off that stool where he's sitting now.'

Louisa went to the music shelf, took down a book of Liszt, thumbed through it quickly, and chose another of his finer compositions – the B minor Sonata. She had meant to play only the first part of the work, but once she got started and saw how the cat was sitting there literally quivering with pleasure and watching her hands with that rapturous concentrated look, she didn't have the heart to stop. She played it all the way through. When it was finished, she glanced up at her husband and smiled. 'There you are,' she said. 'You can't tell me he wasn't absolutely *loving* it.'

'He just likes the noise, that's all.'

'He was *loving* it. Weren't you, darling?' she said, lifting the cat in her arms. 'Oh, my goodness, if only he could talk. Just think of it, dear – he met Beethoven in his youth! He knew Schubert and Mendelssohn and Schumann and Berlioz and Grieg and Delacroix and Ingres and Heine and Balzac. And let me see ... My heavens, he was Wagner's father-in-law! I'm holding Wagner's father-in-law in my arms!'

'Louisa!' her husband said sharply, sitting up straight. 'Pull yourself together.' There was a new edge to his voice now, and he spoke louder.

Louisa glanced up quickly. 'Edward, I do believe you're jealous!'

'Of a miserable grey cat!'

'Then don't be so grumpy and cynical about it all. If you're going to behave like this, the best thing you can do is to go back to your gardening and leave the two of us together in peace. That will be best for all of us, won't it, darling?' she said, addressing the cat, stroking its head. 'And later on this evening, we shall have some more music together, you and I, some more of your own work. Oh, yes,' she said, kissing the creature several times on the neck, 'and we might have a little Chopin, too. You needn't tell me – I happen to know you adore Chopin. You used to be great friends with him, didn't you, darling? As a matter of fact – if I remember rightly – it was in Chopin's apartment that you met the great love of your life, Madame Something-or-Other. Had three illegitimate children by her, too, didn't you? Yes, you did, you naughty thing, and don't go trying to deny it. So you shall have some Chopin,' she said, kissing the cat again, 'and that'll probably bring back all sorts of lovely memories to you, won't it?'

'Louisa, stop this at once!'

'Oh, don't be so stuffy, Edward.'

'You're behaving like a perfect idiot, woman. And anyway, you forget we're going out this evening, to Bill and Betty's for canasta.'

'Oh, but I couldn't *possibly* go out now. There's no question of that.'

Edward got up slowly from his chair, then bent down and stubbed his cigarette hard into the ash-tray. 'Tell me something,' he said quietly. 'You don't really believe this – this twaddle you're talking, do you?'

'But of course I do. I don't think there's any question about it now. And, what's more, I consider that it puts a tremendous responsibility upon us, Edward – upon both of us. You as well.'

'You know what I think,' he said. 'I think you ought to see a doctor. And damn quick, too.'

With that, he turned and stalked out of the room, through the french windows, back into the garden.

Louisa watched him striding across the lawn towards his bonfire and his brambles, and she waited until he was out of sight before she turned and ran to the front door, still carrying the cat.

Soon she was in the car, driving to town.

She parked in front of the library, locked the cat in the car, hurried up the steps into the building, and headed straight for the reference room. There she began searching the cards for books on two subjects – REINCARNATION and LISZT.

Under REINCARNATION she found something called *Recurring Earth-Lives – How and Why*, by a man called F. Milton Willis, published in 1921. Under LISZT she found two biographical volumes. She took out all three books, returned to the car, and drove home.

Back in the house, she placed the cat on the sofa, sat herself down beside it with her books, and prepared to do some serious reading. She would begin, she decided, with Mr F. Milton Willis's work. The volume was thin and a trifle soiled, but it had a good heavy feel to it, and the author's name had an authoritative ring.

The doctrine of reincarnation, she read, states that spiritual souls pass from higher to higher forms of animals. 'A man can, for instance, no more be reborn as an animal than an adult can re-become a child.'

She read this again. But how did he know? How could he be so sure? He couldn't. No one could possibly be certain about a thing like that. At the same time, the statement took a good deal of the wind out of her sails.

'Around the centre of consciousness of each of us, there are, besides the dense outer body, four other bodies, invisible to the eye of flesh, but perfectly visible to people whose faculties of perception of superphysical things have undergone the requisite development ...'

She didn't understand that one at all, but she read on, and soon she came to an interesting passage that told how long a soul usually stayed away from the earth before returning in someone else's body. The time varied according to type, and Mr Willis gave the following breakdown:

Drunkards and the unemployable	40/50 YEARS
Unskilled labourers	60/100 ,,
Skilled workers	100/200 ,,
The *bourgeoisie*	200/300 ,,
The upper-middle classes	500 ,,
The highest class of gentleman farmers	600/1,000 ,,
Those in the Path of Initiation	1,500/2,000 ,,

Quickly she referred to one of the other books, to find out how long Liszt had been dead. It said he died in Bayreuth in 1886. That was sixty-seven years ago. Therefore, according to Mr Willis, he'd have to have been an unskilled labourer to come back so soon. That didn't seem to fit at all. On the other hand, she didn't think much of the author's methods of grading. According to him, 'the highest class of gentleman farmer' was just about the most superior being on the earth. Red jackets and stirrup cups and the bloody, sadistic murder of the fox. No, she thought, that isn't right. It was a pleasure to find herself beginning to doubt Mr Willis.

Later in the book, she came upon a list of some of the more famous reincarnations. Epictetus, she was told, returned to earth as Ralph Waldo Emerson. Cicero came back as Gladstone, Alfred the Great as Queen Victoria, William the Conqueror as Lord Kitchener. Ashoka Vardhana, King of India in 272 BC, came back as Colonel Henry Steel Olcott, an esteemed American lawyer. Pythagoras returned as Master Koot Hoomi, the gentleman who founded the Theosophical Society with Mme Blavatsky and Colonel H. S. Olcott (the esteemed American lawyer, alias Ashoka Vardhana, King of India). It didn't say who Mme Blavatsky had been. But 'Theodore Roosevelt,' it said, 'has for numbers of incarnations played great parts as a leader of men ... From him descended the royal line of ancient Chaldea, he having been, about 30,000 BC, appointed Governor of Chaldea by the Ego we know as Caesar who was then ruler of Persia ... Roosevelt and Caesar have been together time after time as military and administrative leaders; at one time, many thousands of years ago, they were husband and wife ...'

That was enough for Louisa. Mr F. Milton Willis was clearly nothing but a guesser. She was not impressed by his dogmatic assertions. The fellow was probably on the right track, but his pronouncements were extravagant, especially the first one of all, about animals. Soon she hoped to be able to confound the whole Theosophical Society with her proof that man could indeed reappear as a lower animal. Also that he did not have to be an unskilled labourer to come back within a hundred years.

She now turned to one of the Liszt biographies, and she was glancing through it casually when her husband came in again from the garden.

'What are you doing now?' he asked.

'Oh – just checking up a little here and there. Listen, my dear, did you know that Theodore Roosevelt once was Caesar's wife?'

'Louisa,' he said, 'look – why don't we stop this nonsense? I don't like to see you making a fool of yourself like this. Just give me that goddamn cat and I'll take it to the police station myself.'

Louisa didn't seem to hear him. She was staring open-mouthed at a picture of Liszt in the book that lay on her lap. 'My God!' she cried. 'Edward, look!'

'What?'

'Look! The warts on his face! I forgot all about them! He had these great warts on his face and it was a famous thing. Even his students used to cultivate little tufts of hair on their own faces in the same spots, just to be like him.'

'What's that got to do with it?'

'Nothing. I mean not the students. But the warts have.'

'Oh, Christ,' the man said. 'Oh, Christ God Almighty.'

'The cat has them, too! Look, I'll show you.'

She took the animal on to her lap and began examining his face. 'There! There's one! And there's another! Wait a minute! I do believe they're in the same places! Where's that picture?'

It was a famous portrait of the musician in his old age, showing the fine powerful face framed in a mass of long grey hair that covered his ears and came half-way down his neck. On the face itself, each large wart had been faithfully reproduced, and there were five of them in all.

'Now, in the picture there's *one* above the right eyebrow.' She looked above the right eyebrow of the cat. 'Yes! It's there! In exactly the same place! And another on the left, at the top of the nose. That one's there, too! And one just below it on the cheek. And two fairly close together under the chin on the right side. Edward! Edward! Come and look! They're exactly the same.'

'It doesn't prove a thing.'

She looked up at her husband who was standing in the centre of the room in his green sweater and khaki slacks, still perspiring freely. 'You're scared, aren't you, Edward? Scared of losing your precious dignity and having people think you might be making a fool of yourself just for once.'

'I refuse to get hysterical about it, that's all.'

Louisa turned back to the book and began reading some more. 'This is interesting,' she said. 'It says here that Liszt loved all of Chopin's work except one – the Scherzo in B flat minor. Apparently he hated that. He called it the "Governess Scherzo", and said that it ought to be reserved solely for people in that profession.'

'So what?'

'Edward, listen. As you insist on being so horrid about all this, I'll tell you what I'm going to do. I'm going to play this scherzo right now and you can stay here and see what happens.'

'And then maybe you will deign to get us some supper.'

Louisa got up and took from the shelf a large green volume containing all of Chopin's works. 'Here it is. Oh yes, I remember it. It *is* rather awful. Now, listen – or, rather, watch. Watch to see what he does.'

She placed the music on the piano and sat down. Her husband remained standing. He had his hands in his pockets and a cigarette in his mouth, and in spite of himself he was watching the cat, which was now dozing on the sofa. When Louisa began to play, the first effect was as dramatic as ever. The animal jumped up as though it had been stung, and it stood motionless for at least a minute, the ears pricked up, the whole body quivering. Then it became restless and began to walk back and forth along the length of the sofa. Finally, it hopped down on to the floor, and with its nose and tail held high in the air, it marched slowly, majestically, from the room.

'There!' Louisa cried, jumping up and running after it. 'That does it! That really proves it!' She came back carrying the cat which she put down again on the sofa. Her whole face was shining with excitement now, her fists were clenched white, and the little bun on top of her head was loosening and going over to one side. 'What about it, Edward? What d'you think?' She was laughing nervously as she spoke.

'I must say it was quite amusing.'

'*Amusing!* My dear Edward, it's the most wonderful thing that's ever happened! Oh, goodness me!' she cried, picking up the cat again and hugging it to her bosom. 'Isn't it marvellous to think we've got Franz Liszt staying in the house?'

'Now, Louisa. Don't let's get hysterical.'

'I can't help it, I simply can't. And to *imagine* that he's actually going to live with us for always!'

'I beg your pardon?'

'Oh, Edward! I can hardly talk from excitement. And d'you know what I'm going to do next? Every musician in the whole world is going to want to meet him, that's a fact, and ask him about the people he knew – about Beethoven and Chopin and Schubert –'

'He can't talk,' her husband said.

'Well – all right. But they're going to want to meet him anyway, just to see him and touch him and to play their own music to him, modern music he's never heard before.'

'He wasn't that great. Now, if it had been Bach or Beethoven ...'

'Don't interrupt, Edward, please. So what I'm going to do is to notify all the important living composers everywhere. It's my duty. I'll tell them Liszt is here, and invite them to visit him. And you know what? They'll come flying in from every corner of the earth!'

'To see a grey cat?'

'Darling, it's the same thing. It's *him*. No one cares what he *looks* like. Oh, Edward, it'll be the most exciting thing there ever was!'

'They'll think you're mad.'

'You wait and see.' She was holding the cat in her arms and petting it tenderly but looking across at her husband, who now walked over to the french windows and stood there staring out into the garden. The evening was beginning, and the lawn was turning slowly from green to black, and in the distance he could see the smoke from his bonfire rising up in a white column.

'No,' he said, without turning round, 'I'm not having it. Not in this house. It'll make us both look perfect fools.'

'Edward, what do you mean?'

'Just what I say. I absolutely refuse to have you stirring up a lot of publicity about a foolish thing like this. You happen to have found a trick cat. OK – that's fine. Keep it, if it pleases you. I don't mind. But I don't wish you to go any further than that. Do you understand me, Louisa?'

'Further than what?'

'I don't want to hear any more of this crazy talk. You're acting like a lunatic.'

Louisa put the cat slowly down on the sofa. Then slowly she raised herself to her full small height and took one pace forward. '*Damn* you, Edward!' she shouted, stamping her foot. 'For the first time in our lives something really exciting comes along and you're scared to death of having anything to do with it because someone may laugh at you! That's right, isn't it? You can't deny it, can you?'

'Louisa,' her husband said. 'That's quite enough of that. Pull yourself together now and stop this at once.' He walked over and took a cigarette from the box on the table, then lit it with the enormous patent lighter. His wife stood watching him, and now the tears were beginning to trickle out of the inside corners of her eyes, making two little shiny rivers where they ran through the powder on her cheeks.

'We've been having too many of these scenes just lately, Louisa,' he was saying. 'No no, don't interrupt. Listen to me. I make full allowance for the fact that this may be an awkward time of life for you, and that –'

'Oh, my God! You idiot! You pompous idiot! Can't you see that this is different, this is – this is something miraculous? Can't you see *that*?'

At that point, he came across the room and took her firmly by the shoulders. He had the freshly lit cigarette between his lips, and she could see faint contours on his skin where the heavy perspiration had dried up in patches. 'Listen,' he said. 'I'm hungry. I've given up my golf and I've been working all day in the garden, and I'm tired and hungry and I want some supper. So do you. Off you go now to the kitchen and get us both something good to eat.'

Louisa stepped back and put both hands to her mouth. 'My heavens!' she cried. 'I forgot all about it. He must be absolutely famished. Except for some milk, I haven't given him a thing to eat since he arrived.'

'Who?'

'Why, *him* of course. I must go at once and cook something really special. I wish I knew what his favourite dishes used to be. What do you think he would like best, Edward?'

'*Goddamn* it, Louisa!'

'Now, Edward, please. I'm going to handle this *my* way just for once. You stay here,' she said, bending down and touching the cat gently with her fingers. 'I won't be long.'

Louisa went into the kitchen and stood for a moment, wondering what special dish she might prepare. How about a soufflé? A nice cheese soufflé? Yes, that would be rather special. Of course, Edward didn't much care for them, but that couldn't be helped.

She was only a fair cook, and she couldn't be sure of always having a soufflé come out well, but she took extra trouble this time and waited a long while to make certain the oven had heated fully to the correct temperature. While the soufflé was baking and she was searching around for something to go with it, it occurred to her that Liszt had probably never in his life tasted either avocado pears or grapefruit, so she decided to give him both of them at once in a salad. It would be fun to watch his reaction. It really would.

When it was all ready, she put it on a tray and carried it into the living-room. At the exact moment she entered, she saw her husband coming in through the french windows from the garden.

'Here's his supper,' she said, putting it on the table and turning towards the sofa. 'Where is he?'

Her husband closed the garden door behind him and walked across the room to get himself a cigarette.

'Edward, where is he?'

'Who?'

'You know who.'

'Ah, yes. Yes, that's right. Well – I'll tell you.' He was bending forward to light the cigarette, and his hands were cupped around the enormous patent lighter. He glanced up and saw Louisa looking at him – at his shoes and the buttons of his khaki slacks, which were damp from walking in long grass.

'I just went out to see how the bonfire was going,' he said.

Her eyes travelled slowly upward and rested on his hands.

'It's still burning fine,' he went on. 'I think it'll keep going all night.'

But the way she was staring made him uncomfortable.

'What is it?' he said, lowering the lighter. Then he looked down and noticed for the first time the long thin scratch that ran diagonally clear across the back of one hand, from the knuckle to the wrist.

'*Edward!*'

'Yes,' he said, 'I know. Those brambles are terrible. They tear you to pieces. Now, just a minute, Louisa. What's the matter?'

'*Edward!*'

'Oh, for God's sake, woman, sit down and keep calm. There's nothing to get worked up about, Louisa! Louisa, *sit down!*'

PIG

Once upon a time, in the City of New York, a beautiful baby boy was born into this world, and the joyful parents named him Lexington.

No sooner had the mother returned home from the hospital carrying Lexington in her arms than she said to her husband, 'Darling, now you must take me out to a most marvellous restaurant for dinner so that we can celebrate the arrival of our son and heir.'

Her husband embraced her tenderly and told her that any woman who could produce such a beautiful child as Lexington deserved to go absolutely anywhere she wanted. But was she strong enough yet, he inquired, to start running around the city late at night?

'No,' she said, she wasn't. But what the hell.

So that evening they both dressed themselves up in fancy clothes, and leaving little Lexington in care of a trained infant's nurse who was costing them twenty dollars a day and was Scottish into the bargain, they went out to the finest and most expensive restaurant in town. There they each ate a giant lobster and drank a bottle of champagne between them, and after that, they went on to a nighclub, where they drank another bottle of champagne and then sat holding hands for several hours while they recalled and discussed and admired each individual physical feature of their lovely newborn son.

They arrived back at their house on the East Side of Manhattan at around two o'clock in the morning and the husband paid off the taxi driver and then began feeling in his pockets for the key to the front door. After a while, he announced that he must have left it in the pocket of his other suit, and he suggested they ring the bell and get the nurse to come down and let them in. An infant's nurse at twenty dollars a day must expect to be hauled out of bed occasionally in the night, the husband said.

So he rang the bell. They waited. Nothing happened. He rang it again, long and loud. They waited another minute. Then they both stepped back on to the street and shouted the nurse's name (McPottle) up at the nursery windows on the third floor, but there was still no response. The house was dark and silent. The wife began to grow apprehensive. Her baby was imprisoned in this place, she told herself.

Alone with McPottle. And who was McPottle? They had known her
for two days, that was all, and she had a thin mouth, a small
disapproving eye, and a starchy bosom, and quite clearly she was in
the habit of sleeping too soundly for safety. If she couldn't hear the
front-door bell, then how on earth did she expect to hear a baby
crying? Why, this very second the poor thing might be swallowing its
tongue or suffocating on its pillow.

'He doesn't use a pillow,' the husband said. 'You are not to worry.
But I'll get you in if that's what you want.' He was feeling rather
superb after all the champagne, and now he bent down and undid
the laces of one of his black patent-leather shoes, and took it off. Then,
holding it by the toe, he flung it hard and straight through the dining-
room window on the ground floor.

'There you are,' he said, grinning. 'We'll deduct it from McPottle's
wages.'

He stepped forward and very carefully put a hand through the hole
in the glass and released the catch. Then he raised the window.

'I shall lift you in first, little mother,' he said, and he took his wife
around the waist and lifted her off the ground. This brought her big
red mouth up level with his own, and very close, so he started kissing
her. He knew from experience that women like very much to be kissed
in this position, with their bodies held tight and their legs dangling in
the air, so he went on doing it for quite a long time, and she wiggled
her feet, and made loud gulping noises down in her throat. Finally,
the husband turned her round and began easing her gently through
the open window into the dining-room. At this point, a police patrol
car came nosing silently along the street towards them. It stopped
about thirty yards away, and three cops of Irish extraction leaped out
of the car and started running in the direction of the husband and
wife, brandishing revolvers.

'Stick 'em up!' the cops shouted. 'Stick 'em up!' But it was impossible
for the husband to obey this order without letting go of his wife, and
had he done this she would either have fallen to the ground or would
have been left dangling half in and half out of the house, which is a
terribly uncomfortable position for a woman; so he continued gallantly
to push her upward and inward through the window. The cops, all of
whom had received medals before for killing robbers, opened fire
immediately, and although they were still running, and although the
wife in particular was presenting them with a very small target indeed,
they succeeded in scoring several direct hits on each body – sufficient
anyway to prove fatal in both cases.

Thus, when he was no more than twelve days old, little Lexington
became an orphan.

The news of this killing, for which the three policemen subsequently received citations, was eagerly conveyed to all relatives of the deceased couple of newspaper reporters, and the next morning the closest of these relatives, as well as a couple of undertakers, three lawyers, and a priest, climbed into taxis and set out for the house with the broken window. They assembled in the living-room, men and women both, and they sat around in a circle on the sofas and armchairs, smoking cigarettes and sipping sherry and debating what on earth should be done now with the baby upstairs, the orphan Lexington.

It soon became apparent that none of the relatives was particularly keen to assume responsibility for the child, and the discussions and arguments continued all through the day. Everybody declared an enormous, almost an irresistible desire to look after him, and would have done so with the greatest of pleasure were it not for the fact that their apartment was too small, or that they already had one baby and couldn't possibly afford another, or that they wouldn't know what to do with the poor little thing when they went abroad in the summer, or that they were getting on in years, which surely would be most unfair to the boy when he grew up, and so on and so forth. They all knew, of course, that the father had been heavily in debt for a long time and that the house was mortgaged and that consequently there would be no money at all to go with the child.

They were still arguing like mad at six in the evening when suddenly, in the middle of it all, an old aunt of the deceased father (her name was Glosspan) swept in from Virginia, and without even removing her hat and coat, not even pausing to sit down, ignoring all offers of a martini, a whisky, a sherry, she announced firmly to the assembled relatives that she herself intended to take sole charge of the infant boy from then on. What was more, she said, she would assume full financial responsibility on all counts, including education, and everyone else could go back home where they belonged and give their consciences a rest. So saying, she trotted upstairs to the nursery and snatched Lexington from his cradle and swept out of the house with the baby clutched tightly in her arms, while the relatives simply sat and stared and smiled and looked relieved, and McPottle the nurse stood stiff with disapproval at the head of the stairs, her lips compressed, her arms folded across her starchy bosom.

And thus it was that the infant Lexington, when he was thirteen days old, left the City of New York and travelled southward to live with his Great Aunt Glosspan in the State of Virginia.

Aunt Glosspan was nearly seventy when she became guardian to Lexington, but to look at her you would never have guessed it for one minute. She was as sprightly as a woman half her age, with a small, wrinkled, but still quite beautiful face and two lovely brown eyes that sparkled at you in the nicest way. She was also a spinster, though you would never have guessed that either, for there was nothing spinsterish about Aunt Glosspan. She was never bitter or gloomy or irritable; she didn't have a moustache; and she wasn't in the least bit jealous of other people, which in itself is something you can seldom say about either a spinster or a virgin lady, although of course it is not known for certain whether Aunt Glosspan qualified on both counts.

But she was an eccentric old woman, there was no doubt about that. For the past thirty years she had lived a strange isolated life all by herself in a tiny cottage high up on the slopes of the Blue Ridge Mountains, several miles from the nearest village. She had five acres of pasture, a plot for growing vegetables, a flower garden, three cows, a dozen hens, and a fine cockerel.

And now she had little Lexington as well.

She was a strict vegetarian and regarded the consumption of animal flesh as not only unhealthy and disgusting, but horribly cruel. She lived upon lovely clean foods like milk, butter, eggs, cheese, vegetables, nuts, herbs, and fruit, and she rejoiced in the conviction that no living creature would be slaughtered on her account, not even a shrimp. Once, when a brown hen of hers passed away in the prime of life from being eggbound, Aunt Glosspan was so distressed that she nearly gave up egg-eating altogether.

She knew not the first thing about babies, but that didn't worry her in the least. At the railway station in New York, while waiting for the train that would take her and Lexington back to Virginia, she bought six feeding-bottles, two dozen diapers, a box of safety pins, a carton of milk for the journey, and a small paper-covered book called *The Care of Infants*. What more could anyone want? And when the train got going, she fed the baby some milk, changed its nappies after a fashion, and laid it down on the seat to sleep. Then she read *The Care of Infants* from cover to cover.

'There is no problem here,' she said, throwing the book out of the window. 'No problem at all.'

And curiously enough there wasn't. Back home in the cottage everything went just as smoothly as could be. Little Lexington drank his milk and belched and yelled and slept exactly as a good baby should, and Aunt Glosspan glowed with joy whenever she looked at him and showered him with kisses all day long.

4

By the time he was six years old, young Lexington had grown into a most beautiful boy with long golden hair and deep blue eyes the colour of cornflowers. He was bright and cheerful, and already he was learning to help his old aunt in all sorts of different ways around the property, collecting the eggs from the chicken house, turning the handle of the butter churn, digging up potatoes in the vegetable garden, and searching for wild herbs on the side of the mountain. Soon, Aunt Glosspan told herself, she would have to start thinking about his education.

But she couldn't bear the thought of sending him away to school. She loved him so much now that it would kill her to be parted from him for any length of time. There was, of course, that village school down in the valley, but it was a dreadful-looking place, and if she sent him there she just knew they would start forcing him to eat meat the very first day he arrived.

'You know what, my darling?' she said to him one day when he was sitting on a stool in the kitchen watching her make cheese. 'I don't really see why I shouldn't give you your lessons myself.'

The boy looked up at her with his large blue eyes, and gave her a lovely trusting smile. 'That would be nice,' he said.

'And the very first thing I should do would be to teach you how to cook.'

'I think I would like that, Aunt Glosspan.'

'Whether you like it or not, you're going to have to learn some time,' she said. 'Vegetarians like us don't have nearly so many foods to choose from as ordinary people, and therefore they must learn to be doubly expert with what they have.'

'Aunt Glosspan,' the boy said, 'what *do* ordinary people eat that we don't?'

'Animals,' she answered, tossing her head in disgust.

'You mean *live* animals?'

'No,' she said. 'Dead ones.'

The boy considered this for a moment.

'You mean when they die they *eat* them instead of *burying* them?'

'They don't wait for them to die, my pet. They kill them.'

'How do they kill them, Aunt Glosspan?'

'They usually slit their throats with a knife.'

'But what *kind* of animals?'

'Cows and pigs mostly, and sheep.'

'Cows!' the boy cried. 'You mean like Daisy and Snowdrop and Lily?'

'Exactly, my dear.'

'But *how* do they eat them, Aunt Glosspan?'

'They cut them up into bits and they cook the bits. They like it best when it's all red and bloody and sticking to the bones. They love to eat lumps of cow's flesh with the blood oozing out of it.'

'Pigs too?'

'They adore pigs.'

'Lumps of bloody pig's meat,' the boy said. 'Imagine that. What else do they eat, Aunt Glosspan?'

'Chickens.'

'Chickens!'

'Millions of them.'

'Feathers and all?'

'No, dear, not the feathers. Now run along outside and get Aunt Glosspan a bunch of chives, will you, my darling.'

Shortly after that, the lessons began. They covered five subjects, reading, writing, geography, arithmetic, and cooking, but the latter was by far the most popular with both teacher and pupil. In fact, it very soon became apparent that young Lexington possessed a truly remarkable talent in this direction. He was a born cook. He was dextrous and quick. He could handle his pans like a juggler. He could slice a single potato into twenty paper-thin slivers in less time than it took his aunt to peel it. His palate was exquisitely sensitive, and he could taste a pot of strong onion soup and immediately detect the presence of a single tiny leaf of sage. In so young a boy, all this was a bit bewildering to Aunt Glosspan, and to tell the truth she didn't quite know what to make of it. But she was proud as proud could be, all the same, and predicted a brilliant future for the child.

'What a mercy it is,' she said, 'that I have such a wonderful little fellow to look after me in my dotage.' And a couple of years later, she retired from the kitchen for good, leaving Lexington in sole charge of all household cooking. The boy was now ten years old, and Aunt Glosspan was nearly eighty.

With the kitchen to himself, Lexington straight away began experimenting with dishes of his own invention. The old favourites no longer interested him. He had a violent urge to create. There were hundreds of fresh ideas in his head. 'I will begin,' he said, 'by devising a chestnut soufflé.' He made it and served it up for supper that very night. It was terrific. 'You are a genius!' Aunt Glosspan cried, leaping up from her chair and kissing him on both cheeks. 'You will make history!'

From then on, hardly a day went by without some new delectable creation being set upon the table. There was Brazilnut soup, hominy cutlets, vegetable ragout, dandelion omelette, cream-cheese fritters, stuffed-cabbage surprise, stewed foggage, shallots *à la bonne femme*, beetroot mousse piquant, prunes Stroganoff, Dutch rarebit, turnips on horseback, flaming spruce-needle tarts, and many many other beautiful compositions. Never before in her life, Aunt Glosspan declared, had she tasted such food as this; and in the mornings, long before lunch was due, she would go out on to the porch and sit there in her rocking-chair, speculating about the coming meal, licking her chops, sniffing the aromas that came wafting out through the kitchen window.

'What's that you're making in there today, boy?' she would call out.

'Try to guess, Aunt Glosspan.'

'Smells like a bit of salsify fritters to me,' she would say, sniffing vigorously.

Then out he would come, this ten-year-old child, a little grin of triumph on his face, and in his hands a big steaming pot of the most heavenly stew made entirely of parsnips and lovage.

'You know what you ought to do,' his aunt said to him, gobbling the stew. 'You ought to set yourself down this very minute with paper and pencil and write a cooking-book.'

He looked at her across the table, chewing his parsnips slowly.

'Why not?' she cried. 'I've taught you how to write and I've taught you how to cook and now all you've got to do is put the two things together. You write a cooking-book, my darling, and it'll make you famous the whole world over.'

'All right,' he said. 'I will.'

And that very day, Lexington began writing the first page of that monumental work which was to occupy him for the rest of his life. He called it *Eat Good and Healthy*.

Seven years later, by the time he was seventeen, he had recorded over nine thousand different recipes, all of them original, all of them delicious.

But now, suddenly, his labours were interrupted by the tragic death of Aunt Glosspan. She was afflicted in the night by a violent seizure, and Lexington, who had rushed into her bedroom to see what all the noise was about, found her lying on her bed yelling and cussing and twisting herself up into all manner of complicated knots. Indeed, she was a terrible sight to behold, and the agitated youth danced around her in his pyjamas, wringing his hands, and wondering what on earth he should do. Finally, in an effort to cool her down, he fetched a bucket of water from the pond in the cow field and tipped it over her head, but this only intensified the paroxysms, and the old lady expired within the hour.

'This is really too bad,' the poor boy said, pinching her several times to make sure that she was dead. 'And how sudden! How quick and sudden! Why only a few hours ago she seemed in the very best of spirits. She even took three large helpings of my most recent creation, devilled mushroomburgers, and told me how succulent it was.'

After weeping bitterly for several minutes, for he had loved his aunt very much, he pulled himself together and carried her outside and buried her behind the cowshed.

The next day, while tidying up her belongings, he came across an envelope that was addressed to him in Aunt Glosspan's handwriting. He opened it and drew out two fifty-dollar bills and a letter.

Darling boy [the letter said], I know that you have never yet been down the mountain since you were thirteen days old, but as soon as I die you must put on a pair of shoes and a clean shirt and walk down to the village and find the doctor. Ask the doctor to give you a death certificate to prove that I am dead. Then take this certificate to my lawyer, a man called Mr Samuel Zuckermann, who lives in New York City and who has a copy of my will. Mr Zuckermann will arrange everything. The cash in this envelope is to pay the doctor for the certificate and to cover the cost of your journey to New York. Mr Zuckermann will give you more money when you get there, and it is my earnest wish that you use it to further your researches into culinary and vegetarian matters, and that you continue to work upon that great book of yours until you are satisfied that it is complete in every way. Your loving aunt – Glosspan.

Lexington, who had always done everything his aunt told him, pocketed the money, put on a pair of shoes and a clean shirt, and went down the mountain to the village where the doctor lived.

'Old Glosspan?' the doctor said. 'My God, is *she* dead?'

'Certainly she's dead,' the youth answered. 'If you will come back home with me now I'll dig her up and you can see for yourself.'

'How deep did you bury her?' the doctor asked.

'Six or seven feet down, I should think.'

'And how long ago?'

'Oh, about eight hours.'

'Then she's dead,' the doctor announced. 'Here's the certificate.'

7

Our hero now sets out for the City of New York to find Mr Samuel Zuckermann. He travelled on foot, and he slept under hedges, and he lived on berries and wild herbs, and it took him sixteen days to reach the metropolis.

'What a fabulous place this is!' he cried as he stood at the corner of Fifty-seventh Street and Fifth Avenue, staring around him. 'There are no cows or chickens anywhere, and none of the women looks in the least like Aunt Glosspan.'

As for Mr Samuel Zuckermann, he looked like nothing that Lexington had ever seen before.

He was a small spongy man with livid jowls and a huge magenta nose, and when he smiled, bits of gold flashed at you marvellously from lots of different places inside his mouth. In his luxurious office, he shook Lexington warmly by the hand and congratulated him upon his aunt's death.

'I suppose you knew that your dearly beloved guardian was a woman of considerable wealth?' he said.

'You mean the cows and the chickens?'

'I mean half a million bucks,' Mr Zuckermann said.

'How much?'

'Half a million dollars, my boy. And she's left it all to you.' Mr Zuckermann leaned back in his chair and clasped his hands over his spongy paunch. At the same time, he began secretly working his right forefinger in through his waistcoat and under his shirt so as to scratch the skin around the circumference of his navel – a favourite exercise of his, and one that gave him a peculiar pleasure. 'Of course, I shall have to deduct fifty per cent for my services,' he said, 'but that still leaves you with two hundred and fifty grand.'

'I am rich!' Lexington cried. 'This is wonderful! How soon can I have the money?'

'Well,' Mr Zuckermann said, 'luckily for you, I happen to be on rather cordial terms with the tax authorities around here, and I am confident that I shall be able to persuade them to waive all death duties and back taxes.'

'How kind you are,' murmured Lexington.

'I should naturally have to give somebody a small honorarium.'

'Whatever you say, Mr Zuckermann.'

'I think a hundred thousand would be sufficient.'

'Good gracious, isn't that rather excessive?'

'Never undertip a tax inspector or a policeman,' Mr Zuckermann said. 'Remember that.'

'But how much does it leave for me?' the youth asked meekly.

'One hundred and fifty thousand. But then you've got the funeral expenses to pay out of that.'

'*Funeral* expenses?'

'You've got to pay the funeral parlour. Surely you know that?'

'But I buried her myself, Mr Zuckermann, behind the cowshed.'

'I don't doubt it,' the lawyer said. 'So what?'

'I never used a funeral parlour.'

'Listen,' Mr Zuckermann said patiently. 'You may not know it, but there is a law in this State which says that no beneficiary under a will may receive a single penny of his inheritance until the funeral parlour has been paid in full.'

'You mean that's a *law*?'

'Certainly, it's a law, and a very good one it is, too. The funeral parlour is one of our great national institutions. It must be protected at all costs.'

Mr Zuckermann himself, together with a group of public-spirited doctors, controlled a corporation that owned a chain of nine lavish funeral parlours in the city, not to mention a casket factory in Brooklyn and a postgraduate school for embalmers in Washington Heights. The celebration of death was therefore a deeply religious affair in Mr Zuckermann's eyes. In fact, the whole business affected him profoundly, almost as profoundly, one might say, as the birth of Christ affected the shopkeeper.

'You had no right to go out and bury your aunt like that,' he said. 'None at all.'

'I'm very sorry, Mr Zuckermann.'

'Why, it's downright subversive.'

'I'll do whatever you say, Mr Zuckermann. All I want to know is how much I'm going to get in the end, when everything's paid.'

There was a pause. Mr Zuckermann sighed and frowned and continued secretly to run the tip of his finger around the rim of his navel.

'Shall we say fifteen thousand?' he suggested, flashing a big gold smile. 'That's a nice round figure.'

'Can I take it with me this afternoon?'

'I don't see why not.'

So Mr Zuckermann summoned his chief cashier and told him to give Lexington fifteen thousand dollars out of the petty cash, and to obtain a receipt. The youth, who by this time was delighted to be getting anything at all, accepted the money gratefully and stowed it away in his knapsack. Then he shook Mr Zuckermann warmly by the hand, thanked him for all his help, and went out of the office.

'The whole world is before me!' our hero cried as he emerged into the street. 'I now have fifteen thousand dollars to see me through until my book is published. And after that, of course, I shall have a great deal more.' He stood on the pavement, wondering which way to go. He turned left and began strolling slowly down the street, staring at the sights of the city.

'What a revolting smell,' he said, sniffing the air. 'I can't stand this.' His delicate olfactory nerves, tuned to receive only the most delicious kitchen aromas, were being tortured by the stench of the diesel-oil fumes pouring out of the backs of the buses.

'I must get out of this place before my nose is ruined altogether,' he said. 'But first, I've simply got to have something to eat. I'm starving.' The poor boy had had nothing but berries and wild herbs for the past two weeks, and now his stomach was yearning for solid food. I'd like a nice hominy cutlet, he told himself. Or maybe a few juicy salsify fritters.

He crossed the street and entered a small restaurant. The place was hot inside, and dark and silent. There was a strong smell of cooking-fat and cabbage water. The only other customer was a man with a brown hat on his head, crouching intently over his food, who did not look up as Lexington came in.

Our hero seated himself at a corner table and hung his knapsack on the back of his chair. This, he told himself, is going to be most interesting. In all my seventeen years I have tasted only the cooking of two people, Aunt Glosspan and myself – unless one counts Nurse McPottle, who must have heated my bottle a few times when I was an infant. But I am now about to sample the art of a new chef altogether, and perhaps, if I am lucky, I may pick up a couple of useful ideas for my book.

A waiter approached out of the shadows at the back, and stood beside the table.

'How do you do,' Lexington said. 'I should like a large hominy cutlet please. Do it twenty-five seconds each side, in a very hot skillet with sour cream, and sprinkle a pinch of lovage on it before serving – unless of course your chef knows of a more original method, in which case I should be delighted to try it.'

The waiter laid his head over to one side and looked carefully at his customer. 'You want the roast pork and cabbage?' he asked. 'That's all we got left.'

'Roast what and cabbage?'

The waiter took a soiled handkerchief from his trouser pocket and shook it open with a violent flourish, as though he were cracking a whip. Then he blew his nose loud and wet.

'You want it or don't you?' he said, wiping his nostrils.

'I haven't the foggiest idea what it is,' Lexington replied, 'but I should love to try it. You see, I am writing a cooking-book and ...'

'One pork and cabbage!' the waiter shouted, and somewhere in the back of the restaurant, far away in the darkness, a voice answered him.

The waiter disappeared. Lexington reached into his knapsack for his personal knife and fork. These were a present from Aunt Glosspan, given him when he was six years old, made of solid silver, and he had never eaten with any other instruments since. While waiting for the food to arrive, he polished them lovingly with a piece of soft muslin.

Soon the waiter returned carrying a plate on which there lay a thick greyish-white slab of something hot. Lexington leaned forward anxiously to smell it as it was put down before him. His nostrils were wide open to receive the scent, quivering and sniffing.

'But this is absolute heaven!' he exclaimed. 'What an aroma! It's tremendous!'

The waiter stepped back a pace, watching his customer carefully.

'Never in my life have I smelled anything as rich and wonderful as this!' our hero cried, seizing his knife and fork. 'What on earth is it made of?'

The man in the brown hat looked around and stared, then returned to his eating. The waiter was backing away towards the kitchen.

Lexington cut off a small piece of the meat, impaled it on his silver fork, and carried it up to his nose so as to smell it again. Then he popped it into his mouth and began to chew it slowly, his eyes half closed, his body tense.

'This is fantastic!' he cried. 'It is a brand-new flavour! Oh, Glosspan, my beloved Aunt, how I wish you were with me now so you could taste this remarkable dish! Waiter! Come here at once! I want you!'

The astonished waiter was now watching from the other end of the room, and he seemed reluctant to move any closer.

'If you will come and talk to me I will give you a present,' Lexington said, waving a hundred-dollar-bill. 'Please come over here and talk to me.'

The waiter sidled cautiously back to the table, snatched away the money, and held it up close to his face, peering at it from all angles. Then he slipped it quickly into his pocket.

'What can I do for you, my friend?' he asked.

'Look,' Lexington said. 'If you will tell me what this delicious dish is made of, and exactly how it is prepared, I will give you another hundred.'

'I already told you,' the man said. 'It's pork.'

'And what exactly is pork?'

'You never had roast pork before?' the waiter asked, staring.

'For heaven's sake, man, tell me what it is and stop keeping me in suspense like this.'

'It's pig,' the waiter said. 'You just bung it in the oven.'

'*Pig!*'

'All pork is pig. Didn't you know that?'

'You mean *this* is *pig's* meat?'

'I guarantee it.'

'But ... but ... that's impossible,' the youth stammered. 'Aunt Glosspan, who knew more about food than anyone else in the world, said that meat of any kind was disgusting, revolting, horrible, foul, nauseating, and beastly. And yet this piece that I have here on my plate is without doubt the most delicious thing that I have ever tasted. Now how on earth do you explain that? Aunt Glosspan certainly wouldn't have told me it was revolting if it wasn't.'

'Maybe your aunt didn't know how to cook it,' the waiter said.

'Is that possible?'

'You're damned right it is. Especially with pork. Pork has to be very well done or you can't eat it.'

'Eureka!' Lexington cried. 'I'll bet that's exactly what happened! She did it wrong!' He handed the man another hundred-dollar bill. 'Lead me to the kitchen,' he said. 'Introduce me to the genius who prepared this meat.'

Lexington was at once taken into the kitchen, and there he met the cook who was an elderly man with a rash on one side of his neck.

'This will cost you another hundred,' the waiter said.

Lexington was only too glad to oblige, but this time he gave the money to the cook. 'Now listen to me,' he said. 'I have to admit that I am really rather confused by what the waiter has just been telling me. Are you quite positive that the delectable dish which I have just been eating was prepared from pig's flesh?'

The cook raised his right hand and began scratching the rash on his neck.

'Well,' he said, looking at the waiter and giving him a sly wink, 'all I can tell you is that I *think* it was pig's meat.'

'You mean you're not sure?'

'One can't ever be sure.'

'Then what else could it have been?'

'Well,' the cook said, speaking very slowly and still staring at the waiter. 'There's just a chance, you see, that it might have been a piece of human stuff.'

'You mean a man?'

'Yes.'

'Good heavens.'

'Or a woman. It could have been either. They both taste the same.'

'Well – now you really do surprise me,' the youth declared.

'One lives and learns.'

'Indeed one does.'

'As a matter of fact, we've been getting an awful lot of it just lately from the butcher's in place of pork,' the cook declared.

'Have you really?'

'The trouble is, it's almost impossible to tell which is which. They're both very good.'

'The piece I had just now was simply superb.'

'I'm glad you liked it,' the cook said. 'But to be quite honest, I think that was a bit of pig. In fact, I'm almost sure it was.'

'You are?'

'Yes, I am.'

'In that case, we shall have to assume that you are right,' Lexington said. 'So now will you please tell me – and here is another hundred dollars for your trouble – will you please tell me precisely how you prepared it?'

The cook, after pocketing the money, launched out upon a colourful description of how to roast a loin of pork, while the youth, not wanting to miss a single word of so great a recipe, sat down at the kitchen table and recorded every detail in his notebook.

'Is that all?' he asked when the cook had finished.

'That's all.'

'But there must be more to it than that, surely?'

'You got to get a good piece of meat to start off with,' the cook said. 'That's half the battle. It's got to be a good hog and it's got to be butchered right, otherwise it'll turn out lousy whichever way you cook it.'

'Show me how,' Lexington said. 'Butcher me one now so I can learn.'

'We don't butcher pigs in the kitchen,' he cook said. 'That lot you just ate came from a packing-house over in the Bronx.'

'Then give me the address!'

The cook gave him the address, and our hero, after thanking them both many times for all their kindnesses, rushed outside and leapt into a taxi and headed for the Bronx.

8

The packing-house was a big four-storey brick building, and the air around it smelled sweet and heavy, like musk. At the main entrance gates, there was a large notice which said VISITORS WELCOME AT ANY TIME, and thus encouraged, Lexington walked through the gates and entered a cobbled yard which surrounded the building itself. He then followed a series of signposts (THIS WAY FOR THE GUIDED TOURS), and came eventually to a small corrugated-iron shed set well apart from the main building (VISITORS' WAITING-ROOM). After knocking politely on the door, he went in.

There were six other people ahead of him in the waiting-room. There was a fat mother with her two little boys aged about nine and eleven. There was a bright-eyed young couple who looked as though they might be on their honeymoon. And there was a pale woman with long white gloves, who sat very upright, looking straight ahead, with her hands folded on her lap. Nobody spoke. Lexington wondered whether they were all writing cooking-books, like himself, but when he put this question to them aloud, he got no answer. The grown-ups merely smiled mysteriously to themselves and shook their heads, and the two children stared at him as though they were seeing a lunatic.

Soon, the door opened and a man with a merry pink face popped his head into the room and said, 'Next, please.' The mother and the two boys got up and went out.

About ten minutes later, the same man returned. 'Next, please,' he said again, and the honeymoon couple jumped up and followed him outside.

Two new visitors came in and sat down – a middle-aged husband and a middle-aged wife, the wife carrying a wicker shopping-basket containing groceries.

'Next, please,' said the guide, and the woman with the long white gloves got up and left.

Several more people came in and took their places on the stiff-backed wooden chairs.

Soon the guide returned for the third time, and now it was Lexington's turn to go outside.

'Follow me, please,' the guide said, leading the youth across the yard towards the main building.

'How exciting this is!' Lexington cried, hopping from one foot to the other. 'I only wish that my dear Aunt Glosspan could be with me now to see what I am going to see.'

'I myself only do the preliminaries,' the guide said. 'Then I shall hand you over to someone else.'

'Anything you say,' cried the ecstatic youth.

First they visited a large penned-in area at the back of the building where several hundred pigs were wandering around. 'Here's where they start,' the guide said. 'And over there's where they go in.'

'Where?'

'Right there.' The guide pointed to a long wooden shed that stood against the outside wall of the factory. 'We call it the shackling-pen. This way, please.'

Three men wearing long rubber boots were driving a dozen pigs into the shackling-pen just as Lexington and the guide approached, so they all went in together.

'Now,' the guide said, 'watch how they shackle them.'

Inside, the shed was simply a bare wooden room with no roof, and there was a steel cable with hooks on it that kept moving slowly along the length of one wall, parallel with the ground, about three feet up. When it reached the end of the shed, this cable suddenly changed direction and climbed vertically upward through the open roof towards the top floor of the main building.

The twelve pigs were huddled together at the far end of the pen, standing quietly, looking apprehensive. One of the men in rubber boots pulled a length of metal chain down from the wall and advanced upon the nearest animal, approaching it from the rear. Then he bent down and quickly looped one end of the chain around one of the animal's hind legs. The other end he attached to a hook on the moving cable as it went by. The cable kept moving. The chain tightened. The pig's leg was pulled up and back, and then the pig itself began to be dragged backwards. But it didn't fall down. It was rather a nimble pig, and somehow it managed to keep its balance on three legs, hopping from foot to foot and struggling against the pull of the chain, but going back and back all the time until at the end of the pen where the cable changed direction and went vertically upward, the creature was suddenly jerked off its feet and borne aloft. Shrill protests filled the air.

'Truly a fascinating process,' Lexington said. 'But what was the funny cracking noise it made as it went up?'

'Probably the leg,' the guide answered. 'Either that or the pelvis.'

'But doesn't that matter?'

'Why should it matter?' the guide asked. 'You don't eat the bones.'

The rubber-booted men were busy shackling the rest of the pigs, and one after another they were hooked to the moving cable and hoisted up through the roof, protesting loudly as they went.

'There's a good deal more to this recipe than just picking herbs,' Lexington said. 'Aunt Glosspan would never have made it.'

At this point, while Lexington was gazing skyward at the last pig to go up, a man in rubber boots approached him quietly from behind and looped one end of a chain around the youth's own ankle, hooking the other end to the moving belt. The next moment, before he had time to realize what was happening, our hero was jerked off his feet and dragged backwards along the concrete floor of the shackling-pen.

'Stop!' he cried. 'Hold everything! My leg is caught!'

But nobody seemed to hear him, and five seconds later, the unhappy young man was jerked off the floor and hoisted vertically upward through the open roof of the pen, dangling upside down by one ankle, and wriggling like a fish.

'Help!' he shouted. 'Help! There's been a frightful mistake! Stop the engines! Let me down!'

The guide removed a cigar from his mouth and looked up serenely at the rapidly ascending youth, but he said nothing. The men in rubber boots were already on their way out to collect the next batch of pigs.

'Oh, save me!' our hero cried. 'Let me down! Please let me down!' But he was now approaching the top floor of the building where the moving belt curled over like a snake and entered a large hole in the wall, a kind of doorway without a door; and there, on the threshold, waiting to greet him, clothed in a dark-stained yellow rubber apron, and looking for all the world like Saint Peter at the Gates of Heaven, the sticker stood.

Lexington saw him only from upside down, and very briefly at that, but even so he noticed at once the expression of absolute peace and benevolence on the man's face, the cheerful twinkle in the eyes, the little wistful smile, the dimples in his cheeks – and all this gave him hope.

'Hi there,' the sticker said, smiling.

'Quick! Save me!' our hero cried.

'With pleasure,' the sticker said, and taking Lexington gently by one ear with his left hand, he raised his right hand and deftly slit open the boy's jugular vein with a knife.

The belt moved on. Lexington went with it. Everything was still upside down and the blood was pouring out of his throat and getting into his eyes, but he could still see after a fashion, and he had a blurred impression of being in an enormously long room, and at the far end of the room there was a great smoking cauldron of water, and there were dark figures, half hidden in the steam, dancing around the edge of it, brandishing long poles. The conveyor-belt seemed to be travelling right over the top of the cauldron, and the pigs seemed to be dropping one by one into the boiling water, and one of the pigs seemed to be wearing long white gloves on its front feet.

Suddenly our hero started to feel very sleepy, but it wasn't until his good strong heart had pumped the last drop of blood from his body that he passed on out of this, the best of all possible worlds, into the next.

THE CHAMPION OF THE WORLD

All day, in between serving customers, we had been crouching over the table in the office of the filling-station, preparing the raisins. They were plump and soft and swollen from being soaked in water, and when you nicked them with a razor-blade the skin sprang open and the jelly stuff inside squeezed out as easily as you could wish.

But we had a hundred and ninety-six of them to do altogether and the evening was nearly upon us before we had finished.

'Don't they look marvellous!' Claud cried, rubbing his hands together hard. 'What time is it, Gordon?'

'Just after five.'

Through the window we could see a station-wagon pulling up at the pumps with a woman at the wheel and about eight children in the back eating ice-creams.

'We ought to be moving soon,' Claud said. 'The whole thing'll be a washout if we don't arrive before sunset, you realize that.' He was getting twitchy now. His face had the same flushed and pop-eyed look it got before a dog-race or when there was a date with Clarice in the evening.

We both went outside and Claud gave the woman the number of gallons she wanted. When she had gone, he remained standing in the middle of the driveway squinting anxiously up at the sun which was now only the width of a man's hand above the line of trees along the crest of the ridge on the far side of the valley.

'All right,' I said. 'Lock up.'

He went quickly from pump to pump, securing each nozzle in its holder with a small padlock.

'You'd better take off that yellow pullover,' he said.

'Why should I?'

'You'll be shining like a bloody beacon out there in the moonlight.'

'I'll be all right.'

'You will not,' he said. 'Take it off, Gordon, please. I'll see you in three minutes.' He disappeared into his caravan behind the filling-station, and I went indoors and changed my yellow pullover for a blue one.

When we met again outside, Claud was dressed in a pair of black trousers and a dark-green turtleneck sweater. On his head he wore a brown cloth cap with the peak pulled down low over his eyes, and he looked like an apache actor out of a nightclub.

'What's under there?' I asked, seeing the bulge at his waistline.

He pulled up his sweater and showed me two thin but very large white cotton sacks which were bound neat and tight around his belly. 'To carry the stuff,' he said darkly.

'I see.'

'Let's go,' he said.

'I still think we ought to take the car.'

'It's too risky. They'll see it parked.'

'But it's over three miles up to that wood.'

'Yes,' he said. 'And I suppose you realize we can get six months in the clink if they catch us.'

'You never told me that.'

'Didn't I?'

'I'm not coming,' I said. 'It's not worth it.'

'The walk will do you good, Gordon. Come on.'

It was a calm sunny evening with little wisps of brilliant white cloud hanging motionless in the sky, and the valley was cool and very quiet as the two of us began walking together along the grass verge on the side of the road that ran between the hills towards Oxford.

'You got the raisins?' Claud asked.

'They're in my pocket.'

'Good,' he said. 'Marvellous.'

Ten minutes later we turned left off the main road into a narrow lane with high hedges on either side and from now on it was all uphill.

'How many keepers are there?' I asked.

'Three.'

Claud threw away a half-finished cigarette. A minute later he lit another.

'I don't usually approve of new methods,' he said. 'Not on this sort of a job.'

'Of course.'

'But by God, Gordon, I think we're on to a hot one this time.'

'You do?'

'There's no question about it.'

'I hope you're right.'

'It'll be a milestone in the history of poaching,' he said. 'But don't you go telling a single soul how we've done it, you understand. Because if this ever leaked out we'd have every bloody fool in the district doing the same thing and there wouldn't be a pheasant left.'

'I won't say a word.'

'You ought to be very proud of yourself,' he went on. 'There's been men with brains studying this problem for hundreds of years and not one of them's ever come up with anything even a quarter as artful as you have. Why didn't you tell me about it before?'

'You never invited my opinion,' I said.

And that was the truth. In fact, up until the day before, Claud had never even offered to discuss with me the sacred subject of poaching. Often enough, on a summer's evening when work was finished, I had seen him with cap on head sliding quietly out of his caravan and disappearing up the road towards the woods; and sometimes, watching him through the windows of the filling-station, I would find myself wondering exactly what he was going to do, what wily tricks he was going to practise all alone up there under the trees in the dead of night. He seldom came back until very late, and never, absolutely never did he bring any of the spoils with him personally on his return. But the following afternoon – and I couldn't imagine how he did it – there would always be a pheasant or a hare or a brace of partridges hanging up in the shed behind the filling-station for us to eat.

This summer he had been particularly active, and during the last couple of months he had stepped up the tempo to a point where he was going out four and sometimes five nights a week. But that was not all. It seemed to me that recently his whole attitude towards poaching had undergone a subtle and mysterious change. He was more purposeful about it now, more tight-lipped and intense than before, and I had the impression that this was not so much a game any longer as a crusade, a sort of private war that Claud was waging single-handed against an invisible and hated enemy.

But who?

I wasn't sure about this, but I had a suspicion that it was none other than the famous Mr Victor Hazel himself, the owner of the land and the pheasants. Mr Hazel was a local brewer with an unbelievably arrogant manner. He was rich beyond words, and his property stretched for miles along either side of the valley. He was a self-made man with no charm at all and precious few virtues. He loathed all persons of humble station, having once been one of them himself, and he strove desperately to mingle with what he believed were the right kind of folk. He rode to hounds and gave shooting-parties and wore fancy waistcoats, and every weekday he drove an enormous black Rolls-Royce past the filling-station on his way to the brewery. As he flashed by, we would sometimes catch a glimpse of the great glistening brewer's face above the wheel, pink as a ham, all soft and inflamed from drinking too much beer.

Anyway, yesterday afternoon, right out of the blue, Claud had suddenly said to me, 'I'll be going on up to Hazel's woods again tonight. Why don't you come along?'

'Who, me?'

'It's about the last chance this year for pheasants,' he had said. 'The shooting-season opens Saturday and the birds'll be scattered all over the place after that – if there's any left.'

'Why the sudden invitation?' I had asked, greatly suspicious.

'No special reason, Gordon. No reason at all.'

'Is it risky?'

He hadn't answered this.

'I suppose you keep a gun or something hidden away up there?'

'A gun!' he cried, disgusted. 'Nobody ever *shoots* pheasants, didn't you know that? You've only got to fire a *cap-pistol* in Hazel's woods and the keepers'll be on you.'

'Then how do you do it?'

'Ah,' he said, and the eyelids drooped over the eyes, veiled and secretive.

There was a long pause. Then he said, 'Do you think you could keep your mouth shut if I was to tell you a thing or two?'

'Definitely.'

'I've never told this to anyone else in my whole life, Gordon.'

'I am greatly honoured,' I said. 'You can trust me completely.'

He turned his head, fixing me with pale eyes. The eyes were large and wet and ox-like, and they were so near to me that I could see my own face reflected upside down in the centre of each.

'I am now about to let you in on the three best ways in the world of poaching a pheasant,' he said. 'And seeing that you're the guest on this little trip, I am going to give you the choice of which one you'd like us to use tonight. How's that?'

'There's a catch in this.'

'There's no catch, Gordon. I swear it.'

'All right, go on.'

'Now, here's the thing,' he said. 'Here's the first big secret.' He paused and took a long suck at his cigarette. 'Pheasants,' he whispered softly, 'is *crazy* about raisins.'

'Raisins?'

'Just ordinary raisins. It's like a mania with them. My dad discovered that more than forty years ago just like he discovered all three of these methods I'm about to describe to you now.'

'I thought you said your dad was a drunk.'

'Maybe he was. But he was also a great poacher, Gordon. Possibly the greatest there's ever been in the history of England. My dad studied poaching like a scientist.'

'Is that so?'

'I mean it. I really mean it.'

'I believe you.'

'Do you know,' he said, 'my dad used to keep a whole flock of prime cockerels in the back yard purely for experimental purposes.'

'Cockerels?'

'That's right. And whenever he thought up some new stunt for catching a pheasant, he'd try it out on a cockerel first to see how it worked. That's how he discovered about raisins. It's also how he invented the horsehair method.'

Claud paused and glanced over his shoulder as though to make sure that there was nobody listening. 'Here's how it's done,' he said. 'First you take a few raisins and you soak them overnight in water to make them nice and plump and juicy. Then you get a bit of good stiff horsehair and you cut it up into half-inch lengths. Then you push one of these lengths of horsehair through the middle of each raisin so that there's about an eighth of an inch of it sticking out on either side. You follow?'

'Yes.'

'Now – the old pheasant comes along and eats one of these raisins. Right? And you're watching him from behind a tree. So what then?'

'I imagine it sticks in his throat.'

'That's obvious, Gordon. But here's the amazing thing. Here's what my dad discovered. The moment this happens, the bird *never moves his feet again!* He becomes absolutely rooted to the spot, and there he stands pumping his silly neck up and down just like it was a piston, and all you've got to do is walk calmly out from the place where you're hiding and pick him up in your hands.'

'I don't believe that.'

'I swear it,' he said. 'Once a pheasant's had the horsehair you can fire a rifle in his ear and he won't even jump. It's just one of those unexplainable little things. But it takes a genius to discover it.'

He paused, and there was a gleam of pride in his eye now as he dwelt for a moment or two upon the memory of his father, the great inventor.

'So that's Method Number One,' he said. 'Method Number Two is even more simple still. All you do is you have a fishing line. Then you bait the hook with a raisin and you fish for the pheasant just like you fish for a fish. You pay out the line about fifty yards and you lie there on your stomach in the bushes waiting till you get a bite. Then you haul him in.'

'I don't think your father invented that one.'

'It's very popular with fishermen,' he said, choosing not to hear me. 'Keen fishermen who can't get down to the seaside as often as they want. It gives them a bit of the old thrill. The only trouble is it's rather noisy. The pheasant squawks like hell as you haul him in, and then every keeper in the wood comes running.'

'What is Method Number Three?' I asked.

'Ah,' he said. 'Number Three's a real beauty. It was the last one my dad ever invented before he passed away.'

'His final great work?'

'Exactly, Gordon. And I can even remember the very day it happened, a Sunday morning it was, and suddenly my dad comes into the kitchen holding a huge white cockerel in his hands and he says, "I think I've got it!" There's a little smile on his face and a shine of glory in his eyes and he comes in very soft and quiet and he puts the bird down right in the middle of the kitchen table and he says, "By God I think I've got a good one this time!" "A good what?" Mum says, looking up from the sink. "Horace, take that filthy bird off my table." The cockerel has a funny little paper hat over its head, like an ice-cream cone upside down, and my dad is pointing to it proudly. "Stroke him," he says. "He won't move an inch." The cockerel starts scratching away at the paper hat with one of its feet, but the hat seems to be stuck on with glue and it won't come off. "No bird in the world is going to run away once you cover up his eyes," my dad says, and he starts poking the cockerel with his finger and pushing it around on the table, but it doesn't take the slightest bit of notice. "You can have this one," he says, talking to Mum. "You can kill it and dish it up for dinner as a celebration of what I have just invented." And then straight away he takes me by the arm and marches me quickly out the door and off we go over the fields and up into the big forest the other side of Haddenham which used to belong to the Duke of Buckingham, and in less than two hours we get five lovely fat pheasants with no more trouble than it takes to go out and buy them in a shop.'

Claud paused for breath. His eyes were huge and moist and dreamy as they gazed back into the wonderful world of his youth.

'I don't quite follow this,' I said. 'How did he get the paper hats over the pheasants' heads up in the woods?'

'You'd never guess it.'

'I'm sure I wouldn't.'

'Then here it is. First of all you dig a little hole in the ground. Then you twist a piece of paper into the shape of a cone and you fit this into the hole, hollow end upward, like a cup. Then you smear the paper cup all around the inside with bird-lime and drop in a few raisins. At the same time you lay a trail of raisins along the ground leading up to it. Now – the old pheasant comes pecking along the trail, and when he gets to the hole he pops his head inside to gobble the raisins and the next thing he knows he's got a paper hat stuck over his eyes and he can't see a thing. Isn't it marvellous what some people think of, Gordon? Don't you agree?'

'Your dad was a genius,' I said.

'Then take your pick. Choose whichever one of the three methods you fancy and we'll use it tonight.'

'You don't think they're all just a trifle on the crude side, do you?'

'Crude!' he cried, aghast. 'Oh my God! And who's been having roasted pheasant in the house nearly every single day for the last six months and not a penny to pay?'

He turned and walked away towards the door of the workshop. I could see that he was deeply pained by my remark.

'Wait a minute,' I said. 'Don't go.'

'You want to come or don't you?'

'Yes, but let me ask you something first. I've just had a bit of an idea.'

'Keep it,' he said. 'You are talking about a subject you don't know the first thing about.'

'Do you remember that bottle of sleeping-pills the doc gave me last month when I had a bad back?'

'What about them?'

'Is there any reason why those wouldn't work on a pheasant?'

Claud closed his eyes and shook his head pityingly from side to side.

'Wait,' I said.

'It's not worth discussing,' he said. 'No pheasant in the world is going to swallow those lousy red capsules. Don't you know any better than that?'

'You are forgetting the raisins,' I said. 'Now listen to this. We take a raisin. Then we soak it till it swells. Then we make a tiny slit in one side of it with a razor-blade. Then we hollow it out a little. Then we open up one of my red capsules and pour all the powder into the raisin. Then we get a needle and cotton and very carefully we sew up the slit. Now ...'

Out of the corner of my eye, I saw Claud's mouth slowly beginning to open.

'Now,' I said. 'We have a nice clean-looking raisin with two and a half grains of seconal inside it, and let me tell *you* something now. That's enough dope to knock the average *man* unconscious, never mind about *birds*!'

I paused for ten seconds to allow the full impact of this to strike home.

'What's more, with this method we could operate on a really grand scale. We could prepare *twenty* raisins if we felt like it, and all we'd have to do is scatter them around the feeding-grounds at sunset and then walk away. Half an hour later we'd come back, and the pills would be beginning to work, and the pheasants would be up in the trees by then, roosting, and they'd be starting to feel groggy, and they'd be wobbling and trying to keep their balance, and soon every pheasant that had eaten *one single raisin* would keel over unconscious and fall to the ground. My dear boy, they'd be dropping out of the trees like apples, and all we'd have to do is walk around picking them up!'

Claud was staring at me, rapt.

'Oh Christ,' he said softly.

'And they'd never catch us either. We'd simply stroll through the woods dropping a few raisins here and there as we went, and even if they were *watching* us they wouldn't notice anything.'

'Gordon,' he said, laying a hand on my knee and gazing at me with eyes large and bright as two stars. 'If this thing works, it will *revolutionize* poaching.'

'I'm glad to hear it.'

'How many pills have you got left?' he asked.

'Forty-nine. There were fifty in the bottle and I've only used one.'

'Forty-nine's not enough. We want at least two hundred.'

'Are you mad!' I cried.

He walked slowly away and stood by the door with his back to me, gazing at the sky.

'Two hundred's the bare minimum,' he said quietly. 'There's really not much point in doing it unless we have two hundred.'

What is it now, I wondered. What the hell's he trying to do?

'This is the last chance we'll have before the season opens,' he said. 'I couldn't possibly get any more.'

'You wouldn't want us to come back empty-handed, would you?'

'But why so *many*?'

Claud turned his head and looked at me with large innocent eyes. 'Why not?' he said gently. 'Do you have any objection?'

My God, I thought suddenly. The crazy bastard is out to wreck Mr Victor Hazel's opening-day shooting-party.

'You get us two hundred of those pills,' he said, 'and then it'll be worth doing.'

'I can't.'

'You could try, couldn't you?'

Mr Hazel's party took place on the first of October every year and it was a very famous event. Debilitated gentlemen in tweed suits, some with titles and some who were merely rich, motored in from miles around with their gun-bearers and dogs and wives, and all day long the noise of shooting rolled across the valley. There were always enough pheasants to go round, for each summer the woods were methodically restocked with dozens and dozens of young birds at incredible expense. I had heard it said that the cost of rearing and keeping each pheasant up to the time when it was ready to be shot was well over five pounds (which is approximately the price of two hundred loaves of bread). But to Mr Hazel it was worth every penny of it. He became, if only for a few hours, a big cheese in a little world and even the Lord Lieutenant of the County slapped him on the back and tried to remember his first name when he said good-bye.

'How would it be if we just reduced the dose?' Claud asked. 'Why couldn't we divide the contents of one capsule among four raisins?'

'I suppose you could if you wanted to.'

'But would a quarter of a capsule be strong enough for each bird?'

One simply had to admire the man's nerve. It was dangerous enough to poach a single pheasant up in those woods at this time of year and here he was planning to knock off the bloody lot.

'A quarter would be plenty,' I said.

'You're sure of that?'

'Work it out for yourself. It's all done by bodyweight. You'd still be giving about twenty times more than is necessary.'

'Then we'll quarter the dose,' he said, rubbing his hands. He paused and calculated for a moment. 'We'll have one hundred and ninety-six raisins!'

'Do you realize what that involves?' I said. 'They'll take hours to prepare.'

'What of it!' he cried. 'We'll go tomorrow instead. We'll soak the raisins overnight and then we'll have all morning and afternoon to get them ready.'

And that was precisely what we did.

Now, twenty-four hours later, we were on our way. We had been walking steadily for about forty minutes and we were nearing the point where the lane curved round to the right and ran along the crest of the hill towards the big wood where the pheasants lived. There was about a mile to go.

'I don't suppose by any chance these keepers might be carrying guns?' I asked.

'All keepers carry guns,' Claud said.

I had been afraid of that.

'It's for the vermin mostly.'

'Ah.'

'Of course there's no guarantee they won't take a pot at a poacher now and again.'

'You're joking.'

'Not at all. But they only do it from behind. Only when you're running away. They like to pepper you in the legs at about fifty yards.'

'They can't do that!' I cried. 'It's a criminal offence!'

'So is poaching,' Claud said.

We walked on awhile in silence. The sun was below the high hedge on our right now and the lane was in shadow.

'You can consider yourself lucky this isn't thirty years ago,' he went on. 'They used to shoot you on sight in those days.'

'Do you believe that?'

'I know it,' he said. 'Many's the night when I was a nipper I've gone into the kitchen and seen my old dad lying face downward on the table and Mum standing over him digging the grapeshot out of his buttocks with a potato knife.'

'Stop,' I said. 'It makes me nervous.'

'You believe me, don't you?'

'Yes, I believe you.'

'Towards the end he was so covered in tiny little white scars he looked exactly like it was snowing.'

'Yes,' I said. 'All right.'

'Poacher's arse, they used to call it,' Claud said. 'And there wasn't a man in the whole village who didn't have a bit of it one way or another. But my dad was the champion.'

'Good luck to him,' I said.

'I wish to hell he was here now,' Claud said, wistful. 'He'd have given anything in the world to be coming with us on this job tonight.'

'He could take my place,' I said. 'Gladly.'

We had reached the crest of the hill and now we could see the wood ahead of us, huge and dark with the sun going down behind the trees and little sparks of gold shining through.

'You'd better let me have those raisins,' Claud said.

I gave him the bag and he slid it gently into his trouser pocket.

'No talking once we're inside,' he said. 'Just follow me and try not to go snapping any branches.'

Five minutes later we were there. The lane ran right up to the wood itself and then skirted the edge of it for about three hundred yards with only a little hedge between. Claud slipped through the hedge on all fours and I followed.

It was cool and dark inside the wood. No sunlight came in at all.

'This is spooky,' I said.

'Ssshh!'

Claud was very tense. He was walking just ahead of me, picking his feet up high and putting them down gently on the moist ground. He kept his head moving all the time, the eyes sweeping slowly from side to side, searching for danger. I tried doing the same, but soon I began to see a keeper behind every tree, so I gave it up.

Then a large patch of sky appeared ahead of us in the roof of the forest and I knew that this must be the clearing. Claud had told me that the clearing was the place where the young birds were introduced into the woods in early July, where they were fed and watered and guarded by the keepers, and where many of them stayed from force of habit until the shooting began.

'There always plenty of pheasants in the clearing,' he had said.

'Keepers too, I suppose.'

'Yes, but there's thick bushes all around and that helps.'

We were now advancing in a series of quick crouching spurts, running from tree to tree and stopping and waiting and listening and running on again, and then at last we were kneeling safely behind a big clump of alder right on the edge of the clearing and Claud was grinning and nudging me in the ribs and pointing through the branches at the pheasants.

The place was absolutely stiff with birds. There must have been two hundred of them at least strutting around among the tree-stumps.

'You see what I mean?' Claud whispered.

It was an astonishing sight, a sort of poacher's dream come true. And how close they were! Some of them were not more than ten paces from where we knelt. The hens were plump and creamy-brown and they were so fat their breast-feathers almost brushed the ground as they walked. The cocks were slim and beautiful, with long tails and brilliant red patches around the eyes, like scarlet spectacles. I glanced at Claud. His big ox-like face was transfixed in ecstasy. The mouth was slightly open and the eyes had a kind of glazy look about them as they stared at the pheasants.

I believe that all poachers react in roughly the same way as this on sighting game. They are like women who sight large emeralds in a jeweller's window, the only difference being that the women are less dignified in the methods they employ later on to acquire the loot. Poacher's arse is nothing to the punishment that a female is willing to endure.

'Ah-ha,' Claud said softly. 'You see the keeper?'

'Where?'

'Over the other side, by that big tree. Look carefully.'

'My God!'

'It's all right. He can't see *us*.'

We crouched close to the ground, watching the keeper. He was a smallish man with a cap on his head and a gun under his arm. He never moved. He was like a little post standing there.

'Let's go,' I whispered.

The keeper's face was shadowed by the peak of his cap, but it seemed to me that he was looking directly at us.

'I'm not staying here,' I said.

'Hush,' Claud said.

Slowly, never taking his eyes from the keeper, he reached into his pocket and brought out a single raisin. He placed it in the palm of his right hand, and then quickly, with a little flick of the wrist, he threw the raisin high into the air. I watched it as it went sailing over the bushes and I saw it land within a yard or so of two henbirds standing together beside an old tree-stump. Both birds turned their heads sharply at the drop of the raisin. Then one of them hopped over and made a quick peck at the ground and that must have been it.

I glanced up at the keeper. He hadn't moved.

Claud threw a second raisin into the clearing; then a third, and a fourth, and a fifth.

At this point, I saw the keeper turn away his head in order to survey the wood behind him.

Quick as a flash, Claud pulled the paper bag out of his pocket and tipped a huge pile of raisins into the cup of his right hand.

'Stop,' I said.

But with a great sweep of the arm he flung the whole handful high over the bushes into the clearing.

They fell with a soft little patter, like raindrops on dry leaves, and every single pheasant in the place must either have seen them coming or heard them fall. There was a flurry of wings and a rush to find the treasure.

The keeper's head flicked round as though there were a spring inside his neck. The birds were all pecking away madly at the raisins. The keeper took two quick paces forward and for a moment I thought he was going in to investigate. But then he stopped, and his face came up and his eyes began travelling slowly around the perimeter of the clearing.

'Follow me,' Claud whispered. 'And *keep down.*' He started crawling away swiftly on all fours, like some kind of a monkey.

I went after him. He had his nose close to the ground and his huge tight buttocks were winking at the sky and it was easy to see now how poacher's arse had come to be an occupational disease among the fraternity.

We went along like this for about a hundred yards.

'Now run,' Claud said.

We got to our feet and ran, and a few minutes later we emerged through the hedge into the lovely open safety of the lane.

'It went marvellous,' Claud said, breathing heavily. 'Didn't it go absolutely marvellous?' The big face was scarlet and glowing with triumph.

'It was a mess,' I said.

'What!' he cried.

'Of course it was. We can't possibly go back now. That keeper knows there was someone there.'

'He knows nothing,' Claud said. 'In another five minutes it'll be pitch dark inside the wood and he'll be sloping off home to his supper.'

'I think I'll join him.'

'You're a great poacher,' Claud said. He sat down on the grassy bank under the hedge and lit a cigarette.

The sun had set now and the sky was a pale smoke blue, faintly glazed with yellow. In the woods behind us the shadows and the spaces in between the trees were turning from grey to black.

'How long does a sleeping-pill take to work?' Claud asked.

'Look out,' I said. 'There's someone coming.'

The man had appeared suddenly and silently out of the dusk and he was only thirty yards away when I saw him.

'Another bloody keeper,' Claud said.

We both looked at the keeper as he came down the lane towards us. He had a shotgun under his arm and there was a black Labrador walking at his heels. He stopped when he was a few paces away and the dog stopped with him and stayed behind him, watching us through the keeper's legs.

'Good evening,' Claud said, nice and friendly.

This one was a tall bony man about forty with a swift eye and a hard cheek and hard dangerous hands.

'I know you,' he said softly, coming closer. 'I know the both of you.'

Claud didn't answer this.

'You're from the fillin'-station. Right?'

His lips were thin and dry, with some sort of a brownish crust over them.

'You're Cubbage and Hawes and you're from the fillin'-station on the main road. Right?'

'What are we playing?' Claud said. 'Twenty Questions?'

The keeper spat out a big gob of spit and I saw it go floating through the air and land with a plop on a patch of dry dust six inches from Claud's feet. It looked like a little baby oyster lying there.

'Beat it,' the man said. 'Go on. Get out.'

Claud sat on the bank smoking his cigarette and looking at the gob of spit.

'Go on,' the man said. 'Get out.'

When he spoke, the upper lip lifted above the gum and I could see a row of small discoloured teeth, one of them black, the others quince and ochre.

'This happens to be a public highway,' Claud said. 'Kindly do not molest us.'

The keeper shifted the gun from his left arm to his right.

'You're loiterin',' he said, 'with intent to commit a felony. I could run you in for that.'

'No you couldn't,' Claud said.

All this made me rather nervous.

'I've had my eye on you for some time,' the keeper said, looking at Claud.

'It's getting late,' I said. 'Shall we stroll on?'

Claud flipped away his cigarette and got slowly to his feet. 'All right,' he said. 'Let's go.'

We wandered off down the lane the way we had come, leaving the keeper standing there, and soon the man was out of sight in the half-darkness behind us.

'That's the head keeper,' Claud said. 'His name is Rabbetts.'

'Let's get the hell out,' I said.

'Come in here,' Claud said.

There was a gate on our left leading into a field and we climbed over it and sat down behind the hedge.

'Mr Rabbetts is also due for his supper,' Claud said. 'You mustn't worry about him.'

We sat quietly behind the hedge waiting for the keeper to walk past us on his way home. A few stars were showing and a bright three-quarter moon was coming up over the hills behind us in the east.

'Here he is,' Claud whispered. 'Don't move.'

The keeper came loping softly up the lane with the dog padding quick and soft-footed at his heels, and we watched them through the hedge as they went by.

'He won't be coming back tonight,' Claud said.

'How do you know that?'

'A keeper never waits for you in the wood if he knows where you live. He goes to your house and hides outside and watches for you to come back.'

'That's worse.'

'No, it isn't, not if you dump the loot somewhere else before you go home. He can't touch you then.'

'What about the other one, the one in the clearing?'

'He's gone too.'

'You can't be sure of that.'

'I've been studying these bastards for months, Gordon, honest I have. I know all their habits. There's no danger.'

Reluctantly I followed him back into the wood. It was pitch dark in there now and very silent, and as we moved cautiously forward the noise of our footsteps seemed to go echoing around the walls of the forest as though we were walking in a cathedral.

'Here's where we threw the raisins,' Claud said.

I peered through the bushes.

The clearing lay dim and milky in the moonlight.

'You're quite sure the keeper's gone?'

'I *know* he's gone.'

I could just see Claud's face under the peak of his cap, the pale lips, the soft pale cheeks, and the large eyes with a little spark of excitement dancing slowly in each.

'Are they roosting?'

'Yes.'

'Whereabouts?'

'All around. They don't go far.'

'What do we do next?'

'We stay here and wait. I brought you a light,' he added, and he handed me one of those small pocket flashlights shaped like a fountain-pen. 'You may need it.'

I was beginning to feel better. 'Shall we see if we can spot some of them sitting in the trees?' I said.

'No.'

'I should like to see how they look when they're roosting.'

'This isn't a nature-study,' Claud said. 'Please be quiet.'

We stood there for a long time waiting for something to happen.

'I've just had a nasty thought,' I said. 'If a bird can keep its balance on a branch when it's asleep, then surely there isn't any reason why the pills should make it fall down.'

Claud looked at me quick.

'After all,' I said, 'it's not dead. It's still only sleeping.'

'It's doped,' Claud said.

'But that's just a *deeper* sort of sleep. Why should we expect it to fall down just because it's in a *deeper* sleep?'

There was a gloomy silence.

'We should've tried it with chickens,' Claud said. 'My dad would've done that.'

'Your dad was a genius,' I said.

At that moment there came a soft thump from the wood behind us.

'Hey!'

'Ssshh!'

We stood listening.

Thump.

'There's another!'

It was a deep muffled sound as though a bag of sand had been dropped from about shoulder height.

Thump!

'They're pheasants!' I cried.

'Wait!'

'I'm sure they're pheasants!'

Thump! Thump!

'You're right!'

We ran back into the wood.

'Where were they?'

'Over here! Two of them were over here!'

'I thought they were this way.'

'Keep looking!' Claud shouted. 'They can't be far.'

We searched for about a minute.

'Here's one!' he called.

When I got to him he was holding a magnificent cock-bird in both hands. We examined it closely with our flashlights.

'It's doped to the gills,' Claud said. 'It's still alive, I can feel its heart, but it's doped to the bloody gills.'

Thump!
'There's another!'
Thump! Thump!
'Two more!'
Thump!
Thump! Thump! Thump!
'Jesus Christ!'
Thump! Thump! Thump! Thump!
Thump! Thump!

All around us the pheasants were starting to rain down out of the trees. We began rushing around madly in the dark, sweeping the ground with our flashlights.

Thump! Thump! Thump! This lot fell almost on top of me. I was right under the tree as they came down and I found all three of them immediately – two cocks and a hen. They were limp and warm, the feathers wonderfully soft in the hand.

'Where shall I put them?' I called out. I was holding them by the legs.

'Lay them here, Gordon! Just pile them up here where it's light!'

Claud was standing on the edge of the clearing with the moonlight streaming down all over him and a great bunch of pheasants in each hand. His face was bright, his eyes big and bright and wonderful, and he was staring around him like a child who has just discovered that the whole world is made of chocolate.

Thump!
Thump! Thump!
'I don't like it,' I said. 'It's too many.'

'It's beautiful!' he cried and he dumped the birds he was carrying and ran off to look for more.

Thump! Thump! Thump! Thump!
Thump!

It was easy to find them now. There were one or two lying under every tree. I quickly collected six more, three in each hand, and ran back and dumped them with the others. Then six more. Then six more after that.

And still they kept falling.

Claud was in a whirl of ecstasy now, dashing about like a mad ghost under the trees. I could see the beam of his flashlight waving around in the dark and each time he found a bird he gave a little yelp of triumph.

Thump! Thump! Thump!
'That bugger Hazel ought to hear this!' he called out.
'Don't shout,' I said. 'It frightens me.'
'What's that?'
'Don't *shout*. There might be keepers.'

'Screw the keepers!' he cried. 'They're all eating!'

For three or four minutes, the pheasants kept on falling. Then suddenly they stopped.

'Keep searching!' Claud shouted. 'There's plenty more on the ground!'

'Don't you think we ought to get out while the going's good?'

'No,' he said.

We went on searching. Between us we looked under every tree within a hundred yards of the clearing, north, south, east, and west, and I think we found most of them in the end. At the collecting-point there was a pile of pheasants as big as a bonfire.

'It's a miracle,' Claud was saying. 'It's a bloody miracle.' He was staring at them in a kind of trance.

'We'd better just take half a dozen each and get out quick,' I said.

'I would like to count them, Gordon.'

'There's no time for that.'

'I must count them.'

'No,' I said. 'Come on.'

'One . . .

'Two . . .

'Three . . .

'Four . . .'

He began counting them very carefully, picking up each bird in turn and laying it carefully to one side. The moon was directly overhead now and the whole clearing was brilliantly illuminated.

'I'm not standing around here like this,' I said. I walked back a few paces and hid myself in the shadows, waiting for him to finish.

'A hundred and seventeen . . . a hundred and eighteen . . . a hundred and nineteen . . . *a hundred and twenty*!' he cried. '*One hundred and twenty birds!* It's an all-time record!'

I didn't doubt it for a moment.

'The most my dad ever got in one night was fifteen and he was drunk for a week afterwards!'

'You're the champion of the world,' I said. 'Are you ready now?'

'One minute,' he answered and he pulled up his sweater and proceeded to unwind the two big white cotton sacks from around his belly. 'Here's yours,' he said, handing one of them to me. 'Fill it up quick.'

The light of the moon was so strong I could read the small print along the base of the sack. J. W. CRUMP, it said. KESTON FLOUR MILLS, LONDON SW17.

'You don't think that bastard with the brown teeth is watching us this very moment from behind a tree?'

'There's no chance of that,' Claud said. 'He's down at the filling-station like I told you, waiting for us to come home.'

We started loading the pheasants into the sacks. They were soft and floppy-necked and the skin underneath the feathers was still warm.

'There'll be a taxi waiting for us in the lane,' Claud said.

'What?'

'I always go back in a taxi, Gordon, didn't you know that?'

I told him I didn't.

'A taxi is anonymous,' Claud said. 'Nobody knows who's inside a taxi except the driver. My dad taught me that.'

'Which driver?'

'Charlie Kinch. He's only too glad to oblige.'

We finished loading the pheasants, and I tried to hump my bulging sack on to my shoulder. My sack had about sixty birds inside it, and it must have weighed a hundredweight and a half, at least. 'I can't carry this,' I said. 'We'll have to leave some of them behind.'

'Drag it,' Claud said. 'Just pull it behind you.'

We started off through the pitch-black woods, pulling the pheasants behind us. 'We'll never make it all the way back to the village like this,' I said.

'Charlie's never let me down yet,' Claud said.

We came to the margin of the wood and peered through the hedge into the lane. Claud said, 'Charlie boy' very softly and the old man behind the wheel of the taxi not five yards away poked his head out into the moonlight and gave us a sly toothless grin. We slid through the hedge, dragging the sacks after us along the ground.

'Hullo!' Charlie said. 'What's this?'

'It's cabbages,' Claud told him. 'Open the door.'

Two minutes later we were safely inside the taxi, cruising slowly down the hill towards the village.

It was all over now bar the shouting. Claud was triumphant, bursting with pride and excitement, and he kept leaning forward and tapping Charlie Kinch on the shoulder and saying, 'How about it, Charlie? How about this for a haul?' and Charlie kept glancing back popeyed at the huge bulging sacks lying on the floor between us and saying, 'Jesus Christ, man, how did you do it?'

'There's six brace of them for you, Charlie,' Claud said. And Charlie said, 'I reckon pheasants is going to be a bit scarce up at Mr Victor Hazel's opening-day shoot this year,' and Claud said, 'I imagine they are, Charlie, I imagine they are.'

'What in God's name are you going to do with a hundred and twenty pheasants?' I asked.

'Put them in cold storage for the winter,' Claud said. 'Put them in with the dogmeat in the deep-freeze at the filling-station.'

'Not tonight, I trust?'

'No, Gordon, not tonight. We leave them at Bessie's house tonight.'

'Bessie who?'

'Bessie Organ.'

'Bessie *Organ*!'

'Bessie always delivers my game, didn't you know that?'

'I don't know anything,' I said. I was completely stunned. Mrs Organ was the wife of the Reverend Jack Organ, the local vicar.

'Always choose a respectable woman to deliver your game,' Claud announced. 'That's correct, Charlie, isn't it?'

'Bessie's a right smart girl,' Charlie said.

We were driving through the village now and the street-lamps were still on and the men were wandering home from the pubs. I saw Will Prattley letting himself in quietly by the side-door of his fishmonger's shop and Mrs Prattley's head was sticking out of the window just above him, but he didn't know it.

'The vicar is very partial to roasted pheasant,' Claud said.

'He hangs it eighteen days,' Charlie said, 'then he gives it a couple of good shakes and all the feathers drop off.'

The taxi turned left and swung in through the gates of the vicarage. There were no lights on in the house and nobody met us. Claud and I dumped the pheasants in the coal shed at the rear, and then we said good-bye to Charlie Kinch and walked back in the moonlight to the filling-station, empty-handed. Whether or not Mr Rabbetts was watching us as we went in, I do not know. We saw no sign of him.

'Here she comes,' Claud said to me the next morning.

'Who?'

'Bessie – Bessie Organ.' He spoke the name proudly and with a slight proprietary air, as though he were a general referring to his bravest officer.

I followed him outside.

'Down there,' he said, pointing.

Far away down the road I could see a small female figure advancing towards us.

'What's she pushing?' I asked.

Claud gave me a sly look.

'There's only one safe way of delivering game,' he announced, 'and that's under a baby.'

'Yes,' I murmured, 'yes, of course.'

'That'll be young Christopher Organ in there, aged one and a half. He's a lovely child, Gordon.'

I could just make out the small dot of a baby sitting high up in the pram, which had its hood folded down.

'There's sixty or seventy pheasants at least under that little nipper,' Claud said happily. 'You just imagine that.'

'You can't put sixty or seventy pheasants in a pram.'

'You can if it's got a deep well underneath it, and if you take out the mattress and pack them in tight, right up to the top. All you need then is a sheet. You'll be surprised how little room a pheasant takes up when it's limp.'

We stood beside the pumps waiting for Bessie Organ to arrive. It was one of those warm windless September mornings with a darkening sky and a smell of thunder in the air.

'Right through the village bold as brass,' Claud said. 'Good old Bessie.'

'She seems in rather a hurry to me.'

Claud lit a new cigarette from the stub of the old one. 'Bessie is never in a hurry,' he said.

'She certainly isn't walking normal,' I told him. 'You look.'

He squinted at her through the smoke of his cigarette. Then he took the cigarette out of his mouth and looked again.

'Well?' I said.

'She does seem to be going a tiny bit quick, doesn't she?' he said carefully.

'She's going damn quick.'

There was a pause. Claud was beginning to stare very hard at the approaching woman.

'Perhaps she doesn't want to be caught in the rain, Gordon. I'll bet that's exactly what it is, she thinks it's going to rain and she don't want the baby to get wet.'

'Why doesn't she put the hood up?'

He didn't answer this.

'She's *running*!' I cried. 'Look!' Bessie had suddenly broken into a full sprint.

Claud stood very still, watching the woman; and in the silence that followed I fancied I could hear a baby screaming.

'What's up?'

He didn't answer.

'There's something wrong with that baby,' I said. 'Listen.'

At this point, Bessie was about two hundred yards away from us but closing fast.

'Can you hear him now?' I said.

'Yes.'

'He's yelling his head off.'

The small shrill voice in the distance was growing louder every second, frantic, piercing, nonstop, almost hysterical.

'He's having a fit,' Claud announced.

'I think he must be.'

'That's why she's running, Gordon. She wants to get him in here quick and put him under a cold tap.'

'I'm sure you're right,' I said. 'In fact I know you're right. Just listen to that noise.'

'If it isn't a fit, you can bet your life it's something like it.'

'I quite agree.'

Claud shifted his feet uneasily on the gravel of the driveway. 'There's a thousand and one different things keep happening every day to little babies like that,' he said.

'Of course.'

'I knew a baby once who caught his fingers in the spokes of the pram wheel. He lost the lot. It cut them clean off.'

'Yes.'

'Whatever it is,' Claud said, 'I wish to Christ she'd stop running.'

A long truck loaded with bricks came up behind Bessie and the driver slowed down and poked his head out of the window to stare. Bessie ignored him and flew on, and she was so close now I could see her big red face with the mouth wide open, panting for breath. I noticed she was wearing white gloves on her hands, very prim and dainty, and there was a funny little white hat to match perched right on the top of her head, like a mushroom.

Suddenly, out of the pram, straight up into the air, flew an enormous pheasant!

Claud let out a cry of horror.

The fool in the truck going along beside Bessie started roaring with laughter.

The pheasant flapped around drunkenly for a few seconds, then it lost height and landed in the grass by the side of the road.

A grocer's van came up behind the truck and began hooting to get by. Bessie kept running.

Then – *whoosh!* – a second pheasant flew up out of the pram.

Then a third, and a fourth. Then a fifth.

'My God!' I said. 'It's the pills! They're wearing off!'

Claud didn't say anything.

Bessie covered the last fifty yards at a tremendous pace, and she came swinging into the driveway of the filling-station with birds flying up out of the pram in all directions.

'What the hell's going on?' she cried.

'Go round the back!' I shouted. 'Go round the back!' But she pulled up sharp against the first pump in the line, and before we could reach her she had seized the screaming infant in her arms and dragged him clear.

'No! No!' Claud cried, racing towards her. 'Don't lift the baby! Put him back! Hold down the sheet!' But she wasn't even listening, and with the weight of the child suddenly lifted away, a great cloud of pheasants rose up out of the pram, fifty or sixty of them, at least, and the whole sky above us was filled with huge brown birds flapping their wings furiously to gain height.

Claud and I started running up and down the driveway waving our arms to frighten them off the premises. 'Go away!' we shouted. 'Shoo! Go away!' But they were too dopey still to take any notice of us and within half a minute down they came again and settled themselves like a swarm of locusts all over the front of my filling-station. The place was covered with them. They sat wing to wing along the edges of the roof and on the concrete canopy that came out over the pumps, and a dozen at least were clinging to the sill of the office window. Some had flown down on to the rack that held the bottles of lubricating-oil, and others were sliding about on the bonnets of my second-hand cars. One cock-bird with a fine tail was perched superbly on top of a petrol pump, and quite a number, those that were too drunk to stay aloft, simply squatted in the driveway at our feet, fluffing their feathers and blinking their small eyes.

Across the road, a line of cars had already started forming behind the brick-lorry and the grocery-van, and people were opening their doors and getting out and beginning to cross over to have a closer look. I glanced at my watch. It was twenty to nine. Any moment now, I thought, a large black car is going to come streaking along the road from the direction of the village, and the car will be a Rolls, and the face behind the wheel will be the great glistening brewer's face of Mr Victor Hazel.

'They near pecked him to pieces!' Bessie was shouting, clasping the screaming baby to her bosom.

'You go on home, Bessie,' Claud said, white in the face.

'Lock up,' I said. 'Put out the sign. We've gone for the day.'

OVER TO YOU

DEATH OF AN OLD OLD MAN

Oh God, how I am frightened.

Now that I am alone I don't have to hide it; I don't have to hide anything any longer. I can let my face go because no one can see me; because there's twenty-one thousand feet between me and them and because now that it's happening again I couldn't pretend any more even if I wanted to. Now I don't have to press my teeth together and tighten the muscles of my jaw as I did during lunch when the corporal brought in the message; when he handed it to Tinker and Tinker looked up at me and said, 'Charlie, it's your turn. You're next up.' As if I didn't know that. As if I didn't know that I was next up. As if I didn't know it last night when I went to bed, and at midnight when I was still awake and all the way through the night, at one in the morning and at two and three and four and five and six and at seven o'clock when I got up. As if I didn't know it while I was dressing and while I was having breakfast and while I was reading the magazines in the mess, playing shove-halfpenny in the mess, reading the notices in the mess, playing billiards in the mess. I knew it then and I knew it when we went in to lunch, while we were eating that mutton for lunch. And when the corporal came into the room with the message – it wasn't anything at all. It wasn't anything more than when it begins to rain because there is a black cloud in the sky. When he handed the paper to Tinker I knew what Tinker was going to say before he had opened his mouth. I knew exactly what he was going to say.

So that wasn't anything either.

But when he folded the message up and put it in his pocket and said, 'Finish your pudding. You've got plenty of time,' that was when it got worse, because I knew for certain then that it was going to happen again, that within half an hour I would be strapping myself in and testing the engine and signalling to the airmen to pull away the chocks. The others were all sitting around eating their pudding; mine was still on my plate in front of me, and I couldn't take another mouthful. But it was fine when I tightened my jaw muscles and said, 'Thank God for that. I'm tired of sitting around here picking my nose.' It was certainly fine when I said that. It must have sounded like any of the others just before they started off. And when I got up to leave the table and said, 'See you at tea time,' that must have sounded all right too.

But now I don't have to do any of that. Thank Christ I don't have to do that now. I can just loosen up and let myself go. I can do or say anything I want so long as I fly this aeroplane properly. It didn't use to be like this. Four years ago it was wonderful. I loved doing it because it was exciting, because the waiting on the aerodrome was nothing more than the waiting before a football game or before going in to bat; and three years ago it was all right too. But then always the three months of resting and the going back again and the resting and the going back; always going back and always getting away with it, everyone saying what a fine pilot, no one knowing what a near thing it was that time near Brussels and how lucky it was that time over Dieppe and how bad it was that other time over Dieppe and how lucky and bad and scared I've been every minute of every trip every week this year. No one knows that. They all say, 'Charlie's a great pilot,' 'Charlie's a born flyer,' 'Charlie's terrific.'

I think he was once, but not any longer.

Each time now it gets worse. At first it begins to grow upon you slowly, coming upon you slowly, creeping up on you from behind, making no noise, so that you do not turn round and see it coming. If you saw it coming, perhaps you could stop it, but there is no warning. It creeps closer and closer, like a cat creeps closer stalking a sparrow, and then when it is right behind you, it doesn't spring like the cat would spring; it just leans forward and whispers in your ear. It touches you gently on the shoulder and whispers to you that you are young, that you have a million things to do and a million things to say, that if you are not careful you will buy it, that you are almost certain to buy it sooner or later, and that when you do you will not be anything any longer; you will just be a charred corpse. It whispers to you about how your corpse will look when it is charred, how black it will be and how it will be twisted and brittle, with the face and the fingers black and the shoes off the feet because the shoes always come off the feet when you die like that. At first it whispers to you only at night, when you are lying awake in bed at night. Then it whispers to you at odd moments during the day, when you are doing your teeth or drinking a beer or when you are walking down the passage; and in the end it becomes so that you hear it all day and all night all the time.

There's Ijmuiden. Just the same as ever, with the little knob sticking out just beside it. There are the Frisians, Texel, Vlieland, Terschelling, Ameland, Juist and Norderney. I know them all. They look like bacteria under a microscope. There's the Zuider Zee, there's Holland, there's the North Sea, there's Belgium, and there's the world; there's the whole bloody world right there, with all the people who aren't going to get killed and all the houses and the towns and the sea with all the fish. The fish aren't going to get killed either. I'm the only one that's going to get killed. I don't want to die. Oh God, I don't want to die. I don't want to die today anyway. And it isn't the pain. Really it isn't the pain. I don't mind having my leg mashed or my arm burnt off; I swear to you that I don't mind that. But I don't want to die. Four years ago I didn't mind. I remember distinctly not minding about it four years ago. I didn't mind about it three years ago either. It was all fine and exciting; it always is when it looks as though you may be going to lose, as it did then. It is always fine to fight when you are going to lose everything anyway, and that was how it was four years ago. But now we're going to win. It is so different when you are going to win. If I die now I lose fifty years of life, and I don't want to lose that. I'll lose anything except that because that would be all the things I want to do and all the things I want to see; all the things like going on sleeping with Joey. Like going home sometimes. Like walking through a wood. Like pouring out a drink from a bottle. Like looking forward to week ends and like being alive every hour every day every year for fifty years. If I die now I will miss all that, and I will miss everything else. I will miss the things that I don't know about. I think those are really the things I am frightened of missing. I think the reason I do not want to die is because of the things I hope will happen. Yes, that's right. I'm sure that's right. Point a revolver at a tramp, at a wet shivering tramp on the side of the road and say, 'I'm going to shoot you,' and he will cry, 'Don't shoot. Please don't shoot.' The tramp clings to life because of the things he hopes will happen. I am clinging to it for the same reason; but I have clung for so long now that I cannot hold on much longer. Soon I will have to let go. It is like hanging over the edge of a cliff, that's what it is like; and I've been hanging on too long now, holding on to the top of the cliff with my fingers, not being able to pull myself back up, with my fingers getting more and more tired, beginning to hurt and to ache, so that I know that sooner or later I will have to let go. I dare not cry out for help; that is one thing that I dare not do; so I go on hanging over the side of this cliff, and as I hang I keep kicking a little with my feet against the side of the cliff, trying desperately to find a foothold, but it is steep and smooth like the side of a ship, and there isn't any foothold. I am kicking now, that's what I am doing. I am kicking against the smooth side of the cliff, and there isn't any foothold. Soon I shall have to let go. The longer I hang on the more certain I am of that, and so each hour, each day, each night, each week, I become more and more frightened. Four years ago I wasn't hanging over the edge like this. I was running about in the field above, and although I knew that there was a cliff somewhere and that I might fall over it, I did not mind. Three years ago it was the same, but now it is different.

I know that I am not a coward. I am certain of that. I will always keep going. Here I am today, at two o'clock in the afternoon, sitting here flying a course of one hundred and thirty-five at three hundred and sixty miles an hour and flying well; and although I am so frightened that I can hardly think, yet I am going on to do this thing. There was never any question of not going or of turning back. I would rather die than turn back. Turning back never enters into it. It would be easier if it did. I would prefer to have to fight that than to have to fight this fear.

There's Wassalt. Little camouflaged group of buildings and great big camouflaged aerodrome, probably full of one-o-nines and one-nineties. Holland looks wonderful. It must be a lovely place in the summer. I expect they are haymaking down there now. I expect the German soldiers are watching the Dutch girls haymaking. Bastards. Watching them haymaking, then making them come home with them afterwards. I would like to be haymaking now. I would like to be haymaking and drinking cider.

The pilot was sitting upright in the cockpit. His face was nearly hidden by his goggles and by his oxygen mask. His right hand was resting lightly upon the stick, and his left hand was forward on the throttle. All the time he was looking around him into the sky. From force of habit his head never ceased to move from one side to the other, slowly, mechanically, like clockwork, so that each moment almost, he searched every part of the blue sky, above, below and all around. But it was into the light of the sun itself that he looked twice as long as he looked anywhere else; for that is the place where the enemy hides and waits before he jumps upon you. There are only two places in which you can hide yourself when you are up in the sky. One is in cloud and the other is in the light of the sun.

He flew on; and although his mind was working upon many things and although his brain was the brain of a frightened man, yet his instinct was the instinct of a pilot who is in the sky of the enemy. With a quick glance, without stopping the movement of his head, he looked down and checked his instruments. The glance took no more than a second, and like a camera can record a dozen things at once with the opening of a shutter, so he at a glance recorded with his eyes his oil pressure, his petrol, his oxygen, his rev counter, boost and his airspeed, and in the same instant almost he was looking up again into the sky. He looked at the sun, and as he looked, as he screwed up his eyes and searched into the dazzling brightness of the sun, he thought that he saw something. Yes, there it was; a small black speck moving slowly across the bright surface of the sun, and to him the speck was not a speck but a life-size German pilot sitting in a Focke Wulf which had cannon in its wings.

He knew that he had been seen. He was certain that the one above was watching him, taking his time, sure of being hidden in the brightness of the sun, watching the Spitfire and waiting to pounce. The man in the Spitfire did not take his eye away from the small speck of black. His head was quite still now. He was watching the enemy, and as he watched, his left hand came away from the throttle and began to move delicately around the cockpit. It moved quickly and surely, touching this thing and that, switching on his reflector sight, turning his trigger button from 'safe' over to 'fire' and pressing gently with his thumb upon a lever which increased, ever so slightly, the pitch of the airscrew.

There was no thought in his head now save for the thought of battle. He was no longer frightened or thinking of being frightened. All that was a dream, and as a sleeper who opens his eyes in the morning and forgets his dream, so this man had seen the enemy and had forgotten that he was frightened. It was always the same. It had happened a hundred times before, and now it was happening again. Suddenly, in an instant he had become cool and precise, and as he prepared himself, as he made ready his cockpit, he watched the German, waiting to see what he would do.

This man was a great pilot. He was great because when the time came, whenever the moment arrived, his coolness was great and his courage was great, and more than anything else his instinct was great, greater by far than his coolness or his courage or his experience. Now he eased open the throttle and pulled the stick gently backwards, trying to gain height, trying to gain a little of the five-thousand-feet advantage which the German had over him. But there was not much time. The Focke Wulf came out of the sun with its nose down and it came fast. The pilot saw it coming and he kept going straight on, pretending that he had not seen it, and all the time he was looking over his shoulder, watching the German, waiting for the moment to turn. If he turned too soon, the German would turn with him, and he would be duck soup. If he turned too late, the German would get him anyway provided that he could shoot straight, and he would be duck soup then too. So he watched and waited, turning his head and looking over his shoulder, judging his distance; and as the German came within range, as he was about to press his thumb upon the trigger button, the pilot swerved. He yanked the stick hard back and over to the left, he kicked hard with his left foot upon the rudder-bar, and like a leaf which is caught up and carried away by a gust of wind, the Spitfire flipped over on to its side and changed direction. The pilot blacked out.

As his sight came back, as the blood drained away from his head and from his eyes, he looked up and saw the German fighter 'way ahead, turning with him, banking hard, trying to turn tighter and tighter in order to get back on the tail of the Spitfire. The fight was on. 'Here we go,' he said to himself. 'Here we go again,' and he smiled once, quickly, because he was confident and because he had done this so many times before and because each time he had won.

The man was a beautiful pilot. But the German was good too, and when the Spitfire applied a little flap in order to turn in tighter circles, the Focke Wulf appeared to do the same, and they turned together. When the Spitfire throttled back suddenly and got on his tail, the Focke Wulf half-rolled and dived out and under and was away, pulling up again in a loop and rolling off the top, so that he came in again from behind. The Spitfire half-rolled and dived away, but the Focke Wulf anticipated him, and half-rolled and dived with him, behind him on his tail, and here he took a quick shot at the Spitfire, but he missed. For at least fifteen minutes the two small aircraft rolled and dived around each other in the sky. Sometimes they would separate, wheeling around and around in tight turns, watching one another, circling and watching like two boxers circling each other in the ring, waiting for an opening or for the dropping of a guard; then there would be a stall-turn and one would attack the other, and the diving and the rolling and the zooming would start all over again.

All the time the pilot of the Spitfire sat upright in his cockpit, and he flew his aircraft not with his hands but with the tips of his fingers, and the Spitfire was not a Spitfire but a part of his own body; the muscles of his arms and legs were in the wings and in the tail of the machine so that when he banked and turned and dived and climbed he was not moving his hands and his legs, but only the wings and the tail and the body of the aeroplane; for the body of the Spitfire was the body of the pilot, and there was no difference between the one and the other.

So it went on, and all the while, as they fought and as they flew, they lost height, coming down nearer and nearer to the fields of Holland, so that soon they were fighting only three thousand feet above the ground, and one could see the hedges and the small trees and shadows which the small trees made upon the grass.

Once the German tried a long shot, from a thousand yards, and the pilot of the Spitfire saw the tracer streaming past in front of the nose of his machine. Once, when they flew close past each other, he saw, for a moment, the head and shoulders of the German under the glass roof of his cockpit, the head turned towards him, with the brown helmet, the goggles, the nose and the white scarf. Once when he blacked out from a quick pull-out, the black-out lasted longer than usual. It lasted maybe five seconds, and when his sight came back, he looked quickly around for the Focke Wulf and saw it half a mile away, flying straight at him on the beam, a thin inch-long black line which grew quickly, so that almost at once it was no longer an inch, but an inch and a half, then two inches, then six and then a foot. There was hardly any time. There was a second or perhaps two at the most, but it was enough because he did not have to think or to wonder what to do; he had only to allow his instinct to control his arms and his legs and the wings and the body of the aeroplane. There was only one thing to do, and the Spitfire did it. It banked steeply and turned at right-angles towards the Focke Wulf, facing it and flying straight towards it for a head-on attack.

The two machines flew fast towards each other. The pilot of the Spitfire sat upright in his cockpit, and now, more than ever, the aircraft was a part of his body. His eye was upon the reflector sight, the small yellow electric-light dot which was projected up in front of the windshield, and it was upon the thinness of the Focke Wulf beyond. Quickly, precisely, he moved his aircraft a little this way and that, and the yellow dot, which moved with the aircraft, danced and jerked this way and that, and then suddenly it was upon the thin line of the Focke Wulf and there it stayed. His right thumb in the leather glove felt for the firing-button; he squeezed it gently, as a rifleman squeezes a trigger, his guns fired, and at the same time, he saw the small spurts of flame from the cannon in the nose of the Focke Wulf. The whole thing, from beginning to end, took perhaps as long as it would take you to light a cigarette. The German pilot came straight on at him and he had a sudden, vivid, colourless view of the round nose and the thin outstretched wings of the Focke Wulf. Then there was a crack as their wing-tips met, and there was a splintering as the port wing of the Spitfire came away from the body of the machine.

The Spitfire was dead. It fell like a dead bird falls, fluttering a little as it died; continuing in the direction of its flight as it fell. The hands of the pilot, almost in a single movement, undid his straps, tore off his helmet and slid back the hood of the cockpit; then they grasped the edges of the cockpit and he was out and away, falling, reaching for the ripcord, grasping it with his right hand, pulling on it so that his parachute billowed out and opened and the straps jerked him hard between the fork of his legs.

All of a sudden the silence was great. The wind was blowing on his face and in his hair and he reached up a hand and brushed the hair away from his eyes. He was about a thousand feet up, and he looked down and saw flat green country with fields and hedges and no trees. He could see some cows in the field below him. Then he looked up, and as he looked, he said 'Good God,' and his right hand moved quickly to his right hip, feeling for his revolver which he had not brought with him. For there, not more than five hundred yards away, parachuting down at the same time and at the same height, was another man, and he knew when he saw him that it could be only the German pilot. Obviously his plane had been damaged at the same time as the Spitfire in the collision. He must have got out quickly too; and now here they were, both of them parachuting down so close to each other that they might even land in the same field.

He looked again at the German, hanging there in his straps with his legs apart, his hands above his head grasping the cords of the parachute. He seemed to be a small man, thickly built and by no means young. The German was looking at him too. He kept looking, and when his body swung around the other way, he turned his head, looking over his shoulder.

So they went on down. Both men were watching each other, thinking about what would happen soon, and the German was the king because he was landing in his own territory. The pilot of the Spitfire was coming down in enemy country; he would be taken prisoner, or he would be killed, or he would kill the German, and if he did that, he would escape. I will escape anyway, he thought. I'm sure I can run faster than the German. He does not look as though he could run very fast. I will race him across the fields and get away.

The ground was close now. There were not many seconds to go. He saw that the German would almost certainly land in the same field as he, the field with the cows. He looked down to see what the field was like and whether the hedges were thick and whether there was a gate in the hedge, and as he looked, he saw below him in the field a small pond, and there was a small stream running through the pond. It was a cow-drinking pond, muddy round the edges and muddy in the water. The pond was right below him. He was no more than the height of a horse above it and he was dropping fast; he was dropping right into the middle of the pond. Quickly he grasped the cords above his head and tried to spill the parachute to one side so that he would change direction, but he was too late; it wasn't any good. All at once something brushed the surface of his brain and the top of his stomach, and the fear which he had forgotten in the fighting was upon him again. He saw the pond and the black surface of the water of the pond, and the pond was not a pond, and the water was not water; it was a small black hole in the surface of the earth which went on down and down for miles and miles, with steep smooth sides like the sides of a ship, and it was so deep that when you fell into it, you went on falling and falling and you fell for ever. He saw the mouth of the hole and the deepness of it, and he was only a small brown pebble which someone had picked up and thrown into the air so that it would fall into the hole. He was a pebble which someone had picked up in the grass of the field. That was all he was and now he was falling and the hole was below him.

Splash. He hit the water. He went through the water and his feet hit the bottom of the pond. They sank into the mud on the bottom and his head went under the water, but it came up again and he was standing with the water up to his shoulders. The parachute was on top of him; his head was tangled in a mass of cords and white silk and he pulled at them with his hands, first this way and then that, but it only got worse, and the fear got worse because the white silk was covering his head so that he could see nothing but a mass of white cloth and a tangle of cords. Then he tried to move towards the bank, but his feet were stuck in the mud; he had sunk up to his knees in the mud. So he fought the parachute and the tangled cords of the parachute, pulling at them with his hands and trying to get them clear of his head; and as he did so he heard the sound of footsteps running on the grass. He heard the noise of the footsteps coming closer and the German must have jumped, because there was a splash and he was knocked over by the weight of a man's body.

He was under the water, and instinctively he began to struggle. But his feet were still stuck in the mud, the man was on top of him and there were hands around his neck holding him under and squeezing his neck with strong fingers. He opened his eyes and saw brown water. He noticed the bubbles in the water, small bright bubbles rising slowly upward in the brown water. There was no noise or shouting or anything else, but only the bright bubbles moving upward in the water, and suddenly, as he watched them, his mind became clear and calm like a sunny day. I won't struggle, he thought. There is no point in struggling, for when there is a black cloud in the sky, it is bound to rain.

He relaxed his body and all the muscles in his body because he had no further wish to struggle. How nice it is not to struggle, he thought. There is no point in struggling. I was a fool to have struggled so much and for so long; I was a fool to have prayed for the sun when there was a black cloud in the sky. I should have prayed for rain; I should have shouted for rain. I should have shouted, Let it rain, let it rain in solid sheets and I will not care. Then it would have been easy. It would have been so easy then. I have struggled for five years and now I don't have to do it any more. This is so much better; this is ever so much better, because there is a wood somewhere that I wish to walk through, and you cannot walk struggling through a wood. There is a girl somewhere that I wish to sleep with, and you cannot sleep struggling with a girl. You cannot do anything struggling; especially you cannot live struggling, and so now I am going to do all the things that I want to do, and there will be no more struggling.

See how calm and lovely it is like this. See how sunny it is and what a beautiful field this is, with the cows and the little pond and the green hedges with primroses growing in the hedges. Nothing will worry me any more now, nothing nothing nothing; not even that man splashing in the water of the pond over there. He seems very puffed and out of breath. He seems to be dragging something out of the pond, something heavy. Now he's got it to the side and he's pulling it up on to the grass. How funny; it's a body. It's a body of a man. As a matter of fact, I think it's me. Yes, it is me. I know it is because of that smudge of yellow paint on the front of my flying suit. Now he's kneeling down, searching in my pockets, taking out my money and my identification card. He's found my pipe and the letter I got this morning from my mother. He's taking off my watch. Now he's getting up. He's going away. He's going to leave my body behind, lying on the grass beside the pond. He's walking quickly away across the field towards the gate. How wet and excited he looks. He ought to relax a bit. He ought to relax like me. He can't be enjoying himself that way. I think I will tell him.

'Why don't you relax a bit?'

Goodness, how he jumped when I spoke to him. And his face; just look at his face. I've never seen a man look as frightened as that. He's starting to run. He keeps looking back over his shoulder, but he keeps on running. But just look at his face; just look how unhappy and frightened he is. I do not want to go with him. I think I'll leave him. I think I'll stay here for a bit. I think I'll go along the hedges and find some primroses, and if I am lucky I may find some white violets. Then I will go to sleep. I will go to sleep in the sun.

AN AFRICAN STORY

For England, the war began in September, 1939. The people on the island knew about it at once and began to prepare themselves. In farther places the people heard about it a few minutes afterwards, and they too began to prepare themselves.

And in East Africa, in Kenya Colony, there was a young man who was a white hunter, who loved the plains and the valleys and the cool nights on the slopes of Kilimanjaro. He too heard about the war and began to prepare himself. He made his way over the country to Nairobi, and he reported to the RAF and asked that they make him a pilot. They took him in and he began his training at Nairobi airport, flying in little Tiger Moths and doing well with his flying.

After five weeks he nearly got court-martialled because he took his plane up and instead of practising spins and stall-turns as he had been ordered to do, he flew off in the direction of Nakuru to look at the wild animals on the plain. On the way, he thought he saw a Sable antelope, and because these are rare animals, he became excited and flew down low to get a better view. He was looking down at the antelope out of the left side of the cockpit, and because of this he did not see the giraffe on the other side. The leading edge of the starboard wing struck the neck of the giraffe just below the head and cut clean through it. He was flying as low as that. There was damage to the wing, but he managed to get back to Nairobi, and as I said, he was nearly court-martialled, because you cannot explain away a thing like that by saying you hit a large bird, not when there are pieces of giraffe skin and giraffe hair sticking to the wing and the stays.

After six weeks he was allowed to make his first solo cross-country flight, and he flew off from Nairobi to a place called Eldoret, which is a little town eight thousand feet up in the Highlands. But again he was unlucky. This time he had engine failure on the way, due to water in the fuel tanks. He kept his head and made a beautiful forced landing without damaging the aircraft, not far from a little shack which stood alone on the highland plain with no other habitation in sight. That is lonely country up there.

He walked over to the shack, and there he found an old man, living alone, with nothing but a small patch of sweet potatoes, some brown chickens and a black cow.

The old man was kind to him. He gave him food and milk and a place to sleep, and the pilot stayed with him for two days and two nights, until a rescue plane from Nairobi spotted his aircraft on the ground, landed beside it, found out what was wrong, went away and came back with clean petrol which enabled him to take off and return.

But during his stay, the old man, who was lonely and had seen no one for many months, was glad of his company and of the opportunity to talk. He talked much and the pilot listened. He talked of the lonely life, of the lions that came in the night, of the rogue elephant that lived over the hill in the west, of the hotness of the days and of the silence that came with the cold at midnight.

On the second night he talked about himself. He told a long, strange story, and as he told it, it seemed to the pilot that the old man was lifting a great weight off his shoulders in the telling. When he had finished, he said that he had never told that to anyone before, and that he would never tell it to anyone again, but the story was so strange that the pilot wrote it down on paper as soon as he got back to Nairobi. He wrote it not in the old man's words, but in his own words, painting it as a picture with the old man as a character in the picture, because that was the best way to do it. He had never written a story before, and so naturally there were mistakes. He did not know any of the tricks with words which writers use, which they have to use just as painters have to use tricks with paint, but when he had finished writing, when he put down his pencil and went over to the airmen's canteen for a pint of beer, he left behind him a rare and powerful tale.

We found it in his suitcase two weeks later when we were going through his belongings after he had been killed in training, and because he seemed to have no relatives, and because he was my friend, I took the manuscript and looked after it for him.

This is what he wrote.

The old man came out of the door into the bright sunshine, and for a moment he stood leaning on his stick, looking around him, blinking at the strong light. He stood with his head on one side, looking up, listening for the noise which he thought he had heard.

He was small and thick and well over seventy years old, although he looked nearer eighty-five, because rheumatism had tied his body into knots. His face was covered with grey hair, and when he moved his mouth, he moved it only on one side of his face. On his head, whether indoors or out, he wore a dirty white topee.

He stood quite still in the bright sunshine, screwing up his eyes, listening for the noise.

Yes, there it was again. The head of the old man flicked around and he looked towards the small wooden hut standing a hundred yards away on the pasture. This time there was no doubt about it: the yelp of a dog, the high-pitched, sharp-piercing yelp of pain which a dog gives when he is in great danger. Twice more it came and this time the noise was more like a scream than a yelp. The note was higher and more sharp, as though it were wrenched quickly from some small place inside the body.

The old man turned and limped fast across the grass towards the wooden shed where Judson lived, pushed open the door and went in.

The small white dog was lying on the floor and Judson was standing over it, his legs apart, his black hair falling all over his long, red face; standing there tall and skinny, muttering to himself and sweating through his greasy white shirt. His mouth hung open in an odd way, lifeless way, as though his jaw was too heavy for him, and he was dribbling gently down the middle of his chin. He stood there looking at the small white dog which was lying on the floor, and with one hand he was slowly twisting his left ear; in the other he held a heavy bamboo.

The old man ignored Judson and went down on his knees beside his dog, gently running his thin hands over its body. The dog lay still, looking up at him with watery eyes. Judson did not move. He was watching the dog and the man.

Slowly the old man got up, rising with difficulty, holding the top of his stick with both hands and pulling himself to his feet. He looked around the room. There was a dirty rumpled mattress lying on the floor in the far corner; there was a wooden table made of packing cases and on it a Primus stove and a chipped blue-enamelled saucepan. There were chicken feathers and mud on the floor.

The old man saw what he wanted. It was a heavy iron bar standing against the wall near the mattress, and he hobbled over towards it, thumping the hollow wooden floorboards with his stick as he went. The eyes of the dog followed his movements as he limped across the room. The old man changed his stick to his left hand, took the iron bar in his right, hobbled back to the dog and without pausing, he lifted the bar and brought it down hard upon the animal's head. He threw the bar to the ground and looked up at Judson, who was standing there with his legs apart, dribbling down his chin and twitching around the corners of his eyes. He went right up to him and began to speak. He spoke very quietly and slowly, with a terrible anger, and as he spoke he moved only one side of his mouth.

'You killed him,' he said. 'You broke his back.'

Then, as the tide of anger rose and gave him strength, he found more words. He looked up and spat them into the face of the tall Judson, who twitched around the corners of his eyes and backed away towards the wall.

'You lousy, mean, dog-beating bastard. That was my dog. What the hell right have you got beating my dog, tell me that. Answer me, you slobbering madman. Answer me.'

Judson was slowly rubbing the palm of his left hand up and down on the front of his shirt, and now the whole of his face began to twitch. Without looking up, he said, 'He wouldn't stop licking that old place on his paw. I couldn't stand the noise it made. You know I can't stand noises like that, licking, licking, licking. I told him to stop. He looked up and wagged his tail; but then he went on licking. I couldn't stand it any longer, so I beat him.'

The old man did not say anything. For a moment it looked as though he were going to hit this creature. He half raised his arm, dropped it again, spat on the floor, turned around and hobbled out of the door into the sunshine. He went across the grass to where a black cow was standing in the shade of a small acacia tree, chewing its cud, and the cow watched him as he came limping across the grass from the shed. But it went on chewing, munching its cud, moving its jaws regularly, mechanically, like a metronome in slow time. The old man came limping up and stood beside it, stroking its neck. Then he leant against its shoulder and scratched its back with the butt end of his stick. He stood there for a long time, leaning against the cow, scratching it with his stick; and now and again he would speak to it, speaking quiet little words, whispering them almost, like a person telling a secret to another.

It was shady under the acacia tree, and the country around him looked lush and pleasant after the long rains, for the grass grows green up in the Highlands of Kenya; and at this time of the year, after the rains, it is as green and rich as any grass in the world. Away in the north stood Mount Kenya itself, with snow upon its head, with a thin white plume trailing from its summit where the city winds made a storm and blew the white powder from the top of the mountain. Down below, upon the slopes of that same mountain there were lion and elephant, and sometimes during the night one could hear the roar of the lions as they looked at the moon.

The days passed and Judson went about his work on the farm in a silent, mechanical kind of way, taking in the corn, digging the sweet potatoes and milking the black cow, while the old man stayed indoors away from the fierce African sun. Only in the late afternoon when the air began to get cool and sharp, did he hobble outside, and always he went over to his black cow and spent an hour with it under the acacia tree. One day when he came out he found Judson standing beside the cow, regarding it strangely, standing in a peculiar attitude with one foot in front of the other and gently twisting his ear with his right hand.

'What is it now?' said the old man as he came limping up.

'Cow won't stop chewing,' said Judson.

'Chewing her cud,' said the old man. 'Leave her alone.'

Judson said, 'It's the noise, can't you hear it? Crunchy noise like she was chewing pebbles, only she isn't; she's chewing grass and spit. Look at her, she goes on and on crunching, crunching, crunching, and it's just grass and spit. Noise goes right into my head.'

'Get out,' said the old man. 'Get out of my sight.'

At dawn the old man sat, as he always did, looking out of his window, watching Judson coming across from his hut to milk the cow. He saw him coming sleepily across the field, talking to himself as he walked, dragging his feet, making a dark green trail in the wet grass, carrying in his hand the old four-gallon kerosene tin which he used as a milk pail. The sun was coming up over the escarpment and making long shadows behind the man, the cow and the little acacia tree. The old man saw Judson put down the tin and he saw him fetch the box from beside the acacia tree and settle himself upon it, ready for the milking. He saw him suddenly kneeling down, feeling the udder of the cow with his hands and at the same time the old man noticed from where he sat that the animal had no milk. He saw Judson get up and come walking fast towards the shack. He came and stood under the window where the old man was sitting and looked up.

'Cow's got no milk,' he said.

The old man leaned through the open window, placing both his hands on the sill.

'You lousy bastard, you've stole it.'

'I didn't take it,' said Judson. 'I bin asleep.'

'You stole it.' The old man was leaning farther out of the window, speaking quietly with one side of his mouth. 'I'll beat the hell out of you for this,' he said.

Judson said, 'Someone stole it in the night, a native, one of the Kikuyu. Or maybe she's sick.'

It seemed to the old man that he was telling the truth. 'We'll see,' he said, 'if she milks this evening; and now for Christ's sake, get out of my sight.'

By evening the cow had a full udder and the old man watched Judson draw two quarts of good thick milk from under her.

The next morning she was empty. In the evening she was full. On the third morning she was empty once more.

On the third night the old man went on watch. As soon as it began to get dark, he stationed himself at the open window with an old twelve-bore shot gun lying on his lap, waiting for the thief who came and milked his cow in the night. At first it was pitch dark and he could not see the cow even, but soon a three-quarter moon came over the hills and it became light, almost as though it was day time. But it was bitter cold because the Highlands are seven thousand feet up, and the old man shivered at his post and pulled his brown blanket closer around his shoulders. He could see the cow well now, just as well as in daylight, and the little acacia tree threw a deep shadow across the grass, for the moon was behind it.

All through the night the old man sat there watching the cow, and save when he got up once and hobbled back into the room to fetch another blanket, his eyes never left her. The cow stood placidly under the small tree, chewing her cud and gazing at the moon.

An hour before dawn her udder was full. The old man could see it; he had been watching it the whole time, and although he had not seen the movement of its swelling any more than one can see the movement of the hour hand of a watch, yet all the time he had been conscious of the filling as the milk came down. It was an hour before dawn. The moon was low, but the light had not gone. He could see the cow and the little tree and the greenness of the grass around the cow. Suddenly he jerked his head. He heard something. Surely that was a noise he heard. Yes, there it was again, a rustling in the grass right underneath the window where he was sitting. Quickly he pulled himself up and looked over the sill on to the ground.

Then he saw it. A large black snake, a Mamba, eight feet long and as thick as a man's arm, was gliding through the wet grass, heading straight for the cow and going fast. Its small pear-shaped head was raised slightly off the ground and the movement of its body against the wetness made a clear hissing sound like gas escaping from a jet. He raised his gun to shoot. Almost at once he lowered it again, why he did not know, and he sat there not moving, watching the Mamba as it approached the cow, listening to the noise it made as it went, watching it come up close to the cow and waiting for it to strike.

But it did not strike. It lifted its head and for a moment let it sway gently back and forth; then it raised the front part of its black body into the air under the udder of the cow, gently took one of the thick teats into its mouth and began to drink.

The cow did not move. There was no noise anywhere, and the body of the Mamba curved gracefully up from the ground and hung under the udder of the cow. Black snake and black cow were clearly visible out there in the moonlight.

For half an hour the old man watched the Mamba taking the milk of the cow. He saw the gentle pulsing of its black body as it drew the liquid out of the udder and he saw it, after a time, change from one teat to another, until at last there was no longer any milk left. Then the Mamba gently lowered itself to the ground and slid back through the grass in the direction whence it came. Once more it made a clear hissing noise as it went, and once more it passed underneath the window where the old man sat, leaving a thin dark trail in the wet grass where it had gone. Then it disappeared behind the shack.

Slowly the moon went down behind the ridge of Mount Kenya. Almost at the same time the sun rose up out of the escarpment in the east and Judson came out of his hut with the four-gallon kerosene tin in his hand, walking sleepily towards the cow, dragging his feet in the heavy dew as he went. The old man watched him coming and waited. Judson bent down and felt the udder with his hand and as he did so, the old man shouted at him. Judson jumped at the sound of the old man's voice.

'It's gone again,' said the old man.

Judson said, 'Yes, cow's empty.'

'I think,' said the old man slowly, 'I think that it was a Kikuyu boy. I was dozing a bit and only woke up as he was making off. I couldn't shoot because the cow was in the way. He made off behind the cow. I'll wait for him tonight. I'll get him tonight,' he added.

Judson did not answer. He picked up his four-gallon tin and walked back to his hut.

That night the old man sat up again by the window watching the cow. For him there was this time a certain pleasure in the anticipation of what he was going to see. He knew that he would see the Mamba again, but he wanted to make quite certain. And so, when the great black snake slid across the grass towards the cow an hour before sunrise, the old man leaned over the window sill and followed the movements of the Mamba as it approached the cow. He saw it wait for a moment under the belly of the animal, letting its head sway slowly backwards and forwards half a dozen times before finally raising its body from the ground to take the teat of the cow into its mouth. He saw it drink the milk for half an hour, until there was none left, and he saw it lower its body and slide smoothly back behind the shack whence it came. And while he watched these things, the old man began laughing quietly with one side of his mouth.

Then the sun rose up from behind the hills, and Judson came out of his hut with the four-gallon tin in his hand, but this time he went straight to the window of the shack where the old man was sitting wrapped up in his blankets.

'What happened?' said Judson.

The old man looked down at him from his window. 'Nothing,' he said. 'Nothing happened. I dozed off again and the bastard came and took it while I was asleep. Listen, Judson,' he added, 'we got to catch this boy, otherwise you'll be going short of milk, not that that would do you any harm. But we got to catch him. I can't shoot because he's too clever; the cow's always in the way. You'll have to get him.'

'Me get him? How?'

The old man spoke very slowly. 'I think,' he said, 'I think you must hide beside the cow, right beside the cow. That is the only way you can catch him.'

Judson was rumpling his hair with his left hand.

'Today,' continued the old man, 'you will dig a shallow trench right beside the cow. If you lie in it and if I cover you over with hay and grass, the thief won't notice you until he's right alongside.'

'He may have a knife,' Judson said.

'No, he won't have a knife. You take your stick. That's all you'll need.'

Judson said, 'Yes, I'll take my stick. When he comes, I'll jump up and beat him with my stick.' Then suddenly he seemed to remember something. 'What about her chewing?' he said. 'Couldn't stand her chewing all night, crunching and crunching, crunching spit and grass like it was pebbles. Couldn't stand that all night,' and he began twisting again at his left ear with his hand.

'You'll do as you're bloody well told,' said the old man.

That day Judson dug his trench beside the cow which was to be tethered to the small acacia tree so that she could not wander about the field. Then, as evening came and as he was preparing to lie down in the trench for the night, the old man came to the door of his shack and said, 'No point in doing anything until early morning. They won't come till the cow's full. Come in here and wait; it's warmer than your filthy little hut.'

Judson had never been invited into the old man's shack before. He followed him in, happy that he would not have to lie all night in the trench. There was a candle burning in the room. It was stuck into the neck of a beer bottle and the bottle was on the table.

'Make some tea,' said the old man, pointing to the Primus stove standing on the floor. Judson lit the stove and made tea. The two of them sat down on a couple of wooden boxes and began to drink. The old man drank his hot and made loud sucking noises as he drank. Judson kept blowing on his, sipping it cautiously and watching the old man over the top of his cup. The old man went on sucking away at his tea until suddenly Judson said, 'Stop.' He said it quietly, plaintively almost, and as he said it he began to twitch around the corners of his eyes and around his mouth.

'What?' said the old man.

Judson said, 'That noise, that sucking noise you're making.'

The old man put down his cup and regarded the other quietly for a few moments, then he said, 'How many dogs you killed in your time, Judson?'

There was no answer.

'I said how many? How many dogs?'

Judson began picking the tea leaves out of his cup and sticking them on to the back of his left hand. The old man was leaning forward on his box.

'How many dogs, Judson?'

Judson began to hurry with his tea leaves. He jabbed his fingers into his empty cup, picked out a tea leaf, pressed it quickly on to the back of his hand and quickly went back for another. When there were not many left and he did not find one immediately, he bent over and peered closely into the cup, trying to find the ones that remained. The back of the hand which held the cup was covered with wet black tea leaves.

'Judson!' The old man shouted, and one side of his mouth opened and shut like a pair of tongs. The candle flame flickered and became still again.

Then quietly and very slowly, coaxingly, as someone to a child. 'In all your life, how many dogs has it been?'

Judson said, 'Why should I tell you?' He did not look up. He was picking the tea leaves off the back of his hand one by one and returning them to the cup.

'I want to know, Judson.' The old man was speaking very gently. 'I'm getting keen about this too. Let's talk about it and make some plans for more fun.'

Judson looked up. A ball of saliva rolled down his chin, hung for a moment in the air, snapped and fell to the floor.

'I only kill 'em because of a noise.'

'How often've you done it? I'd love to know how often.'

'Lots of times long ago.'

'How? Tell me how you used to do it. What did you like best?'

No answer.

'Tell me, Judson. I'd love to know.'

'I don't see why I should. It's a secret.'

'I won't tell. I swear I won't tell.'

'Well, if you'll promise.' Judson shifted his seat closer and spoke in a whisper. 'Once I waited till one was sleeping, then I got a big stone and dropped it on his head.'

The old man got up and poured himself a cup of tea. 'You didn't kill mine like that.'

'I didn't have time. The noise was so bad, the licking, and I just had to do it quick.'

'You didn't even kill him.'

'I stopped the noise.'

The old man went over to the door and looked out. It was dark. The moon had not yet risen, but the night was clear and cold with many stars. In the east there was a little paleness in the sky, and as he watched, the paleness grew and it changed from a paleness into a brightness, spreading over the sky so that the light was reflected and held by the small drops of dew upon the grass along the highlands; and slowly, the moon rose up over the hills. The old man turned and said, 'Better get ready. Never know; they might come early tonight.'

Judson got up and the two of them went outside. Judson lay down in the shallow trench beside the cow and the old man covered him over with grass, so that only his head peeped out above the ground. 'I shall be watching, too,' he said, 'from the window. If I give a shout, jump up and catch him.'

He hobbled back to the shack, went upstairs, wrapped himself in blankets and took up his position by the window. It was early still. The moon was nearly full and it was climbing. It shone upon the snow on the summit of Mount Kenya.

After an hour the old man shouted out of the window:

'Are you still awake, Judson?'

'Yes,' he answered, 'I'm awake.'

'Don't go to sleep,' said the old man. 'Whatever you do, don't go to sleep.'

'Cow's crunching all the time,' said Judson.

'Good, and I'll shoot you if you get up now,' said the old man.

'You'll shoot me?'

'I said I'll shoot you if you get up now.'

A gentle sobbing noise came up from where Judson lay, a strange gasping sound as though a child was trying not to cry, and in the middle of it, Judson's voice, 'I've got to move; please let me move. This crunching.'

'If you get up,' said the old man, 'I'll shoot you in the belly.'

For another hour or so the sobbing continued, then quite suddenly it stopped.

Just before four o'clock it began to get very cold and the old man huddled deeper into his blankets and shouted, 'Are you cold out there, Judson? Are you cold?'

'Yes,' came the answer. 'So cold. But I don't mind because cow's not crunching any more. She's asleep.'

The old man said, 'What are you going to do with the thief when you catch him?'

'I don't know.'

'Will you kill him?'

A pause.

'I don't know. I'll just go for him.'

'I'll watch,' said the old man. 'It ought to be fun.' He was leaning out of the window with his arms resting on the sill.

Then he heard the hiss under the window sill, and looked over and saw the black Mamba, sliding through the grass towards the cow, going fast and holding its head just a little above the ground as it went.

When the Mamba was five yards away, the old man shouted. He cupped his hands to his mouth and shouted, 'Here he comes, Judson; here he comes. Go and get him.'

Judson lifted his head quickly and looked up. As he did so he saw the Mamba and the Mamba saw him. There was a second, or perhaps two, when the snake stopped, drew back and raised the front part of its body in the air. Then the stroke. Just a flash of black and a slight thump as it took him in the chest. Judson screamed, a long, high-pitched scream which did not rise nor fall, but held its note until gradually it faded into nothingness and there was silence. Now he was standing up, ripping open his shirt, feeling for the place in his chest, whimpering quietly, moaning and breathing hard with his mouth wide open. And all the while the old man sat quietly at the open window, leaning forward and never taking his eyes away from the one below.

Everything comes very quick when one is bitten by a black Mamba, and almost at once the poison began to work. It threw him to the ground, where he lay humping his back and rolling around on the grass. He no longer made any noise. It was all very quiet, as though a man of great strength was wrestling with a giant whom one could not see, and it was as though the giant was twisting him and not letting him get up, stretching his arms through the fork of his legs and pushing his knees up under his chin.

Then he began pulling up the grass with his hands and soon after that he lay on his back kicking gently with his legs. But he didn't last very long. He gave a quick wriggle, humped his back again, turning over as he did it, then he lay on the ground quite still, lying on his stomach with his right knee drawn up underneath his chest and his hands stretched out above his head.

Still the old man sat by the window, and even after it was all over, he stayed where he was and did not stir. There was a movement in the shadow under the acacia tree and the Mamba came forward slowly towards the cow. It came forward a little, stopped, raised its head, waited, lowered its head, and slid forward again right under the belly of the animal. It raised itself into the air and took one of the brown teats in its mouth and began to drink. The old man sat watching the Mamba taking the milk of the cow, and once again he saw the gentle pulsing of its body as it drew the liquid out of the udder.

While the snake was still drinking, the old man got up and moved away from the window.

'You can have his share,' he said quietly. 'We don't mind you having his share,' and as he spoke he glanced back and saw again the black body of the Mamba curving upward from the ground, joining with the belly of the cow.

'Yes,' he said again, 'we don't mind your having his share.'

A PIECE OF CAKE

I do not remember much of it; not beforehand anyway; not until it happened.

There was the landing at Fouka, where the Blenheim boys were helpful and gave us tea while we were being refuelled. I remember the quietness of the Blenheim boys, how they came into the mess-tent to get some tea and sat down to drink it without saying anything; how they got up and went out when they had finished drinking and still they did not say anything. And I knew that each one was holding himself together because the going was not very good right then. They were having to go out too often, and there were no replacements coming along.

We thanked them for the tea and went out to see if they had finished refuelling our Gladiators. I remember that there was a wind blowing which made the windsock stand out straight, like a signpost, and the sand was blowing up around our legs and making a rustling noise as it swished against the tents, and the tents flapped in the wind so that they were like canvas men clapping their hands.

'Bomber boys unhappy,' Peter said.

'Not unhappy,' I answered.

'Well, they're browned off.'

'No. They've had it, that's all. But they'll keep going. You can see they're trying to keep going.'

Our two old Gladiators were standing beside each other in the sand and the airmen in their khaki shirts and shorts seemed still to be busy with the refuelling. I was wearing a thin white cotton flying suit and Peter had on a blue one. It wasn't necessary to fly with anything warmer.

Peter said, 'How far away is it?'

'Twenty-one miles beyond Charing Cross,' I answered, 'on the right side of the road.' Charing Cross was where the desert road branched north to Mersah Matruh. The Italian army was outside Mersah, and they were doing pretty well. It was about the only time, so far as I know, that the Italians have done pretty well. Their morale goes up and down like a sensitive altimeter, and right then it was at forty thousand because the Axis was on top of the world. We hung around waiting for the refuelling to finish.

Peter said, 'It's a piece of cake.'

'Yes. It ought to be easy.'

We separated and I climbed into my cockpit. I have always remembered the face of the airman who helped me to strap in. He was oldish, about forty, and bald except for a neat patch of golden hair at the back of his head. His face was all wrinkles, his eyes were like my grandmother's eyes, and he looked as though he had spent his life helping to strap in pilots who never came back. He stood on the wing pulling my straps and said, 'Be careful. There isn't any sense not being careful.'

'Piece of cake,' I said.

'Like hell.'

'Really. It isn't anything at all. It's a piece of cake.'

I don't remember much about the next bit; I only remember about later on. I suppose we took off from Fouka and flew west towards Mersah, and I suppose we flew at about eight hundred feet. I suppose we saw the sea to starboard, and I suppose – no, I am certain – that it was blue and that it was beautiful, especially where it rolled up on to the sand and made a long thick white line east and west as far as you could see. I suppose we flew over Charing Cross and flew on for twenty-one miles to where they had said it would be, but I do not know. I know only that there was trouble, lots and lots of trouble, and I know that we had turned round and were coming back when the trouble got worse. The biggest trouble of all was that I was too low to bale out, and it is from that point on that my memory comes back to me. I remember the dipping of the nose of the aircraft and I remember looking down the nose of the machine at the ground and seeing a little clump of camel-thorn growing there all by itself. I remember seeing some rocks lying in the sand beside the camel-thorn, and the camel-thorn and the sand and the rocks leapt out of the ground and came to me. I remember that very clearly.

Then there was a small gap of not-remembering. It might have been one second or it might have been thirty; I do not know. I have an idea that it was very short, a second perhaps, and next I heard a *crumph* on the right as the starboard wing tank caught fire, then another *crumph* on the left as the port tank did the same. To me that was not significant, and for a while I sat still, feeling comfortable, but a little drowsy. I couldn't see with my eyes, but that was not significant either. There was nothing to worry about. Nothing at all. Not until I felt the hotness around my legs. At first it was only a warmness and that was all right too, but all at once it was a hotness, a very stinging scorching hotness up and down the sides of each leg.

I knew that the hotness was unpleasant, but that was all I knew. I disliked it, so I curled my legs up under the seat and waited. I think there was something wrong with the telegraph system between the body and the brain. It did not seem to be working very well. Somehow it was a bit slow in telling the brain all about it and in asking for instructions. But I believe a message eventually got through, saying, 'Down here there is a great hotness. What shall we do? (Signed) Left Leg and Right Leg.' For a long time there was no reply. The brain was figuring the matter out.

Then slowly, word by word, the answer was tapped over the wires. 'The – plane – is – burning. Get – out – repeat – get – out – get – out.' The order was relayed to the whole system, to all the muscles in the legs, arms and body, and the muscles went to work. They tried their best; they pushed a little and pulled a little, and they strained greatly, but it wasn't any good. Up went another telegram, 'Can't get out. Something holding us in.' The answer to this one took even longer in arriving, so I just sat there waiting for it to come, and all the time the hotness increased. Something was holding me down and it was up to the brain to find out what it was. Was it giants' hands pressing on my shoulders, or heavy stones or houses or steam rollers or filing cabinets or gravity or was it ropes? Wait a minute. Ropes – ropes. The message was beginning to come through. It came very slowly. 'Your – straps. Undo – your – straps.' My arms received the message and went to work. They tugged at the straps, but they wouldn't undo. They tugged again and again, a little feebly, but as hard as they could, and it wasn't any use. Back went the message, 'How do we undo the straps?'

This time I think that I sat there for three or four minutes waiting for the answer. It wasn't any use hurrying or getting impatient. That was the one thing of which I was sure. But what a long time it was all taking. I said aloud, 'Bugger it. I'm going to be burnt. I'm ...' but I was interrupted. The answer was coming – no, it wasn't – yes, it was, it was slowly coming through. 'Pull – out – the – quick – release – pin – you – bloody – fool – and – hurry.'

Out came the pin and the straps were loosed. Now, let's get out. Let's get out, let's get out. But I couldn't do it. I simply lift myself out of the cockpit. Arms and legs tried their best but it wasn't any use. A last desperate message was flashed upwards and this time it was marked 'Urgent.'

'Something else is holding us down,' it said. 'Something else, something else, something heavy.'

Still the arms and legs did not fight. They seemed to know instinctively that there was no point in using up their strength. They stayed quiet and waited for the answer, and oh what a time it took. Twenty, thirty, forty hot seconds. None of them really white hot yet, no sizzling of flesh or smell of burning meat, but that would come any moment now, because those old Gladiators aren't made of stressed steel like a Hurricane or a Spit. They have taut canvas wings, covered with magnificently inflammable dope, and underneath there are hundreds of small thin sticks, the kind you put under the logs for kindling, only these are drier and thinner. If a clever man said, 'I am going to build a big thing that will burn better and quicker than anything else in the world,' and if he applied himself diligently to his task, he would probably finish up by building something very like a Gladiator. I sat still waiting.

Then suddenly the reply, beautiful in its briefness, but at the same time explaining everything. 'Your – parachute – turn – the – buckle.'

I turned the buckle, released the parachute harness and with some effort hoisted myself up and tumbled over the side of the cockpit. Something seemed to be burning, so I rolled about a bit in the sand, then crawled away from the fire on all fours and lay down.

I heard some of my machine-gun ammunition going off in the heat and I heard some of the bullets thumping into the sand near by. I did not worry about them; I merely heard them.

Things were beginning to hurt. My face hurt most. There was something wrong with my face. Something had happened to it. Slowly I put up a hand to feel it. It was sticky. My nose didn't seem to be there. I tried to feel my teeth, but I cannot remember whether I came to any conclusion about them. I think I dozed off.

All of a sudden there was Peter. I heard his voice and I heard him dancing around and yelling like a madman and shaking my hand and saying, 'Jesus, I thought you were still inside. I came down half a mile away and ran like hell. Are you all right?'

I said, 'Peter, what has happened to my nose?'

I heard him striking a match in the dark. The night comes quickly in the desert. There was a pause.

'It actually doesn't seem to be there very much,' he said. 'Does it hurt?'

'Don't be a bloody fool, of course it hurts.'

He said he was going back to his machine to get some morphia out of his emergency pack, but he came back again soon, saying he couldn't find his aircraft in the dark.

'Peter,' I said, 'I can't see anything.'

'It's night,' he answered. 'I can't see either.'

It was cold now. It was bitter cold, and Peter lay down close alongside so that we could both keep a little warmer. Every now and then he would say, 'I've never seen a man without a nose before,' I kept spewing a lot of blood and every time I did it, Peter lit a match. Once he gave me a cigarette, but it got wet and I didn't want it anyway.

I do not know how long we stayed there and I remember only very little more. I remember that I kept telling Peter that there was a tin of sore throat tablets in my pocket, and that he should take one,

otherwise he would catch my sore throat. I remember asking him
where we were and him saying, 'We're between the two armies,' and
then I remember English voices from an English patrol asking if we
were Italians. Peter said something to them; I cannot remember what
he said.

Later I remember hot thick soup and one spoonful making me sick.
And all the time the pleasant feeling that Peter was around, being
wonderful, doing wonderful things and never going away. That is all
that I can remember.

The men stood beside the airplane painting away and talking about
the heat.

'Painting pictures on the aircraft,' I said.

'Yes,' said Peter. 'It's a great idea. It's subtle.'

'Why?' I said. 'Just you tell me.'

'They're funny pictures,' he said. 'The German pilots will all laugh
when they see them; they'll shake so with their laughing that they
won't be able to shoot straight.'

'Oh baloney baloney baloney.'

'No, it's a great idea. It's fine. Come and have a look.'

We ran towards the line of aircraft. 'Hop, skip, jump,' said Peter.
'Hop skip jump, keep in time.'

'Hop skip jump,' I said, 'Hop skip jump,' and we danced along.

The painter on the first aeroplane had a straw hat on his head and
a sad face. He was copying the drawing out of a magazine, and when
Peter saw it he said, 'Boy oh boy look at that picture,' and he began
to laugh. His laugh began with a rumble and grew quickly into a
belly-roar and he slappped his thighs with his hands both at the same
time and went on laughing with his body doubled up and his mouth
wide open and his eyes shut. His silk top hat fell off his head on to
the sand.

'That's not funny,' I said.

'Not funny!' he cried. 'What d'you mean "not funny"? Look at me.
Look at me laughing. Laughing like this I couldn't hit anything. I
couldn't hit a hay wagon or a house or a louse.' And he capered about
on the sand, gurgling and shaking with laughter. Then he seized me
by the arm and we danced over to the next aeroplane. 'Hop skip
jump,' he said. 'Hop skip jump.'

There was a small man with a crumpled face writing a long story
on the fuselage with a red crayon. His straw hat was perched right on
the back of his head and his face was shiny with sweat.

'Good morning,' he said. 'Good morning, good morning,' and he
swept his hat off his head in a very elegant way.

Peter said, 'Shut up,' and bent down and began to read what the
little man had been writing. All the time Peter was spluttering and

rumbling with laughter, and as he read he began to laugh afresh. He rocked from one side to the other and danced around on the sand slapping his thighs with his hands and bending his body. 'Oh my, what a story, what a story, what a story. Look at me. Look at me laughing,' and he hopped about on his toes, shaking his head and chortling like a madman. Then suddenly I saw the joke and I began to laugh with him. I laughed so much that my stomach hurt and I fell down and rolled around on the sand and roared and roared because it was so funny that there was nothing else I could do.

'Peter, you're marvellous,' I shouted. 'But can all those German pilots read English?'

'Oh hell,' he said. 'Oh hell. Stop,' he shouted. 'Stop your work,' and the painters all stopped their painting and turned round slowly and looked at Peter. They did a little caper on their toes and began to chant in unison. 'Rubbishy things – on all the wings, on all the wings, on all the wings,' they chanted.

'Shut up,' said Peter. 'We're in a jam. We must keep calm. Where's my top hat?'

'What?' I said.

'You can speak German,' he said. 'You must translate for us. He will translate for you,' he shouted to the painters. 'He will translate.'

Then I saw his black top hat lying in the sand. I looked away, then I looked around and saw it again. It was a silk opera hat and it was lying there on its side in the sand.

'You're mad,' I shouted. 'You're madder than hell. You don't know what you're doing. You'll get us all killed. You're absolutely plumb crazy, do you know that? You're crazier than hell. My God, you're crazy.'

'Goodness, what a noise you're making. You mustn't shout like that; it's not good for you.' This was a woman's voice. 'You've made yourself all hot,' she said, and I felt someone wiping my forehead with a handkerchief. 'You mustn't work yourself up like that.'

Then she was gone and I saw only the sky, which was pale blue. There were no clouds and all around were the German fighters. They were above, below and on every side and there was no way I could go; there was nothing I could do. They took it in turns to come in to attack and they flew their aircraft carelessly, banking and looping and dancing in the air. But I was not frightened, because of the funny pictures on my wings. I was confident and I thought, 'I am going to fight a hundred of them alone and I'll shoot them all down. I'll shoot them while they are laughing; that's what I'll do.'

Then they flew closer. The whole sky was full of them. There were so many that I did not know which ones to watch and which ones to attack. There were so many that they made a black curtain over the sky and only here and there could I see a little of the blue showing through. But there was enough to patch a Dutchman's trousers, which was all that mattered. So long as there was enough to do that, then everything was all right.

Still they flew closer. They came nearer and nearer, right up in front of my face so that I saw only the black crosses which stood out brightly against the colour of the Messerschmitts and against the blue of the sky; and as I turned my head quickly from one side to the other I saw more aircraft and more crosses and then I saw nothing but the arms of the crosses and the blue of the sky. The arms had hands and they joined together and made a circle and danced around my Gladiator, while the engines of the Messerschmitts sang joyfully in a deep voice. They were playing Oranges and Lemons and every now and then two would detach themselves and come out into the middle of the floor and make an attack and I knew then that it was Oranges and Lemons. They banked and swerved and danced upon their toes and they leant against the air first to one side, then to the other. 'Oranges and Lemons said the bells of St Clements,' sang the engines.

But I was still confident. I could dance better than they and I had a better partner. She was the most beautiful girl in the world. I looked down and saw the curve of her neck and the gentle slope of her pale shoulders and I saw her slender arms, eager and outstretched.

Suddenly I saw some bullet holes in my starboard wing and I got angry and scared both at the same time; but mostly I got angry. Then I got confident and I said, 'The German who did that had no sense of humour. There's always one man in a party who has no sense of humour. But there's nothing to worry about; there's nothing at all to worry about.'

Then I saw more bullet holes and I got scared. I slid back the hood of the cockpit and stood up and shouted, 'You fools, look at the funny pictures. Look at the one on my tail; look at the story on my fuselage. Please look at the story on my fuselage.'

But they kept on coming. They tripped into the middle of the floor in twos, shooting at me as they came. And the engines of the Messerschmitts sang loudly. 'When will you pay me, said the bells of Old Bailey?' sang the engines, and as they sang the black crosses danced and swayed to the rhythm of the music. There were more holes in my wings, in the engine cowling and in the cockpit.

Then suddenly there were some in my body.

But there was no pain, even when I went into a spin, when the wings of my plane went flip, flip, flip flip, faster and faster, when the blue sky and the black sea chased each other round and round until there was no longer any sky or sea but just the flashing of the sun as I turned. But the black crosses were following me down, still dancing and still holding hands and I could still hear the singing of their engines. 'Here comes a candle to light you to bed, here comes a chopper to chop off your head,' sang the engines.

Still the wings went flip flip, flip flip, and there was neither sky nor sea around me, but only the sun.

Then there was only the sea. I could see it below me and I could see the white horses, and I said to myself, 'Those are white horses riding a rough sea.' I knew then that my brain was going well because of the white horses and because of the sea. I knew that there was not much time because the sea and the white horses were nearer, the white horses were bigger and the sea was like a sea and like water, not like a smooth plate. Then there was only one white horse, rushing forward madly with his bit in his teeth, foaming at the mouth, scattering the spray with his hooves and arching his neck as he ran. He galloped on madly over the sea, riderless and uncontrollable, and I could tell that we were going to crash.

After that it was warmer, and there were no black crosses and there was no sky. But it was only warm because it was not hot and it was not cold. I was sitting in a great red chair made of velvet and it was evening. There was a wind blowing from behind.

'Where am I?' I said.

'You are missing. You are missing, believed killed.'

'Then I must tell my mother.'

'You can't. You can't use that phone.'

'Why not?'

'It goes only to God.'

'What did you say I was?'

'Missing, believed killed.'

'That's not true. It's a lie. It's a lousy lie because here I am and I'm not missing. You're just trying to frighten me and you won't succeed. You won't succeed, I tell you, because I know it's a lie and I'm going back to my squadron. You can't stop me because I'll just go. I'm going, you see, I'm going.'

I got up from the red chair and began to run.

'Let me see those X-rays again, nurse.'

'They're here, doctor.' This was the woman's voice again, and now it came closer. 'You have been making a noise tonight, haven't you? Let me straighten your pillow for you, you're pushing it on to the floor.' The voice was close and it was very soft and nice.

'Am I missing?'

'No, of course not. You're fine.'

'They said I was missing.'

'Don't be silly; you're fine.'

Oh everyone's silly, silly, silly, but it was a lovely day, and I did not want to run but I couldn't stop because my legs were carrying me and I had no control over them. It was as if they did not belong to me, although when I looked down I saw that they were mine, that the shoes on the feet were mine and that the legs were joined to my body. But they would not do what I wanted; they just went on running across the field and I had to go with them. I ran and ran and ran, and although in some places the field was rough and bumpy, I never stumbled. I ran past trees and hedges and in one field there were some sheep which stopped their eating and scampered off as I ran past them. Once I saw my mother in a pale grey dress bending down picking mushrooms, and as I ran past she looked up and said, 'My basket's nearly full; shall we go home soon?' but my legs wouldn't stop and I had to go on.

Then I saw the cliff ahead and I saw how dark it was beyond the cliff. There was this great cliff and beyond it there was nothing but darkness, although the sun was shining in the field where I was running. The light of the sun stopped dead at the edge of the cliff and there was only darkness beyond. 'That must be where the night begins,' I thought, and once more I tried to stop but it was not any good. My legs began to go faster towards the cliff and they began to take longer strides, and I reached down with my hand and tried to stop them by clutching the cloth of my trousers, but it did not work; then I tried to fall down. But my legs were nimble, and each time I threw myself I landed on my toes and went on running.

Now the cliff and the darkness were much nearer and I could see that unless I stopped quickly I should go over the edge. Once more I tried to throw myself to the ground and once more I landed on my toes and went on running.

I was going fast as I came to the edge and I went straight on over it into the darkness and began to fall.

At first it was not quite dark. I could see little trees growing out of the face of the cliff, and I grabbed at them with my hands as I went down. Several times I managed to catch hold of a branch, but it always broke off at once because I was so heavy and because I was falling so fast, and once I caught a thick branch with both hands and the tree leaned forward and I heard the snapping of the roots one by one until it came away from the cliff and I went on falling. Then it became darker because the sun and the day were in the fields far away at the top of the cliff, and as I fell I kept my eyes open and watched the darkness turn from grey-black to black, from black to jet black and from jet black to pure liquid blackness which I could touch with my hands but which I could not see. But I went on falling, and it was so black that there was nothing anywhere and it was not any use doing anything or caring or thinking because of the blackness and because of the falling. It was not any use.

'You're better this morning. You're much better.' It was the woman's voice again.

'Hallo.'

'Hallo; we thought you were never going to get conscious.'

'Where am I?'

'In Alexandria; in hospital.'

'How long have I been here?'

'Four days.'

'What time is it?'

'Seven o'clock in the morning.'

'Why can't I see?'

I heard her walking a little closer.

'Oh, we've just put a bandage around your eyes for a bit.'

'How long for?'

'Just for a while. Don't worry. You're fine. You were very lucky, you know.'

I was feeling my face with my fingers but I couldn't feel it; I could only feel something else.

'What's wrong with my face?'

I heard her coming up to the side of my bed and I felt her hand touching my shoulder.

'You mustn't talk any more. You're not allowed to talk. It's bad for you. Just lie still and don't worry. You're fine.'

I heard the sound of her footsteps as she walked across the floor and I heard her open the door and shut it again.

'Nurse,' I said. 'Nurse.'

But she was gone.

MADAME ROSETTE

'Oh Jesus, this is wonderful,' said the Stag.

He was lying back in the bath with a Scotch and soda in one hand and a cigarette in the other. The water was right up to the brim and he was keeping it warm by turning the tap with his toes.

He raised his head and took a little sip of his whisky, then he lay back and closed his eyes.

'For God's sake, get out,' said a voice from the next room. 'Come on, Stag, you've had over an hour.' Stuffy was sitting on the edge of the bed with no clothes on, drinking slowly and waiting his turn.

The Stag said, 'All right. I'm letting the water out now,' and he stretched out a leg and flipped up the plug with his toes.

Stuffy stood up and wandered into the bathroom holding his drink in his hand. The Stag lay in the bath for a few moments more, then, balancing his glass carefully on the soap rack, he stood up and reached for a towel. His body was short and square, with strong thick legs and exaggerated calf muscles. He had coarse curly ginger hair and a thin, rather pointed face covered with freckles. There was a layer of pale ginger hair on his chest.

'Jesus,' he said, looking down into the bathtub, 'I've brought half the desert with me.'

Stuffy said, 'Wash it out and let me get in. I haven't had a bath for five months.'

This was back in the early days when we were fighting the Italians in Libya. One flew very hard in those days because there were not many pilots. They certainly could not send any out from England because there they were fighting the Battle of Britain. So one remained for long periods out in the desert, living the strange unnatural life of the desert, living in the same dirty little tent, washing and shaving every day in a mug full of one's own spat-out tooth water, all the time picking flies out of one's tea and out of one's food, having sandstorms which were as much in the tents as outside them so that placid men became bloody-minded and lost their tempers with their friends and with themselves; having dysentery and gippy tummy and mastoid and desert sores, having some bombs from the Italian S-79s, having no water and no women; having no flowers growing out of the ground; having very little except sand sand sand. One flew old Gloster

Gladiators against the Italian CR42s, and when one was not flying, it was difficult to know what to do.

Occasionally one would catch scorpions, put them in empty petrol cans and match them against each other in fierce mortal combat. Always there would be a champion scorpion in the squadron, a sort of Joe Louis who was invincible and won all his fights. He would have a name; he would become famous and his training diet would be a great secret known only to the owner. Training diet was considered very important with scorpions. Some were trained on corned beef, some on a thing called Machonachies, which is an unpleasant canned meat stew, some on live beetles and there were others who were persuaded to take a little beer just before the fight, on the premise that it made the scorpion happy and gave him confidence. These last ones always lost. But there were great battles and great champions, and in the afternoons when the flying was over, one could often see a group of pilots and airmen standing around in a circle on the sand, bending over with their hands on their knees, watching the fight, exhorting the scorpions and shouting at them as people shout at boxers or wrestlers in a ring. Then there would be a victory, and the man who owned the winner would become excited. He would dance around in the sand yelling, waving his arms in the air and extolling in a loud voice the virtues of the victorious animal. The greatest scorpion of all was owned by a sergeant called Wishful who fed him only on marmalade. The animal had an unmentionable name, but he won forty-two consecutive fights and then died quietly in training just when Wishful was considering the problem of retiring him to stud.

So you can see that because there were no great pleasures while living in the desert, the small pleasures became great pleasures and the pleasures of children became the pleasures of grown men. That was true for everyone; for the pilots, the fitters, the riggers, the corporals who cooked the food, and the men who kept the stores. It was true for the Stag and for Stuffy, so true that when the two of them wangled a forty-eight hour pass and a lift by air into Cairo, and when they got to the hotel, they were feeling about having a bath rather as you would feel on the first night of your honeymoon.

The Stag had dried himself and was lying on the bed with a towel round his waist, with his hands up behind his head, and Stuffy was in the bath, lying with his head against the back of the bath, groaning and sighing with ecstasy.

The Stag said, 'Stuffy.'

'Yes.'

'What are we going to do now?'

'Women,' said Stuffy. 'We must find some women to take out to supper.'

The Stag said, 'Later. That can wait till later.' It was early afternoon.

'I don't think it can wait,' said Stuffy.

'Yes,' said the Stag, 'it can wait.'

The Stag was very old and wise; he never rushed any fences. He was twenty-seven, much older than anyone else in the squadron, including the CO, and his judgement was much respected by the others.

'Let's do a little shopping first,' he said.

'Then what?' said the voice from the bathroom.

'Then we can consider the other situation.'

There was a pause.

'Stag?'

'Yes.'

'Do you know any women here?'

'I used to. I used to know a Turkish girl with very white skin called Wenka, and a Yugoslav girl who was six inches taller than I, called Kiki, and another who I think was Syrian. I can't remember her name.'

'Ring them up,' said Stuffy.

'I've done it. I did it while you were getting the whisky. They've all gone. It isn't any good.'

'It's never any good,' Stuffy said.

The Stag said, 'We'll go shopping first. There is plenty of time.'

In an hour Stuffy got out of the bath. They both dressed themselves in clean khaki shorts and shirts and wandered downstairs, through the lobby of the hotel and out into the bright hot street. The Stag put on his sunglasses.

Stuffy said, 'I know. I want a pair of sunglasses.'

'All right. We'll go and buy some.'

They stopped a gharry, got in and told the driver to go to Cicurel's. Stuffy bought his sunglasses and the Stag bought some poker dice, then they wandered out again on to the hot crowded street.

'Did you see that girl?' said Stuffy.

'The one that sold us the sunglasses?'

'Yes. That dark one.'

'Probably Turkish,' said Stag.

Stuffy said, 'I don't care what she was. She was terrific. Didn't you think she was terrific?'

They were walking along the Sharia Kasr-el-Nil with their hands in their pockets, and Stuffy was wearing the sunglasses which he had just bought. It was a hot dusty afternoon, and the sidewalk was crowded with Egyptians and Arabs and small boys with bare feet. The flies followed the small boys and buzzed around their eyes, trying to get at the inflammation which was in them, which was there because their mothers had done something terrible to those eyes when the boys were young, so that they would not be eligible for military conscription when they grew older. The small boys pattered along beside the Stag and Stuffy shouting, 'Baksheesh, baksheesh,' in shrill insistent voices, and the flies followed the small boys. There was the smell of Cairo, which is not like the smell of any other city. It comes not from any one thing or from any one place; it comes from everything everywhere; from the gutters and the sidewalks, from the houses and the shops and the things in the shops and the food cooking in the shops, from the horses and the dung of the horses in the streets and from the drains; it comes from the people and the way the sun bears down upon the people and the way the sun bears down upon the gutters and the drains and the horses and the food and the refuse in the streets. It is a rare, pungent smell, like something which is sweet and rotting and hot and salty and bitter all at the same time, and it is never absent, even in the cool of the early morning.

The two pilots walked along slowly among the crowd.

'Didn't you think she was terrific?' said Stuffy. He wanted to know what the Stag thought.

'She was all right.'

'Certainly she was all right. You know what, Stag?'

'What?'

'I would like to take that girl out tonight.'

They crossed over a street and walked on a little farther.

The Stag said, 'Well, why don't you? Why don't you ring up Rosette?'

'Who in the hell's Rosette?'

'Madame Rosette,' said the Stag. 'She is a great woman.'

They were passing a place called Tim's Bar. It was run by an Englishman called Tim Gilfillan who had been a quartermaster sergeant in the last war and who had somehow managed to get left behind in Cairo when the army went home.

'Tim's,' said the Stag. 'Let's go in.'

There was no one inside except for Tim, who was arranging his bottles on shelves behind the bar.

'Well, well, well,' he said, turning around. 'Where you boys been all this time?'

'Hello, Tim.'

He did not remember them, but he knew by their looks that they were in from the desert.

'How's my old friend Graziani?' he said, leaning his elbows on the counter.

'He's bloody close,' said the Stag. 'He's outside Mersah.'

'What you flying now?'

'Gladiators.'

'Hell, they had those here eight years ago.'

'Same ones still here,' said the Stag. 'They're clapped out.' They got their whisky and carried the glasses over to a table in the corner.

Stuffy said, 'Who's this Rosette?'

The Stag took a long drink and put down the glass.

'She's a great woman,' he said.

'Who is she?'

'She's a filthy old Syrian Jewess.'

'All right,' said Stuffy, 'all right, but what about her.'

'Well,' said Stag, 'I'll tell you. Madame Rosette runs the biggest brothel in the world. It is said that she can get you any girl that you want in the whole of Cairo.'

'Bullshit.'

'No, it's true. You just ring her up and tell her where you saw the woman, where she was working, what shop and at which counter, together with an accurate description, and she will do the rest.'

'Don't be such a bloody fool,' said Stuffy.

'It's true. It's absolutely true. Thirty-three squadron told me about her.'

'They were pulling your leg.'

'All right. You go and look her up in the phone book.'

'She wouldn't be in the phone book under that name.'

'I'm telling you she is,' said Stag. 'Go and look her up under Rosette. You'll see I'm right.'

Stuffy did not believe him, but he went over to Tim and asked him for a telephone directory and brought it back to the table. He opened it and turned the pages until he came to R-o-s. He ran his finger down the column. Roseppi ... Rosery ... Rosette. There it was, Rosette, Madame and the address and number, clearly printed in the book. The Stag was watching him.

'Got it?' he said.

'Yes, here it is. Madame Rosette.'

'Well, why don't you go and ring her up?'

'What shall I say?'

The Stag looked down into his glass and poked the ice with his finger.

'Tell her you are a Colonel,' he said. 'Colonel Higgins; she mistrusts pilot officers. And tell her that you have seen a beautiful dark girl selling sunglasses at Cicurel's and that you would like, as you put it, to take her out to dinner.'

'There isn't a telephone here.'

'Oh yes there is. There's one over there.'

Stuffy looked around and saw the telephone on the wall at the end of the bar.

'I haven't got a piastre piece.'

'Well, I have,' said Stag. He fished in his pocket and put a piastre on the table.

'Tim will hear everything I say.'

'What the hell does that matter? He probably rings her up himself. You're windy,' he added.

'You're a shit,' said Stuffy.

Stuffy was just a child. He was nineteen; seven whole years younger than the Stag. He was fairly tall and he was thin, with a lot of black hair and a handsome wide-mouthed face which was coffee brown from the sun of the desert. He was unquestionably the finest pilot in the squadron, and already in these early days, his score was fourteen Italians confirmed destroyed. On the ground he moved slowly and lazily like a tired person and he thought slowly and lazily like a sleepy child, but when he was up in the air his mind was quick and his movements were quick, so quick that they were like reflex actions. It seemed, when he was on the ground, almost as though he was resting, as though he was dozing a little in order to make sure that when he got into the cockpit he would wake up fresh and quick, ready for that two hours of high concentration. But Stuffy was away from the aerodrome now and he had something on his mind which had waked him up almost like flying. It might not last, but for the moment anyway, he was concentrating.

He looked again in the book for the number, got up and walked slowly over to the telephone. He put in the piastre, dialled the number and heard it ringing the other end. The Stag was sitting at the table looking at him and Tim was still behind the bar arranging his bottles. Tim was only about five yards away and he was obviously going to listen to everything that was said. Stuffy felt rather foolish. He leaned against the bar and waited, hoping that no one would answer.

Then click, the receiver was lifted at the other end and he heard a woman's voice saying, 'Allo.'

He said, 'Hello, is Madame Rosette there?' He was watching Tim. Tim went on arranging his bottles, pretending to take no notice, but Stuffy knew that he was listening.

'This ees Madame Rosette. Oo ees it?' Her voice was petulant and gritty. She sounded as if she did not want to be bothered with anyone just then.

Stuffy tried to sound casual. 'This is Colonel Higgins.'

'Colonel oo?'

'Colonel Higgins.' He spelled it.

'Yes, Colonel. What do you want?' She sounded impatient. Obviously this was a woman who stood no nonsense. He still tried to sound casual.

'Well, Madame Rosette, I was wondering if you could help me over a little matter.'

Stuffy was watching Tim. He was listening all right. You can always tell if someone is listening when he is pretending not to. He is careful not to make any noise about what he is doing and he pretends that he is concentrating very hard upon his job. Tim was like that now, moving the bottles quickly from one shelf to another, watching the bottles, making no noise, never looking around into the room. Over in the far corner the Stag was leaning forward with his elbows on the table, smoking a cigarette. He was watching Stuffy, enjoying the whole business and knowing that Stuffy was embarrassed because of Tim. Stuffy had to go on.

'I was wondering if you could help me,' he said. 'I was in Cicurel's today buying a pair of sunglasses and I saw a girl there whom I would very much like to take out to dinner.'

'What's 'er name?' The hard, rasping voice was more business-like than ever.

'I don't know,' he said sheepishly.

'What's she look like?'

'Well, she's got dark hair, and tall and, well, she's very beautiful.'

'What sort of dress was she wearing?'

'Er, let me see. I think it was a kind of white dress with red flowers printed all over it.' Then, as a brilliant afterthought, he added, 'She had a red belt.' He remembered that she had been wearing a shiny red belt.

There was a pause. Stuffy watched Tim who wasn't making any noise with the bottles; he was picking them up carefully and putting them down carefully.

Then the loud gritty voice again, 'It may cost you a lot.'

'That's all right.' Suddenly he didn't like the conversation any more. He wanted to finish it and get away.

'Might cost you six pounds, might cost you eight or ten. I don't know till I've seen her. That all right?'

'Yes yes, that's all right.'

'Where you living, Colonel?'

'Metropolitan Hotel,' he said without thinking.

'All right, I give you a ring later.' And she put down the receiver, bang.

Stuffy hung up, went slowly back to the table and sat down.

'Well,' said Stag, 'that was all right, wasn't it?'

'Yes, I suppose so.'

'What did she say?'

'She said that she would call me back at the hotel.'

'You mean she'll call Colonel Higgins at the hotel.'

Stuffy said, 'Oh Christ.'

Stag said, 'It's all right. We'll tell the desk that the Colonel is in our room and to put his calls through to us. What else did she say?'

'She said it may cost me a lot, six or ten pounds.'

'Rosette will take ninety per cent of it,' said Stag. 'She's a filthy old Syrian Jewess.'

'How will she work it?' Stuffy said.

He was really a gentle person and now he was feeling worried about having started something which might become complicated.

'Well,' said Stag, 'she'll dispatch one of her pimps to locate the girl and find out who she is. If she's already on the books, then it's easy. If she isn't, the pimp will proposition her there and then over the counter at Cicurel's. If the girl tells him to go to hell, he'll up the price, and if she still tells him to go to hell, he'll up the price still more, and in the end she'll be tempted by the cash and probably agree. Then Rosette quotes you a price three times as high and takes the balance herself. You have to pay her, not the girl. Of course, after that the girl goes on Rosette's books, and once she's in her clutches she's finished. Next time Rosette will dictate the price and the girl will not be in a position to argue.'

'Why?'

'Because if she refuses, Rosette will say, "All right, my girl, I shall see that your employers, that's Cicurel's, are told about what you did last time, how you've been working for me and using their shop as a market place. Then they'll fire you." That's what Rosette will say, and the wretched girl will be frightened and do what she's told.'

Stuffy said, 'Sounds like a nice person.'

'Who?'

'Madame Rosette.'

'Charming,' said Stag. 'She's a charming person.'

It was hot. Stuffy wiped his face with his handkerchief.

'More whisky,' said Stag. 'Hi, Tim, two more of those.'

Tim brought the glasses over and put them on the table without saying anything. He picked up the empty glasses and went away at once. To Stuffy it seemed as though he was different from what he had been when they first came in. He wasn't cheery any more, he was quiet and offhand. There wasn't any more 'Hi, you fellows, where you been all this time' about him now, and when he got back behind the counter he turned his back and went on arranging the bottles.

The Stag said, 'How much money you got?'

'Nine pounds, I think.'

'May not be enough. You gave her a free hand, you know. You ought to have set a limit. She'll sting you now.'

'I know,' Stuffy said.

They went on drinking for a little while without talking. Then Stag said, 'What you worrying about, Stuffy?'

'Nothing,' he answered. 'Nothing at all. Let's go back to the hotel. She may ring up.'

They paid for their drinks and said good-bye to Tim, who nodded but didn't say anything. They went back to the Metropolitan and as they went past the desk, the Stag said to the clerk, 'If a call comes in for Colonel Higgins, put it through to our room. He'll be there.' The Egyptian said, 'Yes, sir,' and made a note of it.

In the bedroom, the Stag lay down on his bed and lit a cigarette. 'And what am I going to do tonight?' he said.

Stuffy had been quiet all the way back to the hotel. He hadn't said a word. Now he sat down on the edge of the other bed with his hands still in his pockets and said, 'Look, Stag, I'm not very keen on this Rosette deal any more. It may cost too much. Can't we put it off?'

The Stag sat up. 'Hell no,' he said. 'You're committed. You can't fool about with Rosette like that. She's probably working on it at this moment. You can't back out now.'

'I may not be able to afford it,' Stuffy said.

'Well, wait and see.'

Stuffy got up, went over to the parachute bag and took out the bottle of whisky. He poured out two, filled the glasses with water from the tap in the bathroom, came back and gave one to the Stag.

'Stag,' he said. 'Ring up Rosette and tell her that Colonel Higgins has had to leave town urgently, to rejoin his regiment in the desert. Ring her up and tell her that. Say the Colonel asked you to deliver the message because he didn't have time.'

'Ring her up yourself.'

'She'd recognize my voice. Come on, Stag, you ring her.'

'No,' he said, 'I won't.'

'Listen,' said Stuffy suddenly. It was the child Stuffy speaking. 'I don't want to go out with that woman and I don't want to have any dealings with Madame Rosette tonight. We can think of something else.'

The Stag looked up quickly. Then he said, 'All right. I'll ring her.'

He reached for the phone book, looked up her number and spoke it into the telephone. Stuffy heard him get her on the line and he heard him giving her the message from the Colonel. There was a pause, then the Stag said, 'I'm sorry Madame Rosette, but it's nothing to do with me. I'm merely delivering a message.' Another pause; then the Stag said the same thing over again and that went on for quite a long time, until he must have got tired of it, because in the end he put down the receiver and lay back on his bed. He was roaring with laughter.

'The lousy old bitch,' he said, and he laughed some more.

Stuffy said, 'Was she angry?'

'Angry,' said Stag. 'Was she angry? You should have heard her. Wanted to know the Colonel's regiment and God knows what else and said he'd have to pay. She said you boys think you can fool around with me but you can't.'

'Hooray,' said Stuffy. 'The filthy old Jewess.'

'Now what are we going to do?' said the Stag. 'It's six o'clock already.'

'Let's go out and do a little drinking in some of those Gyppi places.'

'Fine. We'll do a Gyppi pub crawl.'

They had one more drink, then they went out. They went to a place called the Excelsior, then they went to a place called the Sphinx, then to a small place called by an Egyptian name, and by ten o'clock they were sitting happily in a place which hadn't got a name at all, drinking beer and watching a kind of stage show. At the Sphinx they had picked up a pilot from Thirty-three squadron, who said that his name was William. He was about the same age as Stuffy, but his face was younger, for he had not been flying so long. It was especially around his mouth that he was younger. He had a round schoolboy face and a small turned-up nose and his skin was brown from the desert.

The three of them sat happily in the place without a name drinking beer, because beer was the only thing that they served there. It was a long wooden room with an unpolished wooden sawdust floor and wooden tables and chairs. At the far end there was a raised wooden stage where there was a show going on. The room was full of Egyptians, sitting drinking black coffee with the red tarbooshes on their heads. There were two fat girls on the stage dressed in shiny silver pants and silver brassieres. One was waggling her bottom in time to the music. The other was waggling her bosom in time to the music. The bosom waggler was most skilful. She could waggle one bosom without waggling the other and sometimes she would waggle her bottom as well. The Egyptians were spellbound and kept giving her a big hand. The more they clapped the more she waggled and the more she waggled the faster the music played, and the faster the music played, the faster she waggled, faster and faster and faster, never losing the tempo, never losing the fixed brassy smile that was upon her face, and the Egyptians clapped more and more and louder and louder as the speed increased. Everyone was very happy.

When it was over William said, 'Why do they always have those dreary fat women? Why don't they have beautiful women?'

The Stag said, 'The Gyppies like them fat. They like them like that.'

'Impossible,' said Stuffy.

'It's true,' Stag said. 'It's an old business. It comes from the days when there used to be lots of famines here, and all the poor people were thin and all the rich people and the aristocracy were well fed and fat. If you got someone fat you couldn't go wrong; she was bound to be high-class.'

'Bullshit,' said Stuffy.

William said, 'Well, we'll soon find out. I'm going to ask those Gyppies.' He jerked his thumb towards two middle-aged Egyptians who were sitting at the next table, only about four feet away.

'No,' said Stag. 'No, William. We don't want them over here.'

'Yes,' said Stuffy.

'Yes,' said William. 'We've got to find out why the Gyppies like fat woman.'

He was not drunk. None of them was drunk, but they were happy with a fair amount of beer and whisky, and William was the happiest. His brown schoolboy face was radiant with happiness, his turned-up nose seemed to have turned up a little more, and he was probably relaxing for the first time in many weeks. He got up, took three paces over to the table of the Egyptians and stood in front of them, smiling.

'Gentlemen,' he said, 'my friends and I would be honoured if you would join us at our table.'

The Egyptians had dark greasy skins and podgy faces. They were wearing the red hats and one of them had a gold tooth. At first, when William addressed them, they looked a little alarmed. Then they caught on, looked at each other, grinned and nodded.

'Pleess,' said one.

'Pleess,' said the other, and they got up, shook hands with William and followed him over to where the Stag and Stuffy were sitting.

William said, 'Meet my friends. This is the Stag. This is Stuffy. I am William.'

The Stag and Stuffy stood up, they all shook hands, the Egyptians said 'Pleess' once more and then everyone sat down.

The Stag knew that their religion forbade them to drink. 'Have a coffee,' he said.

The one with the gold tooth grinned broadly, raised his palms upward and hunched his shoulders a little. 'For me,' he said, 'I am accustomed. But for my frient,' and he spread out his hands towards the other, 'for my frient – I cannot speak.'

The Stag looked at the friend. 'Coffee?' he asked.

'Pleess,' he answered. 'I am accustomed.'

'Good,' said Stag. 'Two coffees.'

He called a waiter. 'Two coffees,' he said. 'And, wait a minute. Stuffy, William, more beer?'

'For me,' Stuffy said, 'I am accustomed. But for my friend,' and he turned towards William, 'for my friend – I cannot speak.'

William said, 'Please. I am accustomed.' None of them smiled.

The Stag said, 'Good. Waiter, two coffees and three beers.' The waiter fetched the order and the Stag paid. The Stag lifted his glass towards the Egyptians and said, 'Bung ho.'

'Bung ho,' said Stuffy.

'Bung ho,' said William.

The Egyptians seemed to understand and they lifted their coffee cups. 'Pleess,' said the one. 'Thank you,' said the other. They drank.

The Stag put down his glass and said, 'It is an honour to be in your country.'

'You like?'

'Yes,' said the Stag. 'Very fine.'

The music had started again and the two fat women in silver tights were doing an encore. The encore was a knockout. It was surely the most remarkable exhibition of muscle control that has ever been witnessed; for although the bottom-waggler was still just waggling her bottom, the bosom-waggler was standing like an oak tree in the centre of the stage with her arms above her head. Her left bosom she was rotating in a clockwise direction and her right bosom in an anticlockwise direction. At the same time she was waggling her bottom and it was all in time to the music. Gradually the music increased its speed, and as it got faster, the rotating and the waggling got faster and some of the Egyptians were so spellbound by the contra-rotating bosoms of the woman that they were unconsciously following the movements of the bosoms with their hands, holding their hands up in front of them and describing circles in the air. Everyone stamped their feet and screamed with delight and the two women on the stage continued to smile their fixed brassy smiles.

Then it was over. The applause gradually died down.

'Remarkable,' said the Stag.

'You like?'

'Please, it was remarkable.'

'Those girls,' said the one with the gold tooth, 'very special.'

William couldn't wait any longer. He leaned across the table and said, 'Might I ask you a question?'

'Pleess,' said Golden Tooth. 'Pleess.'

'Well,' said William, 'How do you like your women? Like this – slim?' and he demonstrated with his hands. 'Or like this – fat?'

The gold tooth shone brightly behind a big grin. 'For me, I like like this, fat,' and a pair of podgy hands drew a big circle in the air.

'And your friend?' said William.

'For my frient,' he answered, 'I cannot speak.'

'Pleess,' said the friend. 'Like this.' He grinned and drew a fat girl in the air with his hands.

Stuffy said, 'Why do you like them fat?'

Golden Tooth thought for a moment, then he said, 'You like them slim, eh?'

'Please,' said Stuffy. 'I like them slim.'

'Why you like them slim? You tell me.'

Stuffy rubbed the back of his neck with the palm of his hand. 'William,' he said, 'why do we like them slim?'

'For me,' said William, 'I am accustomed.'

'So am I,' Stuffy said. 'But why?'

William considered. 'I don't know,' he said. 'I don't know why we like them slim.'

'Ha,' said Golden Tooth, 'You don't know.' He leaned over the table towards William and said triumphantly, 'And me, I do not know either.'

But that wasn't good enough for William. 'The Stag,' he said, 'says that all rich people in Egypt used to be fat and all poor people were thin.'

'No,' said Golden Tooth, 'No no no. Look those girls up there. Very fat; very poor. Look queen of Egypt, Queen Farida. Very thin; very rich. Quite wrong.'

'Yes, but what about years ago?' said William.

'What is this, years ago?'

William said, 'Oh all right. Let's leave it.'

The Egyptians drank their coffee and made noises like the last bit of water running out of the bathtub. When they had finished, they got up to go.

'Going?' said the Stag.

'Pleess,' said Golden Tooth.

William said, 'Thank you.' Stuffy said, 'Pleess.' The other Egyptian said, 'Pleess' and the Stag said, 'Thank you.' They all shook hands and the Egyptians departed.

'Ropey types,' said William.

'Very,' said Stuffy. 'Very ropey types.'

The three of them sat on drinking happily until midnight, when the waiter came up and told them that the place was closing and that there were no more drinks. They were still not really drunk because they had been taking it slowly, but they were feeling healthy.

'He says we've got to go.'

'All right. Where shall we go? Where shall we go, Stag?'

'I don't know. Where do you want to go?'

'Let's go to another place like this,' said William. 'This is a fine place.'

There was a pause. Stuffy was stroking the back of his neck with his hand. 'Stag,' he said slowly, 'I know where I want to go. I want to go to Madame Rosette's and I want to rescue all the girls there.'

'Who's Madame Rosette?' William said.

'She's a great woman,' said the Stag.

'She's a filthy old Syrian Jewess,' said Stuffy.

'She's a lousy old bitch,' said the Stag.

'All right,' said William. 'Let's go. But who is she?'

They told him who she was. They told him about their telephone calls and about Colonel Higgins, and William said, 'Come on, let's go. Let's go and rescue all the girls.'

They got up and left. When they went outside, they remembered that they were in a rather remote part of the town.

'We'll have to walk a bit,' said Stag. 'No gharries here.'

It was a dark starry night with no moon. The street was narrow and blacked-out. It smelled strongly with the smell of Cairo. It was quiet as they walked along, and now and again they passed a man or sometimes two men standing back in the shadow of a house, leaning against the wall of the house, smoking.

'I say,' said William, 'ropey, what?'

'Very,' said Stuffy. 'Very bad types.'

They walked on, the three of them walking abreast; square short ginger-haired Stag, tall dark Stuffy, and tall young William who went barehead because he had lost his cap. They headed roughly towards the centre of the town where they knew that they would find a gharry to take them on to Rosette.

Stuffy said, 'Oh, won't the girls be pleased when we rescue them?'

'Jesus,' said the Stag, 'it ought to be a party.'

'Does she actually keep them locked up?' William said.

'Well, no,' said Stag. 'Not exactly. But if we rescue them now, they won't have to work any more tonight anyway. You see, the girls she has at her place are nothing but ordinary shop girls who still work during the day in the shops. They have all of them made some mistake or other which Rosette either engineered or found out about, and now she has put the screws on them; she makes them come along in the evening. But they hate her and they do not depend on her for a living. They would kick her in the teeth if they got the chance.'

Stuffy said, 'We'll give them the chance.'

They crossed over a street. William said, 'How many girls will there be there, Stag?'

'I don't know. I suppose there might be thirty.'

'Good God,' said William. 'This *will* be a party. Does she really treat them very badly?'

The Stag said, 'Thirty-three squadron told me that she pays them nothing, about twenty akkers a night. She charges the customers a hundred or two hundred akkers each. Every girl earns for Rosette between five hundred and a thousand akkers every night.'

'Good God,' said William. 'A thousand piastres a night and thirty girls. She must be a millionaire.'

'She is. Someone calculated that not even counting her outside business, she makes the equivalent of about fifteen hundred pounds a week. That's, let me see, that's between five and six thousand pounds a month. Sixty thousand pounds a year.'

Stuffy came out of his dream. 'Jesus,' he said, 'Jesus Christ. The filthy old Syrian Jewess.'

'The lousy old bitch,' said William.

They were coming into a more civilized section of the town, but still there were no gharries.

The Stag said, 'Did you hear about Mary's House?'

'What's Mary's House?' said William.

'It's a place in Alexandria. Mary is the Rosette of Alex.'

'Lousy old bitch,' said William.

'No,' Stag said. 'They say she's a good woman. But anyway, Mary's House was hit by a bomb last week. The navy was in port at the time and the place was full of sailors, nautic types.'

'Killed?'

'Lots of them killed. And d'you know what happened? They posted them as killed in action.'

'The Admiral is a gentleman,' said Stuffy.

'Magnificent,' said William.

Then they saw a gharry and hailed it.

Stuffy said, 'We don't know the address.'

'He'll know it,' said Stag. 'Madame Rosette,' he said to the driver.

The driver grinned and nodded. Then William said, 'I'm going to drive. Give me the reins, driver, and sit up here beside me and tell me where to go.'

The driver protested vigorously, but when William gave him ten piastres, he gave him the reins. William sat high up on the driver's seat with the driver beside him. The Stag and Stuffy got in the back of the carriage.

'Take off,' said Stuffy. William took off. The horses began to gallop.

'No good,' shrieked the driver. 'No good. Stop.'

'Which way Rosette?' shouted William.

'Stop,' shrieked the driver.

William was happy. 'Rosette,' he shouted. 'Which way?'

The driver made a decision. He decided that the only way to stop this madman was to get him to his destination. 'This way,' he shrieked. 'Left.' William pulled hard on the left rein and the horses swerved around the corner. The gharry took it on one wheel.

'Too much bank,' shouted Stuffy from the back seat.

'Which way now?' shouted William.

'Left,' shrieked the driver. They took the next street to the left, then they took one to the right, two more to the left, then one to the right again and suddenly the driver yelled, 'Here pleess, here Rosette. Stop.'

William pulled hard on the reins and gradually the horses raised their heads with the pulling and slowed down to a trot.

'Where?' said William.

'Here,' said the driver. 'Pleess.' He pointed to a house twenty yards ahead. William brought the horses to a stop right in front of it.

'Nice work, William,' said Stuffy.

'Jesus,' said the Stag. 'That was quick.'

'Marvellous,' said William. 'Wasn't it?' He was very happy.

The driver was sweating through his shirt and he was too frightened to be angry.

William said, 'How much?'

'Pleess, twenty piastres.'

William gave him forty and said, 'Thank you very much. Fine horses.' The little man took the money, jumped up on to the gharry, and drove off. He was in a hurry to get away.

They were in another of those narrow, dark streets, but the houses, what they could see of them, looked huge and prosperous. The one which the driver had said was Rosette's was wide and thick and three storeys high, built of grey concrete, and it had a large thick front door which stood wide open. As they went in, the Stag said, 'Now leave this to me. I've got a plan.'

Inside there was a cold grey dusty stone hall, lit by a bare electric light bulb in the ceiling, and there was a man standing in the hall. He was a mountain of a man, a huge Egyptian with a flat face and two cauliflower ears. In his wrestling days he had probably been billed as Abdul the Killer or The Poisonous Pasha, but now he wore a dirty white cotton suit.

The Stag said, 'Good evening. Is Madame Rosette here?'

Abdul looked hard at the three pilots, hesitated, then said, 'Madame Rosette top floor.'

'Thank you,' said Stag. 'Thank you very much.' Stuffy noticed that the Stag was being polite. There was always trouble for somebody when he was like that. Back in the squadron, when he was leading a flight, when they sighted the enemy and when there was going to be a battle, the Stag never gave an order without saying 'Please' and he never received a message without saying 'Thank you'. He was saying 'Thank you' now to Abdul.

They went up the bare stone steps which had iron railings. They went past the first landing and the second landing, and the place was as bare as a cave. At the top of the third flight of steps, there was no landing; it was walled off, and the stairs ran up to a door. The Stag pressed the bell. They waited a while, then a little panel in the door slid back and a pair of small black eyes peeked through. A woman's voice said, 'What you boys want?' Both the Stag and Stuffy recognized the voice from the telephone. The Stag said, 'We would like to see Madame Rosette.' He pronounced the Madame in the French way because he was being polite.

'You officers? Only officers here,' said the voice. She had a voice like a broken board.

'Yes,' said Stag. 'We are officers.'

'You don't look like officers. What kind of officers?'

'RAF.'

There was a pause. The Stag knew that she was considering. She had probably had trouble with pilots before, and he hoped only that she would not see William and the light that was dancing in his eyes; for William was still feeling the way he had felt when he drove the gharry. Suddenly the panel closed and the door opened.

'All right, come in,' she said. She was too greedy, this woman, even to pick her customers carefully.

They went in and there she was. Short, fat, greasy, with wisps of untidy black hair straggling over her forehead; a large, mud-coloured face, a large wide nose and a small fish mouth, with just the trace of a black moustache above the mouth. She had on a loose black satin dress.

'Come into the office, boys,' she said, and started to waddle down the passage to the left. It was a long wide passage, about fifty yards long and four or five yards wide. It ran through the middle of the house, parallel with the street, and as you came in from the stairs, you had to turn left along it. All the way down there were doors, about eight or ten of them on each side. If you turned right as you came in from the stairs, you ran into the end of the passage, but there was one door there too, and as the three of them walked in, they heard a babble of female voices from behind that door. The Stag noted that it was the girls' dressing room.

'This way, boys,' said Rosette. She turned left and slopped down the passage, away from the door with the voices. The three followed her, Stag first, then Stuffy, then William, down the passage which had a red carpet on the floor and huge pink lampshades hanging from the ceiling. They got about halfway down the passage when there was a yell from the dressing room behind them. Rosette stopped and looked around.

'You go on, boys,' she said, 'into the office, last door on the left. I won't be a minute.' She turned and went back towards the dressing-room door. They didn't go on. They stood and watched her, and just as she got to the door, it opened and a girl rushed out. From where they stood, they could see that her fair hair was all over her face and that she had on an untidy-looking green evening dress. She saw Rosette in front of her and she stopped. They heard Rosette say something, something angry and quick spoken, and they heard the girl shout something back at her. They saw Rosette raise her right arm and they saw her hit the girl smack on the side of the face with the palm of her hand. They saw her draw back her hand and hit her again in the same place. She hit her hard. The girl put her hands up to her face and began to cry. Rosette opened the door of the dressing room and pushed her back inside.

'Jesus,' said the Stag. 'She's tough.' William said, 'So am I.' Stuffy didn't say anything.

Rosette came back to them and said, 'Come along, boys. Just a bit of trouble, that's all.' She led them to the end of the passage and in through the last door on the left. This was the office. It was a medium-sized room with two red plush sofas, two or three red plush armchairs and a thick red carpet on the floor. In one corner was a small desk, and Rosette sat herself behind it, facing the room.

'Sit down, boys,' she said.

The Stag took an armchair, Stuffy and William sat on a sofa.

'Well,' she said, and her voice became sharp and urgent. 'Let's do business.'

The Stag leaned forward in his chair. His short ginger hair looked somehow wrong against the bright red plush. 'Madame Rosette,' he said, 'it is a great pleasure to meet you. We have heard so much about you.' Stuffy looked at the Stag. He was being polite again. Rosette looked at him too, and her little black eyes were suspicious. 'Believe me,' the Stag went on, 'we've really been looking forward to this for quite a time now.'

His voice was so pleasant and he was so polite that Rosette took it.

'That's nice of you boys,' she said. 'You'll always have a good time here. I see to that. Now – business.'

William couldn't wait any longer. He said slowly, 'The Stag says that you're a great woman.'

'Thanks, boys.'

Stuffy said, 'The Stag says that you're a filthy old Syrian Jewess.'

William said quickly, 'The Stag says that you're a lousy old bitch.'

'And I know what I'm talking about,' said the Stag.

Rosette jumped to her feet. 'What's this?' she shrieked, and her face was no longer the colour of mud; it was the colour of red clay. The men did not move. They did not smile or laugh; they sat quite still, leaning forward a little in their seats, watching her.

Rosette had had trouble before, plenty of it, and she knew how to deal with it. But this was different. They didn't seem drunk, it wasn't about money and it wasn't about one of her girls. It was about herself and she didn't like it.

'Get out,' she yelled. 'Get out unless you want trouble.' But they did not move.

For a moment she paused, then she stepped quickly from behind her desk and made for the door. But the Stag was there first and when she went for him, Stuffy and William each caught one of her arms from behind.

'We'll lock her in,' said the Stag. 'Let's get out.'

Then she really started yelling and the words which she used cannot
be written down on paper, for they were terrible words. They poured
out of her small fish mouth in one long unbroken high-pitched stream,
and little bits of spit and saliva came out with them. Stuffy and William
pulled her back by the arms towards one of the big chair and she
fought and yelled like a large fat pig being dragged to the slaughter.
They got her in front of the chair and gave her a quick push so that
she fell backwards into it. Stuffy nipped across to her desk, bent down
quickly and jerked the telephone cord from its connection. The Stag
had the door open and all three of them were out of the room before
Rosette had time to get up. The Stag had taken the key from the
inside of the door, and now he locked it. The three of them stood
outside in the passage.

'Jesus,' said the Stag. 'What a woman!'

'Mad as hell,' William said. 'Listen to her.'

They stood outside in the passage and they listened. They heard
her yelling, then she began banging on the door, but she went on
yelling and her voice was not the voice of a woman, it was the voice
of an enraged but articulate bull.

The Stag said, 'Now quick. The girls. Follow me. And from now
on you've got to act serious. You've got to act serious as hell.'

He ran down the passage towards the dressing room, followed by
Stuffy and William. Outside the door he stopped, the other two stopped
and they could still hear Rosette yelling from her office. The Stag said,
'Now don't say anything. Just act serious as hell,' and he opened the
door and went in.

There were about a dozen girls in the room. They all looked up.
They stopped talking and looked up at the Stag, who was standing in
the doorway. The Stag clicked his heels and said, 'This is the Military
Police. *Les Gendarmes Militaires.*' He said it in a stern voice and with a
straight face and he was standing there in the doorway at attention
with his cap on his head. Stuffy and William stood behind him.

'This is the Military Police,' he said again, and he produced his
identification card and held it up between two fingers.

The girls didn't move or say anything. They stayed still in the
middle of what they were doing and they were like a tableau because
they stayed so still. One had been pulling on a stocking and she stayed
like that, sitting on a chair with her leg out straight and the stocking
up to her knee with her hands on the stocking. One had been doing
her hair in front of a mirror and when she looked round she kept her
hands up to her hair. One was standing up and had been applying
lipstick and she raised her eyes to the Stag but still held the lipstick
to her mouth. Several were just sitting around on plain wooden chairs,
doing nothing, and they raised their heads and turned them to the

door, but they went on sitting. Most of them were in some sort of shiny evening dress, one or two were half-clothed, but most of them were in shiny green or shiny blue or shiny red or shiny gold, and when they turned to look at the Stag, they were so still that they were like a tableau.

The Stag paused. Then he said, 'I am to state on behalf of the authorities that they are sorry to disturb you. My apologies, mesd'moiselles. But it is necessary that you come with us for purposes of registration, et cetera. Afterwards you will be allowed to go. It is a mere formality. But now you must come, please. I have conversed with Madame.'

The Stag stopped speaking, but still the girls did not move.

'Please,' said the Stag, 'get your coats. We are the military.' He stepped aside and held open the door. Suddenly the tableau dissolved, the girls got up, puzzled and murmuring, and two or three of them moved towards the door. The others followed. The ones that were half-clothed quickly slipped into dresses, patted their hair with their hands and came too. None of them had coats.

'Count them,' said the Stag to Stuffy as they filed out of the door. Stuffy counted them aloud and there were fourteen.

'Fourteen, sir,' said Stuffy, who was trying to talk like a sergeant-major.

The Stag said, 'Correct,' and he turned to the girls who were crowded in the passage. 'Now, mesd'moiselles, I have the list of your names from Madame, so please do not try to run away. And do not worry. This is merely a formality of the military.'

William was out in the passage opening the door which led to the stairs, and he went out first. The girls followed and the Stag and Stuffy brought up the rear. The girls were quiet and puzzled and worried and a little frightened and they didn't talk, none of them talked except for a tall one with black hair who said, 'Mon Dieu, a formality of the military. Mon Dieu, mon Dieu, what next.' But that was all and they went on down. In the hall they met the Egyptian who had a flat face and two cauliflower ears. For a moment it looked as though there would be trouble. But the Stag waved his identification card in his face and said, 'The Military Police,' and the man was so surprised that he did nothing and let them pass.

And so they came out into the street and the Stag said, 'It is necessary to walk a little way, but only a very little way,' and they turned right and walked along the sidewalk with the Stag leading, Stuffy at the rear and William walking out on the road guarding the flank. There was some moon now. One could see quite well and William tried to keep in step with Stag and Stuffy tried to keep in step with William, and they swung their arms and held their heads up high and looked very military, and the whole thing was a sight to behold. Fourteen girls in shiny evening dresses, fourteen girls in the moonlight in shiny green, shiny blue, shiny red, shiny black and shiny gold, marching along the street with the Stag in front, William alongside and Stuffy at the rear. It was a sight to behold.

The girls had started chattering. The Stag could hear them, although he didn't look around. He marched on at the head of the column and when they came to the crossroads he turned right. The others followed and they had walked fifty yards down the block when they came to an Egyptian café. The Stag saw it and he saw the lights burning behind the blackout curtains. He turned around and shouted 'Halt!' The girls stopped, but they went on chattering and anyone could see that there was mutiny in the ranks. You can't make fourteen girls in high heels and shiny evening dresses march all over town with you at night, not for long anyway, not for long, even if it is a formality of the military. The Stag knew it and now he was speaking.

'Mesd'moiselles,' he said, 'listen to me.' But there was mutiny in the ranks and they went on talking and the tall one with dark hair was saying, 'Mon Dieu, what is this? What in hell's name sort of a thing is this, oh mon Dieu?'

'Quiet,' said the Stag. 'Quiet!' and the second time he shouted it as a command. The talking stopped.

'Mesd'moiselles,' he said, and now he became polite. He talked to them in his best way and when the Stag was polite there wasn't anyone who didn't take it. It was an extraordinary thing because he could make a kind of smile with his voice without smiling with his lips. His voice smiled while his face remained serious. It was a most forcible thing because it gave people the impression that he was being serious about being nice.

'Mesd'moiselles,' he said, and his voice was smiling. 'With the military there always has to be formality. It is something unavoidable. It is something that I regret exceedingly. But there can be chivalry also. And you must know that with the RAF there is great chivalry. So now it will be a pleasure if you will all come in here and take with us a glass of beer. It is the chivalry of the military.' He stepped forward, opened the door of the café and said, 'Oh for God's sake, let's have a drink. Who wants a drink?'

Suddenly the girls saw it all. They saw the whole thing as it was, all of them at once. It took them by surprise. For a second they considered. Then they looked at one another, then they looked at the Stag, then they looked around at Stuffy and at William, and when they looked at those two they caught their eyes and the laughter that was in them. All at once the girls began to laugh and William laughed and Stuffy laughed and they moved forward and poured into the café.

The tall one with dark hair took the Stag by the arm and said, 'Mon Dieu, Military Police, mon Dieu, oh mon Dieu,' and she threw her head back and laughed and the Stag laughed with her. William said, 'It is the chivalry of the military,' and they moved into the café.

The place was rather like the one that they had been in before, wooden and sawdusty, and there were a few coffee-drinking Egyptians sitting around with the red tarbooshes on their heads. William and Stuffy pushed three round tables together and fetched chairs. The girls sat down. The Egyptians at the other tables put down their coffee cups, turned around in their chairs and gaped. They gaped like so many fat muddy fish, and some of them shifted their chairs round facing the party so that they could get a better view and they went on gaping.

A waiter came up and the Stag said, 'Seventeen beers. Bring us seventeen beers.' The waiter said 'Pleess' and went away.

As they sat waiting for the drinks the girls looked at the three pilots and the pilots looked at the girls. William said, 'It is the chivalry of the military,' and the tall dark girl said, 'Mon Dieu, you are crazy people, oh mon Dieu.'

The waiter brought the beer. William raised his glass and said, 'To the chivalry of the military.' The dark girl said, 'Oh mon Dieu.' Stuffy didn't say anything. He was busy looking around at the girls, sizing them up, trying to decide now which one he liked best so that he could go to work at once. The Stag was smiling and the girls were sitting there in their shiny evening dresses, shiny red, shiny gold, shiny blue, shiny green, shiny black and shiny silver, and once again it was almost a tableau, certainly it was a picture, and the girls were sitting there sipping their beer, seeming quite happy, not seeming suspicious any more because to them the whole thing now appeared exactly as it was and they understood.

'Jesus,' said the Stag. He put down his glass and looked around him. 'Oh Jesus, there's enough here for the whole squadron. How I wish the whole squadron was here!' He took another drink, stopped in the middle of it and put down his glass quickly. 'I know what,' he said. 'Waiter, oh waiter.'

'Pleess.'

'Get me a big piece of paper and a pencil.'

'Pleess.' The waiter went away and came back with a sheet of paper. He took a pencil from behind his ear and handed it to the Stag. The Stag banged the table for silence.

'Mesd'moiselles,' he said, 'for the last time there is a formality. It is the last of all the formalities.'

'Of the military,' said William.

'Oh mon Dieu,' said the dark girl.

'It is nothing,' the Stag said. 'You are require to write your name and your telephone number on this piece of paper. It is for my friends in the squadron. It is so that they can be as happy as I am now, but without the same trouble beforehand.' The Stag's voice was smiling again. One could see that the girls liked his voice. 'You would be very kind if you would do that,' he went on, 'for they too would like to meet you. It would be a pleasure.'

'Wonderful,' said William.

'Crazy,' said the dark girl, but she wrote her name and number on the paper and passed it on. The Stag ordered another round of beer. The girls certainly looked funny sitting there in their dresses, but they were writing their names down on the paper. They looked happy and William particularly looked happy, but Stuffy looked serious because the problem of choosing was a weighty one and it was heavy on his mind. They were good-looking girls, young and good-looking, all different, completely different from each other because they were Greek and Syrian and French and Italian and light Egyptian and Yugoslav and many other things, but they were good-looking, all of them were good-looking and handsome.

The piece of paper had come back to the Stag now and they had all written on it; fourteen strangely written names and fourteen telephone numbers. The Stag looked at it slowly. 'This will go on the squadron notice-board,' he said, 'and I will be regarded as a great benefactor.'

William said, 'It should go to headquarters. It should be mimeographed and circulated to all squadrons. It would be good for morale.'

'Oh mon Dieu,' said the dark girl. 'You are crazy.'

Slowly Stuffy got to his feet, picked up his chair, carried it round to the other side of the table and pushed it between two of the girls. All he said was, 'Excuse me. Do you mind if I sit here?' At last he had made up his mind, and now he turned towards the one on his right and quietly went to work. She was very pretty; very dark and very pretty and she had plenty of shape. Stuffy began to talk to her, completely oblivious to the rest of the company, turning towards her and leaning his head on his hand. Watching him, it was not so difficult to understand why he was the greatest pilot in the squadron. He was a young concentrator, this Stuffy; an intense athletic concentrator who moved towards what he wanted in a dead straight line. He took hold of winding roads and carefully he made them straight, then he moved over them with great speed and nothing stopped him. He was like that, and now he was talking to the pretty girl but no one could hear what he was saying.

Meanwhile the Stag was thinking. He was thinking about the next move, and when everyone was getting towards the end of their third beer, he banged the table again for silence.

'Mesd'moiselles,' he said. 'It will be a pleasure for us to escort you home. I will take five of you,' – he had worked it all out – 'Stuffy will take five, and Jamface will take four. We will take three gharries and

I will take five of you in mine and I will drop you home one at a time.'

William said, 'It is the chivalry of the military.'

'Stuffy,' said the Stag. 'Stuffy, is that all right? You take five. It's up to you whom you drop off last.'

Stuffy looked around. 'Yes,' he said. 'Oh yes. That suits me.'

'William, you take four. Drop them home one by one; you understand.'

'Perfectly,' said William. 'Oh perfectly.'

They all got up and moved towards the door. The tall one with dark hair took the Stag's arm and said, 'You take me?'

'Yes,' he answered. 'I take you.'

'You drop me off last?'

'Yes. I drop you off last.'

'Oh mon Dieu,' she said. 'That will be fine.'

Outside they got three gharries and they split up into parties. Stuffy was moving quickly. He got his girls into the carriage quickly, climbed in after them and the Stag saw the gharry drive off down the street. Then he saw William's gharry move off, but it seemed to start away with a sudden jerk, with the horses breaking into a gallop at once. The Stag looked again and he saw William perched high up on the driver's seat with the reins in his hands.

The Stag said, 'Let's go,' and his five girls got into their gharry. It was a squash, but everyone got in. The Stag sat back in his seat and then he felt an arm pushing up and under and linking with his. It was the tall one with dark hair. He turned and looked at her.

'Hello,' he said. 'Hello, you.'

'Ah,' she whispered. 'You are such goddam crazy people.' And the Stag felt a warmness inside him and he began to hum a little tune as the gharry rattled on through the dark streets.

KATINA

Some brief notes about the last days of RAF
fighters in the first Greek campaign.

Peter saw her first.

She was sitting on a stone, quite still, with her hands resting on her lap. She was staring vacantly ahead, seeing nothing, and all around, up and down the little street, people were running backward and forward with buckets of water, emptying them through the windows of the burning houses.

Across the street on the cobblestones, there was a dead boy. Someone had moved his body close in to the side so that it would not be in the way.

A little farther down an old man was working on a pile of stones and rubble. One by one he was carrying the stones away and dumping them to the side. Sometimes he would bend down and peer into the ruins, repeating a name over and over again.

All around there was shouting and running and fires and buckets of water and dust. And the girl sat quietly on the stone, staring ahead, not moving. There was blood running down the left side of her face. It ran down from her forehead and dropped from her chin on to the dirty print dress she was wearing.

Peter saw her and said, 'Look at that little girl.'

We went up to her and Fin put his hand on her shoulder, bending down to examine the cut. 'Looks like a piece of shrapnel,' he said. 'She ought to see the Doc.'

Peter and I made a chair with our hands and Fin lifted her up on to it. We started back through the streets and out towards the aerodrome, the two of us walking a little awkwardly, bending down, facing our burden. I could feel Peter's fingers clasping tightly in mine and I could feel the buttocks of the little girl resting lightly on my wrists. I was on the left side and the blood was dripping down from her face on to the arm of my flying suit, running down the waterproof cloth on to the back of my hand. The girl never moved or said anything.

Fin said, 'She's bleeding rather fast. We'd better walk a bit quicker.'

I couldn't see much of her face because of the blood, but I could tell that she was lovely. She had high cheekbones and large round eyes, pale blue like an autumn sky, and her hair was short and fair. I guessed she was about nine years old.

This was in Greece in early April, 1941, at Paramythia. Our fighter squadron was stationed on a muddy field near the village. We were in a deep valley and all around us were the mountains. The freezing winter had passed, and now, almost before anyone knew it, spring had come. It had come quietly and swiftly, melting the ice on the lakes and brushing the snow off the mountain tops; and all over the airfield we could see the pale green shoots of grass pushing up through the mud, making a carpet for our landings. In our valley there were warm winds and wild flowers.

The Germans, who had pushed in through Yugoslavia a few days before, were now operating in force, and that afternoon they had come over very high with about thirty-five Dorniers and bombed the village. Peter and Fin and I were off duty for a while, and the three of us had gone down to see if there was anything we could do in the way of rescue work. We had spent a few hours digging around in the ruins and helping to put out fires, and we were on our way back when we saw the girl.

Now, as we approached the landing field, we could see the Hurricanes circling around coming in to land, and there was the Doc standing out in front of the dispersal tent, just as he should have been, waiting to see if anyone had been hurt. We walked towards him, carrying the child, and Fin, who was a few yards in front, said,

'Doc, you lazy old devil, here's a job for you.'

The Doc was young and kind and morose except when he got drunk. When he got drunk he sang very well.

'Take her into the sick bay,' he said. Peter and I carried her in and put her down on a chair. Then we left her and wandered over to the dispersal tent to see how the boys had got along.

It was beginning to get dark. There was a sunset behind the ridge over in the west, and there was a full moon, a bombers' moon, climbing up into the sky. The moon shone upon the shoulders of the tents and made them white; small white pyramids, standing up straight, clustering in little orderly groups around the edges of the aerodrome. They had a scared-sheep look about them the way they clustered themselves together, and they had a human look about them the way they stood up close to one another, and it seemed almost as though they knew that there was going to be trouble, as though someone had warned them that they might be forgotten and left behind. Even as I looked, I thought I saw them move. I thought I saw them huddle just a fraction nearer together.

And then, silently, without a sound, the mountains crept a little closer into our valley.

For the next two days there was much flying. There was the getting up at dawn, there was the flying, the fighting and the sleeping; and there was the retreat of the army. That was about all there was or all there was time for. But on the third day the clouds dropped down over the mountains and slid into the valley. And it rained. So we sat around in the mess-tent drinking beer and resinato, while the rain made a noise like a sewing machine on the roof. Then lunch. For the first time in days the whole squadron was present. Fifteen pilots at a long table with benches on either side and Monkey, the CO sitting at the head.

We were still in the middle of our fried corned beef when the flap of the tent opened and in came the Doc with an enormous dripping raincoat over his head. And with him, under the coat, was the little girl. She had a bandage round her head.

The Doc said, 'Hello. I've brought a guest.' We looked around and suddenly, automatically, we all stood up.

The Doc was taking off his raincoat and the little girl was standing there with her hands hanging loose by her sides looking at the men, and the men were all looking at her. With her fair hair and pale skin she looked less like a Greek than anyone I've ever seen. She was frightened by the fifteen scruffy-looking foreigners who had suddenly stood up when she came in, and for a moment she half-turned as if she were going to run away out into the rain.

Monkey said, 'Hallo. Hallo there. Come and sit down.'

'Talk Greek,' the Doc said. 'She doesn't understand.'

Fin and Peter and I looked at one another and Fin said, 'Good God, it's our little girl. Nice work, Doc.'

She recognized Fin and walked round to where he was standing. He took her by the hand and sat her down on the bench, and everyone else sat down too. We gave her some fried corned beef and she ate it slowly, looking down at her plate while she ate. Monkey said, 'Get Pericles.'

Pericles was the Greek interpreter attached to the squadron. He was a wonderful man we'd picked up at Yanina, where he had been the local school teacher. He had been out of work ever since the war started. 'The children do not come to school,' he said. 'They are up in the mountains and fight. I cannot teach sums to the stones.'

Pericles came in. He was old, with a beard, a long pointed nose and sad grey eyes. You couldn't see his mouth, but his beard had a way of smiling when he talked.

'Ask her her name,' said Monkey.

He said something to her in Greek. She looked up and said, 'Katina.' That was all she said.

'Look, Pericles,' Peter said, 'ask her what she was doing sitting by that heap of ruins in the village.'

Fin said, 'For God's sake leave her alone.'

'Ask her, Pericles,' said Peter.

'What should I ask?' said Pericles, frowning.

Peter said, 'What she was doing sitting on that heap of stuff in the village when we found her.'

Pericles sat down on the bench beside her and he talked to her again. He spoke gently and you could see that his beard was smiling a little as he spoke, helping her. She listened and it seemed a long time before she answered. When she spoke, it was only a few words, and the old man translated: 'She says that her family were under the stones.'

Outside the rain was coming down harder than ever. It beat upon the roof of the mess-tent so that the canvas shivered as the water bounced upon it. I got up and walked over and lifted the flap of the tent. The mountains were invisible behind the rain, but I knew they were around us on every side. I had a feeling that they were laughing at us, laughing at the smallness of our numbers and at the hopeless courage of the pilots. I felt that it was the mountains, not us, who were the clever ones. Had not the hills that very morning turned and looked northward towards Tepelene where they had seen a thousand German aircraft gathered under the shadow of Olympus? Was it not true that the snow on the top of Dodona had melted away in a day, sending little rivers of water running down across our landing field? Had not Kataphidi buried his head in a cloud so that our pilots might be tempted to fly through the whiteness and crash against his rugged shoulders?

And as I stood there looking at the rain through the tent flap, I knew for certain that the mountains had turned against us. I could feel it in my stomach.

I went back into the tent and there was Fin, sitting beside Katina, trying to teach her English words. I don't know whether he made much progress, but I do know that once he made her laugh and that was a wonderful thing for him to have done. I remember the sudden sound of her high laughter and how we all looked up and saw her face; how we saw how different it was to what it had been before. No one but Fin could have done it. He was so gay himself that it was difficult to be serious in his presence. He was gay and tall and black-haired, and he was sitting there on the bench, leaning forward, whispering and smiling, teaching Katina to speak English and teaching her how to laugh.

The next day the skies cleared and once again we saw the mountains. We did a patrol over the troops which were already retreating slowly towards Thermopylae, and we met some Messerschmitts and Ju-87s dive-bombing the soldiers. I think we got a few of them, but they got

Sandy. I saw him going down. I sat quite still for thirty seconds and watched his plane spiralling gently downward. I sat and waited for the parachute. I remember switching over my radio and saying quietly, 'Sandy, you must jump now. You must jump; you're getting near the ground.' But there was no parachute.

When we landed and taxied in there was Katina, standing outside the dispersal tent with the Doc; a tiny shrimp of a girl in a dirty print dress, standing there watching the machines as they came in to land. To Fin, as he walked in, she said, 'Tha girisis xana.'

Fin said, 'What does it mean, Pericles?'

'It just means "you are back again",' and he smiled.

The child had counted the aircraft on her fingers as they took off, and now she noticed that there was one missing. We were standing around taking off our parachutes and she was trying to ask us about it, when suddenly someone said, 'Look out. Here they come.' They came through a gap in the hills, a mass of thin, black silhouettes, coming down upon the aerodrome.

There was a scramble for the slit trenches and I remember seeing Fin catch Katina round the waist and carry her off with us, and I remember seeing her fight like a tiger the whole way to the trenches.

As soon as we got into the trench and Fin had let her go, she jumped out and ran over on to the airfield. Down came the Messerschmitts with their guns blazing, swooping so low that you could see the noses of the pilots sticking out under their goggles. Their bullets threw up spurts of dust all around and I saw one of our Hurricanes burst into flames. I saw Katina standing right in the middle of the field, standing firmly with her legs astride and her back to us, looking up at the Germans as they dived past. I have never seen anything smaller and more angry and more fierce in my life. She seemed to be shouting at them, but the noise was great and one could hear nothing at all except the engines and the guns of the aeroplanes.

Then it was over. It was over as quickly as it had begun, and no one said very much except Fin, who said, 'I wouldn't have done that, ever; not even if I was crazy.'

Then evening Monkey got out the squadron records and added Katina's name to the list of members, and the equipment officer was ordered to provide a tent for her. So, on the eleventh of April, 1941, she became a member of the squadron.

In two days she knew the first name or nickname of every pilot and Fin had already taught her to say 'Any luck?' and 'Nice work.'

But that was a time of much activity, and when I try to think of it hour by hour, the whole period becomes hazy in my mind. Mostly, I remember, it was escorting the Blenheims to Valona, and if it wasn't that, it was a ground-strafe of Italian trucks on the Albanian border or an SOS from the Northumberland Regiment saying they were having the hell bombed out of them by half the aircraft in Europe.

None of that can I remember. I can remember nothing of that time clearly, save for two things. The one was Katina and how she was with us all the time; how she was everywhere and how wherever she went the people were pleased to see her. The other thing that I remember was when the Bull came into the mess-tent one evening after a lone patrol. The Bull was an enormous man with massive, slightly hunched shoulders and his chest was like the top of an oak table. Before the war he had done many things, most of them things which one could not do unless one conceded beforehand that there was no difference between life and death. He was quiet and casual and when he came into a room or into a tent, he always looked as though he had made a mistake and hadn't really meant to come in at all. It was getting dark and we were sitting round in the tent playing shove-halfpenny when the Bull came in. We knew that he had just landed.

He glanced around a little apologetically, then he said, 'Hello,' and wandered over to the bar and began to get out a bottle of beer.

Someone said, 'See anything, Bull?'

The Bull said, 'Yes,' and went on fiddling with the bottle of beer.

I suppose we were all very interested in our game of shove-halfpenny because no one said anything else for about five minutes. Then Peter said, 'What did you see, Bull?'

The Bull was leaning against the bar, alternately sipping his beer and trying to make a hooting noise by blowing down the neck of the empty bottle.

Peter said, 'What did you see?'

The Bull put down the bottle and looked up. 'Five S-79s,' he said.

I remember hearing him say it, but I remember also that our game was exciting and that Fin had one more shove to win. We all watched him miss it and Peter said, 'Fin, I think you're going to lose.' And Fin said, 'Go to hell.'

We finished the game, then I looked up and saw the Bull still leaning against the bar making noises with his beer bottle.

He said, 'This sounds like the old Mauretania coming into New York harbour,' and he started blowing into the bottle again.

'What happened with the S-79s?' I said.

He stopped his blowing and put down the bottle.

'I shot them down.'

Everyone heard it. At that moment eleven pilots in that tent stopped what they were doing and eleven heads flicked around and looked at the Bull. He took another drink of his beer and said quietly, 'At one time I counted eighteen parachutes in the air together.'

A few days later he went on patrol and did not come back.

Shortly afterwards Monkey got a message from Athens. It said that the squadron was to move down to Elevsis and from there do a defence of Athens itself and also cover the troops retreating through the Thermopylae Pass.

Katina was to go with the trucks and we told the Doc he was to see that she arrived safely. It would take them a day to make the journey. We flew over the mountains towards the south, fourteen of us, and at two-thirty we landed at Elevsis. It was a lovely aerodrome with runways and hangars; and best of all, Athens was only twenty-five minutes away by car.

That evening, as it was getting dark, I stood outside my tent. I stood with my hands in my pockets watching the sun go down and thinking of the work which we were to do. The more that I thought of it, the more impossible I knew it to be. I looked up, and once again I saw the mountains. They were closer to us here, crowding in upon us on all sides, standing shoulder to shoulder, tall and naked, with their heads in the clouds, surrounding us everywhere save in the south, where lay Piraeus and the open sea. I knew that each night, when it was very dark, when we were all tired and sleeping in our tents, those mountains would move forward, creeping a little closer, making no noise, until at last on the appointed day they would tumble forward with one great rush and push us into the sea.

Fin emerged from his tent.

'Have you seen the mountains?' I said.

'They're full of gods. They aren't any good,' he answered.

'I wish they'd stand still,' I said.

Fin looked up at the great crags of Parnes and Pentelikon.

'They're full of gods,' he said. 'Sometimes, in the middle of the night, when there is a moon, you can see the gods sitting on the summits. There was one on Kataphidi when we were at Paramythia. He was huge, like a house but without any shape and quite black.'

'You saw him?'

'Of course I saw him.'

'When?' I said. 'When did you see him, Fin?'

Fin said, 'Let's go into Athens. Let's go and look at the women in Athens.'

The next day the trucks carrying the ground staff and the equipment rumbled on to the aerodrome, and there was Katina sitting in the front seat of the leading vehicle with the Doc beside her. She waved to us as she jumped down, and she came running towards us, laughing and calling our names in a curious Greek way. She still had on the same dirty print dress and she still had a bandage round her forehead; but the sun was shining in her hair.

We showed her the tent which we had prepared for her and we showed her the small cotton nightdress which Fin had obtained in some mysterious way the night before in Athens. It was white with a lot of little blue birds embroidered on the front and we all thought that it was very beautiful. Katina wanted to put it on at once and it took a long time to persuade her that it was meant only for sleeping in. Six times Fin had to perform a complicated act which consisted of pretending to put on the nightdress, then jumping on to the bed and falling fast asleep. In the end she nodded vigorously and understood.

For the next two days nothing happened, except that the remnants of another squadron came down from the north and joined us. They brought six Hurricanes, so that altogether we had about twenty machines.

Then we waited.

On the third day German reconnaissance aircraft appeared, circling high over Piraeus, and we chased after them but never got up in time to catch them. This was understandable, because our radar was of a very special type. It is obsolete now, and I doubt whether it will ever be used again. All over the country, in all the villages, up on the mountains and out on the islands, there were Greeks, all of whom were connected to our small operations room by field telephone.

We had no operations officer, so we took it in turns to be on duty for the day. My turn came on the fourth day, and I remember clearly what happened.

At six-thirty in the morning the phone buzzed.

'This is A-7,' said a very Greek voice. 'This is A-7. There are noises overhead.'

I looked at the map. There was a little ring with 'A-7' written inside it just beside Yanina. I put a cross on the celluloid which covered the map and wrote 'Noises' beside it, as well as the time: '0631 hours.'

Three minutes later the phone went again.

'This is A-4. This is A-4. There are many noises above me,' said an old quavering voice, 'but I cannot see because there are thick clouds.'

I looked at the map. A-4 was Mt Karava. I made another cross on the celluloid and wrote 'Many noises – 0634,' and then I drew a line between Yanina and Karava. It pointed towards Athens, so I signalled the 'readiness' crew to scramble, and they took off and circled the city. Later they saw a Ju-88 on reconnaissance high above them, but they never caught it. It was in such a way that one worked the radar.

That evening when I came off duty I could not help thinking of the old Greek, sitting all alone in a hut up at A-4; sitting on the slope of Karava looking up into the whiteness and listening all day and all night for noises in the sky. I imagined the eagerness with which he seized the telephone when he heard something, and the joy he must have felt when the voice at the other end repeated his message and thanked him. I thought of his clothes and wondered if they were warm enough and I thought, for some reason, of his boots, which almost certainly had no soles left upon them and were stuffed with tree bark and paper.

That was April seventeenth. It was the evening when Monkey said, 'They say the Germans are at Lamia, which means that we're within range of their fighters. Tomorrow the fun should start.'

It did. At dawn the bombers came over, with the fighters circling around overhead, watching the bombers, waiting to pounce, but doing nothing unless someone interfered with the bombers.

I think we got eight Hurricanes into the air just before they arrived. It was not my turn to go up, so with Katina standing by my side I watched the battle from the ground. The child never said a word. Now and again she moved her head as she followed the little specks of silver dancing high above in the sky. I saw a plane coming down in a trail of black smoke and I looked at Katina. The hatred which was on the face of the child was the fierce burning hatred of an old woman who has hatred in her heart; it was an old woman's hatred and it was strange to see it.

In that battle we lost a sergeant called Donald.

At noon Monkey got another message from Athens. It said that morale was bad in the capital and that every available Hurricane was to fly in formation low over the city in order to show the inhabitants how strong we were and how many aircraft we had. Eighteen of us took off. We flew in tight formation up and down the main streets just above the roofs of the houses. I could see the people looking up, shielding their eyes from the sun, looking at us as we flew over, and in one street I saw an old woman who never looked up at all. None of them waved, and I knew then that they were resigned to their fate. None of them waved, and I knew, although I could not see their faces, that they were not even glad as we flew past.

Then we headed out towards Thermopylae, but on the way we circled the Acropolis twice. It was the first time I had seen it so close.

I saw a little hill – a mound almost, it seemed – and on the top of it I saw the white columns. There were a great number of them, grouped together in perfect order, not crowding one another, white in the sunshine, and I wondered, as I looked at them, how anyone could have put so much on top of so small a hill in such an elegant way.

Then we flew up the great Thermopylae Pass and I saw long lines of vehicles moving slowly southwards towards the sea. I saw occasional puffs of white smoke where a shell landed in the valley and I saw a direct hit on the road which made a gap in the line of trucks. But we saw no enemy aircraft.

When we landed Monkey said, 'Refuel quickly and get in the air again; I think they're waiting to catch us on the ground.'

But it was no use. They came down out of the sky five minutes after we had landed. I remember I was in the pilots' room in Number Two

Hangar, talking to Fin and to a big tall man with rumpled hair called Paddy. We heard the bullets on the corrugated-iron roof of the hangar, then we heard explosions and the three of us dived under the little wooden table in the middle of the room. But the table upset. Paddy set it up again and crawled underneath. 'There's something about being under a table,' he said. 'I don't feel safe unless I'm under a table.'

Fin said, 'I never feel safe.' He was sitting on the floor watching the bullets making holes in the corrugated-iron wall of the room. There was a great clatter as the bullets hit the tin.

Then we became brave and got up and peeped outside the door. There were many Messerschmitt 109s circling the aerodrome, and one by one they straightened out and dived past the hangars, spraying the ground with their guns. But they did something else. They slid back their cockpit hoods and as they came past they threw out small bombs which exploded when they hit the ground and fiercely flung quantities of large lead balls in every direction. Those were the explosions which we had heard, and it was a great noise that the lead balls made as they hit the hangar.

Then I saw the men, the ground crews, standing up in their slit trenches firing at the Messerschmitts with rifles, reloading and firing as fast as they could, cursing and shouting as they shot, aiming ludicrously, hopelessly, aiming at an aeroplane with just a rifle. At Elevsis there were no other defences.

Suddenly the Messerschmitts all turned and headed for home, all except one, which glided down and made a smooth belly landing on the aerodrome.

Then there was chaos. The Greeks around us raised a shout and jumped on to the fire tender and headed out towards the crashed German aeroplane. At the same time more Greeks streamed out from every corner of the field, shouting and yelling and crying for the blood of the pilot. It was a mob intent upon vengeance and one could not blame them; but there were other considerations. We wanted the pilot for questioning, and we wanted him alive.

Monkey, who was standing on the tarmac, shouted to us, and Fin and Paddy and I raced with him towards the station wagon which was standing fifty yards away. Monkey was inside like a flash, started the engine and drove off just as the three of us jumped on the running board. The fire tender with the Greeks on it was not fast and it still had two hundred yards to go, and the other people had a long way to run. Monkey drove quickly and we beat them by about fifty yards.

We jumped up and ran over to the Messerschmitt, and there, sitting in the cockpit, was a fair-haired boy with pink cheeks and blue eyes. I have never seen anyone whose face showed so much fear.

He said to Monkey in English, 'I am hit in the leg.'

We pulled him out of the cockpit and got him into the car, while the Greeks stood around watching. The bullet had shattered the bone in his shin.

We drove him back and as we handed him over to the Doc, I saw Katina standing close, looking at the face of the German. This kid of nine was standing there looking at the German and she could not speak; she could not even move. She clutched the skirt of her dress in her hands and stared at the man's face. 'There is a mistake somewhere,' she seemed to be saying. 'There must be a mistake. This one has pink cheeks and fair hair and blue eyes. This cannot possibly be one of them. This is an ordinary boy.' She watched him as they put him on a stretcher and carried him off, then she turned and ran across the grass to her tent.

In the evening at supper I ate my fried sardines, but I could not eat the bread or the cheese. For three days I had been conscious of my stomach, of a hollow feeling such as one gets just before an operation or while waiting to have a tooth out in the dentist's house. I had had it all day for three days, from the moment I woke up to the time I fell asleep. Peter was sitting opposite me and I asked him about it.

'I've had it for a week,' he said. 'It's good for the bowels. It loosens them.'

'German aircraft are like liver pills,' said Fin from the bottom of the table. 'They are very good for you, aren't they, Doc?'

The Doc said, 'Maybe you've had an overdose.'

'I have,' said Fin, 'I've had an overdose of German liver pills. I didn't read the instructions on the bottle. Take two before retiring.'

Peter said, 'I would love to retire.'

After supper three of us walked down to the hangars with Monkey, who said, 'I'm worried about this ground-strafing. They never attack the hangars because they know that we never put anything inside them. Tonight I think we'll collect four of the aircraft and put them into Number Two Hangar.'

That was a good idea. Normally the Hurricanes were dispersed all over the edge of the aerodrome, but they were being picked off one by one, because it was impossible to be in the air the whole time. The four of us took a machine each and taxied it into Number Two Hangar, and then we pulled the great sliding doors together and locked them.

The next morning, before the sun had risen from behind the mountains, a flock of Ju-87s came over and blew Number Two Hangar right off the face of the earth. Their bombing was good and they did not even hit the hangars on either side of it.

That afternoon they got Peter. He went off towards a village called Khalkis, which was being bombed by Ju-88s, and no one ever saw him again. Gay, laughing Peter, whose mother lived on a farm in

Kent and who used to write to him in long, pale-blue envelopes which he carried about in his pockets.

I had always shared a tent with Peter, ever since I came to the squadron, and that evening after I had gone to bed he came back to that tent. You need not believe me; I do not expect you to, but I am telling you what happened.

I always went to bed first, because there is not room in one of those tents for two people to be turning around at the same time. Peter usually came in two or three minutes afterwards. That evening I went to bed and I lay thinking that tonight he would not be coming. I wondered whether his body lay tangled in the wreckage of his aircraft on the side of some bleak mountain or whether it was at the bottom of the sea, and I hoped only that he had had a decent funeral.

Suddenly I heard a movement. The flap of the tent opened and it shut again. But there were no footsteps. Then I heard him sit down on his bed. It was a noise that I had heard every night for weeks past and always it had been the same. It was just a thump and a creaking of the wooden legs of the camp bed. One after the other the flying boots were pulled off and dropped upon the ground, and as always one of them took three times as long to get off as the other. After that there was the gentle rustle of a blanket being pulled back and then the creakings of the rickety bed as it took the weight of a man's body.

They were sounds I had heard every night, the same sounds in the same order, and now I sat up in bed and said, 'Peter.' It was dark in the tent. My voice sounded very loud.

'Hallo, Peter. That was tough luck you had today.' But there was no answer.

I did not feel uneasy or frightened, but I remember at the time touching the tip of my nose with my finger to make sure that I was there; then because I was very tired, I went to sleep.

In the morning I looked at the bed and saw it had been slept in. But I did not show it to anyone, not even to Fin. I put the blankets back in place myself and patted the pillow.

It was on that day, the twentieth of April, 1941, that we fought the Battle of Athens. It was perhaps the last of the great dog-fighting air battles that will ever be fought, because nowadays the planes fly always in great formation of wings and squadrons, and attack is carried out methodically and scientifically upon the orders of the leader. Nowadays one does not dog-fight at all over the sky except upon very rare occasions. But the Battle of Athens was a long and beautiful dog-fight in which fifteen Hurricanes fought for half an hour with between one hundred and fifty and two hundred German bombers and fighters.

The bombers started coming over early in the afternoon. It was a lovely spring day and for the first time the sun had in it a trace of real summer warmth. The sky was blue, save for a few wispy clouds here and there and the mountains stood out black and clear against the blue of the sky.

Pentelikon no longer hid his head in the clouds. He stood over us, grim and forbidding, watching every move and knowing that each thing we did was of little purpose. Men were foolish and were made only so that they should die, while mountains and rivers went on for ever and did not notice the passing of time. Had not Pentelikon himself many years ago looked down upon Thermopylae and seen a handful of Spartans defending the pass against the invaders; seen them fight until there was not one man left alive among them? Had he not seen the Persians cut to pieces by Leonidas at Marathon, and had he not looked down upon Salamis and upon the sea when Themistocles and the Athenians drove the enemy from their shores, causing them to lose more than two hundred sail? All these things and many more he had seen, and now he looked down upon us, we were as nothing in his eyes. Almost there was a look of scorn upon the face of the mountain, and I thought for a moment that I could hear the laughter of the gods. They knew so well that we were not enough and that in the end we must lose.

The bombers came over just after lunch, and at once we saw that there were a great number of them. We looked up and saw that the sky was full of little silver specks and the sunlight danced and sparkled upon a hundred different pairs of wings.

There were fifteen Hurricanes in all and they fought like a storm in the sky. It is not easy to remember much about such a battle, but I remember looking up and seeing in the sky a mass of small black dots. I remember thinking to myself that those could not be aeroplanes; they simply could not be aeroplanes, because there were not so many aeroplanes in the world.

Then they were on us, and I remember that I applied a little flap so that I should be able to turn in tighter circles; then I remember only one or two small incidents which photographed themselves upon my mind. There were the spurts of flame from the guns of a Messerschmitt as he attacked from the frontal quarter of my starboard side. There was the German whose parachute was on fire as it opened. There was the German who flew up beside me and made rude signs at me with his fingers. There was the Hurricane which collided with a Messerschmitt. There was the aeroplane which collided with a man who was descending in a parachute, and which went into a crazy frightful spin towards the earth with the man and the parachute dangling from its port wing. There were the two bombers which collided while swerving to avoid a fighter, and I remember distinctly seeing a man being thrown clear out of the smoke and debris of the collision, hanging in mid-air with his arms outstretched and his legs apart. I tell you there was nothing that did not happen in that battle.

There was the moment when I saw a single Hurricane doing tight turns around the summit of Mt Parnes with nine Messerschmitts on its tail and then I remember that suddenly the skies seemed to clear. There were no longer any aircraft in sight. The battle was over. I turned around and headed back towards Elevsis, and as I went I looked down and saw Athens and Piraeus and the rim of the sea as it curved around the gulf and travelled southward towards the Mediterranean. I saw the port of Piraeus where the bombs had fallen and I saw the smoke and fire rising above the docks. I saw the narrow coastal plain, and on it I saw tiny bonfires, thin columns of black smoke curling upward and drifting away to the east. They were the fires of aircraft which had been shot down, and I hoped only that none of them were Hurricanes.

Just then I ran straight into a Junkers 88; a straggler, the last bomber returning from the raid. He was in trouble and there was black smoke streaming from one of his engines. Although I shot at him, I don't think that it made any difference. He was coming down anyway. We were over the sea and I could tell that he wouldn't make the land. He didn't. He came down smoothly on his belly in the blue Gulf of Piraeus, two miles from the shore. I followed him and circled, waiting to make sure that the crew got out safely into their dinghy.

Slowly the machine began to sink, dipping its nose under the water and lifting its tail into the air. But there was no sign of the crew. Suddenly, without any warning, the rear gun started to fire. They opened up with their rear gun and the bullets made small jagged holes in my starboard wing. I swerved away and I remember shouting at them. I slid back the hood of the cockpit and shouted, 'You lousy brave bastards. I hope you drown.' The bomber sank soon backwards.

When I got back they were all standing around outside the hangars counting the score, and Katina was sitting on a box with tears rolling down her cheeks. But she was not crying, and Fin was kneeling down beside her, talking to her in English, quietly and gently, forgetting that she could not understand.

We lost one third of our Hurricanes in that battle, but the Germans lost more.

The Doc was dressing someone who had been burnt and he looked up and said, 'You should have heard the Greeks on the aerodrome cheering as the bombers fell out of the sky.'

As we stood around talking, a truck drove up and a Greek got out and said that he had some pieces of body inside. 'This is the watch,' he said, 'that was on the arm.' It was a silver wrist watch with a luminous dial, and on the back there were some initials. We did not look inside the truck.

Now we had, I think, nine Hurricanes left.

That evening a very senior RAF officer came out from Athens and said, 'Tomorrow at dawn you will all fly to Megara. It is about ten miles down the coast. There is a small field there on which you can land. The Army is working on it throughout the night. They have two big rollers there and they are rolling it smooth. The moment you land you must hide your aircraft in the olive grove which is on the south side of the field. The ground staff are going farther south to Argos and you can join them later, but you may be able to operate from Megara for a day or two.'

Fin said, 'Where's Katina? Doc, you must find Katina and see that she gets to Argos safely.'

The Doc said, 'I will,' and we knew that we could trust him.

At dawn the next morning, when it was still dark, we took off and flew to the little field at Megara, ten miles away. We landed and hid our Hurricanes in the olive grove and broke off branches of the trees and put them over the aircraft. Then we sat down on the slope of a small hill and waited for orders.

As the sun rose up over the mountains we looked across the field and saw a mass of Greek villagers coming down from the village of Megara, coming down towards our field. There were many hundreds of them, women and children mostly, and they all came down towards our field, hurrying as they came.

Fin said, 'What the hell,' and we sat up on our little hill and watched, wondering what they were going to do.

They dispersed all around the edge of the field and gathered armfuls of heather and bracken. They carried it out on to the field, and forming themselves into long lines, they began to scatter the heather and the bracken over the grass. They were camouflaging our landing field. The rollers, when they had rolled out the ground and made it flat for landing, had left marks which were easily visible from above, and so the Greeks came out of their village, every man, woman and child, and began to put matters right. To this day I do not know who told them to do it. They stretched in a long line across the field, walking forward slowly and scattering the heather, and Fin and I went out and walked among them.

They were old women and old men mostly, very small and very sad-looking, with dark, deeply wrinkled faces and they worked slowly scattering the heather. As we walked by, they would stop their work and smile, saying something in Greek which we could not understand. One of the children gave Fin a small pink flower and he did not know what to do with it, but walked around carrying it in his hand.

Then we went back to the slope of the hill and waited. Soon the field telephone buzzed. It was the very senior officer speaking. He said that someone must fly back to Elevsis at once and collect important messages and money. He said also that all of us must leave our little field at Megara and go to Argos that evening. The others said that they would wait until I came back with the money so that we could all fly to Argos together.

At the same time, someone had told the two Army men who were still rolling our field, to destroy their rollers so that the Germans would not get them. I remember, as I was getting into my Hurricane, seeing the two huge rollers charging towards each other across the field and I remember seeing the Army men jump aside just before they collided. There was a great crash and I saw all the Greeks who were scattering heather stop in their work and look up. For a moment they stood rock still, looking at the rollers. Then one of them started to run. It was an old woman and she started to run back to the village as fast as she could, shouting something as she went, and instantly every man, woman and child in the field seemed to take fright and ran after her. I wanted to get out and run beside them and explain to them; to say I was sorry but that there was nothing else we could do. I wanted to tell them that we would not forget them and that one day we would come back. But it was no use. Bewildered and frightened, they ran back to their homes, and they did not stop running until they were out of sight, not even the old men.

I took off and flew to Elevsis. I landed on a dead aerodrome. There was not a soul to be seen. I parked my Hurricane, and as I walked over to the hangars the bombers came over once again. I hid in a ditch until they had finished their work, then got up and walked over to the small operations room. The telephone was still on the table, so for some reason I picked up the receiver and said, 'Hallo.'

A rather German voice at the other end answered.

I said, 'Can you hear me?' and the voice said:

'Yes, yes, I can hear you.'

'All right,' I said, 'listen carefully.'

'Yes, continue please.'

'This is the RAF speaking. And one day we will come back, do you understand. One day we will come back.'

Then I tore the telephone from its socket and threw it through the glass of the closed window. When I went outside there was a small man in civilian clothes standing near the door. He had a revolver in one hand and a small bag in the other.

'Do you want anything?' he said in quite good English.

I said, 'Yes, I want important messages and papers which I am to carry back to Argos.'

'Here you are,' he said, as he handed me the bag. 'And good luck.'

I flew back to Megara. There were two Greek destroyers standing offshore, burning and sinking. I circled our field and the others taxied out, took off and we all flew off towards Argos.

The landing ground at Argos was just a kind of small field. It was surrounded by thick olive groves into which we taxied our aircraft for hiding. I don't know how long the field was, but it was not easy to land upon it. You had to come in low hanging on the prop, and the moment you touched down you had to start putting on brake, jerking it on and jerking it off again the moment she started to nose over. But only one man overshot and crashed.

The ground staff had arrived already and as we got out of our aircraft Katina came running up with a basket of black olives, offering them to us and pointing to our stomachs, indicating that we must eat.

Fin bent down and ruffled her hair with his hand. He said, 'Katina, one day we must go into town and buy you a new dress.' She smiled at him but did not understand and we all started to eat black olives.

Then I looked around and saw that the wood was full of aircraft. Around every corner there was an aeroplane hidden in the trees, and when we asked about it we learned that the Greeks had brought the whole of their air force down to Argos and parked them in that little wood. They were peculiar ancient models, not one of them less than five years old, and I don't know how many dozen there were there.

That night we slept under the trees. We wrapped Katina up in a large flying suit and gave her a flying helmet for a pillow, and after she had gone to sleep we sat around eating black olives and drinking resinato out of an enormous cask. But we were very tired, and soon we fell asleep.

All the next day we saw the truckloads of troops moving down the road towards the sea, and as often as we could we took off and flew above them.

The Germans kept coming over and bombing the road near by, but they had not yet spotted our airfield.

Later in the day we were told that every available Hurricane was to take off at six p.m. to protect an important shipping move, and the nine machines, which were all that were now left, were refuelled and got ready. At three minutes to six we began to taxi out of the olive grove on to the field.

The first two machines took off, but just as they left the ground something black swept down out of the sky and shot them both down in flames. I looked around and saw at least fifty Messerschmitt 110s circling our field, and even as I looked some of them turned and came down upon the remaining seven Hurricanes which were waiting to take off.

There was no time to do anything. Each one of our aircraft was hit in that first swoop, although funnily enough only one of the pilots was hurt. It was impossible now to take off, so we jumped out of our aircraft, hauled the wounded pilot out of his cockpit and ran with him back to the slit trenches, to the wonderful big, deep zig-zagging slit trenches which had been dug by the Greeks.

The Messerschmitts took their time. There was no opposition either from the ground or from the air, except that Fin was firing his revolver.

It is not a pleasant thing to be ground-strafed especially if they have cannon in their wings; and unless one has a deep slit trench in which to lie, there is no future in it. For some reason, perhaps because they thought it was a good joke, the German pilots went for the slit trenches before they bothered about the aircraft. The first ten minutes was spent rushing madly around the corners of the trenches so as not to be caught in a trench which ran parallel with the line of flight of the attacking aircraft. It was a hectic, dreadful ten minutes, with everyone shouting 'Here comes another,' and scrambling and rushing to get around the corner into the other section of the trench.

Then the Germans went for the Hurricanes and at the same time for the mass of old Greek aircraft parked all around the olive grove, and one by one, methodically and systematically, they set them on fire. The noise was terrific, and everywhere – in the trees, on the rocks and on the grass – the bullets splattered.

I remember peeping cautiously over the top of our trench and seeing a small white flower growing just a few inches away from my nose. It was pure white and it had three petals. I remember looking past it and seeing three of the Germans diving on my own Hurricane which was parked on the other side of the field and I remember shouting at them, although I do not know what I said.

Then suddenly I saw Katina. She was running out from the far corner of the aerodrome, running right out into the middle of this mass of blazing guns and burning aircraft, running as fast as she could. Once she stumbled, but she scrambled to her feet again and went on running. Then she stopped and stood looking up, raising her fists at the planes as they flew past.

Now as she stood there, I remember seeing one of the Messerschmitts turning and coming in low straight towards her and I remember thinking that she was so small that she could not be hit. I remember seeing the spurts of flame from his guns as he came, and I remember seeing the child, for a split second, standing quite still, facing the machine. I remember that the wind was blowing in her hair.

Then she was down.

The next moment I shall never forget. On every side, as if by magic, men appeared out of the ground. They swarmed out of their trenches and like a crazy mob poured on to the aerodrome, running towards the tiny little bundle which lay motionless in the middle of the field. They ran fast, crouching as they went, and I remember jumping up out of my slit trench and joining with them. I remember thinking of nothing at all and watching the boots of the man in front of me, noticing that he was a little bow-legged and that his blue trousers were much too long.

I remember seeing Fin arrive first, followed closely by a sergeant called Wishful, and I remember seeing the two of them pick up Katina and start running with her back towards the trenches. I saw her leg, which was just a lot of blood and bones, and I saw her chest where the blood was spurting out on to her white print dress; I saw, for a moment, her face, which was white as the snow on top of Olympus.

I ran beside Fin, and as he ran, he kept saying, 'The lousy bastards, the lousy, bloody bastards'; and then as we got to our trench I remember looking round and finding that there was no longer any noise or shooting. The Germans had gone.

Fin said, 'Where's the Doc?' and suddenly there he was, standing beside us, looking at Katina – looking at her face.

The Doc gently touched her wrist and without looking up he said, 'She is not alive.'

They put her down under a little tree, and when I turned away I saw on all sides the fires of countless burning aircraft. I saw my own Hurricane burning near by and I stood staring hopelessly into the flames as they danced around the engine and licked against the metal of the wings.

I stood staring into the flames, and as I stared, the fire became a deeper red and I saw beyond it not a tangled mass of smoking wreckage, but the flames of a hotter and intenser fire which now burned and smouldered in the hearts of the people of Greece.

Still I stared, and as I stared I saw in the centre of the fire, whence the red flames sprang, a bright, white heat, shining bright and without any colour.

As I stared, the brightness diffused and became soft and yellow like sunlight, and through it, beyond it, I saw a young child standing in the middle of a field with the sunlight shining in her hair. For a moment she stood looking up into the sky, which was clear and blue and without any clouds; then she turned and looked towards me, and as she turned I saw that the front of her white print dress was stained deep red, the colour of blood.

Then there was no longer any fire or any flames and I saw before me only the glowing twisted wreckage of a burned-out plane. I must have been standing there for quite a long time.

YESTERDAY WAS BEAUTIFUL

He bent down and rubbed his ankle where it had been sprained with the walking so that he couldn't see the ankle bone. Then he straightened up and looked around him. He felt in his pocket for a packet of cigarettes, took one out and lit it. He wiped the sweat from his forehead with the back of his hand and he stood in the middle of the street looking around him.

'Dammit, there must be someone here,' he said aloud, and he felt better when he heard the sound of his voice.

He walked on, limping, walking on the toe of his injured foot, and when he turned the next corner he saw the sea and the way the road curved around between the ruined houses and went on down the hill to the edge of the water. The sea was calm and black. He could clearly make out the line of hills on the mainland in the distance and he estimated that it was about eight miles away. He bent down again to rub his ankle. 'God dammit,' he said. 'There must be some of them still alive.' But there was no noise anywhere, and there was a stillness about the buildings and about the whole village which made it seem as though the place had been dead for a thousand years.

Suddenly he heard a little noise as though someone had moved his feet on the gravel and when he looked around he saw the old man. He was sitting in the shade on a stone beside a water trough, and it seemed strange that he hadn't seen him before.

'Health to you,' said the pilot. 'Ghia sou,'

He had learned Greek from the people up around Larissa and Yanina.

The old man looked up slowly, turning his head but not moving his shoulders. He had a greyish-white beard. He had a cloth cap on his head and he wore a shirt which had no collar. It was a grey shirt with thin black stripes. He looked at the pilot and he was like a blind man who looks towards something but does not see.

'Old man, I am glad to see you. Are there no other people in the village?'

There was no answer.

The pilot sat down on the edge of the water trough to rest his ankle.

'I am Inglese,' he said. 'I am an aviator who has been shot down and jumped out by the parachute. I am Inglese.'

The old man moved his head slowly up and down. 'Inglesus,' he said quietly. 'You are Inglesus.'

'Yes, I am looking for someone who has a boat. I wish to go back to the mainland.'

There was a pause, and when he spoke, the old man seemed to be talking in his sleep. 'They come over all the time,' he said. 'The Germanoi they come over all the time.' The voice had no expression. He looked up into the sky, then he turned and looked behind him in the sky. 'They will come again today, Inglese. They will come again soon.' There was no anxiety in his voice. There was no expression whatsoever. 'I do not understand why they come to us,' he added.

The pilot said, 'Perhaps not today. It is late now. I think they have finished for today.'

'I do not understand why they come to us, Inglese. There is no one here.'

The pilot said, 'I am looking for a man who has a boat who can take me across to the mainland. Is there a boat owner now in the village?'

'A boat?'

'Yes.' There was a pause while the question was considered.

'There is such a man.'

'Could I find him? Where does he live?'

'There is a man in the village who owns a boat.'

'Please tell me what is his name?'

The old man looked up again at the sky. 'Joannis is the one here who has a boat.'

'Joannis who?'

'Joannis Spirakis,' and he smiled. The name seemed to have a significance for the old man and he smiled.

'Where does he live?' the pilot said. 'I am sorry to be giving you this trouble.'

'Where he lives?'

'Yes.'

The old man considered this too. Then he turned and looked down the street towards the sea. 'Joannis was living in the house nearest to the water. But his house isn't any more. The Germanoi hit it this morning. It was early and it was still dark. You can see the house isn't any more. It isn't any more.'

'Where is he now?'

'He is living in the house of Antonina Angelou. That house there with the red colour on the window.' He pointed down the street.

'Thank you very much. I will go and call on the boat owner.'

'Ever since he was a boy,' the old man went on, 'Joannis has had a boat. His boat is white with a blue line around the top,' and he smiled again. 'But at the moment I do not think he will be in the house. His wife will be there. Anna will be there, with Antonina Angelou. They will be home.'

'Thank you again. I will go and speak to his wife.'

The pilot got up and started to go down the street, but almost at once the man called after him, 'Inglese.'

The pilot turned.

'When you speak to the wife of Joannis – when you speak to Anna ... you should remember something.' He paused, searching for words. His voice wasn't expressionless any longer and he was looking up at the pilot.

'Her daughter was in the house when the Germanoi came. It is just something that you should remember.'

The pilot stood on the road waiting.

'Maria. Her name was Maria.'

'I will remember,' answered the pilot. 'I am sorry.'

He turned away and walked down the hill to the house with the red windows. He knocked and waited. He knocked again louder and waited. There was the noise of footsteps and the door opened.

It was dark in the house and all he could see was that the woman had black hair and that her eyes were black like her hair. She looked at the pilot who was standing out in the sunshine.

'Health to you,' he said. 'I am Inglese.'

She did not move.

'I am looking for Joannis Spirakis. They say that he owns a boat.'

Still she did not move.

'Is he in the house?'

'No.'

'Perhaps his wife is here. She could know where he is.'

At first there was no answer. Then the woman stepped back and held open the door. 'Come in, Inglesus,' she said.

He followed her down the passage and into a back room. The room was dark because there was no glass in the windows – only patches of cardboard. But he could see the old woman who was sitting on the bench with her arms resting on the table. She was tiny. She was small like a child and her face was like a little screwed-up ball of brown paper.

'Who is it?' she said in a high voice.

The first woman said, 'This is an Inglesus. He is looking for your husband because he requires a boat.'

'Health to you, Inglesus,' the old woman said.

The pilot stood by the door, just inside the room. The first woman stood by the window and her arms hung down by her sides.

The old woman said, 'Where are the Germanoi?' Her voice seemed bigger than her body.

'Now they are around Lamia.'

'Lamia.' She nodded. 'Soon they will be here. Perhaps tomorrow they will be here. But I do not care. Do you hear me, Inglesus, I do not care.' She was leaning forward a little in her chair and the pitch of her voice was becoming higher. 'When they come it will be nothing new. They have already been here. Every day they have been here. Every day they come over and they bom bom bom and you shut your eyes and you open them again and you get up and you go outside and the houses are just dust – and the people.' Her voice rose and fell.

She paused, breathing quickly, then she spoke more quietly. 'How many have you killed, Inglesus?'

The pilot put out a hand and leaned against the door to rest his ankle.

'I have killed some,' he said quietly.

'How many?'

'As many as I could, old woman. We cannot count the number of men.'

'Kill them all,' she said softly. 'Go and kill every man and every woman and every baby. Do you hear me, Inglesus? You must kill them all.' The little brown ball of paper became smaller and more screwed up. 'The first one I see I shall kill.' She paused. 'And then, Inglesus, and then later, his family will hear that he is dead.'

The pilot did not say anything. She looked up at him and her voice was different. 'What is it you want Inglesus?'

He said, 'About the Germanoi, I am sorry. But there is not much we can do.'

'No,' she answered, 'there is nothing. And you?'

'I am looking for Joannis. I wish to use his boat.'

'Joannis,' she said quietly, 'he is not here. He is out.'

Suddenly she pushed back the bench, got to her feet and went out of the room. 'Come,' she said. He followed her down the passage towards the front door. She looked even smaller when she was standing than when she was sitting down and she walked quickly down the passage towards the door and opened it. She stepped out into the sunshine and for the first time he saw how very old she was.

She had no lips. Her mouth was just wrinkled skin like the rest of her face and she screwed up her eyes at the sun and looked up the road.

'There he is,' she said. 'That's him.' She pointed at the old man who was sitting beside the drinking trough.

The pilot looked at the man. Then he turned to speak to the old woman, but she had disappeared into the house.

THEY SHALL NOT GROW OLD

The two of us sat outside the hangar on wooden boxes.

It was noon. The sun was high and the heat of the sun was like a close fire. It was hotter than hell out there by the hangar. We could feel the hot air touching the inside of our lungs when we breathed and we found it better if we almost closed our lips and breathed in quickly; it was cooler that way. The sun was upon our shoulders and upon our backs, and all the time the sweat seeped out from our skin, trickled down our necks, over our chests and down our stomachs. It collected just where our belts were tight around the tops of our trousers and it filtered under the tightness of our belts where the wet was very uncomfortable and made prickly heat on the skin.

Our two Hurricanes were standing a few yards away, each with that patient, smug look which fighter planes have when the engine is not turning, and beyond them the thin black strip of the runway sloped down towards the beaches and towards the sea. The black surface of the runway and the white grassy sand on the sides of the runway shimmered and shimmered in the sun. The heat haze hung like a vapour over the aerodrome.

The Stag looked at his watch.

'He ought to be back,' he said.

The two of us were on readiness, sitting there for orders to take off. The Stag moved his feet on the hot ground.

'He ought to be back,' he said.

It was two and a half hours since Fin had gone and he certainly should have come back by now. I looked up into the sky and listened. There was the noise of airmen talking beside the petrol wagon and there was the faint pounding of the sea upon the beaches; but there was no sign of an aeroplane. We sat a little while longer without speaking.

'It looks as though he's had it,' I said.

'Yep,' said the Stag. 'It looks like it.'

The Stag got up and put his hands into the pockets of his khaki shorts. I got up too. We stood looking northwards into the clear sky, and we shifted our feet on the ground because of the softness of the tar and because of the heat.

'What was the name of that girl?' said the Stag without turning his head.

'Nikki,' I answered.

The Stag sat down again on his wooden box, still with his hands in his pockets and he looked down at the ground between his feet. The Stag was the oldest pilot in the squadron; he was twenty-seven. He had a mass of coarse ginger hair which he never brushed. His face was pale, even after all this time in the sun, and covered with freckles. His mouth was wide and tight closed. He was not tall but his shoulders under his khaki shirt were broad and thick like those of a wrestler. He was a quiet person.

'He'll probably be all right,' he said, looking up. 'And anyway, I'd like to meet the Vichy Frenchman who can get Fin.'

We were in Palestine fighting the Vichy French in Syria. We were at Haifa, and three hours before the Stag, Fin and I had gone on readiness. Fin had flown off in response to a urgent call from the Navy, who had phoned up and said that there were two French destroyers moving out of Beyrouth harbour. Please go at once and see where they are going, said the Navy. Just fly up the coast and have a look and come back quickly and tell us where they are going.

So Fin had flown off in his Hurricane. The time had gone by and he had not returned. We knew that there was no longer much hope. If he hadn't been shot down, he would have run out of petrol some time ago.

I looked down and I saw his blue RAF cap which was lying on the ground where he had thrown it as he ran to his aircraft, and I saw the oil stains on top of the cap and the shabby bent peak. It was difficult now to believe that he had gone. He had been in Egypt, in Libya and in Greece. On the aerodrome and in the mess we had had him with us all of the time. He was gay and tall and full of laughter, this Fin, with black hair and a long straight nose which he used to stroke up and down with the tip of his finger. He had a way of listening to you while you were telling a story, leaning back in his chair with his face to the ceiling but with his eyes looking down on the ground, and it was only last night at supper that he had suddenly said, 'You know, I wouldn't mind marrying Nikki. I think she's a good girl.'

The Stag was sitting opposite him at the time, eating baked beans.

'You mean just occasionally,' he said.

Nikki was in a cabaret in Haifa.

'No,' said Fin. 'Cabaret girls make fine wives. They are never unfaithful. There is no novelty for them in being unfaithful; that would be like going back to the old job.'

The Stag had looked up from his beans. 'Don't be such a bloody fool,' he said. 'You wouldn't really marry Nikki.'

'Nikki,' said Fin with great seriousness, 'comes of a fine family. She is a good girl. She never uses a pillow when she sleeps. Do you know why she never uses a pillow when she sleeps?'

'No.'

The others at the table were listening now. Everyone was listening to Fin talking about Nikki.

'Well, when she was very young she was engaged to be married to an officer in the French Navy. She loved him greatly. Then one day when they were sunbathing together on the beach he happened to mention to her that he never used a pillow when he slept. It was just one of those little things which people say to each other for the sake of conversation. But Nikki never forgot it. From that time onwards she began to practise sleeping without a pillow. One day the French officer was run over by a truck and killed; but although to her it was very uncomfortable, she still went on sleeping without a pillow to preserve the memory of her lover.'

Fin took a mouthful of beans and chewed them slowly. 'It is a sad story,' he said. 'It shows that she is a good girl. I think I would like to marry her.'

That was what Fin had said last night at supper. Now he was gone and I wondered what little thing Nikki would do in his memory.

The sun was hot on my back and I turned instinctively in order to take the heat upon the other side of my body. As I turned, I saw Carmel and the town of Haifa. I saw the steep pale-green slope of the mountain as it dropped down towards the sea, and below it I saw the town and the bright colours of the houses shining in the sun. The houses with their white-washed walls covered the sides of Carmel and the red roofs of the houses were like a rash on the face of the mountain.

Walking slowly towards us from the grey corrugated iron hangar, came the three men who were the next crew on readiness. They had their yellow Mae Wests slung over their shoulders and they came walking slowly towards us, holding their helmets in their hands as they came.

When they were close, the Stag said, 'Fin's had it,' and they said, 'Yes, we know.' They sat down on the wooden boxes which we had been using, and immediately the sun was upon their shoulders and upon their backs and they began to sweat. The Stag and I walked away.

The next day was a Sunday and in the morning we flew up the Lebanon valley to ground-strafe an aerodrome called Rayak. We flew past Hermon who had a hat of snow upon his head, and we came down out of the sun on to Rayak and on to the French bombers on the aerodrome and began our strafing. I remember that as we flew past, skimming low over the ground, the doors of the French bombers opened. I remember seeing a whole lot of women in white dresses running out across the aerodrome; I remember particularly their white dresses.

You see, it was a Sunday and the French pilots had asked their ladies out from Beyrouth to look over the bombers. The Vichy pilots had said, come out on Sunday morning and we will show you our aeroplanes. It was a very Vichy French thing for them to do.

So when we started shooting, they all tumbled out and began to run across the aerodrome in their white Sunday dresses.

I remember hearing Monkey's voice over the radio, saying, 'Give them a chance, give them a chance,' and the whole squadron wheeled around and circled the aerodrome once while the women ran over the grass in every direction. One of them stumbled and fell twice and one of them was limping and being helped by a man, but we gave them time. I remember watching the small bright flashes of a machine gun on the ground and thinking that they should at least have stopped their shooting while we were waiting for their white-dressed women to get out of the way.

That was the day after Fin had gone. The next day the Stag and I sat once more at readiness on the wooden boxes outside the hangar. Paddy, a big fair-haired boy, had taken Fin's place and was sitting with us.

It was noon. The sun was high and the heat of the sun was like a close fire. The sweat ran down our necks, down inside our shirts, over our chests and stomachs, and we sat there waiting for the time when we would be relieved. The Stag was sewing the strap on to his helmet with a needle and cotton and telling of how he had seen Nikki the night before in Haifa and of how he had told her about Fin.

Suddenly we heard the noise of an aeroplane. The Stag stopped his talking and we all looked up. The noise was coming from the north, and it grew louder and louder as the aeroplane flew closer, and then the Stag said suddenly, 'It's a Hurricane.'

The next moment it was circling the aerodrome, lowering its wheels to land.

'Who is it?' said the fair-haired Paddy. 'No one's gone out this morning.'

Then, as it glided past us on to the runway, we saw the number on the tail of the machine, H.4427, and we knew that it was Fin.

We were standing up now, watching the machine as it taxied towards us, and when it came up close and swung round for parking we saw Fin in the cockpit. He waved his hand at us, grinned and got out. We ran up and shouted at him, 'Where've you been?' 'Where in the hell have you been?' 'Did you force-land and get away again?' 'Did you find a woman in Beyrouth?' 'Fin, where in the hell have you been?'

Others were coming up and crowding around him now, fitters and riggers and the men who drove the fire tender, and they all waited to hear what Fin would say. He stood there pulling off his helmet, pushing back his black hair with his hand, and he was so astonished at our behaviour that at first he merely looked at us and did not speak. Then he laughed and he said, 'What in the hell's the matter? What's the matter with all of you?'

'Where have you been?' we shouted. 'Where have you been for two days?'

Upon the face of Fin there was a great and enormous astonishment. He looked quickly at his watch.

'Five past twelve,' he said. 'I left at eleven, one hour and five minutes ago. Don't be a lot of damn fools. I must go and report quickly. The Navy will want to know that those destroyers are still in the harbour at Beyrouth.'

He started to walk away; I caught his arm.

'Fin,' I said quietly, 'you've been away since the day before yesterday. What's the matter with you?'

He looked at me and laughed.

'I've seen you organize much better jokes than this one,' he said. 'It isn't so funny. It isn't a bit funny.' And he walked away.

We stood there, the Stag, Paddy and I, the fitters, the riggers and the men who drove the fire-engine, watching Fin as he walked away. We looked at each other, not knowing what to say or to think, understanding nothing, knowing nothing except that Fin had been serious when he spoke and that what he said he had believed to be true. We knew this because we knew Fin, and we knew it because when one has been together as we had been together, then there is never any doubting of anything that anyone says when he is talking about his flying; there can only be a doubting of one's self. These men were doubting themselves, standing there in the sun doubting themselves, and the Stag was standing by the wing of Fin's machine peeling off with his fingers little flakes of paint which had dried up and cracked in the sun.

Someone said, 'Well, I'll be buggered,' and the men turned and started to walk quietly back to their jobs. The next three pilots on readiness came walking slowly towards us from the grey corrugated-iron hangar, walking slowly under the heat of the sun and swinging their helmets in their hands as they came. The Stag, Paddy and I walked over to the pilots' mess to have a drink and lunch.

The mess was a small white wooden building with a verandah. Inside there were two rooms, one a sitting room with armchairs and magazines and a hole in the wall through which you could buy drinks, and the other a dining room with one long wooden table. In the sitting room we found Fin talking to Monkey, our CO. The other pilots were sitting around listening and everybody was drinking beer. We knew that it was really a serious business in spite of the beer and the armchairs; that Monkey was doing what he had to do and doing it in the only way possible. Monkey was a rare man, tall with a handsome face, an Italian bullet wound in his leg and a casual friendly efficiency. He never laughed out loud, he just choked and grunted deep in his throat.

Fin was saying, 'You must go easy, Monkey; you must help me to stop thinking that I've gone mad.'

Fin was being serious and sensible, but he was worried as hell.

'I have told you all I know,' he said. 'That I took off at eleven o'clock, that I climbed up high, that I flew to Beyrouth, saw the two French destroyers and came back, landing at five past twelve. I swear to you that that is all I know.'

He looked around at us, at the Stag and me, at Paddy and Johnny and the half-dozen other pilots in the room, and we smiled at him and nodded to show him that we were with him, not against him, and that we believed what he said.

Monkey said, 'What in the hell am I going to say to Headquarters at Jerusalem? I reported you missing. Now I've got to report your return. They'll insist on knowing where you've been.'

The whole thing was getting to be too much for Fin. He was sitting upright, tapping with the fingers of his left hand on the leather arm of his chair, tapping with quick sharp taps, leaning forward, thinking, thinking, fighting to think, tapping on the arm of the chair and then he began tapping the floor with his foot as well. The Stag could stand it no longer.

'Monkey,' he said, 'Monkey, let's just leave it all for a bit. Let's leave it and perhaps Fin will remember something later on.'

Paddy, who was sitting on the arm of the Stag's chair, said, 'Yes, and meanwhile we could tell HQ that Fin had force-landed in a field in Syria, taken two days to repair his aircraft, then flown home.'

Everybody was helping Fin. The pilots were all helping him. In the mind of each of us was the certain knowledge that here was something that concerned us greatly. Fin knew it, although that was all he knew, and the others knew it because one could see it upon their faces. There was a tension, a fine high-drawn tension in the room, because here for the first time was something which was neither bullets nor fire nor the coughing of an engine nor burst tyres nor blood in the cockpit nor yesterday nor today, nor even tomorrow. Monkey felt it too, and he said, 'Yes, let's have another drink and leave it for a bit. I'll tell HQ that you force-landed in Syria and managed to get off again later.'

We had some more beer and went in to lunch. Monkey ordered bottles of Palestine white wine with the meal to celebrate Fin's return.

After that no one mentioned the thing at all; we did not even talk about it when Fin wasn't there. But each one of us continued to think about it secretly, knowing for certain that it was something important and that it was not finished. The tension spread quickly through the squadron and it was with all the pilots.

Meanwhile the days went by and the sun shone upon the aerodrome and upon the aircraft and Fin took his place among us flying in the normal way.

Then one day, I think it was about a week later, we did another ground-strafe of Rayak aerodrome. There were six of us, with Monkey leading and Fin flying on his starboard side. We came in low over Rayak and there was plenty of light flak, and as we went in on the first run, Paddy's machine was hit. As we wheeled for the second run we saw his Hurricane wing gently over and dive straight to the ground at the edge of the aerodrome. There was a great billow of white smoke as it hit, then the flames, and as the flames spread the smoke turned from white to black and Paddy was with it. Immediately there was a crackle over the radio and I heard Fin's voice, very excited, shouting into his microphone, shouting, 'I've remembered it. Hello, Monkey, I've remembered it all,' and Monkey's calm slow reply, 'OK Fin, OK; don't forget it.'

We did our second run and then Monkey led us quickly away, weaving in and out of the valleys, with the bare grey brown hills far above us on either side, and all the way home, all through the half-hour's flight, Fin never stopped shouting over the RT. First he would call to Monkey and say, 'Hello, Monkey, I've remembered it, all of it; every bit of it.' Then he would say, 'Hello, Stag, I've remembered it, all of it; I can't forget it now.' He called me and he called Johnny and he called Wishful; he called us all separately over and over again, and he was so excited that sometimes he shouted too loudly into his mike and we could not hear what he was saying.

When we landed, we dispersed our aircraft and because Fin for some reason had to park his at the far side of the aerodrome, the rest of us were in the Operations room before him.

The Ops room was beside the hangar. It was a bare place with a large table in the middle of the floor on which there was a map of the area. There was another smaller table with a couple of telephones, a few wooden chairs and benches and at one end the floor was stacked with Mae Wests, parachutes and helmets. We were standing there taking off our flying clothing and throwing it on to the floor at the end of the room when Fin arrived. He came quickly into the doorway and stopped. His black hair was standing up straight and untidy because of the way in which he had pulled off his helmet; his face was shiny with sweat and his khaki shirt was dark and wet. His mouth was open and he was breathing quickly. He looked as though he had been running. He looked like a child who had rushed downstairs into a room full of grown-ups to say that the cat has had kittens in the nursery and who does not know how to begin.

We had all heard him coming because that was what we had been waiting for. Everyone stopped what they were doing and stood still, looking at Fin.

Monkey said, 'Hello Fin,' and Fin said, 'Monkey, you've got to believe this because it's what happened.'

Monkey was standing over by the table with the telephones; the Stag was near him, square short ginger-haired Stag, standing up straight, holding a Mae West in his hand, looking at Fin. The others were at the far end of the room. When Fin spoke, they began to move up quietly until they were closer to him, until they reached the edge of the big map table which they touched with their hands. There they stood, looking at Fin, waiting for him to begin.

He started at once, talking quickly, then calming down and talking more slowly as he got into his story. He told everything, standing there by the door of the Ops room, with his yellow Mae West still on him and with his helmet and oxygen mask in his hand. The others stayed where they were and listened, and as I listened to him, I forgot that it was Fin speaking and that we were in the Ops room at Haifa; I forgot everything and went with him on his journey, and did not come back until he had finished.

'I was flying at about twenty thousand,' he said. 'I flew over Tyre and Sidon and over the Damour River and then I flew inland over the Lebanon hills, because I intended to approach Beyrouth from the east. Suddenly I flew into cloud, thick white cloud which was so thick and dense that I could see nothing except the inside of my cockpit. I couldn't understand it, because a moment before everything had been clear and blue and there had been no cloud anywhere.

'I started to lose height to get out of the cloud and I went down and down and still I was in it. I knew that I must not go too low because of the hills, but at six thousand the cloud was still around me. It was so thick that I could see nothing, not even the nose of my machine nor the wings, and the cloud condensed on the windshield and little rivers of water ran down the glass and got blown away by the slipstream. I have never seen cloud like that before. It was thick and white right up to the edges of the cockpit. I felt like a man on a magic carpet, sitting there alone in this little glass-topped cockpit, with no wings, no tail, no engine and no aeroplane.

'I knew that I must get out of this cloud, so I turned and flew west over the sea away from the mountains; then I came down low by my altimeter. I came down to five hundred feet, four hundred, three hundred, two hundred, one hundred, and the cloud was still around me. For a moment I paused. I knew that it was unsafe to go lower. Then, quite suddenly, like a gust of wind, came the feeling that there was nothing below me; no sea nor earth nor anything else and slowly, deliberately, I opened the throttle, pushed the stick hard forward and dived.

'I did not watch the altimeter; I looked straight ahead through the windshield at the whiteness of the cloud and I went on diving. I sat there pressing the stick forward, keeping her in the dive, watching the vast clinging whiteness of the cloud and I never once wondered where I was going. I just went.

'I do not know how long I sat there; it may have been minutes and it may have been hours; I know only that as I sat there and kept her diving, I was certain that what was below me was neither mountains nor rivers nor earth nor sea and I was not afraid.

'Then I was blinded. It was like being half asleep in bed when someone turns on the light.

'I came out of the cloud so suddenly and so quickly that I was blinded. There was no space of time between being in it and being out of it. One moment I was in it and the whiteness was thick around me and in that same moment I was out of it and the light was so bright that I was blinded. I screwed up my eyes and held them tight closed for several seconds.

'When I opened them everything was blue, more blue than anything that I had ever seen. It was not a dark blue, nor was it a bright blue; it was a blue blue, a pure shining colour which I had never seen before and which I cannot describe. I looked around. I looked up above me and behind me. I sat up and peered below me through the glass of the cockpit and everywhere it was blue. It was bright and clear, like pleasant sunlight, but there was no sun.

'Then I saw them.

'Far ahead and above I saw a long thin line of aircraft flying across the sky. They were moving forward in a single black line, all at the same speed, all in the same direction, all close up, following one behind the other, and the line stretched across the sky as far as the eye could see. It was the way they moved ahead, the urgent way in which they pressed forward forward forward like ships sailing before a great wind, it was from this that I knew everything. I do not know why or how I knew it, but I knew as I looked at them that these were the pilots and air crews who had been killed in battle, who now, in their own aircraft were making their last flight, their last journey.

'As I flew higher and closer I could recognize the machines themselves. I saw in that long procession nearly every type there was. I saw Lancasters and Dorniers, Halifaxes and Hurricanes, Messerschmitts, Spitfires, Stirlings, Savoia 79s, Junker 88s, Gladiators, Hampdens, Macchi 200s, Blenheims, Focke Wulfs, Beaufighters, Swordfish and Heinkels. All these and many more I saw, and the moving line reached across the blue sky both to the one side and to the other until it faded from sight.

'I was close to them now and I began to sense that I was being sucked towards them regardless of what I wished to do. There was a wind which took hold of my machine, blew it over and tossed it about like a leaf and I was pulled and sucked as by a giant vortex towards the other aeroplanes. There was nothing I could do for I was in the vortex and in the arms of the wind. This all happened very quickly, but I remember it clearly. I felt the pull on my aircraft becoming stronger; I was whisked forward faster and faster, and then suddenly I was flying in the procession itself, moving forward with the others, at the same speed and on the same course. Ahead of me, close enough for me to see the colour of the paint on its wings, was a Swordfish, an old Fleet Air Arm Swordfish. I could see the heads and helmets of the observer and the pilot as they sat in their cockpits, the one behind the other. Ahead of the Swordfish there was a Dornier, a Flying Pencil, and beyond the Dornier there were others which I could not recognize from where I was.

'We flew on and on. I could not have turned and flown away even if I had wanted to. I do not know why, although it may have been something to do with the vortex and with the wind, but I knew that it was so. Moreover, I was not really flying my aircraft; it flew itself. There was no manoeuvring to reckon with, no speed, no height, no throttle, no stick, no nothing. Once I glanced down at my instruments and saw that they were all dead, just as they are when the machine is sitting on the ground.

'So we flew on. I had no idea how fast we went. There was no sensation of speed and for all I know, it was a million miles an hour. Now I come to think of it, I never once during that time felt either hot or cold or hungry or thirsty; I felt none of those things. I felt no fear, because I knew nothing of which to be afraid. I felt no worry, because I could remember nothing or think of nothing about which to be worried. I felt no desire to do anything that I was not doing or to have anything that I did not have, because there was nothing that I wished to do and there was nothing that I wished to have. I felt only pleasure at being where I was, at seeing the wonderful light and the beautiful colour around me. Once I caught sight of my face in the cockpit mirror and I saw that I was smiling, smiling with my eyes and with my mouth, and when I loooked away I knew that I was still smiling, simply because that was the way I felt. Once, the observer in the Swordfish ahead of me turned and waved his hand. I slid back the roof of my cockpit and waved back. I remember that even when I opened the cockpit, there was no rush of air and no rush of cold or heat, nor was there any pressure of the slipstream on my hand. Then I noticed that they were all waving at each other, like children on a roller-coaster and I turned and waved at the man in the Macchi behind me.

'But there was something happening along the line. Far up in front I could see that the aeroplanes had changed course, were wheeling around to the left and losing height. The whole procession, as it reached a certain point, was banking around and gliding downwards in a wide, sweeping circle. Instinctively I glanced down over the cockpit, and there I saw spread out below me a vast green plain. It was green and smooth and beautiful; it reached to the far edges of the horizon where the blue of the sky came down and merged with the green of the plain.

'And there was the light. Over to the left, far away in the distance was a bright white light, shining bright and without any colour. It was as though the sun, but something far bigger than the sun, something without shape or form whose light was bright but not blinding, was lying on the far edge of the green plain. The light spread outwards from a centre of brilliance and it spread far up into the sky and far out over the plain. When I saw it, I could not at first look away from it. I had no desire to go towards it, into it, and almost at once the desire and the longing became so intense that several times I tried to pull my aircraft out of the line and fly straight towards it; but it was not possible and I had to fly with the rest.

'As they banked around and lost height I went with them, and we began to glide down towards the green plain below. Now that I was closer, I could see the great mass of aircraft upon the plain itself. They were everywhere, scattered over the ground like currants upon a green carpet. There were hundreds and hundreds of them, and each minute, each second almost, their numbers grew as those in front of me landed and taxied to a standstill.

'Quickly we lost height. Soon I saw that the ones just in front of me were lowering their wheels and preparing to land. The Dornier next but one to me levelled off and touched down. Then the old Swordfish. The pilot turned a little to the left out of the way of the Dornier and landed beside him. I turned to the left of the Swordfish and levelled off. I looked out of the cockpit at the ground, judging the height, and I saw the green of the ground blurred as it rushed past me and below me.

'I waited for my aircraft to sink and to touch down. It seemed to take a long time. "Come on," I said. "Come on, come on." I was only about six feet up, but she would not sink. "Get down," I shouted, "please *get down*." I began to panic. I became frightened. Suddenly I noticed that I was gaining speed. I cut all the switches but it made no difference. The aircraft was gathering speed, going faster and faster, and I looked around and saw behind me the long procession of aircraft dropping down out of the sky and sweeping in to land. I saw the mass of machines upon the ground, scattered far across the plain and away on one side I saw the light, that shining white light which shone so brightly over the great plain and to which I longed to go. I know that had I been able to land, I would have started to run towards that light the moment I got out of my aircraft.

'And now I was flying away from it. My fear grew. As I flew faster and farther away, the fear took hold of me until soon I was fighting crazy mad, pulling at the stick, wrestling with the aeroplane, trying to turn it around, back towards the light. When I saw that it was impossible, I tried to kill myself. I really wanted to kill myself then. I tried to dive the aircraft into the ground, but it flew on straight. I tried to jump out of the cockpit, but there was a hand upon my shoulder which held me down. I tried to bang my head against the sides of the cockpit, but it made no difference and I sat there fighting with my machine and with everything until suddenly I noticed that I was in cloud. I was in the same thick white cloud as before; and I seemed to be climbing. I looked behind me, but the cloud had closed in all round. There was nothing now but this vast impenetrable whiteness. I began to feel sick and giddy. I did not care any longer what happened one way or the other, I just sat there limply, letting the machine fly on by itself.

'It seemed a long time and I am sure that I sat there for many hours. I must have gone to sleep. As I slept, I dreamed. I dreamed not of the things that I had just seen, but of the things of my ordinary life, of the squadron, of Nikki and of the aerodrome here at Haifa. I dreamed that I was sitting at readiness outside the hangar with two others, that a request came from the Navy for someone to do a quick recco over Beyrouth; and because I was first up, I jumped into my Hurricane and went off. I dreamed that I passed over Tyre and Sidon and over the Damour River, climbing up to twenty thousand as I went. Then I turned inland over the Lebanon hills, swung around and approached Beyrouth from the east. I was above the town, peering over the side of the cockpit, looking for the harbour and trying to find the two French destroyers. Soon I saw them, saw them clearly, tied up close alongside each other by the wharf, and I banked around and dived for home as fast as I could.

'The Navy's wrong, I thought to myself as I flew back. The destroyers are still in the harbour. I looked at my watch. An hour and a half. "I've been quick," I said. "They'll be pleased." I tried to call up on the radio to give the information, but I couldn't get through.

'Then I came back here. When I landed, you all crowded around me and asked me where I had been for two days, but I could remember nothing. I did not remember anything except the flight to Beyrouth until just now, when I saw Paddy being shot down. As his machine hit the ground, I found myself saying, "You lucky bastard. You lucky,

lucky bastard," and as I said it, I knew why I was saying it and remembered everything. That was when I shouted to you over the radio. That was when I remembered.'

Fin had finished. No one had moved or said anything all the time that he had been talking. Now it was only Monkey who spoke. He shuffled his feet on the floor, turned and looked out of the window and said quietly, almost in a whisper, 'Well, I'll be damned,' and the rest of us went slowly back to the business of taking off our flying clothing and stacking it in the corner of the room on the floor; all except the Stag, square short Stag, who stood there watching Fin as Fin walked slowly across the room to put away his clothing.

After Fin's story, the squadron returned to normal. The tension which had been with us for over a week, disappeared. The aerodrome was a happier place in which to be. But no one every mentioned Fin's journey. We never once spoke about it together, not even when we got drunk in the evening at the Excelsior in Haifa.

The Syrian campaign was coming to an end. Everyone could see that it must finish soon, although the Vichy people were still fighting fiercely south of Beyrouth. We were still flying. We were flying a great deal over the fleet, which was bombarding the coast, for we had the job of protecting them from the Junker 88s which came over from Rhodes. It was on the last one of these flights over the fleet that Fin was killed.

We were flying high above the ships when the Ju-88s came over in force and there was a battle. We had only six Hurricanes in the air; there were many of the Junkers and it was a good fight. I do not remember much about what went on at the time. One never does. But I remember that it was a hectic, chasing fight, with the Junkers diving for the ships, with the ships barking at them, throwing up everything into the air so that the sky was full of white flowers which blossomed quickly and grew and blew away with the wind. I remember the German who blew up in mid-air, quickly, with just a white flash, so that where the bomber had been, there was nothing left except tiny little pieces falling slowly downwards. I remember the one that had its rear turret shot away, which flew along with the gunner hanging out of the tail by his straps, struggling to get back into the machine. I remember one, a brave one who stayed up above to fight us while the others went down to dive-bomb. I remember that we shot him up and I remember seeing him turn slowly over on to his back, pale green belly upwards like a dead fish, before finally he spun down.

And I remember Fin.

I was close to him when his aircraft caught fire. I could see the flames coming out of the nose of his machine and dancing over the engine cowling. There was black smoke coming from the exhaust of his Hurricane.

I flew up close and I called to him over the RT. 'Hello, Fin,' I called, 'you'd better jump.'

His voice came back, calm and slow. 'It's not so easy.'

'Jump,' I shouted, 'jump quickly.'

I could see him sitting there under the glass roof of the cockpit. He looked towards me and shook his head.

'It's not so easy,' he answered. 'I'm a bit shot up. My arms are shot up and I can't undo the straps.'

'Get out,' I shouted. 'For God's sake, get out,' but he did not answer. For a moment his aircraft flew on, straight and level, then gently, like a dying eagle, it dipped a wing and dived towards the sea. I watched it as it went; I watched the thin trail of black smoke which it made across the sky, and as I watched, Fin's voice came again over the radio, clear and slow. 'I'm a lucky bastard,' he was saying. 'A lucky, lucky bastard.'

BEWARE OF THE DOG

Down below there was only a vast white undulating sea of cloud. Above there was the sun, and the sun was white like the clouds, because it is never yellow when one looks at it from high in the air.

He was still flying the Spitfire. His right hand was on the stick and he was working the rudder-bar with his left leg alone. It was quite easy. The machine was flying well. He knew what he was doing.

Everything is fine, he thought. I'm doing all right. I'm doing nicely. I know my way home. I'll be there in half an hour. When I land I shall taxi in and switch off my engine and I shall say, help me to get out, will you. I shall make my voice sound ordinary and natural and none of them will take any notice. Then I shall say, someone help me to get out. I can't do it alone because I've lost one of my legs. They'll all laugh and think that I'm joking and I shall say, all right, come and have a look, you unbelieving bastards. Then Yorky will climb up on to the wing and look inside. He'll probably be sick because of all the blood and the mess. I shall laugh and say, for God's sake, help me get out.

He glanced down again at his right leg. There was not much of it left. The cannon-shell had taken him on the thigh, just above the knee, and now there was nothing but a great mess and a lot of blood. But there was no pain. When he looked down, he felt as though he were seeing something that did not belong to him. It had nothing to do with him. It was just a mess which happened to be there in the cockpit; something strange and unusual and rather interesting. It was like finding a dead cat on the sofa.

He really felt fine, and because he still felt fine, he felt excited and unafraid.

I won't even bother to call up on the radio for the blood-wagon, he thought. It isn't necessary. And when I land I'll sit there quite normally and say, some of you fellows come and help me out, will you, because I've lost one of my legs. That will be funny. I'll laugh a little while I'm saying it; I'll say it calmly and slowly, and they'll think I'm joking. When Yorky comes up on to the wing and gets sick, I'll say, Yorky you old son of a bitch, have you fixed my car yet. Then when I get out I'll make my report. Later I'll go up to London. I'll take that half bottle of whisky with me and I'll give it to Bluey. We'll

sit in her room and drink it. I'll get the water out of the bathroom
tap. I won't say much until it's time to go to bed, then I'll say, Bluey
I've got a surprise for you. I lost a leg today. But I don't mind so long
as you don't. It doesn't even hurt. We'll go everywhere in cars. I
always hated walking except when I walked down the street of the
coppersmiths in Baghdad, but I could go in a rickshaw. I could go
home and chop wood, but the head always flies off the axe. Hot water,
that's what it needs; put it in the bath and make the handle swell. I
chopped lots of wood last time I went home and I put the axe in the
bath ...

Then he saw the sun shining on the engine cowling of his machine.
He saw the sun shining on the rivets in the metal, and he remembered
the aeroplane and he remembered where he was. He realized that he
was no longer feeling good; that he was sick and giddy. His head kept
falling forward on to his chest because his neck seemed no longer to
have any strength. But he knew that he was flying the Spitfire. He
could feel the handle of the stick between the fingers of his right hand.

I'm going to pass out, he thought. Any moment now I'm going to
pass out.

He looked at his altimeter. Twenty-one thousand. To test himself
he tried to read the hundreds as well as the thousands. Twenty-one
thousand and what? As he looked the dial became blurred and he
could not even see the needle. He knew then that he must bale out;
that there was not a second to lose, otherwise he would become
unconscious. Quickly, frantically, he tried to slide back the hood with
his left hand, but he had not the strength. For a second he took his
right hand off the stick and with both hands he managed to push the
hood back. The rush of cold air on his face seemed to help. He had a
moment of great clearness. His actions became orderly and precise.
That is what happens with a good pilot. He took some quick deep
breaths from his oxygen mask, and as he did so, he looked out over
the side of the cockpit. Down below there was only a vast white sea
of cloud and he realized that he did not know where he was.

It'll be the Channel, he thought. I'm sure to fall in the drink.

He throttled back, pulled off his helmet, undid his straps and pushed
the stick hard over to the left. The Spitfire dipped its port wing and
turned smoothly over on to its back. The pilot fell out.

As he fell, he opened his eyes, because he knew that he must not
pass out before he had pulled the cord. On one side he saw the sun;
on the other he saw the whiteness of the clouds, and as he fell, as he
somersaulted in the air, the white clouds chased the sun and the sun
chased the clouds. They chased each other in a small circle; they ran
faster and faster and there was the sun and the clouds and the clouds
and the sun, and the clouds came nearer until suddenly there was no
longer any sun but only a great whiteness. The whole world was white

and there was nothing in it. It was so white that sometimes it looked black, and after a time it was either white or black, but mostly it was white. He watched it as it turned from white to black, then back to white again, and the white stayed for a long time, but the black lasted only for a few seconds. He got into the habit of going to sleep during the white periods, of waking up just in time to see the world when it was black. The black was very quick. Sometimes it was only a flash, a flash of black lightning. The white was slow and in the slowness of it, he always dozed off.

One day, when it was white, he put out a hand and he touched something. He took it between his fingers and crumpled it. For a time he lay there, idly letting the tips of his fingers play with the thing which they had touched. Then slowly he opened his eyes, looked down at his hand and saw that he was holding something which was white. It was the edge of a sheet. He knew it was a sheet because he could see the texture of the material and the stitchings on the hem. He screwed up his eyes and opened them again quickly. This time he saw the room. He saw the bed in which he was lying; he saw the grey walls and the door and the green curtains over the window. There were some roses on the table by his bed.

Then he saw the basin on the table near the roses. It was a white enamel basin and beside it there was a small medicine glass.

This is a hospital, he thought. I am in a hospital. But he could remember nothing. He lay back on his pillow, looking at the ceiling and wondering what had happened. He was gazing at the smooth greyness of the ceiling which was so clean and grey, and then suddenly he saw a fly walking upon it. The sight of this fly, the suddenness of seeing this small black speck on a sea of grey, brushed the surface of his brain, and quickly, in that second, he remembered everything. He remembered the Spitfire and he remembered the altimeter showing twenty-one thousand feet. He remembered the pushing back of the hood with both hands and he remembered the baling out. He remembered his leg.

It seemed all right now. He looked down at the end of the bed, but he could not tell. He put one hand underneath the bedclothes and felt for his knees. He found one of them, but when he felt for the other, his hand touched something which was soft and covered in bandages.

Just then the door opened and a nurse came in.

'Hello,' she said. 'So you've waked up at last.'

She was not good-looking, but she was large and clean. She was between thirty and forty and she had fair hair. More than that he did not notice.

'Where am I?'

'You're a lucky fellow. You landed in a wood near the beach. You're in Brighton. They brought you in two days ago, and now you're all fixed up. You look fine.'

'I've lost a leg,' he said.

'That's nothing. We'll get you another one. Now you must go to sleep. The doctor will be coming to see you in about an hour.' She picked up the basin and the medicine glass and went out.

But he did not sleep. He wanted to keep his eyes open because he was frightened that if he shut them again everything would go away. He lay looking at the ceiling. The fly was still there. It was very energetic. It would run forward very fast for a few inches, then it would stop. Then it would run forward again, stop, run forward, and every now and then it would take off and buzz around viciously in small circles. It always landed back in the same place on the ceiling and started running and stopping all over again. He watched it for so long that after a while it was no longer a fly, but only a black speck upon a sea of grey, and he was still watching it when the nurse opened the door, and stood aside while the doctor came in. He was an Army doctor, a major, and he had some last war ribbons on his chest. He was bald and small, but he had a cheerful face and kind eyes.

'Well, well,' he said. 'So you've decided to wake up at last. How are you feeling?'

'I feel all right.'

'That's the stuff. You'll be up and about in no time.'

The doctor took his wrist to feel his pulse.

'By the way,' he said, 'some of the lads from your squadron were ringing up and asking about you. They wanted to come along and see you, but I said that they'd better wait a day or two. Told them you were all right and that they could come and see you a little later on. Just lie quiet and take it easy for a bit. Got something to read?' He glanced at the table with the roses. 'No. Well, nurse will look after you. She'll get you anything you want.' With that he waved his hand and went out, followed by the large clean nurse.

When they had gone, he lay back and looked at the ceiling again. The fly was still there and as he lay watching it he heard the noise of an aeroplane in the distance. He lay listening to the sound of its engines. It was a long way away. I wonder what it is, he thought. Let me see if I can place it. Suddenly he jerked his head sharply to one side. Anyone who has been bombed can tell the noise of a Junkers 88. They can tell most other German bombers for that matter, but especially a Junkers 88. The engines seem to sing a duet. There is a deep vibrating bass voice and with it there is a high pitched tenor. It is the singing of the tenor which makes the sound of a Ju-88 something which one cannot mistake.

He lay listening to the noise and he felt quite certain about what it was. But where were the sirens and where the guns? That German pilot certainly had a nerve coming near Brighton alone in daylight.

The aircraft was always far away and soon the noise faded away into the distance. Later on there was another. This one, too, was far away, but there was the same deep undulating bass and the high swinging tenor and there was no mistaking it. He had heard that noise every day during the Battle.

He was puzzled. There was a bell on the table by the bed. He reached out his hand and rang it. He heard the noise of footsteps down the corridor. The nurse came in.

'Nurse, what were those aeroplanes?'

'I'm sure I don't know. I didn't hear them. Probably fighters or bombers. I expect they were returning from France. Why, what's the matter?'

'They were Ju-88s. I'm sure they were Ju-88s. I know the sound of the engines. There were two of them. What were they doing over here?'

The nurse came up to the side of his bed and began to straighten out the sheets and tuck them in under the mattress.

'Gracious me, what things you imagine. You mustn't worry about a thing like that. Would you like me to get you something to read?'

'No, thank you.'

She patted his pillow and brushed back the hair from his forehead with her hand.

'They never come over in daylight any longer. You know that. They were probably Lancasters or Flying Fortresses.'

'Nurse.'

'Yes.'

'Could I have a cigarette?'

'Why certainly you can.'

She went out and came back almost at once with a packet of Players and some matches. She handed one to him and when he had put it in his mouth, she struck a match and lit it.

'If you want me again,' she said, 'just ring the bell,' and she went out.

Once towards evening he heard the noise of another aircraft. It was far away, but even so he knew that it was a single-engined machine. It was going fast; he could tell that. He could not place it. It wasn't a Spit, and it wasn't a Hurricane. It did not sound like an American engine either. They make more noise. He did not know what it was, and it worried him greatly. Perhaps I am very ill, he thought. Perhaps I am imagining things. Perhaps I am a little delirious. I simply do not know what to think.

That evening the nurse came in with a basin of hot water and began to wash him.

'Well,' she said, 'I hope you don't think that we're being bombed.'

She had taken off his pyjama top and was soaping his right arm with a flannel. He did not answer.

She rinsed the flannel in the water, rubbed more soap on it, and began to wash his chest.

'You're looking fine this evening,' she said. 'They operated on you as soon as you came in. They did a marvellous job. You'll be all right. I've got a brother in the RAF,' she added. 'Flying bombers.'

He said, 'I went to school in Brighton.'

She looked up quickly. 'Well, that's fine,' she said. 'I expect you'll know some people in the town.'

'Yes,' he said, 'I know quite a few.'

She had finished washing his chest and arms. Now she turned back the bedclothes so that his left leg was uncovered. She did it in such a way that his bandaged stump remained under the sheets. She undid the cord of his pyjama trousers and took them off. There was no trouble because they had cut off the right trouser leg so that it could not interfere with the bandages. She began to wash his left leg and the rest of his body. This was the first time he had had a bed-bath and he was embarrassed. She laid a towel under his leg and began washing his foot with the flannel. She said, 'This wretched soap won't lather at all. It's the water. It's as hard as nails.'

He said, 'None of the soap is very good now and, of course, with hard water it's hopeless.' As he said it he remembered something. He remembered the baths which he used to take at school in Brighton, in the long stone-floored bathroom which had four baths in a row. He remembered how the water was so soft that you had to take a shower afterwards to get all the soap off your body, and he remembered how the foam used to float on the surface of the water, so that you could not see your legs underneath. He remembered that sometimes they were given calcium tablets because the school doctor used to say that soft water was bad for the teeth.

'In Brighton,' he said, 'the water isn't . . .'

He did not finish the sentence. Something had occurred to him; something so fantastic and absurd that for a moment he felt like telling the nurse about it and having a good laugh.

She looked up. 'The water isn't what?' she said.

'Nothing,' he answered. 'I was dreaming.'

She rinsed the flannel in the basin, wiped the soap off his leg and dried him with a towel.

'It's nice to be washed,' he said. 'I feel better.' He was feeling his face with his hand. 'I need a shave.'

'We'll do that tomorrow,' she said. 'Perhaps you can do it yourself then.'

That night he could not sleep. He lay awake thinking of the Junkers

88s and of the hardness of the water. He could think of nothing else. They were Ju-88s, he said to himself. I know they were. And yet it is not possible, because they would not be flying around so low over here in broad daylight. I know that it is true and yet I know that it is impossible. Perhaps I am ill. Perhaps I am behaving like a fool and do not know what I am doing or saying. Perhaps I am delirious. For a long time he lay awake thinking these things, and once he sat up in bed and said aloud, 'I will prove that I am not crazy. I will make a little speech about something complicated and intellectual. I will talk about what to do with Germany after the war.' But before he had time to begin, he was asleep.

He woke just as the first light of day was showing through the slit in the curtains over the window. The room was still dark, but he could tell that it was already beginning to get light outside. He lay looking at the grey light which was showing through the slit in the curtain and as he lay there he remembered the day before. He remembered the Junkers 88s and the hardness of the water; he remembered the large pleasant nurse and the kind doctor, and now a small grain of doubt took root in his mind and it began to grow.

He looked around the room. The nurse had taken the roses out the night before. There was nothing except the table with a packet of cigarettes, a box of matches and an ashtray. The room was bare. It was no longer warm or friendly. It was not even comfortable. It was cold and empty and very quiet.

Slowly the grain of doubt grew, and with it came fear, a light, dancing fear that warned but did not frighten; the kind of fear that one gets not because one is afraid, but because one feels that there is something wrong. Quickly the doubt and the fear grew so that he became restless and angry, and when he touched his forehead with his hand, he found that it was damp with sweat. He knew then that he must do something; that he must find some way of proving to himself that he was either right or wrong, and he looked up and saw again the window and the green curtains. From where he lay, that window was right in front of him, but it was fully ten yards away. Somehow he must reach it and look out. The idea became an obsession with him and soon he could think of nothing except the window. But what about his leg? He put his hand underneath the bedclothes and felt the thick bandaged stump which was all that was left on the right hand side. It seemed all right. It didn't hurt. But it would not be easy.

He sat up. Then he pushed the bedclothes aside and put his left leg on the floor. Slowly, carefully, he swung his body over until he had both hands on the floor as well; then he was out of bed, kneeling on the carpet. He looked at the stump. It was very short and thick, covered with bandages. It was beginning to hurt and he could feel it throbbing. He wanted to collapse, lie down on the carpet and do nothing, but he knew that he must go on.

With two arms and one leg, he crawled over towards the window. He would reach forward as far as he could with his arms, then he would give a little jump and slide his left leg along after them. Each time he did it, it jarred his wound so that he gave a soft grunt of pain, but he continued to crawl across the floor on two hands and one knee. When he got to the window he reached up, and one at a time he placed both hands on the sill. Slowly he raised himself up until he was standing on his left leg. Then quickly he pushed aside the curtains and looked out.

He saw a small house with a grey tiled roof standing alone beside a narrow lane, and immediately behind it there was a ploughed field. In front of the house there was an untidy garden, and there was a green hedge separating the garden from the lane. He was looking at the hedge when he saw the sign. It was just a piece of board nailed to the top of a short pole, and because the hedge had not been trimmed for a long time, the branches had grown out around the sign so that it seemed almost as though it had been placed in the middle of the hedge. There was something written on the board with white paint. He pressed his head against the glass of the window, trying to read what it said. The first letter was a G, he could see that. The second was an A, and the third was an R. One after another he managed to see what the letters were. There were three words, and slowly he spelled the letters out aloud to himself as he managed to read them. G-A-R-D-E A-U C-H-I-E-N, *Garde au chien*. That is what it said.

He stood there balancing on one leg and holding tightly to the edges of the window sill with his hands, staring at the sign and at the whitewashed lettering of the words. For a moment he could think of nothing at all. He stood there looking at the sign, repeating the words over and over to himself. Slowly he began to realize the full meaning of the thing. He looked up at the cottage and at the ploughed field. He looked at the small orchard on the left of the cottage and he looked at the green countryside beyond. 'So this is France,' he said. 'I am in France.'

Now the throbbing in his right thigh was very great. It felt as though someone was pounding the end of his stump with a hammer and suddenly the pain became so intense that it affected his head. For a moment he thought he was going to fall. Quickly he knelt down again, crawled back to the bed and hoisted himself in. He pulled the bedclothes over himself and lay back on the pillow, exhausted. He could still think of nothing at all except the small sign by the hedge and the ploughed field and the orchard. It was the words on the sign that he could not forget.

It was some time before the nurse came in. She came carrying a basin of hot water and she said, 'Good morning, how are you today?'

He said, 'Good morning, nurse.'

The pain was still great under the bandages, but he did not wish to tell this woman anything. He looked at her as she busied herself with getting the washing things ready. He looked at her more carefully now. Her hair was very fair. She was tall and big-boned and her face seemed pleasant. But there was something a little uneasy about her eyes. They were never still. They never looked at anything for more than a moment and they moved too quickly from one place to another in the room. There was something about her movements also. They were too sharp and nervous to go well with the casual manner in which she spoke.

She set down the basin, took off his pyjama top and began to wash him.

'Did you sleep well?'

'Yes.'

'Good,' she said. She was washing his arms and his chest.

'I believe there's someone coming down to see you from the Air Ministry after breakfast,' she went on. 'They want a report or something. I expect you know all about it. How you got shot down and all that. I won't let him stay long, so don't worry.'

He did not answer. She finished washing him and gave him a toothbrush and some toothpowder. He brushed his teeth, rinsed his mouth and spat the water out into the basin.

Later she brought him his breakfast on a tray, but he did not want to eat. He was still feeling weak and sick and he wished only to lie still and think about what had happened. And there was a sentence running through his head. It was a sentence which Johnny, the Intelligence Officer of his squadron, always repeated to the pilots every day before they went out. He could see Johnny now, leaning against the wall of the dispersal hut with his pipe in his hand, saying, 'And if they get you, don't forget, 'just your name, rank and number. Nothing else. For God's sake, say nothing else.'

'There you are,' she said as she put the tray on his lap. 'I've got you an egg. Can you manage all right?'

'Yes.'

She stood beside the bed. 'Are you feeling all right?'

'Yes.'

'Good. If you want another egg I might be able to get you one.'

'This is all right.'

'Well, just ring the bell if you want any more.' And she went out.

He had just finished eating, when the nurse came in again.

She said, 'Wing Commander Roberts is here. I've told him that he can only stay for a few minutes.'

She beckoned with her hand and the Wing Commander came in.

'Sorry to bother you like this,' he said.

He was an ordinary RAF officer, dressed in a uniform which was a little shabby. He wore wings and a DFC. He was fairly tall and thin with plenty of black hair. His teeth, which were irregular and widely spaced, stuck out a little even when he closed his mouth. As he spoke he took a printed form and a pencil from his pocket and he pulled up a chair and sat down.

'How are you feeling?'

There was no answer.

'Tough luck about your leg. I know how you feel. I hear you put up a fine show before they got you.'

The man in the bed was lying quite still, watching the man in the chair.

The man in the chair said, 'Well, let's get this stuff over. I'm afraid you'll have to answer a few questions so that I can fill in this combat report. Let me see now, first of all, what was your squadron?'

The man in the bed did not move. He looked straight at the Wing Commander and he said, 'My name is Peter Williamson, my rank is Squadron Leader and my number is nine seven two four five seven.'

ONLY THIS

That night the frost was very heavy. It covered the hedges and whitened the grass in the fields so that it seemed almost as though it had been snowing. But the night was clear and beautiful and bright with stars, and the moon was nearly full.

The cottage stood alone in a corner of the big field. There was a path from the front door which led across the field to a stile and on over the next field to a gate which opened on to the lane about three miles from the village. There were no other houses in sight and the country around was open and flat and many of the fields were under the plough because of the war.

The light of the moon shone upon the cottage. It shone through the open window into the bedroom where the woman was asleep. She slept lying on her back, with her face upturned to the ceiling, with her long hair spread out around her on the pillow, and although she was asleep, her face was not the face of someone who is resting. Once she had been beautiful, but now there were thin furrows running across her forehead and there was a tightness about the way in which her skin was stretched over the cheekbones. But her mouth was still gentle, and as she slept, she did not close her lips.

The bedroom was small, with a low ceiling, and for furniture there was a dressing-table and an armchair. The clothes of the woman lay over the back of the armchair where she had put them when she undressed. Her black shoes were on the floor beside the chair. On the dressing-table there was a hairbrush, a letter and a large photograph of a young boy in uniform who wore a pair of wings on the left side of his tunic. It was a smiling photograph, the kind that one likes to send to one's mother and it had a thin, black frame made of wood. The moon shone through the open window and the woman slept her restless sleep. There was no noise anywhere save for the soft, regular noise of her breathing and the rustle of the bedclothes as she stirred in her sleep.

Then, from far away, there came a deep, gentle rumble which grew and grew and became louder and louder until soon the whole sky seemed to be filled with a great noise which throbbed and throbbed and kept on throbbing and did not stop.

Right at the beginning, even before it came close, the woman had heard the noise. In her sleep she had been waiting for it, listening for the noise and dreading the moment when it would come. When she heard it, she opened her eyes and for a while she lay quite still, listening. Then she sat up, pushed the bedclothes aside and got out of bed. She went over to the window and placing her hands on the window sill, she leaned out, looking up into the sky; and her long hair fell down over her shoulders, over the thin cotton nightdress which she wore. For many minutes she stood there in the cold, leaning out of the window, hearing the noise, looking up and searching the sky; but she saw only the bright moon and the stars.

'God keep you,' she said aloud. 'Oh dear God keep you safe.'

Then she turned and went quickly over to the bed, pulled the blankets away and wrapped them round her shoulders like a shawl. She slipped her bare feet into the black shoes and walked over to the armchair and pushed it forward so that it was right up in front of the window. Then she sat down.

The noise and the throbbing overhead was very great. For a long time it continued as the huge procession of bombers moved towards the south. All the while the woman sat huddled in her blankets, looking out of the window into the sky.

Then it was over. Once more the night became silent. The frost lay heavy on the field and on the hedges and it seemed as though the whole countryside was holding its breath. An army was marching in the sky. All along the route people had heard the noise and knew what it was; they knew that soon, even before they had gone to sleep, there would be a battle. Men drinking beer in the pubs had stopped their talking in order to listen. Families in their houses had turned off the radio and gone out into their gardens, where they stood looking up into the sky. Soldiers arguing in their tents had stopped their shouting, and men and women walking home at night from the factories had stood still on the road, listening to the noise.

It is always the same. As the bombers move south across the country at night, the people who hear them become strangely silent. For those women whose men are with the planes, the moment is not an easy one to bear.

Now they had gone, and the woman lay back in the armchair and closed her eyes, but she did not sleep. Her face was white and the skin seemed to have been drawn tightly over her cheeks and gathered up in wrinkles around her eyes. Her lips were parted and it was as though she were listening to someone talking. Almost she could hear the sound of his voice as he used to call to her from outside the window when he came back from working in the fields. She could hear him saying he was hungry and asking what there was for supper, and then when he came in he would put his arm around her shoulder and talk to her about what he had been doing all day. She would bring in the supper and he would sit down and start to eat and always he would say, why don't you have some and she never knew what to answer except that she wasn't hungry. She would sit and watch him and pour out his tea, and after a while she would take his plate and go out into the kitchen to get him some more.

It was not easy having only one child. The emptiness when he was not there and the knowing all the time that something might happen; the deep conscious knowing that there was nothing else to live for except this; that if something did happen, then you too would be dead. There would be no use in sweeping the floor or washing the dishes or cleaning the house; there would be no use in gathering wood for the fire or in feeding the hens; there would be no use in living.

Now, as she sat there by the open window she did not feel the cold; she felt only a great loneliness and a great fear. The fear took hold of her and grew upon her so that she could not bear it, and she got up from the chair and leaned out of the window again, looking up into the sky. And as she looked the night was no longer beautiful; it was cold and clear and immensely dangerous. She did not see the fields or the hedges or the carpet of frost upon the countryside; she saw only the depths of the sky and the danger that was there.

Slowly she turned and sank down again into her chair. Now the fear was great. She could think of nothing at all except that she must see him and be with him, that she must see him now because tomorrow would be too late. She let her head rest against the back of the chair and when she closed her eyes she saw the aircraft; she saw it clearly in the moonlight, moving forward through the night like a great, black bird. She was close to it and she could see the way in which the nose of the machine reached out far ahead of everything, as though the bird was craning its neck in the eagerness of its passage. She could see the markings on the wings and on the body and she knew that he was inside. Twice she called to him, but there was no answer; then the fear and the longing welled up within her so that she could stand it no longer and it carried her forward through the night and on and on until she was with him, beside him, so close that she could have touched him had she put out her hand.

He was sitting at the controls with gloves on his hands, dressed in a great bulky flying-suit which made his body look huge and shapeless and twice its normal size. He was looking straight ahead at the instruments on the panel, concentrating upon what he was doing and thinking of nothing except flying the machine.

Now she called to him again and he heard her. He looked around and when he saw her, he smiled and stretched out a hand and touched her shoulder, and then all the fear and the loneliness and the longing went out of her and she was happy.

For a long time she stood beside him watching him as he flew the machine. Every now and then he would look around and smile at her, and once he said something, but she could not hear what it was because of the noise of the engines. Suddenly he pointed ahead through the glass windshield of the aeroplane and she saw that the sky was full of searchlights. There were many hundreds of them; long white fingers of light travelling lazily across the sky, swaying this way and that, working in unison so that sometimes several of them would come together and meet in the same spot and after a while they would separate and meet again somewhere else, all the time searching the night for the bombers which were moving in on the target.

Behind the searchlights she saw the flak. It was coming up from the town in a thick many-coloured curtain, and the flash of the shells as they burst in the sky lit up the inside of the bomber.

He was looking straight ahead now, concentrating upon the flying, weaving through the searchlights and going directly into this curtain of flak, and she watched and waited and did not dare to move or to speak lest she distract him from his task.

She knew that they had been hit when she saw the flames from the nearest engine on the left side. She watched them through the glass of the side panel, licking against the surface of the wing as the wind blew them backwards, and she watched them take hold of the wing and come dancing over the black surface until they were right up under the cockpit itself. At first she was not frightened. She could see him sitting there, very cool, glancing continually to one side, watching the flames and flying the machine, and once he looked quickly around and smiled at her and she knew then that there was no danger. All around she saw the searchlights and the flak and the explosions of the flak and the colours of the tracer, and the sky was not a sky but just a small confined space which was so full of lights and explosions that it did not seem possible that one could fly through it.

But the flames were brighter now on the left wing. They had spread over the whole surface. They were alive and active, feeding on the fabric, leaning backwards in the wind which fanned them and encouraged them and gave them no chance of going out.

Then came the explosion. There was a blinding white flash and a hollow *crumph* as though someone had burst a blown-up paper bag; then there was nothing but flames and thick whitish-grey smoke. The flames were coming up through the floor and through the sides of the cockpit; the smoke was so thick that it was difficult to see and almost impossible to breathe. She became terrified and panicky because he was still sitting there at the controls, flying the machine, fighting to keep it on an even keel, turning the wheel first to one side, then to the other, and suddenly there was a blast of cold air and she had a vague impression of urgent crouching figures scrambling past her and throwing themselves away from the burning aircraft.

Now the whole thing was a mass of flames and through the smoke she could see him still sitting there, fighting with the wheel while the crew got out, and as he did so he held one arm up over his face because the heat was so great. She rushed forward and took him by the shoulders and shook him and shouted, 'Come on, quickly, you must get out, quickly, quickly.'

Then she saw that his head had fallen forward upon his chest and that he was limp and unconscious. Frantically she tried to pull him out of the seat and towards the door, but he was too limp and heavy. The smoke was filling her lungs and her throat so that she began to retch and gasp for breath. She was hysterical now, fighting against death and against everything and she managed to get her hands under his arms and drag him a little way towards the door. But it was impossible to get him farther. His legs were tangled around the wheel and there was a buckle somewhere which she could not undo. She knew then that it was impossible, that there was no hope because of the smoke and the fire and because there was no time; and suddenly all the strength drained out of her body. She fell down on top of him and began to cry as she had never cried before.

Then came the spin and the fierce rushing dive downwards and she was thrown forward into the fire so that the last she knew was the bright yellow of the flames and the smell of the burning.

Her eyes were closed and her head was resting against the back of the chair. Her hands were clutching the edges of the blankets as though she were trying to pull them tighter around her body and her long hair fell down over her shoulders.

Outside the moon was low in the sky. The frost lay heavier than ever on the fields and on the hedges and there was no noise anywhere. Then from far away in the south came a deep gentle rumble which grew and grew and became louder and louder until soon the whole sky was filled with the noise and the singing of those who were coming back.

But the woman who sat by the window never moved. She had been dead for some time.

SOMEONE LIKE YOU

'Beer?'

'Yes, beer.'

I gave the order and the waiter brought the bottles and two glasses. We poured out our own, tipping the glasses and holding the tops of the bottles close to the glass.

'Cheers,' I said.

He nodded. We lifted our glasses and drank.

It was five years since I had seen him, and during that time he had been fighting the war. He had been fighting it right from the beginning up to now and I saw at once how he had changed. From being a young, bouncing boy, he had become someone old and wise and gentle. He had become gentle like a wounded child. He had become old like a tired man of seventy years. He had become so different and he had changed so much that at first it was embarrassing for both of us and it was not easy to know what to say.

He had been flying in France in the early days and he was in Britain during the Battle. He was in the Western Desert when we had nothing and he was in Greece and Crete. He was in Syria and he was at Habbaniya during the rebellion. He was at Alamein. He had been flying in Sicily and in Italy and then he had gone back and flown again from England. Now he was an old man.

He was small, not more than five feet six, and he had a pale, wide-open face which did not hide anything, and a sharp pointed chin. His eyes were bright and dark. They were never still unless they were looking into your own. His hair was black and untidy. There was a wisp of it always hanging down over his forehead; he kept pushing it back with his hand.

For a while we were awkward and did not speak. He was sitting opposite me at the table, leaning forward a little, drawing lines on the dew of the cold beer-glass with his finger. He was looking at the glass, pretending to concentrate upon what he was doing, and to me it seemed as though he had something to say, but that he did not know how to say it. I sat there and picked nuts out of the plate and munched them noisily, pretending that I did not care about anything, not even about making a noise while eating.

Then without stopping his drawing on the glass and without looking up, he said quietly and very slowly, 'Oh God, I wish I was a waiter or a whore or something.'

He picked up his glass and drank the beer slowly and all at once, in two swallows. I knew now that there was something on his mind and I knew that he was gathering courage so that he could speak.

'Let's have another,' I said.

'Yes, let's have a whisky.'

'All right, whisky.'

I ordered two double Scotches and some soda, and we poured the soda into the Scotch and drank. He picked up his glass and drank, put it down, picked it up again and drank some more. As he put down the glass the second time, he leaned forward and quite suddenly he began to talk.

'You know,' he said, 'you know I keep thinking during a raid, when we are running over the target, just as we are going to release our bombs, I keep thinking to myself, shall I just jink a little; shall I swerve a fraction to one side, then my bombs will fall on someone else. I keep thinking, whom shall I make them fall on; whom shall I kill tonight. Which ten, twenty or a hundred people shall I kill tonight. It is all up to me. And now I think about this every time I go out.'

He had taken a small nut and was splitting it into pieces with his thumb-nail as he spoke, looking down at what he was doing because he was embarrassed by his own talk.

He was speaking very slowly. 'It would just be a gentle pressure with the ball of my foot upon the rudder-bar; a pressure so slight that I would hardly know that I was doing it, and it would throw the bombs on to a different house and on to other people. It is all up to me, the whole thing is up to me, and each time that I go out I have to decide which ones shall be killed. I can do it with the gentle pressure of the ball of my foot upon the rudder-bar. I can do it so that I don't even notice that it is being done. I just lean a little to one side because I am shifting my sitting position. That is all I am doing, and then I kill a different lot of people.'

Now there was no dew left upon the face of the glass, but he was still running the fingers of his right hand up and down the smooth surface.

'Yes,' he said, 'it is a complicated thought. It is very far-reaching; and when I am bombing I cannot get it out of my mind. You see it is such a gentle pressure with the ball of the foot; just a touch on the rudder-bar and the bomb-aimer wouldn't even notice. Each time I go out, I say to myself, shall it be these or shall it be those? Which ones are the worst? Perhaps if I make a little skid to the left I will get a houseful of lousy women-shooting German soldiers, or perhaps if I make that little skid I will miss getting the soldiers and get an old man in a shelter. How can I know? How can anyone know these things?'

He paused and pushed his empty glass away from him into the middle of the table.

'And so I never jink,' he added, 'at least hardly ever.'

'I jinked once,' I said, 'ground-strafing. I thought I'd kill the ones on the other side of the road instead.'

'Everybody jinks,' he said. 'Shall we have another drink?'

'Yes, let's have another.'

I called the waiter and gave the order, and while we were waiting, we sat looking around the room at the other people. The place was starting to fill up because it was about six o'clock and we sat there looking at the people who were coming in. They were standing around looking for tables, sitting down, laughing and ordering drinks.

'Look at that woman,' I said. 'The one just sitting down over there.'

'What about her?'

'Wonderful figure,' I said. 'Wonderful bosom. Look at her bosom.'

The waiter brought the drinks.

'Did I ever tell you about Stinker?' he said.

'Stinker who?'

'Stinker Sullivan in Malta.'

'No.'

'About Stinker's dog?'

'No.'

'Stinker had a dog, a great big Alsatian, and he loved that dog as though it was his father and his mother and everything else he had, and the dog loved Stinker. It used to follow him around everywhere he went, and when he went on ops it used to sit on the tarmac outside the hangars waiting for him to come back. It was called Smith. Stinker really loved that dog. He loved it like his mother and he used to talk to it all day long.'

'Lousy whisky,' I said.

'Yes, let's have another.'

We got some more whisky.

'Well anyway,' he went on, 'one day the squadron got orders to fly to Egypt. We had to go at once; not in two hours or later in the day, but at once. And Stinker couldn't find his dog. Couldn't find Smith anywhere. Started running all over the aerodrome yelling for Smith and going mad yelling at everyone asking where he was and yelling Smith Smith all over the aerodrome. Smith wasn't anywhere.'

'Where was he?' I said.

'He wasn't there and we had to go. Stinker had to go without Smith and he was mad as a hatter. His crew said he kept calling up over the radio asking if they'd found him. All the way to Heliopolis he kept calling up Malta saying, have you got Smith, and Malta kept saying no, they hadn't.'

'This whisky is really terrible,' I said.

'Yes. We must have some more.'

We had a waiter who was very quick.

'I was telling you about Stinker,' he said.

'Yes, tell me about Stinker.'

'Well, when we got to Egypt he wouldn't talk about anything except Smith. He used to walk around acting as though the dog was always with him. Damn fool walked around saying, "Come on, Smith, old boy, come on," and he kept looking down and talking to him as he walked along. Kept reaching down and patting the air and stroking this bloody dog that wasn't there.'

'Where was it?'

'Malta, I suppose. Must have been in Malta.'

'Isn't this awful whisky?'

'Terrible. We must have some more when we've finished this.'

'Cheers.'

'Cheers.'

'Waiter. Oh waiter. Yes; again.'

'So Smith was in Malta.'

'Yes,' he said. 'And this damn fool Stinker Sullivan went on like this right up to the time he was killed.'

'Must have been mad.'

'He was. Mad as a hatter. You know once he walked into the Sporting Club at Alexandria at drinking time.'

'That wasn't so mad.'

'He walked into the big lounge and as he went in he held the door open and started calling his dog. Then when he thought the dog had come in, he closed the door and started walking right down the length of the room, stopping every now and then and looking round and saying, "Come on, Smith, old boy, come on." He kept flipping his fingers. Once he got down under a table where two men and two women were drinking. He got on to his hands and knees and said, "Smith, come on out of there; come here at once," and he put out his hand and started dragging nothing at all from under the table. Then he apologized to the people at the table. "This is the hell of a dog," he said to them. You should have seen their faces. He went on like that all down the room and when he came to the other end he held the door open for the dog to go out and then went out after it.'

'Man was mad.'

'Mad as a hatter. And you should have seen their faces. It was full of people drinking and they didn't know whether it was them who were crazy or whether it was Stinker. They kept looking up at each other to make sure that they weren't the only ones who couldn't see the dog. One man dropped his drink.'

'That was awful.'

'Terrible.'

The waiter came and went. The room was full of people now, all sitting at little tables, talking and drinking and wearing their uniforms. The pilot poked the ice down into his glass with his finger.

'He used to jink too,' he said.

'Who?'

'Stinker. He used to talk about it.'

'Jinking isn't anything,' I said. 'It's like not touching the cracks on the pavement when you're walking along.'

'Balls. That's just personal. Doesn't affect anyone else.'

'Well, it's like car-waiting.'

'What's car-waiting?'

'I always do it,' I said.

'What is it?'

'Just as you're going to drive off, you sit back and count twenty, then you drive off.'

'You're mad too,' he said. 'You're like Stinker.'

'It's a wonderful way to avoid accidents. I've never had one in a car yet; at least, not a bad one.'

'You're drunk.'

'No, I always do it.'

'Why?'

'Because then if someone was going to have stepped off the kerb in front of your car, you won't hit them because you started later. You were delayed because you counted twenty, and the person who stepped off the kerb whom you would have hit – you missed him.'

'Why?'

'He stepped off the kerb long before you got there because you counted twenty.'

'That's a good idea.'

'I know it's a good idea.'

'It's a bloody marvellous idea.'

'I've saved lots of lives. And you can drive straight across intersections because the car you would have hit has already gone by. It went by just a little earlier because you delayed yourself by counting twenty.'

'Marvellous.'

'Isn't it?'

'But it's like jinking,' he said. 'You never really know what would have happened.'

'I always do it,' I said.

We kept right on drinking.

'Look at that woman,' I said.

'The one with the bosom?'

'Yes, marvellous bosom.'

He said slowly, 'I bet I've killed lots of women more beautiful than that one.'

'Not lots with bosoms like that.'

'I'll bet I have. Shall we have another drink?'

'Yes, one for the road.'

'There aren't any other women with bosoms like that,' I said. 'Not in Germany anyway.'

'Oh yes there are. I've killed lots of them.'

'All right. You've killed lots of women with wonderful bosoms.'

He leaned back and waved his hand around the room. 'See all the people in this room,' he said.

'Yes.'

'Wouldn't there be a bloody row if they were all suddenly dead; if they all suddenly fell off their chairs on to the floor dead?'

'What about it?'

'Wouldn't there be a bloody row?'

'Certainly there'd be a row.'

'If all the waiters got together and put stuff in all the drinks and everyone died.'

'There'd be a godalmighty row.'

'Well, I've done that hundreds of times. I've killed more people than there are in this room hundreds of times. So have you.'

'Lots more,' I said. 'But that's different.'

'Same sort of people. Men and women and waiters. All drinking in a pub.'

'That's different.'

'Like hell it is. Wouldn't there be a bloody row if it happened here?'

'Bloody awful row.'

'But we've done it. Lots of times.'

'Hundreds of times,' I said. 'This is nothing.'

'This is a lousy place.'

'Yes, it's lousy. Let's go somewhere else.'

'Finish our drinks.'

We finished our drinks and we both tried to pay the bill, so we tossed for it and I won. It came to sixteen dollars and twenty-five cents. He gave the waiter a two-dollar tip.

We got up and walked around the tables and over to the door.

'Taxi,' he said.

'Yes, must have a taxi.'

There wasn't a doorman. We stood out on the kerb waiting for a taxi to come along and he said, 'This is a good town.'

'Wonderful town,' I said. I felt fine. It was dark outside, but there were a few street-lamps, and we could see the cars going by and the people walking on the other side of the street. There was a thin, quiet drizzle falling, and the wetness on the black street shone yellow under the lights of the cars and under the street-lamps. The tyres of the cars hissed on the wet surface.

'Let's go to a place which has lots of whisky,' he said. 'Lots of whisky and a man with egg on his beard serving it.'

'Fine.'

'Somewhere where there are no other people but just us and the man with egg on his beard. Either that.'

'Yes,' I said. 'Either that or what?'

'Or a place with a hundred thousand people in it.'

'Yes,' I said. 'OK.'

We stood there waiting and we could see the lights of the cars as they came round the bend over to the left, coming towards us with the tyres swishing on the wet surface and going past us up the road to the bridge which goes over the river. We could see the drizzle falling through the beams of their headlights and we stood there waiting for a taxi.

SWITCH
BITCH

THE VISITOR

Not long ago, a large wooden case was deposited at the door of my house by the railway delivery service. It was an unusually strong and well-constructed object, and made of some kind of dark-red hardwood, not unlike mahogany. I lifted it with great difficulty on to a table in the garden, and examined it carefully. The stencilling on one side said that it had been shipped from Haifa by the m/v *Waverley Star*, but I could find no sender's name or address. I tried to think of somebody living in Haifa or thereabouts who might be wanting to send me a magnificent present. I could think of no one. I walked slowly to the toolshed, still pondering the matter deeply, and returned with a hammer and screwdriver. Then I began gently to prise open the top of the case.

Behold, it was filled with books! Extraordinary books! One by one, I lifted them all out (not yet looking inside any of them) and stacked them in three tall piles on the table. There were twenty-eight volumes altogether, and very beautiful they were indeed. Each of them was identically and superbly bound in rich green morocco, with the initials O.H.C. and a Roman numeral (I to XXVIII) tooled in gold upon the spine.

I took up the nearest volume, number XVI, and opened it. The unlined white pages were filled with a neat small handwriting in black ink. On the title page was written '1934'. Nothing else. I took up another volume, number XXI. It contained more manuscript in the same handwriting, but on the title page it said '1939'. I put it down and pulled out Volume I, hoping to find a preface of some kind there, or perhaps the author's name. Instead, I found an envelope inside the cover. The envelope was addressed to me. I took out the letter it contained and glanced quickly at the signature. *Oswald Hendryks Cornelius*, it said.

It was Uncle Oswald!

No member of the family had heard from Uncle Oswald for over thirty years. This letter was dated 10 March 1964, and until its arrival, we could only assume that he still existed. Nothing was really known about him except that he lived in France, that he travelled a great deal, that he was a wealthy bachelor with unsavoury but glamorous habits who steadfastly refused to have anything to do with his own relatives. The rest was all rumour and hearsay, but the rumours were so splendid and the hearsay so exotic that Oswald had long since become a shining hero and a legend to us all.

'My dear boy,' the letter began,

I believe that you and your three sisters are my closest surviving blood relations. You are therefore my rightful heirs, and because I have made no will, all that I leave behind me when I die will be yours. Alas, I have nothing to leave. I used to have quite a lot, and the fact that I have recently disposed of it all in my own way is none of your business. As consolation, though, I am sending you my private diaries. These, I think, ought to remain in the family. They cover all the best years of my life, and it will do you no harm to read them. But if you show them around or lend them to strangers, you do so at your own great peril. If you publish them, then that, I should imagine, would be the end of both you and your publisher simultaneously. For you must understand that thousands of the heroines whom I mention in the diaries are still only half dead, and if you were foolish enough to splash their lilywhite reputation with scarlet print, they would have your head on a salver in two seconds flat, and probably roast it in the oven for good measure. So you'd better be careful. I only met you once. That was years ago, in 1921, when your family was living in that large ugly house in South Wales. I was your big uncle and you were a very small boy, about five years old. I don't suppose you remember the young Norwegian nursemaid you had then. A remarkably clean, well-built girl she was, and exquisitely shaped even in her uniform with its ridiculously starchy white shield concealing her lovely bosom. The afternoon I was there, she was taking you for a walk in the woods to pick bluebells, and I asked if I might come along. And when we got well into the middle of the woods, I told you I'd give you a bar of chocolate if you could find your own way home. And you did (see Vol. III). You were a sensible child. Farewell – Oswald Hendryks Cornelius.

The sudden arrival of the diaries caused much excitement in the family, and there was a rush to read them. We were not disappointed. It was astonishing stuff – hilarious, witty, exciting, and often quite touching as well. The man's vitality was unbelievable. He was always on the move, from city to city, from country to country, from woman to woman, and in between the women, he would be searching for spiders in Kashmir or tracking down a blue porcelain vase in Nanking. But the women always came first. Wherever he went, he left an endless trail of females in his wake, females ruffled and ravished beyond words, but purring like cats.

Twenty-eight volumes with exactly three hundred pages to each volume takes a deal of reading, and there are precious few writers who could hold an audience over a distance like that. But Oswald did it. The narrative never seemed to lose its flavour, the pace seldom slackened, and almost without exception, every single entry, whether it was long or short, and whatever the subject, became a marvellous little individual story that was complete in itself. And at the end of it all, when the last page of the last volume had been read, one was left with the rather breathless feeling that this might just possibly be one of the major autobiographical works of our time.

If it were regarded solely as a chronicle of a man's amorous adventures, then without a doubt there was nothing to touch it. Casanova's *Memoirs* read like a Parish Magazine in comparison, and the famous lover himself, beside Oswald, appears positively undersexed.

There was social dynamite on every page; Oswald was right about that. But he was surely wrong in thinking that the explosions would all come from the women. What about their husbands, the humiliated cock-sparrows, the cuckolds? The cuckold, when aroused, is a very fierce bird indeed, and there would be thousands upon thousands of them rising up out of the bushes if The Cornelius Diaries, unabridged, saw the light of day while they were still alive. Publication, therefore, was right out of the question.

A pity, this. Such a pity, in fact, that I thought something ought to be done about it. So I sat down and re-read the diaries from beginning to end in the hope that I might discover at least one complete passage which could be printed and published without involving both the publisher and myself in serious litigation. To my joy, I found no less than six. I showed them to a lawyer. He said he thought they *might* be 'safe', but he wouldn't guarantee it. One of them – The Sinai Desert Episode – seemed 'safer' than the other five, he added.

So I have decided to start with that one and to offer it for publication right away, at the end of this short preface. If it is accepted and all goes well, then perhaps I shall release one or two more.

The Sinai entry is from the last volume of all, Vol. XXVIII, and is dated 24 August 1946. In point of fact, it is the *very last entry* of the last volume of all, the last thing Oswald ever wrote, and we have no record of where he went or what he did after that date. One can only guess. You shall have the entry verbatim in a moment, but first of all, and so that you may more easily understand some of the things Oswald says and does in his story, let me try to tell you a little about the man himself. Out of the mass of confession and opinion contained in those twenty-eight volumes, there emerges a fairly clear picture of his character.

At the time of the Sinai episode, Oswald Hendryks Cornelius was fifty-one years old, and he had, of course, never been married. 'I am afraid,' he was in the habit of saying, 'that I have been blessed or should I call it burdened, with an uncommonly fastidious nature.'

In some ways, this was true, but in others, and especially in so far as marriage was concerned, the statement was the exact opposite of the truth.

The real reason Oswald had refused to get married was simply that he had never in his life been able to confine his attentions to one particular woman for longer than the time it took to conquer her. When that was done, he lost interest and looked around for another victim.

A normal man would hardly consider this a valid reason for remaining single, but Oswald was not a normal man. He was not even a normal polygamous man. He was, to be honest, such a wanton and incorrigible philanderer that no bride on earth would have put up with him for more than a few days, let alone for the duration of a honeymoon – although heaven knows there were enough who would have been willing to give it a try.

He was a tall, narrow person with a fragile and faintly aesthetic air. His voice was soft, his manner was courteous, and at first sight he seemed more like a gentleman-in-waiting to the queen than a celebrated rapscallion. He never discussed his amorous affairs with other men, and a stranger, though he sit and talk with him all evening, would be unable to observe the slightest sign of deceit in Oswald's clear blue eyes. He was, in fact, precisely the sort of man that an anxious father would be likely to choose to escort his daughter safely home.

But sit Oswald beside a *woman*, a woman who interested him, and instantaneously his eyes would change, and as he looked at her, a small dangerous spark would begin dancing slowly in the very centre of each pupil; and then he would set about her with his conversation, talking to her rapidly and cleverly and almost certainly more wittily than anyone else had ever done before. This was a gift he had, a most singular talent, and when he put his mind to it, he could make his words coil themselves around and around the listener until they held her in some sort of a mild hypnotic spell.

But it wasn't only his fine talk and the look in his eyes that fascinated the women. It was also his nose. (In Vol. XIV, Oswald includes, with obvious relish, a note written to him by a certain lady in which she describes such things as this in great detail.) It appears that when Oswald was aroused, something odd would begin to happen around the edges of his nostrils, a tightening of the rims, a visible flaring which enlarged the nostril holes and revealed whole areas of the bright red skin inside. This created a queer, wild, animalistic impression, and although it may not sound particularly attractive when described on paper, its effect upon the ladies was electric.

Almost without exception, women were drawn toward Oswald. In the first place, he was a man who refused to be owned at any price, and this automatically made him desirable. Add to this the unusual combination of a first-rate intellect, an abundance of charm, and a reputation for excessive promiscuity, and you have a potent recipe.

Then again, and forgetting for a moment the disreputable and licentious angle, it should be noted that there were a number of other surprising facets to Oswald's character that in themselves made him a rather intriguing person. There was, for example, very little that he did not know about nineteenth-century Italian opera, and he had written a curious little manual upon the three composers Donizetti, Verdi, and Ponchielli. In it, he listed by name all the important mistresses that these men had had during their lives, and he went on to examine, in a most serious vein, the relationship between creative passion and carnal passion, and the influence of the one upon the other, particularly as it affected the works of these composers.

Chinese porcelain was another of Oswald's interests, and he was acknowledged as something of an international authority in this field. The blue vases of the Tchin-Hoa period were his special love, and he had a small but exquisite collection of these pieces.

He also collected spiders and walking sticks.

His collection of spiders, or more accurately his collection of Arachnida, because it included scorpions and pedipalps, was possibly as comprehensive as any outside a museum, and his knowledge of the hundreds of genera and species was impressive. He maintained, incidentally (and probably correctly), that the spider's silk was superior in quality to the ordinary stuff spun by silkworms, and he never wore a tie that was made of any other material. He possessed about forty of these ties altogether, and in order to acquire them in the first place, and in order also to be able to add two new ties a year to his wardrobe, he had to keep thousands and thousands of *Arana* and *Epeira diademata* (the common English garden spiders) in an old conservatory in the garden of his country house outside Paris, where they bred and multiplied at approximately the same rate as they ate one another. From them, he collected the raw thread himself – no one else would enter that ghastly glasshouse – and sent it to Avignon, where it was reeled and thrown and scoured and dyed and made into cloth. From Avignon, the cloth was delivered directly to Sulka, who were enchanted by the whole business, and only too glad to fashion ties out of such a rare and wonderful material.

'But you can't *really* like spiders?' the women visitors would say to Oswald as he displayed his collection.

'Oh, but I adore them,' he would answer. 'Especially the females.

They remind me so much of certain human females that I know. They remind me of my very favourite human females.'

'What nonsense, darling.'

'Nonsense? I think not.'

'It's rather insulting.'

'On the contrary, my dear, it is the greatest compliment I could pay. Did you not know, for instance, that the female spider is so savage in her lovemaking that the male is very lucky indeed if he escapes with his life at the end of it all. Only if he is exceedingly agile and marvellously ingenious will he get away in one piece.'

'Now, *Oswald!*'

'And the crab spider, my beloved, the teeny-weeny little crab spider is so dangerously passionate that her lover has to tie her down with intricate loops and knots of his own thread before he dares to embrace her ...'

'Oh, *stop* it, Oswald, this *minute!*' the women would cry, their eyes shining.

Oswald's collection of walking sticks was something else again. Every one of them had belonged either to a distinguished or a disgusting person, and he kept them all in his Paris apartment, where they were displayed in two long racks standing against the walls of the passage (or should one call it the highway?) which led from the living-room to the bed-room. Each stick had its own ivory label above it, saying Sibelius, Milton, King Farouk, Dickens, Robespierre, Puccini, Oscar Wilde, Franklin Roosevelt, Goebbels, Queen Victoria, Toulouse-Lautrec, Hindenburg, Tolstoy, Laval, Sarah Bernhardt, Goethe, Voroshiloff, Cézanne, Toho ... There must have been over a hundred of them in all, some very beautiful, some very plain, some with gold or silver tops, and some with curly handles.

'Take down the Tolstoy,' Oswald would say to a pretty visitor. 'Go on, take it down ... that's right ... and now ... now rub your own palm gently over the knob that has been worn to a shine by the great man himself. Is it not rather wonderful, the mere contact of your skin with that spot?'

'It is, rather, isn't it.'

'And now take the Goebbels and do the same thing. Do it properly, though. Allow your palm to fold tightly over the handle ... good ... and now ... now lean your weight on it, lean hard, exactly as the little deformed doctor used to do ... there ... that's it ... now stay like that for a minute or so and then tell me if you do not feel a thin finger of ice creeping all the way up your arm and into your chest?'

'It's terrifying!'

'Of course it is. Some people pass out completely. They keel right over.'

Nobody ever found it dull to be in Oswald's company, and perhaps that, more than anything else, was the reason for his success.

We come now to the Sinai episode. Oswald, during that month, had been amusing himself by motoring at a fairly leisurely pace down from Khartoum to Cairo. His car was a superlative pre-war Lagonda which had been carefully stored in Switzerland during the war years, and as you can imagine, it was fitted with every kind of gadget under the sun. On the day before Sinai (23 August 1946), he was in Cairo, staying at Shepheard's Hotel, and that evening, after a series of impudent manoeuvres, he had succeeded in getting hold of a Moorish lady of supposedly aristocratic descent, called Isabella. Isabella happened to be the jealously guarded mistress of none other than a certain notorious and dyspeptic Royal Personage (there was still a monarchy in Egypt then). This was a typically Oswaldian move.

But there was more to come. At midnight, he drove the lady out to Giza and persuaded her to climb with him in the moonlight right to the very top of the great pyramid of Cheops.

'. . . There can be no safer place,' he wrote in the diary, 'nor a more romantic one, than the apex of a pyramid on a warm night when the moon is full. The passions are stirred not only by the magnificent view but also by that curious sensation of power that surges within the body whenever one surveys the world from a great height. And as for safety – this pyramid is exactly 481 feet high, which is 115 feet higher than the dome of St Paul's Cathedral, and from the summit one can observe all the approaches with the greatest of ease. No other boudoir on earth can offer this facility. None has so many emergency exits, either, so that if some sinister figure should happen to come clambering up in pursuit on one side of the pyramid, one has only to slip calmly and quietly down the other . . .'

As it happened, Oswald had a very narrow squeak indeed that night. Somehow, the palace must have got word of the little affair, for Oswald, from his lofty moonlit pinnacle, suddenly observed *three* sinister figures, not one, closing in on three different sides, and starting to climb. But luckily for him, there is a fourth side to the great pyramid of Cheops, and by the time those Arab thugs had reached the top, the two lovers were already at the bottom and getting into the car.

The entry for 24 August takes up the story at exactly this point. It is reproduced here word for word and comma for comma as Oswald wrote it. Nothing has been altered or added or taken away:

24 August 1946

'He'll chop off Isabella's head if he catch her now,' Isabella said.

'Rubbish,' I answered, but I reckoned she was probably right.

'He'll chop off Oswald's head, too,' she said.

'Not mine, dear lady. I shall be a long way away from here

when daylight comes. I'm heading straight up the Nile for Luxor immediately.'

We were driving quickly away from the pyramids now. It was about two thirty a.m.

'To Luxor?' she said.

'Yes.'

'And Isabella is going with you.'

'No,' I said.

'Yes,' she said.

'It is against my principles to travel with a lady,' I said.

I could see some lights ahead of us. They came from the Mena House Hotel, a place where tourists stay out in the desert, not far from the pyramids. I drove fairly close to the hotel and stopped the car.

'I'm going to drop you here,' I said. 'We had a fine time.'

'So you won't take Isabella to Luxor?'

'I'm afraid not,' I said. 'Come on, hop it.'

She started to get out of the car, then she paused with one foot on the road, and suddenly she swung round and poured out upon me a torrent of language so filthy yet so fluent that I had heard nothing like it from the lips of a lady since ... well, since 1931, in Marrakesh, when the greedy old Duchess of Glasgow put her hand into a chocolate box and got nipped by a scorpion I happened to have placed there for safe-keeping (Vol. XIII, 5 June 1931).

'You are disgusting,' I said.

Isabella leapt out and slammed the door so hard the whole car jumped on its wheels. I drove off very fast. Thank heaven I was rid of her. I cannot abide bad manners in a pretty girl.

As I drove, I kept one eye on the mirror, but as yet no car seemed to be following me. When I came to the outskirts of Cairo, I began threading my way through the side roads, avoiding the centre of the city. I was not particularly worried. The royal watchdogs were unlikely to carry the matter much further. All the same, it would have been foolhardy to go back to Shepheard's at this point. It wasn't necessary, anyway, because all my baggage, except for a small valise, was with me in the car. I never leave suitcases behind me in my room when I go out of an evening in a foreign city. I like to be mobile.

I had no intention, of course, of going to Luxor. I wanted now to get away from Egypt altogether. I didn't like the country at all. Come to think of it, I never had. The place made me feel uncomfortable in my skin. It was the dirtiness of it all, I think, and the putrid smells. But then let us face it, it really is a squalid country; and I have a powerful suspicion, though I hate to say it, that the Egyptians wash themselves less thoroughly than any other peoples in the world – with the possible exception of the Mongolians. Certainly they do not wash their crockery to my taste. There was, believe it or not, a long, crusted, coffee-coloured lipmark stamped upon the rim of the cup they placed before me at breakfast yesterday. Ugh! It was repulsive! I kept staring at it and wondering whose slobbery lower lip had done the deed.

I was driving now through the narrow dirty streets of the eastern suburbs of Cairo. I knew precisely where I was going. I had made up my mind about that before I was even halfway down the pyramid with Isabella. I was going to Jerusalem. It was no distance to speak of, and it was a city that I always enjoyed. Furthermore, it was the quickest way out of Egypt. I would proceed as follows:

1. Cairo to Ismailia. About three hours driving. Sing an opera on the way, as usual. Arrive Ismailia 6–7 a.m. Take a room and have a two-hour sleep. Then shower, shave, and breakfast.

2. At 10 a.m., cross over the Suez Canal by the Ismailia bridge and take the desert road across Sinai to the Palestine border. Make a search for scorpions *en route* in the Sinai Desert. Time, about four hours, arriving Palestine border 2 p.m.

3. From there, continue straight on to Jerusalem via Beersheba, reaching The King David Hotel in time for cocktails and dinner.

It was several years since I had travelled that particular road, but I remembered that the Sinai Desert was an outstanding place for scorpions. I badly wanted another female opisthophthalmus, a large one. My present specimen had the fifth segment of its tail missing, and I was ashamed of it.

It didn't take me long to find the main road to Ismailia, and as soon as I was on it, I settled the Lagonda down to a steady sixty-five miles per hour. The road was narrow, but it had a smooth surface, and there was no traffic. The Delta country lay bleak and dismal around me in the moonlight, the flat treeless fields, the ditches running between, and the black black soil everywhere. It was inexpressibly dreary.

But it didn't worry *me*. I was no part of it. I was completely isolated in my own luxurious little shell, as snug as a hermit crab and travelling a lot faster. Oh, how I do love to be on the move, winging away to new people and new places and leaving the old ones far behind! Nothing in the world exhilarates me more than that. And how I despise the average citizen, who settles himself down upon one tiny spot of land with one asinine woman, to breed and stew and rot in that condition unto his life's end. And always with the same woman! I cannot *believe* that any man in his senses would put up with just one female day after day and year after year. Some of them, of course, don't. But millions pretend they do.

I myself have never, absolutely never permitted an intimate relationship to last for more than twelve hours. That is the farthest limit. Even eight hours is stretching it a bit, to my mind. Look what happened, for example, with Isabella. While we were upon the summit of the pyramid, she was a lady of scintillating parts, as pliant and playful as a puppy, and had I left her there to the mercy of those three Arab thugs, and skipped down on my own, all would have been well. But I foolishly stuck by her and helped her to descend, and as a result, the lovely lady turned into a vulgar screeching trollop, disgusting to behold.

What a world we live in! One gets no thanks these days for being chivalrous.

The Lagonda moved on smoothly through the night. Now for an opera. Which one should it be this time? I was in the mood for a Verdi. What about *Aida*? Of course! It must be *Aida* – the Egyptian opera! Most appropriate.

I began to sing. I was in exceptionally good voice tonight. I let myself go. It was delightful; and as I drove through the small town of Bilbeis, I was Aida herself, singing '*Numei pietà*', the beautiful concluding passage of the first scene.

Half an hour later, at Zagazig, I was Amonasro begging the King of Egypt to save the Ethiopian captives with '*Ma tu, re, tu signore possente*'.

Passing through El Abbasa, I was Rhadames, rendering '*Fuggiam gli adori nospiti*', and now I opened all the windows of the car so that this incomparable love song might reach the ears of the fellaheen snoring in their hovels along the roadside, and perhaps mingle with their dreams.

As I pulled into Ismailia, it was six o'clock in the morning and the sun was already climbing high in a milky-blue heaven, but I myself was in the terrible sealed-up dungeon with Aida, singing '*O, terra, addio; addio valle di pianti!*'

How swiftly the journey had gone. I drove to an hotel. The staff was just beginning to stir. I stirred them up some more and got the best room available. The sheets and blanket on the bed looked as though they had been slept in by twenty-five unwashed Egyptians on twenty-five consecutive nights, and I tore them off with my own hands (which I scrubbed immediately afterwards with antiseptic soap) and replaced them with my personal bedding. Then I set my alarm and slept soundly for two hours.

For breakfast I ordered a poached egg on a piece of toast. When the dish arrived – and I tell you, it makes my stomach curdle just to write about it – there was a *gleaming, curly, jet-black human hair*, three inches long, lying diagonally across the yolk of my poached egg. It was too much. I leaped up from the table and rushed out of the dining-room. '*Addio!*' I cried, flinging some money at the cashier as I went by, '*addio valle di pianti!*' And with that I shook the filthy dust of the hotel from my feet.

Now for the Sinai Desert. What a welcome change that would be. A real desert is one of the least contaminated places on earth, and Sinai was no exception. The road across it was a narrow strip of black tarmac about a hundred and forty miles long, with only a single filling station and a group of huts at the halfway mark, at a place called B'ir Rawd Salim. Otherwise there was nothing but pure uninhabited desert all the way. It would be very hot at this time of the year, and it was essential to carry drinking water in case of a breakdown. I therefore pulled up outside a kind of general store in the main street of Ismailia to get my emergency canister refilled.

I went in and spoke to the proprietor. The man had a nasty case of trachoma. The granulation on the under surfaces of his eyelids was so acute that the lids themselves were raised right up off the eyeballs – a beastly sight. I asked him if he would sell me a gallon of *boiled* water. He thought I was mad, and madder still when I insisted on following him back into his grimy kitchen to make sure that he did things properly. He filled a kettle with tap-water and placed it on a paraffin stove. The stove had a tiny little smoky yellow flame. The proprietor seemed very proud of the stove and of its performance. He stood admiring it, his head on one side. Then he suggested that I might prefer to go back and wait in the shop. He would bring me the water, he said, when it was ready. I refused to leave. I stood there watching the kettle like a lion, waiting for the water to boil; and while I was doing this, the breakfast scene suddenly started coming back to me in all its horror – the egg, the yolk, and the hair. Whose hair was it that had lain embedded in the slimy yolk of my egg at breakfast? Undoubtedly it was the cook's hair. And when, pray, had the cook last washed his head? He had probably never washed his head. Very well, then. He was almost certainly verminous. But that in itself would not cause a hair to fall out. What *did* cause the cook's hair, then, to fall out on to my poached egg this morning as he transferred the egg from the pan to the plate. There is a reason for all things, and in this case the reason was obvious. The cook's scalp was infested with purulent seborrhoeic impetigo. And the hair itself, the long black hair that I might so easily have swallowed had I been less alert, was therefore swarming with millions and millions of loving pathogenic cocci whose exact scientific name I have, happily, forgotten.

Can I, you ask, be absolutely sure that the cook had purulent seborrhoeic impetigo? Not absolutely sure – no. But if he hadn't, then he certainly had ringworm instead. And what did that mean? I knew only too well what it meant. It meant that ten million microsporons had been clinging and clustering around that awful hair, waiting to go into my mouth.

I began to feel sick.

'The water boils,' the shopkeeper said triumphantly.

'Let it boil,' I told him. 'Give it eight minutes more. What is it you want me to get – typhus?'

Personally, I never drink water by itself if I can help it, however pure it may be. Plain water has no flavour at all. I take it, of course, as tea or as coffee, but even then I try to arrange for bottled Vichy or Malvern to be used in the preparation. I avoid tap-water. Tap-water is diabolical stuff. Often it is nothing more nor less than reclaimed sewage.

'Soon this water will be boiled away in steam,' the proprietor said, grinning at me with green teeth.

I lifted the kettle myself and poured the contents into my canister.

Back in the shop, I bought six oranges, a small water-melon, and a slab of well-wrapped English chocolate. Then I returned to the Lagonda. Now at last I was away.

A few minutes later, I had crossed the sliding bridge that went over the Suez Canal just above Lake Timsah, and ahead of me lay the flat blazing desert and the little tarmac road stretching out before me like a black ribbon all the way to the horizon. I settled the Lagonda to the usual steady sixty-five miles an hour, and I opened the windows wide. The air that came in was like the breath of an oven. The time was almost noon, and the sun was throwing its heat directly on to the roof of the car. My thermometer inside registered 103°. But as you know, a touch of warmth never bothers me so long as I am sitting still and am wearing suitable clothes – in this case a pair of cream-coloured linen slacks, a white aertex shirt, and a spider's-silk tie of the loveliest rich moss-green. I felt perfectly comfortable and at peace with the world.

For a minute or two I played with the idea of performing another opera *en route* – I was in the mood for *La Gioconda* – but after singing a few bars of the opening chorus, I began to perspire slightly; so I rang down the curtain, and lit a cigarette instead.

I was now driving through some of the finest scorpion country in the world, and I was eager to stop and make a search before I reached the halfway filling-station at B'ir Rawd Salim. I had so far met not a single vehicle or seen a living creature since leaving Ismailia an hour before. This pleased me. Sinai was authentic desert. I pulled up on the side of the road and switched off the engine. I was thirsty, so I ate an orange. Then I put my white topee on my head, and eased myself slowly out of the car, out of my comfortable hermit-crab shell, and into the sunlight. For a full minute I stood motionless in the middle of the road, blinking at the brilliance of the surroundings.

There was a blazing sun, a vast hot sky, and beneath it all on every side a great pale sea of yellow sand that was not quite of this world.

There were mountains now in the distance on the south side of the road, bare, pale-brown, tanagra-coloured mountains faintly glazed with blue and purple, that rose up suddenly out of the desert and faded away in a haze of heat against the sky. The stillness was overpowering. There was no sound at all, no voice of a bird or insect anywhere, and it gave me a queer godlike feeling to be standing there alone in the middle of such a splendid, hot, inhuman landscape – as though I were on another planet altogether, on Jupiter or Mars, or in some place more distant and desolate still, where never would the grass grow or the clouds turn red.

I went to the boot of the car and took out my killing-box, my net, and my towel. Then I stepped off the road into the soft burning sand. I walked slowly for about a hundred yards into the desert, my eyes searching the ground. I was not looking for scorpions but the lairs of scorpions. The scorpion is a cryptozoic and nocturnal creature that hides all through the day either under a stone or in a burrow, according to its type. Only after the sun has gone down does it come out to hunt for food.

The one I wanted, opisthophthalmus, was a burrower, so I wasted no time turning over stones. I searched only for burrows. After ten or fifteen minutes, I had found none; but already the heat was getting to be too much for me, and I decided reluctantly to return to the car. I walked back very slowly, still watching the ground, and I had reached the road and was in the act of stepping on to it when all at once, in the sand, not more than twelve inches from the edge of the tarmac, I caught sight of a scorpion's burrow.

I put the killing-box and the net on the ground beside me. Then, with my little trowel, I began very cautiously to scrape away the sand all around the hole. This was an operation that never failed to excite me. It was like a treasure hunt – a treasure hunt with just the right amount of danger accompanying it to stir the blood. I could feel my heart beating away in my chest as I probed deeper and deeper into the sand.

And suddenly ... there she was!

Oh, my heavens, what a whopper. A gigantic female scorpion, not opisthophthalmus, as I saw immediately, but pandinus, the other large African burrower. And clinging to her back – this was too good to be true! – swarming all over her, were one, two, three, four, five ... a total of fourteen tiny babies! The mother was six inches long at least! Her children were the size of small revolver bullets. She had seen me now, the first human she had ever seen in her life, and her pincers were wide open, her tail was curled high over her back like a question mark, ready to strike. I took up the net, and slid it swiftly underneath her, and scooped her up. She twisted and squirmed, striking wildly in all directions with the end of her tail. I saw a single large drop of venom fall through the mesh into the sand. Quickly, I transferred her, together with the offspring, to the killing-box, and closed the lid. Then I fetched the ether from the car, and poured it through the little gauze hole in the top of the box until the pad inside was well soaked.

How splendid she would look in my collection! The babies would, of course, fall away from her as they died, but I would stick them on again with glue in more or less their correct positions; and then I would be the proud possessor of a huge female pandinus with her own fourteen offspring on her back! I was extremely pleased. I lifted the killing-box (I could feel her thrashing about furiously inside) and placed it in the boot, together with the net and trowel. Then I returned to my seat in the car, lit a cigarette, and drove on.

The more contented I am, the slower I drive. I drove quite slowly now, and it must have taken me nearly an hour more to reach B'ir Rawd Salim, the halfway station. It was a most unenticing place. On the left, there was a single gasoline pump and a wooden shack. On the right, there were three more shacks, each about the size of a potting-shed. The rest was desert. There was not a soul in sight. The time was twenty minutes before two in the afternoon, and the temperature inside the car was 106°.

What with the nonsense of getting the water boiled before leaving Ismailia, I had forgotten completely to fill up with gasoline before leaving, and my gauge was now registering slightly less than two gallons. I'd cut it rather fine – but no matter. I pulled in alongside the pump, and waited. Nobody appeared. I pressed the horn button, and the four tuned horns on the Lagonda shouted their wonderful '*Son gia mille e tre!*' across the desert. Nobody appeared. I pressed again.

sang the horns. Mozart's phrase sounded magnificent in these surroundings. But still nobody appeared. The inhabitants of B'ir Rawd Salim didn't give a damn, it seemed, about my friend Don Giovanni and the 1,003 women he had deflowered in Spain.

At last, after I had played the horns no less than six times, the door of the hut behind the gasoline pump opened and a tallish man emerged and stood on the threshold, doing up his buttons with both hands. He took his time over this, and not until he had finished did he glance up at the Lagonda. I looked back at him through my open window. I saw him take the first step in my direction ... he took it very, very slowly ... Then he took a second step ...

My God! I thought at once. The spirochetes have got him!

He had the slow, wobbly walk, the loose-limbed, high-stepping gait of a man with locomotor ataxia. With each step he took, the front foot was raised high in the air before him and brought down violently to the ground, as though he were stamping on a dangerous insect.

I thought: I had better get out of here. I had better start the motor and get the hell out of here before he reaches me. But I knew I couldn't. I *had* to have the gasoline. I sat in the car staring at the awful creature as he came stamping laboriously over the sand. He must have had the revolting disease for years and years, otherwise it wouldn't have developed into ataxis. *Tabes dorsalis* they call it in professional circles, and pathologically this means that the victim is suffering from degeneration of the posterior columns of the spinal chord. But ah my foes and oh my friends, it is really a lot worse than that; it is a slow and merciless consuming of the actual nerve fibres of the body by syphilitic toxins.

The man – the Arab, I shall call him – came right up to the door of my side of the car and peered in through the open window. I leaned away from him, praying that he would not come an inch closer. Without a doubt, he was one of the most blighted humans I had ever seen. His face had the eroded, eaten-away look of an old wood-carving when the worm has been at it, and the sight of it made me wonder how many other diseases the man was suffering from, besides syphilis.

'Salaam,' he mumbled.

'Fill up the tank,' I told him.

He didn't move. He was inspecting the interior of the Lagonda with great interest. A terrible feculent odour came wafting in from his direction.

'Come along!' I said sharply. 'I want some gasoline!'

He looked at me and grinned. It was more of a leer than a grin, an insolent mocking leer that seemed to be saying, 'I am the king of the gasoline pump at B'ir Rawd Salim! Touch me if you dare!' A fly had settled in the corner of one of his eyes. He made no attempt to brush it away.

'You want gasoline?' he said, taunting me.

I was about to swear at him, but I checked myself just in time, and answered politely, 'Yes please, I would be very grateful.'

He watched me slyly for a few moments to be sure I wasn't mocking him, then he nodded as though satisfied now with my behaviour. He turned away and started slowly toward the rear of the car. I reached into the door-pocket for my bottle of Glenmorangie. I poured myself a stiff one, and sat sipping it. That man's face had been within a yard of my own; his foetid breath had come pouring into the car ... and who knows how many billions of airborne viruses might not have come pouring in with it? On such an occasion it is a fine thing to sterilize the mouth and throat with a drop of Highland whisky. The whisky is also a solace. I emptied the glass, and poured myself another. Soon I began to feel less alarmed. I noticed the watermelon lying on the seat beside me. I decided that a slice of it at this moment would be refreshing. I took my knife from its case and cut out a thick section. Then, with the point of the knife, I carefully picked out all the black seeds, using the rest of the melon as a receptacle.

I sat drinking the whisky and eating the melon. Both very delicious.

'Gasoline is done,' the dreadful Arab said, appearing at the window. 'I check water now, and oil.'

I would have preferred him to keep his hands off the Lagonda altogether, but rather than risk an argument, I said nothing. He went clumping off toward the front of the car, and his walk reminded me of a drunken Hitler Stormtrooper doing the goosestep in very slow motion.

Tabes dorsalis, as I live and breathe.

The only other disease to induce that queer high-stepping gait is chronic beriberi. Well – he probably had that one, too. I cut myself another slice of watermelon, and concentrated for a minute or so on taking out the seeds with the knife. When I looked up again, I saw that the Arab had raised the bonnet of the car on the righthand side, and was bending over the engine. His head and shoulders were out of sight, and so were his head and arms. What on earth was the man doing? The oil dipstick was on the other side. I rapped on the windshield. He seemed not to hear me. I put my head out of the window and shouted, 'Hey! Come out of there!'

Slowly, he straightened up, and as he drew his right arm out of the bowels of the engine, I saw that he was holding in his fingers something that was long and black and curly and very thin.

'Good God!' I thought. 'He's found a snake in there!'

He came round to the window, grinning at me and holding the object out for me to see; and only then, as I got a closer look, did I realize that it was not a snake at all – *it was the fan-belt of my Lagonda!*

All the awful implications of suddenly being stranded in this outlandish place with this disgusting man came flooding over me as I sat there staring dumbly at my broken fanbelt.

'You can see,' the Arab was saying, 'it was hanging on by a single thread. A good thing I noticed it.'

I took it from him and examined it closely. 'You cut it!' I cried.

'Cut it?' he answered softly. 'Why should I cut it?'

To be perfectly honest, it was impossible for me to judge whether he had or had not cut it. If he had, then he had also taken the trouble to fray the severed ends with some instrument to make it look like an ordinary break. Even so, my guess was that he *had* cut it, and if I was right then the implications were more sinister than ever.

'I suppose you know I can't go on without a fan-belt?' I said.

He grinned again with that awful mutilated mouth, showing ulcerated gums. 'If you go now,' he said, 'you will boil over in three minutes.'

'So what do you suggest?'

'I shall get you another fan-belt.'

'You will?'

'Of course. There is a telephone here, and if you will pay for the call, I will telephone to Ismailia. And if they haven't got one in Ismailia, I will telephone to Cairo. There is no problem.'

'No problem!' I shouted, getting out of the car. 'And when pray, do you think the fan-belt is going to arrive in this ghastly place?'

'There is a mail-truck comes through every morning about ten o'clock. You would have it tomorrow.'

The man had all the answers. He never even had to think before replying.

This bastard, I thought, *has cut fan-belts before.*

I was very alert now, and watching him closely.

'They will not have a fan-belt for a machine of this make in Ismailia,' I said. 'It would have to come from the agents in Cairo. I will telephone them myself.' The fact that there was a telephone gave me some comfort. The telephone poles had followed the road all the way across the desert, and I could see the two wires leading into the hut from the nearest pole. 'I will ask the agents in Cairo to set out immediately for this place in a special vehicle,' I said.

The Arab looked along the road toward Cairo, some two hundred miles away. 'Who is going to drive six hours here and six hours back to bring a fan-belt?' he said. 'The mail will be just as quick.'

'Show me the telephone,' I said, starting toward the hut. Then a nasty thought struck me, and I stopped.

How could I possibly use this man's contaminated instrument? The earpiece would have to be pressed against my ear, and the mouthpiece would almost certainly touch my mouth; and I didn't give a damn what the doctors said about the impossibility of catching syphilis from remote contact. A syphilitic mouthpiece was a syphilitic mouthpiece, and you wouldn't catch *me* putting it anywhere near *my* lips, thank you very much. I wouldn't even enter his hut.

I stood there in the sizzling heat of the afternoon and looked at the Arab with his ghastly diseased face, and the Arab looked back at me, as cool and unruffled as you please.

'You want the telephone?' he asked.

'No,' I said. 'Can you read English?'

'Oh, yes.'

'Very well. I shall write down for you the name of the agents and the name of this car, and also my own name. They know me there. You will tell them what is wanted. And listen ... tell them to dispatch a special car immediately at my expense. I will pay them well. And if they won't do that, tell them they *have* to get the fan-belt to Ismailia in time to catch the mailtruck. You understand?'

'There is no problem,' the Arab said.

So I wrote down what was necessary on a piece of paper and gave it to him. He walked away with that slow, stamping tread toward the hut, and disappeared inside. I closed the bonnet of the car. Then I went back and sat in the driver's seat to think things out.

I poured myself another whisky, and lit a cigarette. There must be *some* traffic on this road. Somebody would surely come along before nightfall. But would that help me? No, it wouldn't – unless I were prepared to hitch a ride and leave the Lagonda and all my baggage behind to the tender mercies of the Arab. Was I prepared to do that? I didn't know. Probably yes. But if I were forced to stay the night, I would lock myself in the car and try to keep awake as much as possible. On no account would I enter the shack where that creature lived. Nor would I touch his food. I had whisky and water, and I had half a watermelon and a slab of chocolate. That was ample.

The heat was pretty bad. The thermometer in the car was still around 104°. It was hotter outside in the sun. I was perspiring freely. My God, what a place to get stranded in! And what a companion!

After about fifteen minutes, the Arab came out of the hut. I watched him all the way to the car.

'I talked to the garage in Cairo,' he said, pushing his face through the window. 'Fan-belt will arrive tomorrow by mailtruck. Everything arranged.'

'Did you ask them about sending it at once?'

'They said impossible,' he answered.

'You're sure you asked them?'

He inclined his head to one side and gave me that sly insolent grin. I turned away and waited for him to go. He stayed where he was. 'We have house for visitors,' he said. 'You can sleep there very nice. My wife will make food, but you will have to pay.'

'Who else is here besides you and your wife?'

'Another man,' he said. He waved an arm in the direction of the three shacks across the road, and I turned and saw a man standing in the doorway of the middle shack, a short wide man who was dressed in dirty khaki slacks and shirt. He was standing absolutely motionless in the shadow of the doorway, his arms dangling at his sides. He was looking at me.

'Who is he?' I said.

'Saleh.'

'What does he do?'

'He helps.'

'I will sleep in the car,' I said. 'And it will not be necessary for your wife to prepare food. I have my own.' The Arab shrugged and turned away and started back toward the shack where the telephone was. I stayed in the car. What else could I do? It was just after two-thirty. In three or four hours' time it would start to get a little cooler. Then I could take a stroll and maybe hunt up a few scorpions. Meanwhile, I must make the best of things as they were. I reached into the back of the car where I kept my box of books and, without looking, I took out the first one I touched. The box contained thirty or forty of the best books in the world, and all of them could be re-read a hundred times and would improve with each reading. It was immaterial which one I got. It turned out to be *The Natural History of Selborne*. I opened it at random ...

'... We had in this village more than twenty years ago an idiot boy, whom I well remember, who, from a child, showed a strong propensity to bees; they were his food, his amusement, his sole object. And as people of this cast have seldom more than one point of view, so this lad exerted all his few faculties on this one pursuit. In winter he dozed away his time, within his father's house, by the fireside, in a kind of torpid state, seldom departing from the chimney-corner; but in the summer he was all alert, and in quest of his game in the fields, and on sunny banks. Honey-bees, bumble-bees, wasps, were his prey wherever he found them; he had no apprehensions from their stings, but would seize them *nudis manibus*, and at once disarm them of their weapons, and suck their bodies for the sake of their honey-bags. Sometimes he would fill his bosom, between his shirt and skin, with a number of these captives, and sometimes confine them to bottles. He was a very *merops apiaster*, or bee-bird, and very injurious to men that kept bees; for he would slide into their bee-gardens, and, sitting down before the stools, would rap with his fingers on the hives, and so take the bees as they came out. He has been known to overturn hives for the sake of honey, of which he is passionately fond. Where metheglin was making, he would linger round the tubs and vessels, begging a draught of what he called bee-wine. As he ran about, he used to make a humming noise with his lips, resembling the buzzing of bees ...'

I glanced up from the book and looked around me. The motionless man across the road had disappeared. There was nobody in sight. The silence was eerie, and the stillness, the utter stillness and desolation of the place was profoundly oppressive. I knew I was being watched. I knew that every little move I made, every sip of whisky and every puff of a cigarette, was being carefully noticed. I detest violence and I never carry a weapon. But I could have done with one now. For a while, I toyed with the idea of starting the motor and driving on down the road until the engine boiled over. But how far would I get? Not very far in this heat and without a fan. One mile, perhaps, or two at the most ...

No – to hell with it. I would stay where I was and read my book.

It must have been about an hour later that I noticed a small dark speck moving toward me along the road in the far distance, coming from the Jerusalem direction. I laid aside my book without taking my eyes away from the speck. I watched it growing bigger and bigger. It was travelling at a great speed, at a really amazing speed. I got out of the Lagonda and hurried to the side of the road and stood there, ready to signal the driver to stop.

Closer and closer it came, and when it was about a quarter of a mile away, it began to slow down. Suddenly, I noticed the shape of its radiator. It was a *Rolls-Royce*! I raised an arm and kept it raised, and the big green car with a man at the wheel pulled in off the road and stopped beside my Lagonda.

I felt absurdly elated. Had it been a Ford or a Morris, I would have been pleased enough, but I would not have been elated. The fact that it was a Rolls – a Bentley would have done equally well, or an Isotta, or another Lagonda – was a virtual guarantee that I would receive all the assistance I required; for whether you know it or not, there is a powerful brotherhood existing among people who own very costly automobiles. They respect one another automatically, and the reason they respect one another is simply that wealth respects wealth. In point of fact, there is nobody in the world that a very wealthy person respects more than another very wealthy person, and because of this, they naturally seek each other out wherever they go. Recognition signals of many kinds are used among them. With the female, the wearing of massive jewels is perhaps the most common; but the costly automobile is also much favoured, and is used by both sexes. It is a travelling placard, a public declaration of affluence, and as such, it is also a card of membership to that excellent unofficial society, the Very-Wealthy-Peoples Union. I am a member myself of long standing, and am delighted to be one. When I meet another member, as I was about to do now, I feel an immediate rapport. I respect him. We speak the same language. He is one of *us*. I had good reason, therefore, to be elated.

The driver of the Rolls climbed out and came toward me. He was a small dark man with olive skin, and he wore an immaculate white linen suit. Probably a Syrian, I thought. Just possibly a Greek. In the heat of the day he looked as cool as could be.

'Good afternoon,' he said. 'Are you having trouble?'

I greeted him, and then bit by bit, I told him everything that had happened.

'My dear fellow,' he said in perfect English, 'but my *dear fellow*, how very distressing. What rotten luck. This is no place to get stranded in.'

'It isn't, is it?'

'And you say that a new fan-belt has definitely been ordered?'

'Yes,' I answered, 'if I can rely upon the proprietor of this establishment.'

The Arab, who had emerged from his shack almost before the Rolls had come to a stop, had now joined us, and the stranger proceeded to question him swiftly in Arabic about the steps he had taken on my behalf. It seemed to me that the two knew each other pretty well, and it was clear that the Arab was in great awe of the new arrival. He was practically crawling along the ground in his presence.

'Well – that seems to be all right,' the stranger said at last, turning to me. 'But quite obviously you won't be able to move on from here until tomorrow morning. Where were you headed for?'

'Jerusalem,' I said. 'And I don't relish the idea of spending the night in this infernal spot.'

'I should say not, my dear man. That would be most uncomfortable.' He smiled at me, showing exceptionally white teeth. Then he took out a cigarette case, and offered me a cigarette. The case was gold, and on the outside of it there was a thin line of green jade inlaid diagonally from corner to corner. It was a beautiful thing. I accepted the cigarette. He lit it for me, then lit his own.

The stranger took a long pull at his cigarette, inhaling deeply. Then he tilted back his head and blew the smoke up into the sun. 'We shall both get heat-stroke if we stand around here much longer,' he said. 'Will you permit me to make a suggestion?'

'But of course.'

'I do hope you won't consider it presumptuous, coming from a complete stranger ...'

'Please ...'

'You can't possibly remain here, so I suggest you come back and stay the night in my house.'

There! The Rolls-Royce was smiling at the Lagonda – smiling at it as it would never have smiled at a Ford or a Morris!

'You mean in Ismailia?' I said.

'No, no,' he answered, laughing. 'I live just around the corner, just over there.' He waved a hand in the direction he had come from.

'But surely you were going to Ismailia? I wouldn't want you to change your plans on my behalf.'

'I wasn't going to Ismailia at all,' he said. 'I was coming down here to collect the mail. My house – and this may surprise you – is quite close to where we are standing. You see that mountain. That's Maghara. I'm immediately behind it.'

I looked at the mountain. It lay ten miles to the north, a yellow rocky lump, perhaps two thousand feet high. 'Do you really mean that you have a house in the middle of all this ... this wasteland?' I asked.

'You don't believe me?' he said, smiling.

'Of course I believe you,' I answered. 'Nothing surprises me any more. Except, perhaps,' and here I smiled back at him, 'except when I meet a stranger in the middle of the desert, and he treats me like a brother. I am overwhelmed by your offer.'

'Nonsense, my dear fellow. My motives are entirely selfish. Civilized company is not easy to come by in these parts. I am quite thrilled at the thought of having a guest for dinner. Permit me to introduce myself – Abdul Aziz.' He made a quick little bow.

'Oswald Cornelius,' I said. 'It is a great pleasure.' We shook hands.

'I live partly in Beirut,' he said.

'I live in Paris.'

'Charming. And now – shall we go? Are you ready?'

'But my car,' I said. 'Can I leave it here safely?'

'Have no fear about that. Omar is a friend of mine. He's not much to look at, poor chap, but he won't let you down if you're with me. And the other one, Saleh, is a good mechanic. He'll fit your new fanbelt when it arrives tomorrow. I'll tell him now.'

Saleh, the man from across the road, had walked over while we were talking. Mr Aziz gave him his instructions. He then spoke to both men about guarding the Lagonda. He was brief and incisive. Omar and Saleh stood bowing and scraping. I went across to the Lagonda to get a suitcase. I needed a change of clothes badly.

'Oh, by the way,' Mr Aziz called over to me, 'I usually put on a black tie for dinner.'

'Of course,' I murmured, quickly pushing back my first choice of suitcase and taking another.

'I do it for the ladies mostly. They seem to like dressing themselves up for dinner.'

I turned sharply and looked at him, but he was already getting into his car.

'Ready?' he said.

I took the briefcase and placed it in the back of the Rolls. Then I climbed into the front seat beside him, and we drove off.

During the drive, we talked casually about this and that. He told me that his business was in carpets. He had offices in Beirut and Damascus. His forefathers, he said, had been in the trade for hundreds of years.

I mentioned that I had a seventeenth-century Damascus carpet on the floor of my bedroom in Paris.

'You don't mean it!' he cried, nearly swerving off the road with excitement. 'Is it silk and wool, with the warp made entirely of silk? And has it got a ground of gold and silver threads?'

'Yes,' I said. 'Exactly.'

'But my dear fellow! You mustn't put a thing like that on the floor!'

'It is touched only by bare feet,' I said.

That pleased him. It seemed that he loved carpets almost as much as I loved the blue vases of Tchin-Hoa.

Soon we turned left off the tarred road on to a hard stony track and headed straight over the desert toward the mountain. 'This is my private driveway,' Mr Aziz said. 'It is five miles long.'

'You are even on the telephone,' I said, noticing the poles that branched off the main road to follow his private drive.

And then suddenly a queer thought struck me.

That Arab at the filling-station ... he also was on the telephone ...

Might not this, then, explain the fortuitous arrival of Mr Aziz?

Was it possible that my lonely host had devised a clever method of shanghai-ing travellers off the road in order to provide himself with what he called 'civilized company' for dinner? Had he, in fact, given the Arab standing instructions to immobilize the cars of all likely-looking persons one after the other as they came along? 'Just cut the fan-belt, Omar. Then phone me up quick. But make sure it's a decent-looking fellow with a good car. Then I'll pop along and see if I think he's worth inviting to the house ...'

It was ridiculous of course.

'I think,' my companion was saying, 'that you are wondering why in the world I should choose to have a house out here in a place like this.'

'Well, yes, I am a bit.'

'Everyone does,' he said.

'*Everyone*,' I said.

'Yes,' he said.

Well, well, I thought – everyone.

'I live here,' he said, 'because I have a peculiar affinity with the desert. I am drawn to it the same way as a sailor is drawn to the sea. Does that seem so very strange to you?'

'No,' I answered, 'it doesn't seem strange at all.'

He paused and took a pull at his cigarette. Then he said, 'That is one reason. But there is another. Are you a family man, Mr Cornelius?'

'Unfortunately not,' I answered cautiously.

'I am,' he said. 'I have a wife and a daughter. Both of them, in my eyes at any rate, are very beautiful. My daughter is just eighteen. She has been to an excellent boarding-school in England, and she is now ...' he shrugged ... 'she is now just sitting around and waiting until she is old enough to get married. But this waiting period – what does one do with a beautiful young girl during that time? I can't let her loose. She is far too desirable for that. When I take her to Beirut, I see the men hanging around her like wolves waiting to pounce. It drives me nearly out of my mind. I know all about men, Mr Cornelius. I know how they behave. It is true, of course, that I am not the only father who has had this problem. But the others seem somehow able to face it and accept it. They let their daughters go. They just turn them out of the house and look the other way. I cannot do that. I simply *cannot bring* myself to do it! I refuse to allow her to be mauled by every Achmed, Ali, and Hamil that comes along. And that, you see, is the other reason why I live in the desert – to protect my lovely child for a few more years from the wild beasts. Did you say that you had no family at all, Mr Cornelius?'

'I'm afraid that's true.'

'Oh.' He seemed disappointed. 'You mean you've never been married?'

'Well ... no,' I said. 'No. I haven't.' I waited for the next inevitable question. It came about a minute later.

'Have you never *wanted* to get married and have children?'

They all asked that one. It was simply another way of saying, 'Are you, in that case, homosexual?'

'Once,' I said. 'Just once.'

'What happened?'

'There was only one person ever in my life, Mr Aziz ... and after she went ...' I sighed.

'You mean she died?'

I nodded, too choked up to answer.

'My dear fellow,' he said. 'Oh, I am so sorry. Forgive me for intruding.'

We drove on for a while in silence.

'It's amazing,' I murmured, 'how one loses all interest in matters of the flesh after a thing like that. I suppose it's the shock. One never gets over it.'

He nodded sympathetically, swallowing it all.

'So now I just travel around trying to forget. I've been doing it for years ...'

We had reached the foot of Mount Maghara now and were following the track as it curved around the mountain toward the side that was invisible from the road – the north side. 'As soon as we round the next bend you'll see the house,' Mr Aziz said.

We rounded the bend ... and there it was! I blinked and stared, and I tell you that for the first few seconds I literally could not believe my eyes. I saw before me a white castle – I mean it – a *tall, white castle* with turrets and towers and little spires all over it, standing like a fairy-tale in the middle of a splash of green vegetation on the lower slope of the blazing-hot, bare, yellow mountain! It was fantastic! It was straight out of Hans Christian Andersen or Grimm. I had seen plenty of romantic-looking Rhine and Loire valley castles in my time, but never before had I seen anything with such a slender, graceful, fairy-tale quality as this! The greenery, as I observed when we drew closer, was a pretty garden of lawns and date-palms, and there was a high white wall going all the way round to keep out the desert.

'Do you approve?' my host asked, smiling.

'It's fabulous!' I said. 'It's like all the fairy-tale castles in the world made into one.'

'That's exactly what it is!' he cried. 'It's a fairy-tale castle! I built it especially for my daughter, my beautiful Princess.'

And the beautiful Princess is imprisoned within its walls by her strict and jealous father, King Abdul Aziz, who refuses to allow her the pleasures of masculine company. But watch out, for here comes Prince Oswald Cornelius to the rescue! Unbeknownst to the King, he is going to ravish the beautiful Princess, and make her very happy.

'You have to admit it's different,' Mr Aziz said.

'It is that.'

'It is also nice and private. I sleep very peacefully here. So does the Princess. No unpleasant young men are likely to come climbing in through *those* windows during the night.'

'Quite so,' I said.

'It used to be a small oasis,' he went on. 'I bought it from the government. We have ample water for the house, the swimming-pool, and three acres of garden.'

We drove through the main gates, and I must say it was wonderful to come suddenly into a miniature paradise of green lawns and flower-beds and palm-trees. Everything was in perfect order, and water-sprinklers were playing on the lawns. When we stopped at the front door of the house, two servants in spotless gallabiyahs and scarlet tarbooshes ran out immediately, one to each side of the car, to open the doors for us.

Two servants? But would both of them have come out like that unless they'd been expecting *two* people? I doubted it. More and more, it began to look as though my odd little theory about being shanghaied as a dinner guest was turning out to be correct. It was all very amusing.

My host ushered me in through the front door, and at once I got that lovely shivery feeling that comes over the skin as one walks suddenly out of intense heat into an air-conditioned room. I was standing in the hall. The floor was of green marble. On my right, there was a wide archway leading to a large room, and I received a fleeting impression of cool white walls, fine pictures, and superlative Louis XV furniture. What a place to find oneself in, in the middle of the Sinai Desert!

And now a woman was coming slowly down the stairs. My host had turned away to speak to the servants, and he didn't see her at once, so when she reached the bottom step, the woman paused, and she laid her naked arm like a white anaconda along the rail of the banister, and there she stood, looking at me as though she were Queen Semiramis on the steps of Babylon, and I was a candidate who might or might not be to her taste. Her hair was jet-black, and she had a figure that made me wet my lips.

When Mr Aziz turned and saw her, he said, 'Oh darling, there you are. I've brought you a guest. His car broke down at the filling-station – such rotten luck – so I asked him to come back and stay the night. Mr Cornelius ... my wife.'

'How very nice,' she said quietly, coming forward.

I took her hand and raised it to my lips. 'I am overcome by your kindness, madame,' I murmured. There was, upon that hand of hers, a diabolical perfume. It was almost exclusively animal. The subtle, sexy secretions of the sperm-whale, the male musk-deer, and the beaver were all there, pungent and obscene beyond words; they dominated the blend completely, and only faint traces of the clean vegetable oils – lemon, cajuput, and zeroli – were allowed to come through. It was superb! And another thing I noticed in the flash of that first moment was this: When I took her hand, she did not, as other women do, let it lie limply across my palm like a fillet of raw fish. Instead, she placed her thumb *underneath* my hand, with the fingers on top; and thus she was able to – and I swear she did – exert a gentle but suggestive pressure upon my hand as I administered the conventional kiss.

'Where is Diana?' asked Mr Aziz.

'She's out by the pool,' the woman said. And turning to me, 'Would *you* like a swim, Mr Cornelius? You must be roasted after hanging around that awful filling-station.'

She had huge velvet eyes, so dark they were almost black, and when she smiled at me, the end of her nose moved upwards, distending the nostrils.

There and then, Prince Oswald Cornelius decided that he cared not one whit about the beautiful Princess who was held captive in the castle by the jealous King. He would ravish the Queen instead.

'Well ...' I said.

'I'm going to have one,' Mr Aziz said.

'Let's all have one,' his wife said. 'We'll lend you a pair of trunks.'

I asked if I might go up to my room first and get out a clean shirt and clean slacks to put on after the swim, and my hostess said, 'Yes, of course,' and told one of the servants to show me the way. He took me up two flights of stairs, and we entered a large white bedroom which had in it an exceptionally large double-bed. There was a well-equipped bathroom leading off to one side, with a pale-blue bathtub and a bidet to match. Everywhere, things were scrupulously clean and very much to my liking. While the servant was unpacking my case, I went over to the window and looked out, and I saw the great blazing desert sweeping in like a yellow sea all the way from the horizon until it met the white garden wall just below me, and there, within the wall,

I could see the swimming-pool, and beside the pool there was a girl lying on her back in the shade of a big pink parasol. The girl was wearing a white swimming costume, and she was reading a book. She had long slim legs and black hair. She was the Princess.

What a set-up, I thought. The white castle, the comfort, the cleanliness, the air-conditioning, the two dazzlingly beautiful females, the watchdog husband, and a whole evening to work in! The situation was so perfectly designed for my entertainment that it would have been impossible to improve upon it. The problems that lay ahead appealed to me very much. A simple straightforward seduction did not amuse me any more. There was no artistry in that sort of thing; and I can assure you that had I been able, by waving a magic wand, to make Mr Abdul Aziz, the jealous watchdog, disappear for the night, I would not have done so. I wanted no pyrrhic victories.

When I left the room, the servant accompanied me. We descended the first flight of stairs, and then, on the landing of the floor below my own, I paused and said casually, 'Does the whole family sleep on this floor?'

'Oh, yes,' the servant said. 'That is the master's room there' – indicating a door – 'and next to it is Mrs Aziz. Miss Diana is opposite.'

Three separate rooms. All very close together. Virtually impregnable. I tucked the information away in my mind and went on down to the pool. My host and hostess were there before me.

'This is my daughter, Diana,' my host said.

The girl in the white swimming-suit stood up and I kissed her hand. 'Hello, Mr Cornelius,' she said.

She was using the same heavy animal perfume as her mother – ambergris, musk, and castor! What a smell it had – bitchy, brazen, and marvellous! I sniffed at it like a dog. She was, I thought, even more beautiful than the parent, if that were possible. She had the same large velvety eyes, the same black hair, and the same shape of face; but her legs were unquestionably longer, and there was something about her body that gave it a slight edge over the older woman's: it was more sinuous, more snaky, and almost certain to be a good deal more flexible. But the older woman, who was probably thirty-seven and looked no more than twenty-five, had a spark in her eye that the daughter could not possibly match.

Eeeny, meeny, miny, mo – just a little while ago, Prince Oswald had sworn that he would ravish the Queen alone, and to hell with the Princess. But now that he had seen the Princess in the flesh, he did not know which one to prefer. Both of them, in their different ways, held forth a promise of innumerable delights, the one innocent and eager, the other expert and voracious. The truth of the matter was that he would like to have them both – the Princess as an hors d'oeuvre, and the Queen as the main dish.

'Help yourself to a pair of trunks in the changing-room, Mr

Cornelius,' Mrs Aziz was saying, so I went into the hut and changed, and when I came out again the three of them were already splashing about in the water. I dived in and joined them. The water was so cold it made me gasp.

'I thought that would surprise you,' Mr Aziz said, laughing. 'It's cooled. I keep it at sixty-five degrees. It's more refreshing in this climate.'

Later, when the sun began dropping lower in the sky, we all sat around in our wet swimming-clothes while a servant brought us pale, ice-cold martinis, and it was at this point that I began, very slowly, very cautiously, to seduce the two ladies in my own particular fashion. Normally, when I am given a free hand, this is not especially difficult for me to do. The curious little talent that I happen to possess – the ability to hypnotize a woman with words – very seldom lets me down. It is not, of course, done only with words. The words themselves, the innocuous, superficial words, are spoken only by the mouth, whereas the real message, the improper and exciting promise, comes from all the limbs and organs of the body, and is transmitted through the eyes. More than that I cannot honestly tell you about how it is done. The point is that it works. It works like cantharides. I believe that I could sit down opposite the Pope's wife, if he had one, and within fifteen minutes, were I to try hard enough, she would be leaning toward me over the table with her lips apart and her eyes glazed with desire. It is a minor talent, not a great one, but I am nonetheless thankful to have had it bestowed upon me, and I have done my best at all times to see that it has not been wasted.

So the four of us, the two wondrous women, the little man, and myself, sat close together in a semi-circle beside the swimming-pool, lounging in deck-chairs and sipping our drinks and feeling the warm six o'clock sunshine upon our skin. I was in good form. I made them laugh a great deal. The story about the greedy old Duchess of Glasgow putting her hand in the chocolate-box and getting nipped by one of my scorpions had the daughter falling out of her chair with mirth; and when I described in detail the interior of my spider breeding-house in the garden outside Paris, both ladies began wriggling with revulsion and pleasure.

It was at this stage that I noticed the eyes of Mr Abdul Aziz resting upon me in a good-humoured, twinkling kind of way. 'Well, well,' the eyes seemed to be saying, 'we are glad to see that you are not quite so disinterested in women as you led us to believe in the car ... Or is it, perhaps, that these congenial surroundings are helping you to forget that great sorrow of yours at last ...' Mr Aziz smiled at me, showing his pure white teeth. It was a friendly smile. I gave him a friendly smile back. What a friendly little fellow he was. He was genuinely delighted to see me paying so much attention to the ladies. So far, then, so good.

I shall skip very quickly over the next few hours, for it was not until after midnight that anything really tremendous happened to me. A few brief notes will suffice to cover the intervening period:

At seven o'clock, we all left the swimming-pool and returned to the house to dress for dinner.

At eight o'clock, we assembled in the big living-room to drink another cocktail. The two ladies were both superbly turned out, and sparkling with jewels. Both of them wore low-cut, sleeveless evening-dresses which had come, without any doubt at all, from some great fashion house in Paris. My hostess was in black, her daughter in pale blue, and the scent of that intoxicating perfume was everywhere about them. What a pair they were! The older woman had that slight forward hunch to her shoulders which one sees only in the most passionate and practised of females; for in the same way as a horsey woman will become bandy-legged from sitting constantly upon a horse, so a woman of great passion will develop a curious roundness of the shoulders from continually embracing men. It is an occupational deformity, and the noblest of them all.

The daughter was not yet old enough to have acquired this singular badge of honour, but with her it was enough for me simply to stand back and observe the shape of her body and to notice the splendid sliding motion of her thighs underneath the tight silk dress as she wandered about the room. She had a line of tiny soft golden hairs growing all the way up the exposed length of her spine, and when I stood behind her it was difficult to resist the temptation of running my knuckles up and down those lovely vertebrae.

At eight thirty, we moved into the dining-room. The dinner that followed was a really magnificent affair, but I shall waste no time here describing food or wine. Throughout the meal I continued to play most delicately and insidiously upon the sensibilities of the women, employing every skill that I possessed; and by the time the dessert arrived, they were melting before my eyes like butter in the sun.

After dinner we returned to the living-room for coffee and brandy, and then, at my host's suggestion, we played a couple of rubbers of bridge.

By the end of the evening, I knew for certain that I had done my work well. The old magic had not let me down. Either of the two ladies, should circumstances permit, was mine for the asking. I was not deluding myself over this. It was a straightforward, obvious fact. It stood out a mile. The face of my hostess was bright with excitement, and whenever she looked at me across the card-table, those huge dark velvety eyes would grow bigger and bigger, and the nostrils would dilate, and the mouth would open slightly to reveal the tip of a moist pink tongue squeezing through between the teeth. It was a marvellously lascivious gesture, and more than once it caused me to trump my own trick. The daughter was less daring but equally direct. Each time her eyes met mine, and that was often enough, she would raise her brows just the tiniest fraction of a centimetre, as though asking a question; then she would make a quick sly little smile, supplying the answer.

'I think it's time we all went to bed,' Mr Aziz said, examining his watch. 'It's after eleven. Come along, my dears.'

Then a queer thing happened. At once, without a second's hesitation and without another glance in my direction, both ladies rose and made for the door! It was astonishing. It left me stunned. I didn't know what to make of it. It was the quickest thing I'd ever seen. And yet it wasn't as though Mr Aziz had spoken angrily. His voice, to me at any rate, had sounded as pleasant as ever. But now he was already turning out the lights, indicating clearly that he wished me also to retire. What a blow! I had expected at least to receive a whisper from either the wife or the daughter before we separated for the night, just a quick three or four words telling me where to go and when; but instead, I was left standing like a fool beside the card-table while the two ladies glided out of the room.

My host and I followed them up the stairs. On the landing of the first floor, the mother and daughter stood side by side, waiting for me.

'Good night, Mr Cornelius,' my hostess said.

'Good night, Mr Cornelius,' the daughter said.

'Good night, my dear fellow,' Mr Aziz said. 'I do hope you have everything you want.'

They turned away, and there was nothing for me to do but continue slowly, reluctantly, up the second flight of stairs to my own room. I entered it and closed the door. The heavy brocade curtains had already been drawn by one of the servants but I parted them and leaned out of the window to take a look at the night. The air was still and warm, and a brilliant moon was shining over the desert. Below me, the swimming-pool in the moonlight looked something like an enormous glass mirror lying flat on the lawn, and beside it I could see the four deck-chairs we had been sitting in earlier.

Well, well, I thought. What happens now?

One thing I knew I must not do in this house was to venture out of my room and go prowling around the corridors. That would be suicide. I had learned many years ago that there are three breeds of husband with whom one must never take unnecessary risks – the Bulgarian, the Greek, and the Syrian. None of them, for some reason, resents you flirting quite openly with his wife, but he will kill you at once if he catches you getting into her bed. Mr Aziz was a Syrian. A degree of prudence was therefore essential, and if any move were going to be made now, it must be made not by me but by one of the two women, for only she (or they) would know precisely what was safe and what was dangerous. Yet I had to admit that after witnessing the way in which my host had called them both to heel four minutes ago, there was little hope of further action in the near future. The trouble was, though, that I had got myself so infernally steamed up.

I undressed and took a long cold shower. That helped. Then, because I have never been able to sleep in the moonlight, I made sure that the curtains were tightly drawn together. I got into bed, and for the next hour or so I lay reading some more of Gilbert White's *Natural History of Selborne*. That also helped, and at last, somewhere between midnight and one a.m., there came a time when I was able to switch out the light and prepare myself for sleep without altogether too many regrets.

I was just beginning to doze off when I heard some tiny sounds. I recognized them at once. They were sounds that I had heard many times before in my life, and yet they were still, for me, the most thrilling and evocative in the whole world. They consisted of a series of little soft metallic noises, of metal grating gently against metal, and they were made, they were always made by somebody who was very slowly, very cautiously, turning the handle of one's door from the outside. Instantly, I became wide awake. But I did not move. I simply opened my eyes and stared in the direction of the door; and I can remember wishing at that moment for a gap in the curtain, for just a small thin shaft of moonlight to come in from outside so that I could at least catch a glimpse of the shadow of the lovely form that was about to enter. But the room was as dark as a dungeon.

I did not hear the door open. No hinge squeaked. But suddenly a little gust of air swept through the room and rustled the curtains, and a moment later I heard the soft thud of wood against wood as the door was carefully closed again. Then came the click of the latch as the handle was released.

Next, I heard feet tiptoeing toward me over the carpet.

For one horrible second, it occurred to me that this might just possibly be Mr Abdul Aziz creeping in upon me with a long knife in his hand, but then all at once a warm extensile body was bending over mine, and a woman's voice was whispering in my ear, '*Don't make a sound!*'

'My dearest beloved,' I said, wondering which one of them it was, 'I knew you'd ...' Instantly her hand came over my mouth.

'*Please!*' she whispered. '*Not another word!*'

I didn't argue. My lips had many better things to do than that. So had hers.

Here I must pause. This is not like me at all – I know that. But just for once, I wish to be excused a detailed description of the great scene that followed. I have my own reasons for this and I beg you to respect them. In any case, it will do you no harm to exercise your own imagination for a change, and if you wish, I shall stimulate it a little by saying simply and truthfully that of the many thousands and thousands of women I have known in my time, none has transported me to greater extremes of ecstasy than this lady of the Sinai Desert. Her dexterity was amazing. Her passion was intense. Her range was unbelievable. At every turn, she was ready with some new and intricate manoeuvre. And to cap it all, she possessed the subtlest and most recondite style I have ever encountered. She was a great artist. She was a genius.

All this, you will probably say, indicated clearly that my visitor must have been the older woman. You would be wrong. It indicated nothing. True genius is a gift of birth. It has very little to do with age; and I can assure you I had no way of knowing for certain which of them it was in the darkness of that room. I wouldn't have bet a penny on it either way. At one moment, after some particularly boisterous cadenza, I would be convinced it was the wife. *It must be the wife!* Then suddenly the whole tempo would begin to change, and the melody would become so childlike and innocent that I found myself swearing it was the daughter. *It must be the daughter!*

Maddening it was not to know the true answer. It tantalized me. It also humbled me, for, after all, a connoisseur, a supreme connoisseur, should always be able to guess the vintage without seeing the label on the bottle. But this one really had me beat. At one point, I reached for cigarettes, intending to solve the mystery in the flare of a match, but her hand was on me in a flash, and cigarettes and matches were snatched away and flung across the room. More than once, I began to whisper the question itself into her ear, but I never got three words out before the hand shot up again and smacked itself over my mouth. Rather violently, too.

Very well, I thought. Let it be for now. Tomorrow morning, downstairs in the daylight, I shall know for certain which one of you it was. I shall know by the glow on the face, by the way the eyes look back into mine, and by a hundred other little telltale signs. I shall also know by the marks that my teeth have made on the left side of the neck, above the dress line. A rather wily move, that one, I thought, and so perfectly timed – my vicious bite was administered during the height of her passion – that she never for one moment realized the significance of the act.

It was altogether a most memorable night, and at least four hours must have gone by before she gave me a final fierce embrace, and slipped out of the room as quickly as she had come in.

The next morning I did not awaken until after ten o'clock. I got out of bed and drew open the curtains. It was another brilliant, hot, desert day. I took a leisurely bath, then dressed myself as carefully as ever. I felt relaxed and chipper. It made me very happy to think that I could still summon a woman to my room with my eyes alone, even in middle age. And what a woman! It would be fascinating to find out which one of them she was. I would soon know.

I made my way slowly down the two flights of stairs.

'Good morning, my dear fellow, good morning!' Mr Aziz said, rising from a small desk he had been writing at in the living-room. 'Did you have a good night?'

'Excellent, thank you,' I answered, trying not to sound smug.

He came and stood close to me, smiling with his very white teeth. His shrewd little eyes rested on my face and moved over it slowly, as though searching for something.

'I have good news for you,' he said. 'They called up from B'ir Rawd Salim five minutes ago and said your fan-belt had arrived by the mail-truck. Saleh is fitting it on now. It'll be ready in an hour. So when you've had some breakfast, I'll drive you over and you can be on your way.'

I told him how grateful I was.

'We'll be sorry to see you go,' he said. 'It's been an immense pleasure for all of us having you drop in like this, an immense pleasure.'

I had my breakfast alone in the dining-room. Afterwards, I returned to the living-room to smoke a cigarette while my host continued writing at his desk.

'Do forgive me,' he said. 'I just have a couple of things to finish here. I won't be long. I've arranged for your case to be packed and put in the car, so you have nothing to worry about. Sit down and enjoy your cigarette. The ladies ought to be down any minute now.'

The wife arrived first. She came sailing into the room looking more than ever like the dazzling Queen Semiramis of the Nile, and the first thing I noticed about her was the pale-green chiffon scarf knotted casually around her neck! Casually but carefully! So carefully that no part of the skin of the neck was visible. The woman went straight over to her husband and kissed him on the cheek. 'Good morning, my darling,' she said.

You cunning beautiful bitch, I thought.

'Good *morning*, Mr Cornelius,' she said gaily, coming over to sit in the chair opposite mine. 'Did you have a good night? I do hope you had everything you wanted.'

Never in my life have I seen such a sparkle in a woman's eyes as I saw in hers that morning, nor such a glow of pleasure in a woman's face.

'I had a very good night indeed, thank *you*,' I answered, showing her that I knew.

She smiled and lit a cigarette. I glanced over at Mr Aziz, who was still writing away busily at the desk with his back to us. He wasn't paying the slightest attention to his wife or to me. He was, I thought, exactly like all the other poor cuckolds that I ever created. Not one of them would believe that it could happen to him, not right under his own nose.

'Good morning, everybody!' cried the daughter, sweeping into the room. 'Good morning, daddy! Good morning, mummy!' She gave them each a kiss. 'Good morning, Mr Cornelius!' She was wearing a pair of pink slacks and a rust-coloured blouse, and I'll be damned if she didn't also have a scarf tied carelessly but carefully around her neck! A chiffon scarf!

'Did you have a decent night?' she asked, perching herself like a young bride on the arm of my chair, arranging herself in such a way that one of her thighs rested against my forearm. I leaned back and looked at her closely. She looked back at me and winked. She actually winked! Her face was glowing and sparkling every bit as much as her mother's, and if anything, she seemed even more pleased with herself than the older woman.

I felt pretty confused. Only one of them had a bite mark to conceal, yet both of them had covered their necks with scarves. I conceded that this might be a coincidence, but on the face of it, it looked much more like a conspiracy to me. It looked as though they were both working closely together to keep me from discovering the truth. But what an extraordinary screwy business! And what was the purpose of it all? And in what other peculiar ways, might I ask, did they plot and plan together among themselves? Had they drawn lots or something the night before? Or did they simply take it in turns with visitors? I *must* come back again, I told myself, for another visit as soon as possible just to see what happens the next time. In fact, I might motor down specially from Jerusalem in a day or two. It would be easy, I reckoned, to get myself invited again.

'Are you ready, Mr Cornelius?' Mr Aziz said, rising from his desk.

'Quite ready,' I answered.

The ladies, sleek and smiling, led the way outside to where the big green Rolls-Royce was waiting. I kissed their hands and murmured a million thanks to each of them. Then I got into the front seat beside my host, and we drove off. The mother and daughter waved. I lowered my window and waved. Then we were out of the garden and into the desert, following the stony yellow track as it skirted the base of Mount Maghara, with the telegraph poles marching along beside us.

During the journey, my host and I conversed pleasantly about this and that. I was at pains to be as agreeable as possible because my one object now was to get myself invited to stay at the house again. If I didn't succeed in getting *him* to ask *me*, then *I* should have to ask *him*. I would do it at the last moment. 'Good-bye, my dear friend,' I would say, gripping him warmly by the throat. 'May I have the pleasure of dropping in to see you again if I happen to be passing this way?' And of course he would say yes.

'Did you think I exaggerated when I told you my daughter was beautiful?' he asked me.

'You understated it,' I said. 'She's a raving beauty. I do congratulate you. But your wife is no less lovely. In fact, between the two of them they almost swept me off my feet,' I added, laughing.

'I noticed that,' he said, laughing with me. 'They're a couple of very naughty girls. They do so love to flirt with other men. But why should I mind. There's no harm in flirting.'

'None whatsoever,' I said.

'I think it's gay and fun.'

'It's charming,' I said.

In less than half an hour we had reached the main Ismailia– Jerusalem road. Mr Aziz turned the Rolls on to the black tarmac strip and headed for the filling-station at seventy miles an hour. In a few minutes we would be there. So now I tried moving a little closer to the subject of another visit, fishing gently for an invitation. 'I can't get over your house,' I said. 'I think it's simply wonderful.'

'It is nice, isn't it?'

'I suppose you're bound to get pretty lonely out there, on and off, just the three of you together?'

'It's no worse than anywhere else,' he said. 'People get lonely wherever they are. A desert, or a city – it doesn't make much difference, really. But we do have visitors, you know. You'd be surprised at the number of people who drop in from time to time. Like you, for instance. It was a great pleasure having you with us, my dear fellow.'

'I shall never forget it,' I said. 'It is a rare thing to find kindness and hospitality of that order nowadays.'

I waited for him to tell me that I must come again, but he didn't. A little silence sprang up between us, a slightly uneasy little silence. To bridge it, I said, 'I think yours is the most thoughtful paternal gesture I've ever heard of in my life.'

'Mine?

'Yes. Building a house right out there in the back of beyond and living in it just for your daughter's sake, to protect her. I think it's remarkable.'

I saw him smile, but he kept his eyes on the road and said nothing. The filling-station and the group of huts were now in sight about a mile ahead of us. The sun was high and it was getting hot inside the car.

'Not many fathers would put themselves out to that extent,' I went on.

Again he smiled, but somewhat bashfully, this time, I thought. And then he said, 'I don't deserve *quite* as much credit as you like to give

me, really I don't. To be absolutely honest with you, that pretty
daughter of mine isn't the only reason for my living in such splendid
isolation.'

'I know that.'

'You do?'

'You told me. You said the other reason was the desert. You loved
it, you said, as a sailor loves the sea.'

'So I did. And it's quite true. But there's still a third reason.'

'Oh, and what is that?'

He didn't answer me. He sat quite still with his hands on the wheel
and his eyes fixed on the road ahead.

'I'm sorry,' I said. 'I shouldn't have asked the question. It's none
of my business.'

'No, no, that's quite all right,' he said. 'Don't apologize.'

I stared out of the window at the desert. 'I think it's hotter than
yesterday,' I said. 'It must be well over a hundred already.'

'Yes.'

I saw him shifting a little in his seat, as though trying to get
comfortable, and then he said, 'I don't really see why I shouldn't tell
you the truth about that house. You don't strike me as being a gossip.'

'Certainly not,' I said.

We were close to the filling-station now, and he had slowed the car
down almost to walking-speed to give himself time to say what he had
to say. I could see the two Arabs standing beside my Lagonda,
watching us.

'That daughter,' he said at length, 'the one you met – she isn't the
only daughter I have.'

'Oh, really?'

'I've got another who is five years older than she.'

'And just as beautiful, no doubt,' I said. 'Where does she live? In
Beirut?'

'No, she's in the house.'

'In which house? Not the one we've just left?'

'Yes.'

'But I never saw her!'

'Well,' he said, turning suddenly to watch my face, 'maybe not.'

'But why?'

'She has leprosy.'

I jumped.

'Yes, I know,' he said, 'it's a terrible thing. She has the worst kind,
too, poor girl. It's called anaesthetic leprosy. It is highly resistant, and
almost impossible to cure. If only it were the nodular variety, it would
be much easier. But it isn't, and there you are. So when a visitor comes
to the house, she keeps to her own apartment, on the third floor ...'

The car must have pulled into the filling-station about then because the next thing I can remember was seeing Mr Abdul Aziz sitting there looking at me with those small clever black eyes of his, and he was saying, 'But my dear fellow, you mustn't alarm yourself like this. Calm yourself down, Mr Cornelius, calm yourself down! There's absolutely nothing in the world for you to worry about. It is not a very contagious disease. You have to have the most *intimate* contact with the person in order to catch it . . .'

I got out of the car very slowly and stood in the sunshine. The Arab with the diseased face was grinning at me and saying, 'Fan-belt all fixed now. Everything fine.' I reached into my pocket for cigarettes, but my hand was shaking so violently I dropped the packet on the ground. I bent down and retrieved it. Then I got a cigarette out and managed to light it. When I looked up again, I saw the green Rolls-Royce already half a mile down the road, and going away fast.

THE GREAT SWITCHEROO

There were about forty people at Jerry and Samantha's cocktail-party that evening. It was the usual crowd, the usual discomfort, the usual appalling noise. People had to stand very close to one another and shout to make themselves heard. Many were grinning, showing capped white teeth. Most of them had a cigarette in the left hand, a drink in the right.

I moved away from my wife Mary and her group. I headed for the small bar in the far corner, and when I got there, I sat down on a bar-stool and faced the room. I did this so that I could look at the women. I settled back with my shoulders against the bar-rail, sipping my Scotch and examining the women one by one over the rim of my glass.

I was studying not their figures but their faces, and what interested me there was not so much the face itself but the big red mouth in the middle of it all. And even then, it wasn't the whole mouth but only the lower lip. The lower lip, I had recently decided, was the great revealer. It gave away more than the eyes. The eyes hid their secrets. The lower lip hid very little. Take, for example, the lower lip of Jacinth Winkleman, who was standing nearest to me. Notice the wrinkles on that lip, how some were parallel and some radiated outward. No two people had the same pattern of lip-wrinkles, and come to think of it, you could catch a criminal that way if you had his lip-print on file and he had taken a drink at the scene of the crime. The lower lip is what you suck and nibble when you're ruffled, and Martha Sullivan was doing that right now as she watched from a distance her fatuous husband slobbering over Judy Martinson. You lick it when lecherous. I could see Ginny Lomax licking hers with the tip of her tongue as she stood beside Ted Dorling and gazed up into his face. It was a deliberate lick, the tongue coming out slowly and making a slow wet wipe along the entire length of the lower lip. I saw Ted Dorling looking at Ginny's tongue, which was what she wanted him to do.

It really does seem to be a fact, I told myself, as my eyes wandered from lower lip to lower lip across the room, that all the less attractive traits of the human animal, arrogance, rapacity, gluttony, lasciviousness, and the rest of them, are clearly signalled in that little carapace of scarlet skin. But you have to know the code. The protuberant or bulging lower lip is supposed to signify sensuality. But this is only half true in men and wholly untrue in women. In women, it is the thin line you should look for, the narrow blade with the sharply delineated bottom edge. And in the nymphomaniac there is a tiny just visible crest of skin at the top centre of the lower lip.

Samantha, my hostess, had that.

Where was she now, Samantha?

Ah, there she was, taking an empty glass out of a guest's hand. Now she was heading my way to refill it.

'Hello, Vic,' she said: 'You all alone?'

She's a nympho-bird all right, I told myself. But a very rare example of the species, because she is entirely and utterly monogamous. She is a married monogamous nympho-bird who stays for ever in her own nest.

She is also the fruitiest female I have ever set eyes upon in my whole life.

'Let me help you,' I said, standing up and taking the glass from her hand. 'What's wanted in here?'

'Vodka on the rocks,' she said. 'Thanks, Vic.' She laid a lovely long white arm upon the top of the bar and she leaned forward so that her bosom rested on the bar-rail, squashing upward. 'Oops,' I said, pouring vodka outside the glass.

Samantha looked at me with huge brown eyes, but said nothing.

'I'll wipe it up,' I said.

She took the refilled glass from me and walked away. I watched her go. She was wearing black pants. They were so tight around the buttocks that the smallest mole or pimple would have shown through the cloth. But Samantha Rainbow had not a blemish on her bottom. I caught myself licking my own lower lip. That's right, I thought. I want her. I lust after that woman. But it's too risky to try. It would be suicide to make a pass at a girl like that. First of all, she lives next door, which is too close. Secondly, as I have already said, she is monogamous. Thirdly, she is thick as a thief with Mary, my own wife. They exchange dark female secrets. Fourthly, her husband Jerry is my very old and good friend, and not even I, Victor Hammond, though I am churning with lust, would dream of trying to seduce the wife of a man who is my very old and trusty friend.

Unless . . .

It was at this point, as I sat on the bar-stool letching over Samantha Rainbow, that an interesting idea began to filter quietly into the centre of my brain. I remained still, allowing the idea to expand. I watched Samantha across the room, and began fitting her into the framework of the idea. Oh, Samantha, my gorgeous and juicy little jewel, I shall have you yet.

But could anybody seriously hope to get away with a crazy lark like that?

No, not in a million nights.

One couldn't even *try* it unless Jerry agreed. So why think about it?

Samantha was standing about six yards away, talking to Gilbert Mackesy. The fingers of her right hand were curled around a tall glass. The fingers were long and almost certainly dexterous.

Assuming, just for the fun of it, that Jerry did agree, then even so, there would still be gigantic snags along the way. There was, for example, the little matter of physical characteristics. I had seen Jerry many times at the club having a shower after tennis, but right now I couldn't for the life of me recall the necessary details. It wasn't the sort of thing one noticed very much. Usually, one didn't even look.

Anyway, it would be madness to put the suggestion to Jerry point-blank. I didn't know him *that* well. He might be horrified. He might even turn nasty. There could be an ugly scene. I must test him out, therefore, in some subtle fashion.

'You know something,' I said to Jerry about an hour later when we were sitting together on the sofa having a last drink. The guests were drifting away and Samantha was by the door saying goodbye to them. My own wife Mary was out on the terrace talking to Bob Swain. I could see through the open french windows. 'You know something funny?' I said to Jerry as we sat together on the sofa.

'What's funny?' Jerry asked me.

'A fellow I had lunch with today told me a fantastic story. Quite unbelievable.'

'What story?' Jerry said. The whisky had begun to make him sleepy.

'This man, the one I had lunch with, had a terrific letch after the wife of his friend who lived nearby. And his friend had an equally big letch after the wife of the man I had lunch with. Do you see what I mean?'

'You mean two fellers who lived close to each other both fancied each other's wives.'

'Precisely,' I said.

'Then there was no problem,' Jerry said.

'There was a very big problem,' I said. 'The wives were both very faithful and honourable women.'

'Samantha's the same,' Jerry said. 'She wouldn't look at another man.'

'Nor would Mary,' I said. 'She's a fine girl.'

Jerry emptied his glass and set it down carefully on the sofa-table. 'So what happened in your story?' he said. 'It sounds dirty.'

'What happened,' I said, 'was that these two randy sods cooked up a plan which made it possible for each of them to ravish the other's wife without the wives ever knowing it. If you can believe such a thing.'

'With chloroform?' Jerry said.

'Not at all. They were fully conscious.'

'Impossible,' Jerry said. 'Someone's been pulling your leg.'

'I don't think so,' I said. 'From the way this man told it to me, with all the little details and everything, I don't think he was making it up. In fact, I'm sure he wasn't. And listen, they didn't do it just once, either. They've been doing it every two or three weeks for months!'

'And the wives don't know?'

'They haven't a clue.'

'I've got to hear this,' Jerry said. 'Let's get another drink first.'

We crossed to the bar and refilled our glasses, then returned to the sofa.

'You must remember,' I said, 'that there had to be a tremendous lot of preparation and rehearsal beforehand. And many intimate details had to be exchanged to give the plan a chance of working. But the essential part of the scheme was simple:

'They fixed a night, call it Saturday. On that night the husbands and wives were to go up to bed as usual, at say eleven or eleven thirty.

'From then on, normal routine would be preserved. A little reading, perhaps, a little talking, then out with the lights.

'After lights out, the husbands would at once roll over and pretend to go to sleep. This was to discourage their wives from getting fresh, which at this stage must on no account be permitted. So the wives went to sleep. But the husbands stayed awake. So far so good.

'Then at precisely one a.m., by which time the wives would be in a good deep sleep, each husband would slip quietly out of bed, put on a pair of bedroom slippers and creep downstairs in his pyjamas. He would open the front door and go out into the night, taking care not to close the door behind him.

'They lived,' I went on, 'more or less across the street from one another. It was a quiet suburban neighbourhood and there was seldom anyone about at that hour. So these two furtive pyjama-clad figures would pass each other as they crossed the street, each one heading for another house, another bed, another woman.'

Jerry was listening to me carefully. His eyes were a little glazed from drink, but he was listening to every word.

'The next part,' I said, 'had been prepared very thoroughly by both men. Each knew the inside of his friend's house almost as well as he knew his own. He knew how to find his way in the dark downstairs and up without knocking over the furniture. He knew his way to the stairs and exactly how many steps there were to the top and which of them creaked and which didn't. He knew on which side of the bed the woman upstairs was sleeping.

'Each took off his slippers and left them in the hall, then up the stairs he crept in his bare feet and pyjamas. This part of it, according to my friend, was rather exciting. He was in a dark silent house that wasn't his own, and on his way to the main bedroom he had to pass no less than three children's bedrooms where the doors were always left slightly open.'

'Children!' Jerry cried. 'My God, what if one of them had woken up and said, "Daddy, is that you?"'

'That was all taken care of,' I said. 'Emergency procedure would then come into effect immediately. Also if the wife, just as he was creeping into her room, woke up and said, "Darling, what's wrong? Why are you wandering about?"; then again, emergency procedure.'

'What emergency procedure?' Jerry said.

'Simple,' I answered. 'The man would immediately dash downstairs and out the front door and across to his own house and ring the bell. This was a signal for the other character, no matter what he was doing at the time, also to rush downstairs at full speed and open the door and let the other fellow in while he went out. This would get them both back quickly to their proper houses.'

'With egg all over their faces,' Jerry said.

'Not at all,' I said.

'That doorbell would have woken the whole house,' Jerry said.

'Of course,' I said. 'And the husband, returning upstairs in his pyjamas, would merely say, "I went to see who the hell was ringing the bell at this ungodly hour. Couldn't find anyone. It must have been a drunk."'

'What about the other guy?' Jerry asked. 'How does he explain why he rushed downstairs when his wife or child spoke to him?'

'He would say, "I heard someone prowling about outside, so I rushed down to get him, but he escaped." "Did you actually see him?" his wife would ask anxiously. "Of course I saw him," the husband would answer. "He ran off down the street. He was too damn fast for me." Whereupon the husband would be warmly congratulated for his bravery.'

'Okay,' Jerry said. 'That's the easy part. Everything so far is just a matter of good planning and good timing. But what happens when these two horny characters actually climb into bed with each other's wives?'

'They go right to it,' I said.

'The wives are sleeping,' Jerry said.

'I know,' I said. 'So they proceed immediately with some very gentle but very skilful love-play, and by the time these dames are fully awake, they're as randy as rattlesnakes.'

'No talking, I presume,' Jerry said.

'Not a word.'

'Okay, so the wives are awake,' Jerry said. 'And their hands get to work. So just for a start, what about the simple question of body size? What about the difference between the new man and the husband? What about tallness and shortness and fatness and thinness? You're not telling me these men were physically identical?'

'Not identical, obviously,' I said. 'But they were more or less similar in build and height. That was essential. They were both clean-shaven and had roughly the same amount of hair on their heads. That sort of similarity is commonplace. Look at you and me, for instance. We're roughly the same height and build, aren't we?'

'Are we?' Jerry said.

'How tall are you?' I said.

'Six foot exactly.'

'I'm five eleven,' I said. 'One inch difference. What do you weigh?'

'One hundred and eighty-seven.'

'I'm a hundred and eighty-four,' I said. 'What's three pounds among friends?'

There was a pause. Jerry was looking out throught the french windows on to the terrace where my wife, Mary, was standing. Mary was still talking to Bob Swain and the evening sun was shining in her hair. She was a dark pretty girl with a bosom. I watched Jerry. I saw his tongue come out and go sliding along the surface of his lower lip.

'I guess you're right,' Jerry said, still looking at Mary. 'I guess we are about the same size, you and me.' When he turned back and faced me again, there was a little red rose high up on each cheek. 'Go on about these two men,' he said. 'What about some of the other differences?'

'You mean faces?' I said. 'No one's going to see faces in the dark.'

'I'm not talking about faces,' Jerry said.

'What are you talking about, then?'

'I'm talking about their cocks,' Jerry said. 'That's what it's all about isn't it? And you're not going to tell me ...'

'Oh yes, I am,' I said. 'Just so long as both men were either circumcised or uncircumcised, then there was really no problem.'

'Are you seriously suggesting that all men have the same size in cocks?' Jerry said. 'Because they don't.'

'I know they don't,' I said.

'Some are enormous,' Jerry said. 'And some are titchy.'

'There are always exceptions,' I told him. 'But you'd be surprised at the number of men whose measurements are virtually the same, give or take a centimetre. According to my friend, ninety per cent are normal. Only ten per cent are notably large or small.'

'I don't believe that,' Jerry said.

'Check on it sometime,' I said. 'Ask some well-travelled girl.'

Jerry took a long slow sip of his whisky, and his eyes over the top

of his glass were looking again at Mary on the terrace. 'What about
the rest of it?' he said.

'No problem,' I said.

'No problem, my arse,' he said. 'Shall I tell you why this is a phony
story?'

'Go ahead.'

'Everybody knows that a wife and husband who have been married
for some years develop a kind of routine. It's inevitable. My God, a
new operator would be spotted instantly. You know damn well he
would. You can't suddenly wade in with a totally different style and
expect the woman not to notice it, and I don't care how randy she
was. She'd smell a rat in the first minute!'

'A routine can be duplicated,' I said. 'Just so long as every detail
of that routine is described beforehand.'

'A bit personal, that,' Jerry said.

'The whole thing's personal,' I said. 'So each man tells his story.
He tells precisely what he usually does. He tells everything. The lot.
The works. The whole routine from beginning to end.'

'Jesus,' Jerry said.

'Each of these men,' I said, 'had to learn a new part. He had, in
effect, to become an actor. He was impersonating another character.'

'Not so easy, that,' Jerry said.

'No problem at all, according to my friend. The only thing one had
to watch out for was not to get carried away and start improvising.
One had to follow the stage directions very carefully and stick to
them.'

Jerry took another pull at his drink. He also took another look at
Mary on the terrace. Then he leaned back against the sofa, glass in
hand.

'These two characters,' he said. 'You mean they actually pulled it
off?'

'I'm damn sure they did,' I said. 'They're still doing it. About once
every three weeks.'

'Fantastic story,' Jerry said. 'And a damn crazy dangerous thing to
do. Just imagine the sort of hell that would break loose if you were
caught. Instant divorce. Two divorces, in fact. One on each side of
the street. Not worth it.'

'Takes a lot of guts,' I said.

'The party's breaking up,' Jerry said. 'They're all going home with
their goddam wives.'

I didn't say any more after that. We sat there for a couple of minutes
sipping our drinks while the guests began drifting towards the hall.

'Did he say it was fun, this friend of yours?' Jerry asked suddenly.

'He said it was a gas,' I answered. 'He said all the normal pleasures
got intensified one hundred per cent because of the risk. He swore it

was the greatest way of doing it in the world, impersonating the husband and the wife not knowing it.'

At that point, Mary came in through the french windows with Bob Swain. She had an empty glass in one hand and a flame-coloured azalea in the other. She had picked the azalea on the terrace.

'I've been watching you,' she said, pointing the flower at me like a pistol. 'You've hardly stopped talking for the last ten minutes. What's he been telling you, Jerry?'

'A dirty story,' Jerry said, grinning.

'He does that when he drinks,' Mary said.

'Good story,' Jerry said. 'But totally impossible. Get him to tell it to you sometime.'

'I don't like dirty stories,' Mary said. 'Come along, Vic. It's time we went.'

'Don't go yet,' Jerry said, fixing his eyes upon her splendid bosom. 'Have another drink.'

'No thanks,' she said. 'The children'll be screaming for their supper. I've had a lovely time.'

'Aren't you going to kiss me good night?' Jerry said, getting up from the sofa. He went for her mouth, but she turned her head quickly and he caught only the edge of her cheek.

'Go away, Jerry,' she said. 'You're drunk.'

'Not drunk,' Jerry said. 'Just lecherous.'

'Don't you get lecherous with me, my boy,' Mary said sharply. 'I hate that sort of talk.' She marched away across the room, carrying her bosom before her like a battering-ram.

'So long, Jerry,' I said. 'Fine party.'

Mary, full of dark looks, was waiting for me in the hall. Samantha was there, too, saying goodbye to the last guests – Samantha with her dexterous fingers and her smooth skin and her smooth, dangerous thighs. 'Cheer up, Vic,' she said to me, her white teeth showing. She looked like the creation, the beginning of the world, the first morning. 'Good night, Vic darling,' she said, stirring her fingers in my vitals.

I followed Mary out of the house. 'You feeling all right?' she asked.

'Yes,' I said. 'Why not?'

'The amount you drink is enough to make anyone feel ill,' she said.

There was a scrubby old hedge dividing our place from Jerry's and there was a gap in it we always used. Mary and I walked through the gap in silence. We went into the house and she cooked up a big pile of scrambled eggs and bacon, and we ate it with the children.

After the meal, I wandered outside. The summer evening was clear and cool and because I had nothing else to do I decided to mow the grass in the front garden. I got the mower out of the shed and started it up. Then I began the old routine of marching back and forth behind it. I like mowing grass. It is a soothing operation, and on our front lawn I could always look at Samantha's house going one way and thinking about her going the other.

I had been at it for about ten minutes when Jerry came strolling through the gap in the hedge. He was smoking a pipe and had his hands in his pockets and he stood on the edge of the grass, watching me. I pulled up in front of him, but left the motor ticking over.

'Hi, sport,' he said. 'How's everything?'

'I'm in the doghouse,' I said. 'So are you.'

'Your little wife,' he said, 'is just too goddamn prim and prissy to be true.'

'Oh, I know that.'

'She rebuked me in my own house,' Jerry said.

'Not very much.'

'It was enough,' he said, smiling slightly.

'Enough for what?'

'Enough to make me want to get a little bit of my own back on her. So what would you think if I suggested you and I have a go at that thing your friend told you about at lunch?'

When he said this, I felt such a surge of excitement my stomach nearly jumped out of my mouth. I gripped the handles of the mower and started revving the engine.

'Have I said the wrong thing?' Jerry asked.

I didn't answer.

'Listen,' he said. 'If you think it's a lousy idea, let's just forget I ever mentioned it. You're not mad at me, are you?'

'I'm not mad at you, Jerry,' I said. 'It's just that it never entered my head that *we* should do it.'

'It entered mine,' he said. 'The set-up is perfect. We wouldn't even have to cross the street.' His face had gone suddenly bright and his eyes were shining like two stars. 'So what do you say, Vic?'

'I'm thinking,' I said.

'Maybe you don't fancy Samantha.'

'I don't honestly know,' I said.

'She's lots of fun,' Jerry said. 'I guarantee that.'

At this point, I saw Mary come out on to the front porch. 'There's Mary,' I said. 'She's looking for the children. We'll talk some more tomorrow.'

'Then it's a deal?'

'It could be, Jerry. But only on condition we don't rush it. I want to be dead sure everything is right before we start. Damn it all, this is a whole brand-new can of beans!'

'No, it's not!' he said. 'Your friend said it was a gas. He said it was easy.'

'Ah, yes,' I said, 'My friend. Of course. But each case is different.' I opened the throttle on the mower and went whirring away across the lawn. When I got to the far side and turned around, Jerry was already through the gap in the hedge and walking up to his front door.

The next couple of weeks was a period of high conspiracy for Jerry and me. We held secret meetings in bars and restaurants to discuss strategy, and sometimes he dropped into my office after work and we had a planning session behind the closed door. Whenever a doubtful point arose, Jerry would always say, 'How did your friend do it?' And I would play for time and say, 'I'll call him up and ask him about that one.'

After many conferences and much talk, we agreed upon the following main points:

1. That D Day should be a Saturday.

2. That on D Day evening we should take our wives out to a good dinner, the four of us together.

3. That Jerry and I should leave our houses and cross over through the gap in the hedge at precisely one a.m. Sunday morning.

4. That instead of lying in bed in the dark until one a.m. came along, we should both, as soon as our wives were asleep, go quietly downstairs to the kitchen and drink coffee.

5. That we should use the front doorbell idea if an emergency arose.

6. That the return cross-over time was fixed for two a.m.

7. That while in the wrong bed, questions (if any) from the woman must be answered by an 'Uh-uh' sounded with the lips closed tight.

8. That I myself must immediately give up cigarettes and take to a pipe so that I would 'smell' the same as Jerry.

9. That we should at once start using the same brand of hair oil and after-shave lotion.

10. That as both of us normally wore our wrist-watches in bed, and they were much the same shape, it was decided not to exchange. Neither of us wore rings.

11. That each man must have something unusual about him that the woman would identify positively with her own husband. We therefore invented what became known as 'The Sticking Plaster Ploy'. It worked like this: on D Day evening, when the couples arrived back in their own homes immediately after the dinner, each husband would make a point of going to the kitchen to cut himself a piece of cheese. At the same time, he would carefully stick a large piece of plaster over the tip of the forefinger of his right hand. Having done this, he would hold up the finger and say to his wife, 'I cut myself. It's nothing, but it was bleeding a bit.' Thus, later on, when the men have switched beds, each woman will be made very much aware of the plaster-covered finger (the man would see to that), and will associate it directly with her own husband. An important psychological ploy, this,

calculated to dissipate any tiny suspicion that might enter the mind of either female.

So much for the basic plans. Next came what we referred to in our notes as 'Familiarization with the Layout'. Jerry schooled me first. He gave me three hours' training in his own house one Sunday afternoon when his wife and children were out. I had never been into their bedroom before. On the dressing table were Samantha's perfumes, her brushes, and all her other little things. A pair of her stockings was draped over the back of a chair. Her nightdress, white and blue, was hanging behind the door leading to the bathroom.

'Okay,' Jerry said. 'It'll be pitch dark when you come in. Samantha sleeps on this side, so you must tiptoe around the end of the bed and slide in on the other side, over there. I'm going to blindfold you and let you practise.'

At first, with the blindfold on, I wandered all over the room like a drunk. But after about an hour's work, I was able to negotiate the course pretty well. But before Jerry would finally pass me out, I had to go blindfold all the way from the front door through the hall, up the stairs, past the children's rooms, into Samantha's room and finish up in exactly the right place. And I had to do it silently, like a thief. All this took three hours of hard work, but I got it in the end.

The following Sunday morning when Mary had taken our children to church, I was able to give Jerry the same sort of work-out in my house. He learned the ropes faster than me, and within an hour he had passed the blindfold test without placing a foot wrong.

It was during this session that we decided to disconnect each woman's bedside lamp as we entered the bedroom. So Jerry practised finding the plug and pulling it out with his blindfold on, and the following week-end, I was able to do the same in Jerry's house.

Now came by far the most important part of our training. We called it 'Spilling the Beans', and it was here that both of us had to describe in every detail the procedure we adopted when making love to our own wives. We agreed not to worry ourselves with any exotic variations that either of us might or might not occasionally practise. We were concerned only with teaching one another the most commonly used routine, the one least likely to arouse suspicion.

The session took place in my office at six o'clock on a Wednesday evening, after the staff had gone home. At first, we were both slightly embarrassed, and neither of us wanted to begin. So I got out the bottle of whisky, and after a couple of stiff drinks, we loosened up and the teach-in started. While Jerry talked I took notes, and vice versa. At the end of it all, it turned out that the only real difference between Jerry's routine and my own was one of tempo. But what a difference it was! He took things (if what he said was to be believed) in such a leisurely fashion and he prolonged the moments to such an extravagant degree that I wondered privately to myself whether his partner did not sometimes go to sleep in the middle of it all. My job, however, was not to criticize but to copy, and I said nothing.

Jerry was not so discreet. At the end of my personal description, he had the temerity to say, 'Is that really what you do?'

'What do you mean?' I asked.

'I mean is it all over and done with as quickly as that?'

'Look,' I said. 'We aren't here to give each other lessons. We're here to learn the facts.'

'I know that,' he said. 'But I'm going to feel a bit of an ass if I copy your style exactly. My God, you go through it like an express train whizzing through a country station!'

I stared at him, mouth open.

'Don't look so surprised,' he said. 'The way you told it to me, anyone would think . . .'

'Think what?' I said.

'Oh, forget it,' he said.

'Thank you,' I said. I was furious. There are two things in this world at which I happen to know I excel. One is driving an automobile and the other is you-know-what. So to have him sit there and tell me I didn't know how to behave with my own wife was a monstrous piece of effrontery. It was he who didn't know, not me. Poor Samantha. What she must have had to put up with over the years.

'I'm sorry I spoke,' Jerry said. He poured more whisky into our glasses. 'Here's to the great switcheroo!' he said. 'When do we go?'

'Today is Wednesday,' I said. 'How about this coming Saturday?'

'Christ,' Jerry said.

'We ought to do it while everything's still fresh in our minds,' I said. 'There's an awful lot to remember.'

Jerry walked to the window and looked down at the traffic in the street below. 'Okay,' he said, turning around. 'Next Saturday it shall be!' Then we drove home in our separate cars.

'Jerry and I thought we'd take you and Samantha out to dinner Saturday night,' I said to Mary. We were in the kitchen and she was cooking hamburgers for the children.

She turned around and faced me, frying-pan in one hand, spoon in the other. Her blue eyes looked straight into mine. 'My Lord, Vic,' she said. 'How nice. But what are we celebrating?'

I looked straight back at her and said, 'I thought it would be a change to see some new faces. We're always meeting the same old bunch of people in the same old houses.'

She took a step forward and kissed me on the cheek. 'What a good man you are,' she said. 'I love you.'

'Don't forget to phone the baby-sitter.'

'No, I'll do it tonight,' she said.

Thursday and Friday passed very quickly, and suddenly it was Saturday. It was D Day. I woke up feeling madly excited. After breakfast, I couldn't sit still, so I decided to go out and wash the car. I was in the middle of this when Jerry came strolling through the gap in the hedge, pipe in mouth.

'Hi, sport,' he said. 'This is the day.'

'I know that,' I said. I also had a pipe in my mouth. I was forcing myself to smoke it, but I had trouble keeping it alight, and the smoke burned my tongue.

'How're you feeling?' Jerry asked.

'Terrific,' I said. 'How about you?'

'I'm nervous,' he said.

'Don't be nervous, Jerry.'

'This is one hell of a thing we're trying to do,' he said. 'I hope we pull it off.'

I went on polishing the windshield. I had never known Jerry to be nervous of anything before. It worried me a bit.

'I'm damn glad we're not the first people ever to try it,' he said. 'If no one had ever done it before, I don't think I'd risk it.'

'I agree,' I said.

'What stops me being too nervous,' he said, 'is the fact that your friend found it so fantastically easy.'

'My friend said it was a cinch,' I said. 'But for Chris-sake, Jerry, don't be nervous when the time comes. That would be disastrous.'

'Don't worry,' he said. 'But Jesus, it's exciting, isn't it?'

'It's exciting all right,' I said.

'Listen,' he said. 'We'd better go easy on the booze tonight.'

'Good idea,' I said. 'See you at eight thirty.'

At half past eight, Samantha, Jerry, Mary, and I drove in Jerry's car to Billy's Steak House. The restaurant, despite its name, was high-class and expensive, and the girls had put on long dresses for the occasion. Samantha was wearing something green that didn't start until it was halfway down her front, and I had never seen her looking lovelier. There were candles on our table. Samantha was seated opposite me and whenever she leaned forward with her face close to the flame, I could see that tiny crest of skin at the top centre of her lower lip. 'Now,' she said as she accepted a menu from the waiter, 'I wonder what I'm going to have tonight.'

Ho-ho-ho, I thought, that's a good question.

Everything went fine in the restaurant and the girls enjoyed themselves. When we arrived back at Jerry's house, it was eleven forty-five, and Samantha said, 'Come in and have a nightcap.'

'Thanks,' I said, 'but it's a bit late. And the baby-sitter has to be driven home.' So Mary and I walked across to our house, and *now*, I told myself as I entered the front door, *from now on* the count-down begins. I must keep a clear head and forget nothing.

While Mary was paying the baby-sitter, I went to the fridge and found a piece of Canadian cheddar. I took a knife from the drawer and a strip of plaster from the cupboard. I stuck the plaster around the tip of the forefinger of my right hand and waited for Mary to turn around.

'I cut myself,' I said holding up the finger for her to see. 'It's nothing, but it was bleeding a bit.'

'I'd have thought you'd had enough to eat for the evening,' was all she said. But the plaster registered on her mind and my first little job had been done.

I drove the baby-sitter home and by the time I got back up to the bedroom it was round about midnight and Mary was already half asleep with her light out. I switched out the light on my side of the bed and went into the bathroom to undress. I pottered about in there for ten minutes or so and when I came out, Mary, as I had hoped, was well and truly sleeping. There seemed no point in getting into bed beside her. So I simply pulled back the covers a bit on my side to make it easier for Jerry, then with my slippers on, I went downstairs to the kitchen and switched on the electric kettle. It was now twelve seventeen. Forty-three minutes to go.

At twelve thirty-five, I went upstairs to check on Mary and the kids. Everyone was sound asleep.

At twelve fifty-five, five minutes before zero hour, I went up again for a final check. I went right up close to Mary's bed and whispered her name. There was no answer. Good. *That's it! Let's go!*

I put a brown raincoat over my pyjamas. I switched off the kitchen light so that the whole house was in darkness. I put the front door lock on the latch. And then, feeling an enormous sense of exhilaration, I stepped silently out into the night.

There were no lamps on our street to lighten the darkness. There was no moon or even a star to be seen. It was a black black night, but the air was warm and there was a little breeze blowing from somewhere.

I headed for the gap in the hedge. When I got very close, I was able to make out the hedge itself and find the gap. I stopped there, waiting. Then I heard Jerry's footsteps coming toward me.

'Hi, sport,' he whispered. 'Everything okay?'

'All ready for you,' I whispered back.

He moved on. I heard his slippered feet padding softly over the grass as he went toward my house. I went toward his.

I opened Jerry's front door. It was even darker inside than out. I closed the door carefully. I took off my raincoat and hung it on the door knob. I removed my slippers and placed them against the wall

by the door. I literally could not see my hands before my face.
Everything had to be done by touch.

My goodness, I was glad Jerry had made me practise blindfold for
so long. It wasn't my feet that guided me now but my fingers. The
fingers of one hand or another were never for a moment out of contact
with something, a wall, the banister, a piece of furniture, a window-
curtain. And I knew or thought I knew exactly where I was all the
time. But it was an awesome eerie feeling trespassing on tiptoe through
someone else's house in the middle of the night. As I fingered my way
up the stairs, I found myself thinking of the burglars who had broken
into our front room last winter and stolen the television set. When the
police came next morning, I pointed out to them an enormous turd
lying in the snow outside the garage. 'They nearly always do that,'
one of the cops told me. 'They can't help it. They're scared.'

I reached the top of the stairs. I crossed the landing with my right
fingertips touching the wall all the time. I started down the corridor,
but paused when my hand found the door of the first children's room.
The door was slightly open. I listened. I could hear young Robert
Rainbow, aged eight, breathing evenly inside. I moved on. I found
the door to the second children's bedroom. This one belonged to Billy,
aged six and Amanda, three. I stood listening. All was well.

The main bedroom was at the end of the corridor, about four yards
on. I reached the door. Jerry had left it open, as planned. I went in.
I stood absolutely still just inside the door, listening for any sign that
Samantha might be awake. All was quiet. I felt my way around the
wall until I reached Samantha's side of the bed. Immediately, I knelt
on the floor and found the plug connecting her bedside lamp. I drew
it from its socket and laid it on the carpet. Good. Much safer now. I
stood up. I couldn't see Samantha, and at first I couldn't hear anything
either. I bent low over the bed. Ah yes, I could hear her breathing.
Suddenly I caught a whiff of the heavy musky perfume she had been
using that evening, and I felt the blood rushing to my groin. Quickly
I tiptoed around the big bed, keeping two fingers in gentle contact
with the edge of the bed the whole way.

All I had to do now was get in. I did so, but as I put my weight
upon the mattress, the creaking of the springs underneath sounded as
though someone was firing a rifle in the room. I lay motionless, holding
my breath. I could hear my heart thumping away like an engine in
my throat. Samantha was facing away from me. She didn't move. I
pulled the covers up over my chest and turned toward her. A female
glow came out of her to me. Here we go, then! *Now!*

I slid a hand over and touched her body. Her nightdress was warm
and silky. I rested the hand gently on her hips. Still she didn't move.
I waited a minute or so, then I allowed the hand that lay upon the

hip to steal onward and go exploring. Slowly, deliberately, and very accurately, my fingers began the process of setting her on fire.

She stirred. She turned on to her back. Then she murmured sleepily, 'Oh, dear ... Oh, my goodness me ... Good heavens, darling!'

I, of course, said nothing. I just kept on with the job.

A couple of minutes went by.

She was lying quite still.

Another minute passed. Then another. She didn't move a muscle.

I began to wonder how much longer it would be before she caught alight.

I persevered.

But why the silence? Why this absolute and total immobility, this frozen posture?

Suddenly it came to me. I had forgotten completely about Jerry! I was so hotted up, I had forgotten all about his own personal routine! I was doing it my way, not his! His way was far more complex than mine. It was ridiculously elaborate. It was quite unnecessary. But it was what she was used to. And now she was noticing the difference and trying to figure out what on earth was going on.

But it was too late to change direction now. I must keep going.

I kept going. The woman beside me was like a coiled spring lying there. I could feel the tension under her skin. I began to sweat.

Suddenly, she uttered a queer little groan.

More ghastly thoughts rushed through my mind. Could she be ill? Was she having a heart attack? Ought I to get the hell out quick?

She groaned again, louder this time. Then all at once, she cried out, 'Yes-yes-yes-yes-yes!' and like a bomb whose slow fuse had finally reached the dynamite, she exploded into life. She grabbed me in her arms and went for me with such incredible ferocity, I felt I was being set upon by a tiger.

Or should I say tigress?

I never dreamed a woman could do the things Samantha did to me then. She was a whirlwind, a dazzling frenzied whirlwind that tore me up by the roots and spun me around and carried me high into the heavens, to places I did not know existed.

I myself did not contribute. How could I? I was helpless. I was in the palm-tree spinning in the heavens, the lamb in the claws of the tiger. It was as much as I could do to keep breathing.

Thrilling it was, all the same, to surrender to the hands of a violent woman, and for the next ten, twenty, thirty minutes – how would I know? – the storm raged on. But I have no intention here of regaling the reader with bizarre details. I do not approve of washing juicy linen in public. I am sorry, but there it is. I only hope that my reticence will not create too strong a sense of anticlimax. Certainly, there was nothing anti about my own climax, and in the final searing paroxysm

I gave a shout which should have awakened the entire neighbourhood. Then I collapsed. I crumpled up like a drained wineskin.

Samantha, as though she had done no more than drink a glass of water, simply turned away from me and went right back to sleep.

Phew!

I lay still, recuperating slowly.

I had been right, you see, about that little thing on her lower lip, had I not?

Come to think of it, I had been right about more or less everything that had to do with this incredible escapade. What a triumph! I felt wonderfully relaxed and well-spent.

I wondered what time it was. My watch was not a luminous one. I'd better go. I crept out of bed. I felt my way, a trifle less cautiously this time, around the bed, out of the bedroom, along the corridor, down the stairs and into the hall of the house. I found my raincoat and slippers. I put them on. I had a lighter in the pocket of my raincoat. I used it and read the time. It was eight minutes before two. Later than I thought, I opened the front door and stepped out into the black night.

My thoughts now began to concentrate upon Jerry. Was he all right? Had he gotten away with it? I moved through the darkness toward the gap in the hedge.

'Hi, sport,' a voice whispered beside me.

'Jerry!'

'Everything okay?' Jerry asked.

'Fantastic,' I said. 'Amazing. What about you?'

'Same with me,' he said. I caught the flash of his white teeth grinning at me in the dark. 'We made it, Vic!' he whispered, touching my arm. 'You were right! It worked! It was sensational!'

'See you tomorrow,' I whispered. 'Go home.'

We moved apart. I went through the hedge and entered my house. Three minutes later, I was safely back in my own bed, and my own wife was sleeping soundly alongside me.

The next morning was Sunday. I was up at eight thirty and went downstairs in pyjamas and dressing-gown, as I always do on a Sunday, to make breakfast for the family. I had left Mary sleeping. The two boys, Victor, aged nine, and Wally, seven, were already down.

'Hi, daddy,' Wally said.

'I've got a great new breakfast,' I announced.

'What?' both boys said together. They had been into town and fetched the Sunday paper and were now reading the comics.

'We make some buttered toast and we spread orange marmalade on it,' I said. 'Then we put strips of crisp bacon on top of the marmalade.'

'*Bacon!*' Victor said. 'With *orange marmalade!*'

'I know. But you wait till you try it. It's wonderful.'

I dished out the grapefruit juice and drank two glasses of it myself. I set another on the table for Mary when she came down. I switched on the electric kettle, put the bread in the toaster, and started to fry the bacon. At this point, Mary came into the kitchen. She had a flimsy peach-coloured chiffon thing over her nightdress.

'Good morning,' I said, watching her over my shoulder as I manipulated the frying-pan.

She did not answer. She went to her chair at the kitchen table and sat down. She started to sip her juice. She looked neither at me nor at the boys. I went on frying the bacon.

'Hi, mummy,' Wally said.

She didn't answer this either.

The smell of the bacon fat was beginning to turn my stomach.

'I'd like some coffee,' Mary said, not looking around. Her voice was very odd.

'Coming right up,' I said. I pushed the frying-pan away from the heat and quickly made a cup of black instant coffee. I placed it before her.

'Boys,' she said, addressing the children, 'would you please do your reading in the other room till breakfast is ready.'

'Us?' Victor said. 'Why?'

'Because I say so.'

'Are we doing something wrong?' Wally asked.

'No, honey, you're not. I just want to be left alone for a moment with daddy.'

I felt myself shrink inside my skin. I wanted to run. I wanted to rush out the front door and go running down the street and hide.

'Get yourself a coffee, Vic,' she said, 'and sit down.' Her voice was quite flat. There was no anger in it. There was just nothing. And she still wouldn't look at me. The boys went out, taking the comic section with them.

'Shut the door,' Mary said to them.

I put a spoonful of powdered coffee into my cup and poured boiling water over it. I added milk and sugar. The silence was shattering. I crossed over and sat down in my chair opposite her. It might just as well have been an electric chair, the way I was feeling.

'Listen, Vic,' she said, looking into her coffee cup. 'I want to get this said before I lose my nerve and then I won't be able to say it.'

'For heaven's sake, what's all the drama about?' I asked. 'Has something happened?'

'Yes, Vic, it has.'

'What?'

Her face was pale and still and distant, unconscious of the kitchen around her.

'Come on, then, out with it,' I said bravely.

'You're not going to like this very much,' she said, and her big blue haunted-looking eyes rested a moment on my face, then travelled away.

'What am I not going to like very much?' I said. The sheer terror of it all was beginning to stir my bowels. I felt the same way as those burglars the cops had told me about.

'You know I hate talking about love-making and all that sort of thing,' she said. 'I've never once talked to you about it all the time we've been married.'

'That's true,' I said.

She took a sip of her coffee, but she wasn't tasting it. 'The point is this,' she said. 'I've never liked it. If you really want to know, I've hated it.'

'Hated what?' I asked.

'Sex,' she said. 'Doing it.'

'Good Lord!' I said.

'It's never given me even the slightest little bit of pleasure.'

This was shattering enough in itself, but the real cruncher was still to come, I felt sure of that.

'I'm sorry if that surprises you,' she added.

I couldn't think of anything to say, so I kept quiet.

Her eyes rose again from the coffee cup and looked into mine, watchful, as if calculating something, then fell again. 'I wasn't ever going to tell you,' she said. 'And I never would have if it hadn't been for last night.'

I said very slowly, 'What about last night?'

'Last night,' she said, 'I suddenly found out what the whole crazy thing is all about.'

'You did?'

She looked full at me now, and her face was as open as a flower. 'Yes,' she said. 'I surely did.'

I didn't move.

'Oh darling!' she cried, jumping up and rushing over and giving me an enormous kiss. 'Thank you so much for last night! You were marvellous! And I was marvellous! We were both marvellous! Don't look so embarrassed, my darling! You ought to be proud of yourself! You were fantastic! I love you! I do! I do!'

I just sat there.

She leaned close to me and put an arm around my shoulders. 'And now,' she said softly, 'now that you have ... I don't quite know how to say this ... now that you have sort of discovered what it is I *need*, everything is going to be marvellous from now on!'

I sat there. She went slowly back to her chair. A big tear was running down one of her cheeks. I couldn't think why.

'I was right to tell you, wasn't I?' she said, smiling through her tears.

'Yes,' I said. 'Oh, yes.' I stood up and went over to the cooker so that I wouldn't be facing her. Through the kitchen window, I caught sight of Jerry crossing his garden with the Sunday paper under his arm. There was a lilt in his walk, a little prance of triumph in each pace he took, and when he reached the steps of his front porch, he ran up them two at a time.

THE LAST ACT

Anna was in the kitchen washing a head of Boston lettuce for the family supper when the doorbell rang. The bell itself was on the wall directly above the sink, and it never failed to make her jump if it rang when she happened to be near. For this reason, neither her husband nor any of the children ever used it. It seemed to ring extra loud this time, and Anna jumped extra high.

When she opened the door, two policemen were standing outside. They looked at her out of pale waxen faces, and she looked back at them, waiting for them to say something.

She kept looking at them, but they didn't speak or move. They stood so still and so rigid that they were like two wax figures somebody had put on her doorstep as a joke. Each of them was holding his helmet in front of him in his two hands.

'What is it?' Anna asked.

They were both young, and they were wearing leather gauntlets up to their elbows. She could see their enormous motor-cycles propped up along the edge of the sidewalk behind them, and dead leaves were falling around the motor-cycles and blowing along the sidewalk and the whole of the street was brilliant in the yellow light of a clear, gusty September evening. The taller of the two policemen shifted uneasily on his feet. Then he said quietly, 'Are you Mrs Cooper, ma'am?'

'Yes, I am.'

The other said, 'Mrs Edmund J. Cooper?'

'Yes.' And then slowly it began to dawn upon her that these men, neither of whom seemed anxious to explain his presence, would not be behaving as they were unless they had some distasteful duty to perform.

'Mrs Cooper,' she heard one of them saying, and from the way he said it, as gently and softly as if he were comforting a sick child, she knew at once that he was going to tell her something terrible. A great wave of panic came over her, and she said, 'What happened?'

'We have to inform you, Mrs Cooper ...'

The policemen paused, and the woman, watching him, felt as though her whole body were shrinking and shrinking and shrinking inside its skin.

'... that your husband was involved in an accident on the Hudson

River Parkway at approximately five forty-five this evening, and died in the ambulance ...'

The policeman who was speaking produced the crocodile wallet she had given Ed on their twentieth wedding anniversary, two years back, and as she reached out to take it, she found herself wondering whether it might not still be warm from having been close to her husband's chest only a short while ago.

'If there's anything we can do,' the policeman was saying, 'like calling up somebody to come over ... some friend or relative maybe ...'

Anna heard his voice drifting away, then fading out altogether, and it must have been about then that she began to scream. Soon she became hysterical, and the two policemen had their hands full trying to control her until the doctor arrived some forty minutes later and injected something into her arm.

She was no better, though, when she woke up the following morning. Neither her doctor nor her children were able to reason with her in any way at all, and had she not been kept under almost constant sedation for the next few days, she would undoubtedly have taken her own life. In the brief lucid periods between drug-takings, she acted as though she were demented, calling out her husband's name and telling him that she was coming to join him as soon as she possibly could. It was terrible to listen to her. But in defence of her behaviour, it should be said at once that this was no ordinary husband she had lost.

Anna Greenwood had married Ed Cooper when they were both eighteen, and over the time they were together, they grew to be closer and more dependent upon each other than it is possible to describe in words. Every year that went by, their love became more intense and overwhelming, and toward the end, it had reached such a ridiculous peak that it was almost impossible for them to endure the daily separation caused by Ed's departure for the office in the mornings. When he returned at night he would rush through the house to seek her out, and she, who had heard the noise of the front door slamming, would drop everything and rush simultaneously in his direction, meeting him head on, recklessly, at full speed, perhaps halfway up the stairs, or on the landing, or between the kitchen and the hall; and as they came together, he would take her in his arms and hug her and kiss her for minutes on end as though she were yesterday's bride. It was wonderful. It was so utterly unbelievably wonderful that one is very nearly able to understand why she should have had no desire and no heart to continue living in a world where her husband did not exist any more.

Her three children, Angela (twenty), Mary (nineteen) and Billy (seventeen and a half), stayed around her constantly right from the start of the catastrophe. They adored their mother, and they certainly had no intention of letting her commit suicide if they could help it. They worked hard and with loving desperation to convince her that life could still be worth living, and it was due entirely to them that she managed in the end to come out of the nightmare and climb back slowly into the ordinary world.

Four months after the disaster, she was pronounced 'moderately safe' by the doctors, and she was able to return, albeit rather listlessly, to the old routine of running the house and doing the shopping and cooking the meals for her grown-up children.

But then what happened?

Before the snows of that winter had melted away, Angela married a young man from Rhode Island and went off to live in the suburbs of Providence.

A few months later, Mary married a fair-haired giant from a town called Slayton, in Minnesota, and away she flew for ever and ever and ever. And although Anna's heart was now beginning to break all over again into tiny pieces, she was proud to think that neither of the two girls had the slightest inkling of what was happening to her. ('Oh, Mummy, isn't it wonderful!' 'Yes, my darling, I think it's the most beautiful wedding there's ever been! I'm even more excited than you are!' etc., etc.)

And then, to put the lid on everything, her beloved Billy, who had just turned eighteen, went off to begin his first year at Yale.

So all at once, Anna found herself living in a completely empty house.

It is an awful feeling, after twenty-three years of boisterous, busy, magical family life, to come down alone to breakfast in the mornings, to sit there in silence with a cup of coffee and a piece of toast, and to wonder what you are going to do with the day that lies ahead. The room you are sitting in, which has heard so much laughter, and seen so many birthdays, so many Christmas trees, so many presents being opened, is quiet now and feels curiously cold. The air is heated and the temperature itself is normal, but the place still makes you shiver. The clock has stopped because you were never the one who wound it in the first place. A chair stands crooked on its legs, and you sit staring at it, wondering why you hadn't noticed it before. And when you glance up again, you have a sudden panicky feeling that all the four walls of the room have begun creeping in upon you very very slowly when you weren't looking.

In the beginning, she would carry her coffee cup over to the telephone and start calling up friends. But all her friends had husbands and children, and although they were always as nice and warm and cheerful as they could possibly be, they simply could not spare the time to sit and chat with a desolate lady from across the way first thing in the morning. So then she started calling up her married daughters instead.

They, also, were sweet and kind to her at all times, but Anna detected, very soon, a subtle change in their attitudes toward her. She was no longer number one in their lives. They had husbands now, and were concentrating everything upon them. Gently but firmly, they were moving their mother into the background. It was quite a shock. But she knew they were right. They were absolutely right. She was no longer entitled to impinge upon their lives or to make them feel guilty for neglecting her.

She saw Dr Jacobs regularly, but he wasn't really any help. He tried to get her to talk and she did her best, and sometimes he made little speeches to her full of oblique remarks about sex and sublimation. Anna never properly understood what he was driving at, but the burden of his song appeared to be that she should get herself another man.

She took to wandering around the house and fingering things that used to belong to Ed. She would pick up one of his shoes and put her hand into it and feel the little dents that the ball of his foot and his toes had made upon the sole. She found a sock with a hole in it, and the pleasure it gave her to darn that sock was indescribable. Occasionally, she took out a shirt, a tie, and a suit, and laid them on the bed, all ready for him to wear, and once, one rainy Sunday morning, she made an Irish stew ...

It was hopeless to go on.

So how many pills would she need to make absolutely sure of it this time? She went upstairs to her secret store and counted them. There were only nine. Was that enough? She doubted that it was. Oh, hell. The one thing she was not prepared to face all over again was failure – the rush to the hospital, the stomach-pump, the seventh floor of the Payne Whitney Pavilion, the psychiatrists, the humiliation, the misery of it all ...

In that case, it would have to be the razor-blade. But the trouble with the razor-blade was that it had to be done properly. Many people failed miserably when they tried to use the razor-blade on the wrist. In fact, nearly all of them failed. They didn't cut deep enough. There was a big artery down there somewhere that simply had to be reached. Veins were no good. Veins made plenty of mess, but they never quite managed to do the trick. Then again, the razor-blade was not an easy thing to hold, not if one had to make a firm incision, pressing it right home all the way, deep deep down. But *she* wouldn't fail. The ones who failed were the ones who actually *wanted* to fail. She wanted to succeed.

She went to the cupboard in the bathroom, searching for blades. There weren't any. Ed's razor was still there, and so was hers. But there was no blade in either of them, and no little packet lying alongside. That was understandable. Such things had been removed from the house on an earlier occasion. But there was no problem. Anyone could buy a packet of razor-blades.

She returned to the kitchen and took the calendar down from the wall. She chose September 23rd, which was Ed's birthday, and wrote r-b (for razor-blades) against the date. She did this on September 9th, which gave her exactly two weeks' grace to put her affairs in order. There was much to be done – old bills to be paid, a new will to be written, the house to be tidied up, Billy's college fees to be taken care of for the next four years, letters to the children, to her own parents, to Ed's mother, and so on and so forth.

Yet, busy as she was, she found that those two weeks, those fourteen long days, were going far too slowly for her liking. She wanted to use the blade, and eagerly every morning she counted the days that were left. She was like a child counting the days before Christmas. For wherever it was that Ed Cooper had gone when he died, even if it were only to the grave, she was impatient to join him.

It was in the middle of this two-week period that her friend Elizabeth Paoletti came calling on her at eight thirty one morning. Anna was making coffee in the kitchen at the time, and she jumped when the bell rang and jumped again when it gave a second long blast.

Liz came sweeping in through the front door, talking non-stop as usual. 'Anna, my darling woman, I need your help! Everyone's down with flu at the office. You've *got* to come! Don't argue with me! I know you can type and I know you haven't got a damn thing in the world to do all day except mope. Just grab your hat and purse and let's get going. Hurry up, girl, hurry up! I'm late as it is!'

Anna said, 'Go away, Liz. Leave me alone.'

'The cab is waiting.' Liz said.

'Please,' Anna said, 'don't try to bully me now. I'm not coming.'

'You are coming,' Liz said. 'Pull yourself together. Your days of glorious martyrdom are over.'

Anna continued to resist, but Liz wore her down, and in the end she agreed to go along just for a few hours.

Elizabeth Paoletti was in charge of an adoption society, one of the best in the city. Nine of the staff were down with flu. Only two were left, excluding herself. 'You don't know a thing about the work,' she said in the cab, 'but you're just going to have to help us all you can ...'

The office was bedlam. The telephones alone nearly drove Anna mad. She kept running from one cubicle to the next, taking messages that she did not understand. And there were girls in the waiting room, young girls with ashen stony faces, and it became part of her duty to type their answers on an official form.

'The father's name?'

'Don't know.'

'You've no idea?'

'What's the father's name got to do with it?'

'My dear, if the father is known, then his consent has to be obtained as well as yours before the child can be offered for adoption.'

'You're quite sure about that?'

'Jesus, I told you, didn't I?'

At lunchtime, somebody brought her a sandwich, but there was no time to eat it. At nine o'clock that night, exhausted and famished and considerably shaken by some of the knowledge she had aquired, Anna staggered home, took a stiff drink, fried up some eggs and bacon, and went to bed.

'I'll call for you at eight o'clock tomorrow morning,' Liz had said. 'And for God's sake be ready.' Anna was ready. And from then on she was hooked.

It was as simple as that.

All she'd needed right from the beginning was a good hard job of work to do, and plenty of problems to solve – other people's problems instead of her own.

The work was arduous and often quite shattering emotionally, but Anna was absorbed by every moment of it, and within about – we are skipping right forward now – within about a year and a half, she began to feel moderately happy once again. She was finding it more and more difficult to picture her husband vividly, to see him precisely as he was when he ran up the stairs to meet her, or when he sat across from her at supper in the evenings. The exact sound of his voice was becoming less easy to recall, and even the face itself, unless she glanced at a photograph, was no longer sharply etched in the memory. She still thought about him constantly, but she discovered that she could do so now without bursting into tears, and when she looked back on the way she had behaved a while ago, she felt slightly embarrassed. She started taking a mild interest in her clothes and in her hair, she returned to using lipstick and to shaving the hair from her legs. She enjoyed her food, and when people smiled at her, she smiled right back at them and meant it. In other words, she was back in the swim once again. She was pleased to be alive.

It was at this point that Anna had to go down to Dallas on office business.

Liz's office did not normally operate beyond state lines, but in this instance, a couple who had adopted a baby through the agency had subsequently moved away from New York and gone to live in Texas. Now, five months after the move, the wife had written to say that she no longer wanted to keep the child. Her husband, she announced, had died of a heart attack soon after they'd arrived in Texas. She herself had remarried almost at once, and her new husband 'found it impossible to adjust to an adopted baby ...'

Now this was a serious situation, and quite apart from the welfare of the child itself, there were all manner of legal obligations involved.

Anna flew down to Dallas in a plane that left New York very early, and she arrived before breakfast. After checking in at her hotel, she spent the next eight hours with the persons concerned in the affair, and by the time she had done all that could be done that day, it was around four thirty in the afternoon and she was utterly exhausted. She took a cab back to the hotel, and went up to her room. She called Liz on the phone to report the situation, then she undressed and soaked herself for a long time in a warm bath. Afterwards, she wrapped up in a towel and lay on the bed, smoking a cigarette.

Her efforts on behalf of the child had so far come to nothing. There had been two lawyers there who had treated her with absolute contempt. How she hated them. She detested their arrogance and their softly spoken hints that nothing she might do would make the slightest difference to their client. One of them kept his feet up on the table all the way through the discussion, and both of them had rolls of fat on their bellies, and the fat spilled out into their shirts like liquid and hung in huge folds over their belted trouser-tops.

Anna had visited Texas many times before in her life, but until now she had never gone there alone. Her visits had always been with Ed, keeping him company on business trips; and during those trips, he and she had often spoken about the Texans in general and about how difficult it was to like them. One could ignore their coarseness and their vulgarity. It wasn't that. But there was, it seemed, a quality of ruthlessness still surviving among these people, something quite brutal, harsh, inexorable, that it was impossible to forgive. They had no bowels of compassion, no pity, no tenderness. The only so-called virtue they possessed – and this they paraded ostentatiously and endlessly to strangers – was a kind of professional benevolence. It was plastered all over them. Their voices, their smiles, were rich and syrupy with it. But it left Anna cold. It left her quite, quite cold inside.

'Why do they love acting so tough?' she used to ask.

'Because they're children,' Ed would answer. 'They're dangerous children who go about trying to imitate their grandfathers. Their grandfathers *were* pioneers. These people aren't.'

It seemed that they lived, these present-day Texans, by a sort of egotistic will, push and be pushed. Everybody was pushing. Everybody was being pushed. And it was all very fine for a stranger in their midst to step aside and announce firmly, 'I will *not* push, and I will *not* be pushed.' That was impossible. It was especially impossible in Dallas. Of all the cities in the state, Dallas was the one that had always disturbed Anna the most. It was such a godless city, she thought, such a rapacious, gripped, iron, godless city. It was a place that had run amok with its money, and no amount of gloss and phony culture and syrupy talk could hide the fact that the great golden fruit was rotten inside.

Anna lay on the bed with her bath towel around her. She was alone in Dallas this time. There was no Ed with her now to envelope her in his incredible strength and love; and perhaps it was because of this that she began, all of a sudden, to feel slightly uneasy. She lit a second cigarette and waited for the uneasiness to pass. It didn't pass; it got worse. A hard little knot of fear was gathering itself in the top of her stomach, and there it stayed, growing bigger every minute. It was an unpleasant feeling, the kind one might experience if one were alone in the house at night and heard, or thought one heard, a footstep in the next room.

In this place there were a million footsteps, and she could hear them all.

She got off the bed and went over to the window, still wrapped in her towel. Her room was on the twenty-second floor, and the window was open. The great city lay pale and milky-yellow in the evening sunshine. The street below was solid with automobiles. The sidewalk was filled with people. Everybody was hustling home from work, pushing and being pushed. She felt the need of a friend. She wanted very badly to have someone to talk to at this moment. She would have liked a house to go to, a house with a family – a wife and husband and children and rooms full of toys, and the husband and wife would fling their arms around her at the front door and cry out, 'Anna! How marvellous to see you! How long can you stay? A week, a month, a year?'

All of a sudden, as so often happens in situations like this, her memory went *click*, and she said aloud, 'Conrad Kreuger! Good heavens above! *He* lives in Dallas ... at least he used to ...'

She hadn't seen Conrad since they were classmates in high school, in New York. They were both about seventeen then, and Conrad had been her beau, her love, her everything. For over a year they had gone around together, and each of them had sworn eternal loyalty to the other, with marriage in the near future. Then suddenly Ed Cooper had flashed into her life, and that, of course, had been the end of the romance with Conrad. But Conrad did not seem to have taken the break too badly. It certainly couldn't have *shattered* him, because not more than a month or two later he had started going strong with another girl in the class ...

Now what was *her* name?

A big handsome bosomy girl she was, with flaming red hair and a peculiar name, a very old-fashioned name. What was it? Arabella? No, not Arabella. Ara- something, though. Araminty? Yes! Araminty it was! And what is more, within a year or so, Conrad Kreuger had married Araminty and had carried her back with him to Dallas, the place of his birth.

Anna went over to the bedside table and picked up the telephone directory.

Kreuger, Conrad P., M.D.

That was Conrad all right. He had always said he was going to be a doctor. The book gave an office number and a residence number.

Should she phone him?

Why not?

She glanced at her watch. It was five twenty. She lifted the receiver and gave the number of his office.

'Doctor Kreuger's surgery,' a girl's voice answered.

'Hello,' Anna said. 'Is Doctor Kreuger there?'

'The doctor is busy right now. May I ask who's calling?'

'Will you please tell him that Anna Greenwood telephoned him.'

'Who?'

'Anna Greenwood.'

'Yes, Miss Greenwood. Did you wish for an appointment?'

'No, thank you.'

'Is there something I can do for you?'

Anna gave the name of her hotel, and asked her to pass it on to Dr Kreuger.

'I'll be very glad to,' the secretary said. 'Goodbye, Miss Greenwood.'

'Goodbye,' Anna said. She wondered whether Dr Conrad P. Kreuger would remember her name after all these years. She believed he would. She lay back again on the bed and began trying to recall what Conrad himself used to look like. Extraordinarily handsome, that he was. Tall ... lean ... big-shouldered ... with almost pure-black hair ... and a marvellous face ... a strong carved face like one of those Greek heroes, Perseus or Ulysses. Above all, though, he had been a very gentle boy, a serious, decent, quiet, gentle boy. He had never kissed her much – only when he said goodbye in the evenings. And he'd never gone in for necking, as all the others had. When he took her home from the movies on Saturday nights, he used to park his old Buick outside her house and sit there in the car beside her, just talking and talking about the future, his future and hers, and how he was going to go back to Dallas to become a famous doctor. His refusal to indulge in necking and all the nonsense that went with it had impressed her no end. He respects me, she used to say. He loves me. And she was probably right. In any event, he had been a nice man, a nice good man. And had it not been for the fact that Ed Cooper was a super-nice, super-good man, she was sure she would have married Conrad Kreuger.

The telephone rang. Anna lifted the receiver. 'Yes,' she said. 'Hello.'

'Anna Greenwood?'

'Conrad Kreuger!'

'My dear Anna! What a fantastic surprise. Good gracious me. After all these years.'

'It's a long time, isn't it.'

'It's a lifetime. Your voice sounds just the same.'

'So does yours.'

'What brings you to our fair city? Are you staying long?'

'No, I have to go back tomorrow. I hope you didn't mind my calling you.'

'Hell, no, Anna. I'm delighted. Are you all right?'

'Yes, I'm fine. I'm fine now. I had a bad time of it for a bit after Ed died ...'

'What!'

'He was killed in an automobile two and a half years ago.'

'Oh gee, Anna, I *am* sorry. How terrible. I ... I don't know what to say ...'

'Don't say anything.'

'You're okay now?'

'I'm fine. Working like a slave.'

'That's the girl ...'

'How's ... how's Araminty?'

'Oh, she's fine.'

'Any children?'

'One,' he said. 'A boy. How about you?'

'I have three, two girls and a boy.'

'Well, well, what d'you know! Now listen, Anna ...'

'I'm listening.'

'Why don't I run over to the hotel and buy you a drink? I'd like to do that. I'll bet you haven't changed one iota.'

'I look old, Conrad.'

'You're lying.'

'I feel old, too.'

'You want a good doctor?'

'Yes. I mean no. Of course I don't. I don't want any more doctors. All I need is ... well ...'

'Yes?'

'This place worries me, Conrad. I guess I need a friend. That's all I need.'

'You've got one. I have just one more patient to see, and then I'm free. I'll meet you down in the bar, the something room, I've forgotten what it's called, at six, in about half an hour. Will that suit you?'

'Yes,' she said. 'Of course. And ... thank you, Conrad.' She replaced the receiver, then got up from the bed, and began to dress.

She felt mildly flustered. Not since Ed's death had she been out and had a drink alone with a man. Dr Jacobs would be pleased when she told him about it on her return. He wouldn't congratulate her madly, but he would certainly be pleased. He'd say it was a step in the right direction, a beginning. She still went to him regularly, and now that she had gotten so much better, his oblique references had become far less oblique and he had more than once told her that her depressions and suicidal tendencies would never completely disappear until she had actually and physically 'replaced' Ed with another man.

'But it is impossible to replace a person one has loved to distraction,' Anna had said to him the last time he had brought up the subject. 'Heavens above, doctor, when Mrs Crummlin-Brown's parakeet died last month, her *parakeet*, mind you, not her husband, she was so shook up about it, she swore she'd never have another bird again!'

'Mrs Cooper,' Dr Jacobs had said, 'one doesn't normally have sexual intercourse with a parakeet.'

'Well ... no ...'

'That's why it doesn't have to be replaced. But when a husband dies, and the surviving wife is still an active and a healthy woman, she will invariably get a replacement within three years if she possibly can. And vice versa.'

Sex. It was about the only thing that sort of doctor ever thought about. He had sex on the brain.

By the time Anna had dressed and taken the elevator downstairs, it was ten minutes after six. The moment she walked into the bar, a man stood up from one of the tables. It was Conrad. He must have been watching the door. He came across the floor to meet her. He was smiling nervously. Anna was smiling, too. One always does.

'Well, well,' he said. 'Well well well,' and she, expecting the usual peck on the cheek, inclined her face upward toward his own, still smiling. But she had forgotten how formal Conrad was. He simply took her hand in his and shook it – once. 'This *is* a surprise,' he said. 'Come and sit down.'

The room was the same as any other hotel drinking-room. It was lit by dim lights, and filled with many small tables. There was a saucer of peanuts on each table, and there were leather bench-seats all around the walls. The waiters were rigged out in white jackets and maroon pants. Conrad led her to a corner table, and they sat down facing each other. A waiter was standing over them at once.

'What will you have?' Conrad asked.

'Could I have a martini?'

'Of course. Vodka?'

'No, gin, please.'

'One gin martini,' he said to the waiter. 'No. Make it two. I've never been much of a drinker, Anna, as you probably remember, but I think this calls for a celebration.'

The waiter went away. Conrad leaned back in his chair and studied her carefully. 'You look pretty good,' he said.

'You look pretty good yourself, Conrad,' she told him. And so he did. It was astonishing how little he had aged in twenty-five years. He was just as lean and handsome as he'd ever been – in fact, more so. His black hair was still black, his eye was clear, and he looked altogether like a man who was no more than thirty years old.

'You *are* older than me, aren't you?' he said.

'What sort of a question is that?' she said, laughing. 'Yes Conrad, I am exactly one year older than you. I'm forty-two.'

'I thought you were.' He was still studying her with the utmost care, his eyes travelling all over her face and neck and shoulders. Anna felt herself blushing.

'Are you an enormously successful doctor?' she asked. 'Are you the best in town?'

He cocked his head over to one side, right over, so that the ear almost touched the top of the shoulder. It was a mannerism that Anna had always liked. 'Successful?' he said. 'Any doctor can be successful these days in a big city – financially, I mean. But whether or not I am absolutely first rate at my job is another matter. I only hope and pray that I am.'

The drinks arrived and Conrad raised his glass and said, 'Welcome to Dallas, Anna. I'm so pleased you called me up. It's good to see you again.'

'It's good to see you, too, Conrad,' she said, speaking the truth.

He looked at her glass. She had taken a huge first gulp, and the glass was now half empty. 'You prefer gin to vodka?' he asked.

'I do,' she said, 'yes.'

'You ought to change over.'

'Why?'

'Gin is not good for females.'

'It's not?'

'It's very bad for them.'

'I'm sure it's just as bad for males,' she said.

'Actually, no. It isn't nearly so bad for males as it is for females.'

'Why is it bad for females?'

'It just is,' he said. 'It's the way they're built. What kind of work are you engaged in, Anna? And what brought you all the way down to Dallas? Tell me about you.'

'Why is gin bad for females?' she said, smiling at him.

He smiled back at her and shook his head, but he didn't answer.

'Go on,' she said.

'No, let's drop it.'

'You can't leave me up in the air like this,' she said. 'It's not fair.'

After a pause, he said, 'Well, if you really want to know, gin contains a certain amount of the oil which is squeezed out of juniper berries. They use it for flavouring.'

'What does it do?'

'Plenty.'

'Yes, but what?'

'Horrible things.'

'Conrad, don't be shy. I'm a big girl now.'

He was still the same old Conrad, she thought, still as diffident, as scrupulous, as shy as ever. For that she liked him. 'If this drink is really doing horrible things to me,' she said, 'then it is unkind of you not to tell me what those things are.'

Gently, he pinched the lobe of his left ear with the thumb and forefinger of his right hand. Then he said, 'Well, the truth of the matter is, Anna, oil of juniper has a direct inflammatory effect upon the uterus.'

'Now come on!'

'I'm not joking.'

'Mother's ruin,' Anna said. 'It's an old wives' tale.'

'I'm afraid not.'

'But you're talking about women who are pregnant.'

'I'm talking about all women, Anna.' He had stopped smiling now, and he was speaking quite seriously. He seemed to be concerned about her welfare.

'What do you specialize in?' she asked him. 'What kind of medicine? You haven't told me that.'

'Gynaecology and obstetrics.'

'Ah-ha!'

'Have you been drinking gin for many years?' he asked.

'Oh, about twenty,' Anna said.

'Heavily?'

'For heaven's sake, Conrad, stop worrying about my insides. I'd like another martini, please.'

'Of course.'

He called the waiter and said, 'One vodka martini.'

'No,' Anna said, 'gin.'

He sighed and shook his head and said, 'Nobody listens to her doctor these days.'

'You're not my doctor.'

'No,' he said. 'I'm your friend.'

'Let's talk about your wife,' Anna said. 'Is she still as beautiful as ever?'

He waited a few moments, then he said, 'Actually, we're divorced.'

'Oh, no!'

'Our marriage lasted for the grand total of two years. It was hard work to keep it going even that long.'

For some reason, Anna was profoundly shocked. 'But she was such a beautiful girl,' she said. 'What happened?'

'Everything happened, everything you could possibly think of that was bad.'

'And the child?'

'She got him. They always do.' He sounded very bitter. 'She took him back to New York. He comes to see me once a year, in the summer. He's twenty years old now. He's at Princeton.'

'Is he a fine boy?'

'He's a wonderful boy,' Conrad said. 'But I hardly know him. It isn't much fun.'

'And you never married again?'

'No, never. But that's enough about me. Let's talk about you.'

Slowly, gently, he began to draw her out on the subject of her health and the bad times she had gone through after Ed's death. She found she didn't mind talking to him about it, and she told him more or less the whole story.

'But what makes your doctor think you're not completely cured?' he said. 'You don't look very suicidal to me.'

'I don't think I am. Except that sometimes, not often, mind you, but just occasionally, when I get depressed, I have the feeling that it wouldn't take such a hell of a big push to send me over the edge.'

'In what way?'

'I kind of start edging toward the bathroom cupboard.'

'What do you have in the bathroom cupboard?'

'Nothing very much. Just the ordinary equipment a girl has for shaving her legs.'

'I see.' Conrad studied her face for a few moments, then he said, 'Is that how you were feeling just now when you called me?'

'Not quite. But I'd been thinking about Ed. And that's always a bit dangerous.'

'I'm glad you called.'

'So am I,' she said.

Anna was getting to the end of her second martini. Conrad changed the subject and began talking about his practice. She was watching him rather than listening to him. He was so damned handsome it was impossible not to watch him. She put a cigarette between her lips, then offered the pack to Conrad.

'No thanks,' he said. 'I don't.' He picked up a book of matches from the table and gave her a light, then he blew out the match and said, 'Are those cigarettes mentholated?'

'Yes, they are.'

She took a deep drag, and blew the smoke slowly up into the air. 'Now go ahead and tell me that they're going to shrivel up my entire reproductive system,' she said.

He laughed and shook his head.

'Then why did you ask?'

'Just curious, that's all.'

'You're lying. I can tell it from your face. You were about to give me the figures for the incidence of lung cancer in heavy smokers.'

'Lung cancer has nothing to do with menthol, Anna,' he said, and he smiled and took a tiny sip of his original martini, which he had so far hardly touched. He set the glass back carefully on the table. 'You still haven't told me what work you are doing,' he went on, 'or why you came to Dallas.'

'Tell me about menthol first. If it's even half as bad as the juice of the juniper berry, I think I ought to know about it quick.'

He laughed and shook his head.

'Please!'

'No, ma'am.'

'Conrad, you simply cannot start things up like this and then drop them. It's the second time in five minutes.'

'I don't want to be a medical bore,' he said.

'You're not being a bore. These things are fascinating. Come on! Tell! Don't be mean.'

It was pleasant to be sitting there feeling moderately high on two big martinis, and making easy talk with this graceful man, this quiet, comfortable, graceful person. He was not being coy. Far from it. He was simply being his normal scrupulous self.

'Is it something shocking?' she asked.

'No. You couldn't call it that.'

'Then go ahead.'

He picked up the packet of cigarettes lying in front of her, and studied the label. 'The point is this,' he said. 'If you inhale menthol, you absorb it into the bloodstream. And that isn't good, Anna. It does things to you. It has certain very definite effects upon the central nervous system. Doctors still prescribe it occasionally.'

'I know that,' she said. 'Nose-drops and inhalations.'

'That's one of its minor uses. Do you know the other?'

'You rub it on the chest when you have a cold.'

'You can if you like, but it wouldn't help.'

'You put it in ointment and it heals cracked lips.'

'That's camphor.'

'So it is.'

He waited for her to have another guess.

'Go ahead and tell me,' she said.

'It may surprise you a bit.'

'I'm ready to be surprised.'

'Menthol,' Conrad said, 'is a well-known anti-aphrodisiac.'

'A what?'

'It suppresses sexual desire.'

'Conrad, you're making these things up.'

'I swear to you I'm not.'

'Who uses it?'

'Very few people nowadays. It has too strong a flavour. Saltpetre is much better.'

'Ah yes. I know about saltpetre.'

'What do you know about saltpetre?'

'They give it to prisoners,' Anna said. 'They sprinkle it on their cornflakes every morning to keep them quiet.'

'They also use it in cigarettes,' Conrad said.

'You mean prisoners' cigarettes?'

'I mean *all* cigarettes.'

'That's nonsense.'

'Is it?'

'Of course it is.'

'Why do you say that?'

'Nobody would stand for it,' she said.

'They stand for cancer.'

'That's quite different, Conrad. How do you know they put saltpetre in cigarettes?'

'Have you never wondered,' he said, 'what makes a cigarette go on burning when you lay it in the ashtray? Tobacco doesn't burn of its own accord. Any pipe smoker will tell you that.'

'They use special chemicals,' she said.

'Exactly; they use saltpetre.'

'Does saltpetre burn?'

'Sure it burns. It used to be one of the prime ingredients of old-fashioned gunpowder. Fuses, too. It makes very good fuses. That cigarette of yours is a first-rate slow-burning fuse, is it not?'

Ann looked at her cigarette. Though she hadn't drawn on it for a couple of minutes, it was still smouldering away and the smoke was curling upward from the tip in a slim blue-grey spiral.

'So this has menthol in it *and* saltpetre?' she said.

'Absolutely.'

'And they're *both* anti-aphrodisiacs?'

'Yes. You're getting a double dose.'

'It's ridiculous, Conrad. It's too little to make any difference.'

He smiled but didn't answer this.

'There's not enough there to inhibit a cockroach,' she said.

'That's what you think, Anna. How many do you smoke a day?'

'About thirty.'

'Well,' he said, 'I guess it's none of my business.' He paused, and then he added, 'But you and I would be a lot better off today if it was.'

'Was what?'

'My business.'

'Conrad, what *do* you mean?'

'I'm simply saying that if you, once upon a time, hadn't suddenly decided to drop me, none of this misery would have happened to either of us. We'd still be happily married to each other.'

His face had suddenly taken on a queer sharp look.

'Drop you?'

'It was quite a shock, Anna.'

'Oh dear,' she said, 'but everybody drops everybody else at that age, don't they?'

'I wouldn't know,' Conrad said.

'You're not cross with me still, are you, for doing that?'

'Cross!' he said. 'Good God, Anna! Cross is what children get when they lose a toy! I lost a wife!'

She stared at him, speechless.

'Tell me,' he went on, 'didn't you have any idea how I felt at the time?'

'But Conrad, we were so *young*.'

'It destroyed me, Anna. It just about destroyed me.'

'But how ...'

'How what?'

'How, if it meant so much, could you turn right around and get engaged to somebody else a few weeks later?'

'Have you never heard of the rebound?' he asked.

She nodded, gazing at him in dismay.

'I was wildly in love with you, Anna.'

She didn't answer.

'I'm sorry,' he said. 'That was a silly outburst. Please forgive me.'

There was a long silence.

Conrad was leaning back in his chair, studying her from a distance. She took another cigarette from the pack, and lit it. Then she blew out the match and placed it carefully in the ashtray. When she glanced up again, he was still watching her. There was an intent, far look in his eyes.

'What are you thinking about?' she asked.

He didn't answer.

'Conrad,' she said, 'do you still hate me for doing what I did?'

'Hate you?'

'Yes, hate me. I have a queer feeling that you do. I'm sure you do, even after all these years.'

'Anna,' he said.

'Yes, Conrad?'

He hitched his chair closer to the table, and leaned forward. 'Did it ever cross your mind ...'

He stopped.

She waited.

He was looking so intensely earnest all of a sudden that she leaned forward herself.

'Did what cross my mind?' she asked.

'The fact that you and I ... that both of us ... have a bit of unfinished business.'

She stared at him.

He looked back at her, his eyes as bright as two stars. 'Don't be shocked,' he said, 'please.'

'Shocked?'

'You look as though I'd just asked you to jump out of the window with me.'

The room was full of people now, and it was very noisy. It was like being at a cocktail party. You had to shout to be heard.

Conrad's eyes waited on her, impatient, eager.

'I'd like another martini,' she said.

'Must you?'

'Yes,' she said, 'I must.'

In her whole life, she had been made love to by only one man – her husband, Ed.

And it had always been wonderful.

Three thousand times?

She thought more. Probably a good deal more. Who counts?

Assuming, though, for the sake of argument, that the exact figure (for there has to be an exact figure) was three thousand six hundred and eighty ...

... and knowing that every single time it happened it was an act of pure, passionate, authentic love-making between the same man and the same woman ...

... then how in heaven's name could an entirely new man, an unloved stranger, hope to come in suddenly on the three thousand, six hundred and eighty-*first* time and be even halfway acceptable?

He'd be a trespasser.

All the memories would come rushing back. She would be lying there suffocated by memories.

She had raised this very point with Dr Jacobs during one of her sessions a few months back, and old Jacobs had said, 'There will be no nonsense about memories, my dear Mrs Cooper. I wish you would forget that. Only the present will exist.'

'But how do I get there?' she had said. 'How can I summon up enough nerve suddenly to go upstairs to a bedroom and take off my clothes in front of a new man, a stranger, in cold blood...?'

'Cold blood!' he had cried. 'Good God, woman, it'll be boiling hot!' And later he had said, 'Do at any rate try to believe me, Mrs Cooper, when I tell you that any woman who has been deprived of sexual congress after more than twenty years of practice – of uncommonly frequent practice in your case, if I understand you correctly – any woman in those circumstances is going to suffer continually from severe psychological disturbances until the routine is re-established. You are feeling a lot better, I know that, but it is my duty to inform you that you are by no means back to normal ...'

To Conrad, Anna said, 'This isn't by any chance a therapeutic suggestion, is it?'

'A *what?*'

'A therapeutic suggestion.'

'What in the world do you mean?'

'It sounds exactly like a plot hatched up by my Dr Jacobs.'

'Look,' he said, and now he leaned right across the table and touched her left hand with the tip of one finger. 'When I knew you before, I was too damn young and nervous to make that sort of proposition, much as I wanted to. I didn't think there was any particular hurry then, anyway. I figured we had a whole lifetime before us. I wasn't to know you were going to drop me.'

Her martini arrived. Anna picked it up and began to drink it fast. She knew exactly what it was going to do to her. It was going to make her float. A third martini always did that. Give her a third martini and within seconds her body would become completely weightless and she would go floating around the room like a wisp of hydrogen gas.

She sat there holding the glass with both hands as though it were a sacrament. She took another gulp. There was not much of it left now. Over the rim of her glass she could see Conrad watching her with disapproval as she drank. She smiled at him radiantly.

'You're not against the use of anaesthetics when you operate, are you?' she asked.

'Please, Anna, don't talk like that.'

'I am beginning to float,' she said.

'So I see,' he answered. 'Why don't you stop there?'

'What did you say?'

'I said, why don't you stop?'

'Do you want me to tell you why?'

'No,' he said. He made a little forward movement with his hands as though he were going to take her glass away from her, so she quickly put it to her lips and tipped it high, holding it there for a few seconds to allow the last drop to run out. When she looked at Conrad again, he was placing a ten-dollar bill on the waiter's tray, and the waiter was saying, 'Thank *you*, sir. Thank you indeed,' and the next thing she knew she was floating out of the room and across the lobby of the hotel with Conrad's hand cupped lightly under one of her elbows, steering her toward the elevators. They floated up to the twenty-second floor, and then along the corridor to the door of her bedroom. She fished the key out of her purse and unlocked the door and floated inside. Conrad followed, closing the door behind him. Then very suddenly, he grabbed hold of her and folded her up in his enormous arms and started kissing her with great gusto.

She let him do it.

He kissed her all over her mouth and cheeks and neck, taking deep breaths in between the kisses. She kept her eyes open, watching him in a queer detached sort of way, and the view she got reminded her vaguely of the blurry close-up view of a dentist's face when he is working on an upper back tooth.

Then all of a sudden, Conrad put his tongue into one of her ears. The effect of this upon her was electric. It was as though a live two-hundred-volt plug had been pushed into an empty socket, and all the lights came on and the bones began to melt and the hot molten sap went running down into her limbs and she exploded into a frenzy. It was the kind of marvellous, wanton, reckless, flaming frenzy that Ed used to provoke in her so very often in the olden days by just a touch of the hand here and there. She flung her arms around Conrad's neck and started kissing him back with far more gusto than he had ever kissed her, and although he looked at first as though he thought she was going to swallow him alive, he soon recovered his balance.

Anna hadn't the faintest idea how long they stood there embracing and kissing with such violence, but it must have been for quite a while. She felt such happiness, such ... such *confidence* again at last, such sudden overwhelming confidence in herself that she wanted to tear off her clothes and do a wild dance for Conrad in the middle of the room. But she did no such foolish thing. Instead, she simply floated away to the edge of the bed and sat down to catch her breath. Conrad quickly sat down beside her. She leaned her head against his chest and sat there glowing all over while he gently stroked her hair. Then she undid one button of his shirt and slid her hand inside and laid it against his chest. Through his ribs, she could feel the beating of his heart.

'What do I see here?' Conrad said.

'What do you see where, my darling?'

'On your scalp. You want to watch this, Anna.'

'You watch it for me, dearest.'

'Seriously,' he said, 'you know what this looks like? It looks like a tiny touch of androgenic alopecia.'

'Good.'

'No, it is not good. It's actually an inflammation of the hair follicles, and it causes baldness. It's quite common on women in their later years.'

'Oh shut up, Conrad,' she said, kissing him on the side of the neck. 'I have the most gorgeous hair.'

She sat up and pulled off his jacket. Then she undid his tie and threw it across the room.

'There's a little hook on the back of my dress,' she said. 'Undo it, please.'

Conrad unhooked the hook, then unzipped the zipper and helped her to get out of the dress. She had on a rather nice pale-blue slip. Conrad was wearing an ordinary white shirt, as doctors do, but it was now open at the neck, and this suited him. His neck had a little ridge of sinewy muscle running up vertically on either side, and when he turned his head the muscle moved under the skin. It was the most beautiful neck Anna had ever seen.

'Let's do this very very slowly,' she said. 'Let's drive ourselves crazy with anticipation.'

His eyes rested a moment on her face, then travelled away, all the way down the length of her body, and she saw him smile.

'Shall we be very stylish and dissipated, Conrad, and order a bottle of champagne? I can ask room service to bring it up, and you can hide in the bathroom when they come in.'

'No,' he said. 'You've had enough to drink already. Stand up, please.'

The tone of his voice caused her to stand up at once.

'Come here,' he said.

She went close to him. He was still sitting on the bed, and now, without getting up, he reached forward and began to take off the rest of her clothes. He did this slowly and deliberately. His face had become suddenly rather pale.

'Oh, darling,' she said, 'how marvellous! You've got that famous thing! A real thick clump of hair growing out of each of your ears! You know what that means, don't you? It's *the* absolutely positive sign of enormous virility!' She bent down and kissed him on the ear. He went on taking off her clothes – the bra, the shoes, the girdle, the pants, and finally the stockings, all of which he dropped in a heap on the floor. The moment he had peeled off her last stocking and dropped it, he turned away. He turned right away from her as though she didn't exist, and now he began to undress himself.

It was rather odd to be standing so close to him in nothing but her own skin and him not even giving her a second look. But perhaps men did these things. Ed might have been an exception. How could *she* know? Conrad took off his white shirt first, and after folding it very carefully, he stood up and carried it to a chair and laid it on one of the arms. He did the same with his undershirt. Then he sat down again on the edge of the bed and started removing his shoes. Anna remained quite still, watching him. His sudden change of mood, his silence, his curious intensity, were making her a bit afraid. But they were also exciting her. There was a stealth, almost a menace in his movements, as though he were some splendid animal treading softly toward the kill. A leopard.

She became hypnotized watching him. She was watching his fingers, the surgeon's fingers, as they untied and loosened the laces of the left shoe, easing it off the foot, and placing it neatly half under the bed. The right shoe came next. Then the left sock and the right sock, both of them being folded together and laid with the utmost precision across the toes of the shoes. Finally the fingers moved up to the top of the trousers, where they undid one button and then began to manipulate the zipper. The trousers, when taken off, were folded along the creases, then carried over to the chair. The underpants followed.

Conrad, now naked, walked slowly back to the edge of the bed, and sat. Then at last, he turned his head and noticed her. She stood waiting ... and trembling. He looked her slowly up and down. Then abruptly, he shot out a hand and took her by the wrist, and with a sharp pull he had her sprawled across the bed.

The relief was enormous. Anna flung her arms around him and held on to him tightly, oh so tightly, for fear that he might go away. She was in mortal fear that he might go away and not come back. And there they lay, she holding on to him as though he were the only thing left in the world to hold on to, and he, strangely quiet, watchful, intent, slowly disentangling himself and beginning to touch her now in a number of different places with those fingers of his, those expert surgeon's fingers. And once again she flew into a frenzy.

The things he did to her during the next few moments were terrible and exquisite. He was, she knew, merely getting her ready, preparing her, or as they say in the hospital, prepping her for the operation itself, but oh God, she had never known or experienced anything even remotely like this. And it was all exceedingly quick, for in what seemed to her no more than a few seconds, she had reached that excruciating point of no return where the whole room becomes compressed into a single tiny blinding speck of light that is going to explode and tear one to pieces at the slightest extra touch. At this stage, in a swift rapacious parabola, Conrad swung his body on top of her for the final act.

And now Anna felt her passion being drawn out of her as if a long live nerve were being drawn slowly out of her body, a long live thread of electric fire, and she cried out to Conrad to go on and on and on, and as she did so, in the middle of it all, somewhere above her, she heard another voice, and this other voice grew louder and louder, more and more insistent, demanding to be heard:

'I said are you *wearing* something?' the voice wanted to know.

'Oh darling, what is it?'

'I keep asking you, are you *wearing* something?'

'Who, me?'

'There's an obstruction here. You must be wearing a diaphragm or some other appliance.'

'Of course not, darling. Everything's wonderful. Oh, do be quiet.'

'Everything is *not* wonderful, Anna.'

Like a picture on the screen, the room swam back into focus. In the foreground was Conrad's face. It was suspended above her, on naked shoulders. The eyes were looking directly into hers. The mouth was still talking.

'If you're going to use a device, then for heaven's sake learn to introduce it in the proper manner. There is nothing so aggravating as careless positioning. The diaphragm has to be placed right back against the cervix.'

'But I'm not wearing anything!'

'You're not? Well, there's still an obstruction.'

Not only the room but the whole world as well seemed slowly to be sliding away from under her now.

'I feel sick,' she said.

'You what?'

'I feel sick.'

'Don't be childish, Anna.'

'Conrad, I'd like you to go, please. Go now.'

'What on earth are you talking about?'

'Go away from me, Conrad!'

'That's ridiculous, Anna. Okay, I'm sorry I spoke. Forget it.'

'Go away!' she cried. *'Go away! Go away! Go away!'*

She tried to push him away from her, but he was huge and strong and he had her pinned.

'Calm yourself,' he said. 'Relax. You can't suddenly change your mind like this, in the middle of everything. And for heaven's sake, don't start weeping.'

'Leave me alone, Conrad, I beg you.'

He seemed to be gripping her with everything he had, arms and elbows, hands and fingers, thighs and knees, ankles and feet. He was like a toad the way he gripped her. He was exactly like an enormous clinging toad, gripping and grasping and refusing to let go. She had seen a toad once doing precisely this. It was copulating with a frog on a stone beside a stream, and there it sat, motionless, repulsive, with an evil yellow gleam in its eye, gripping the frog with its two powerful front paws and refusing to let go ...

'Now stop struggling, Anna. You're acting like a hysterical child. For God's sake, woman, what's eating you?'

'You're hurting me!' she cried.

'Hurting you?'

'It's hurting me terribly!'

She told him this only to get him away.

'You know why it's hurting?' he said.

'Conrad! Please!'

'Now wait a minute, Anna. Allow me to explain ...'

'No!' she cried. 'I've had enough explaining!'

'My dear woman ...'

'No!' She was struggling desperately to free herself, but he still had her pinned.

'The reason it hurts,' he went on, 'is that you are not manufacturing any fluid. The mucosa is virtually dry ...'

'Stop!'

'The actual name is senile atrophic vaginitis. It comes with age, Anna. That's why it's called *senile* vaginitis. There's not much one can do ...'

At that point, she started to scream. The screams were not very loud, but they were screams nevertheless, terrible, agonized stricken screams, and after listening to them for a few seconds, Conrad, in a single graceful movement, suddenly rolled away from her and pushed her to one side with both hands. He pushed her with such force that she fell on to the floor.

She climbed slowly to her feet, and as she staggered into the bathroom, she was crying 'Ed! ... Ed! ... Ed! ...' in a queer supplicating voice. The door shut.

Conrad lay very still listening to the sounds that came from behind the door. At first, he heard only the sobbing of the woman, but a few seconds later, above the sobbing, he heard the sharp metallic click of a cupboard being opened. Instantly, he sat up and vaulted off the bed and began to dress himself with great speed. His clothes, so neatly folded, lay ready at hand, and it took him no more than a couple of minutes to put them on. When that was done, he crossed to the mirror and wiped the lipstick off his face with a handkerchief. He took a comb from his pocket and ran it through his fine black hair. He walked once round the bed to see if he had forgotten anything, and then, carefully, like a man who is tiptoeing from a room where a child is sleeping, he moved out into the corridor, closing the door softly behind him.

BITCH

I have so far released for publication only one episode from Uncle Oswald's diaries. It concerned, as some of you may remember, a carnal encounter between my uncle and a Syrian female leper in the Sinai Desert. Six years have gone by since its publication and nobody has yet come forward to make trouble. I am therefore encouraged to release a second episode from these curious pages. My lawyer has advised against it. He points out that some of the people are still living and are easily recognizable. He says I will be sued mercilessly. Well, let them sue. I am proud of my uncle. He knew how life should be lived. In a preface to the first episode I said that Casanova's *Memoirs* read like a Parish Magazine beside Uncle Oswald's diaries, and that the great lover himself, when compared with my uncle, appears positively undersexed. I stand by that, and given time I shall prove it to the world. Here then is a little episode from Volume XXIII, precisely as Uncle Oswald wrote it:

PARIS
Wednesday

Breakfast at ten. I tried the honey. It was delivered yesterday in an early Sèvres sucrier which had that lovely canary-coloured ground known as *jonquille*. 'From Suzie,' the note said, 'and thank you.' It is nice to be appreciated. And the honey was interesting. Suzie Jolibois had, among other things, a small farm south of Casablanca, and was fond of bees. Her hives were set in the midst of a plantation of *cannabis indica*, and the bees drew their nectar exclusively from this source. They lived, those bees, in a state of perpetual euphoria and were disinclined to work. The honey was therefore very scarce. I spread a third piece of toast. The stuff was almost black. It had a pungent aroma. The telephone rang. I put the receiver to my ear and waited. I never speak first when called. After all, I'm not phoning them. They're phoning me.

'Oswald! Are you there?'

I knew the voice. 'Yes, Henri,' I said. 'Good morning.'

'Listen!' he said, speaking fast and sounding excited. 'I think I've got it! I'm almost certain I've got it! Forgive me if I'm out of breath, but I've just had a rather fantastic experience. It's all right now. Everything's fine. Will you come over?'

'Yes,' I said. 'I'll come over.' I replaced the receiver and poured myself another cup of coffee. Had Henri really done it at last? If he had, then I wanted to be around to share the fun.

I must pause here to tell you how I met Henri Biotte. Some three years ago I drove down to Provence to spend a summer weekend with a lady who was interesting to me simply because she possessed an extraordinarily powerful muscle in a region where other women have no muscles at all. An hour after my arrival, I was strolling alone on the lawn beside the river when a small dark man approached me. He had black hairs on the backs of his hands and he made me a little bow and said, 'Henri Biotte, a fellow guest.'

'Oswald Cornelius,' I said.

Henry Biotte was as hairy as a goat. His chin and cheeks were covered with bristly black hair and thick tufts of it were sprouting from his nostrils. 'May I join you?' he said, falling into step beside me and starting immediately to talk. And what a talker he was! How Gallic, how excitable. He walked with a mad little hop, and his fingers flew as if he wanted to scatter them to the four winds of heaven, and his words went off like firecrackers, with terrific speed. He was a Belgian chemist, he said, working in Paris. He was an olfactory chemist. He had devoted his life to the study of olfaction.

'You mean smell?' I said.

'Yes, yes!' he cried. 'Exactly! I am an expert on smells. I know more about smells than anyone else in the world!'

'Good smells or bad?' I asked, trying to slow him down.

'Good smells, lovely smells, glorious smells!' he said. 'I make them! I can make any smell you want!'

He went on to tell me he was the chief perfume blender to one of the great couturiers in the city. And his nose, he said, placing a hairy finger on the tip of his hairy proboscis, probably looked just like any other nose, did it not? I wanted to tell him it had more hairs sprouting from the noseholes than wheat from the prairies and why didn't he get his barber to snip them out, but instead I confessed politely that I could see nothing unusual about it.

'Quite so,' he said. 'But in actual fact it is a smelling organ of phenomenal sensitivity. With two sniffs it can detect the presence of a single drop of macroylic musk in a gallon of geranium oil.'

'Extraordinary,' I said.

'On the Champs Elysées,' he went on, 'which is a wide thoroughfare, my nose can identify the precise perfume being used by a woman walking on the other side of the street.'

'With the traffic in between?'

'With heavy traffic in between,' he said.

He went on to name two of the most famous perfumes in the world, both of them made by the fashion-house he worked for. 'Those are my personal creations,' he said modestly. 'I blended them myself. They have made a fortune for the celebrated old bitch who runs the business.'

'But not for you?'

'Me! I am but a poor miserable employee on a salary,' he said, spreading his palms and hunching his shoulders so high they touched his earlobes. 'One day, though, I shall break away and pursue my dream.'

'You have a dream?'

'I have a glorious, tremendous, exciting dream, my dear sir!'

'Then why don't you pursue it?'

'Because first I must find a man farsighted enough and wealthy enough to back me.'

Ah-ha, I thought, so that's what it's all about. 'With a reputation like yours, that shouldn't be too difficult,' I said.

'The sort of rich man I seek is hard to find,' he said. 'He must be a sporty gambler with a very keen appetite for the bizarre.'

That's me, you clever little bugger, I thought. 'What is this dream you wish to pursue?' I asked him. 'Is it making perfumes?'

'My dear fellow!' he cried. 'Anyone can make *perfumes*! I'm talking about *the* perfume! The *only* one that counts!'

'Which would that be?'

'Why, the *dangerous* one, of course! And when I have made it, I shall rule the world!'

'Good for you,' I said.

'I am not joking, Monsieur Cornelius. Would you permit me to explain what I am driving at?'

'Go ahead.'

'Forgive me if I sit down,' he said, moving toward a bench. 'I had a heart attack last April and I have to be careful.'

'I'm sorry to hear that.'

'Oh, don't be sorry. All will be well so long as I don't overdo things.'

It was a lovely afternoon and the bench was on the lawn near the riverbank and we sat down on it. Beside us, the river flowed slow and smooth and deep, and there were little clouds of waterflies hovering over the surface. Across the river there were willows along the bank and beyond the willows an emerald-green meadow, yellow with buttercups, and a single cow grazing. The cow was brown and white.

'I will tell you what kind of perfume I wish to make,' he said. 'But it is essential I explain a few other things to you on the way or you will not fully understand. So please bear with me a while.' One hand lay limp upon his lap, the hairy part upward. It looked like a black rat. He was stroking it gently with the fingers of the other hand.

'Let us consider first,' he said, 'the phenomenon that occurs when a dog meets a bitch in heat. The dog's sexual drive is tremendous. All self-control disappears. He has only one thought in his head, which is to fornicate on the spot, and unless he is prevented by force, he will do so. But do you know what it is that causes this tremendous sex-drive in a dog?'

'Smell,' I said.

'Precisely, Monsieur Cornelius. Odorous molecules of a special conformation enter the dog's nostrils and stimulate his olfactory nerve-endings. This causes urgent signals to be sent to the olfactory bulb and thence to the higher brain centres. It is *all* done by smell. If you sever a dog's olfactory nerve, he will lose interest in sex. This is also true of many other mammals, but it is not true of man. Smell has nothing to do with the sexual appetite of the human male. He is stimulated in this respect by sight, by tactility, and by his lively imagination. Never by smell.'

'What about perfume?' I said.

'It's all rubbish!' he answered. 'All those expensive scents in small bottles, the ones I make, they have no aphrodisiac effect at all upon a man. Perfume was never intended for that purpose. In the old days, women used it to conceal the fact that they stank. Today, when they no longer stink, they use it purely for narcissistic reasons. They enjoy putting it on and smelling their own good smells. Men hardly notice the stuff. I promise you that.'

'I do,' I said.

'Does it stir you physically?'

'No, not physically. Aesthetically, yes.'

'You enjoy the smell. So do I. But there are plenty of other smells I enjoy more – the bouquet of a good Lafite, the scent of a fresh Comice pear, or the smell of the air blowing in from the sea on the Brittany coast.'

A trout jumped high in midstream and the sunlight flashed on its body. 'You must forget,' said Monsieur Biotte, 'all the nonsense about musk and ambergris and the testicular secretions of the civet cat. We make our perfumes from chemicals these days. If I want a musky odour I will use ethylene sebacate. Phenylacetic acid will give me civet and benzaldehyde will provide the smell of almonds. No sir, I am no longer interested in mixing up chemicals to make pretty smells.'

For some minutes his nose had been running slightly, wetting the black hairs in his nostrils. He noticed it and produced a handkerchief and gave it a blow and a wipe. 'What I intend to do,' he said, 'is to produce a perfume which will have the same electrifying effect upon a man as the scent of a bitch in heat has upon a dog! One whiff and that'll be it! The man will lose all control. He'll rip off his pants and ravish the lady on the spot!'

'We could have some fun with that,' I said.

'We could rule the world!' he cried.

'Yes, but you told me just now that smell has nothing to do with the sexual appetite of the human male.'

'It doesn't,' he said. 'But it used to. I have evidence that in the period of the post-glacial drift, when primitive man was far more closely related to the ape than he is now, he still retained the ape-like characteristic of jumping on any right-smelling female he ran across. And later, in the Palaeolithic and Neolithic periods, he continued to become sexually animated by smell, but to a lesser and lesser degree. By the time the higher civilizations had come along in Egypt and China around 10,000 BC, evolution had played its part and had completely suppressed man's ability to be stimulated sexually by smell. Am I boring you?'

'Not at all. But tell me, does that mean an actual physical change has taken place in man's smelling apparatus?'

'Absolutely not,' he said, 'otherwise there'd be nothing we could do about it. The little mechanism that enabled our ancestors to smell these subtle odours is still there. I happen to know it is. Listen, you've seen how some people can make their ears move a tiny bit?'

'I can do it myself,' I said, doing it.

'You see,' he said, 'the ear-moving muscle is still there. It's a leftover from the time when man used to be able to cock his ears forward for better hearing, like a dog. He lost that ability over a hundred thousand years ago, but the muscle remains. And the same applies to our smelling apparatus. The mechanism for smelling those secret smells is still there, but we have lost the ability to use it.'

'How can you be so certain it's still there?' I asked.

'Do you know how our smelling system works?' he said.

'Not really.'

'Then I shall tell you, otherwise I cannot answer your question. Attend closely, please. Air is sucked in through the nostrils and passes the three baffle-shaped turbinate bones in the upper part of the nose. There it gets warmer and filtered. This warm air now travels up and over two clefts that contain the smelling organs. These organs are patches of yellowish tissue, each about an inch square. In this tissue are embedded the nerve-fibres and nerve-endings of the olfactory nerve. Every nerve-ending consists of an olfactory cell bearing a cluster of tiny hair-like filaments. These filaments act as receivers. "Receptors" is a better word. And when the receptors are tickled or stimulated by odorous molecules, they send signals to the brain. If, as you come downstairs in the morning, you sniff into your nostrils the odorous molecules of frying bacon, these will stimulate your receptors, the receptors will flash a signal along the olfactory nerve to the brain, and the brain will interpret it in terms of the character and intensity of the odour. And that is when you cry out, "Ah-ha, bacon for breakfast!" '

'I never eat bacon for breakfast,' I said.

He ignored this.

'These receptors,' he went on, 'these tiny hair-like filaments are what concern us. And now you are going to ask me how on earth they can tell the difference between one odorous molecule and another, between say peppermint and camphor?'

'How can they?' I said. I was interested in this.

'Attend more closely than ever now, please,' he said. 'At the end of each receptor is an indentation, a sort of cup, except that it isn't round. This is the "receptor site". Imagine now thousands of these little hair-like filaments with tiny cups at their extremities, all waving about like the tendrils of sea anemones and waiting to catch in their cups any odorous molecules that pass by. That, you see, is what actually happens. When you sniff a certain smell, the odorous molecules of the substance which made that smell go rushing around inside your nostrils and get caught by the little cups, the receptor sites. Now the important thing to remember is this. Molecules come in all shapes and sizes. Equally, the little cups or receptor sites are also differently shaped. Thus, the molecules lodge only in the receptor sites which fit them. Pepperminty molecules go only into special pepperminty receptor sites. Camphor molecules, which have a quite different shape, will fit only into the special camphor receptor sites, and so on. It's rather like those toys for small children where they have to fit variously shaped pieces into the right holes.'

'Let me see if I understand you,' I said. 'Are you saying that my brain will know it is a pepperminty smell simply because the molecule has lodged in a pepperminty reception site?'

'Precisely.'

'But you are surely not suggesting there are differently shaped receptor sites for every smell in the world?'

'No,' he said, 'as a matter of fact, man has only seven differently shaped sites.'

'Why only seven?'

'Because our sense of smell recognizes only seven "pure primary odours". All the rest are "complex odours" made up by mixing the primaries.'

'Are you sure of that?'

'Positive. Our sense of taste has even less. It recognizes only four primaries – sweet, sour, salt, and bitter! All other tastes are mixtures of these.'

'What are the seven pure primary odours?' I asked him.

'Their names are of no importance to us,' he said. 'Why confuse the issue.'

'I'd like to hear them.'

'All right,' he said. 'They are camphoraceous, pungent, musky, ethereal, floral, pepperminty, and putrid. Don't look so sceptical, please. This isn't *my* discovery. Very learned scientists have worked on it for years. And their conclusions are quite accurate, *except in one respect.*'

'What's that?'

'*There is an eighth pure primary odour which they don't know about, and an eight receptor site to receive the curiously shaped molecules of that odour!*'

'Ah-ha-ha!' I said. 'I see what you're driving at.'

'Yes,' he said, 'the eighth pure primary odour is the sexual stimulant that caused primitive man to behave like a dog thousands of years ago. It has a very peculiar molecular structure.'

'Then you know what it is?'

'Of course I know what it is.'

'And you say we still retain the receptor sites for these peculiar molecules to fit in to?'

'Absolutely.'

'This mysterious smell,' I said, 'does it ever reach our nostrils nowadays?'

'Frequently.'

'Do we smell it? I mean, are we aware of it?'

'No.'

'You mean the molecules don't get caught in the receptor sites?'

'They do, my dear fellow, they do. But nothing happens. No signal is sent off to the brain. The telephone line is out of action. It's like that ear muscle. The mechanism is still there, but we've lost the ability to use it properly.'

'And what do you propose to do about that?' I asked.

'I shall reactivate it,' he said. 'We are dealing with nerves here, not muscles. And these nerves are not dead or injured, they're merely dormant. I shall probably increase the intensity of the smell a thousandfold, and add a catalyst.'

'Go on,' I said.

'That's enough.'

'I should like to hear more,' I said.

'Forgive me for saying so Monsieur Cornelius, but I don't think you know enough about organoleptic quality to follow me any further. The lecture is over.'

Henri Biotte sat smug and quiet on the bench beside the river stroking the back of one hand with the fingers of the other. The tufts of hair sprouting from his nostrils gave him a pixie look, but that was camouflage. He struck me rather as a dangerous and dainty little creature, someone who lurked behind stones with a sharp eye and a sting in his tail, waiting for the lone traveller to come by. Surreptitiously I searched his face. The mouth interested me. The lips had a magenta tinge, possibly something to do with his heart trouble. The lower lip

,was caruncular and pendulous. It bulged out in the middle like a purse, and could easily have served as a receptacle for small coins. The skin of the lip seemed to be blown up very tight, as though by air, and it was constantly wet, not from licking but from an excess of saliva in the mouth.

And there he sat, this Monsieur Henri Biotte, smiling a wicked little smile and waiting patiently for me to react. He was a totally amoral man, that much was clear, but then so was I. He was also a wicked man, and although I cannot in all honesty claim wickedness as one of my own virtues, I find it irresistible in others. A wicked man has a lustre all his own. Then again, there was something diabolically splendid about a person who wished to set back the sex habits of civilized man half a million years.

Yes, he had me hooked. So there and then, sitting beside the river in the garden of the lady from Provence, I made an offer to Henri. I suggested he should leave his present employment forthwith and set himself up in a small laboratory. I would pay all the bills for this little venture as well as making good his salary. It would be a five-year contract, and we would go fifty-fifty on anything that came out of it.

Henri was ecstatic. 'You mean it?' he cried. 'You are serious?'

I held out my hand. He grasped it in both of his and shook it vigorously. It was like shaking hands with a yak. 'We shall control mankind!' he said. 'We'll be the gods of the earth!' He flung his arms around me and embraced me and kissed me first on one cheek, then on the other. Oh, this awful Gallic kissing. Henry's lower lip felt like the wet underbelly of a toad against my skin. 'Let's keep the celebrations until later,' I said, wiping myself dry with a linen handkerchief.

Henri Biotte made apologies and excuses to his hostess and rushed back to Paris that night. Within a week he had given up his old job and had rented three rooms to serve as a laboratory. These were on the third floor of a house on the Left Bank, on the Rue de Cassette, just off the Boulevard Raspaille. He spent a great deal of my money equipping the place with complicated apparatus, and he even installed a large cage into which he put two apes, a male and a female. He also took on an assistant, a clever and moderately presentable young lady called Jeanette. And with all that, he set to work.

You should understand that for me this little venture was of no great importance. I had plenty of other things to amuse me. I used to drop in on Henri maybe a couple of times a month to see how things were going, but otherwise I left him entirely to himself. My mind wasn't on his job. I hadn't the patience for that kind of research. And when results failed to come quickly, I began to lose all interest. Even the pair of over-sexed apes ceased to amuse me after a while.

Only once did I derive any pleasure from my visits to his laboratory. As you must know by now, I can seldom resist even a moderately presentable woman. And so, on a certain rainy Thursday afternoon, while Henri was busy applying electrodes to the olfactory organs of a frog in one room, I found myself applying something infinitely more agreeable to Jeanette in the other room. I had not, of course, expected anything out of the ordinary from this little frolic. I was acting more out of habit than anything else. But my goodness, what a surprise I got! Beneath her white overall, this rather austere research chemist turned out to be a sinewy and flexible female of immense dexterity. The experiments she performed, first with the oscillator, then with the high-speed centrifuge, were absolutely breathtaking. In fact, not since that Turkish tightrope walker in Ankara (see Vol. XXI) had I experienced anything quite like it. Which all goes to show for the thousandth time that women are as inscrutable as the ocean. You never know what you have under your keel, deep water or shallow, until you have heaved the lead.

I did not bother to visit the laboratory again after that. You know my rule. I never return to a female a second time. With me at any rate, women invariably pull out all the stops during the first encounter, and a second meeting can therefore be nothing more than the same old tune on the same old fiddle. Who wants that? Not me. So when I suddenly heard Henri's voice calling urgently to me over the telephone that morning at breakfast, I had almost forgotten his existence.

I drove through the fiendish Paris traffic to the Rue de Cassette. I parked the car and took the tiny elevator to the third floor. Henri opened the door of the laboratory. 'Don't move!' he cried. 'Stay right where you are!' He scuttled away and returned in a few seconds holding a little tray upon which lay two greasy-looking red rubber objects. 'Noseplugs,' he said. 'Put them in, please. Like me. Keep out the molecules. Go on, ram them in tight. You'll have to breathe through your mouth, but who cares?'

Each noseplug had a short length of blue string attached to its blunt lower end, presumably for pulling it back out of the nostril. I could see the two bits of blue string dangling from Henri's nostrils. I inserted my own noseplugs. Henri inspected them. He rammed them in tighter with his thumb. Then he went dancing back into the lab, waving his hairy hands and crying out, 'Come in now, my dear Oswald! Come in, come in! Forgive my excitement, but this is a great day for me!' The plugs in his nose made him speak as though he had a bad cold. He hopped over to a cupboard and reached inside. He brought out one of those small square bottles made of very thick glass that hold about an ounce of perfume. He carried it over to where I stood, cupping his hands around it as though it were a tiny bird. 'Look! Here it is! The most precious fluid in the entire world!'

This is the sort of rubbishy overstatement I dislike intensely. 'So you think you've done it?' I said.

'I know I've done it, Oswald! I am certain I've done it!'

'Tell me what happened.'

'That's not so easy,' he said. 'But I can try.'

He placed the little bottle carefully on the bench. 'I had left this particular blend, Number 1076, to distil overnight,' he went on. 'That was because only one drop of distillate is produced every half hour. I had it dripping into a sealed beaker to prevent evaporation. All these fluids are extremely volatile. And so, soon after I arrived at eight thirty this morning, I went over to Number 1076 and lifted the seal from the beaker. I took a tiny sniff. Just one tiny sniff. Then I replaced the seal.'

'And then?'

'Oh, my God, Oswald, it was fantastic! I completely lost control of myself! I did things I would never in a million years have dreamed of doing!'

'Such as what?'

'My dear fellow, I went completely wild! I was like a wild beast, an animal! I was not human! The civilizing influences of centuries simply dropped away! I was Neolithic!'

'What did you do?'

'I can't remember the next bit very clearly. It was all so quick and violent. But I became overwhelmed by the most terrifying sensation of lust it is possible to imagine. Everything else was blotted out of my mind. All I wanted was a woman. I felt that if I didn't get hold of a woman immediately, I would explode.'

'Lucky Jeanette,' I said, glancing toward the next room. 'How is she now?'

'Jeanette left me over a year ago,' he said. 'I replaced her with a brilliant young chemist called Simone Gautier.'

'Lucky Simone, then.'

'No, no!' Henri cried. 'That was the awful thing! She hadn't arrived! Today of all days, she was late for work! I began to go mad. I dashed out into the corridor and down the stairs. I was like a dangerous animal. I was hunting for a woman, any woman, and heaven help her when I found her!'

'And who did you find?'

'Nobody, thank God. Because suddenly, I regained my senses. The effect had worn off. It was very quick, and I was standing alone on the second-floor landing. I felt cold. But I knew at once exactly what had happened. I ran back upstairs and re-entered this room with my nostrils pinched tightly between finger and thumb. I went straight to the drawer where I stored the noseplugs. Ever since I started working on this project, I have kept a supply of noseplugs ready for just such an occasion. I rammed in the plugs. Now I was safe.'

'Can't the molecules get up into the nose through the mouth?' I asked him.

'They can't reach the receptor sites,' he said. 'That's why you can't smell through your mouth. So I went over to the apparatus and switched off the heat. I then transferred the tiny quantity of precious fluid from the beaker to this very solid airtight bottle you see here. In it there are precisely eleven cubic centimetres of Number 1076.'

'Then you telephoned me.'

'Not immediately, no. Because at that point, Simone arrived. She took one look at me and ran into the next room, screaming.'

'Why did she do that?'

'My God, Oswald, I was standing there stark naked and I hadn't realized it. I must have ripped off all my clothes!'

'Then what?'

'I got dressed again. After that, I went and told Simone exactly what had happened. When she heard the truth, she became as excited as me. Don't forget, we've been working on this together for over a year now.'

'Is she still here?'

'Yes. She's next door in the other lab.'

It was quite a story Henri had told me. I picked up the little square bottle and held it against the light. Through the thick glass I could see about half an inch of fluid, pale and pinkish-grey, like the juice of a ripe quince.

'Don't drop it,' Henri said. 'Better put it down.' I put it down. 'The next step,' he went on, 'will be to make an accurate test under scientific conditions. For that I shall have to spray a measured quantity on to a woman and then let a man approach her. It will be necessary for me to observe the operation at close range.'

'You are a dirty old man,' I said.

'I am an olfactory chemist,' he said primly.

'Why don't I go out into the street with my noseplugs in,' I said, 'and spray some on to the first woman who comes along. You can watch from the window here. It ought to be fun.'

'It would be fun all right,' Henri said. 'But not very scientific. I must make the tests indoors under controlled conditions.'

'And I will play the male part,' I said.

'No, Oswald.'

'What do you mean, no. I insist.'

'Now listen to me,' Henri said. 'We have not yet found out what will happen when a woman is present. This stuff is very powerful, I am certain of that. And you, my dear sir, are not exactly young. It could be extremely dangerous. It could drive you beyond the limit of your endurance.'

I was stung. 'There are no limits to my endurance,' I said.

'Rubbish,' Henri said. 'I refuse to take chances. That is why I have engaged the fittest and strongest young man I could find.'

'You mean you've already done this?'

'Certainly I have,' Henri said. 'I am excited and impatient. I want to get on. The boy will be here any minute.'

'Who is he?'

'A professional boxer.'

'Good God.'

'His name is Pierre Lacaille. I am paying him one thousand francs for the job.'

'How did you find him?'

'I know a lot more people than you think, Oswald. I am not a hermit.'

'Does the man know what he's in for?'

'I have told him that he is to participate in a scientific experiment that has to do with the psychology of sex. The less he knows the better.'

'And the woman? Who will you use there?'

'Simone, of course,' Henri said. 'She is a scientist in her own right. She will be able to observe the reactions of the male even more closely than me.'

'That she will,' I said. 'Does she realize what might happen to her?'

'Very much so. And I had one hell of a job persuading her to do it. I had to point out that she would be participating in a demonstration that will go down in history. It will be talked about for hundreds of years.'

'Nonsense,' I said.

'My dear sir, through the centuries there are certain great epic moments of scientific discovery that are never forgotten. Like the time when Dr Horace Wells of Hartford, Connecticut, had a tooth pulled out in 1844.'

'What was so historic about that?'

'Dr Wells was a dentist who had been playing about with nitrous oxide gas. One day, he got a terrible toothache. He knew the tooth would have to come out, and he called in another dentist to do the job. But first he persuaded his colleague to put a mask over his face and turn on the nitrous oxide. He became unconscious and the tooth was extracted and he woke up again as fit as a flea. Now *that*, Oswald, was the first operation ever performed in the world under general anaesthesia. It started something big. We shall do the same.'

At this point, the doorbell rang. Henri grabbed a pair of noseplugs and carried them with him to the door. And there stood Pierre, the boxer. But Henri would not allow him to enter until the plugs were rammed firmly up his nostrils. I believe the fellow came thinking he was going to act in a blue film, but the business with the plugs must have quickly disillusioned him. Pierre Lacaille was a bantamweight, small, muscular, and wiry. He had a flat face and a bent nose. He was about twenty-two and not very bright.

Henri introduced me, then ushered us straight into the adjoining laboratory where Simone was working. She was standing by the lab bench in a white overall, writing something in a notebook. She looked up at us through thick glasses as we came in. The glasses had a white plastic frame.

'Simone,' Henri said, 'this is Pierre Lacaille.' Simone looked at the boxer but said nothing. Henri didn't bother to introduce me.

Simone was a slim thirtyish woman with a pleasant scrubbed face. Her hair was brushed back and plaited into a bun. This, together with the white spectacles, the white overall, and the white skin of her face, gave her a quaint antiseptic air. She looked as though she had been sterilised for thirty minutes in an autoclave and should be handled with rubber gloves. She gazed at the boxer with large brown eyes.

'Let's get going,' Henri said. 'Are you ready?'

'I don't know what's going to happen,' the boxer said. 'But I'm ready.' He did a little dance on his toes.

Henri was also ready. He had obviously worked the whole thing out before I arrived. 'Simone will sit in that chair,' he said, pointing to a plain wooden chair set in the middle of the laboratory. 'And you, Pierre, will stand on the six-metre mark with your noseplugs still in.'

There were chalk lines on the floor indicating various distances from the chair, from half a metre up to six metres.

'I shall begin by spraying a small quantity of liquid on to the lady's neck,' Henri went on addressing the boxer. 'You will then remove your noseplugs and start walking slowly toward her.' To me he said, 'I wish first of all to discover the effective range, the exact distance he is from the subject when the molecules hit.'

'Does he start with his clothes on?' I asked.

'Exactly as he is now.'

'And is the lady expected to cooperate or to resist?'

'Neither. She must be a purely passive instrument in his hands.'

Simone was still looking at the boxer. I saw her slide the end of her tongue slowly over her lips.

'This perfume,' I said to Henri, 'does it have any effect upon a woman?'

'None whatsoever,' he said. 'That is why I am sending Simone out now to prepare the spray.' The girl went into the main laboratory, closing the door behind her.

'So you spray something on the girl and I walk toward her,' the boxer said. 'What happens then?'

'We shall have to wait and see,' Henri said. 'You are not worried, are you?'

'Me, worried?' the boxer said. 'About a woman?'

'Good boy,' Henri said. Henri was becoming very excited. He went hopping from one end of the room to the other, checking and rechecking the position of the chair on its chalk mark and moving all breakables such as glass beakers and bottles and test-tubes off the bench on to a high shelf. 'This isn't the ideal place,' he said, 'but we must make the best of it.' He tied a surgeon's mask over the lower part of his face, then handed one to me.

'Don't you trust the noseplugs?'

'It's just an extra precaution,' he said. 'Put it on.'

The girl returned carrying a tiny stainless-steel spray-gun. She gave the gun to Henri. Henri took a stop watch from his pocket. 'Get ready, please,' he said. 'You Pierre, stand over there on the six-metre mark.' Pierre did so. The girl seated herself in the chair. It was a chair without arms. She sat very prim and upright in her spotless white overall with her hands folded on her lap, her knees together. Henri stationed himself behind the girl. I stood to one side. 'Are we ready?' Henri cried.

'Wait,' said the girl. It was the first word she had spoken. She stood up, removed her spectacles, placed them on a high shelf, then returned to her seat. She smoothed the white overall along her thighs, then clasped her hands together and laid them again on her lap.

'Are we ready now?' Henri said.

'Let her have it,' I said. 'Shoot.'

Henri aimed the little spray-gun at an area of bare skin just below Simone's ear. He pulled the trigger. The gun made a soft hiss and a fine misty spray came out of its nozzle.

'Pull your noseplugs out!' Henri called to the boxer as he skipped quickly away from the girl and took up a position next to me. The boxer caught hold of the strings dangling from his nostrils and pulled. The vaselined plugs slid out smoothly.

'Come on, come on!' Henri shouted. 'Start moving! Drop the plugs on the floor and come forward slowly!' The boxer took a pace forward. 'Not so fast!' Henri cried. 'Slowly does it! That's better! Keep going! Keep going! Don't stop!' He was crazy with excitement, and I must admit I was getting a bit worked up myself. I glanced at the girl. She was crouching in the chair, just a few yards away from the boxer, tense, motionless, watching his every move, and I found myself thinking about a white female rat I had once seen in a cage with a huge python. The python was going to swallow the rat and the rat knew it, and the rat was crouching very low and still, hypnotized, transfixed, utterly fascinated by the slow advancing movements of the snake.

The boxer edged forward.

As he passed the five-metre mark, the girl unclasped her hands. She laid them palms downwards on her thighs. Then she changed her mind and placed them more or less underneath her buttocks, gripping the seat of the chair on either side, bracing herself, as it were, against the coming onslaught.

The boxer had just passed the two-metre mark when the smell hit him. He stopped dead. His eyes glazed and he swayed on his legs as though he had been tapped on the head with a mallet. I thought he was going to keel over but he didn't. He stood there swaying gently from side to side like a drunk. Suddenly he started making noises through his nostrils, queer little snorts and grunts that reminded me of a pig sniffing around its trough. Then without any warning at all, he sprang at the girl. He ripped off her white overall, her dress, and her underclothes. After that, all hell broke loose.

There is little point in describing exactly what went on during the next few minutes. You can guess most of it anyway. I do have to admit, though, that Henri had probably been right in choosing an exceptionally fit and healthy young man. I hate to say it, but I doubt my middle-aged body could have stood up to the incredibly violent gymnastics the boxer seemed driven to perform. I am not a voyeur. I hate that sort of thing. But in this case, I stood there absolutely transfixed. The sheer animal ferocity of the man was frightening. He was like a wild beast. And right in the middle of it all, Henri did an interesting thing. He produced a revolver and rushed up to the boxer and shouted, 'Get away from that girl! Leave her alone or I'll shoot you!' The boxer ignored him, so Henri fired a shot just over the top of his head and yelled, 'I mean it, Pierre! I shall kill you if you don't stop!' The boxer didn't even look up.

Henri was hopping and dancing about the room and shouting, 'It's fantastic! It's magnificent! Unbelievable! It works! It works! We've done it, my dear Oswald! We've done it!'

The action stopped as quickly as it had begun. The boxer suddenly let go of the girl, stood up, blinked a few times, and then said, 'Where the hell am I? What happened?'

Simone, who seemed to have come through it all with no bones broken, jumped up, grabbed her clothes, and ran into the next room. 'Thank you, mademoiselle,' said Henri as she flew past him.

The interesting thing was that the bemused boxer hadn't the faintest idea what he had been doing. He stood there naked and covered with sweat, gazing around the room and trying to figure out how in the world he came to be in that condition.

'What did I do?' he asked. 'Where's the girl?'

'You were terrific!' Henri shouted, throwing him a towel. 'Don't worry about a thing! The thousand francs is all yours!'

Just then the door flew open and Simone, still naked, ran back into the lab. 'Spray me again!' she cried. 'Oh, Monsieur Henri, spray me just one more time!' Her face was alight, her eyes shining brilliantly.

'The experiment is over,' Henri said. 'Go away and dress yourself.'
He took her firmly by the shoulders and pushed her back into the
other room. Then he locked the door.

Half an hour later, Henri and I sat celebrating our success in a
small café down the street. We were drinking coffee and brandy. 'How
long did it go on?' I asked.

'Six minutes and thirty-two seconds,' Henri said.

I sipped my brandy and watched the people strolling by on the
sidewalk. 'What's the next move?'

'First, I must write up my notes,' Henri said. 'Then we shall talk
about the future.'

'Does anyone else know the formula?'

'Nobody.'

'What about Simone?'

'She doesn't know it.'

'Have you written it down?'

'Not so anyone else could understand it. I shall do that tomorrow.'

'Do it first thing,' I said. 'I'll want a copy. What shall we call the
stuff? We need a name.'

'What do you suggest?'

'*Bitch*,' I said. 'Let's call it *Bitch*.' Henri smiled and nodded his head
slowly. I ordered more brandy. 'It would be great stuff for stopping a
riot,' I said. 'Much better than tear-gas. Imagine the scene if you
sprayed it on an angry mob.'

'Nice,' Henri said. 'Very nice.'

'Another thing we could do, we could sell it to very fat, very rich
women at fantastic prices.'

'We could do that,' Henri answered.

'Do you think it would cure loss of virility in men?' I asked him.

'Of course,' Henri said. 'Impotence would go out the window.'

'What about octogenarians?'

'Them, too,' he said, 'though it would kill them at the same time.'

'And marriages on the rocks?'

'My dear fellow,' Henri said. 'The possibilities are legion.'

At that precise moment, the seed of an idea came sneaking slowly
into my mind. As you know, I have a passion for politics. And my
strongest passion, although I am English, is for the politics of the
United States of America. I have always thought it is over there, in
that mighty and mixed-up nation, that the destinies of mankind must
surely lie. And right now, there was a President in office whom I could
not stand. He was an evil man who pursued evil policies. Worse than
that, he was a humourless and unattractive creature. So why didn't
I, Oswald Cornelius, remove him from office?

The idea appealed to me.

'How much *Bitch* have you got in the lab at the moment?' I asked.

'Exactly ten cubic centimetres,' Henri said.

'And how much is one dose?'

'We used one cc for our test.'

'That's all I want,' I said. 'One cc. I'll take it home with me today. And a set of noseplugs.'

'No,' Henri said. 'Let's not play around with it at this stage. It's too dangerous.'

'It is my property,' I said. 'Half of it is mine. Don't forget our agreement.'

In the end, he had to give in. But he hated doing it. We went back to the lab, inserted our noseplugs, and Henri measured out precisely one cc of *Bitch* into a small scent-bottle. He sealed the stopper with wax and gave me the bottle. 'I implore you to be discreet,' he said. 'This is probably the most important scientific discovery of the century, and it must not be treated as a joke.'

From Henri's place, I drove directly to the workshop of an old friend, Marcel Brossollet. Marcel was an inventor and manufacturer of tiny precise scientific gadgets. He did a lot of work for surgeons, devising new types of heart-valves and pacemakers and those little one-way valves that reduce intracranial pressure in hydrocephalics.

'I want you to make me,' I said to Marcel, 'a capsule that will hold exactly one cc of liquid. To this little capsule, there must be attached a timing device that will split the capsule and release the liquid at a predetermined moment. The entire thing must not be more than half an inch long and half an inch thick. The smaller the better. Can you manage that?'

'Very easily,' Marcel said. 'A thin plastic capsule, a tiny section of razor-blade to split the capsule, a spring to flip the razor-blade, and the usual pre-set alarm system on a very small ladies' watch. Should the capsule be fillable?'

'Yes. Make it so I myself can fill it and seal it up. Can I have it in a week?'

'Why not?' Marcel said. 'It is very simple.'

The next morning brought dismal news. That lecherous little slut Simone had apparently sprayed herself with the entire remaining stock of *Bitch*, over nine cubic centimetres of it, the moment she arrived at the lab! She had then sneaked up behind Henri, who was just settling himself at his desk to write up his notes.

I don't have to tell you what happened next. And worse of all, the silly girl had forgotten that Henri had a serious heart condition. Damn it, he wasn't even allowed to climb a flight of stairs. So when the molecules hit him the poor fellow didn't stand a chance. He was dead within a minute, killed in action as they say, and that was that.

The infernal woman might at least have waited until he had written down the formula. As it was, Henri left not a single note. I searched the lab after they had taken away his body, but I found nothing. So now more than ever, I was determined to make good use of the only remaining cubic centimetre of *Bitch* in the world.

A week later, I collected from Marcel Brossollet a beautiful little gadget. The timing device consisted of the smallest watch I had ever seen, and this, together with the capsule and all the other parts, had been secured to a tiny aluminium plate three eighths of an inch square. Marcel showed me how to fill and seal the capsule and set the timer. I thanked him and paid the bill.

As soon as possible, I travelled to New York. In Manhattan, I put up at the Plaza Hotel. I arrived there at about three in the afternoon. I took a bath, had a shave, and asked room service to send me up a bottle of Glenlivet and some ice. Feeling clean and comfortable in my dressing-gown, I poured myself a good strong drink of the delicious malt whisky, then settled down in a deep chair with the morning's *New York Times*. My suite overlooked Central Park, and through the open window I could hear the hum of traffic and the blaring of cab-drivers' horns on Central Park South. Suddenly, one of the smaller headlines on the front page of the paper caught my eye. It said, PRESIDENT ON TV TONIGHT. I read on.

> The President is expected to make an important foreign policy statement when he speaks tonight at the dinner to be given in his honour by the Daughters of the American Revolution in the ballroom of the Waldorf Astoria . . .

My God, what a piece of luck!

I had been prepared to wait in New York for many weeks before I got a chance like this. The President of the United States does not often appear with a bunch of women on television. And that was exactly how I had to have him. He was an extraordinarily slippery customer. He had fallen into many a sewer and had always come out smelling of shit. Yet he managed every time to convince the nation that the smell was coming from someone else, not him. So the way I figured it was this. A man who rapes a woman in full sight of twenty million viewers across the country would have a pretty hard time denying he ever did it.

I read on.

> The President will speak for approximately twenty minutes, commencing at nine p.m. and all major TV networks will carry the speech. He will be introduced by Mrs Elvira Ponsonby, the incumbent President of the Daughters of the American Revolution. When interviewed in her suite at the Waldorf Towers, Mrs Ponsonby said . . .

It was perfect! Mrs Ponsonby would be seated on the President's right. At ten past nine precisely, with the President well into his speech and half the population of the United States watching, a little capsule nestling secretly in the region of Mrs Ponsonby's bosom would be punctured and half a centimetre of *Bitch* would come oozing out on to her gilt lamé ball-gown. The President's head would come up, and he would sniff and sniff again, his eyes would bulge, his nostrils would flare, and he would start snorting like a stallion. Then suddenly he would turn and grab hold of Mrs Ponsonby. She would be flung across the dining-table and the President would leap on top of her, with the pie à la mode and strawberry shortcake flying in all directions.

I leaned back and closed my eyes, savouring the delicious scene. I saw the headlines in the papers the next morning:

PRESIDENT'S BEST PERFORMANCE TO DATE

PRESIDENTIAL SECRETS REVEALED TO NATION

PRESIDENT INAUGURATES BLUE TV

and so on.

He would be impeached the next day and I would slip quietly out of New York and head back to Paris. Come to think of it, I would be leaving tomorrow!

I checked the time. It was nearly four o'clock. I dressed myself without hurrying. I took the elevator down to the main lobby and strolled across to Madison Avenue. Somewhere around Sixty-second Street, I found a good florist's shop. There I bought a corsage of three massive orchid blooms all fastened together. The orchids were cattleyas, white and mauve splotches on them. They were particularly vulgar. So, undoubtedly, was Mrs Elvira Ponsonby. I had the shop pack them in a handsome box tied up with gold string. Then I strolled back to the Plaza, carrying the box, and went up to my suite.

I locked all doors leading to the corridor in case the maid should come in to turn back the bed. I got out the noseplugs and vaselined them carefully. I inserted them in my nostrils, ramming them home very hard. I tied a surgeon's mask over my lower face as an extra precaution, just as Henri had done. I was ready now for the next step.

With an ordinary nose-dropper, I transferred my precious cubic centimetre of *Bitch* from the scent bottle to the tiny capsule. The hand holding the dropper shook a little as I did this, but all went well. I sealed the capsule. After that, I wound up the tiny watch and set it to the correct time. It was three minutes after five o'clock. Lastly, I set the timer to go off and break the capsule at ten minutes past nine.

The stems of the three huge orchid blooms had been tied together by the florist with a broad one-inch-wide white ribbon and it was a simple matter for me to remove the ribbon and secure my little capsule and timer to the orchid stems with cotton thread. When that was done, I wound the ribbon back around the stems and over my gadget. Then I retied the bow. It was a nice job.

Next, I telephone the Waldorf and learned that the dinner was to begin at eight o'clock, but that the guests must be assembled in the ballroom by seven thirty, before the President arrived.

At ten minutes to seven, I paid off my cab outside the Waldorf Towers entrance and walked into the building. I crossed the small lobby and placed my orchid box on the reception desk. I leaned over the desk, getting as close as possible to the clerk. 'I have to deliver this package to Mrs Elvira Ponsonby,' I whispered, using a slight American accent. 'It is a gift from the President.'

The clerk looked at me suspiciously.

'Mrs Ponsonby is introducing the President before he speaks tonight in the ballroom,' I added. 'The President wishes her to have this corsage right away.'

'Leave it here and I'll have it sent up to her suite,' the clerk said.

'No, you won't,' I told him. 'My orders are to deliver it in person. What's the number of her suite?'

The man was impressed. 'Mrs Ponsonby is in five-o-one,' he said.

I thanked him and went into the elevator. When I got out at the fifth floor and walked along the corridor, the elevator operator stayed and watched me. I rang the bell to five-o-one.

The door was opened by the most enormous female I had ever seen in my life. I have seen giant women in circuses. I have seen lady wrestlers and weight-lifters. I have seen the huge Masai women in the plains below Kilimanjaro. But never had I seen a female so tall and broad and thick as this one. Nor so thoroughly repugnant. She was groomed and dressed for the greatest occasion of her life, and in the two seconds that elapsed before either of us spoke, I was able to take most of it in – the metallic silver-blue hair with every strand glued into place, the brown pig-eyes, the long sharp nose sniffing for trouble, the curled lips, the prognathous jaw, the powder, the mascara, the scarlet lipstick and, most shattering of all, the massive shored-up bosom that projected like a balcony in front of her. It stuck out so far it was a miracle she didn't topple forward with the weight of it all. And there she stood, this pneumatic giant, swathed from neck to ankles in the stars and stripes of the American flag.

'Mrs Elvira Ponsonby?' I murmured.

'I am Mrs Ponsonby,' she boomed. 'What do you want? I am extremely busy.'

'Mrs Ponsonby,' I said. 'The President has ordered me to deliver this to you in person.'

She melted immediately. 'The dear man!' she shouted. 'How

perfectly gorgeous of him!' Two massive hands reached out to grab
the box. I let her have it.

'My instructions are to make sure you open it before you go to the
banquet,' I said.

'Sure I'll open it,' she said. 'Do I have to do it in front of you?'

'If you wouldn't mind.'

'Okay, come on in. But I don't have much time.'

I followed her into the living-room of the suite. 'I am to tell you,'
I said, 'that it comes with all good wishes from one President to
another.'

'Ha!' she roared. 'I like that! What a gorgeous man he is!' She
untied the gold string of the box and lifted the lid. 'I guessed it!' she
shouted. 'Orchids! How splendid! They're far grander than this poor
little thing I'm wearing!'

I had been so dazzled by the galaxy of stars across her bosom that
I hadn't noticed the single orchid pinned to the left-hand side.

'I must change over at once,' she said. 'The President will be
expecting me to wear his gift.'

'He certainly will,' I said.

Now to give you an idea of how far her chest stuck out in front of
her, I must tell you that when she reached forward to unpin the flower,
she was only just able to touch it even with her arms fully extended.
She fiddled around with the pin for quite a while, but she couldn't
really see what she was doing and it wouldn't come undone. 'I'm
terrified of tearing this gorgeous gown,' she said. 'Here, you do it.'
She swung around and thrust her mammoth bust in my face. I
hesitated. 'Go on!' she boomed. 'I don't have all night!' I went to it,
and in the end I managed to get the pin unhooked from her dress.

'Now let's get the other one on,' she said.

I put aside the single orchid and lifted my own flowers carefully
from the box.

'Have they got a pin?' she asked.

'I don't believe they have,' I said. That was something I'd forgotten.

'No matter,' she said. 'We'll use the old one,' She removed the
safety-pin from the first orchid, and then, before I could stop her, she
seized the three orchids I was holding and jabbed the pin hard into
the white ribbon around the stems. She jabbed it almost exactly into
the spot where my little capsule of *Bitch* was lying hidden. The pin
struck something hard and wouldn't go through. She jabbed it again.
Again it struck metal. 'What the hell's under here?' she snorted.

'Let me do it!' I cried, but it was too late, because the wet stain of
Bitch from the punctured capsule was already spreading over the white
ribbon and one hundredth of a second later the smell hit me. It caught
me smack under the nose and it wasn't actually like a smell at all
because a smell is something intangible. You cannot feel a smell. But

this stuff was palpable. It was solid. It felt as though some kind of fiery liquid were being squirted up my nostrils under high pressure. It was exceedingly uncomfortable. I could feel it pushing higher and higher, penetrating far beyond the nasal passages, forcing its way up behind the forehead and reaching for the brain. Suddenly the stars and stripes on Mrs Ponsonby's dress began to wobble and bobble about and then the whole room started wobbling and I could hear my heart thumping in my head. It felt as though I were going under an anaesthetic.

At that point, I must have blacked out completely, if only for a couple of seconds.

When I came round again, I was standing naked in a rosy room and there was a funny feeling in my groin. I looked down and saw that my beloved sexual organ was three feet long and thick to match. It was still growing. It was lengthening and swelling at a tremendous rate. At the same time, my body was shrinking. Smaller and smaller shrank my body. Bigger and bigger grew my astonishing organ, and it went on growing, by God, until it had enveloped my entire body and absorbed it within itself. I was now a gigantic perpendicular penis, seven feet tall and as handsome as they come.

I did a little dance around the room to celebrate my splendid new condition. On the way I met a maiden in a star-spangled dress. She was very big as maidens go. I drew myself up to my full height and declaimed in a loud voice:

> 'The summer's flower is to the summer sweet,
> It flourishes despite the summer's heat.
> But tell me truly, did you ever see
> A sexual organ quite so grand as me?'

The maiden leapt up and flung her arms as far around me as she could. Then cried out:

> 'Shall I compare thee to a summer's day?
> Shall I ... Oh dear, I know not what to say.
> But all my life I've had an itch to kiss
> A man who could erect himself like this.

A moment later, the two of us were millions of miles up in outer space, flying through the universe in a shower of meteorites all red and gold. I was riding her bareback, crouching forward and gripping her tightly between my thighs. 'Faster!' I shouted, jabbing long spurs into her flanks. 'Go faster!' Faster and still faster she flew, spurting and spinning around the rim of the sky, her mane streaming with sun, and snow waving out of her tail. The sense of power I had was overwhelming. I was unassailable, supreme. I was the Lord of the Universe, scattering the planets and catching the stars in the palm of my hand and tossing them away as though they were ping-pong balls.

Oh, ecstasy and ravishment! Oh, Jericho and Tyre and Sidon! The walls came tumbling down and the firmament disintegrated, and out of the smoke and fire of the explosion, the sitting-room in the Waldorf Towers came swimming slowly back into my consciousness like a rainy day. The place was a shambles. A tornado would have done less damage. My clothes were on the floor. I started dressing myself very quickly. I did it in about thirty seconds flat. And as I ran toward the door, I heard a voice that seemed to be coming from somewhere behind an upturned table in the far corner of the room. 'I don't know who you are, young man,' it said. 'But you've certainly done me a power of good.'

SOMEONE
LIKE
YOU

TASTE

There were six of us to dinner that night at Mike Schofield's house in London: Mike and his wife and daughter, my wife and I, and a man called Richard Pratt.

Richard Pratt was a famous gourmet. He was president of a smalll society known as the Epicures, and each month he circulated privately to its members a pamphlet on food and wines. He organized dinners where sumptuous dishes and rare wines were served. He refused to smoke for fear of harming his palate, and when discussing a wine, he had a curious, rather droll habit of referring to it as though it were a living being. 'A prudent wine,' he would say, 'rather diffident and evasive, but quite prudent.' Or, 'A good-humoured wine, benevolent and cheerful – slightly obscene, perhaps, but none the less good-humoured.'

I had been to dinner at Mike's twice before when Richard Pratt was there, and on each occasion Mike and his wife had gone out of their way to produce a special meal for the famous gourmet. And this one, clearly, was to be no exception. The moment we entered the dining-room, I could see that the table was laid for a feast. The tall candles, the yellow roses, the quantity of shining silver, the three wineglasses to each person, and above all, the faint scent of roasting meat from the kitchen brought the first warm oozings of saliva to my mouth.

As we sat down, I remembered that on both Richard Pratt's previous visits Mike had played a little betting game with him over the claret, challenging him to name its breed and its vintage. Pratt had replied that that should not be too difficult provided it was one of the great years. Mike had then bet him a case of the wine in question that he could not do it. Pratt had accepted, and had won both times. Tonight I felt sure that the little game would be played over again, for Mike was quite willing to lose the bet in order to prove that his wine was good enough to be recognized, and Pratt, for his part, seemed to take a grave, restrained pleasure in displaying his knowledge.

The meal began with a plate of whitebait, fried very crisp in butter, and to go with it there was a Moselle. Mike got up and poured the wine himself, and when he sat down again, I could see that he was watching Richard Pratt. He had set the bottle in front of me so that

I could read the label. It said, 'Geierslay Ohligsberg, 1945'. He leaned over and whispered to me that Geierslay was a tiny village in the Moselle, almost unknown outside Germany. He said that this wine we were drinking was something unusual, that the output of the vineyard was so small that it was almost impossible for a stranger to get any of it. He had visited Geierslay personally the previous summer in order to obtain the few bottles that they had finally allowed him to have.

'I doubt whether anyone else in the country has any of it at the moment,' he said. I saw him glance again at Richard Pratt. 'Great thing about Moselle,' he continued, raising his voice, 'it's the perfect wine to serve before a claret. A lot of people serve a Rhine wine instead, but that's because they don't know any better. A Rhine wine will kill a delicate claret, you know that? It's barbaric to serve a Rhine before a claret. But a Moselle – ah! – a Moselle is exactly right.'

Mike Schofield was an amiable, middle-aged man. But he was a stockbroker. To be precise, he was a jobber in the stock market, and like a number of his kind, he seemed to be somewhat embarrassed, almost ashamed to find that he. had made so much money with so slight a talent. In his heart he knew that he was not really much more than a bookmaker – an unctuous, infinitely respectable, secretly unscrupulous bookmaker – and he knew that his friends knew it, too. So he was seeking now to become a man of culture, to cultivate a literary and aesthetic taste, to collect paintings, music, books, and all the rest of it. His little sermon about Rhine wine and Moselle was a part of this thing, this culture that he sought.

'A charming little wine, don't you think?' he said. He was still watching Richard Pratt. I could see him give a rapid furtive glance down the table each time he dropped his head to take a mouthful of whitebait. I could almost *feel* him waiting for the moment when Pratt would take his first sip, and look up from his glass with a smile of pleasure, of astonishment, perhaps even of wonder, and then there would be a discussion and Mike would tell him about the village of Geierslay.

But Richard Pratt did not taste his wine. He was completely engrossed in conversation with Mike's eighteen-year-old daughter, Louise. He was half turned towards her, smiling at her, telling her, so far as I could gather, some story about a chef in a Paris restaurant. As he spoke, he leaned closer and closer to her, seeming in his eagerness almost to impinge upon her, and the poor girl leaned as far as she could away from him nodding politely, rather desperately, and looking not at his face but at the topmost button of his dinner jacket.

We finished our fish, and the maid came round removing the plates. When she came to Pratt, she saw that he had not yet touched his food, so she hesitated, and Pratt noticed her. He waved her away, broke off his conversation, and quickly began to eat, popping the little crisp brown fish quickly into his mouth with rapid jabbing movements of his fork. Then, when he had finished, he reached for his glass, and in two short swallows he tipped the wine down his throat and turned immediately to resume his conversation with Louise Schofield.

Mike saw it all. I was conscious of him sitting there, very still, containing himself, looking at his guest. His round jovial face seemed to loosen slightly and to sag, but he contained himself and was still and said nothing.

Soon the maid came forward with the second course. This was a large roast beef. She placed it on the table in front of Mike who stood up and carved it, cutting the slices very thin, laying them gently on the plates for the maid to take around. When he had served everyone, including himself, he put down the carving knife and leaned forward with both hands on the edge of the table.

'Now,' he said, speaking to all of us but looking at Richard Pratt. 'Now for the claret. I must go and fetch the claret, if you'll excuse me.'

'You go and fetch it, Mike?' I said. 'Where is it?'

'In my study, with the cork out – breathing.'

'Why the study?'

'Acquiring room temperature, of course. It's been there twenty-four hours.'

'But why the study?'

'It's the best place in the house. Richard helped me choose it last time he was here.'

At the sound of his name, Pratt looked round.

'That's right, isn't it?' Mike said.

'Yes,' Pratt answered, nodding gravely. 'That's right.'

'On top of the green filing cabinet in my study,' Mike said. 'That's the place we chose. A good draught-free spot in a room with an even temperature. Excuse me now, will you, while I fetch it.'

The thought of another wine to play with had restored his humour, and he hurried out of the door, to return a minute later more slowly, walking softly, holding in both hands a wine basket in which a dark bottle lay. The label was out of sight, facing downwards. 'Now!' he cried as he came towards the table. 'What about this one, Richard? You'll never name this one!'

Richard Pratt turned slowly and looked up at Mike, then his eyes travelled down to the bottle nestling in its small wicker basket, and he raised his eyebrows; a slight, supercilious arching of the brows, and with it a pushing outward of the wet lower lip, suddenly imperious and ugly.

'You'll never get it,' Mike said. 'Not in a hundred years.'

'A claret?' Richard Pratt asked, condescending.

'Of course.'

'I assume, then, that it's from one of the smaller vineyards?'

'Maybe it is, Richard. And then again, maybe it isn't.'

'But it's a good year? One of the great years?'

'Yes, I guarantee that.'

'Then it shouldn't be too difficult,' Richard Pratt said, drawling his words, looking exceedingly bored. Except that, to me, there was something strange about his drawling and his boredom: between the eyes a shadow of something evil, and in his bearing an intentness that gave me a faint sense of uneasiness as I watched him.

'This one is really rather difficult,' Mike said. 'I won't force you to bet on this one.'

'Indeed. And why not?' Again the slow arching of the brows, the cool, intent look.

'Because it's difficult.'

'That's not very complimentary to me, you know.'

'My dear man,' Mike said, 'I'll bet you with pleasure, if that's what you wish.'

'It shouldn't be too hard to name it.'

'You mean you want to bet?'

'I'm perfectly willing to bet,' Richard Pratt said.

'All right, then, we'll have the usual. A case of the wine itself.'

'You don't think I'll be able to name it, do you?'

'As a matter of fact, and with all due respect, I don't,' Mike said. He was making some effort to remain polite, but Pratt was not bothering overmuch to conceal his contempt for the whole proceeding. And yet, curiously, his next question seemed to betray a certain interest.

'You like to increase the bet?'

'No, Richard. A case is plenty.'

'Would you like to bet fifty cases?'

'That would be silly.'

Mike stood very still behind his chair at the head of the table, carefully holding the bottle in its ridiculous wicker basket. There was a trace of whiteness around his nostrils now, and his mouth was shut very tight.

Pratt was lolling back in his chair, looking up at him, the eyebrows raised, the eyes half closed, a little smile touching the corners of his lips. And again I saw, or thought I saw, something distinctly disturbing about the man's face, that shadow of intentness between the eyes, and in the eyes themselves, right in their centres where it was black, a small slow spark of shrewdness, hiding.

'So you don't want to increase the bet?'

'As far as I'm concerned, old man, I don't give a damn,' Mike said. 'I'll bet you anything you like.'

The three women and I sat quietly, watching the two men. Mike's wife was becoming annoyed; her mouth had gone sour and I felt that at any moment she was going to interrupt. Our roast beef lay before us on our plates, slowly steaming.

'So you'll bet me anything I like?'

'That's what I told you. I'll bet you anything you damn well please, if you want to make an issue out of it.'

'Even ten thousand pounds?'

'Certainly I will, if that's the way you want it.' Mike was more confident now. He knew quite well that he could call any sum Pratt cared to mention.

'So you say I can name the bet?' Pratt asked again.

'That's what I said.'

There was a pause while Pratt looked slowly around the table, first at me, then at the three women, each in turn. He appeared to be reminding us that we were witness to the offer.

'Mike!' Mrs Schofield said. 'Mike, why don't we stop this nonsense and eat our food. It's getting cold.'

'But it isn't nonsense,' Pratt told her evenly. 'We're making a little bet.'

I noticed the maid standing in the background holding a dish of vegetables, wondering whether to come forward with them or not.

'All right, then,' Pratt said. 'I'll tell you what I want you to bet.'

'Come on, then,' Mike said, rather reckless. 'I don't give a damn what it is – you're on.'

Pratt nodded, and again the little smile moved the corners of his lips, and then, quite slowly, looking at Mike all the time, he said, 'I want you to bet me the hand of your daughter in marriage.'

Louise Schofield gave a jump. 'Hey!' she cried. 'No! That's not funny! Look here, Daddy, that's not funny at all.'

'No, dear,' her mother said. 'They're only joking.'

'I'm not joking,' Richard Pratt said.

'It's ridiculous,' Mike said. He was off balance again now.

'You said you'd bet anything I liked.'

'I meant money.'

'You didn't *say* money.'

'That's what I meant.'

'Then it's a pity you didn't say it. But anyway, if you wish to go back on your offer, that's quite all right with me.'

'It's not a question of going back on my offer, old man. It's a no-bet any way, because you can't match the stake. You yourself don't happen to have a daughter to put up against mine in case you lose. And if you had, I wouldn't want to marry her.'

'I'm glad of that, dear,' his wife said.

'I'll put up anything you like,' Pratt announced. 'My house, for example. How about my house?'

'Which one?' Mike asked, joking now.

'The country one.'

'Why not the other one as well?'

'All right then, if you wish it. Both my houses.'

At that point I saw Mike pause. He took a step forward and placed the bottle in its basket gently down on the table. He moved the salt-cellar to one side, then the pepper, and then he picked up his knife, studied the blade thoughtfully for a moment, and put it down again. His daughter, too, had seen him pause.

'Now, Daddy!' she cried. 'Don't be *absurd!* It's *too* silly for words. I refuse to be betted on like this.'

'Quite right, dear,' her mother said. 'Stop it at once, Mike, and sit down and eat your food.'

Mike ignored her. He looked over at his daughter and he smiled, a slow, fatherly, protective smile. But in his eyes, suddenly, there glimmered a little triumph. 'You know,' he said, smiling as he spoke. 'You know, Louise, we ought to think about this a bit.'

'Now, stop it, Daddy! I refuse even to listen to you! Why, I've never heard anything so ridiculous in my life!'

'No, seriously, my dear. Just wait a moment and hear what I have to say.'

'But I don't *want* to hear it.'

'Louise! Please! It's like this. Richard, here, has offered us a serious bet. He is the one who wants to make it, not me. And if he loses, he will have to hand over a considerable amount of property. Now, wait a minute, my dear, don't interrupt. The point is this. *He cannot possibly win.*'

'He seems to think he can.'

'Now listen to me, because I know what I'm talking about. The expert, when tasting a claret – so long as it is not one of the famous great wines like Lafite or Latour – can only get a certain way towards naming the vineyard. He can, of course, tell you the Bordeaux district from which the wine comes, whether it is from St Emilion, Pomerol, Graves, or Médoc. But them each district has several communes, little counties, and each county has many, many small vineyards. It is impossible for a man to differentiate between them all by taste and smell alone. I don't mind telling you that this one I've got here is a wine from a small vineyard that is surrounded by many other small vineyards, and he'll never get it. It's impossible.'

'You can't be sure of that,' his daughter said.

'I'm telling you I can. Though I say it myself, I understand quite a bit about this wine business, you know. And anyway, heavens alive, girl, I'm your father and you don't think I'd let you in for – for something you didn't want, do you? I'm trying to make you some money.'

'Mike!' his wife said sharply. 'Stop it now, Mike, please!'

Again he ignored her. 'If you will take this bet,' he said to his daughter, 'in ten minutes you will be the owner of two large houses.'

'But I don't want two large houses, Daddy.'

'Then sell them. Sell them back to him on the spot. I'll arrange all that for you. And then, just think of it, my dear, you'll be rich! You'll be independent for the rest of your life!'

'Oh, Daddy, I don't like it. I think it's silly.'

'So do I,' the mother said. She jerked her head briskly up and down as she spoke, like a hen. 'You ought to be ashamed of yourself, Michael, ever suggesting such a thing! Your own daughter, too!'

Mike didn't even look at her. 'Take it!' he said eagerly, staring hard at the girl. 'Take it, quick! I'll guarantee you won't lose.'

'But I don't like it, Daddy.'

'Come on, girl. Take it!'

Mike was pushing her hard. He was leaning towards her, fixing her with two hard bright eyes, and it was not easy for the daughter to resist him.

'But what if I lose?'

'I keep telling you, you can't lose. I'll guarantee it.'

'Oh, Daddy, must I?'

'I'm making you a fortune. So come on now. What do you say, Louise? All right?'

For the last time, she hesitated. Then she gave a helpless little shrug of the shoulders and said, 'Oh, all right, then. Just so long as you swear there's no danger of losing.'

'Good!' Mike cried. 'That's fine! Then it's a bet!'

'Yes,' Richard Pratt said, looking at the girl. 'It's a bet.'

Immediately, Mike picked up the wine, tipped the first thimbleful into his own glass, then skipped excitedly around the table filling up the others. Now everyone was watching Richard Pratt, watching his face as he reached slowly for his glass with his right hand and lifted it to his nose. The man was about fifty years old and he did not have a pleasant face. Somehow, it was all mouth – mouth and lips – the full, wet lips of the professional gourmet, the lower lip hanging downward in the centre, a pendulous, permanemtly open taster's lip, shaped open to receive the rim of a glass or a morsel of food. Like a keyhole, I thought, watching it; his mouth is like a large wet keyhole.

Slowly he lifted the glass to his nose. The point of the nose entered the glass and moved over the surface of the wine, delicately sniffing. He swirled the wine gently around in the glass to receive the bouquet. His concentration was intense. He has closed his eyes, and now the whole top half of his body, the head and neck and chest, seemed to become a kind of huge sensitive smelling-machine, receiving, filtering, analysing the message from the sniffing nose.

Mike, I noticed, was lounging in his chair, apparently unconcerned, but he was watching every move. Mrs Schofield, the wife, sat prim and upright at the other end of the table, looking straight ahead, her face tight with disapproval. The daughter, Louise, had shifted her chair away a little, and sidewise, facing the gourmet, and she, like her father, was watching closely.

For at least a minute, the smelling process continued; then, without opening his eyes or moving his head, Pratt lowered the glass to his mouth and tipped in almost half the contents. He paused, his mouth full of wine, getting the first taste; then, he permitted some of it to trickle down his throat and I saw his Adam's apple move as it passed by. But most of it he retained in his mouth. And now, without swallowing again, he drew in through his lips a thin breath of air which mingled with the fumes of the wine in the mouth and passed on down into his lungs. He held the breath, blew it out through his nose, and finally began to roll the wine around under the tongue, and chewed it, actually chewed it with his teeth as though it were bread.

It was a solemn, impressive performance, and I must say he did it well.

'Um,' he said, putting down the glass, running a pink tongue over his lips, 'Um – yes. A very interesting little wine – gentle and gracious, almost feminine in the after-taste.'

There was an excess of saliva in his mouth, and as he spoke he spat an occasional bright speck of it on to the table.

'Now we can start to eliminate,' he said. 'You will pardon me for doing this carefully, but there is much at stake. Normally I would perhaps take a bit of a chance, leaping forward quickly and landing right in the middle of the vineyard of my choice. But this time – I must move cautiously this time, must I not?' He looked up at Mike and he smiled, a thick-lipped, wet-lipped smile. Mike did not smile back.

'First, then, which district in Bordeaux does this wine come from? That's not too difficult to guess. It is far too light in the body to be from either St Emilion or Graves. It is obviously a Médoc. There's no doubt about *that*.

'Now – from which commune in Médoc does it come? That also, by elimination, should not be too difficult to decide. Margaux? No. It cannot be Margaux. It has not the violent bouquet of a Margaux. Pauillac? It cannot be Pauillac, either. It is too tender, too gentle and wistful for Pauillac. The wine of Pauillac has a character that is almost imperious in its taste. And also, to me, a Pauillac contains just a little pith, a curious dusty, pithy flavour that the grape acquires from the soil of the district. No, no. This – this is a very gentle wine, demure and bashful in the first taste, emerging shyly but quite graciously in the second. A little arch, perhaps, in the second taste, and a little naughty also, teasing the tongue with a trace, just a trace of tannin. Then, in the after-taste, delightful – consoling and feminine, with a certain blithely generous quality that one associates only with the wines of the commune of St Julien. Unmistakably this is a St Julien.'

He leaned back in his chair, held his hands up level with his chest, and placed the fingertips carefully together. He was becoming ridiculously pompous, but I thought that some of it was deliberate, simply to mock his host. I found myself waiting rather tensely for him to go on. The girl Louise was lighting a cigarette. Pratt heard the match strike and he turned on her, flaring suddenly with real anger. 'Please!' he said. 'Please don't do that! It's a disgusting habit, to smoke at table!'

She looked up at him, still holding the burning match in one hand, the big slow eyes settling on his face, resting there a moment, moving away again, slow and contemptuous. She bent her head and blew out the match, but continued to hold the unlighted cigarette in her fingers.

'I'm sorry, my dear,' Pratt said, 'but I simply cannot have smoking at table.'

She didn't look at him again.

'Now, let me see – where were we?' he said. 'Ah, yes. This wine is from Bordeaux, from the commune of St Julien, in the district of Médoc. So far, so good. But now we come to the more difficult part – the name of the vineyard itself. For in St Julien there are many vineyards, and as our host so rightly remarked earlier on, there is often not much difference between the wine of one and wine of another. But we shall see.'

He paused again, closing his eyes. 'I am trying to establish the "growth",' he said. 'If I can do that, it will be half the battle. Now, let me see. This wine is obviously not from a first-growth vineyard – nor even a second. It is not a great wine. The quality, the – the – what do you call it? – the radiance, the power, is lacking. But a third growth – that it could be. And yet I doubt it. We know it is a good year – our host has said so – and this is probably flattering it a little bit. I must be careful. I must be very careful here.'

He picked up his glass and took another small sip.

'Yes,' he said, sucking his lips, 'I was right. It is a fourth growth. Now I am sure of it. A fourth growth from a very good year – from a great year, in fact. And that's what made it taste for a moment like a third – or even a second-growth wine. Good! That's better! Now we are closing in! What are the fourth-growth vineyards in the commune of St Julien?'

Again he paused, took up his glass, and held the rim against that sagging, pendulous lower lip of his. Then I saw the tongue shoot out, pink and narrow, the tip of it dipping into the wine, withdrawing swiftly again – a repulsive sight. When he lowered the glass, his eyes remained closed, the face concentrated, only the lips moving, sliding over each other like two pieces of wet, spongy rubber.

'There it is again!' he cried. 'Tannin in the middle taste, and the quick astringent squeeze upon the tongue. Yes, yes, of course! Now I have it! The wine comes from one of those small vineyards around Beychevelle. I remember now. The Beychevelle district, and the river and the little harbour that has silted up so the wine ships can no longer use it. Beychevelle ... could it actually be a Beychevelle itself? No, I don't think so. Not quite. But it is somewhere very close. Château Talbot? Could it be Talbot? Yes, it could. Wait one moment.'

He sipped the wine again, and out of the side of my eye I noticed Mike Schofield and how he was leaning farther and farther forward over the table, his mouth slightly open, his small eyes fixed upon Richard Pratt.

'No. I was wrong. It is not a Talbot. A Talbot comes forward to you just a little quicker than this one; the fruit is nearer the surface. If it is a '34, which I believe it is, then it couldn't be Talbot. Well, well. Let me think. It is not a Beychevelle and it is not a Talbot, and yet – yet it is so close to both of them, so close, that the vineyard must be almost in between. Now, which could that be?'

He hesitated, and we waited, watching his face. Everyone, even Mike's wife, was watching him now. I heard the maid put down the dish of vegetables on the sideboard behind me, gently, so as not to disturb the silence.

'Ah!' he cried. 'I have it! Yes, I think I have it!'

For the last time, he sipped the wine. Then, still holding the glass up near his mouth, he turned to Mike and he smiled, a slow, silky smile, and he said, 'You know what this is? This is the little Château Branaire-Ducru.'

Mike sat tight, not moving.

'And the year, 1934.'

We all looked at Mike, waiting for him to turn the bottle around in its basket and show the label.

'Is that your final answer?' Mike said.

'Yes, I think so.'

'Well, is it or isn't it?'

'Yes, it is.'

'What was the name again?'

'Château Branaire-Ducru. Pretty little vineyard. Lovely old château. Know it quite well. Can't think why I didn't recognize it at once.'

'Come on, Daddy,' the girl said. 'Turn it round and let's have a peek. I want my two houses.'

'Just a minute,' Mike said. 'Wait just a minute.' He was sitting very quiet, bewildered-looking, and his face was becoming puffy and pale, as though all the force was draining slowly out of him.

'Michael!' his wife called sharply from the other end of the table. 'What's the matter?'

'Keep out of this, Margaret, will you please.'

Richard Pratt was looking at Mike, smiling with his mouth, his eyes small and bright. Mike was not looking at anyone.

'Daddy!' the daughter cried, agonized. 'But, Daddy, you don't mean to say he guessed it right!'

'Now, stop worrying, my dear,' Mike said. 'There's nothing to worry about.'

I think it was more to get away from his family than anything else that Mike then turned to Richard Pratt and said, I'll tell you what, Richard. I think you and I better slip off into the next room and have a little chat.'

'I don't want a little chat,' Pratt said. 'All I want is to see the label on that bottle.' He knew he was a winner now; he had the bearing, the quiet arrogance of a winner, and I could see that he was prepared to become thoroughly nasty if there was any trouble. 'What are you waiting for?' he said to Mike, 'Go on and turn it round.'

Then this happened: the maid, the tiny, erect figure of the maid in her white-and-black uniform, was standing beside Richard Pratt, holding something out in her hand. 'I believe these are yours, sir,' she said.

Pratt glanced around, saw the pair of thin horn-rimmed spectacles that she held out to him, and for a moment he hesitated. 'Are they? Perhaps they are, I don't know.'

'Yes, sir, they're yours.' The maid was an elderly woman – nearer seventy than sixty – a faithful family retainer of many years' standing. She put the spectacles down on the table beside him.

Without thanking her, Pratt took them up and slipped them into his top pocket, behind the white handkerchief.

But the maid didn't go away. She remained standing beside and slightly behind Richard Pratt, and there was something so unusual in her manner and in the way she stood there, small, motionless and erect, that I for one found myself watching her with a sudden apprehension. Her old grey face had a frosty, determined look, the lips were compressed, the little chin was out, and the hands were clasped together tight before her. The curious cap on her head and the flash of white down the front of her uniform made her seem like some tiny, ruffled, white-breasted bird.

'You left them in Mr Schofield's study,' she said. Her voice was unnaturally, deliberately polite. 'On top of the green filing cabinet in his study, sir, when you happened to go in there by yourself before dinner.'

It took a few moments for the full meaning of her words to penetrate, and in the silence that followed I became aware of Mike and how he was slowly drawing himself up in his chair, and the colour coming to his face, and the eyes opening wide, and the curl of the mouth, and the dangerous little patch of whiteness beginning to spread around the area of the nostrils.

'Now, Michael!' his wife said. 'Keep calm now, Michael, dear! Keep calm!'

LAMB TO THE SLAUGHTER

The room was warm and clean, the curtains drawn, the two table lamps alight – hers and the one by the empty chair opposite. On the sideboard behind her, two tall glasses, soda water, whisky. Fresh ice cubes in the Thermos bucket.

Mary Maloney was waiting for her husband to come home from work.

Now and again she would glance up at the clock, but without anxiety, merely to please herself with the thought that each minute gone by made it nearer the time when he would come. There was a slow smiling air about her, and about everything she did. The drop of the head as she bent over her sewing was curiously tranquil. Her skin – for this was her sixth month with child – had acquired a wonderful translucent quality, the mouth was soft, and the eyes, with their new placid look, seemed larger, darker than before.

When the clock said ten minutes to five, she began to listen, and a few moments later, punctually as always, she heard the tyres on the gravel outside, and the car door slamming, the footsteps passing the window, the key turning in the lock. She laid aside her sewing, stood up, and went forward to kiss him as he came in.

'Hullo, darling,' she said.

'Hullo,' he answered.

She took his coat and hung it in the closet. Then she walked over and made the drinks, a strongish one for him, a weak one for herself; and soon she was back again in her chair with the sewing, and he in the other, opposite, holding the tall glass with both his hands, rocking it so the ice cubes tinkled against the side.

For her, this was alway a blissful time of day. She knew he didn't want to speak much until the first drink was finished, and she, on her side, was content to sit quietly, enjoying his company after the long hours alone in the house. She loved to luxuriate in the presence of this man, and to feel – almost as a sunbather feels the sun – that warm male glow that came out of him to her when they were alone together. She loved him for the way he sat loosely in a chair, for the way he came in a door, or moved slowly across the room with long strides. She loved the intent, far look in his eyes when they rested on her, the funny shape of the mouth, and especially the way he remained silent

about his tiredness, sitting still with himself until the whisky had taken
some of it away.

'Tired, darling?'

'Yes,' he said. 'I'm tired.' And as he spoke, he did an unusual thing.
He lifted his glass and drained it in one swallow although there was
still half of it, at least half of it, left. She wasn't really watching him
but she knew what he had done because she heard the ice cubes falling
back against the bottom of the empty glass when he lowered his arm.
He paused a moment, leaning forward in the chair, then he got up
and went slowly over to fetch himself another.

'I'll get it!' she cried, jumping up.

'Sit down,' he said.

When he came back, she noticed that the new drink was dark amber
with the quantity of whisky in it.

'Darling, shall I get your slippers?'

'No.'

She watched him as he began to sip the dark yellow drink, and she
could see little oily swirls in the liquid because it was so strong.

'I think it's a shame,' she said, 'that when a policeman gets to be
as senior as you, they keep him walking about on his feet all day long.'

He didn't answer, so she bent her head again and went on with her
sewing; but each time he lifted the drink to his lips, she heard the ice
cubes clinking against the side of the glass.

'Darling,' she said. 'Would you like me to get you some cheese? I
haven't made any supper because it's Thursday.'

'No,' he said.

'If you're too tired to eat out,' she went on, 'it's still not too late.
There's plenty of meat and stuff in the freezer, and you can have it
right here and not even move out of the chair.'

Her eyes waited on him for an answer, a smile, a little nod, but he
made no sign.

'Anyway,' she went on, 'I'll get you some cheese and crackers first.'

'I don't want it,' he said.

She moved uneasily in her chair, the large eyes still watching his
face. 'But you *must* have supper. I can easily do it here. I'd like to do
it. We can have lamb chops. Or pork. Anything you want. Everything's
in the freezer.'

'Forget it,' he said.

'But, darling, you *must* eat! I'll fix it anyway, and then you can have
it or not, as you like.'

She stood up and placed her sewing on the table by the lamp.

'Sit down,' he said. 'Just for a minute, sit down.'

It wasn't till then that she began to get frightened.

'Go on,' he said. 'Sit down.'

She lowered herself back slowly into the chair, watching him all the time with those large, bewildered eyes. He had finished the second drink and was staring down into the glass frowning.

'Listen,' he said, 'I've got something to tell you.'

'What is it, darling? What's the matter?'

He had become absolutely motionless, and he kept his head down so that the light from the lamp beside him fell across the upper part of his face, leaving the chin and mouth in shadow. She noticed there was a little muscle moving near the corner of his left eye.

'This is going to be a bit of a shock to you, I'm afraid,' he said. 'But I've thought about it a good deal and I've decided the only thing to do is tell you right away. I hope you won't blame me too much.'

And he told her. It didn't take long, four or five minutes at most, and she sat very still through it all, watching him with a kind of dazed horror as he went further and further away from her with each word.

'So there it is,' he added. 'And I know it's kind of a bad time to be telling you, but there simply wasn't any other way. Of course I'll give you money and see you're looked after. But there needn't really be any fuss. I hope not anyway. It wouldn't be very good for my job.'

Her first instinct was not to believe any of it, to reject it all. It occurred to her that perhaps he hadn't even spoken, that she herself had imagined the whole thing. Maybe, if she went about her business and acted as though she hadn't been listening, then later, when she sort of woke up again, she might find none of it had ever happened.

'I'll get the supper,' she managed to whisper, and this time he didn't stop her.

When she walked across the room she couldn't feel her feet touching the floor. She couldn't feel anything at all – except a slight nausea and a desire to vomit. Everything was automatic now – down the stairs to the cellar, the light switch, the deep freeze, the hand inside the cabinet taking hold of the first object it met. She lifted it out, and looked at it. It was wrapped in paper, so she took off the paper and looked at it again.

A leg of lamb.

All right then, they would have lamb for supper. She carried it upstairs, holding the thin bone-end of it with both her hands, and as she went through the living-room, she saw him standing over by the window with his back to her, and she stopped.

'For God's sake,' he said, hearing her, but not turning round. 'Don't make supper for me. I'm going out.'

At that point, Mary Maloney simply walked up behind him and without any pause she swung the big frozen leg of lamb high in the air and brought it down as hard as she could on the back of his head.

She might just as well have hit him with a steel club.

She stepped back a pace, waiting, and the funny thing was that he remained standing there for at least four or five seconds, gently swaying. Then he crashed to the carpet.

The violence of the crash, the noise, the small table overturning, helped bring her out of the shock. She came out slowly, feeling cold and surprised, and she stood for a while blinking at the body, still holding the ridiculous piece of meat tight with both hands.

All right, she told herself. So I've killed him.

It was extraordinary, now, how clear her mind became all of a sudden. She began thinking very fast. As the wife of a detective, she knew quite well what the penalty would be. That was fine. It made no difference to her. In fact, it would be a relief. On the other hand, what about the child? What were the laws about murderers with unborn children? Did they kill them both – mother and child? Or did they wait until the tenth month? What did they do?

Mary Maloney didn't know. And she certainly wasn't prepared to take a chance.

She carried the meat into the kitchen, placed it in a pan, turned the oven on high, and shoved it inside. Then she washed her hands and ran upstairs to the bedroom. She sat down before the mirror, tidied her face, touched up her lips and face. She tried a smile. It came out rather peculiar. She tried again.

'Hullo Sam,' she said brightly, aloud.

The voice sounded peculiar too.

'I want some potatoes please, Sam. Yes, and I think a can of peas.'

That was better. Both the smile and the voice were coming out better now. She rehearsed it several times more. Then she ran downstairs, took her coat, went out the back door, down the garden, into the street.

It wasn't six o'clock yet and the lights were still on in the grocery shop.

'Hullo Sam,' she said brightly, smiling at the man behind the counter.

'Why, good evening, Mrs Maloney. How're *you*?'

'I want some potatoes please, Sam. Yes, and I think a can of peas.'

The man turned and reached up behind him on the shelf for the peas.

'Patrick's decided he's tired and doesn't want to eat out tonight,' she told him. 'We usually go out Thursdays, you know, and now he's caught me without any vegetables in the house.'

'Then how about meat, Mrs Maloney?'

'No, I've got meat, thanks. I got a nice leg of lamb, from the freezer.'

'Oh.'

'I don't much like cooking it frozen, Sam, but I'm taking a chance on it this time. You think it'll be all right?'

'Personally,' the grocer said, 'I don't believe it makes any difference. You want these Idaho potatoes?'

'Oh yes, that'll be fine. Two of those.'

'Anything else?' The grocer cocked his head on one side, looking at her pleasantly. 'How about afterwards? What you going to give him for afterwards?'

'Well – what would you suggest, Sam?'

The man glanced around his shop. 'How about a nice big slice of cheesecake? I know he likes that.'

'Perfect,' she said. 'He loves it.'

And when it was all wrapped and she had paid she put on her brightest smile and said, 'Thank you, Sam. Good night.'

'Good night, Mrs Maloney. And thank *you*.'

And now, she told herself as she hurried back, all she was doing now, she was returning home to her husband and he was waiting for his supper; and she must cook it good, and make it as tasty as possible because the poor man was tired; and if, when she entered the house, she happened to find anything unusual, or tragic, or terrible, then naturally it would be a shock and she'd become frantic with grief and horror. Mind you, she wasn't *expecting* to find anything. She was just going home with the vegetables. Mrs Patrick Maloney going home with the vegetables on Thursday evening to cook supper for her husband.

That's the way, she told herself. Do everything right and natural. Keep things absolutely natural and there'll be no need for any acting at all.

Therefore, when she entered the kitchen by the back door, she was humming a little tune to herself and smiling.

'Patrick!' she called. 'How are you darling?'

She put the parcel down on the table and went through into the living-room; and when she saw him lying there on the floor with his legs doubled up and one arm twisted back underneath his body, it really was rather a shock. All the old love and longing for him welled up inside her, and she ran over to him, knelt down beside him, and began to cry her heart out. It was easy. No acting was necessary.

A few minutes later she got up and went to the phone. She knew the number of the police station, and when the man at the other end answered, she cried to him, 'Quick! Come quick! Patrick's dead!'

'Who's speaking?'

'Mrs Maloney. Mrs Patrick Maloney.'

'You mean Patrick Maloney's dead?'

'I think so,' she sobbed. 'He's lying on the floor and I think he's dead.'

'Be right over,' the man said.

The car came over quickly, and when she opened the front door, two policemen walked in. She knew them both – she knew nearly all the men at that precinct – and she fell right into Jack Noonan's arms, weeping hysterically. He put her gently into a chair, then went over to join the other one, who was called O'Malley, kneeling by the body.

'Is he dead?' she cried.

'I'm afraid he is. What happened?'

Briefly, she told her story about going out to the grocer and coming back to find him on the floor. While she was talking, crying and talking, Noonan discovered a small patch of congealed blood on the dead man's head. He showed it to O'Malley who got up at once and hurried to the phone.

Soon, other men began to come into the house. First a doctor, then two detectives, one of whom she knew by name. Later, a police photographer arrived and took pictures, and a man who knew about fingerprints. There was a great deal of whispering and muttering beside the corpse, and the detectives kept asking her a lot of questions. But they always treated her kindly. She told her story again, this time right from the beginning, when Patrick had come in, and she was sewing, and he was tired, so tired he hadn't wanted to go out for supper. She told how she'd put the meat in the oven – 'it's there now, cooking' – and how she'd slipped out to the grocer for vegetables, and come back to find him lying on the floor.

'Which grocer?' one of the detectives asked.

She told him, and he turned and whispered something to the other detective who immediately went outside into the street.

In fifteen minutes he was back with a page of notes, and there was more whispering, and through her sobbing she heard a few of the whispered phrases – '... acted quite normal ... very cheerful ... wanted to give him a good supper ... peas ... cheesecake ... impossible that she ...'

After a while, the photographer and the doctor departed and two other men came in and took the corpse away on a stretcher. Then the fingerprint man went away. The two detectives remained, and so did the two policemen. They were exceptionally nice to her, and Jack Noonan asked if she wouldn't rather go somewhere else, to her sister's house perhaps, or to his own wife who would take care of her and put her up for the night.

No, she said. She didn't feel she could move even a yard at the moment. Would they mind awfully if she stayed just where she was until she felt better? She didn't feel too good at the moment, she really didn't.

Then hadn't she better lie down on the bed? Jack Noonan asked.

No, she said, she'd like to stay right where she was, in this chair. A little later perhaps, when she felt better, she would move.

So they left her there while they went about their business, searching the house. Occasionally one of the detectives asked her another question. Sometimes Jack Noonan spoke to her gently as he passed by. Her husband, he told her, had been killed by a blow on the back of the head administered with a heavy blunt instrument, almost certainly a large piece of metal. They were looking for the weapon. The murderer may have taken it with him, but on the other hand he may've thrown it away or hidden it somewhere on the premises.

'It's the old story,' he said. 'Get the weapon, and you've got the man.'

Later, one of the detectives came up and sat beside her. Did she know, he asked, of anything in the house that could've been used as the weapon? Would she mind having a look around to see if anything was missing – a very big spanner for example, or a heavy metal vase.

They didn't have any heavy metal vases, she said.

'Or a big spanner?'

She didn't think they had a big spanner. But there might be some things like that in the garage.

The search went on. She knew that there were other policemen in the garden all around the house. She could hear their footsteps on the gravel outside, and sometimes she saw the flash of a torch through a chink in the curtains. It began to get late, nearly nine she noticed by the clock on the mantel. The four men searching the rooms seemed to be growing weary, a trifle exasperated.

'Jack,' she said, the next time Sergeant Noonan went by. 'Would you mind giving me a drink?'

'Sure I'll give you a drink. You mean this whisky?'

'Yes, please. But just a small one. It might make me feel better.'

He handed her the glass.

'Why don't you have one yourself,' she said. 'You must be awfully tired. Please do. You've been very good to me.'

'Well,' he answered. 'It's not strictly allowed, but I might take just a drop to keep me going.'

One by one the others came in and were persuaded to take a little nip of whisky. They stood around rather awkwardly with the drinks in their hands, uncomfortable in her presence, trying to say consoling things to her. Sergeant Noonan wandered into the kitchen, came out quickly and said, 'Look, Mrs Maloney. You know that oven of yours is still on, and the meat still inside.'

'Oh *dear* me!' she cried. 'So it is!'

'I better turn it off for you, hadn't I?'

'Will you do that, Jack. Thank you so much.'

When the sergeant returned the second time, she looked at him with her large, dark, tearful eyes. 'Jack Noonan,' she said.

'Yes?'

'Would you do me a small favour – you and these others?'

'We can try, Mrs Maloney.'

'Well,' she said. 'Here you all are, and good friends of dear Patrick's too, and helping to catch the man who killed him. You must be terribly hungry by now because it's long past your supper time, and I know Patrick would never forgive me, God bless his soul, if I allowed you to remain in his house without offering you decent hospitality. Why don't you eat up that lamb that's in the oven? It'll be cooked just right by now.'

'Wouldn't dream of it,' Sergeant Noonan said.

'Please,' she begged. 'Please eat it. Personally I couldn't touch a thing, certainly not what's been in the house when he was here. But it's all right for you. It'd be a favour to me if you'd eat it up. Then you can go on with your work again afterwards.'

There was a good deal of hesitating among the four policemen, but they were clearly hungry, and in the end they were persuaded to go into the kitchen and help themselves. The woman stayed where she was, listening to them through the open door, and she could hear them speaking among themselves, their voices thick and sloppy because their mouths were full of meat.

'Have some more, Charlie?'

'No. Better not finish it.'

'She *wants* us to finish it. She said so. Be doing her a favour.'

'Okay then. Give me some more.'

'That's the hell of a big club the guy must've used to hit poor Patrick,' one of them was saying. 'The doc says his skull was smashed all to pieces just like from a sledge-hammer.'

'That's why it ought to be easy to find.'

'Exactly what I say.'

'Whoever done it, they're not going to be carrying a thing like that around with them longer than they need.'

One of them belched.

'Personally, I think it's right here on the premises.'

'Probably right under our very noses. What you think, Jack?'

And in the other room, Mary Maloney began to giggle.

MAN FROM THE SOUTH

It was getting on towards six o'clock so I thought I'd buy myself a beer and go out and sit in a deckchair by the swimming pool and have a little evening sun.

I went to the bar and got the beer and carried it outside and wandered down the garden towards the pool.

It was a fine garden with lawns and beds of azaleas and tall coconut palms, and the wind was blowing strongly through the tops of the palm trees, making the leaves hiss and crackle as though they were on fire. I could see the clusters of big brown nuts hanging down underneath the leaves.

There were plenty of deck chairs around the swimming pool and there were white tables and huge brightly coloured umbrellas and sunburned men and women sitting around in bathing suits. In the pool itself there were three or four girls and about a dozen boys, all splashing about and making a lot of noise and throwing a large rubber ball at one another.

I stood watching them. The girls were English girls from the hotel. The boys I didn't know about, but they sounded American, and I thought they were probably naval cadets who'd come ashore from the US naval training vessel which had arrived in harbour that morning.

I went over and sat down under a yellow umbrella where there were four empty seats, and I poured my beer and settled back comfortably with a cigarette.

It was very pleasant sitting there in the sunshine with beer and cigarette. It was pleasant to sit and watch the bathers splashing about in the green water.

The American sailors were getting on nicely with the English girls. They'd reached the stage where they were diving under the water and tipping them up by their legs.

Just then I noticed a small, oldish man walking briskly around the edge of the pool. He was immaculately dressed in a white suit and he walked very quickly with little bouncing strides, pushing himself high up on to his toes with each step. He had on a large creamy Panama hat, and he came bouncing along the side of the pool, looking at the people and the chairs.

He stopped beside me and smiled, showing two rows of very small, uneven teeth, slightly tarnished. I smiled back.

'Excuse pleess, but may I sit here?'

'Certainly,' I said. 'Go ahead.'

He bobbed around to the back of the chair and inspected it for safety, then he sat down and crossed his legs. His white buckskin shoes had little holes punched all over them for ventilation.

'A fine evening,' he said. 'They are all evenings fine here in Jamaica.' I couldn't tell if the accent were Italian or Spanish, but I felt fairly sure he was some sort of a South American. And old too, when you saw him close. Probably around sixty-eight or seventy.

'Yes,' I said. 'It is wonderful here, isn't it.'

'And who, might I ask, are all dese? Dese is no hotel people.' He was pointing at the bathers in the pool.

'I think they're American sailors,' I told him. 'They're Americans who are learning to be sailors.'

'Of course dey are Americans. Who else in de world is going to make as much noise as dat? You are not American no?'

'No,' I said. 'I am not.'

Suddenly one of the American cadets was standing in front of us. He was dripping wet from the pool and one of the English girls was standing there with him.

'Are these chairs taken?' he said.

'No,' I answered.

'Mind if I sit down?'

'Go ahead.'

'Thanks,' he said. He had a towel in his hand and when he sat down he unrolled it and produced a pack of cigarettes and a lighter. He offered the cigarettes to the girl and she refused; then he offered them to me and I took one. The little man said, 'Tank you, no, but I tink I have a cigar.' He pulled out a crocodile case and got himself a cigar, then he produced a knife which had a small scissors in it and he snipped the end off the cigar.

'Here, let me give you a light.' The American boy held up his lighter.

'Dat will not work in dis wind.'

'Sure it'll work. It always works.'

The little man removed his unlighted cigar from his mouth, cocked his head on one side and looked at the boy.

'*All*-ways?' he said slowly.

'Sure, it never fails. Not with me anyway.'

The little man's head was still cocked over on one side and he was still watching the boy. 'Well, well. So you say dis famous lighter it never fails. Iss dat you say?'

'Sure,' the boy said. 'That's right.' He was about nineteen or twenty with a long freckled face and a rather sharp birdlike nose. His chest was not very sunburned and there were freckles there too, and a few wisps of pale-reddish hair. He was holding the lighter in his right hand, ready to flip the wheel. 'It never fails,' he said, smiling now because he was purposely exaggerating his little boast. 'I promise you it never fails.'

'One momint, pleess.' The hand that held the cigar came up high, palm outward, as though it were stopping traffic. 'Now juss one momint.' He had a curiously soft, toneless voice and he kept looking at the boy all the time.

'Shall we not perhaps make a little bet on dat?' He smiled at the boy. 'Shall we not make a little bet on whether your lighter lights?'

'Sure, I'll bet,' the boy said. 'Why not?'

'You like to bet?'

'Sure, I'll always bet.'

The man paused and examined his cigar, and I must say I didn't much like the way he was behaving. It seemed he was already trying to make something out of this, and to embarrass the boy, and at the same time I had the feeling he was relishing a private little secret all his own.

He looked up again at the boy and said slowly, 'I like to bet, too. Why we don't have a good bet on dis ting? A good big bet.'

'Now wait a minute,' the boy said. 'I can't do that. But I'll bet you a quarter. I'll even bet you a dollar, or whatever it is over here – some shillings, I guess.'

The little man waved his hand again. 'Listen to me. Now we have some fun. We make a bet. Den we got up to my room here in de hotel where iss no wind and I bet you you cannot light dis famous lighter of yours ten times running without missing once.'

'I'll bet I can,' the boy said.

'All right. Good. We make a bet, yes?'

'Sure, I'll bet you a buck.'

'No, no. I make you a very good bet. I am rich man and I am sporting man also. Listen to me. Outside de hotel iss my car. Iss very fine car. American car from your country. Cadillac –'

'Hey, now. Wait a minute.' The boy leaned back in his deck-chair and he laughed. 'I can't put up that sort of property. This is crazy.'

'Not crazy at all. You strike lighter successfully ten times running and Cadillac is yours. You like to have dis Cadillac, yes?'

'Sure, I'd like to have a Cadillac.' The boy was still grinning.

'All right. Fine. We make a bet and I put up my Cadillac.'

'And what do I put up?'

The little man carefully removed the red band from his still unlighted cigar. 'I never ask you, my friend, to bet something you cannot afford. You understand?'

'Then what do I bet?'

'I make it very easy for you, yes?'

'Okay. You make it easy.'

'Some small ting you can afford to give away, and if you did happen to lose it you would not feel too bad. Right?'

'Such as what?'

'Such as, perhaps, de little finger on your left hand.'

'My *what*?' The boy stopped grinning.

'Yes. Why not? You win, you take de car. You looss, I take de finger.'

'I don't get it. How d'you mean, you take the finger?'

'I chop it off.'

'Jumping jeepers! That's a crazy bet. I think I'll just make it a dollar.'

The little man leaned back, spread out his hands palms upwards and gave a tiny contemptuous shrug of the shoulders, 'Well, well, well,' he said. 'I do not understand. You say it lights but you will not bet. Den we forget it, yes?'

The boy sat quite still, staring at the bathers in the pool. Then he remembered suddenly he hadn't lighted his cigarette. He put it between his lips, cupped his hands around the lighter and flipped the wheel. The wick lighted and burned with a small, steady, yellow flame and the way he held his hands the wind didn't get to it at all.

'Could I have a light, too?' I said.

'God, I'm sorry, I forgot you didn't have one.'

I held out my hand for the lighter, but he stood up and came over to do it for me.

'Thank you,' I said, and he returned to his seat.

'You having a good time?' I asked.

'Fine,' he answered. 'It's pretty nice here.'

There was a silence then, and I could see that the little man had succeeded in disturbing the boy with his absurd proposal. He was sitting there very still, and it was obvious that a small tension was beginning to build up inside him. Then he started shifting about in his seat, and rubbing his chest, and stroking the back of his neck, and finally he placed both hands on his knees and began tap-tapping with his fingers against the kneecaps. Soon he was tapping with one of his feet as well.

'Now just let me check up on this bet of yours,' he said at last. 'You say we go up to your room and if I make this lighter light ten times running I win a Cadillac. If it misses just once then I forfeit the little finger of my left hand. Is that right?'

'Certainly. Dat is de bet. But I tink you are afraid.'

'What do we do if I lose? Do I have to hold my finger out while you chop it off?'

'Oh, no! Dat would be no good. And you might be tempted to refuse to hold it out. What I should do I should tie one of your hands to de table before we started and I should stand dere with a knife ready to go *chop* de momint your lighter missed.'

'What year is the Cadillac?' the boy asked.

'Excuse. I not understand.'

'What year – how old is the Cadillac?'

'Ah! How old? Yes. It is last year. Quite new car. But I see you are not betting man. Americans never are.'

The boy paused for just a moment and he glanced first at the English girl, then at me. 'Yes,' he said sharply. 'I'll bet you.'

'Good!' The little man clapped his hands together quietly, once. 'Fine,' he said. 'We do it now. And you, sir,' he turned to me, 'you would perhaps be good enough to, what you call it, to – to referee.' He had pale, almost colourless eyes with tiny bright black pupils.

'Well,' I said. 'I think it's a crazy bet. I don't think I like it very much.'

'Nor do I,' said the English girl. It was the first time she'd spoken. 'I think it's a stupid, ridiculous bet.'

'Are you serious about cutting off this boy's finger if he loses?' I said.

'Certainly I am. Also about giving him Cadillac if he win. Come now. We go to my room.'

He stood up. 'You like to put on some clothes first?' he said.

'No,' the boy answered. 'I'll come like this.' Then he turned to me. 'I'd consider it a favour if you'd come along and referee.'

'All right,' I said. 'I'll come along, but I don't like the bet.'

'You come too,' he said to the girl. 'You come and watch.'

The little man led the way back through the garden to the hotel. He was animated now, and excited, and that seemed to make him bounce up higher than ever on his toes as he walked along.

'I live in annexe,' he said. 'You like to see car first? Iss just here.'

He took us to where we could see the front driveway of the hotel and he stopped and pointed to a sleek pale-green Cadillac parked close by.

'Dere she iss. De green one. You like?'

'Say, that's a nice car,' the boy said.

'All right. Now we go up and see if you can win her.'

We followed him into the annexe and up one flight of stairs. He unlocked his door and we all trooped into what was a large pleasant double bedroom. There was a woman's dressing-gown lying across the bottom of one of the beds.

'First,' he said, 'we 'ave a little Martini.'

The drinks were on a small table in the far corner, all ready to be mixed, and there was a shaker and ice and plenty of glasses. He began to make the Martini, but meanwhile he'd rung the bell and now there was a knock on the door and a coloured maid came in.

'Ah!' he said, putting down the bottle of gin, taking a wallet from his pocket and pulling out a pound note. 'You will do something for me now, pleess.' He gave the maid the pound.

'You keep dat,' he said. 'And now we are going to play a little game in here and I want you to go off and find for me two – no tree tings. I want some nails, I want a hammer, and I want a chopping knife, a butcher's chopping knife which you can borrow from de kitchen. You can get, yes?'

'A *chopping knife!*' The maid opened her eyes wide and clasped her hands in front of her. 'You mean a *real* chopping knife?'

'Yes, yes, of course. Come on now, pleess. You can find dose tings surely for me.'

'Yes, sir, I'll try, sir. Surely I'll try to get them.' And she went.

The little man handed round the Martinis. We stood there and sipped them, the boy with the long freckled face and the pointed nose, bare-bodied except for a pair of faded brown bathing shorts; the English girl, a large-boned fair-haired girl wearing a pale blue bathing suit, who watched the boy over the top of her glass all the time; the little man with the colourless eyes standing there in his immaculate white suit drinking his Martini and looking at the girl in her pale blue bathing dress. I didn't know what to make of it all. The man seemed serious about the bet and he seemed serious about the business of cutting off the finger. But hell, what if the boy lost? Then we'd have to rush him to the hospital in the Cadillac that he hadn't won. That would be a fine thing. Now wouldn't that be a really fine thing? It would be a damn silly unnecessary thing so far as I could see.

'Don't you think this is rather a silly bet?' I said.

'I think it's a fine bet,' the boy answered. He had already downed one large Martini.

'I think it's a stupid, ridiculous bet,' the girl said. 'What'll happen if you lose?'

'It won't matter. Come to think of it, I can't remember ever in my life having had any use for the little finger on my left hand. Here he is.' The boy took hold of the finger. 'Here he is and he hasn't ever done a thing for me yet. So why shouldn't I bet him? I think it's a fine bet.'

The little man smiled and picked up the shaker and refilled our glasses.

'Before we begin,' he said, 'I will present to de – to de referee de key of de car.' He produced a car key from his pocket and gave it to me. 'De papers,' he said, 'de owning papers and insurance are in de pocket of de car.'

Then the coloured maid came in again. In one hand she carried a small chopper, the kind used by butchers for chopping meat bones, and in the other a hammer and a bag of nails.

'Good! You get dem all. Tank you, tank you. Now you can go.' He waited until the maid had closed the door, then he put the implements on one of the beds and said, 'Now we prepare ourselves, yes?' And to the boy, 'Help me, pleess, with dis table. We carry it out a little.'

It was the usual kind of hotel writing desk, just a plain rectangular table about four feet by three with a blotting pad, ink, pens and paper. They carried it out into the room away from the wall, and removed the writing things.

'And now,' he said, 'a chair.' He picked up a chair and placed it beside the table. He was very brisk and very animated, like a person organizing games at a children's party. 'And now de nails. I must put in de nails.' He fetched the nails and he began to hammer them into the top of the table.

We stood there, the boy, the girl, and I, holding Martinis in our hands, watching the little man at work. We watched him hammer two nails into the table, about six inches apart. He didn't hammer them right home; he allowed a small part of each one to stick up. Then he tested them for firmness with his fingers.

Anyone would think the son of a bitch had done this before, I told myself. He never hesitates. Table, nails, hammer, kitchen chopper. He knows exactly what he needs and how to arrange it.

'And now,' he said, 'all we want is some string.' He found some string. 'All right, at last we are ready. Will you pleess to sit here at de table?' he said to the boy.

The boy put his glass away and sat down.

'Now place de left hand between dese two nails. De nails are only so I can tie your hand in place. All right, good. Now I tie your hand secure to de table – so.'

He wound the string around the boy's wrist, then several times around the wide part of the hand, then he fastened it tight to the nails. He made a good job of it and when he'd finished there wasn't any question about the boy being able to draw his hand away. But he could move his fingers.

'Now pleess, clench de fist, all except for de little finger. You must leave de little finger sticking out, lying on de table.'

'*Ex*-cellent! *Ex*-cellent! Now we are ready. Wid your right hand you manipulate de lighter. But one momint, pleess.'

He skipped over to the bed and picked up the chopper. He came back and stood beside the table with the chopper in his hand.

'We are all ready?' he said. 'Mister referee, you must say to begin.'

The English girl was standing there in her pale blue bathing costume right behind the boy's chair. She was just standing there, not saying anything. The boy was sitting quite still holding the lighter in his right hand, looking at the chopper. The little man was looking at me.

'Are you ready?' I asked the boy.

'I'm ready.'

'And you?' to the little man.

'Quite ready,' he said and he lifted the chopper up in the air and held it there about two feet above the boy's finger, ready to chop. The boy watched it, but didn't flinch and his mouth didn't move at all. He merely raised his eyebrows and frowned.

'All right,' I said. 'Go ahead.'

The boy said, 'Will you please count aloud the number of times I light it.'

'Yes,' I said. 'I'll do that.'

With his thumb he raised the top of the lighter, and again with the thumb he gave the wheel a sharp flick. The flint sparked and the wick caught fire and burned with a small yellow flame.

'One!' I called.

He didn't blow the flame out; he closed the top of the lighter on it and he waited for perhaps five seconds before opening it again.

He flicked the wheel very strongly and once more there was a small flame burning on the wick.

'Two!'

No one else said anything. The boy kept his eyes on the lighter. The little man held the chopper up in the air and he too was watching the lighter.

'Three!'

'Four!'

'Five!'

'Six!'

'Seven!' Obviously it was one of those lighters that worked. The flint gave a big spark and the wick was the right length. I watched the thumb snapping the top down on to the flame. Then a pause. Then the thumb raising the top once more. This was an all-thumb operation. The thumb did everything. I took a breath, ready to say eight. The thumb flicked the wheel. The flint sparked. The little flame appeared.

'Eight!' I said, and as I said it the door opened. We all turned and we saw a woman standing in the doorway, a small, black-haired woman, rather old, who stood there for about two seconds then rushed forward, shouting, 'Carlos! Carlos!' She grabbed his wrist, took the chopper from him, threw it on the bed, took hold of the little man by the lapels of his white suit and began shaking him very vigorously, talking to him fast and loud and fiercely all the time in some Spanish-sounding language. She shook him so fast you couldn't see him any more. He became a faint, misty, quickly moving outline, like the spokes of a turning wheel.

Then she slowed down and the little man came into view again and she hauled him across the room and pushed him backwards on to one of the beds. He sat on the edge of it blinking his eyes and testing his head to see if it would still turn on his neck.

'I am sorry,' the woman said. 'I am so terribly sorry that this should happen.' She spoke almost perfect English.

'It is too bad,' she went on. 'I suppose it is really my fault. For ten minutes I leave him alone to go and have my hair washed and I come back and he is at it again.' She looked sorry and deeply concerned.

The boy was untying his hand from the table. The English girl and I stood there and said nothing.

'He is a menace,' the woman said. 'Down where we live at home he has taken altogether forty-seven fingers from different people, and has lost eleven cars. In the end they threatened to have him put away somewhere. That's why I brought him up here.'

'We were only having a little bet,' mumbled the little man from the bed.

'I suppose he bet you a car,' the woman said.

'Yes,' the boy answered. 'A Cadillac.'

'He has no car. It's mine. And that makes it worse,' she said, 'that he should bet you when he has nothing to bet with. I am ashamed and very sorry about it all.' She seemed an awfully nice woman.

'Well,' I said, 'then here's the key of your car.' I put it on the table.

'We were only having a little bet,' mumbled the little man.

'He hasn't anything left to bet with,' the woman said. 'He hasn't a thing in the world. Not a thing. As a matter of fact I myself won it all from him a long while ago. It took time, a lot of time, and it was hard work, but I won it all in the end.' She looked up at the boy and she smiled, a slow sad smile, and she came over and put out a hand to take the key from the table.

I can see it now, that hand of hers; it had only one finger on it, and a thumb.

THE SOLDIER

It was one of those nights that made him feel he knew what it was like to be a blind man; not the shadow of an image for his eyes to discern, not even the forms of the trees visible against the sky.

Out of the darkness he became aware of small rustling noises in the hedge, the breathing of a horse some distance away in the field, the soft thud of a hoof as it moved its foot; and once he heard the rush of a bird flying past him low overhead.

'Jock,' he said, speaking loud. 'We'll go home now.' And he turned and began to walk back up the slope of the lane, the dog pulling ahead, showing the way in the dark.

It must be nearly midnight, he thought. That meant that soon it would be tomorrow. Tomorrow was worse than today. Tomorrow was the worst of all because it was going to become today – and today was now.

Today had not been very nice, especially that business with the splinter.

Stop it, he told himself. There isn't any sense thinking about it. It doesn't do anyone any good thinking about things like that. Think about something else for a change. You can kick out a dangerous thought, you know, if you put another in its place. Go right back as far as you can go. Let's have some memories of sweet days. The seaside holidays in the summer, wet sand and red buckets and shrimping nets and the slippery seaweedy rocks and the small clear pools and sea anemones and snails and mussels and sometimes one grey translucent shrimp hovering deep down in the beautiful green water.

But how *could* that splinter have got into the sole of his foot without him feeling it?

It is not important. Do you remember hunting for cowries along the margin of the tide, each one so fine and perfect it became a precious jewel to be held in the hand all the way home; and the little orange-coloured scallops, the pearly oyster shells, the tiny bits of emerald glass, a live hermit crab, a cockle, the spine of a skate, and once, but never to be forgotten, the dry seawashed jawbone of a human being with teeth in it, white and wonderful among the shells and pebbles. Oh Mummy, look what I've found! Look, Mummy, look!

But to go back to the splinter. She had really been rather unpleasant about that.

'What do you mean, you didn't notice?' she had asked, scornful.

'I just didn't notice, that's all.'

'I suppose you're going to tell me if I stick a pin into your foot you won't feel it?'

'I didn't say that.'

And then she had jabbed him suddenly in the ankle with the pin she had been using to take out the splinter, and he hadn't been watching so he didn't know about it till she had cried out in a kind of horror. And when he had looked down, the pin was sticking into the flesh all by itself behind the anklebone, almost half of it buried.

'Take it out,' he had said. 'You can poison someone like that.'

'You mean you can't *feel* it?'

'Take it out, will you?'

'You mean it doesn't hurt?'

'The pain is terrible. Take it out.'

'What's the *matter* with you?'

'I said the pain is terrible. Didn't you hear me?'

Why did they *do* things like that to him?

When I was down beside the sea, a wooden spade they gave to me, to dig the sandy shore. My holes were empty as a cup, and every time the sea came up, till it could come no more.

A year ago the doctor had said, 'Shut your eyes. Now tell me whether I'm pushing this toe up or down.'

'Up,' he had said.

'And now?'

'Down. No, up. I think it's up.'

It was peculiar that a neuro-surgeon should want to play with his toes.

'Did I get them all right, doctor?'

'You did very well.'

But that was a year ago. He had felt pretty good a year ago. The sort of things that happened now never used to happen then. Take, for example, just one item – the bathroom tap.

Why was the hot tap in the bathroom on a different side this morning? That was a new one.

It is not of the least importance, you understand, but it would be interesting to know why.

Do you think she could have changed it over, taken a spanner and a pipe-wrench and sneaked in during the night and changed it over?

Do you? Well – if you really want to know – yes. The way she'd been acting lately, she'd be quite capable of doing that.

A strange and difficult woman, that's what she was. Mind you, she used not to be, but there's no doubt at all that right now she was as strange and difficult as they come. Especially at night.

Yes, at night. That was the worst time of all – the night.

Why, when he put out his right hand in bed at night, could his fingers not feel what they were touching? He had knocked over the lamp and she had woken up and then sat up suddenly while he was feeling for it on the floor in the dark.

'What are you doing now?'

'I knocked over the lamp. I'm sorry.'

'Oh Christ,' she had said. 'Yesterday it was the glass of water. What's the *matter* with you?'

Once, the doctor had stroked the back of his hand with a feather, and he hadn't been able to feel that either. But he had felt it when the man scratched him with a pin.

'Shut your eyes. No – you mustn't look. Shut them tight. Now tell me if this is hot or cold.'

'Hot.'

'And this?'

'Cold.'

'And this?'

'Cold. I mean hot. Yes, it's hot, isn't it?'

'That's right,' the doctor had said. 'You did very well.'

But that was a year ago.

Why were the switches on the walls, just lately, always a few inches away from the well-remembered places when he felt for them in the dark?

Don't think about it, he told himself. The only thing is not to think about it.

And while we're on the subject, why did the walls of the living-room take on a slightly different shade of colour each day?

Green and blue-green and blue; and sometimes – sometimes slowly swimming like colours seen through the heat-haze of a brazier.

One by one, neatly, like index cards out of a machine, the little questions dropped.

Whose face appeared for one second at the window during dinner? Whose eyes?

'What are you staring at?'

'Nothing,' he had answered. 'But it would be nice if we could draw the curtains, don't you think?'

'Robert, what were you staring at?'

'Nothing.'

'Why were you staring at the window like that?'

'It would be nice if we could draw the curtains, don't you think?' he had answered.

He was going past the place where he had heard the horse in the field and now he could hear it again; the breathing, the soft hoof thuds, and the crunch of grass-cropping that was like the noise of a man munching celery.

'Hello old horse,' he said, calling loud into the darkness. 'Hello old horse over there.'

Suddenly he heard the footsteps behind him, slow, long-striding footsteps close behind, and he stopped. The footsteps stopped. He turned around, searching the darkness.

'Good evening,' he said, 'You here again?'

In the quiet that followed he could hear the wind moving the leaves in the hedge.

'Are you going my way?' he said.

Then he turned and walked on, the dog still pulling ahead, and the footsteps started after him again, but more softly now, as though the person were walking on toes.

He stopped and turned again.

'I can't see you,' he said, 'because it's so dark. Are you someone I know?'

Again the silence, and the cool summer wind on his cheeks, and the dog tugging on the leash to get home.

'All right,' he called. 'You don't have to answer if you don't want to. But remember I know you're there.'

Someone trying to be clever.

Far away in the night, over to the west and very high, he heard the faint hum of an aeroplane. He stopped again, head up, listening.

'Miles away,' he said. 'Won't come near here.'

But why, when one of them flew over the house, did everything inside him come to a stop, and his talking and what he was doing, while he sat or stood in a sort of paralysis waiting for the whistle-shriek of the bomb. That one after dinner this evening.

'Why did you duck like that?'she asked.

'Duck?'

'Why did you duck? What are you ducking for?'

'Duck?' he had said again. 'I don't know what you mean.'

'I'll say you don't,' she had answered, staring at him hard with those hard, blue-white eyes, the lids dropping slightly, as always when there was contempt. The drop of her eyelids was something beautiful to him, the half-closed eyes and the way the lids dropped and the eyes became hooded when her contempt was extreme.

Yesterday, lying in bed in the early morning, when the noise of gunfire was just beginning far away down the valley, he had reached out with his left hand and touched her body for a little comfort.

'What on earth are you doing?'

'Nothing, dear.'

'You woke me up.'

'I'm sorry.'

It would be a help if she would only let him lie closer to her in the early mornings when he began to hear the noise of gunfire.

He would soon be home now. Around the last bend of the lane he could see a light glowing pink through the curtain of the living-room window, and he hurried forward to the gate and through it and up the path to the front door, the dog still pulling ahead.

He stood on the porch, feeling around for the door-knob in the dark.

It was on the right when he went out. He distinctly remembered it being on the right-hand side when he shut the door half an hour ago and went out.

It couldn't be that she had changed *that* over too? Just to fox him? Taken a bag of tools and quickly changed it over to the other side while he was out walking the dog?

He moved his hand over to the left – and the moment the fingers touched the knob, something small but violent exploded inside his head and with it a surge of fury and outrage and fear. He opened the door, shut it quickly behind him and shouted 'Edna, are you there?'

There was no answer so he shouted again, and this time she heard him.

'What do you want now? You woke me up.'

'Come down here a moment, will you. I want to talk to you.'

'Oh for heaven's sake,' she answered. 'Be quiet and come on up.'

'Come here!' he shouted. 'Come here at once!'

'I'll be damned if I will. You come here.'

The man paused, head back, looking up the stairs into the dark of the second floor. He could see where the stair-rail curved to the left and went on up out of sight in the black towards the landing and if you went straight on across the landing you came to the bedroom, and it would be black in there too.

'Edna!' he shouted. 'Edna!'

'Oh go to hell.'

He began to move slowly up the stairs, treading quietly, touching the stair-rail for guidance, up and around the lefthand curve into the dark above. At the top he took an extra step that wasn't there; but he was ready for it and there was no noise. He paused awhile then, listening, and he wasn't sure, but he thought he could hear the guns starting up again far away down the valley, heavy stuff mostly, seventy-fives and maybe a couple of mortars somewhere in the background.

Across the landing now and through the open doorway – which was easy in the dark because he knew it so well – through on to the bedroom carpet that was thick and soft and pale grey although he could not feel or see it.

In the centre of the room he waited, listening for sounds. She had gone back to sleep and was breathing rather loud, making the slightest little whistle with the air between her teeth each time she exhaled. The curtain flapped gently against the open window, the alarm-clock tick-tick-ticked beside the bed.

Now that his eyes were becoming accustomed to the dark he could just make out the end of the bed, the white blanket tucked in under the mattress, the bulge of her feet under the bedclothes; and then, as though aware of the presence of the man in the room, the woman stirred. He heard her turn, and turn again. The sound of her breathing stopped. There was a succession of little movement-noises and once the bedsprings creaked, loud as a shout in the dark.

'Is that you, Robert?'

He made no move, no sound.

'Robert, are you there?'

The voice was strange and rather unpleasant to him.

'Robert!' She was wide awake now. 'Where are you?'

Where had he heard that voice before? It had a quality of stridence, dissonance, like two single high notes struck together hard in discord. Also there was an inability to pronounce the R of Robert. Who was it that used to say Wobert to him?

'Wobert,' she said again. 'What are you doing?'

Was it that nurse in the hospital, the tall one with fair hair? No, it was further back. Such an awful voice as that he ought to remember. Give him a little time and he would get the name.

At that moment he heard the snap of the switch of the bedside lamp and in the flood of light he saw the woman half-sitting up in bed, dressed in some sort of a pink nightdress. There was a surprised, wide-eyed expression on her face. Her cheeks and chin were oily with cold cream.

'You better put that thing down,' she was saying, 'before you cut yourself.'

'Where's Edna?' He was staring at her hard.

The woman, half-sitting up in bed, watched him carefully. He was standing at the foot of the bed, a huge, broad man, standing motionless, erect, with heels together, almost at attention, dressed in his dark-brown, woolly, heavy suit.

'Go on,' she ordered. 'Put it down.'

'Where's Edna?'

'What's the matter with you, Wobert?'

'There's nothing the matter with me. I'm just asking you where's my wife?'

The woman was easing herself up gradually into an erect sitting position and sliding her legs towards the edge of the bed. 'Well,' she said at length, the voice changing, the hard blue-white eyes secret and cunning, 'if you really want to know, Edna's gone. She left just now while you were out.'

'Where did she go?'

'She didn't say.'

'And who are you?'

'I'm just a friend of hers.'

'You don't have to shout at me,' he said. 'What's all the excitement?'

'I simply want you to know I'm not Edna.'

The man considered this a moment, then he said, 'How did you know my name?'

'Edna told me.'

Again he paused, studying her closely, still slightly puzzled, but much calmer now, his eyes calm, perhaps even a little amused the way they looked at her.

'I think I prefer Edna.'

In the silence that followed they neither of them moved. The woman was very tense, sitting up straight with her arms tense on either side of her and slightly bent at the elbows, the hands pressing palms downward on the mattress.

'I love Edna, you know. Did she ever tell you I love her?'

The woman didn't answer.

'I think she's a bitch. But it's funny thing I love her just the same.'

The woman was not looking at the man's face; she was watching his right hand.

'Awful cruel little bitch, Edna.'

And a long silence now, the man standing erect, motionless, the woman sitting motionless in the bed, and it was so quiet suddenly that through the open window they could hear the water in the millstream going over the dam far down the valley on the next farm.

Then the man again, speaking calmly, slowly, quite impersonally:

'As a matter of fact, I don't think she even likes me any more.'

The woman shifted closer to the edge of the bed. 'Put that knife down,' she said, 'before you cut yourself.'

'Don't shout, please. Can't you talk nicely?' Now, suddenly, the man leaned forward, staring intently into the woman's face, and he raised his eyebrows. 'That's strange,' he said. 'That's very strange.'

He took a step forward, his knees touching the bed.

'You look a bit like Edna yourself.'

'Edna's gone out. I told you that.'

He continued to stare at her and the woman kept quite still, the palms of her hands pressing deep into the mattress.

'Well,' he said. 'I wonder.'

'I told you Edna's gone out. I'm a friend of hers. My name is Mary.'

'My wife,' the man said, 'has a funny little brown mole just behind her left ear. You don't have that, do you?'

'I certainly don't.'

'Turn your head and let me look.'

'I told you I didn't have it.'

'Just the same, I'd like to make sure.'

The man came slowly around the end of the bed. 'Stay where you are,' he said. 'Please don't move.' And he came towards her slowly, watching her all the time, a little smile touching the corners of his mouth.

The woman waited until he was within reach, and then, with a quick right hand, so quick he never saw it coming, she smacked him hard across the front of the face. And when he sat down on the bed and began to cry, she took the knife from his hand and went swiftly out of the room, down the stairs to the hall, where the telephone was.

MY LADY LOVE, MY DOVE

It has been my habit for many years to take a nap after lunch. I settle myself in a chair in the living-room with a cushion behind my head and my feet up on a small square leather stool, and I read until I drop off.

On this Friday afternoon, I was in my chair and feeling as comfortable as ever with a book in my hands – an old favourite, Doubleday and Westwood's *The Genera of Diurnal Lepidoptera* – when my wife, who has never been a silent lady, began to talk to me from the sofa opposite. 'These two people,' she said, 'what time are they coming?'

I made no answer, so she repeated the question, louder this time.

I told her politely that I didn't know.

'I don't think I like them very much,' she said. 'Especially him.'

'No dear, all right.'

'Arthur. I said I don't think I like them very much.'

I lowered my book and looked across at her lying with her feet up on the sofa, flipping over the pages of some fashion magazine. 'We've only met them once,' I said.

'A dreadful man, really. Never stopped telling jokes, or stories, or something.'

'I'm sure you'll manage them very well, dear.'

'And she's pretty frightful, too. When do you think they'll arrive?'

Somewhere around six o'clock, I guessed.

'But don't *you* think they're awful?' she asked, pointing at me with her finger.

'Well ...'

'They're *too* awful, they really are.'

'We can hardly put them off now, Pamela.'

'They're absolutely the end,' she said.

'Then why did you ask them?' The question slipped out before I could stop myself and I regretted it at once, for it is a rule with me never to provoke my wife if I can help it. There was a pause, and I watched her face, waiting for the answer – the big white face that to me was something so strange and fascinating there were occasions when I could hardly bring myself to look away from it. In the evenings sometimes – working on her embroidery, or painting those small intricate flower pictures – the face would tighten and glimmer with a subtle inward strength that was beautiful beyond words, and I would sit and stare at it minute after minute while pretending to read. Even now, at this moment, with that compressed acid look, the frowning forehead, the petulant curl of the nose, I had to admit that there was a majestic quality about this woman, something splendid, almost stately; and so tall she was, far taller than I – although today, in her fifty-first year, I think one would have to call her big rather than tall.

'You know very well why I asked them,' she answered sharply. 'For bridge, that's all. They play an absolutely first-class game, and for a decent stake.' She glanced up and saw me watching her. 'Well,' she said, 'that's about the way you feel too, isn't it?'

'Well, of course, I ...'

'Don't be a fool, Arthur.'

'The only time I met them I must say they did seem quite nice.'

'So is the butcher.'

'Now Pamela, dear – please. We don't want any of that.'

'Listen,' she said, slapping down the magazine on her lap, 'you saw the sort of people they were as well as I did. A pair of stupid climbers who think they can go anywhere just because they play good bridge.'

'I'm sure you're right dear, but what I don't honestly understand is why–'

'I keep telling you – so that for once we can get a decent game. I'm sick and tired of playing with rabbits. But I really can't see why I should have these awful people in the house.'

'Of course not, my dear, but isn't it a little late now–'

'Arthur?'

'Yes?'

'Why for God's sake do you always argue with me. You *know* you disliked them as much as I did.'

'I really don't think you need worry, Pamela. After all, they seemed quite a nice well-mannered young couple.'

'Arthur, don't be pompous.' She was looking at me hard with those wide grey eyes of hers, and to avoid them – they sometimes made me quite uncomfortable – I got up and walked over to the french windows that led into the garden.

The big sloping lawn out in front of the house was newly mown, striped with pale and dark ribbons of green. On the far side, the two laburnums were in full flower at last, the long golden chains making a blaze of colour against the darker trees beyond. The roses were out too, and the scarlet begonias, and in the long herbaceous border all my lovely hybrid lupins, columbine, delphinium, sweet-william, and the huge, pale, scented iris. One of the gardeners was coming up the drive from his lunch. I could see the roof of his cottage through the trees, and beyond it to one side, the place where the drive went out through the iron gates on the Canterbury road.

My wife's house. Her garden. How beautiful it all was! How peaceful! Now, if only Pamela would try to be a little less solicitous of my welfare, less prone to coax me into doing things for my own good rather than for my own pleasure, then everything would be heaven. Mind you, I don't want to give the impression that I do not love her – I worship the very air she breathes – or that I can't manage her, or that I am not the captain of my ship. All I am trying to say is that she can be a trifle irritating at times, the way she carries on. For example, those little mannerisms of hers – I do wish she would drop them all, especially the way she has of pointing a finger at me to emphasize a phrase. You must remember that I am a man who is built rather small, and a gesture like this, when used to excess by a person like my wife, is apt to intimidate. I sometimes find it difficult to convince myself that she is not an overbearing woman.

'Arthur!' she called. 'Come here.'

'What?'

'I've just had a most marvellous idea. Come here.'

I turned and went over to where she was lying on the sofa.

'Look,' she said, 'do you want to have some fun?'

'What sort of fun?'

'With the Snapes?'

'Who are the Snapes?'

'Come on,' she said. 'Wake up. Henry and Sally Snape. Our week-end guests.'

'Well?'

'Now listen. I was lying here thinking how awful they really are ... the way they behave ... him with his jokes and her like a sort of love-crazed sparrow ...' She hesitated, smiling slyly, and for some reason, I got the impression she was about to say a shocking thing. 'Well – if that's the way they behave when they're in front of us, then what on earth must they be like when they're alone together?'

'Now wait a minute, Pamela –'

'Don't be an ass, Arthur. Let's have some fun – some real fun for once – tonight.' She had half raised herself up off the sofa, her face bright with a kind of sudden recklessness, the mouth slightly open, and she was looking at me with two round grey eyes, a spark dancing slowly in each.

'Why shouldn't we?'

'What do you want to do?'

'Why, it's obvious. Can't you see?'

'No, I can't.'

'All we've got to do is put a microphone in their room.' I admit I was expecting something pretty bad, but when she said this I was so shocked I didn't know what to answer.

'That's exactly what we'll do,' she said.

'Here!' I cried. 'No. Wait a minute. You can't do that.'

'Why not?'

'That's about the nastiest trick I ever heard of. It's like – why, it's like listening at keyholes, or reading letters, only far far worse. You don't mean this seriously, do you?'

'Of course I do.'

I knew how much she disliked being contradicted, but there were times when I felt it necessary to assert myself, even at considerable risk. 'Pamela,' I said, snapping the words out sharply, 'I forbid you to do it!'

She took her feet down from the sofa and sat up straight. 'What in God's name are you trying to pretend to be, Arthur? I simply don't understand you.'

'That shouldn't be too difficult.'

'Tommyrot! I've known you do lots of worse things than this before now.'

'Never!'

'Oh yes I have. What makes you suddenly think you're a so much nicer person than I am?'

'I've never done things like that.'

'All right, my boy,' she said, pointing her finger at me like a pistol. 'What about that time at the Milfords' last Christmas? Remember? You nearly laughed your head off and I had to put my hand over your mouth to stop them hearing us. What about that for one?'

'That was different,' I said. 'It wasn't our house. And they weren't our guests.'

'It doesn't make any difference at all.' She was sitting very upright, staring at me with those round grey eyes, and the chin was beginning to come up high in a peculiarly contemptuous manner. 'Don't be such a pompous hypocrite,' she said. 'What on earth's come over you?'

'I really think it's a pretty nasty thing, you know, Pamela. I honestly do.'

'But listen, Arthur. I'm a *nasty* person. And so are you – in a secret sort of way. That's why we get along together.'

'I never heard such nonsense.'

'Mind you, if you've suddenly decided to change your character completely, that's another story.'

'You've got to stop talking this way, Pamela.'

'You see,' she said, 'if you really *have* decided to reform, then what on earth am I going to do?'

'You don't know what you're saying.'

'Arthur, how could a nice person like you want to associate with a stinker?'

I sat myself down slowly in the chair opposite her, and she was watching me all the time. You understand, she was a big woman, with a big white face, and when she looked at me hard, as she was doing now, I became – how shall I say it – surrounded, almost enveloped by her, as though she were a great tub of cream and I had fallen in.

'You don't honestly want to do this microphone thing, do you?'

'But of course I do. It's time we had a bit of fun around here. Come on, Arthur. Don't be so stuffy.'

'It's not right, Pamela.'

'It's just as right' – up came the finger again – 'just as right as when you found those letters of Mary Probert's in her purse and you read them through from beginning to end.'

'We should never have done that.'

'*We!*'

'You read them afterwards, Pamela.'

'It didn't harm anyone at all. You said so yourself at the time. And this one's no worse.'

'How would *you* like it if someone did it to *you*?'

'How could I *mind* if I didn't know it was being done? Come on, Arthur. Don't be so flabby.'

'I'll have to think about it.'

'Maybe the great radio engineer doesn't know how to connect the mike to the speaker?'

'That's the easiest part.'

'Well, go on then. Go on and do it.'

'I'll think about it and let you know later.'

'There's no time for that. They might arrive any moment.'

'Then I won't do it. I'm not going to be caught red-handed.'

'If they come before you're through, I'll simply keep them down here. No danger. What's the time, anyway?'

It was nearly three o'clock.

'They're driving down from London,' she said, 'and they certainly won't leave till after lunch. That gives you plenty of time.'

'Which room are you putting them in?'

'The big yellow room at the end of the corridor. That's not too far away, is it?'

'I suppose it could be done.'

'And by the by,' she said, 'where are you going to have the speaker?'

'I haven't said I'm going to do it yet.'

'My God!' she cried, 'I'd like to see someone try and stop you now. You ought to see your face. It's all pink and excited at the very prospect. Put the speaker in our bedroom, why not? But go on – and hurry.'

I hesitated. It was something I made a point of doing whenever she tried to order me about, instead of asking nicely. 'I don't like it, Pamela.'

She didn't say any more after that; she just sat there, absolutely still, watching me, a resigned, waiting expression on her face, as though she were in a long queue. This, I knew from experience, was a danger signal. She was like one of those bomb things with the pin pulled out, and it was only a matter of time before – bang! and she would explode. In the silence that followed, I could almost hear her ticking.

So I got up quietly and went out to the workshop and collected a mike and a hundred and fifty feet of wire. Now that I was away from her, I am ashamed to admit that I began to feel a bit of excitement myself, a tiny warm prickling sensation under the skin, near the tips of my fingers. It was nothing much, mind you – really nothing at all. Good heavens, I experience the same thing every morning of my life when I open the paper to check the closing prices on two or three of my wife's larger stockholdings. So I wasn't going to get carried away by a silly joke like this. At the same time, I couldn't help being amused.

I took the stairs two at a time and entered the yellow room at the end of the passage. It had the clean, unlived-in appearance of all guest rooms, with its twin beds, yellow satin bedspreads, pale-yellow walls, and golden-coloured curtains. I began to look around for a good place to hide the mike. This was the most important part of all, for whatever happened, it must not be discovered. I thought first of the basket of logs by the fireplace. Put it under the logs. No not safe enough. Behind the radiator? On top of the wardrobe? Under the desk? None of these seemed very professional to me. All might be subject to chance inspection because of a dropped collar stud or something like that. Finally, with considerable cunning, I decided to put it inside of the springing of the sofa. The sofa was against the wall, near the edge of the carpet, and my lead wire could go straight under the carpet over to the door.

I tipped up the sofa and slit the material underneath. Then I tied the microphone securely up among the springs, making sure that it faced the room. After that, I led the wire under the carpet to the door. I was calm and cautious in everything I did. Where the wire had to emerge from under the carpet and pass out of the door, I made a little groove in the wood so that it was almost invisible.

All this, of course, took time, and when I suddenly heard the crunch of wheels on the gravel of the drive outside, and then the slamming of car doors and the voices of our guests, I was still only half-way down the corridor, tacking the wire along the skirting. I stopped and straightened up, hammer in hand, and I must confess that I felt afraid. You have no idea how unnerving that noise was to me. I experienced the same sudden stomachy feeling of fright as when a bomb once dropped the other side of the village during the war, one afternoon, while I was working quietly in the library with my butterflies.

Don't worry, I told myself. Pamela will take care of these people. She won't let them come up here.

Rather frantically, I set about finishing the job, and soon I had the wire tacked all along the corridor and through into our bedroom. Here, concealment was not so important, although I still did not permit myself to get careless because of the servants. So I laid the wire under the carpet and brought it up unobtrusively into the back of the radio. Making the final connections was an elementary technical matter and took me no time at all.

Well – I had done it. I stepped back and glanced at the little radio. Somehow, now, it looked different – no longer a silly box for making noises but an evil little creature that crouched on the table top with a part of its own body reaching out secretly into a forbidden place far away. I switched it on. It hummed faintly but made no other sound. I took my bedside clock, which had a loud tick, and carried it along to the yellow room and placed it on the floor by the sofa. When I returned, sure enough the radio creature was ticking away as loudly as if the clock were in the room – even louder.

I fetched back the clock. Then I tidied myself up in the bathroom, returned my tools to the workshop, and prepared to meet the guests. But first, to compose myself, and so that I would not have to appear in front of them with the blood, as it were, still wet on my hands, I spent five minutes in the library with my collection. I concentrated on a tray of the lovely *Vanessa cardui* – the 'painted lady' – and made a few notes for a paper I was preparing entitled 'The Relation between Colour Pattern and Framework of Wings', which I intended to read at the next meeting of our society in Canterbury. In this way I soon regained my normal grave, attentive manner.

When I entered the living-room, our two guests, whose names I could never remember, were seated on the sofa. My wife was mixing drinks.

'Oh, *there* you are, Arthur,' she said. 'Where *have* you been?'

I thought this was an unnecessary remark. 'I'm so sorry.' I said to the guests as we shook hands. 'I was busy and forgot the time.'

'We all know what *you've* been doing,' the girl said, smiling wisely. 'But we'll forgive him, won't we, dearest?'

'I think we should,' the husband answered.

I had a frightful, fantastic vision of my wife telling them, amidst roars of laughter, precisely what I had been doing upstairs. She *couldn't* – she *couldn't* have done that! I looked round at her and she too was smiling as she measured out the gin.

'I'm sorry we disturbed you,' the girl said.

I decided that if this was going to be a joke then I'd better join in quickly, so I forced myself to smile with her.

'You must let us see it,' the girl continued.

'See what?'

'Your collection. Your wife says that they are absolutely beautiful.'

I lowered myself slowly into a chair and relaxed. It was ridiculous to be so nervous and jumpy. 'Are you interested in butterflies?' I asked her.

'I'd love to see yours, Mr Beauchamp.'

The Martinis were distributed and we settled down to a couple of hours of talk and drink before dinner. It was from then on that I began to form the impression that our guests were a charming couple. My wife, coming from a titled family, is apt to be conscious of her class and breeding, and is often hasty in her judgement of strangers who are friendly towards her – particularly tall men. She is frequently right, but in this case I felt that she might be making a mistake. As a rule, I myself do not like tall men either; they are apt to be supercilious and omniscient. But Henry Snape – my wife had whispered his name – struck me as being an amiable simple young man with good manners whose main preoccupation, very properly, was Mrs Snape. He was handsome in a long-faced, horsy sort of way, with dark-brown eyes that seemed to be gentle and sympathetic. I envied him his fine mop of black hair, and caught myself wondering what lotion he used to keep it looking so healthy. He did tell us one or two jokes, but they were on a high level and no one could have objected.

'At school,' he said, 'they used to call me Scervix. Do you know why?'

'I haven't the least idea,' my wife answered.

'Because cervix is Latin for nape.'

This was rather deep and it took me a while to work out.

'What school was that, Mr Snape?' my wife asked.

'Eton,' he said, and my wife gave a quick little nod of approval. Now she will talk to him, I thought, so I turned my attention to the other one, Sally Snape. She was an attractive girl with a bosom. Had I met her fifteen years earlier I might well have got myself into some sort of trouble. As it was, I had a pleasant enough time telling her all about my beautiful butterflies. I was observing her closely as I talked, and after a while I began to get the impression that she was not, in fact, quite so merry and smiling a girl as I had been led to believe at first. She seemed to be coiled in herself, as though with a secret she was jealously guarding. The deep-blue eyes moved too quickly about the room, never settling or resting on one thing for more than a moment; and over all her face, though so faint that they might not even have been there, those small downward lines of sorrow.

'I'm so looking forward to our game of bridge,' I said, finally changing the subject.

'Us too,' she answered. 'You know we play almost every night, we love it so.'

'You are extremely expert, both of you. How did you get to be so good?'

'It's practice,' she said. 'That's all. Practice, practice, practice.'

'Have you played in any championships?'

'Not yet, but Henry wants very much for us to do that. It's hard work, you know, to reach that standard. Terribly hard work.' Was there not here, I wondered, a hint of resignation in her voice? Yes, that was probably it; he was pushing her too hard, making her take it too seriously, and the poor girl was tired of it all.

At eight o'clock, without changing, we moved in to dinner. The meal went well, with Henry Snape telling us some very droll stories. He also praised my Richebourg '34 in a most knowledgeble fashion, which pleased me greatly. By the time coffee came, I realized that I had grown to like these two youngsters immensely, and as a result I began to feel uncomfortable about this microphone business. It would have been all right if they had been horrid people, but to play this trick on two such charming young persons as these filled me with a strong sense of guilt. Don't misunderstand me. I was not getting cold feet. It didn't seem necessary to stop the operation. But I refused to relish the prospect openly as my wife seemed now to be doing, with covert smiles and winks and secret little noddings of the head.

Around nine-thirty, feeling comfortable and well fed, we returned to the large living-room to start our bridge. We were playing for a fair stake – ten shillings a hundred – so we decided not to split families, and I partnered my wife the whole time. We all four of us took the game seriously, which is the only way to take it, and we played silently, intently, hardly speaking at all except to bid. It was not the money we played for. Heaven knows, my wife had enough of that, and so apparently did the Snapes. But among experts it is almost traditional that they play for a reasonable stake.

That night the cards were evenly divided, but for once my wife played badly, so we got the worst of it. I could see that she wasn't concentrating fully, and as we came along towards midnight she began not even to care. She kept glancing up at me with those large grey eyes of hers, the eyebrows raised, the nostrils curiously open, a little gloating smile around the corner of her mouth.

Our opponents played a fine game. Their bidding was masterly, and all through the evening they made only one mistake. That was when the girl badly overestimated her partner's hand and bid six spades. I doubled and they went three down, vulnerable, which cost them eight hundred points. It was just a momentary lapse, but I remember that Sally Snape was very put out by it, even though her husband forgave her at once, kissing her hand across the table and telling her not to worry.

Around twelve-thirty my wife announced that she wanted to go to bed.

'Just one more rubber?' Henry Snape said.

'No, Mr Snape. I'm tired tonight. Arthur's tired, too. I can see it. Let's all go to bed.'

She herded us out of the room and we went upstairs, the four of us together. On the way up, there was the usual talk about breakfast and what they wanted and how they were to call the maid. 'I think you'll like your room,' my wife said. 'It has a view right across the valley, and the sun comes to you in the morning around ten o'clock.'

We were in the passage now, standing outside our own bedroom door, and I could see the wire I had put down that afternoon and how it ran along the top of the skirting down to their room. Although it was nearly the same colour as the paint, it looked very conspicuous to me. 'Sleep well,' my wife said. 'Sleep well, Mrs Snape. Good night, Mr Snape.' I followed her into our room and shut the door.

'Quick!' she cried. 'Turn it on!' My wife was always like that, frightened that she was going to miss something. She had a reputation, when she went hunting – I never go myself – of always being right up with the hounds whatever the cost to herself or her horse for fear that she might miss a kill. I could see she had no intention of missing this one.

The little radio warmed up just in time to catch the noise of their door opening and closing again.

'There!' my wife said. 'They've gone in.' She was standing in the centre of the room in her blue dress, her hands clasped before her, her head craned forward, intently listening, and the whole of the big white face seemed somehow to have gathered itself together, tight like a wineskin.

Almost at once the voice of Henry Snape came out of the radio, strong and clear. 'You're just a goddam little fool,' he was saying, and this voice was so different from the one I remembered, so harsh and unpleasant, it made me jump. 'The whole bloody evening wasted! Eight hundred points – that's eight pounds between us!'

'I got mixed up,' the girl answered. 'I won't do it again, I promise.'

'What's *this*?' my wife said. 'What's going on?' Her mouth was wide open now, the eyebrows stretched up high, and she came quickly over to the radio and leaned forward, ear to the speaker. I must say I felt rather excited myself.

'I promise, I promise I won't do it again,' the girl was saying.

'We're not taking any chances,' the man answered grimly. 'We're going to have another practice right now.'

'Oh no, please! I couldn't stand it!'

'Look,' the man said, 'all the way out here to take money off this rich bitch and you have to go and mess it up.'

My wife's turn to jump.

'The second time this week,' he went on.

'I promise I won't do it again.'

'Sit down. I'll sing them out and you answer.'

'No, Henry, *please*! Not all five hundred of them. It'll take three hours.'

'All right, then. We'll leave out the finger positions. I think you're sure of those. We'll just do the basic bids showing honour tricks.'

'Oh, Henry, must we? I'm so tired.'

'It's absolutely essential you get them perfect,' he said. 'We have a game every day next week, you know that. And we've got to eat.'

'What is this?' my wife whispered. 'What on earth is it?'

'Shhh!' I said. 'Listen!'

'All right,' the man's voice was saying. 'Now we'll start from the beginning. Ready?'

'Oh Henry, *please*!' She sounded very near to tears.

'Come on, Sally. Pull yourself together.'

Then, in a quite different voice, the one we had been used to hearing in the living-room, Henry Snape said, '*One* club.' I noticed that there was a curious lilting emphasis on the word 'one', the first part of the word drawn out long.

'Ace queen of clubs,' the girl replied wearily. 'King jack of spades. No hearts, and ace jack of diamonds.'

'And how many cards to each suit? Watch my finger positions carefully.'

'You said we could miss those.'

'Well – if you're quite sure you know them?'

'Yes, I know them.'

A pause, then 'A *club*.'

'King jack of clubs,' the girl recited. 'Ace of spades. Queen jack of hearts, and ace queen of diamonds.'

Another pause, then 'I'll say *one* club.'

'Ace king of clubs . . .'

'My heavens alive!' I cried. 'It's a bidding code! They show every card in the hand!'

'Arthur, it couldn't be!'

'It's like those men who go into the audience and borrow something from you and there's a girl blindfold on the stage, and from the way he phrases the question she can tell him exactly what it is – even a railway ticket, and what station it's from.'

'It's impossible!'

'Not at all. But it's tremendous hard work to learn. Listen to them.'

'I'll go *one heart*,' the man's voice was saying.

'King queen ten of hearts. Ace jack of spades. No diamonds. Queen jack of clubs . . .'

'And you see,' I said, 'he tells her the *number* of cards he has in each suit by the position of his fingers.'

'How?'

'I don't know. You heard him saying about it.'

'My *God*, Arthur! Are you sure that's what they're doing?'

'I'm afraid so.' I watched her as she walked quickly over to the side of the bed to fetch a cigarette. She lit it with her back to me and then swung round, blowing the smoke up at the ceiling in a thin stream. I knew we were going to have to do something about this, but I wasn't quite sure what because we couldn't possibly accuse them without revealing the source of our information. I waited for my wife's decision.

'Why, Arthur,' she said slowly, blowing out clouds of smoke. 'Why, this is a *mar-vellous* idea. D'you think *we* could learn to do it?'

'What!'

'Of course. Why not?'

'Here! No! Wait a minute, Pamela . . .' but she came swiftly across the room, right up close to me where I was standing, and she dropped her head and looked down at me – the old look of a smile that wasn't a smile, at the corners of the mouth, and the curl of the nose, and the big full grey eyes staring at me with their bright black centres, and then they were grey, and all the rest was white flecked with hundreds of tiny red veins – and when she looked at me like this, hard and close, I swear to you it made me feel as though I were drowning.

'Yes,' she said. 'Why not?'

'But Pamela . . . Good heavens . . . No . . . After all . . .'

'Arthur, I do wish you wouldn't *argue* with me all the time. That's exactly what we'll do. Now, go fetch a deck of cards; we'll start right away.'

DIP IN THE POOL

On the morning of the third day, the sea calmed. Even the most delicate passengers – those who had not been seen around the ship since sailing time – emerged from their cabins and crept on to the sun deck where the deck steward gave them chairs and tucked rugs around their legs and left them lying in rows, their faces upturned to the pale, almost heatless January sun.

It had been moderately rough the first two days, and this sudden calm and the sense of comfort that it brought created a more genial atmosphere over the whole ship. By the time evening came, the passengers, with twelve hours of good weather behind them, were beginning to feel confident, and at eight o'clock that night the main dining-room was filled with people eating and drinking with the assured, complacent air of seasoned sailors.

The meal was not half over when the passengers became aware, by the slight friction between their bodies and the seats of their chairs, that the big ship had actually started rolling again. It was very gentle at first, just a slow, lazy leaning to one side, then to the other, but it was enough to cause a subtle, immediate change of mood over the whole room. A few of the passengers glanced up from their food, hesitating, waiting, almost listening for the next roll, smiling nervously, little secret glimmers of apprehension in their eyes. Some were completely unruffled, some were openly smug, a number of the smug ones making jokes about food and weather in order to torture the few who were beginning to suffer. The movement of the ship then became rapidly more and more violent, and only five or six minutes after the first roll had been noticed, she was swinging heavily from side to side, the passengers bracing themselves in their chairs, leaning against the pull as in a car cornering.

At last the really bad roll came, and Mr William Botibol, sitting at the purser's table, saw his plate of poached turbot with hollandaise sauce sliding suddenly away from under his fork. There was a flutter of excitement, everybody reaching for plates and wineglasses. Mrs Renshaw, seated at the purser's right, gave a little scream and clutched that gentleman's arm.

'Going to be a dirty night,' the purser said, looking at Mrs Renshaw.

'I think it's blowing up for a very dirty night.' There was just the faintest suggestion of relish in the way he said it.

A steward came hurrying up and sprinkled water on the table cloth between the plates. The excitement subsided. Most of the passengers continued with their meal. A small number, including Mrs Renshaw, got carefully to their feet and threaded their ways with a kind of concealed haste between the tables and through the doorway.

'Well,' the purser said, 'there she goes.' He glanced around with approval at the remainder of his flock who were sitting quiet, looking complacent, their faces reflecting openly that extraordinary pride that travellers seem to take in being recognized as 'good sailors'.

When the eating was finished and the coffee had been served, Mr Botibol, who had been unusually grave and thoughtful since the rolling started, suddenly stood up and carried his cup of coffee around to Mrs Renshaw's vacant place, next to the purser. He seated himself in her chair, then immediately leaned over and began to whisper urgently in the purser's ear. 'Excuse me,' he said, 'but could you tell me something, please?'

The purser, small and fat and red, bent forward to listen. 'What's the trouble, Mr Botibol?'

'What I want to know is this.' The man's face was anxious and the purser was watching it. 'What I want to know is will the captain already have made his estimate on the day's run – you know, for the auction pool? I mean before it began to get rough like this?'

The purser, who had prepared himself to receive a personal confidence, smiled and leaned back in his seat to relax his full belly. 'I should say so – yes,' he answered. He didn't bother to whisper his reply, although automatically he lowered his voice, as one does when answering a whisperer.

'About how long ago do you think he did it?'

'Some time this afternoon. He usually does it in the afternoon.'

'About what time?'

'Oh, I don't know. Around four o'clock I should guess.'

'Now tell me another thing. How does the captain decide which number it shall be? Does he take a lot of trouble over that?'

The purser looked at the anxious frowning face of Mr Botibol and he smiled, knowing quite well what the man was driving at. 'Well, you see, the captain has a little conference with the navigating officer, and they study the weather and a lot of other things, and then they make their estimate.'

Mr Botibol nodded, pondering this answer for a moment. Then he said, 'Do you think the captain knew there was bad weather coming today?'

'I couldn't tell you,' the purser replied. He was looking into the small black eyes of the other man, seeing the two single little sparks of excitement dancing in their centres. 'I really couldn't tell you, Mr Botibol. I wouldn't know.'

'If this gets any worse it might be worth buying some of the low numbers. What do you think?' The whispering was more urgent, more anxious now.

'Perhaps it will,' the purser said. 'I doubt whether the old man allowed for a really rough night. It was pretty calm this afternoon when he made his estimate.'

The others at the table had become silent and were trying to hear, watching the purser with that intent, half-cocked, listening look that you can see also at the race track when they are trying to overhear a trainer talking about his chance: the slightly open lips, the upstretched eyebrows, the head forward and cocked a little to one side – that desperately straining, half-hypnotized, listening look that comes to all of them when they are hearing something straight from the horse's mouth.

'Now suppose *you* were allowed to buy a number, which one would *you* choose today?' Mr Botibol whispered.

'I don't know what the range is yet,' the purser patiently answered. 'They don't announce the range till the auction starts after dinner. And I'm really not very good at it anyway. I'm only the purser, you know.'

At that point Mr Botibol stood up. 'Excuse me, all,' he said, and he walked carefully away over the swaying floor between the other tables, and twice he had to catch hold of the back of a chair to steady himself against the ship's roll.

'The sun deck, please,' he said to the elevator man.

The wind caught him full in the face as he stepped out on to the open deck. He staggered and grabbed hold of the rail and held on tight with both hands, and he stood there looking out over the darkening sea where the great waves were welling up high and white horses were riding against the wind with plumes of spray behind them as they went.

'Pretty bad out there, wasn't it, sir?' the elevator man said on the way down.

Mr Botibol was combing his hair back into place with a small red comb. 'Do you think we've slackened speed at all on account of the weather?' he asked.

'Oh my word yes, sir. We slackened off considerable since this started. You got to slacken off speed in weather like this or you'll be throwing the passengers all over the ship.'

Down in the smoking-room people were already gathering for the auction. They were grouping themselves politely around the various tables, the men a little stiff in their dinner jackets, a little pink and overshaved and stiff beside their cool white-armed women. Mr Botibol took a chair close to the auctioneer's table. He crossed his legs, folded his arms, and settled himself in his seat with the rather desperate air of a man who has made a tremendous decision and refuses to be frightened.

The pool, he was telling himself, would probably be around seven thousand dollars. That was almost exactly what it had been the last two days with the numbers selling for between three and four hundred apiece. Being a British ship they did it in pounds, but he liked to do his thinking in his own currency. Seven thousand dollars was plenty of money. My goodness, yes! And what he would do he would get them to pay him in hundred-dollar bills and he would take it ashore in the inside pocket of his jacket. No problem there. And right away, yes right away, he would buy a Lincoln convertible. He would pick it up on the way from the ship and drive it home just for the pleasure of seeing Ethel's face when she came out the front door and looked at it. Wouldn't that be something, to see Ethel's face when he glided up to the door in a brand-new pale-green Lincoln convertible! Hello, Ethel, honey, he would say, speaking very casual. I just thought I'd get you a little present. I saw it in the window as I went by, so I thought of you and how you were always wanting one. You like it, honey? he would say. You like the colour? And then he would watch her face.

The auctioneer was standing up behind his table now. 'Ladies and gentlemen!' he shouted. 'The captain has estimated the day's run, ending midday tomorrow, at five hundred and fifteen miles. As usual we will take the ten numbers on either side of it to make up the range. That makes it five hundred and five to five hundred and twenty-five. And of course for those who think the true figure will be still farther away, there'll be "low field" and "high field" sold separately as well. Now, we'll draw the first numbers out of the hat ... here we are ... five hundred and twelve?'

The room became quiet. The people sat still in their chairs, all eyes watching the auctioneer. There was a certain tension in the air, and as the bids got higher, the tension grew. This wasn't a game or a joke; you could be sure of that by the way one man wold look across at another who had raised his bid – smiling perhaps, but only the lips smiling, the eyes bright and absolutely cold.

Number five hundred and twelve was knocked down for one hundred and ten pounds. The next three or four numbers fetched roughly the same amount.

The ship was rolling heavily, and each time she went over, the wooden panelling on the walls creaked as if it were going to split. The passengers held on to the arms of their chairs, concentrating upon the auction.

'Low field!' the auctioneer called out. 'The next number is low field.'

Mr Botibol sat up very straight and tense. He would wait, he had decided, until the others had finished bidding, then he would jump in and make the last bid. He had figured that there must be at least five hundred dollars in his account at the bank at home, probably nearer six. That was about two hundred pounds – over two hundred. This ticket wouldn't fetch more than that.

'As you all know,' the auctioneer was saying, 'low field covers every number *below* the smallest number in the range, in this case every number below five hundred and five. So, if you think this ship is going to cover less than five hundred and five miles in the twenty-four hours ending at noon tomorrow, you better get in and buy this number. So what am I bid?'

It went clear up to one hundred and thirty pounds. Others besides Mr Botibol seemed to have noticed that the weather was rough. One hundred and forty ... fifty ... There it stopped. The auctioneer raised his hammer.

'Going at one hundred and fifty ...'

'Sixty!' Mr Botibol called, and every face in the room turned and looked at him.

'Seventy!'

'Eighty!' Mr Botibol called.

'Ninety!'

'Two hundred!' Mr Botibol called. He wasn't stopping now – not for anyone.

There was a pause.

'Any advance on two hundred pounds?'

Sit still, he told himself. Sit absolutely still and don't look up. It's unlucky to look up. Hold your breath. No one's going to bid you up so long as you hold your breath.

'Going for two hundred pounds ...' The auctioneer had a pink bald head and there were little beads of sweat sparkling on top of it. 'Going ...' Mr Botibol held his breath. 'Going ... Gone!' The man banged the hammer on the table. Mr Botibol wrote out a cheque and handed it to the auctioneer's assistant, then he settled back in his chair to wait for the finish. He did not want to go to bed before he knew how much there was in the pool.

They added it up after the last number had been sold and it came to twenty-one hundred-odd pounds. That was around six thousand dollars. Ninety per cent to go to the winner, ten per cent to seamen's charities. Ninety per cent of six thousand was five thousand four hundred. Well – that was enough. He could buy the Lincoln convertible and there would be something left over, too. With this gratifying thought he went off, happy and excited, to his cabin.

When Mr Botibol awoke the next morning he lay quite still for several minutes with his eyes shut, listening for the sound of the gale, waiting for the roll of the ship. There was no sound of any gale and the ship was not rolling. He jumped up and peered out of the porthole. The sea – Oh Jesus God – was smooth as glass, the great ship was moving through it fast, obviously making up for time lost during the night. Mr Botibol turned away and sat slowly down on the edge of his bunk. A fine electricity of fear was beginning to prickle under the skin of his stomach. He hadn't a hope now. One of the higher numbers was certain to win it after this.

'Oh, my God,' he said aloud. 'What shall I do?'

What, for example, would Ethel say? It was simply not possible to tell her that he had spent almost all of their two years' savings on a ticket in the ship's pool. Nor was it possible to keep the matter secret. To do that he would have to tell her to stop drawing cheques. And what about the monthly instalments on the television set and the *Encyclopaedia Britannica*? Already he could see the anger and contempt in the woman's eyes, the blue becoming grey and the eyes themselves narrowing as they always did when there was anger in them.

'Oh, my God. What *shall* I do?'

There was no point in pretending that he had the slightest chance now – not unless the goddam ship started to go backwards. They'd have to put her in reverse and go full speed astern and keep right on going if he was to have any chance of winning it now. Well, maybe he should ask the captain to do just that. Offer him ten per cent of the profits. Offer him more if he wanted it. Mr Botibol started to giggle. Then very suddenly he stopped, his eyes and mouth both opening wide in a kind of shocked surprise. For it was at this moment that the idea came. It hit him hard and quick, and he jumped up from his bed, terribly excited, ran over to the porthole and looked out again. Well, he thought, why not? Why ever not? The sea was calm and he wouldn't have any trouble keeping afloat until they picked him up. He had a vague feeling that someone had done this thing before, but that didn't prevent him from doing it again. The ship would have to stop and lower a boat, and the boat would have to go back maybe half a mile to get him, and then it would have to return to the ship, the whole thing. An hour was about thirty miles. It would knock thirty miles off the day's run. That would do it. 'Low field' would be sure to win it then. Just so long as he made certain someone saw him falling over; but that would be simple to arrange. And he'd better wear light clothes, something easy to swim in. Sports clothes, that was it. He would dress as though he were going up to play some deck tennis – just a shirt and a pair of shorts and tennis-shoes. And leave his watch behind. What was the time? Nine-fifteen. The sooner the better, then. Do it now and get it over with. Have to do it soon, because the time limit was midday.

Mr Botibol was both frightened and excited when he stepped out on to the sun deck in his sports clothes. His small body was wide at the hips, tapering upward to extremely narrow sloping shoulders, so that it resembled, in shape at any rate, a bollard. His white skinny legs were covered with black hairs, and he came cautiously out on deck, treading softly in his tennis shoes. Nervously he looked around him. There was only one other person in sight, an elderly woman with very thick ankles and immense buttocks who was leaning over tie rail staring at the sea. She was wearing a coat of Persian lamb and the collar was turned up so Mr Botibol couldn't see her face.

He stood still, examining her carefully from a distance. Yes, he told himself, she would probably do. She would probably give the alarm just as quickly as anyone else. But wait one minute, take your time, William Botibol, take your time. Remember what you told yourself a few minutes ago in the cabin when you were changing? You remember that?

The thought of leaping off a ship into the ocean a thousand miles from the nearest land had made Mr Botibol – a cautious man at the best of times – unusually advertent. He was by no means satisfied yet that this woman he saw before him was *absolutely certain* to give the alarm when he made his jump. In his opinion there were two possible reasons why she might fail him. Firstly, she might be deaf and blind. It was not very probable, but on the other hand it *might* be so, and why take a chance? All he had to do was check it by talking to her for a moment beforehand. Secondly – and this will demonstrate how suspicious the mind of a man can become when it is working through self-preservation and fear – secondly, it had occurred to him that the woman might herself be the owner of one of the high numbers in the pool and as such would have a sound financial reason for not wishing to stop the ship. Mr Botibol recalled that people had killed their fellows for far less than six thousand dollars. It was happening every day in the newspapers. So why take a chance on that either? Check on it first. Be sure of your facts. Find out about it by a little polite conversation. Then, provided that the woman appeared also to be a pleasant, kindly human being, the thing was a cinch and he could leap overboard with a light heart.

Mr Botibol advanced casually towards the woman and took up a position beside her, leaning on the rail. 'Hullo,' he said pleasantly.

She turned and smiled at him, a surprisingly lovely, almost a beautiful smile, although the face itself was very plain. 'Hullo,' she answered him.

Check, Mr Botibol told himself, on the first question. She is neither blind nor deaf. 'Tell me,' he said, coming straight to the point, 'what did you think of the auction last night?'

'Auction?' she asked, frowning. 'Auction? What auction?'

'You know, that silly old thing they have in the lounge after dinner, selling numbers on the ship's daily run. I just wondered what you thought about it.'

She shook her head, and again she smiled, a sweet and pleasant smile that had in it perhaps the trace of an apology. 'I'm very lazy,' she said. 'I always go to bed early. I have my dinner in bed. It's so restful to have dinner in bed.'

Mr Botibol smiled back at her and began to edge away. 'Got to go and get my exercise now,' he said. 'Never miss my exercise in the morning. It was nice seeing you. Very nice seeing you . . .' He retreated about ten paces, and the woman let him go without looking around.

Everything was now in order. The sea was calm, he was lightly dressed for swimming, there were almost certainly no man-eating sharks in this part of the Atlantic, and there was this pleasant kindly old woman to give the alarm. It was a question now only of whether the ship would be delayed long enough to swing the balance in his favour. Almost certainly it would. In any event, he could do a little to help in that direction himself. He could make a few difficulties about getting hauled up into the lifeboat. Swim around a bit, back away from them surreptitiously as they tried to come up close to fish him out. Every minute, every second gained would help him win. He began to move forward again to the rail, but now a new fear assailed him. Would he get caught in the propeller? He had heard about that happening to persons falling off the sides of big ships. But then, he wasn't going to fall, he was going to jump, and that was a very different thing. Provided he jumped out far enough he would be sure to clear the propeller.

Mr Botibol advanced slowly to a position at the rail about twenty yards away from the woman. She wasn't looking at him now. So much the better. He didn't want her watching him as he jumped off. So long as no one was watching he would be able to say afterwards that he had slipped and fallen by accident. He peered over the side of the ship. It was a long, long drop. Come to think of it now, he might easily hurt himself badly if he hit the water flat. Wasn't there someone who once split his stomach open that way, doing a belly flop from the high dive? He must jump straight and land feet first. Go in like a knife. Yes, sir. The water seemed cold and deep and grey and it made him shiver to look at it. But it was now or never. Be a man, William Botibol, be a man. All right then . . . now . . . here goes . . .

He climbed up on to the wide wooden top-rail, stood there poised, balancing for three terrifying seconds, then he leaped – he leaped up and out as far as he could go and at the same time he shouted '*Help!*'

'*Help! Help!*' he shouted as he fell. Then he hit the water and went under.

When the first shout for help sounded, the woman who was leaning on the rail started up and gave a little jump of surprise. She looked around quickly and saw sailing past her through the air this small man dressed in white shorts and tennis shoes, spreadeagled and shouting as he went. For a moment she looked as though she weren't quite sure what she ought to do: throw a lifebelt, run away and give the alarm, or simply turn and yell. She drew back a pace from the rail and swung half around facing up to the bridge, and for this brief moment she remained motionless, tense, undecided. Then almost at once she seemed to relax, and she leaned forward far over the rail, staring at the water where it was turbulent in the ship's wake. Soon a tiny round black head appeared in the foam, an arm raised above it, once, twice, vigorously waving, and a small faraway voice was heard calling something that was difficult to understand. The woman leaned still farther over the rail, trying to keep the little bobbing black speck in sight, but soon, so very soon, it was such a long way away that she couldn't even be sure it was there at all.

After a while another woman came out on deck. This one was bony and angular, and she wore horn-rimmed spectacles. She spotted the first woman and walked over to her, treading the deck in the deliberate, military fashion of all spinsters.

'So *there* you are,' she said.

The woman with the fat ankles turned and looked at her, but said nothing.

'I've been searching for you,' the bony one continued. 'Searching all over.'

'It's very odd,' the woman with the fat ankles said. 'A man dived overboard just now, with his clothes on.'

'Nonsense!'

'Oh yes. He said he wanted to get some exercise and he dived in and didn't even bother to take his clothes off.'

'You better come down now,' the bony woman said. Her mouth had suddenly become firm, her whole face sharp and alert, and she spoke less kindly than before. 'And don't you ever go wandering about on deck alone like this again. You know quite well you're meant to wait for me.'

'Yes, Maggie,' the woman with the fat ankles answered, and again she smiled, a tender, trusting smile, and she took the hand of the other one and allowed herself to be led away across the deck.

'Such a nice man,' she said. 'He waved to me.'

GALLOPING FOXLEY

Five days a week, for thirty-six years, I have travelled the eight-twelve train to the City. It is never unduly crowded, and it takes me right in to Cannon Street Station, only an eleven and a half minute walk from the door of my office in Austin Friars.

I have always liked the process of commuting; every phrase of the little journey is a pleasure to me. There is a regularity about it that is agreeable and comforting to a person of habit, and in addition, it serves as a sort of slipway along which I am gently but firmly launched into the waters of daily business routine.

Ours is a smallish country station and only nineteen or twenty people gather there to catch the eight-twelve. We are a group that rarely changes, and when occasionally a new face appears on the platform it causes a certain disclamatory, protestant ripple, like a new bird in a cage of canaries.

But normally, when I arrive in the morning with my usual four minutes to spare, there they all are, these good, solid, steadfast people, standing in their right places with their right umbrellas and hats and ties and faces and their newspapers under their arms, as unchanged and unchangeable through the years as the furniture in my own living-room. I like that.

I like also my corner seat by the window and reading *The Times* to the noise and motion of the train. This part of it lasts thirty-two minutes and it seems to soothe both my brain and my fretful old body like a good long massage. Believe me, there's nothing like routine and regularity for preserving one's peace of mind. I have now made this morning journey nearly ten thousand times in all, and I enjoy it more and more every day. Also (irrelevant, but interesting), I have become a sort of clock. I can tell at once if we are running two, three, or four minutes late, and I never have to look up to know which station we are stopped at.

The walk at the other end from Cannon Street to my office is neither too long nor too short – a healthy little perambulation along streets crowded with fellow commuters all proceeding to their places of work on the same orderly schedule as myself. It gives me a sense of assurance to be moving among these dependable, dignified people who stick to their jobs and don't go gadding about all over the world. Their lives, like my own, are regulated nicely by the minute hand of an accurate watch, and very often our paths cross at the same times and places on the street each day.

For example, as I turn the corner into St Swithin's Lane, I invariably come head on with a genteel middle-aged lady who wears silver pince-nez and carries a black brief-case in her hand – a first-rate accountant, I should say, or possibly an executive in the textile industry. When I cross over Threadneedle Street by the traffic lights, nine times out of ten I pass a gentleman who wears a different garden flower in his buttonhole each day. He dresses in black trousers and grey spats and is clearly a punctual and meticulous person, probably a banker, or perhaps a solicitor like myself; and several times in the last twenty-five years, as we have hurried past one another across the street, our eyes have met in a fleeting glance of mutual approval and respect.

At least half the faces I pass on this little walk are now familar to me. And good faces they are too, my kind of faces, my kind of people – sound, sedulous, businesslike folk with none of that restlessness and glittering eye about them that you see in all these so-called clever types who want to tip the world upside-down with their Labour Governments and socialized medicines and all the rest of it.

So you can see that I am, in every sense of the words, a contented commuter. Or would it be more accurate to say that I *was* a contented commuter? At the time when I wrote the little autobiographical sketch you have just read – intending to circulate it among the staff of my office as an exhortation and an example – I was giving a perfectly true account of my feelings. But that was a whole week ago, and since then something rather peculiar has happened. As a matter of fact, it started to happen last Tuesday, the very morning that I was carrying the rough draft up to Town in my pocket; and this, to me, was so timely and coincidental that I can only believe it to have been the work of God. God had read my little essay and he had said to himself, 'This man Perkins is becoming over-complacent. It is high time I taught him a lesson.' I honestly believe that's what happened.

As I say, it was last Tuesday, the Tuesday afer Easter, a warm yellow spring morning, and I was striding on to the platform of our small country station with *The Times* tucked under my arm and the draft of 'The Contented Commuter' in my pocket, when I immediately became aware that something was wrong. I could actually *feel* that curious little ripple of protest running along the ranks of my fellow commuters. I stopped and glanced around.

The stranger was standing plumb in the middle of the platform, feet apart and arms folded, looking for all the world as though he owned the whole place. He was a biggish, thickset man, and even from behind he somehow managed to convey a powerful impression of arrogance and oil. Very definitely, he was not one of us. He carried a cane instead of an umbrella, his shoes were brown instead of black, the grey hat was cocked at a ridiculous angle, and in one way and another there seemed to be an excess of silk and polish about his person. More than this I did not care to observe. I walked straight past him with my face to the sky, adding, I sincerely hope, a touch of real frost to an atmosphere that was already cool.

The train came in. And now, try if you can to imagine my horror when the new man actually followed me into *my own* compartment! Nobody had done this to me for fifteen years. My colleagues always respect my seniority. One of my special little pleasures is to have the place to myself for at least one, sometimes two or even three stations. But here, if you please, was this fellow, this stranger, straddling the seat opposite and blowing his nose and rustling the *Daily Mail* and lighting a disgusting pipe.

I lowered my *Times* and stole a glance at his face. I suppose he was about the same age as me – sixty-two or three – but he had one of those unpleasantly handsome, brown, leathery countenances that you see nowadays in advertisements for men's shirts – the lion shooter and the polo player and the Everest climber and the tropical explorer and the racing yachtsman all rolled into one; dark eyebrows, steely eyes, strong white teeth clamping the stem of a pipe. Personally, I mistrust all handsome men. The superficial pleasures of this life come too easily to them, and they seem to walk the world as though they themselves were personally responsible for their own good looks. I don't mind a *woman* being pretty. That's different. But in a man, I'm sorry, but somehow or other I find it downright offensive. Anyway, here was this one sitting right opposite me in the carriage, and I was looking at him over the top of my *Times* when suddenly he glanced up and our eyes met.

'D'you mind the pipe?' he asked, holding it up in his fingers. That was all he said. But the sound of his voice had a sudden and extraordinary effect upon me. In fact, I think I jumped. Then I sort of froze up and sat staring at him for at least a minute before I got hold of myself and made an answer.

'This is a smoker,' I said, 'so you may do as you please.'

'I just thought I'd ask.'

There it was again, that curiously crisp, familiar voice, clipping its words and spitting them out very hard and small like a little quick-firing gun shooting out raspberry seeds. Where had I heard it before? and why did every word seem to strike upon some tiny tender spot far back in my memory? Good heavens, I thought. Pull yourself together. What sort of nonsense is this?

The stranger returned to his paper. I pretended to do the same. But by this time I was properly put out and I couldn't concentrate at all. Instead, I kept stealing glances at him over the top of the editorial page. It was really an intolerable face, vulgarly, almost lasciviously handsome, with an oily salacious sheen all over the skin. But had I or had I not seen it before some time in my life? I began to think I had, because now, even when I looked at it I felt a peculiar kind of discomfort that I cannot quite describe – something to do with pain and with violence, perhaps even with fear.

We spoke no more during the journey, but you can well imagine that by then my whole routine had been thoroughly upset. My day was ruined; and more than one of my clerks at the office felt the sharper edge of my tongue, particularly after luncheon when my digestion started acting up on me as well.

The next morning, there he was again standing in the middle of the platform with his cane and his pipe and his silk scarf and his nauseatingly handsome face. I walked past him and approached a certain Mr Grummitt, a stockbroker who has been commuting with me for over twenty-eight years. I can't say I've ever had an actual conversation with him before – we are rather a reserved lot on our station – but a crisis like this will usually break the ice.

'Grummitt,' I whispered. 'Who's this bounder?'

'Search me,' Grummitt said.

'Pretty unpleasant.'

'Very.'

'Not going to be a regular, I trust.'

'Oh God,' Grummitt said.

Then the train came in.

This time, to my great relief, the man got into another compartment.

But the following morning I had him with me again.

'Well,' he said, settling back in the seat directly opposite. 'It's a *topping* day.' And once again I felt that slow uneasy stirring of the memory, stronger than ever this time, closer to the surface but not yet quite within my reach.

Then came Friday, the last day of the week. I remember it had rained as I drove to the station, but it was one of those warm sparkling April showers that last only five or six minutes, and when I walked on to the platform, all the umbrellas were rolled up and the sun was shining and there were big white clouds floating in the sky. In spite of this, I felt depressed. There was no pleasure in this journey for me any longer. I knew the stranger would be there. And sure enough, he was, standing with his legs apart just as though he owned the place, and this time swinging his cane casually back and forth through the air.

The cane! That did it! I stopped like I'd been shot.

'It's Foxley!' I cried under my breath. 'Galloping Foxley! And still swinging his cane!'

I stepped closer to get a better look. I tell you I've never had such

a shock in all my life. It was Foxley all right. Bruce Foxley or Galloping
Foxley as we used to call him. And the last time I'd seen him, let me
see – it was at school and I was no more than twelve or thirteen years
old.

At that point the train came in, and heaven help me if he didn't
get into my compartment once again. He put his hat and cane up on
the rack, then turned and sat down and began lighting his pipe. He
glanced up at me through the smoke with those rather small cold eyes
and he said, '*Ripping* day, isn't it. Just like summer.'

There was no mistaking the voice now. It hadn't changed at all.
Except that the things I had been used to hearing it say were different.

'All right, Perkins,' it used to say. 'All right, you nasty little boy. I
am about to beat you again.'

How long ago was that? It must be nearly fifty years. Extraordinary,
though, how little the features had altered. Still the same arrogant tilt
of the chin, the flaring nostrils, the contemptuous staring eyes that
were too small and a shade too close together for comfort; still the
same habit of thrusting his face forward at you, impinging on you,
pushing you into a corner; and even the hair I could remember –
coarse and slightly wavy, with just a trace of oil all over it, like a well-
tossed salad. He used to keep a bottle of green hair mixture on the
side table in his study – when you have to dust a room you get to
know and to hate all the objects in it – and this bottle had the royal
coat of arms on the label and the name of a shop in Bond Street, and
under that, in small print, it said 'By Appointment - Hairdressers To
His Majesty King Edward VII.' I can remember that particularly
because it seemed so funny that a shop should want to boast about
being hairdresser to someone who was practically bald – even a
monarch.

And now I watched Foxley settle back in his seat and begin reading
the paper. It was a curious sensation, sitting only a yard away from
this man who fifty years before had made me so miserable that I had
once contemplated suicide. He hadn't recognized *me*; there wasn't
much danger of that because of my moustache. I felt fairly sure I was
safe and could sit there and watch him all I wanted.

Looking back on it, there seems little doubt that I suffered very
badly at the hands of Bruce Foxley my first year in school, and
strangely enough, the unwitting cause of it all was my father. I was
twelve and a half when I first went off to this fine old public school.
That was, let me see, in 1907. My father, who wore a silk topper and
morning coat, escorted me to the station, and I can remember how
we were standing on the platform among piles of wooden tuck-boxes
and trunks and what seemed like thousands of very large boys milling
about and talking and shouting at one another, when suddenly

somebody who was wanting to get by us gave my father a great push from behind and nearly knocked him off his feet.

My father, who was a small, courteous, dignified person, turned around with surprising speed and seized the culprit by the wrist.

'Don't they teach you better manners than that at this school, young man?' he said.

The boy, at least a head taller than my father, looked down at him with a cold, arrogant-laughing glare, and said nothing.

'It seems to me,' my father said, staring back at him, 'that an apology would be in order.'

But the boy just kept on looking down his nose at my father with this funny little arrogant smile at the corners of his mouth, and his chin kept coming further and further out.

'You strike me as being an impudent and ill-mannered boy,' my father went on. 'And I can only pray that you are an exception in your school. I would not wish for any son of mine to pick up such habits.'

At this point, the big boy inclined his head slightly in my direction, and a pair of small, cold, rather close together eyes looked down into mine. I was not particularly frightened at the time; I knew nothing about the power of senior boys over junior boys at public schools; and I can remember that I looked straight back at him in support of my father, whom I adored and respected.

When my father started to say something more, the boy simply turned away and sauntered slowly down the platform into the crowd.

Bruce Foxley never forgot this episode; and of course the really unlucky thing about it for me was that when I arrived at school I found myself in the same 'house' as him. Even worse than that – I was in his study. He was doing his last year, and he was a prefect – 'a boazer' we called it – and as such he was officially permitted to beat any of the fags in the house. But being in his study, I automatically became his own particular, personal slave. I was his valet and cook and maid and errand-boy, and it was my duty to see that he never lifted a finger for himself unless absolutely necessary. In no society that I know of in the world is a servant imposed upon to the extent that we wretched little fags were imposed upon by the boazers at school. In frosty or snowy weather I even had to sit on the seat of the lavatory (which was in an unheated outhouse) every morning after breakfast to warm it before Foxley came along.

I could remember how he used to saunter across the room in his loose-jointed, elegant way, and if a chair were in his path he would knock it aside and I would have to run over and pick it up. He wore silk shirts and always had a silk handkerchief tucked up his sleeve, and his shoes were made by someone called Lobb (who also had a royal crest). They were pointed shoes, and it was my duty to rub the leather with a bone for fifteen minutes each day to make it shine.

But the worst memories of all had to do with the changing room.

I could see myself now, a small pale shrimp of a boy standing just inside the door of this huge room in my pyjamas and bedroom slippers and brown camel-hair dressing-gown. A single bright electric bulb was hanging on a flex from the ceiling, and all around the walls the black and yellow football shirts with their sweaty smell filling the room, and the voice, the clipped, pip-spitting voice was saying, 'So which is it to be this time? Six with the dressing-gown on – or four with it off?'

I never could bring myself to answer this question. I would simply stand there staring down at the dirty floor-planks, dizzy with fear and unable to think of anything except that this other larger boy would soon start smashing away at me with his long, thin, white stick, slowly, scientifically, skilfully, legally, and with apparent relish, and I would bleed. Five hours earlier, I had failed to get the fire to light in his study. I had spent my pocket money on a box of special firelighters and I had held a newspaper across the chimney opening to make a draught and I had knelt down in front of it and blown my guts out into the bottom of the grate; but the coals would not burn.

'If you're too obstinate to answer,' the voice was saying, 'then I'll have to decide for you.'

I wanted desperately to answer because I knew which one I had to choose. It's the first thing you learn when you arrive. Always keep the dressing-gown *on* and take the extra strokes. Otherwise you're almost certain to get cut. Even three with it on is better than one with it off.

'Take it off then and get into the far corner and touch your toes. I'm going to give you four.'

Slowly I would take it off and lay it on the ledge above the boot-lockers. And slowly I would walk over to the far corner, cold and naked now in my cotton pyjamas, treading softly and seeing everything around me suddenly very bright and flat and far away, like a magic lantern picture, and very big, and very unreal, and sort of swimming through the water in my eyes.

'Go on and touch your toes. Tighter – much tighter than that.'

Then he would walk down to the far end of the changing-room and I would be watching him upside down between my legs, and he would disappear through a doorway that led down two steps into what we called 'the basin-passage'. This was a stone-floored corridor with wash basins along one wall, and beyond it was the bathroom. When Foxley disappeared I knew he was walking down to the far end of the basin-passage. Foxley always did that. Then, in the distance, but echoing loud among the basins and the tiles, I would hear the noise of his shoes on the stone floor as he started galloping forward, and through my legs I would see him leaping up the two steps into the changing-room and come bounding towards me with his face thrust forward and the cane held high in the air. This was the moment when I shut my eyes and waited for the crack and told myself that whatever happened I must not straighten up.

Anyone who has been properly beaten will tell you that the real pain does not come until about eight or ten seconds after the stroke. The stroke itself is merely a loud crack and a sort of blunt thud against your backside, numbing you completely (I'm told a bullet wound does the same). But later on, oh my heavens, it feels as if someone is laying a red hot poker right across your naked buttocks and it is absolutely impossible to prevent yourself from reaching back and clutching it with your fingers.

Foxley knew all about this time lag, and the slow walk back over a distance that must altogether have been fifteen yards gave each stroke plenty of time to reach the peak of its pain before the next one was delivered.

On the fourth stroke I would invariably straighten up. I couldn't help it. It was an automatic defence reaction from a body that had had as much as it could stand.

'You flinched,' Foxley would say. 'That one doesn't count. Go on – down you get.'

The next time I would remember to grip my ankles.

Afterwards he would watch me as I walked over – very stiff now and holding my backside – to put on my dressing-gown, but I would always try to keep turned away from him so he couldn't see my face. And when I went out, it would be, 'Hey, you! Come back!'

I was in the passage then, and I would stop and turn and stand in the doorway, waiting.

'Come here. Come on, come back here. Now – haven't you forgotten something?'

All I could think of at that moment was the excruciating burning pain in my behind.

'You strike me as being an impudent and ill-mannered boy,' he would say, imitating my father's voice. 'Don't they teach you better manners than that at this school?'

'Thank ... you,' I would stammer. 'Thank ... you ... for the beating.'

And then back up the dark stairs to the dormitory and it became much better then because it was all over and the pain was going and the others were clustering round and treating me with a certain rough sympathy born of having gone through the same thing themselves, many times.

'Hey, Perkins, let's have a look.'

'How many d'you get?'

'Five, wasn't it? We heard them easily from here.'

'Come on, man. Let's see the marks.'

I would take down my pyjamas and stand there while this group of experts solemnly examined the damage.

'Rather far apart, aren't they? Not quite up to Foxley's usual standard.'

'Two of them are close. Actually touching. Look – these two are beauties!'

'That low one was a rotten shot.'

'Did he go right down the basin-passage to start his run?'

'You got an extra one for flinching, didn't you?'

'By golly, old Foxley's really got it in for *you*, Perkins.'

'Bleeding a bit too. Better wash it, you know.'

Then the door would open and Foxley would be there, and everyone would scatter and pretend to be doing his teeth or saying his prayers while I was left standing in the centre of the room with my pants down.

'What's going on here?' Foxley would say, taking a quick look at his own handiwork. 'You – Perkins! Put your pyjamas on properly and get to bed.'

And that was the end of a day.

Through the week, I never had a moment of time to myself. If Foxley saw me in the study taking up a novel or perhaps opening my stamp album, he would immediately find something for me to do. One of his favourites, especially when it was raining outside, was, 'Oh, Perkins, I think a bunch of wild irises would look rather nice on my desk, don't you?'

Wild irises grew only around Orange Ponds. Orange Ponds was two miles down the road and half a mile across the fields. I would get up from my chair, put on my raincoat and my straw hat, take my umbrella – my brolly – and set off on this long and lonely trek. The straw hat had to be worn at all times outdoors, but it was easily destroyed by rain; therefore the brolly was necessary to protect the hat. On the other hand, you can't keep a brolly over your head while scrambling about on a woody bank looking for irises, so to save my hat from ruin I would put it on the ground under my brolly while I searched for flowers. In this way, I caught many colds.

But the most dreaded day was Sunday. Sunday was for cleaning the study, and how well I can remember the terror of those mornings, the frantic dusting and scrubbing, and then the waiting for Foxley to come in to inspect.

'Finished?' he would ask.

'I . . . I think so.'

Then he would stroll over to the drawer of his desk and take out a single white glove, fitting it slowly on to his right hand, pushing each finger well home, and I would stand there watching and trembling as he moved around the room running his white-gloved forefinger along the picture tops, the skirting, the shelves, the window sills, the lamp shades. I never took my eyes off that finger. For me it was an instrument of doom. Nearly always, it managed to discover some tiny crack that I had overlooked or perhaps hadn't even thought about; and when this happened Foxley would turn slowly around, smiling that dangerous little smile that wasn't a smile, holding up the white finger so that I should see for myself the thin smudge of dust that lay along the side of it.

'Well,' he would say. 'So you're a lazy little boy. Aren't you?'

No answer.

'Aren't you?'

'I thought I dusted it all.'

'Are you or are you not a nasty, lazy little boy?'

'Y-yes.'

'But your father wouldn't want you to grow up like that, would he? Your father is very particular about manners, is he not?'

No answer.

'I asked you, is your father particular about manners?'

'Perhaps – yes.'

'Therefore I will be doing him a favour if I punish you, won't I?'

'I don't know.'

'Won't I?'

'Y-yes?'

'We will meet later then, after prayers, in the changing-room.'

The rest of the day would be spent in an agony of waiting for the evening to come.

Oh my goodness, how it was all coming back to me now. Sunday was also letter-writing time. 'Dear Mummy and Daddy – thank you very much for your letter. I hope you are both well. I am, except I have got a cold because I got caught in the rain but it will soon be over. Yesterday we played Shrewsbury and beat them 4–2. I watched and Foxley who you know is the head of our house scored one of our goals. Thank you very much for the cake. With love from William.'

I usually went to the lavatory to write my letter, or to the boot-hole, or the bathroom – any place out of Foxley's way. But I had to watch the time. Tea was at four-thirty and Foxley's toast had to be ready. Every day I had to make toast for Foxley, and on weekdays there were no fires allowed in the studies, so all the fags, each making toast for his own studyholder, would have to crowd around the one small fire in the library, jockeying for position with his toasting-fork. Under these conditions, I still had to see that Foxley's toast was (1) very crisp, (2) not burned at all, (3) hot and ready exactly on time. To fail in any one of these requirements was a 'beatable offence'.

'Hey, you! What's this?'

'It's toast.'

'Is this really your idea of toast?'

'Well ...'

'You're too idle to make it right, aren't you?'

'I try to make it.'

'You know what they do to an idle horse, Perkins?'

'No.'

'Are you a horse?'

'No.'

'Well – anyway, you're an ass – ha, ha – so I think you qualify. I'll be seeing you later.'

Oh, the agony of those days. To burn Foxley's toast was a 'beatable offence'. So was forgetting to take the mud off Foxley's football boots. So was failing to hang up Foxley's football clothes. So was rolling up Foxley's brolly the wrong way round. So was banging the study door when Foxley was working. So was filling Foxley's bath too hot for him. So was not cleaning the buttons properly on Foxley's OTC uniform. So was making those blue metal-polish smudges on the uniform itself. So was failing to shine the *soles* of Foxley's shoes. So was leaving Foxley's study untidy at any time. In fact, so far as Foxley was concerned, I was practically a beatable offence myself.

I glanced out of the window. My goodness, we were nearly there. I must have been dreaming away like this for quite a while, and I hadn't even opened my *Times*. Foxley was still leaning back in the corner seat opposite me reading his *Daily Mail*, and through a cloud of blue smoke from his pipe I could see the top half of his face over the newspaper, the small bright eyes, the corrugated forehead, the wavy, slightly oily hair.

Looking at him now, after all that time, was a peculiar and rather exciting experience. I knew he was no longer dangerous, but the old memories were still there and I didn't feel altogether comfortable in his presence. It was something like being inside the cage with a tame tiger.

What nonsense is this? I asked myself. Don't be so stupid. My heavens, if you wanted to you could go ahead and tell him exactly what you thought of him and he couldn't touch you, Hey – that was an idea!

Except that – well – after all, was it worth it? I was too old for that sort of thing now, and I wasn't sure that I really felt much anger towards him anyway.

So what should I do? I couldn't sit there staring at him like an idiot.

At that point, a little impish fancy began to take a hold of me. What I would like to do, I told myself, would be to lean across and tap him lightly on the knee and tell him who I was. Then I would watch his face. After that, I would begin talking about our schooldays together, making it just loud enough for the other people in the carriage to hear. I would remind him playfully of some of the things he used to do to me, and perhaps even describe the changing-room beatings so as to embarrass him a trifle. A bit of teasing and discomfort wouldn't do him any harm. And it would do *me* an awful lot of good.

Suddenly he glanced up and caught me staring at him. It was the second time this had happened, and I noticed a flicker of irritation in his eyes.

All right, I told myself. Here we go. But keep it pleasant and sociable and polite. It'll be much more effective that way, more embarrassing for him.

So I smiled at him and gave him a courteous little nod. Then, raising my voice, I said, 'I do hope you'll excuse me. I'd like to introduce myself.' I was leaning forward watching him closely so as not to miss the reaction. 'My name is Perkins – William Perkins – and I was at Repton in 1907.'

The others in the carriage were sitting very still, and I could sense that they were all listening and waiting to see what would happen next.

'I'm glad to meet uou,' he said, lowering the paper to his lap. 'Mine's Fortescue – Jocelyn Fortescue, Eton, 1916.'

SKIN

That year – 1946 – winter was a long time going. Although it was April, a freezing wind blew through the streets of the city, and overhead the snow clouds moved across the sky.

The old man who was called Drioli shuffled painfully along the sidewalk of the rue de Rivoli. He was cold and miserable, huddled up like a hedgehog in a filthy black coat, only his eyes and the top of his head visible above the turned-up collar.

The door of a café opened and the faint whiff of roasting chicken brought a pain of yearning to the top of his stomach. He moved on glancing without any interest at the things in the shop windows – perfume, silk ties and shirts, diamonds, porcelain, antique furniture, finely bound books. Then a picture gallery. He had always liked picture galleries. This one had a single canvas on display in the window. He stopped to look at it. He turned to go on. He checked, looked back; and now, suddenly, there came to him a slight uneasiness, a movement of the memory, a distant recollection of something, somewhere, he had seen before. He looked again. It was a landscape, a clump of trees leaning madly over to one side as if blown by a tremendous wind, the sky swirling and twisting all around. Attached to the frame there was a little plaque, and on this it said: CHAIM SOUTINE (1894–1943).

Drioli stared at the picture, wondering vaguely what there was about it that seemed familiar. Crazy painting, he thought. Very strange and crazy – but I like it ... Chaïm Soutine ... Soutine ... 'By God!' he cried suddenly. 'My little Kalmuck, that's who it is! My little Kalmuck with a picture in the finest shop in Paris! Just imagine that!'

The old man pressed his face closer to the window. He could remember the boy – yes, quite clearly he could remember him. But when? The rest of it was not so easy to recollect. It was so long ago. How long? Twenty – no, more like thirty years, wasn't it? Wait a minute. Yes – it was the year before the war, the first war, 1913. That was it. And this Soutine, this ugly little Kalmuck, a sullen brooding boy whom he had liked – almost loved – for no reason at all that he could think of except that he could paint.

And how he could paint! It was coming back more clearly now – the street, the line of refuse cans along the length of it, the rotten smell, the brown cats walking delicately over the refuse, and then the women, moist fat women sitting on the doorsteps with their feet upon the cobblestones of the street. Which street? Where was it the boy had lived?

The Cité Falguière, that was it! The old man nodded his head several times, pleased to have remembered the name. Then there was the studio with the single chair in it, and the filthy red couch that the boy had used for sleeping; the drunken parties, the cheap white wine, the furious quarrels, and always, always the bitter sullen face of the boy brooding over his work.

It was odd, Drioli thought, how easily it all came back to him now, how each single small remembered fact seemed instantly to remind him of another.

There was that nonsense with the tattoo, for instance. Now, *that* was a mad thing if ever there was one. How had it started? Ah, yes – he had got rich one day, that was it, and he had bought lots of wine. He could see himself now as he entered the studio with the parcel of bottles under his arm – the boy sitting before the easel, and his (Drioli's) own wife standing in the centre of the room, posing for her picture.

'Tonight we shall celebrate,' he said. 'We shall have a little celebration, us three.'

'What is it that we celebrate?' the boy asked, without looking up. 'Is it that you have decided to divorce your wife so she can marry me?'

'No,' Drioli said. 'We celebrate because today I have made a great sum of money with my work.'

'And I have made nothing. We can celebrate that also.'

'If you like.' Drioli was standing by the table unwrapping the parcel. He felt tired and he wanted to get at the wine. Nine clients in one day was all very nice, but it could play hell with a man's eyes. He had never done as many as nine before. Nine boozy soldiers – and the remarkable thing was that no fewer than seven of them had been able to pay in cash. This had made him extremely rich. But the work was terrible on the eyes. Drioli's eyes were half closed from fatigue, the whites streaked with little connecting lines of red; and about an inch behind each eyeball there was a small concentration of pain. But it was evening now and he was wealthy as a pig, and in the parcel there were three bottles – one for his wife, one for his friend, and one for him. He had found the corkscrew and was drawing the corks from the bottles, each making a small plop as it came out.

The boy put down his brush. 'Oh, Christ,' he said. 'How can one work with all this going on?'

The girl came across the room to look at the painting. Drioli came over also, holding a bottle in one hand, a glass in the other.

'No!' the boy shouted, blazing up suddenly. 'Please – no!' He snatched the canvas from the easel and stood it against the wall. But Drioli had seen it.

'I like it.'

'It's terrible.'

'It's marvellous. Like all the others that you do, it's marvellous. I love them all.'

'The trouble is,' the boy said, scowling, 'that in themselves they are not nourishing. I cannot eat them.'

'But still they are marvellous.' Drioli handed him a tumblerful of the pale-yellow wine. 'Drink it,' he said. 'It will make you happy.'

Never, he thought, had he known a more unhappy person, or one with a gloomier face. He had spotted him in a café some seven months before, drinking alone, and because he had looked like a Russian or some sort of an Asiatic, Drioli had sat down at his table and talked.

'You are a Russian?'

'Yes.'

'Where from?'

'Minsk.'

Drioli had jumped up and embraced him, crying that he too had been born in that city.

'It wasn't actually Minsk,' the boy had said. 'But quite near.'

'Where?'

'Smilovichi, about twelve miles away.'

'Smilovichi!' Drioli had shouted, embracing him again. 'I walked there several times when I was a boy.' Then he had sat down again, staring affectionately at the other's face. 'You know,' he had said, 'you don't look like a western Russian. You're like a Tartar, or a Kalmuck. You look exactly like a Kalmuck.'

Now, standing in the studio, Drioli looked again at the boy as he took the glass of wine and tipped it down his throat in one swallow. Yes, he did have a face like a Kalmuck – very broad and high-cheeked, with a wide coarse nose. This broadness of the cheeks was accentuated by the ears which stood out sharply from the head. And then he had the narrow eyes, the black hair, the thick sullen mouth of a Kalmuck, but the hands – the hands were always a surprise, so small and white like a lady's, with tiny thin fingers.

'Give me some more,' the boy said. 'If we are to celebrate then let us do it properly.'

Drioli distributed the wine and sat himself on a chair. The boy sat on the old couch with Drioli's wife. The three bottles were placed on the floor between them.

'Tonight we shall drink as much as we possibly can,' Drioli said. 'I am exceptionally rich. I think perhaps I should go out now and buy some more bottles. How many shall I get?'

'Six more,' the boy said. 'Two for each.'

'Good. I shall go now and fetch them.'

'And I will help you.'

In the nearest café Drioli bought six bottles of white wine, and they carried them back to the studio. They placed them on the floor in two rows, and Drioli fetched the corkscrew and pulled the corks, all six of them; then they sat down again and continued to drink.

'It is only the very wealthy,' Drioli said, 'who can afford to celebrate in this manner.'

'That is true,' the boy said. 'Isn't that true, Josie?'

'Of course.'

'How do you feel, Josie?'

'Fine.'

'Will you leave Drioli and marry me?'

'No.'

'Beautiful wine,' Drioli said. 'It is a privilege to drink it.'

Slowly, methodically, they set about getting themselves drunk. The process was routine, but all the same there was a certain ceremony to be observed, and a gravity to be maintained, and a great number of things to be said, then said again – and the wine must be praised, and the slowness was important too, so that there would be time to savour the three delicious stages of transition, especially (for Drioli) the one when he began to float and his feet did not really belong to him. That was the best period of them all – when he could look down at his feet and they were so far away that he would wonder what crazy person they might belong to and why they were lying around on the floor like that, in the distance.

After a while, he got up to switch on the light. He was surprised to see that the feet came with him when he did this, especially because he couldn't feel them touching the ground. It gave him a pleasant sensation of walking on air. Then he began wandering around the room, peeking slyly at the canvases stacked against the walls.

'Listen,' he said at length. 'I have an idea.' He came across and stood before the couch, swaying gently. 'Listen, my little Kalmuck.'

'What?'

'I have a tremendous idea. Are you listening?'

'I'm listening to Josie.'

'Listen to me, *please*. You are my friend – my ugly little Kalmuck from Minsk – and to me you are such an artist that I would like to have a picture, a lovely picture – '

'Have them all. Take all you can find, but do not interrupt me when I am talking with your wife.'

'No, no. Now listen. I mean a picture that I can have with me always ... for ever ... wherever I go ... whatever happens ... but

always with me ... a picture by you.' He reached forward and shook
the boy's knee. 'Now listen to me, *please*.'

'Listen to him,' the girl said.

'It is this. I want you to paint a picture on my skin, on my back.
Then I want you to tattoo over what you have painted so that it will
be there always.'

'You have crazy ideas.'

'I will teach you how to use the tattoo. It is easy. A child could do
it.'

'I am not a child.'

'*Please* ...'

'You are quite mad. What is it you want?' The painter looked up
into the slow, dark, wine-bright eyes of the other man. 'What in
heaven's name is it you want?'

'You could do it easily! You could! You could!'

'You mean with the tattoo?'

'Yes, with the tattoo! I will teach you in two minutes!'

'Impossible!'

'Are you saying I do not know what I am talking about?'

No, the boy could not possibly be saying that because if anyone
knew about the tattoo it was he – Drioli. Had he not, only last month,
covered a man's whole belly with the most wonderful and delicate
design composed entirely of flowers? What about the client who had
had so much hair upon his chest that he had done him a picture of a
grizzly bear so designed that the hair on the chest became the furry
coat of the bear? Could he not draw the likeness of a lady and position
it with such subtlety upon a man's arm that when the muscle of the
arm was flexed the lady came to life and performed some astonishing
contortions?

'All I am saying,' the boy told him, 'is that you are drunk and this
is a drunken idea.'

'We could have Josie for a model. A study of Josie upon my back.
Am I not entitled to a picture of my wife upon my back?'

'Of Josie?'

'Yes.' Drioli knew he only had to mention his wife and the boy's
thick brown lips would loosen and begin to quiver.

'No,' the girl said.

'Darling Josie, *please*. Take this bottle and finish it, then you will
feel more generous. It is an enormous idea. Never in my life have I
had such an idea before.'

'What idea?'

'That he should make a picture of you upon my back. Am I not
entitled to that?'

'A picture of me?'

'A nude study,' the boy said. 'It is an agreeable idea.'

'Not nude,' the girl said.

'It is an enormous idea,' Drioli said.

'It's a damn crazy idea,' the girl said.

'It is in any event an idea,' the boy said. 'It is an idea that calls for a celebration.'

They emptied another bottle among them. Then the boy said, 'It is no good. I could not possibly manage the tattoo. Instead, I will paint this picture on your back and you will have it with you so long as you do not take a bath and wash it off. If you never take a bath again in your life then you will have it always, as long as you live.'

'No,' Drioli said.

'Yes – and on the day that you decide to take a bath I will know that you do not any longer value my picture. It will be a test of your admiration for my art.'

'I do not like the idea,' the girl said. 'His admiration for your art is so great that he would be unclean for many years. Let us have the tattoo. But not nude.'

'Then just the head,' Drioli said.

'I could not manage it.'

'It is immensely simple. I will undertake to teach you in two minutes. You will see. I shall go now and fetch the instruments. The needles and the inks. I have inks of many different colours – as many different colours as you have paints, and far more beautiful ...'

'It is impossible.'

'I have many inks. Have I not many different colours of inks, Josie?'

'Yes.'

'You will see,' Drioli said. 'I will go now and fetch them.' He got up from his chair and walked unsteadily, but with determination, out of the room.

In half an hour Drioli was back. 'I have brought everything,' he cried, waving a brown suitcase. 'All the necessities of the tattooist are here in this bag.'

He placed the bag on the table, opened it, and laid out the electric needles and the small bottles of coloured inks. He plugged in the electric needle, then he took the instrument in his hand and pressed a switch. It made a buzzing sound and the quarter inch of needle that projected from the end of it began to vibrate swiftly up and down. He threw off his jacket and rolled up his left sleeve. 'Now look. Watch me and I will show you how easy it is. I will make a design on my arm, here.'

His forearm was already covered with blue markings, but he selected a small clear patch of skin upon which to demonstrate.

'First, I choose my ink – let us use ordinary blue – and I dip the point of the needle in the ink ... so ... and I hold the needle up straight and I run it lightly over the surface of the skin ... like this

... and with the little motor and the electricity, the needle jumps up and down and punctures the skin and the ink goes in and there you are. See how easy it is ... see how I draw a picture of a greyhound here upon my arm ...'

The boy was intrigued. 'Now let *me* practise a little – on your arm.'

With the buzzing needle he began to draw blue lines upon Drioli's arm. 'It is simple,' he said. 'It is like drawing with pen and ink. There is no difference except that it is slower.'

'There is nothing to it. Are you ready? Shall we begin?'

'At once.'

'The model!' cried Drioli. 'Come on, Josie!' He was in a bustle of enthusiasm now, tottering around the room arranging everything, like a child preparing for some exciting game. 'Where will you have her? Where shall she stand?'

'Let her be standing there, by my dressing-table. Let her be brushing her hair. I will paint her with her hair down over her shoulders and her brushing it.'

'Tremendous. You are a genius.'

Reluctantly, the girl walked over and stood by the dressing table, carrying her glass of wine with her.

Drioli pulled off his shirt and stepped out of his trousers. He retained only his underpants and his socks and shoes, and he stood there swaying gently from side to side, his small body firm, white-skinned, almost hairless. 'Now,' he said, 'I am the canvas. Where will you place your canvas?'

'As always, upon the easel.'

'Don't be crazy. I am the canvas.'

'Then place yourself upon the easel. That is where you belong.'

'How can I?'

'Are you the canvas or are you not the canvas?'

'I am the canvas. Already I begin to feel like a canvas.'

'Then place yourself upon the easel. There should be no difficulty.'

'Truly, it is not possible.'

'Then sit on the chair. Sit back to front, then you can lean your drunken head against the back of it. Hurry now, for I am about to commence.'

'I am ready. I am waiting.'

'First,' the boy said, 'I shall make an ordinary painting. Then, if it pleases me, I shall tattoo over it.' With a wide brush he began to paint upon the naked skin of the man's back.

'Ayee! Ayee!' Drioli screamed. 'A monstrous centipede is marching down my spine!'

'Be still now! Be still!' The boy worked rapidly, applying the paint only in a thin blue wash so that it would not afterwards interfere with the process of tattooing. His concentration, as soon as he began to

paint, was so great that it appeared somehow to supersede his
drunkenness. He applied the brush strokes with quick short jabs of the
arm, holding the wrist stiff, and in less than half an hour it was
finished.

'All right. That's all,' he said to the girl, who immediately returned
to the couch, lay down, and fell asleep.

Drioli remained awake. He watched the boy take up the needle and
dip it in the ink; then he felt the sharp tickling sting as it touched the
skin of his back. The pain, which was unpleasant but never extreme,
kept him from going to sleep. By following the track of the needle and
by watching the different colours of ink that the boy was using, Drioli
amused himself trying to visualize what was going on behind him. The
boy worked with an astonishing intensity. He appeared to have become
completely absorbed in the little machine and in the unusual effects it
was able to produce.

Far into the small hours of the morning the machine buzzed and
the boy worked. Drioli could remember that when the artist finally
stepped back and said, 'It is finished,' there was daylight outside and
the sound of people walking in the street.

'I want to see it,' Drioli said. The boy held up a mirror, at an angle,
and Drioli craned his neck to look.

'Good God!' he cried. It was a startling sight. The whole of his
back, from the top of the shoulders to the base of the spine, was a
blaze of colour – gold and green and blue and black and scarlet. The
tattoo was applied so heavily it looked almost like an impasto. The
boy had followed as closely as possible the original brush strokes, filling
them in solid, and it was marvellous the way he had made use of the
spine and the protrusion of the shoulder blades so that they became
part of the composition. What is more, he had somehow managed to
achieve – even with this slow process – a certain spontaneity. The
portrait was quite alive; it contained much of that twisted, tortured
quality so characteristic of Soutine's other work. It was not a good
likeness. It was a mood rather than a likeness, the model's face vague
and tipsy, the background swirling around her head in a mass of dark-
green curling strokes.

'It's tremendous!'

'I rather like it myself.' The boy stood back, examining it critically.
'You know,' he added, 'I think it's good enough for me to sign.' And
taking up the buzzer again, he inscribed his name in red ink on the
right-hand side, over the place where Drioli's kidney was.

The old man who was called Drioli was standing in a sort of trance,
staring at the painting in the window of the picture-dealer's shop. It
had been so long ago, all that – almost as though it had happened in
another life.

And the boy? What had become of him? He could remember now

that after returning from the war – the first war – he had missed him
and had questioned Josie.

'Where is my little Kalmuck?'

'He is gone,' she had answered. 'I do not know where, but I heard
it said that a dealer had taken him up and sent him away to Céret to
make more paintings.'

'Perhaps he will return.'

'Perhaps he will. Who knows?'

That was the last time they had mentioned him. Shortly afterwards
they had moved to Le Havre where there were more sailors and
business was better. The old man smiled as he remembered Le Havre.
Those were the pleasant years, the years between the wars, with the
small shop near the docks and the comfortable rooms and always
enough work, with every day three, four, five sailors coming and
wanting pictures on their arms. Those were truly the pleasant years.

Then had come the second war, and Josie being killed, and the
Germans arriving, and that was the finish of his business. No one had
wanted pictures on their arms any more after that. And by that time
he was too old for any other kind of work. In desperation he had made
his way back to Paris, hoping vaguely that things would be easier in
the big city. But they were not.

And now, after the war was over, he possessed neither the means
nor the energy to start up his small business again. It wasn't very easy
for an old man to know what to do, especially when one did not like
to beg. Yet how else could he keep alive?

Well, he thought, still staring at the picture. So that is my little
Kalmuck. And how quickly the sight of one small object such as this
can stir the memory. Up to a few moments ago he had even forgotten
that he had a tattoo on his back. It had been ages since he had thought
about it. He put his face closer to the window and looked into the
gallery. On the walls he could see many other pictures and all seemed
to be the work of the same artist. There were a great number of people
strolling around. Obviously it was a special exhibition.

On a sudden impulse, Drioli turned, pushed open the door of the
gallery and went in.

It was a long room with thick wine-coloured carpet, and by God
how beautiful and warm it was! There were all these people strolling
about looking at the pictures, well-washed dignified people, each of
whom held a catalogue in the hand. Drioli stood just inside the door,
nervously glancing around, wondering whether he dared go forward
and mingle with this crowd. But before he had had time to gather his
courage, he heard a voice beside him saying, 'What is it you want?'

The speaker wore a black morning coat. He was plump and short
and had a very white face. It was a flabby face with so much flesh
upon it that the cheeks hung down on either side of the mouth in two

fleshy collops, spanielwise. He came up close to Drioli and said again, 'What is it you want?'

Drioli stood still.

'If you please,' the man was saying, 'take yourself out of my gallery.'

'Am I not permitted to look at the pictures?'

'I have asked you to leave.'

Drioli stood his ground. He felt suddenly, overwhelmingly outraged.

'Let us not have trouble,' the man was saying. 'Come on now, this way.' He put a fat white paw on Drioli's arm and began to push him firmly to the door.

That did it. 'Take your goddam hands off me!' Drioli shouted. His voice rang clear down the long gallery and all the heads jerked around as one – all the startled faces stared down the length of the room at the person who had made this noise. A flunky came running over to help, and the two men tried to hustle Drioli through the door. The people stood still, watching the struggle. Their faces expressed only a mild interest, and seemed to be saying, 'It's all right. There's no danger to us. It's being taken care of.'

'I, too!' Drioli was shouting. 'I, too, have a picture by this painter! He was my friend and I have a picture which he gave me!'

'He's mad.'

'A lunatic. A raving lunatic.'

'Someone should call the police.'

With a rapid twist of the body Drioli suddenly jumped clear of the two men, and before anyone could stop him he was running down the gallery shouting, 'I'll show you! I'll show you! I'll show you!' He flung off his overcoat, then his jacket and shirt, and he turned so that his naked back was towards the people.

'There!' he cried, breathing quickly. 'You see? There it is!'

There was a sudden absolute silence in the room, each person arrested in what he was doing, standing motionless in a kind of shocked, uneasy bewilderment. They were staring at the tattooed picture. It was still there, the colours as bright as ever, but the old man's back was thinner now, the shoulder blades protruded more sharply, and the effect, though not great, was to give the picture a curiously wrinkled, squashed appearance.

Somebody said, 'My God, but it is!'

Then came the excitement and the noise of voices as the people surged forward to crowd around the old man.

'It is unmistakable!'

'His early manner, yes?'

'It is fantastic, fantastic!'

'And look, it is signed!'

'Bend your shoulders forward, my friend, so that the picture stretches out flat.'

'Old one, when was this done?'

'In 1913,' Drioli said, without turning around. 'In the autumn of 1913.'

'Who taught Soutine to tattoo?'

'I taught him.'

'And the woman?'

'She was my wife.'

The gallery owner was pushing through the crowd towards Drioli. He was calm now, deadly serious, making a smile with his mouth. 'Monsieur,' he said, 'I will buy it.' Drioli could see the loose fat upon the face vibrating as he moved his jaw. 'I said I will buy it, Monsieur.'

'How can you buy it?' Drioli asked softly.

'I will give two hundred thousand francs for it.' The dealer's eyes were small and dark, the wings of his broad nose-base were beginning to quiver.

'Don't do it!' someone murmured in the crowd. 'It is worth twenty times as much.'

Drioli opened his mouth to speak. No words came, so he shut it; then he opened it again and said slowly, 'But how can I sell it?' He lifted his hands, let them drop loosely to his sides. 'Monsieur, how can I possibly sell it?' All the sadness in the world was in his voice.

'Yes!' they were saying in the crowd. 'How can he sell it? It is part of himself!'

'Listen,' the dealer said, coming up close. 'I will help you. I will make you rich. Together we shall make some private arrangement over this picture, no?'

Drioli watched him with slow, apprehensive eyes. 'But how can you buy it, Monsieur? What will you do with it when you have bought it? Where will you keep it? Where will you keep it tonight? And where tomorrow?'

'Ah, where will I keep it? Yes, where will I keep it? Now, where will I keep it? Well, now ...' The dealer stroked the bridge of his nose with a fat white finger. 'It would seem,' he said, 'that if I take the picture, I take you also. That is a disadvantage.' He paused and stroked his nose again. 'The picture itself is of no value until you are dead. How old are you, my friend?'

'Sixty-one.'

'But you are perhaps not very robust, no?' The dealer lowered the hand from his nose and looked Drioli up and down, slowly, like a farmer appraising an old horse.

'I do not like this,' Drioli said, edging away. 'Quite honestly, Monsieur, I do not like it.' He edged straight into the arms of a tall man who put out his hands and caught him gently by the shoulders. Drioli glanced around and apologized. The man smiled down at him, patting one of the old fellow's naked shoulders reassuringly with a hand encased in a canary-coloured glove.

'Listen, my friend,' the stranger said, still smiling. 'Do you like to swim and to bask yourself in the sun?'

Drioli looked up at him, rather startled.

'Do you like fine food and red wine from the great châteaux of Bordeaux?' The man was still smiling, showing strong white teeth with a flash of gold among them. He spoke in a soft coaxing manner, one gloved hand still resting on Drioli's shoulder. 'Do you like such things?'

'Well – yes,' Drioli answered, still greatly perplexed. 'Of course.'

'And the company of beautiful women?'

'Why not?'

'And a cupboard full of suits and shirts made to your own personal measurements? It would seem that you are a little lacking for clothes.'

Drioli watched this suave man, waiting for the rest of the proposition.

'Have you ever had a shoe constructed especially for your own foot?'

'No.'

'You would like that?'

'Well ...'

'And a man who will shave you in the mornings and trim your hair?'

Drioli simply stood and gaped.

'And a plump attractive girl to manicure the nails of your fingers?'

Someone in the crowd giggled.

'And a bell beside your bed to summon a maid to bring your breakfast in the morning? Would you like these things, my friend? Do they appeal to you?'

Drioli stood still and looked at him.

'You see, I am the owner of the Hotel Bristol in Cannes. I now invite you to come down there and live as my guest for the rest of your life in luxury and comfort.' The man paused, allowing his listener time to savour this cheerful prospect.

'Your only duty – shall I call it your pleasure – will be to spend your time on my beach in bathing trunks, walking among my guests, sunning yourself, swimming, drinking cocktails. You would like that?'

There was no answer.

'Don't you see – all the guests will thus be able to observe this fascinating picture by Soutine. You will become famous, and men will say, "Look, there is the fellow with ten million francs upon his back." You like this idea, Monsieur? It pleases you?'

Drioli looked up at the tall man in the canary gloves, still wondering whether this was some sort of a joke. 'It is a comical idea,' he said slowly. 'But do you really mean it?'

'Of course I mean it.'

'Wait,' the dealer interrupted. 'See here, old one. Here is the answer to our problem. I will buy the picture, and I will arrange with a surgeon to remove the skin from your back, and then you will be able to go off on your own and enjoy the great sum of money I shall give you for it.'

'With no skin on my back?'

'No, no, please! You misunderstand. This surgeon will put a new piece of skin in the place of the old one. It is simple.'

'Could he do that?'

'There is nothing to it.'

'Impossible!' said the man with the canary gloves. 'He's too old for such a major skin-grafting operation. It would kill him. It would kill you, my friend.'

'It would kill me?'

'Naturally. You would never survive. Only the picture would come through.'

'In the name of God!' Drioli cried. He looked around aghast at the faces of the people watching him, and in the silence that followed, another man's voice, speaking quietly from the back of the group, could be heard saying, 'Perhaps, if one were to offer this old man enough money, he might consent to kill himself on the spot. Who knows?' A few people sniggered. The dealer moved his feet uneasily on the carpet.

Then the hand in the canary glove was tapping Drioli again upon the shoulder. 'Come on,' the man was saying, smiling his broad white smile. 'You and I will go and have a good dinner and we can talk about it some more while we eat. How's that? Are you hungry?'

Drioli watched him, frowning. He didn't like the man's long flexible neck, or the way he craned it forward at you when he spoke, like a snake.

'Roast duck and Chambertin,' the man was saying. He put a rich succulent accent on the words, splashing them out with his tongue. 'And perhaps a soufflé aux marrons, light and frothy.'

Drioli's eyes turned up towards the ceiling, his lips became loose and wet. One could see the poor old fellow beginning literally to drool at the mouth.

'How do you like your duck?' the man went on. 'Do you like it very brown and crisp outside, or shall it be ...'

'I am coming,' Drioli said quickly. Already he had picked up his shirt and was pulling it frantically over his head. 'Wait for me, Monsieur. I am coming.' And within a minute he had disappeared out of the gallery with his new patron.

It wasn't more than a few weeks later that a picture by Soutine, of a woman's head, painted in an unusual manner, nicely framed and heavily varnished, turned up for sale in Buenos Aires. That – and the fact that there is no hotel in Cannes called Bristol – causes one to

wonder a little, and to pray for the old man's health, and to hope
fervently that whereever he may be at this moment, there is a plump
attractive girl to manicure the nails of his fingers, and a maid to bring
him his breakfast in bed in the mornings.

POISON

It must have been around midnight when I drove home, and as I approached the gates of the bungalow I switched off the headlamps of the car so the beam wouldn't swing in through the window of the side bedroom and wake Harry Pope. But I needn't have bothered. Coming up the drive I noticed his light was still on, so he was awake anyway – unless perhaps he'd dropped off while reading.

I parked the car and went up the five steps to the balcony, counting each step carefully in the dark so I wouldn't take an extra one which wasn't there when I got to the top. I crossed the balcony, pushed through the screen doors into the house itself and switched on the light in the hall. I went across to the door of Harry's room, opened it quietly, and looked in.

He was lying on the bed and I could see he was awake. But he didn't move. He didn't even turn his head towards me, but I heard him say, 'Timber, Timber, come here.'

He spoke slowly, whispering each word carefully, separately, and I pushed the door right open and started to go quickly across the room.

'Stop. Wait a moment, Timber.' I could hardly hear what he was saying. He seemed to be straining enormously to get the words out.

'What's the matter, Harry?'

'Sshhh!' he whispered. 'Sshhh! For God's sake don't make a noise. Take your shoes off before you come nearer. *Please* do as I say, Timber.'

The way he was speaking reminded me of George Barling after he got shot in the stomach when he stood leaning against a crate containing a spare aeroplane engine, holding both hands on his stomach and saying things about the German pilot in just the same hoarse straining half whisper Harry was using now.

'Quickly, Timber, but take your shoes off first.'

I couldn't understand about taking off the shoes but I figured that if he was as ill as he sounded I'd better humour him, so I bent down and removed the shoes and left them in the middle of the floor. Then I went over to his bed.

'Don't touch the bed! For God's sake don't touch the bed!' He was still speaking like he'd been shot in the stomach and I could see him lying there on his back with a single sheet covering three-quarters of his body. He was wearing a pair of pyjamas with blue, brown, and white stripes, and he was sweating terribly. It was a hot night and I was sweating a little myself, but not like Harry. His whole face was wet and the pillow around his head was sodden with moisture. It looked like a bad go of malaria to me.

'What is it, Harry?'

'A krait,' he said.

'A *krait*! Oh, my God! Where'd it bite you? How long ago?'

'Shut up,' he whispered.

'Listen, Harry,' I said, and I leaned forward and touched his shoulder. 'We've got to be quick. Come on now, quickly, tell me where it bit you.' He was lying there very still and tense as though he was holding on to himself hard because of sharp pain.

'I haven't been bitten,' he whispered. 'Not yet. It's on my stomach. Lying there asleep.'

I took a quick pace backwards. I couldn't help it, and I stared at his stomach or rather at the sheet that covered it. The sheet was rumpled in several places and it was impossible to tell if there was anything underneath.

'You don't really mean there's a krait lying on your stomach now?'

'I swear it.'

'How did it get there?' I shouldn't have asked the question because it was easy to see he wasn't fooling. I should have told him to keep quiet.

'I was reading,' Harry said, and he spoke very slowly, taking each word in turn and speaking it carefully so as not to move the muscles of his stomach. 'Lying on my back reading and I felt something on my chest, behind the book. Sort of tickling. Then out of the corner of my eye saw this little krait sliding over my pyjamas. Small, about ten inches. Knew I mustn't move. Couldn't have anyway. Lay there watching it. Thought it would go over top of the sheet.' Harry paused and was silent for a few moments. His eyes looked down along his body towards the place where the sheet covered his stomach, and I could see he was watching to make sure his whispering wasn't disturbing the thing that lay there.

'There was a fold in the sheet,' he said, speaking more slowly than ever now and so softly I had to lean close to hear him. 'See it, it's still there. It went under that. I could feel it through my pyjamas, moving on my stomach. Then it stopped moving and now it's lying there in the warmth. Probably asleep. I've been waiting for you.' He raised his eyes and looked at me.

'How long ago?'

'Hours,' he whispered. 'Hours and bloody hours and hours. I can't keep still much longer. I've been wanting to cough.'

There was not much doubt about the truth of Harry's story. As a matter of fact it wasn't a surprising thing for a krait to do. They hang around people's houses and they go for the warm places. The surprising thing was that Harry hadn't been bitten. The bite is quite deadly except sometimes when you catch it at once and they kill a fair number of people each year in Bengal, mostly in the villages.

'All right, Harry,' I said, and now I was whispering too. 'Don't move and don't talk any more unless you have to. You know it won't bite unless it's frightened. We'll fix it in no time.'

I went softly out of the room in my stocking feet and fetched a small sharp knife from the kitchen. I put it in my trouser pocket ready to use instantly in case something went wrong while we were still thinking out a plan. If Harry coughed or moved or did something to frighten the krait and got bitten, I was going to be ready to cut the bitten place and try to suck the venom out. I came back to the bedroom and Harry was still lying very quiet and sweating all over his face. His eyes followed me as I moved across the room to his bed and I could see he was wondering what I'd been up to. I stood beside him, trying to think of the best thing to do.

'Harry,' I said, and now when I spoke I put my mouth almost on his ear so I wouldn't have to raise my voice above the softest whisper, 'I think the best thing to do is for me to draw the sheet back very, very gently. Then we could have a look first. I think I could do that without disturbing it.'

'Don't be a damn fool.' There was no expression in his voice. He spoke each word too slowly, too carefully, and too softly for that. The expression was in the eyes and around the corners of the mouth.

'Why not?'

'The light would frighten him. It's dark under there now.'

'Then how about whipping the sheet back quick and brushing it off before it had time to strike?'

'Why don't you get a doctor?' Harry said. The way he looked at me told me I should have thought of that myself in the first place.

'A doctor. Of course. That's it. I'll get Ganderbai.'

I tiptoed out to the hall, looked up Ganderbai's number in the book, lifted the phone and told the operator to hurry.

'Dr Ganderbai,' I said. 'This is Timber Woods.'

'Hello, Mr Woods. You not in bed yet?'

'Look, could you come round at once? And bring serum – for a krait bite.'

'Who's been bitten?' The question came so sharply it was like a small explosion in my ear.

'No one. No one yet. But Harry Pope's in bed and he's got one lying on his stomach – asleep under the sheet on his stomach.'

For about three seconds there was silence on the line. Then speaking slowly, not like an explosion now but slowly, precisely, Ganderbai said, 'Tell him to keep quite still. He is not to move or to talk. Do you understand?'

'Of course.'

'I'll come at once!' He rang off and I went back to the bedroom. Harry's eyes watched me as I walked across to his bed.

'Ganderbai's coming. He said for you to lie still.'

'What in God's name does he think I'm doing!'

'Look, Harry, he said no talking. Absolutely no talking. Either of us.'

'Why don't you shut up then?' When he said this, one side of his mouth started twitching with rapid little downward movements that continued for a while after he finished speaking. I took out my handkerchief and very gently I wiped the sweat off his face and neck, and I could feel the slight twitching of the muscle – the one he used for smiling – as my fingers passed over it with the handkerchief.

I slipped out to the kitchen, got some ice from the ice-box, rolled it up in a napkin, and began to crush it small. That business of the mouth, I didn't like that. Or the way he talked, either. I carried the ice pack back to the bedroom and laid it across Harry's forehead.

'Keep you cool.'

He screwed up his eyes and drew breath sharply through his teeth. 'Take it away,' he whispered. 'Make me cough.' His smiling-muscle began to twitch again.

The beam of a headlamp shone through the window as Ganderbai's car swung around to the front of the bungalow. I went out to meet him, holding the ice pack with both hands.

'How is it?' Ganderbai asked, but he didn't stop to talk; he walked on past me across the balcony and through the screen doors into the hall. 'Where is he? Which room?'

He put his bag down on a chair in the hall and followed me into Harry's room. He was wearing soft-soled bedroom slippers and he walked across the floor noiselessly, delicately, like a careful cat. Harry watched him out of the sides of his eyes. When Ganderbai reached the bed he looked down at Harry and smiled, confident and reassuring, nodding his head to tell Harry it was a simple matter and he was not to worry but just to leave it to Dr Ganderbai. Then he turned and went back to the hall and I followed him.

'First thing is to try to get some serum into him,' he said, and he opened his bag and started to make preparations. 'Intravenously. But I must do it neatly. Don't want to make him flinch.'

We went into the kitchen and he sterilized a needle. He had a hypodermic syringe in one hand and a small bottle in the other and he stuck the needle through the rubber top of the bottle and began drawing a pale yellow liquid up into the syringe by pulling out the plunger. Then he handed the syringe to me.

'Hold that till I ask for it.'

He picked up the bag and together we returned to the room. Harry's eyes were bright now and wide open. Ganderbai bent over Harry and very cautiously, like a man handling sixteenth-century lace, he rolled up the pyjama sleeve to the elbow without moving the arm. I noticed he stood well away from the bed.

He whispered, 'I'm going to give you an injection. Serum. Just a prick but try not to move. Don't tighten your stomach muscles. Let them go limp.'

Harry looked at the syringe.

Ganderbai took a piece of red rubber tubing from his bag and slid one end under and up and around Harry's biceps; then he tied the tubing tight with a knot. He sponged a small area of the bare forearm with alcohol, handed the swab to me and took the syringe from my hand. He held it up to the light, squinting at the calibrations, squirting out some of the yellow fluid. I stood still beside him, watching. Harry was watching too and sweating all over his face so it shone like it was smeared thick with face cream melting on his skin and running down on to the pillow.

I could see the blue vein on the inside of Harry's forearm, swollen now because of the tourniquet, and then I saw the needle above the vein, Ganderbai holding the syringe almost flat against the arm, sliding the needle in sideways through the skin into the blue vein, sliding it slowly but so firmly it went in smooth as into cheese. Harry looked at the ceiling and closed his eyes and opened them again, but he didn't move.

When it was finished Ganderbai leaned forward putting his mouth close to Harry's ear. 'Now you'll be all right even if you *are* bitten. But don't move. Please don't move. I'll be back in a moment.'

He picked up his bag and went out to the hall and I followed.

'Is he safe now?' I asked.

'No.'

'How safe is he?'

The little Indian doctor stood there in the hall rubbing his lower lip.

'It must give some protection, mustn't it?' I asked.

He turned away and walked to the screen doors that led on to the verandah. I thought he was going through them, but he stopped this side of the doors and stood looking out into the night.

'Isn't the serum very good?' I asked.

'Unfortunately not,' he answered without turning round. 'It might save him. It might not. I am trying to think of something else to do.'

'Shall we draw the sheet back quick and brush it off before it has time to strike?'

'Never! We are not entitled to take a risk.' He spoke sharply and his voice was pitched a little higher than usual.

'We can't very well leave him lying there,' I said. 'He's getting nervous.'

'Please! Please!' he said, turning round, holding both hands up in the air. 'Not so fast, please. This is not a matter to rush into baldheaded.' He wiped his forehead with his handkerchief and stood there, frowning, nibbling his lip.

'You see,' he said at last. 'There is a way to do this. You know what we must do – we must administer an anaesthetic to the creature where it lies.'

It was a splendid idea.

'It is not safe,' he continued, 'because a snake is cold blooded and anaesthetic does not work so well or so quick with such animals, but it is better than any other thing to do. We could use ether ... chloroform ...' He was speaking slowly and trying to think the thing out while he talked.

'Which shall we use?'

'Chloroform,' he said suddenly. 'Ordinary chloroform. That is best. Now quick!' He took my arm and pulled me towards the balcony. 'Drive to my house! By the time you get there I will have waked up my boy on the telephone and he will show you my poisons cupboard. Here is the key of the cupboard. Take a bottle of chloroform. It has an orange label and the name is printed on it. I stay here in case anything happens. Be quick now, hurry! No, no, you don't need your shoes!'

I drove fast and in about fifteen minutes I was back with the bottle of chloroform. Ganderbai came out of Harry's room and met me in the hall. 'You got it?' he said. 'Good, good. I just been telling him what we are going to do. But now we must hurry. It is not easy for him in there like that all this time. I am afraid he might move.'

He went back to the bedroom and I followed, carrying the bottle carefully with both hands. Harry was lying on the bed in precisely the same position as before with the sweat pouring down his cheeks. His face was white and wet. He turned his eyes towards me and I smiled at him and nodded confidently. He continued to look at me. I raised my thumb, giving him the okay signal. He closed his eyes. Ganderbai was squatting down by the bed, and on the floor beside him was the hollow rubber tube that he had previously used as a tourniquet, and he'd got a small paper funnel fitted into one end of the tube.

He began to pull a little piece of the sheet out from under the mattress. He was working directly in line with Harry's stomach, about eighteen inches from it, and I watched his fingers as they tugged gently at the edge of the sheet. He worked so slowly it was almost impossible to discern any movement either in his fingers or in the sheet that was being pulled.

Finally he succeeded in making an opening under the sheet and he took the rubber tube and inserted one end of it in the opening so that it would slide under the sheet along the mattress towards Harry's body. I do not know how long it took him to slide that tube in a few inches. It may have been twenty minutes, it may have been forty. I never once saw the tube move. I knew it was going in because the visible part of it grew gradually shorter, but I doubted that the krait could have felt even the faintest vibration. Ganderbai himself was sweating now, large pearls of sweat standing out all over his forehead and along his upper lip. But his hands were steady and I noticed that his eyes were watching, not the tube in his hands, but the area of crumpled sheet above Harry's stomach.

Without looking up, he held out a hand to me for the chloroform. I twisted out the ground-glass stopper and put the bottle right into his hand, not letting go till I was sure he had a good hold on it. Then he jerked his head for me to come closer and he whispered, 'Tell him I'm going to soak the mattress and that it will be very cold under his body. He must be ready for that and he must not move. Tell him now.'

I bent over Harry and passed on the message.

'Why doesn't he get on with it?' Harry said.

'He's going to now, Harry. But it'll feel very cold, so be ready for it.'

'Oh, God Almighty, get on, get on!' For the first time he raised his voice, and Ganderbai glanced up sharply, watched him for a few seconds, then went back to his business.

Ganderbai poured a few drops of chloroform into the paper funnel and waited while it ran down the tube. Then he poured some more. Then he waited again, and the heavy sickening smell of chloroform spread out over the room bringing with it faint unpleasant memories of white-coated nurses and white surgeons standing in a white room around a long white table. Ganderbai was pouring steadily now and I could see the heavy vapour of the chloroform swirling slowly like smoke above the paper funnel. He paused, held the bottle up to the light, poured one more funnelful and handed the bottle back to me. Slowly he drew out the rubber tube from under the sheet; then he stood up.

The strain of inserting the tube and pouring the chloroform must have been great, and I recollect that when Ganderbai turned and whispered to me, his voice was small and tired. 'We'll give it fifteen minutes. Just to be safe.'

I leaned over to tell Harry. 'We're going to give it fifteen minutes, just to be safe. But it's probably done for already.'

'Then why for God's sake don't you look and see!' Again he spoke loudly and Ganderbai sprang round, his small brown face suddenly very angry. He had almost pure black eyes and he stared at Harry and Harry's smiling-muscle started to twitch. I took my handkerchief and wiped his wet face, trying to stroke his forehead a little for comfort as I did so.

Then we stood and waited beside the bed, Ganderbai watching Harry's face all the time in a curious intense manner. The little Indian was concentrating all his will power on keeping Harry quiet. He never once took his eyes from the patient and although he made no sound, he seemed somehow to be shouting at him all the time, saying: Now listen, you've got to listen, you're not going to go spoiling this now, d'you hear me; and Harry lay there twitching his mouth, sweating, closing his eyes, opening them, looking at me, at the sheet, at the ceiling, at me again, but never at Ganderbai. Yet somehow Ganderbai was holding him. The smell of chloroform was oppressive and it made me feel sick, but I couldn't leave the room now. I had the feeling someone was blowing up a huge balloon and I could see it was going to burst, but I couldn't look away.

At length Ganderbai turned and nodded and I knew he was ready to proceed. 'You go over to one side of the bed,' he said. 'We will each take one side of the sheet and draw it back together, but very slowly, please, and very quietly.'

'Keep still now, Harry,' I said and I went around to the other side of the bed and took hold of the sheet. Ganderbai stood opposite me, and together we began to draw back the sheet, lifting it up clear of Harry's body, taking it back very slowly, both of us standing well away but at the same time bending forward, trying to peer underneath it. The smell of chloroform was awful. I remember trying to hold my breath and when I couldn't do that any longer I tried to breathe shallow so the stuff wouldn't get into my lungs.

The whole of Harry's chest was visible now, or rather the striped pyjama top which covered it, and then I saw the white cord of his pyjama trousers, neatly tied in a bow. A little farther and I saw a button, a mother-of-pearl button, and that was something I had never had on my pyjamas, a fly button, let alone a mother-of-pearl one. This Harry, I thought, he is very refined. It is odd how one sometimes has frivolous thoughts at exciting moments, and I distinctly remember thinking about Harry being very refined when I saw that button.

Apart from the button there was nothing on his stomach.

We pulled the sheet back faster then, and when we had uncovered his legs and feet we let the sheet drop over the end of the bed on to the floor.

'Don't move,' Ganderbai said, 'don't move, Mr Pope'; and he began to peer around along the side of Harry's body and under his legs.

'We must be careful,' he said. 'It may be anywhere. It could be up the leg of his pyjamas.'

When Ganderbai said this, Harry quickly raised his head from the pillow and looked down at his legs. It was the first time he had moved. Then suddenly he jumped up, stood on his bed and shook his legs one after the other violently in the air. At that moment we both thought he had been bitten and Ganderbai was already reaching down into his bag for a scalpel and a tourniquet when Harry ceased his caperings and stood still and looked at the mattress he was standing on and shouted, 'It's not there!'

Ganderbai straightened up and for a moment he too looked at the mattress; then he looked up at Harry. Harry was all right. He hadn't been bitten and now he wasn't going to get bitten and he wasn't going to be killed and everything was fine. But that didn't seem to make anyone feel any better.

'Mr Pope, you are of course *quite* sure you saw it in the first place?' There was a note of sarcasm in Ganderbai's voice that he would never have employed in ordinary circumstances. 'You don't think you might possibly have been dreaming, do you, Mr Pope?' The way Ganderbai was looking at Harry, I realized that the sarcasm was not seriously intended. He was only easing up a bit after the strain.

Harry stood on his bed in his striped pyjamas, glaring at Ganderbai, and the colour began to spread out over his cheeks.

'Are you telling me I'm a liar?' he shouted.

Ganderbai remained absolutely still, watching Harry. Harry took a pace forward on the bed and there was a shining look in his eyes.

'Why, you dirty little Hindu sewer rat!'

'Shut up, Harry!' I said.

'You dirty black –'

'Harry!' I called. 'Shut up, Harry!' It was terrible, the things he was saying.

Ganderbai went out of the room as though neither of us was there and I followed him and put my arm around his shoulder as he walked across the hall and out on to the balcony.

'Don't you listen to Harry,' I said. 'This thing's made him so he doesn't know what he's saying.'

We went down the steps from the balcony to the drive and across the drive in the darkness to where his old Morris car was parked. He opened the door and got in.

'You did a wonderful job,' I said. 'Thank you so very much for coming.'

'All he needs is a good holiday,' he said quietly, without looking at me, then he started the engine and drove off.

THE WISH

Under the palm of one hand the child became aware of the scab of an old cut on his kneecap. He bent forward to examine it closely. A scab was always a fascinating thing; it presented a special challenge he was never able to resist.

Yes, he thought, I will pick it off, even if it isn't ready, even if the middle of it sticks, even if it hurts like anything.

With a fingernail he began to explore cautiously around the edges of the scab. He got the nail underneath it, and when he raised it, but ever so slightly, it suddenly came off, the whole hard brown scab came off beautifully, leaving an interesting little circle of smooth red skin.

Nice. Very nice indeed. He rubbed the circle and it didn't hurt. He picked up the scab, put it on his thigh and flipped it with a finger so that it flew away and landed on the edge of the carpet, the enormous red and black and yellow carpet that stretched the whole length of the hall from the stairs on which he sat to the front door in the distance. A tremendous carpet. Bigger than the tennis lawn. Much bigger than that. He regarded it gravely, settling his eyes upon it with mild pleasure. He had never really noticed it before, but now, all of a sudden, the colours seemed to brighten mysteriously and spring out at him in a most dazzling way.

You see, he told himself, I know how it is. The red parts of the carpet are red-hot lumps of coal. What I must do is this: I must walk all the way along it to the front door without touching them. If I touch the red I will be burnt. As a matter of fact, I will be burnt up completely. And the black parts of the carpet ... yes, the black parts are snakes, poisonous snakes, adders mostly, and cobras, thick like tree-trunks round the middle, and if I touch one of *them*, I'll be bitten and I'll die before tea time. And if I get across safely, without being burnt and without being bitten, I will be given a puppy for my birthday tomorrow.

He got to his feet and climbed higher up the stairs to obtain a better view of this vast tapestry of colour and death. Was it possible? Was there enough yellow? Yellow was the only colour he was allowed to walk on. Could it be done? This was not a journey to be undertaken lightly; the risks were too great for that. The child's face – a fringe of white-gold hair, two large blue eyes, a small pointed chin – peered down anxiously over the banisters. The yellow was a bit thin in places and there were one or two widish gaps, but it did seem to go all the way along to the other end. For someone who had only yesterday triumphantly travelled the whole length of the brick path from the stables to the summer-house without touching the cracks, this carpet thing should not be too difficult. Except for the snakes. The mere thought of snakes sent a fine electricity of fear running like pins down the backs of his legs and under the soles of his feet.

He came slowly down the stairs and advanced to the edge of the carpet. He extended one small sandalled foot and placed it cautiously upon a patch of yellow. Then he brought the other foot up, and there was just enough room for him to stand with the two feet together. There! He had started! His bright oval face was curiously intent, a shade whiter perhaps than before, and he was holding his arms out sideways to assist his balance. He took another step, lifting his foot high over a patch of black, aiming carefully with his toe for a narrow channel of yellow on the other side. When he had completed the second step he paused to rest, standing very stiff and still. The narrow channel of yellow ran forward unbroken for at least five yards and he advanced gingerly along it, bit by bit, as though walking a tightrope. Where it finally curled off sideways, he had to take another long stride, this time over a vicious-looking mixture of black and red. Half-way across he began to wobble. He waved his arms around wildly, windmill fashion, to keep his balance, and he got across safely and rested again on the other side. He was quite breathless now, and so tense he stood high on his toes all the time, arms out sideways, fists clenched. He was on a big safe island of yellow. There was lots of room on it, he couldn't possibly fall off, and he stood there resting, hesitating, waiting, wishing he could stay for ever on this big safe yellow island. But the fear of not getting the puppy compelled him to go on.

Step by step, he edged further ahead, and between each one he paused to decide exactly where next he should put his foot. Once, he had a choice of ways, either to left or right, and he chose the left because although it seemed the more difficult, there was not so much black in that direction. The black was what made him nervous. He glanced quickly over his shoulder to see how far he had come. Nearly half-way. There could be no turning back now. He was in the middle and he couldn't turn back and he couldn't jump off sideways either because it was too far, and when he looked at all the red and all the black that lay ahead of him, he felt that old sudden sickening surge of panic in his chest – like last Easter time, that afternoon when he got lost all alone in the darkest part of Piper's Wood.

He took another step, placing his foot carefully upon the only little piece of yellow within reach, and this time the point of the foot came within a centimetre of some black. It wasn't touching the black, he could see it wasn't touching, he could see the small line of yellow separating the toe of his sandal from the black; but the snake stirred as though sensing the nearness, and raised its head and gazed at the foot with bright beady eyes, watching to see if it was going to touch.

'*I'm not touching you! You mustn't bite me! You know I'm not touching you!*'

Another snake slid up noiselessly beside the first, raised its head, two heads now, two pairs of eyes staring at the foot, gazing at a little naked place just below the sandal strap where the skin showed through. The child went high up on his toes and stayed there, frozen stiff with terror. It was minutes before he dared to move again.

The next step would have to be a really long one. There was this deep curling river of black that ran clear across the width of the carpet, and he was forced by this position to cross it at its widest part. He thought first of trying to jump it, but decided he couldn't be sure of landing accurately on the narrow band of yellow the other side. He took a deep breath, lifted one foot, and inch by inch he pushed it out in front of him, far far out, then down and down until at last the tip of his sandal was across and resting safely on the edge of the yellow. He leaned forward, transferring his weight to his front foot. Then he tried to bring the back foot up as well. He strained and pulled and jerked his body, but the legs were too wide apart and he couldn't make it. He tried to get back again. He couldn't do that either. He was doing the splits and he was properly stuck. He glanced down and saw this deep curling river of black underneath him. Parts of it were stirring now, and uncoiling and sliding and beginning to shine with a dreadfully oily glister. He wobbled, waved his arms frantically to keep his balance, but that seemed to make it worse. He was starting to go over. He was going over to the right, quite slowly he was going over, then faster and faster, and at the last moment, instinctively he put out a hand to break the fall and the next thing he saw was this bare hand of his going right into the middle of a great glistening mass of black and he gave one piercing cry of terror as it touched.

Outside in the sunshine, far away behind the house, the mother was looking for her son.

NECK

When, about eight years ago, old Sir William Turton died and his son Basil inherited *The Turton Press* (as well as the title), I can remember how they started laying bets around Fleet Street as to just how long it would be before some nice young woman managed to persuade the little fellow that she must look after him. That is to say, him and his money.

The new Sir Basil Turton was maybe forty years old at the time, a bachelor, a man of mild and simple character who up to then had shown no interest in anything at all except his collection of modern paintings and sculpture. No woman had disturbed him; no scandal or gossip had ever touched his name. But now that he had become the proprietor of quite a large newspaper and magazine empire, it was necessary for him to emerge from the calm of his father's country house and come up to London.

Naturally, the vultures started gathering at once, and I believe that not only Fleet Street but very nearly the whole of the city was looking on eagerly as they scrambled for the body. It was slow motion, of course, deliberate and deadly slow motion, and therefore not so much like vultures as a bunch of agile crabs clawing for a piece of horsemeat under water.

But to everyone's surprise the little chap proved to be remarkably elusive, and the chase dragged on right through the spring and early summer of that year. I did not know Sir Basil personally, nor did I have any reason to feel friendly towards him, but I couldn't help taking the side of my own sex and found myself cheering loudly every time he managed to get himself off the hook.

Then, round about the beginning of August, apparently at some secret female signal, the girls declared a sort of truce among themselves while they went abroad, and rested, and regrouped, and made fresh plans for the winter kill. This was a mistake because precisely at that moment a dazzling creature called Natalia something or other, whom nobody had heard of before, swept in from the Continent, took Sir Basil firmly by the wrist and led him off in a kind of swoon to the Registry Office at Caxton Hall where she married him before anyone else, least of all the bridegroom, realized what was happening.

You can imagine that the London ladies were indignant, and

naturally they started disseminating a vast amount of fruity gossip about the new Lady Turton ('That dirty poacher,' they called her). But we don't have to go into that. In fact, for the purposes of this story we can skip the next six years, which brings us right up to the present, to an occasion exactly one week ago today when I myself had the pleasure of meeting her ladyship for the first time. By now, as you must have guessed, she was not only running the whole of *The Turton Press*, but as a result had become a considerable political force in the country. I realize that other women have done this sort of thing before, but what made her particular case unusual was the fact that she was a foreigner and that nobody seemed to know precisely what country she came from – Yugoslavia, Bulgaria, or Russia.

So last Thursday I went to this small dinner party at a friend's in London, and while we were standing around in the drawing-room before the meal, sipping good Martinis and talking about the atom bomb and Mr Bevan, the maid popped her head in to announce the last guest.

'Lady Turton,' she said.

Nobody stopped talking; we were too well-mannered for that. No heads were turned. Only our eyes swung round to the door, waiting for the entrance.

She came in fast – tall and slim in a red-gold dress with sparkles on it – the mouth smiling, the hand outstretched towards her hostess, and my heavens, I must say she was a beauty.

'Mildred, good evening!'

'My dear Lady Turton! How nice!'

I believe we *did* stop talking then, and we turned and stared and stood waiting quite meekly to be introduced, just like she might have been the Queen or a famous film star. But she was better looking than either of those. The hair was black, and to go with it she had one of those pale, oval, innocent fifteenth-century Flemish faces, almost exactly a Madonna by Memling or Van Eyck. At least that was the first impression. Later, when my turn came to shake hands, I got a closer look and saw that except for the outline and colouring it wasn't really a Madonna at all – far, far from it.

The nostrils for example were very odd, somehow more open, more flaring than any I had seen before, and excessively arched. This gave the whole nose a kind of open, snorting look that had something of the wild animal about it – the mustang.

And the eyes, when I saw them close, were not wide and round the way the Madonna painters used to make them, but long and half closed, half smiling, half sullen, and slightly vulgar, so that in one way and another they gave her a most delicately dissipated air. What's more, they didn't look at you directly. They came to you slowly from over on one side with a curious sliding motion that made me nervous.

I tried to see their colour, thought it was pale grey, but couldn't be sure.

Then she was led away across the room to meet other people. I stood watching her. She was clearly conscious of her success and of the way these Londoners were deferring to her. 'Here am I,' she seemed to be saying, 'and I only came over a few years ago, but already I am richer and more powerful than any of you.' There was a little prance of triumph in her walk.

A few minutes later we went in to dinner, and to my surprise I found myself seated on her ladyship's right. I presumed that our hostess had done this as a kindness to me, thinking I might pick up some material for the social column I write each day in the evening paper. I settled myself down ready for an interesting meal. But the famous lady took no notice of me at all; she spent her time talking to the man on her left, the host. Until at last, just as I was finishing my ice-cream, she suddenly turned, reached over, picked up my place card and read the name. Then, with that queer sliding motion of the eyes she looked into my face. I smiled and made a little bow. She didn't smile back, but started shooting questions at me, rather personal questions – job, age, family, things like that – in a peculiar lapping voice, and I found myself answering as best I could.

During this inquisition it came out among other things that I was a lover of painting and sculpture.

'Then you should come down to the country some time and see my husband's collection.' She said it casually, merely as a form of conversation, but you must realize that in my job I cannot afford to lose an opportunity like this.

'How kind of you, Lady Turton. But I'd simply love to. When shall I come?'

Her head went up and she hesitated, frowned, shrugged her shoulders, and then said, 'Oh, I don't care. Any time.'

'How about this next week-end? Would that be all right?'

The slow narrow eyes rested a moment on mine, then travelled away. 'I suppose so, if you wish. I don't care.'

And that was how on the following Saturday afternoon I came to be driving down to Wooton with my suitcase in the back of the car. You may think that perhaps I forced the invitation a bit, but I couldn't have got it any other way. And apart from the professional aspect, I personally wanted very much to see the house. As you know, Wooton is one of the truly great stone houses of the early English Renaissance. Like its sisters, Longleat, Wollaton, and Montacute, it was built in the latter half of the sixteenth century when for the first time a great man's house could be designed as a comfortable dwelling, not as a castle, and when a new group of architects such as John Thorpe and the Smithsons were starting to do marvellous things all over the country.

It lies south of Oxford, near a small town called Princes Risborough –
not a long trip from London – and as I swung in through the main
gates the sky was closing overhead and the early winter evening was
beginning.

I went slowly up the long drive, trying to see as much of the grounds
as possible, especially the famous topiary which I had heard such a
lot about. And I must say it was an impressive sight. On all sides there
were massive yew trees, trimmed and clipped into many different
comical shapes – hens, pigeons, bottles, boots, armchairs, castles, egg-
cups, lanterns, old women with flaring petticoats, tall pillars, some
crowned with a ball, others with big rounded roofs and stemless
mushroom finials – and in the half darkness the greens had turned to
black so that each figure, each tree, took on a dark, smooth sculptural
quality. At one point I saw a lawn covered with gigantic chessmen,
each a live yew tree, marvellously fashioned. I stopped the car, got
out and walked among them, and they were twice as tall as me. What's
more, the set was complete, kings, queens, bishops, knights, rooks and
pawns, standing in position as for the start of a game.

Around the next bend I saw the great grey house itself, and in front
of it the large entrance forecourt enclosed by a high balustraded wall
with small pillared pavilions at its outer angles. The piers of the
balustrades were surmounted by stone obelisks – the Italian influence
on the Tudor mind – and a flight of steps at least a hundred feet wide
led up to the house.

As I drove into the forecourt I noticed with rather a shock that the
fountain basin in the middle supported a large statue by Epstein. A
lovely thing, mind you, but surely not quite in sympathy with its
surroundings. Then, looking back as I climbed the stairway to the
front door, I saw that on all the little lawns and terraces round about
there were other modern statues and many kinds of curious sculpture.
In the distance, I thought I recognized Gaudier Brzeska, Brancusi,
Saint-Gaudens, Henry Moore, and Epstein again.

The door was opened by a young footman who led me up to a
bedroom on the first floor. Her ladyship, he explained, was resting, so
were the other guests, but they would all be down in the main drawing-
room in an hour or so, dressed for dinner.

Now in my job it is necessary to do a lot of week-ending. I suppose
I spend around fifty Saturdays and Sundays a year in other people's
houses, and as a result I have become fairly sensitive to unfamiliar
atmosphere. I can tell good or bad almost by sniffing with my nose
the moment I get in the front door; and this one I was in now I did
not like. The place smelled wrong. There was the faint, desiccated
whiff of something troublesome in the air; I was concious of it even as
I lay steaming luxuriously in my great marble bath; and I couldn't

help hoping that no unpleasant things were going to happen before Monday came.

The first of them – though more of a surprise than an unpleasantness – occurred ten minutes later. I was sitting on the bed putting on my socks when softly the door opened, and an ancient lopsided gnome in black tails slid into the room. He was the butler, he explained, and his name was Jelks, and he did so hope I was comfortable and had everything I wanted.

I told him I was and had.

He said he would do all he could to make my week-end agreeable. I thanked him and waited for him to go. He hesitated, and then, in a voice dripping with unction, he begged permission to mention a rather delicate matter. I told him to go ahead.

To be quite frank, he said, it was about tipping. The whole business of tipping made him acutely miserable.

Oh? And why was that?

Well, if I really wanted to know, he didn't like the idea that his guests felt under an obligation to tip him when they left the house – as indeed they did. It was an undignified proceeding both for the tipper and the tipped. Moreover, he was well aware of the anguish that was often created in the minds of guests such as myself, if I would pardon the liberty, who might feel compelled by convention to give more than they could really afford.

He paused, and two small crafty eyes watched my face for a sign. I murmured that he needn't worry himself about such things so far as I was concerned.

On the contrary, he said, he hoped sincerely that I would agree from the beginning to give him no tip at all.

'Well,' I said. 'Let's not fuss about it now, and when the time comes we'll see how we feel.'

'No, sir!' he cried. 'Please, I really must insist.'

So I agreed.

He thanked me, and shuffled a step or two closer. Then, laying his head on one side and clasping his hands before him like a priest, he gave a tiny apologetic shrug of the shoulders. The small sharp eyes were still watching me, and I waited, one sock on, the other in my hands, trying to guess what was coming next.

All that he would ask, he said softly, so softly now that his voice was like music heard faintly in the street outside a great concert hall, all that he would ask was that instead of a tip I should give him thirty-three and a third per cent of my winnings at cards over the week-end. If I lost, there would be nothing to pay.

It was all so soft and smooth and sudden that I was not even surprised.

'Do they play a lot of cards, Jelks?'

'Yes, sir, a great deal.'

'Isn't thirty-three and a third a bit steep?'

'I don't think so, sir.'

'I'll give you ten per cent.'

'No, sir, I couldn't do that.' He was now examining the finger-nails of his left hand, and patiently frowning.

'Then we'll make it fifteen. All right?'

'Thirty-three and a third, sir. It's very reasonable. After all, sir, seeing that I don't even know if you are a good player, what I'm actually doing, not meaning to be personal, is backing a horse and I've never even seen it run.'

No doubt you think I should never have started bargaining with the butler in the first place, and perhaps you are right. But being a liberal-minded person, I always try my best to be affable with the lower classes. Apart from that, the more I thought about it, the more I had to admit to myself that it was an offer no sportsman had the right to reject.

'All right then, Jelks. As you wish.'

'Thank you, sir.' He moved towards the door, walking slowly sideways like a crab; but once more he hesitated, a hand on the knob. 'If I may give you a little advice, sir – may I?'

'Yes?'

'It's simply that her ladyship tends to overbid her hand.'

Now *this was* going too far. I was so startled I dropped my sock. After all, it's one thing to have a harmless little sporting arrangement with the butler about tipping, but when he begins conniving with you to take money away from the hostess then it's time to call a halt.

'All right Jelks. Now that'll do.'

'No offence, sir, I hope. All I mean is you're bound to be playing against her ladyship. She always partners Major Haddock.'

'Major Haddock? You mean Major Jack Haddock?'

'Yes, sir.'

I noticed there was the trace of a sneer around the corners of Jelks's nose when he spoke about this man. And it was worse with Lady Turton. Each time he said 'her ladyship' he spoke the words with the outsides of his lips as though he were nibbling a lemon, and there was a subtle, mocking inflection in his voice.

'You'll excuse me now, sir. *Her ladyship* will be down at seven o'clock. So will *Major Haddock* and the others.' He slipped out of the door leaving behind him a certain dampness in the room and a faint smell of embrocation.

Shortly after seven, I found my way to the main drawing-room, and Lady Turton, as beautiful as ever, got up to greet me.

'I wasn't even sure you were coming,' she said in that peculiar lilting voice. 'What's your name again?'

'I'm afraid I took you at your word, Lady Turton. I hope it's all right.'

'Why not?' she said. 'There's forty-seven bedrooms in the house. This is my husband.'

A small man came around the back of her and said, 'You know, I'm so glad you were able to come.' He had a lovely warm smile and when he took my hand I felt instantly a touch of friendship in his fingers.

'And Carmen La Rosa,' Lady Turton said.

This was a powerfully built woman who looked as though she might have something to do with horses. She nodded at me, and although my hand was already half-way out she didn't give me hers, thus forcing me to convert the movement into a noseblow.

'You have a cold?' she said. 'I'm sorry.'

I did not like Miss Carmen La Rosa.

'And this is Jack Haddock.'

I knew this man slightly. He was a director of companies (whatever that may mean), and a well-known member of society. I had used his name a few times in my column, but I had never liked him, and this I think was mainly because I have a deep suspicion of all people who carry their military titles back with them into private life – especially majors and colonels. Standing there in his dinner-jacket with his full-blooded animal face and black eyebrows and large white teeth, he looked so handsome there was almost something indecent about it. He had a way of raising his upper lip when he smiled, baring his teeth, and he was smiling now as he gave me a hairy brown hand.

'I hope you're going to say some nice things about us in your column.'

'He better had,' Lady Turton said, 'or I'll say some nasty ones about him on my front page.'

I laughed, but the three of them, Lady Turton, Major Haddock, and Carmen La Rosa had already turned away and were settling themselves back on the sofa. Jelks gave me a drink, and Sir Basil drew me gently aside for a quiet chat at the other end of the room. Every now and again Lady Turton would call her husband to fetch her something – another Martini, a cigarette, an ashtray, a handkerchief – and he, half rising from his chair, would be forestalled by the watchful Jelks who fetched it for him.

Clearly, Jelks loved his master; and just as clearly he hated the wife. Each time he did something for her he made a little sneer with his nose and drew his lips together so they puckered like a turkey's bottom.

At dinner, our hostess sat her two friends, Haddock and La Rosa, on either side of her. This unconventional arrangement left Sir Basil and me at the other end of the table where we were able to continue our pleasant talk about painting and sculpture. Of course it was obvious to me by now that the Major was infatuated with her ladyship. And again, although I hate to say it, it seemed as though the La Rosa woman was hunting the same bird.

All this foolishness appeared to delight the hostess. But it did not delight her husband. I could see that he was conscious of the little scene all the time we were talking; and often his mind would wander from our subject and he would stop short in mid-sentence, his eyes travelling down to the other end of the table to settle pathetically for a moment on that lovely head with the black hair and the curiously flaring nostrils. He must have noticed then how exhilarated she was, how the hand that gestured as she spoke rested every now and again on the Major's arm, and how the other woman, the one who perhaps had something to do with horses, kept saying, 'Nata-*li*-a? Now Nata-*li*-a, listen to me!'

'Tomorrow,' I said, 'you must take me round and show me the sculptures you've put up in the garden.'

'Of course,' he said, 'with pleasure.' He glanced again at the wife, and his eyes had a sort of supplicating look that was piteous beyond words. He was so mild and passive a man in every way that even now I could see there was no anger in him, no danger, no chance of an explosion.

After dinner I was ordered straight to the card table to partner Miss Carmen La Rosa against Major Haddock and Lady Turton. Sir Basil sat quietly on the sofa with a book.

There was nothing unusual about the game itself; it was routine and rather dull. But Jelks was a nuisance. All evening he prowled around us, emptying ashtrays and asking about drinks and peering at our hands. He was obviously short-sighted and I doubt whether he saw much of what was going on because as you may or may not know, here in England no butler has ever been permitted to wear spectacles – nor, for that matter, a moustache. This is the golden, unbreakable rule, and a very sensible one it is too, although I'm not quite sure what lies behind it. I presume that a moustache would make him look too much like a gentleman, and spectacles too much like an American, and where would we be then I should like to know? In any event Jelks was a nuisance all evening; and so was Lady Turton who was constantly being called to the phone on newspaper business.

At eleven o'clock she looked up from her cards and said, 'Basil, it's time you went to bed.'

'Yes, my dear, perhaps it is.' He closed the book, got up, and stood for a minute watching the play. 'Are you having a good game?' he asked.

The others didn't answer him, so I said, 'It's a nice game.'

'I'm so glad. And Jelks will look after you and get anything you want.'

'Jelks can go to bed too,' the wife said.

I could hear Major Haddock breathing through his nose beside me, and the soft drop of the cards one by one on to the table, and then the sound of Jelks's feet shuffling over the carpet towards us.

'You wouldn't prefer me to stay, m'lady?'

'No. Go to bed. You too, Basil.'

'Yes, my dear. Good night. Good night all.'

Jelks opened the door for him, and he went slowly out followed by the butler.

As soon as the next rubber was over, I said that I too wanted to go to bed.

'All right,' Lady Turton said. 'Good night.'

I went up to my room, locked the door, took a pill, and went to sleep.

The next morning, Sunday, I got up and dressed around ten o'clock and went down to the breakfast-room. Sir Basil was there before me, and Jelks was serving him with grilled kidneys and bacon and fried tomatoes. He was delighted to see me and suggested that as soon as we had finished eating we should take a long walk around the grounds. I told him nothing would give me more pleasure.

Half an hour later we started out, and you've no idea what a relief it was to get away from that house and into the open air. It was one of those warm shining days that come occasionally in mid-winter after a night of heavy rain, with a bright surprising sun and no breath of wind. Bare trees seemed beautiful in the sunlight, water still dripping from the branches, and wet places all around were sparkling with diamonds. The sky had small faint clouds.

'*What* a lovely day!'

'Yes – isn't it a lovely day!'

We spoke hardly another word during the walk; it wasn't necessary. But he took me everywhere and I saw it all – the huge chess-men and all the rest of the topiary. The elaborate garden houses, the pools, the fountains, the children's maze whose hedges were hornbeam and lime so that it was only good in summer when the leaves were out, and the parterres, the rockeries, the greenhouses with their vines and nectarine trees. And of course, the sculpture. Most of the contemporary European sculptors were there, in bronze, granite, limestone, and wood; and although it was a pleasure to see them warming and glowing in the sun, to me they still looked a trifle out of place in these vast formal surroundings.

'Shall we rest here now a little while?' Sir Basil said after we had walked for more than an hour. So we sat down on a white bench beside a water-lily pond full of carp and goldfish, and lit cigarettes. We were some way from the house, on a piece of ground that was raised above its surroundings, and from where we sat the gardens were spread out below us like a drawing in one of those old books on garden architecture, with the hedges and lawns and terraces and fountains making a pretty pattern of squares and rings.

'My father bought this place just before I was born,' Sir Basil said. 'I've lived here ever since, and I know every inch of it. Each day I grow to love it more.'

'It must be wonderful in summer.'

'Oh, but it is. You should come down and see it in May and June. Will you promise to do that?'

'Of course,' I said. 'I'd love to come,' and as I spoke I was watching the figure of a woman dressed in red moving among the flower-beds in the far distance. I saw her cross over a wide expanse of lawn, and there was a lilt in her walk, a little shadow attending her, and when she was over the lawn, she turned left and went along one side of a high wall of clipped yew until she came to another smaller lawn that was circular and had in its centre a piece of sculpture.

'This garden is younger than the house,' Sir Basil said. 'It was laid out early in the eighteenth century by a Frenchman called Beaumont, the same fellow who did Levens, in Westmorland. For at least a year he had two hundred and fifty men working on it.'

The woman in the red dress had been joined now by a man, and they were standing face to face, about a yard apart, in the very centre of the whole garden panorama, on this little circular patch of lawn, apparently conversing. The man had some small black object in his hand.

'If you're interested, I'll show you the bills that Beaumont put in to the old Duke while he was making it.'

'I'd like very much to see them. They must be fascinating.'

'He paid his labourers a shilling a day and they worked ten hours.'

In the clear sunlight it was not difficult to follow the movements and gestures of the two figures on the lawn. They had turned now towards the piece of sculpture, and were pointing at it in a sort of mocking way, apparently laughing and making jokes about its shape. I recognized it as a being one of the Henry Moores, done in wood, a thin smooth object of singular beauty that had two or three holes in it and a number of strange limbs protruding.

'When Beaumont planted the yew trees for the chess-men and the other things, he knew they wouldn't amount to much for at least a hundred years. We don't seem to possess that sort of patience in our planning these days, do we? What do you think?'

'No,' I said. 'We don't.'

The black object in the man's hand turned out to be a camera, and now he had stepped back and was taking pictures of the woman beside the Henry Moore. She was striking a number of different poses, all of them, so far as I could see, ludicrous and meant to be amusing. Once she put her arms around one of the protruding wooden limbs and hugged it, and another time she climbed up and sat side-saddle on the thing, holding imaginary reins in her hands. A great wall of yew hid these two people from the house, and indeed from all the rest of the garden except the little hill on which we sat. They had every right to believe that they were not overlooked, and even if they had happened to glance our way – which was into the sun – I doubt whether they would have noticed the two small motionless figures sitting on the bench beside the pond.

'You know, I love these yews,' Sir Basil said. 'The colour of them is so wonderful in a garden because it rests the eye. And in the summer it breaks up the areas of brilliance into little patches and makes them more comfortable to admire. Have you noticed the different shades of green on the planes and facets of each clipped tree?'

'It's lovely, isn't it.'

The man now seemed to be explaining something to the woman, and pointing at the Henry Moore, and I could tell by the way they threw back their heads that they were laughing again. The man continued to point, and then the woman walked around the back of the wood carving, bent down and poked her head through one of its holes. The thing was about the size, shall I say, of a small horse, but thinner than that, and from where I sat I could see both sides of it – to the left, the woman's body, to the right, her head protruding through. It was very much like one of those jokes at the seaside where you put your head through a hole in a board and get photographed as a fat lady. The man was photographing her now.

'There's another thing about yews,' Sir Basil said. 'In the early summer when the young shoots come out ...' At that moment he paused and sat up straighter and leaned slightly forward, and I could sense his whole body suddenly stiffening.

'Yes,' I said, 'when the young shoots come out?'

The man had taken the photograph, but the woman still had her head through the hole, and now I saw him put both hands (as well as the camera) behind his back and advance towards her. Then he bent forward so his face was close to hers, touching it, and he held it there while he gave her, I suppose, a few kisses or something like that. In the stillness that followed, I fancied I heard a faint faraway tinkle of female laughter coming to us through the sunlight across the garden.

'Shall we go back to the house?' I asked.

'Back to the house?'

'Yes, shall we go back and have a drink before lunch?'

'A drink? Yes, we'll have a drink.' But he didn't move. He sat very still, gone far away from me now, staring intently at the two figures. I also was staring at them. I couldn't take my eyes away; I *had* to look. It was like seeing a dangerous little ballet in miniature from a great distance, and you knew the dancers and the music but not the end of the story, not the choreography, nor what they were going to do next, and you were fascinated, and you *had* to look.

'Gaudier Brzeska,' I said. 'How great do you think he might've become if he hadn't died so young?'

'Who?'

'Gaudier Brzeska.'

'Yes,' he said. 'Of course.'

I noticed now that something queer was happening. The woman still had her head through the hole, but she was beginning to wriggle her body from side to side in a slow unusual manner, and the man was standing motionless, a pace or so away watching her. He seemed suddenly uneasy the way he stood there, and I could tell by the drop of the head and by the stiff intent set of the body that there was no laughter in him any more. For a while he remained still, then I saw him place his camera on the ground and go forward to the woman, taking her head in his hands; and all at once it was more like a puppet show than a ballet, with tiny wooden figures performing tiny jerky movements, crazy and unreal, on a faraway sunlit stage.

We sat quietly together on the white bench, and we watched while the tiny puppet man began to manipulate the woman's head with his hands. He was doing it gently, there was no doubt about that, slowly and gently, stepping back every now and then to think about it some more, and several times crouching down to survey the situation from another angle. Whenever he left her alone the woman would again start to wriggle her body, and the peculiar way she did it reminded me of a dog that feels a collar round its neck for the first time.

'She's stuck,' Sir Basil said.

And now the man was walking to the other side of the carving, the side where the woman's body was, and he put out his hands and began trying to do something with her neck. Then, as though suddenly exasperated, he gave the neck two or three quick jerky pulls, and this time the sound of the woman's voice, raised high in anger, or pain, or both, came back to us small and clear through the sunlight.

Out of the corner of one eye I could see Sir Basil nodding his head quietly up and down. 'I got my fist caught in a jar of boiled sweets once,' he said, 'and I couldn't get it out.'

The man had retreated a few yards, and was standing with hands on hips, head up, looking furious and sullen. The woman, from her uncomfortable position, appeared to be talking to him, or rather shouting at him, and although the body itself was pretty firmly fixed and could only wriggle, the legs were free and did a good deal of moving and stamping.

'I broke the jar with a hammer and told my mother I'd knocked it off the shelf by mistake.' He seemed calmer now, not tense at all, although his voice was curiously flat. 'I suppose we'd better go down and see if we can help.'

'Perhaps we should.'

But still he didn't move. He took out a cigarette and lit it, putting the used match carefully back in the box.

'I'm sorry,' he said. 'Will you have one?'

'Thanks, I think I will.' He made a little ceremony of giving me the cigarette and lighting it for me, and again he put the used match back in the box. Then we got up and walked slowly down the grass slope.

We came upon them silently, through an archway in the yew hedge, and it was naturally quite a surprise.

'What's the matter here?' Sir Basil asked. He spoke softly, with a dangerous softness that I'm sure his wife had never heard before.

'She's gone and put her head through the hole and now she can't get it out,' Major Haddock said. 'Just for a lark, you know.'

'For a what?'

'Basil!' Lady Turton shouted. 'Don't be such a damn fool! Do something, can't you!' She may not have been able to move much, but she could still talk.

'Pretty obvious we're going to have to break up this lump of wood,' the Major said. There was a small smudge of red on his grey moustache, and this, like the single extra touch of colour that ruins a perfect painting, managed somehow to destroy all his manly looks. It made him comic.

'You mean break the Henry Moore?'

'My dear sir, there's no other way of setting the lady free. God knows how she managed to squeeze it in, but I know for a fact that she can't pull it out. It's the ears get in the way.'

'Oh dear,' Sir Basil said. 'What a terrible pity. My beautiful Henry Moore.'

At this stage Lady Turton began abusing her husband in a most unpleasant manner, and there's no knowing how long it would have gone on had not Jelks suddenly appeared out of the shadows. He came sidling silently on to the lawn and stationed himself at a respectful distance from Sir Basil, as though awaiting instructions. His black clothes looked perfectly ridiculous in the morning sunlight, and with his ancient pink-white face and white hands he was like some small crabby animal that has lived all its life in a hole under the ground.

'Is there anything I can do, Sir Basil?' He kept his voice level, but I didn't think his face was quite straight. When he looked at Lady Turton there was a little exulting glimmer in his eyes.

'Yes Jelks, there is. Go back and get me a saw or something so I can cut out a section of this wood.'

'Shall I call one of the men, Sir Basil? William is a good carpenter.'

'No, I'll do it myself. Just get the tools – and hurry.'

While they were waiting for Jelks, I strolled away because I didn't want to hear any more of the things that Lady Turton was saying to her husband. But I was back in time to see the butler returning, followed now by the other woman, Carmen La Rosa, who made a rush for the hostess.

'Nata-*li*-a! My dear Nata-*li*-a! What *have* they done to you?'

'Oh shut up,' the hostess said. 'And get out of the way, will you.'

Sir Basil took up a position close to his lady's head, waiting for Jelks. Jelks advanced slowly, carrying a saw in one hand, an axe in the other, and he stopped maybe a yard away. He then held out both implements in front of him so his master could choose, and there was a brief moment – no more than two or three seconds – of silence, and of waiting, and it just happened that I was watching Jelks at this time. I saw the hand that was carrying the axe come forward an extra fraction of an inch towards Sir Basil. It was so slight a movement it was barely noticeable – a tiny pushing forward of the hand, slow and secret, a little offer, a little coaxing offer that was accompanied perhaps by an infinitesimal lift of the eyebrow.

I'm not sure whether Sir Basil saw it, but he hesitated, and again the hand that held the axe came edging forward, and it was almost exactly like that card trick where the man says 'Take one, whichever one you want,' and you always get the one he means you to have. Sir Basil got the axe. I saw him reach out in a dreamy sort of way, accepting it from Jelks, and then, the instant he felt the handle in his grasp he seemed to realize what was required of him and he sprang to life.

For me, after that, it was like the awful moment when you see a child running out into the road and a car is coming and all you can do is shut your eyes tight and wait until the noise tells you it has happened. The moment of waiting becomes a long lucid period of time with yellow and red spots dancing on a black field, and even if you open your eyes again and find that nobody has been killed or hurt, it makes no difference because so far as you and your stomach were concerned you saw it all.

I saw this one all right, every detail of it, and I didn't open my eyes again until I heard Sir Basil's voice, even softer than usual, calling in gentle protest to the butler.

'Jelks,' he was saying, and I looked and saw him standing there as calm as you please, still holding the axe. Lady Turton's head was there too, still sticking through the hole, but her face had turned a terrible ashy grey, and the mouth was opening and shutting and making a kind of gurgling sound.

'Look here, Jelks,' Sir Basil was saying. 'What on earth are you

thinking about. This thing's much too dangerous. Give me the saw.'
And as he exchanged implements I noticed for the first time two little
warm roses of colour appearing on his cheeks, and above them, all
around the corners of his eyes, the twinkling tiny wrinkles of a smile.

THE SOUND MACHINE

It was a warm summer evening and Klausner walked quickly through the front gate and around the side of the house and into the garden at the back. He went on down the garden until he came to a wooden shed and he unlocked the door, went inside and closed the door behind him.

The interior of the shed was an unpainted room. Against one wall, on the left, there was a long wooden workbench, and on it, among a littering of wires and batteries and small sharp tools, there stood a black box about three feet long, the shape of a child's coffin.

Klausner moved across the room to the box. The top of the box was open, and he bent down and began to poke and peer inside it among a mass of different-coloured wires and silver tubes. He picked up a piece of paper that lay beside the box, studied it carefully, put it down, peered inside the box and started running his fingers along the wires, tugging gently at them to test the connections, glancing back at the paper, then into the box, then at the paper again, checking each wire. He did this for perhaps an hour.

Then he put a hand around to the front of the box where there were three dials, and he began to twiddle them, watching at the same time the movement of the mechanism inside the box. All the while he kept speaking softly to himself, nodding his head, smiling sometimes, his hands always moving, the fingers moving swiftly, deftly, inside the box, his mouth twisting into curious shapes when a thing was delicate or difficult to do, saying, 'Yes.... Yes.... And now this one.... Yes.... Yes. But is this right? Is it – where's my diagram? ... Ah, yes... Of course.... Yes, yes.... That's right.... And now.... Good.... Good.... Yes.... Yes, yes, yes.' His concentration was intense; his movements were quick; there was an air of urgency about the way he worked, of breathlessness, of strong suppressed excitement.

Suddenly he heard footsteps on the gravel path outside and he straightened and turned swiftly as the door opened and a tall man came in. It was Scott. It was only Scott, the doctor.

'Well, well, well,' the Doctor said. 'So this is where you hide yourself in the evenings.'

'Hullo, Scott,' Klausner said.

'I happened to be passing,' the Doctor told him, 'so I dropped in to see how you were. There was no one in the house, so I came on down here. How's that throat of yours been behaving?'

'It's all right. It's fine.'

'Now I'm here I might as well have a look at it.'

'Please don't trouble. I'm quite cured. I'm fine.'

The Doctor began to feel the tension in the room. He looked at the black box on the bench; then he looked at the man. 'You've got your hat on,' he said.

'Oh, have I?' Klausner reached up, removed the hat and put it on the bench.

The Doctor came up closer and bent down to look into the box. 'What's this?' he said. 'Making a radio?'

'No, just fooling around.'

'It's got rather complicated looking innards.'

'Yes,' Klausner seemed tense and distracted.

'What is it?' the Doctor asked. 'It's rather a frightening-looking thing, isn't it?'

'It's just an idea,'

'Yes?'

'It has to do with sound, that's all.'

'Good heavens, man! Don't you get enough of that sort of thing all day in your work?'

'I like sound.'

'So it seems.' The Doctor went to the door, turned, and said, 'Well, I won't disturb you. Glad your throat's not worrying you any more.' But he kept standing there looking at the box, intrigued by the remarkable complexity of its inside, curious to know what this strange patient of his was up to. 'What's it really for?' he asked. 'You've made me inquisitive.'

Klausner looked down at the box, then at the Doctor, and he reached up and began gently to scratch the lobe of his right ear. There was a pause. The Doctor stood by the door, waiting, smiling.

'All right, I'll tell you, if you're interested.' There was another pause, and the Doctor could see that Klausner was having trouble about how to begin.

He was shifting from one foot to the other, tugging at the lobe of his ear, looking at his feet, and then at last, slowly, he said, 'Well, it's like this ... the theory is very simple really. The human ear ... you know that it can't hear everything. There are sounds that are so low-pitched or so high-pitched that it can't hear them.'

'Yes,' the Doctor said. 'Yes.'

'Well, speaking very roughly, any note so high that it has more than fifteen thousand vibrations a second – we can't hear it. Dogs have better ears than us. You know you can buy a whistle whose note is so high-pitched that you can't hear it at all. But a dog can hear it.'

'Yes, I've seen one,' the Doctor said.

'Of course you have. And up the scale, higher than the note of that whistle, there is another note – a vibration if you like, but I prefer to think of it as a note. You can't hear that one either. And above that there is another and another rising right up the scale for ever and ever and ever, an endless succession of notes ... an infinity of notes ... there is a note – if only our ears could hear it – so high that it vibrates a million times a second ... and another a million times as high as that ... and on and on, higher and higher, as far as numbers go, which is ... infinity ... eternity ... beyond the stars.'

Klausner was becoming more animated every moment. He was a frail man, nervous and twitchy, with always moving hands. His large head inclined towards his left shoulder as though his neck were not quite strong enough to support it rigidly. His face was smooth and pale, almost white, and the pale-grey eyes that blinked and peered from behind a pair of steel spectacles were bewildered, unfocused, remote. He was a frail, nervous, twitchy little man, a moth of a man, dreamy and distracted; suddenly fluttering and animated; and now the Doctor, looking at that strange pale face and those pale-grey eyes, felt that somehow there about this little person a quality of distance, of immense immeasurable distance, as though the mind were far away from where the body was.

The Doctor waited for him to go on. Klausner sighed and clasped his hands tightly together. 'I believe,' he said, speaking more slowly now, 'that there is a whole world of sound about us all the time that we cannot hear. It is possible that up there in those high-pitched inaudible regions there is a new exciting music being made, with subtle harmonies and fierce grinding discords, a music so powerful that it would drive us mad if only our ears were tuned to hear the sound of it. There may be anything ... for all we know there may –'

'Yes,' the Doctor said. 'But it's not very probable.'

'Why not? Why not?' Klausner pointed to a fly sitting on a small roll of copper wire on the workbench. 'You see that fly? What sort of noise is that fly making now? None – that one can hear. But for all we know the creature may be whistling like mad on a very high note, or barking or croaking or singing a song. It's got a mouth, hasn't it? It's got a throat!'

The Doctor looked at the fly and he smiled. He was still standing by the door with his hands on the doorknob. 'Well,' he said. 'So you're going to check up on that?'

'Some time ago,' Klausner said, 'I made a simple instrument that proved to me the existence of many odd inaudible sounds. Often I have sat and watched the needle of my instrument recording the presence of sound vibrations in the air when I myself could hear nothing. And *those* are the sounds I want to listen to. I want to know where they come from and who or what is making them.'

'And that machine on the table there,' the Doctor said, 'is that going to allow you to hear these noises?'

'It may. Who knows? So far, I've had no luck. But I've made some changes in it and tonight I'm ready for another trial. This machine,' he said, touching it with his hands, 'is designed to pick up sound vibrations that are too high-pitched for reception by the human ear, and to convert them to a scale of audible tones. I tune it in, almost like a radio.'

'How d'you mean?'

'It isn't complicated. Say I wish to listen to the squeak of a bat. That's a fairly high-pitched sound – about thirty thousand vibrations a second. The average human ear can't quite hear it. Now, if there were a bat flying around this room and I tuned in to thirty thousand on my machine, I would hear the squeaking of that bat very clearly. I would even hear the correct note – F sharp, or B flat, or whatever it might be – but merely at a much *lower pitch*. Don't you understand?'

The Doctor looked at the long, black coffin-box. 'And you're going to try it tonight?'

'Yes.'

'Well, I wish you luck.' He glanced at his watch. 'My goodness!' he said. 'I must fly. Good-bye, and thank you for telling me. I must call again sometime and find out what happened.' The Doctor went out and closed the door behind him.

For a while longer, Klausner fussed about with the wires in the black box; then he straightened up and in a soft excited whisper said, 'Now we'll try again ... We'll take it out into the garden this time ... and then perhaps ... perhaps ... the reception will be better. Lift it up now ... carefully.... Oh, my God, it's heavy!' He carried the box to the door, found that he couldn't open the door without putting it down, carried it back, put it on the bench, opened the door, and then caried it with some difficulty into the garden. He placed the box carefully on a small wooden table that stood on the lawn. He returned to the shed and fetched a pair of earphones. He plugged the wire connections from the earphones into the machine and put the earphones over his ears. The movements of his hands were quick and precise. He was excited, and breathed loudly and quickly through his mouth. He kept on talking to himself with little words of comfort and encouragement, as though he were afraid – afraid that the machine might not work and afraid also of what might happen if it did.

He stood there in the garden beside the wooden table, so pale, small, and thin that he looked like an ancient, consumptive, bespectacled child. The sun had gone down. There was no wind, no sound at all. From where he stood, he could see over a low fence into the next garden, and there was a woman walking down the garden with a flower-basket on her arm. He watched her for a while without thinking about her at all. Then he turned to the box on the table and pressed a switch on its front. He put his left hand on the volume control and his right hand on the knob that moved a needle across a large central dial, like the wavelength dial of a radio. The dial was marked with many numbers, in a series of bands, starting at 15,000 and going on up to 1,000,000.

And now he was bending forward over the machine. His head was cocked to one side in a tense, listening attitude. His right hand was beginning to turn the knob. The needle was travelling slowly across the dial, so slowly he could hardly see it move, and in the earphones he could hear a faint, spasmodic crackling.

Behind this crackling sound he could hear a distant humming tone which was the noise of the machine itself, but that was all. As he listened, he became conscious of a curious sensation, a feeling that his ears were stretching out away from his head, that each ear was connected to his head by a thin stiff wire, like a tentacle, and that the wires were lengthening, that the ears were going up and up towards a secret and forbidden territory, a dangerous ultrasonic region where ears had never been before and had no right to be.

The little needle crept slowly across the dial, and suddenly he heard a shriek, a frightful piercing shriek, and he jumped and dropped his hands, catching hold of the edge of the table. He stared around him as if expecting to see the person who had shrieked. There was no one in sight except the woman in the garden next door, and it was certainly not she. She was bending down, cutting yellow roses and putting them in her basket.

Again it came – a throatless, inhuman shriek, sharp and short, very clear and cold. The note itself possessed a minor, metallic quality that he had never hear before. Klausner looked around him, searching instinctively for the source of the noise. The woman next door was the only living thing in sight. He saw her reach down; take a rose stem in the fingers of one hand and snip the stem with a pair of scissors. Again he heard the scream.

It came at the exact moment when the rose stem was cut.

At this point, the woman straightened up, put the scissors in the basket with the roses and turned to walk away.

'Mrs Saunders!' Klausner shouted, his voice shrill with excitement. 'Oh, Mrs Saunders!'

And looking round, the woman saw her neighbour standing on his lawn – a fantastic, arm-waving little person with a pair of earphones on his head – calling to her in a voice so high and loud that she became alarmed.

'Cut another one! Please cut another one quickly!'

She stood still, staring at him. 'Why, Mr Klausner,' she said. 'What's the matter?'

'Please do as I ask,' he said. 'Cut just one more rose!'

Mrs Saunders had always believed her neighbour to be a rather peculiar person; now it seemed that he had gone completely crazy. She wondered whether she should run into the house and fetch her husband. No, she thought. No, he's harmless. I'll just humour him. 'Certainly, Mr Klausner, if you like,' she said. She took her scissors from the basket, bent down and snipped another rose.

Again Klausner heard that frightful, throatless shriek in the earphones; again it came at the exact moment the rose stem was cut. He took off the earphones and ran to the fence that separated the two gardens. 'All right,' he said. 'That's enough. No more. Please, no more.'

The woman stood there, a yellow rose in one hand, clippers in the other, looking at him.

'I'm going to tell you something, Mrs Saunders,' he said, 'something that you won't believe.' He put his hands on top of the fence and peered at her intently through his thick spectacles. 'You have, this evening, cut a basketful of roses. You have with a sharp pair of scissors cut through the stems of living things, and each rose that you cut screamed in the most terrible way. Did you know that, Mrs Saunders?'

'No,' she said. 'I certainly didn't know that.'

'It happens to be true,' he said. He was breathing rather rapidly, but he was trying to control his excitement. 'I heard them shrieking. Each time you cut one, I heard the cry of pain. A very high-pitched sound, approximately one hundred and thirty-two thousand vibrations a second. You couldn't possibly have heard it yourself. But *I* heard it.'

'Did you really, Mr Klausner?' She decided she would make a dash for the house in about five seconds.

'You might say,' he went on, 'that a rose bush has no nervous system to feel with, no throat to cry with. You'd be right. It hasn't. Not like ours, anyway. But *how do you know, Mrs Saunders*' – and here he leaned far over the fence and spoke in a fierce whisper – '*how do you know* that a rose bush doesn't feel as much pain when someone cuts its stem in two as you would feel if someone cut your wrist off with a garden shears? *How do you know that? It's alive*, isn't it?'

'Yes, Mr Klausner. Oh, yes – and good night.' Quickly she turned and ran up the garden to her house. Klausner went back to the table. He put on the earphones and stood for a while listening. He could still hear the faint crackling sound and the humming noise of the machine, but nothing more. He bent down and took hold of a small white daisy growing on the lawn. He took it between thumb and forefinger and slowly pulled it upward and sideways until the stem broke.

From the moment that he started pulling to the moment when the stem broke, he heard – he distinctly heard in the earphones – a faint high-pitched cry, curiously inanimate. He took another daisy and did it again. Once more he heard the cry, but he wasn't so sure now that it expressed *pain*. No, it wasn't pain; it was surprise. Or was it? It didn't really express any of the feelings or emotions known to a human being. It was just a cry, a neutral, stony cry – a single emotionless note, expressing nothing. It had been the same with the roses. He had been wrong in calling it a cry of pain. A flower probably didn't feel pain. It felt something else which we didn't know about – something called toin or spurl or plinuckment, or anything you like.

He stood up and removed the earphones. It was getting dark and he could see pricks of light shining in the windows of the houses all around him. Carefully he picked up the black box from the table, carried it into the shed and put it on the workbench. Then he went out, locked the door behind him and walked up to the house.

The next morning Klausner was up as soon as it was light. He dressed and went straight to the shed. He picked up the machine and carried it outside, clasping it to his chest with both hands, walking unsteadily under its weight. He went past the house, out through the front gate, and across the road to the park. There he paused and looked around him; then he went on until he came to a large tree, a beech tree, and he placed the machine on the ground close to the trunk of the tree. Quickly he went back to the house and got an axe from the coal cellar and carried it across the road into the park. He put the axe on the ground beside the three.

Then he looked around him again, peering nervously through his thick glasses in every direction. There was no one about. It was six in the morning.

He put the earphones on his head and switched on the machine. He listened for a moment to the faint familiar humming sound; then he picked up the axe, took a stance with his legs wide apart and swung the axe as hard as he could at the base of the tree trunk. The blade cut deep into the wood and stuck there, and at the instant of impact he heard a most extraordinary noise in the earphones. It was a new noise, unlike any he had heard before – a harsh, noteless, enormous noise, a growling, low-pitched, screaming sound, not quick and short like the noise of the roses, but drawn out like a sob lasting for fully a minute, loudest at the moment when the axe struck, fading gradually fainter and fainter until it was gone.

Klausner stared in horror at the place where the blade of the axe had sunk into the woodflesh of the tree; then gently he took the axe handle, worked the blade loose and threw the thing to the ground. With his fingers he touched the gash that the axe had made in the wood, touching the edges of the gash, trying to press them together to close the wound, and he kept saying, 'Tree ... oh, tree ... I am sorry ... I am sorry ... but it will heal ... it will heal fine ...'

For a while he stood there with his hands upon the trunk of the great tree; then suddenly he turned away and hurried off out of the park, across the road, through the front gate and back into his house. He went to the telephone, consulted the book, dialled a number and waited. He held the receiver tightly in his left hand and tapped the table impatiently with his right. He heard the telephone buzzing at the other end, and then the click of a lifted receiver and a man's voice, a sleepy voice, saying: 'Hullo. Yes.'

'Dr Scott?' he said.

'Yes. Speaking.'

'Dr Scott. You must come at once – quickly, please.'

'Who is it speaking?'

'Klausner here, and you remember what I told you last night about my experience with sound, and how I hoped I might –'

'Yes, yes, of course, but what's the matter? Are you ill?'

'No, I'm not ill, but –'

'It's half-past six in the morning,' the Doctor said, 'and you call me but you are not ill.'

'Please come. Come quickly. I want someone to hear it. It's driving me mad! I can't believe it ...'

The Doctor heard the frantic, almost hysterical note in the man's voice, the same note he was used to hearing in the voices of people who called up and said, 'There's been an accident. Come quickly.' He said slowly, 'You really want me to get out of bed and come over now?'

'Yes, now. At once, please.'

'All right, then – I'll come.'

Klausner sat down beside the telephone and waited. He tried to remember what the shriek of the tree had sounded like, but he couldn't. He could remember only that it had been enormous and frightful and that it had made him feel sick with horror. He tried to imagine what sort of noise a human would make if he had to stand anchored to the ground while someone deliberately swung a small sharp thing at his leg so that the blade cut in deep and wedged itself in the cut. Same sort of noise perhaps? No. Quite different. The noise of the tree was worse than any known human noise because of that frightening, toneless, throatless quality. He began to wonder about other living things, and he thought immediately of a field of wheat standing up straight and yellow and alive, with the mower going through it, cutting the stems, five hundred stems a second, every second. Oh, my God, what would *that* noise be like? Five hundred wheat plants screaming together and every second another five hundred being cut and screaming and – no, he thought, I do not want to go to a wheat field with my machine. I would never eat bread after that. But what about potatoes and cabbages and carrots and onions? And what about apples? Ah, no. Apples are all right. They fall off naturally when they are ripe. Apples are all right if you let them fall off instead of tearing them from the tree branch. But not vegetables. Not a potato for example. A potato would surely shriek; so would a carrot and an onion and a cabbage ...

He heard the click of the front-gate latch and he jumped up and went out and saw the tall doctor coming down the path, little black bag in hand.

'Well,' the Doctor said. 'Well, what's all the trouble?'

'Come with me, Doctor. I want you to hear it. I called you because you're the only one I've told. It's over the road in the park. Will you come now?'

The Doctor looked at him. He seemed calmer now. There was no sign of madness or hysteria; he was merely disturbed and excited.

They went across the road into the park and Klausner led the way to the great beech tree at the foot of which stood the long black coffin-box of the machine – and the axe.

'Why did you bring it out here?' the Doctor asked.

'I wanted a tree. There aren't any big trees in the garden.'

'And why the axe?'

'You'll see in a moment. But now please put on these earphones and listen. Listen carefully and tell me afterwards precisely what you hear. I want to make quite sure ...'

The Doctor smiled and took the earphones and put them over his ears.

Klausner bent down and flicked the switch on the panel of the machine; then he picked up the axe and took his stance with his legs apart, ready to swing. For a moment he paused.

'Can you hear anything?' he said to the Doctor.

'Can I what?'

'Can you *hear* anything?'

'Just a humming noise.'

Klausner stood there with the axe in his hands trying to bring himself to swing, but the thought of the noise that the tree would make made him pause again.

'What are you waiting for?' the Doctor asked.

'Nothing,' Klausner answered, and then lifted the axe and swung it at the tree, and as he swung, he thought he felt, he could swear he felt a movement of the ground on which he stood. He felt a slight shifting of the earth beneath his feet as though the roots of the tree were moving underneath the soil, but it was too late to check the blow and the axe blade struck the tree and wedged deep into the wood. At that moment, high overhead, there was the cracking sound of wood splintering and the swishing sound of leaves brushing against other leaves and they both looked up and the Doctor cried, 'Watch out! Run, man! Quickly, run!'

The Doctor had ripped off the earphones and was running away fast, but Klausner stood spellbound, staring up at the great branch, sixty feet long at least, that was bending slowly downward, breaking and crackling and splintering at its thickest point, where it joined the main trunk of the tree. The branch came crashing down and Klausner leapt aside just in time. It fell upon the machine and smashed it into pieces.

'Great heavens!' shouted the Doctor as he came running back. 'That was a near one! I thought it had got you!'

Klausner was staring at the tree. His large head was leaning to one side and upon his smooth white face there was a tense, horrified expression. Slowly he walked up to the tree and gently he prised the blade loose from the trunk.

'Did you hear it?' he said, turning to the Doctor. His voice was barely audible.

The Doctor was still out of breath from running and the excitement. 'Hear what?'

'In the earphones. Did you hear anything when the axe struck?'

The Doctor began to rub the back of his neck. 'Well,' he said, 'as a matter of fact....' He paused and frowned and bit his lower lip. 'No, I'm not sure. I couldn't be sure. I don't suppose I had the earphones on for more than a second after the axe struck.'

'Yes, yes, but what did you hear?'

'I don't know,' the Doctor said. 'I don't know what I heard. Probably the noise of the branch breaking.' He was speaking rapidly, rather irritably.

'What did it sound like?' Klausner leaned forward slightly, staring hard at the Doctor. '*Exactly* what did it sound like?'

'Oh hell!' the Doctor said. 'I really don't know. I was more interested in getting out of the way. Let's leave it.'

'Dr Scott, *what-did-it-sound-like*?'

'For God's sake, how could I tell, what with half the tree falling on me and having to run for my life?' The Doctor certainly seemed nervous. Klausner had sensed it now. He stood quite still, staring at the Doctor and for fully half a minute he didn't speak. The Doctor moved his feet, shrugged his shoulders and half turned to go. 'Well,' he said, 'we'd better get back.'

'Look,' said the little man, and now his smooth white face became suddenly suffused with colour. 'Look,' he said, 'you stitch this up.' He pointed to the last gash that the axe had made in the tree trunk. 'You stitch this up quickly.'

'Don't be silly,' the Doctor said.

'You do as I say. Stitch it up.' Klausner was gripping the axe handle and he spoke softly, in a curious, almost a threatening tone.

'Don't be silly,' the Doctor said. 'I can't stitch through wood. Come on. Let's get back.'

'So you can't stitch through wood?'

'No, of course not.'

'Have you got any iodine in your bag?'

'What if I have?'

'Then paint the cut with iodine. It'll sting, but that can't be helped.'

'Now look,' the Doctor said, and again he turned as if to go. 'Let's not be ridiculous. Let's get back to the house and then ...'

'Paint-the-cut-with-iodine.'

The Doctor hesitated. He saw Klausner's hands tightening on the handle of the axe. He decided that his only alternative was to run away fast, and he certainly wasn't going to do that.

'All right,' he said. 'I'll paint it with iodine.'

He got his black bag which was lying on the grass about ten yards away, opened it and took out a bottle of iodine and some cotton wool. He went up to the tree trunk, uncorked the bottle, tipped some of the iodine on to the cotton wool, bent down and began to dab it into the cut. He kept one eye on Klausner who was standing motionless with the axe in his hands, watching him.

'Make sure you get it right in.'

'Yes,' the Doctor said.

'Now do the other one – the one just above it!'

The Doctor did as he was told.

'There you are,' he said. 'It's done.'

He straightened up and surveyed his work in a very serious manner. 'That should do nicely.'

Klausner came closer and gravely examined the two wounds.

'Yes,' he said, nodding his huge head slowly up and down. 'Yes, that will do nicely.' He stepped back a pace. 'You'll come and look at them again tomorrow?'

'Oh, yes,' the Doctor said. 'Of course.'

'And put some more iodine on?'

'If necessary, yes.'

'Thank you, Doctor,' Klausner said, and he nodded his head again and he dropped the axe and all at once he smiled, a wild, excited smile, and quickly the Doctor went over to him and gently he took him by the arm and he said, 'Come on, we must go now,' and suddenly they were walking away, the two of them, walking silently, rather hurriedly across the park, over the road, back to the house.

NUNC DIMITTIS

It is nearly midnight, and I can see that if I don't make a start with writing this story now, I never shall. All evening I have been sitting here trying to force myself to begin, but the more I have thought about it, the more appalled and ashamed and distressed I have become by the whole thing.

My idea – and I believe it was a good one – was to try, by a process of confession and analysis, to discover a reason or at any rate some justification for my outrageous behaviour towards Janet de Pelagia. I wanted, essentially, to address myself to an imaginary and sympathetic listener, a kind of mythical *you*, someone gentle and understanding to whom I might tell unashamedly every detail of this unfortunate episode. I can only hope that I am not too upset to make a go of it.

If I am to be quite honest with myself, I suppose I shall have to admit that what is disturbing me most is not so much the sense of my own shame, or even the hurt that I have inflicted upon poor Janet; it is the knowledge that I have made a monstrous fool of myself and that all my friends – if I can still call them that – all those warm and lovable people who used to come so often to my house, must now be regarding me as nothing but a vicious, vengeful old man. Yes, that surely hurts. When I say to you that my friends were my whole life – everything, absolutely everything in it – then perhaps you will begin to understand.

Will you? I doubt it – unless I digress for a minute to tell you roughly the sort of person I am.

Well – let me see. Now that I come to think of it, I suppose I am, after all, a type; a rare one, mark you, but nevertheless a quite definite type – the wealthy, leisurely, middle-aged man of culture, adored (I choose the word carefully) by his many friends for his charm, his money, his air of scholarship, his generosity, and I sincerely hope for himself also. You will find him (this type) only in the big capitals – London, Paris, New York; of that I am certain. The money he has was earned by his dead father whose memory he is inclined to despise. This is not his fault, for there is something in his make-up that compels him secretly to look down upon all people who never had the wit to learn the difference between Rockingham and Spode, Waterford and

Venetian, Sheraton and Chippendale, Monet and Manet, or even Pommard and Montrachet.

He is, therefore, a connoisseur, possessing above all things an exquisite taste. His Constables, Boningtons, Lautrecs, Redons, Vuillards, Matthew Smiths are as fine as anything in the Tate; and because they are so fabulous and beautiful they create an atmosphere of suspense around him in the home, something tantalizing, breathtaking, faintly frightening – frightening to think that he has the power and the right, if he feels inclined, to slash, tear, plunge his fist through a superb Dedham Vale, a Mont Saint-Victoire, an Arles cornfield, a Tahiti maiden, a portrait of Madame Cézanne. And from the walls on which these wonders hang there issues a little golden glow of splendour, a subtle emanation of grandeur in which he lives and moves and entertains with a sly nonchalance that is not entirely unpractised.

He is invariably a bachelor, yet he never appears to get entangled with the women who surround him, who love him so dearly. It is just possible – and this you may or may not have noticed – that there is a frustration, a discontent, a regret somewhere inside him. Even a slight aberration.

I don't think I need say any more. I have been very frank. You should know me well enough by now to judge me fairly – and dare I hope it? – to sympathize with me when you hear my story. You may even decide that much of the blame for what has happened should be placed, not upon me, but upon a lady called Gladys Ponsonby. After all, she was the one who started it. Had I not escorted Gladys Ponsonby back to her house that night nearly six months ago, and had she not spoken so freely to me about certain people, and certain things, then this tragic business could never have taken place.

It was last December, if I remember rightly, and I had been dining with the Ashendens in that lovely house of theirs that overlooks the southern fringe of Regent's Park. There were a fair number of people there, but Gladys Ponsonby was the only one beside myself who had come alone. So when it was time for us to leave, I naturally offered to see her safely back to her house. She accepted and we left together in my car; but unfortunately, when we arrived at her place she insisted that I come in and have 'one for the road', as she put it. I didn't wish to seem stuffy, so I told the chauffeur to wait and followed her in.

Gladys Ponsonby is an unusually short woman, certainly not more than four feet nine or ten, maybe even less than that – one of those tiny persons who gives me, when I am beside her, the comical, rather wobbly feeling that I am standing on a chair. She is a widow, a few years younger than me – maybe fifty-three or four, and it is possible that thirty years ago she was quite a fetching little thing. But now the face is loose and puckered with nothing distinctive about it whatsoever. The individual features, the eyes, the nose, the mouth, the chin, are buried in the folds of fat around the puckered little face and one does not notice them. Except perhaps the mouth, which reminds me – I cannot help it – of a salmon.

In the living-room, as she gave me my brandy, I noticed that her hand was a trifle unsteady. The lady is tired, I told myself, so I mustn't stay long. We sat down together on the sofa and for a while discussed the Ashendens' party and the people who were there. Finally I got up to go.

'Sit down, Lionel,' she said. 'Have another brandy.'

'No, really, I must go.'

'Sit down and don't be so stuffy. *I'm* having another one, and the least you can do is keep me company while I drink it.'

I watched her as she walked over to the sideboard, this tiny woman, faintly swaying, holding her glass out in front of her with both hands as though it were an offering; and the sight of her walking like that, so incredibly short and squat and stiff, suddenly gave me the ludicrous notion that she had no legs at all above the knees.

'Lionel, what are you chuckling about?' She half turned to look at me as she poured the drink, and some of it slopped over the side of the glass.

'Nothing, my dear. Nothing at all.'

'Well, stop it, and tell me what you think of my new portrait.' She indicated a large canvas hanging over the fireplace that I had been trying to avoid with my eye ever since I entered the room. It was a hideous thing, painted, as I well knew, by a man who was now all the rage in London, a very mediocre painter called John Royden. It was a full-length portrait of Gladys, Lady Ponsonby, painted with a certain technical cunning that made her out to be a tall and quite alluring creature.

'Charming,' I said.

'Isn't it, though! I'm so glad you like it.'

'Quite charming.'

'I think John Royden is a genius. Don't you think he's a genius, Lionel?'

'Well – that might be going a bit far.'

'You mean it's a little early to say for sure?'

'Exactly.'

'But listen, Lionel – and I think this will surprise you. John Royden is so sought after now that he won't even *consider* painting anyone for less than a thousand guineas!'

'Really?'

'Oh, yes! And everyone's queueing up, simply *queueing up* to get themselves done.'

'Most interesting.'

'Now take your Mr Cézanne or whatever his name is. I'll bet *he* never got that sort of money in *his* lifetime.'

'Never.'

'And you say *he* was a genius?'

'Sort of – yes.'

'Then so is Royden,' she said, settling herself again on the sofa. 'The money proves it.'

She sat silent for a while, sipping her brandy, and I couldn't help noticing how the unsteadiness of her hand was causing the rim of the glass to jog against her lower lip. She knew I was watching her, and without turning her head she swivelled her eyes and glanced at me cautiously out of the corners of them. 'A penny for your thoughts?'

Now, if there is one phrase in the world I cannot abide, it is this. It gives me an actual physical pain in the chest and I begin to cough.

'Come on, Lionel. A penny for them.'

I shook my head, quite unable to answer. She turned away abruptly and placed the brandy glass on a small table to her left; and the manner in which she did this seemed to suggest – I don't know why – that she felt rebuffed and was now clearing the decks for action. I waited, rather uncomfortable in the silence that followed, and because I had no conversation left in me, I made a great play about smoking my cigar, studying the ash intently and blowing the smoke up slowly towards the ceiling. But she made no move. There was beginning to be something about this lady I did not much like, a mischievous brooding air that made me want to get up quickly and go away. When she looked around again, she was smiling at me slyly with those little buried eyes of hers, but the mouth – oh, just like a salmon's – was absolutely rigid.

'Lionel, I think I'll tell you a secret.'

'Really, Gladys, I simply must get home.'

'Don't be frightened, Lionel. I won't embarrass you. You look so frightened all of a sudden.'

'I'm not very good at secrets.'

'I've been thinking,' she said, 'you're such a great expert on pictures, this ought to interest you.' She sat quite still except for her fingers which were moving all the time. She kept them perpetually twisting and twisting around each other, and they were like a bunch of small white snakes wriggling in her lap.

'Don't you want to hear my secret, Lionel?'

'It isn't that, you know. It's just that it's so awfully late ...'

'This is probably the best-kept secret in London. A woman's secret. I suppose it's known to about – let me see – about thirty or forty women altogether. And not a single man. Except him, of course – John Royden.'

I didn't wish to encourage her, so I said nothing.

'But first of all, promise – *promise* you won't tell a soul?'

'Dear me!'

'You *promise*, Lionel?'

'Yes, Gladys, all right, I promise.'

'Good! Now listen.' She reached for the brandy glass and settled back comfortably in the far corner of the sofa. 'I suppose you know John Royden paints only women?'

'I didn't.'

'And they're always full-length portraits, either standing or sitting – like mine there. Now take a good look at it, Lionel. Do you see how beautifully the dress is painted?'

'Well . . .'

'Go over and look carefully, please.'

I got up reluctantly and went over and examined the painting. To my surprise I noticed that the paint of the dress was laid on so heavily it was actually raised out from the rest of the picture. It was a trick, quite effective in its way, but neither difficult to do nor entirely original.

'You see?' she said. 'It's thick, isn't it, where the dress is?'

'Yes.'

'But there's a bit more to it than that, you know, Lionel. I think the best way is to describe what happened the very first time I went along for a sitting.'

Oh, what a bore this woman is, I thought, and how can I get away?

'That was about a year ago, and I remember how excited I was to be going into the studio of the great painter. I dressed myself up in a wonderful new thing I'd just got from Norman Hartnell, and a special little red hat, and off I went. Mr Royden met me at the door, and of course I was fascinated by him at once. He had a small pointed beard and thrilling blue eyes, and he wore a black velvet jacket. The studio was huge, with red velvet sofas and velvet chairs – he loves velvet – and velvet curtains and even a velvet carpet on the floor. He sat me down, gave me a drink and came straight to the point. He told me about how he painted quite differently from other artists. In his opinion, he said, there was only one method of attaining perfection when painting a woman's body and I mustn't be shocked when I heard what it was.

'"I don't think I'll be shocked, Mr Royden," I told him.

'"I'm sure you won't, either," he said. He had the most marvellous white teeth and they sort of shone through his beard when he smiled. "You see, it's like this," he went on. "You examine any painting you like of a woman – I don't care who it's by – and you'll see that although the dress may be well painted, there is an effect of artificiality, of flatness about the whole thing, as though the dress were draped over a log of wood. And you know why?"'

'"No, Mr Royden, I don't."

'"Because the painters themselves didn't really know what was underneath!"'

Gladys Ponsonby paused to take a few more sips of brandy. 'Don't look so startled, Lionel,' she said to me. 'There's nothing wrong about this. Keep quiet and let me finish. So then Mr Royden said, "That's why I insist on painting my subjects first of all in the nude."

'"Good Heavens, Mr Royden!" I exclaimed.

'"If you object to that, I don't mind making a slight concession, Lady Ponsonby," he said. "But I prefer it the other way."

'"Really, Mr Royden, I don't know."

'"And when I've done you like that," he went on, "we'll have to wait a few weeks for the paint to dry. Then you come back and I paint on your underclothing. And when that's dry, I paint on the dress. You see, it's quite simple."'

'The man's an absolute bounder!' I cried.

'No, Lionel, no! You're quite wrong. If only you could have heard him, so charming about it all, so genuine and sincere. Anyone could see he really *felt* what he was saying.'

'I tell you, Gladys, the man's a bounder!'

'Don't be so silly, Lionel. And anyway, let me finish. The first thing I told him was that my husband (who was alive then) would never agree.

'"Your husband need never know," he answered. "Why trouble him. No one knows my secret except the women I've painted."

'And when I protested a bit more, I remember he said, "My dear Lady Ponsonby, there's nothing immoral about this. Art is only immoral when practised by amateurs. It's the same with medicine. You wouldn't refuse to undress before your doctor, would you?"

'I told him I would if I'd gone to him for ear-ache. That made him laugh. But he kept on at me about it and I must say he was very convincing, so after a while I gave in and that was that. So now, Lionel, my sweet, you know the secret.' She got up and went over to fetch herself some more brandy.

'Gladys, is this really true?'

'Of course it's true.'

'You mean to say that's the way he paints all his subjects?'

'Yes. And the joke is the husbands never know anything about it. All they see is a nice fully clothed portrait of their wives. Of course, there's nothing wrong with being painted in the nude; artists do it all the time. But our silly husbands have a way of objecting to that sort of thing.'

'By gad, the fellow's got a nerve!'

'I think he's a genius.'

'I'll bet he got the idea from Goya.'

'Nonsense, Lionel.'

'Of course he did. But listen, Gladys. I want you to tell me something. Did you by any chance know about this ... this peculiar technique of Royden's before you went to him?'

When I asked the question she was in the act of pouring the brandy, and she hesitated and turned her head to look at me, a little silky smile moving the corners of her mouth. 'Damn you, Lionel,' she said. 'You're far too clever. You never let me get away with a single thing.'

'So you knew?'

'Of course. Hermione Girdlestone told me.'

'Exactly as I thought!'

'There's still nothing wrong.'

'Nothing,' I said. 'Absolutely nothing.' I could see it all quite clearly now. This Royden was indeed a bounder, practising as neat a piece of psychological trickery as ever I'd seen. The man knew only too well that there was a whole set of wealthy indolent women in the city who got up at noon and spent the rest of the day trying to relieve their boredom with bridge and canasta and shopping until the cocktail hour came along. All they craved was a little excitement, something out of the ordinary, and the more expensive the better. Why – the news of an entertainment like this would spread through their ranks like smallpox. I could just see the great plump Hermione Girdlestone leaning over the canasta table and telling them about it ... 'But my dear, it's *simp*-ly fascinating ... I can't *tell* you how intriguing it is ...*much* more fun than going to your doctor ...'

'You won't tell anyone, Lionel, will you? You promised.'

'No, of course not. But now I must go, Gladys, I really must.'

'Don't be so silly. I'm just beginning to enjoy myself. Stay till I've finished this drink, anyway.'

I sat patiently on the sofa while she went on with her interminable brandy sipping. The little buried eyes were still watching me out of their corners in that mischievous, canny way, and I had a strong feeling that the woman was now hatching out some further unpleasantness or scandal. There was the look of serpents in those eyes and a queer curl around the mouth; and in the air – although maybe I only imagined it – the faint smell of danger.

Then suddenly, so suddenly that I jumped, she said, 'Lionel, what's this I hear about you and Janet de Pelagia?'

'Now, Gladys, please ...'

'Lionel, you're blushing!'

'Nonsense.'

'Don't tell me the old bachelor has really taken a tumble at last?'

'Gladys, this is too absurd.' I began making movements to go, but she put a hand on my knee and stopped me.

'Don't you know by now, Lionel, that there *are* no secrets?'

'Janet is a fine girl.'

'You can hardly call her a *girl*.' Gladys Ponsonby paused, staring down into the large brandy glass that she held cupped in both hands. 'But of course, I agree with you, Lionel, she's a wonderful person in every way. Except,' and now she spoke very slowly, 'except that she *does* say some rather peculiar things occasionally.'

'What sort of things?'

'Just things, you know – things about people. About you.'

'What did she say about me?'

'Nothing at all, Lionel. It wouldn't interest you.'

'What did she say about me?'

'It's not even worth repeating, honestly it isn't. It's only that it struck me as being rather odd at the time.'

'Gladys – what did she say?' While I waited for her to answer, I could feel the sweat breaking out all over my body.

'Well now, let me see. Of course, she was only joking or I couldn't dream of telling you, but I suppose she *did* say how it was all a wee bit of a bore.'

'What was?'

'Sort of going out to dinner with you nearly every night – that kind of thing.'

'She said it was a bore?'

'Yes.' Gladys Ponsonby drained the brandy glass with one last big gulp, and sat up straight. 'If you really want to know, she said it was a crashing bore. And then ...'

'What did she say then?'

'Now look, Lionel – there's no need to get excited. I'm only telling you this for your own good.'

'Then please hurry up and tell it.'

'It's just that I happened to be playing canasta with Janet this afternoon and I asked her if she was free to dine with me tomorrow. She said no, she wasn't.'

'Go on.'

'Well – actually what she said was "I'm dining with that crashing old bore Lionel Lampson."'

'Janet said that?'

'Yes, Lionel dear.'

'What else?'

'Now, that's enough. I don't think I should tell the rest.'

'Finish it, please!'

'Why, Lionel, don't keep shouting at me like that. Of course I'll tell you if you insist. As a matter of fact, I wouldn't consider myself a true friend if I didn't. Don't you think it's the sign of true friendship when two people like us ...'

'Gladys! *Please* hurry.'

'Good heavens, you must give me time to *think*. Let me see now – so far as I can remember, what she *actually* said was this ...' – and Gladys Ponsonby, sitting upright on the sofa with her feet not quite touching the floor, her eyes away from me now, looking at the wall, began cleverly to mimic the deep tone of that voice I knew so well – '"Such a bore, my dear, because with Lionel one can *always* tell exactly what will happen *right* from beginning to end. For dinner we'll go to the Savoy Grill – it's *always* the Savoy Grill – and for two hours I'll have to listen to the pompous old ... I mean I'll have to listen to him droning away about pictures and porcelain – *always* pictures and porcelain. Then in the taxi going home he'll reach out for my hand, and he'll lean closer, and I'll get a whiff of stale cigar smoke and brandy, and he'll start burbling about how he wished – oh, how he wished he was just twenty years younger. And I will say, 'Could you open a window, do you mind?' And when we arrive at my house I'll tell him to keep the taxi, but he'll pretend he hasn't heard and pay it off quickly. And then at the front door, while I fish for my key, he'll stand beside me with a sort of silly spaniel look in his eyes, and I'll slowly put the key in the lock, and slowly turn it, and then – very quickly, before he has time to move – I'll say good night and skip inside and shut the door behind me ..." Why, Lionel! What's the matter, dear? You look positively ill ...'

At that point, mercifully, I must have swooned clear away. I can remember practically nothing of the rest of that terrible night except for a vague and disturbing suspicion that when I regained consciousness I broke down completely and permitted Gladys Ponsonby to comfort me in a variety of different ways. Later, I believe I walked out of the house and was driven home, but I remained more or less unconscious of everything around me until I woke up in my bed the next morning.

I awoke feeling weak and shaken. I lay still with my eyes closed, trying to piece together the events of the night before – Gladys Ponsonby's living-room, Gladys on the sofa sipping brandy, the little puckered face, the mouth that was like a salmon's mouth, the things she had said ... What was it she had said? Ah, yes. About me. My God, yes! About Janet and me! Those outrageous, unbelievable remarks! Could Janet really have made them? Could she?

I can remember with what terrifying swiftness my hatred of Janet de Pelagia now began to grow. It all happened in a few minutes – a sudden, violent welling up of a hatred that filled me till I thought I was going to burst. I tried to dismiss it, but it was on me like a fever, and in no time at all I was hunting around, as would some filthy gangster, for a method of revenge.

A curious way to behave, you may say, for a man such as me; to which I would answer – no, not really, if you consider the circumstances. To my mind, this was the sort of thing that could drive a man to murder. As a matter of fact, had it not been for a small sadistic streak that caused me to seek a more subtle and painful punishment for my victim, I might well have become a murderer myself. But mere killing, I decided, was too good for this woman, and far too crude for my own taste. So I began looking for a superior alternative.

I am not normally a scheming person; I consider it an odious business and have had no practice in it whatsoever. But fury and hate can concentrate a man's mind to an astonishing degree, and in no time at all a plot was forming and unfolding in my head – a plot so superior and exciting that I began to be quite carried away at the idea of it. By the time I had filled in the details and overcome one or two minor objections, my brooding vengeful mood had changed to one of extreme elation, and I remember how I started bouncing up and down absurdly on my bed and clapping my hands. The next thing I knew I had the telephone directory on my lap and was searching eagerly for a name. I found it, picked up the phone, and dialled the number.

'Hello,' I said. 'Mr Royden? Mr John Royden?'

'Speaking.'

Well – it wasn't difficult to persuade the man to call around and see me for a moment. I had never met him, but of course he knew my name, both as an important collector of paintings and as a person of some consequence in society. I was a big fish for him to catch.

'Let me see now, Mr Lampson,' he said, 'I think I ought to be free in about a couple of hours. Will that be all right?'

I told him it would be fine, gave my address, and rang off.

I jumped out of bed. It was really remarkable how exhilarated I felt all of a sudden. One moment I had been in an agony of despair, contemplating murder and suicide and I don't know what, the next, I was whistling an aria from Puccini in my bath. Every now and again I caught myself rubbing my hands together in a devilish fashion, and once, during my exercises, when I overbalanced doing a double-knee-bend, I sat on the floor and giggled like a schoolboy.

At the appointed time Mr John Royden was shown in to my library and I got up to meet him. He was a small neat man with a slightly ginger goatee beard. He wore a black velvet jacket, a rust-brown tie, a red pullover, and black suède shoes. I shook his small neat hand.

'Good of you to come along so quickly, Mr Royden.'

'Not at all, sir.' The man's lips – like the lips of nearly all bearded men – looked wet and naked, a trifle indecent, shining pink in among all that hair. After telling him again how much I admired his work, I got straight down to business.

'Mr Royden,' I said. 'I have a rather unusual request to make of you, something quite personal in its way.'

'Yes, Mr Lampson?' He was sitting in the chair opposite me and he cocked his head over to one side, quick and perky like a bird.

'Of course, I know I can trust you to be discreet about anything I say.'

'Absolutely, Mr Lampson.'

'All right. Now my proposition is this: there is a certain lady in town here whose portrait I would like you to paint. I very much want to possess a fine painting of her. But there are certain complications. For example, I have my own reasons for not wishing her to know that it is I who am commissioning the portrait.'

'You mean . . .'

'Exactly, Mr Royden. That is exactly what I mean. As a man of the world I'm sure you will understand.'

He smiled, a crooked little smile that only just came through his beard, and he nodded his head knowingly up and down.

'Is it not possible,' I said, 'that a man might be – how shall I put it? – extremely fond of a lady and at the same time have his own good reasons for not wishing her to know about it yet?'

'More than possible, Mr Lampson.'

'Sometimes a man has to stalk his quarry with great caution, waiting patiently for the right moment to reveal himself.'

'Precisely, Mr Lampson.'

'There are better ways of catching a bird than by chasing it through the woods.'

'Yes, indeed, Mr Lampson.'

'Putting salt on its tail, for instance.'

'Ha-ha?'

'All right, Mr Royden. I think you understand. Now – do you happen by any chance to know a lady called Janet de Pelagia?'

'Janet de Pelagia? Let me see now – yes. At least, what I mean is I've heard of her. I couldn't exactly say I know her.'

'That's a pity. It makes it a little more difficult. Do you think you could get to meet her – perhaps at a cocktail party or something like that?'

'Shouldn't be too tricky, Mr Lampson.'

'Good, because what I suggest is this: that you go up to her and tell her she's the sort of model you've been searching for for years – just the right face, the right figure, the right coloured eyes. You know the sort of thing. Then ask her if she'd mind sitting for you free of charge. Say you'd like to do a picture of her for next year's Academy. I feel sure she'd be delighted to help you, and honoured too, if I may say so. Then you will paint her and exhibit the picture and deliver it to me after the show is over. No one but you need know that I have bought it.'

The small round eyes of Mr Royden were watching me shrewdly,

I thought, and the head was again cocked over to one side. He was sitting on the edge of his chair, and in this position, with the pullover making a flash of red down his front, he reminded me of a robin on a twig listening for a suspicious noise.

'There's really nothing wrong about it at all,' I said. 'Just call it – if you like – a harmless little conspiracy being perpetrated by a ... well ... by a rather romantic old man.'

'I know, Mr Lampson, I know ...' He still seemed to be hesitating, so I said quickly, 'I'll be glad to pay you double your usual fee.'

That did it. The man actually licked his lips. 'Well, Mr Lampson, I must say this sort of thing's not really in my line, you know. But all the same, it'd be a very heartless man who refused such a – shall I say such a romantic assignment?'

'I should like a full-length portrait, Mr Royden, please. A large canvas – let me see – about twice the size of that Manet on the wall there.'

'About sixty by thirty-six?'

'Yes. And I should like her to be standing. That to my mind, is her most graceful attitude.'

'I quite understand, Mr Lampson. And it'll be a pleasure to paint such a lovely lady.'

I expect it will, I told myself. The way you go about it, my boy, I'm quite sure it will. But I said, 'All right, Mr Royden, then I'll leave it all to you. And don't forget, please – this is a little secret between ourselves.'

When he had gone I forced myself to sit still and take twenty-five deep breaths. Nothing else would have restrained me from jumping up and shouting for joy like an idiot. I have never in my life felt so exhilarated. My plan was working! The most difficult part was already accomplished. There would be a wait now, a long wait. The way this man painted, it would take him several months to finish the picture. Well, I would just have to be patient, that's all.

I now decided, on the spur of the moment, that it would be best if I were to go abroad in the interim; and the very next morning, after sending a message to Janet (with whom, you will remember, I was due to dine that night) telling her I had been called away, I left for Italy.

There, as always, I had a delightful time, marred only by a constant nervous excitement caused by the thought of returning to the scene of action.

I eventually arrived back, four months later, in July, on the day after the opening of the Royal Academy, and I found to my relief that everything had gone according to plan during my absence. The picture of Janet de Pelagia had been painted and hung in the Exhibition, and it was already the subject of much favourable comment both by the critics and the public. I myself refrained from going to see it, but Royden told me on the telephone that there had been several inquiries by persons who wished to buy it, all of whom had been informed that it was not for sale. When the show was over, Royden delivered the picture to my house and received his money.

I immediately had it carried up to my workroom, and with mounting excitement I began to examine it closely. The man had painted her standing up in a black evening dress and there was a red-plush sofa in the background. Her left hand was resting on the back of a heavy chair, also of red-plush, and there was a huge crystal chandelier hanging from the ceiling.

My God, I thought, what a hideous thing! The portrait itself wasn't so bad. He had caught the woman's expression – the forward drop of the head, the wide blue eyes, the large, ugly-beautiful mouth with the trace of a smile in one corner. He had flattered her, of course. There wasn't a wrinkle on her face or the slightest suggestion of fat under her chin. I bent forward to examine the painting of the dress. Yes – here the paint was thicker, much thicker. At this point, unable to wait another moment, I threw off my coat and prepared to go to work.

I should mention here that I am myself an expert cleaner and restorer of paintings. The cleaning, particularly, is a comparatively simple process provided one has patience and a gentle touch, and those professionals who make such a secret of their trade and charge such shocking prices get no business from me. Where my own pictures are concerned I always do the job myself.

I poured out the turpentine and added a few drops of alcohol. I dipped a small wad of cotton wool in the mixture, squeezed it out, and then gently, so very gently, with a circular motion, I began to work upon the black paint of the dress. I could only hope that Royden had allowed each layer to dry thoroughly before applying the next, otherwise the two would merge and the process I had in mind would be impossible. Soon I would know. I was working on one square inch of black dress somewhere around the lady's stomach and I took plenty of time, cautiously testing and teasing the paint, adding a drop or two more of alcohol to my mixture, testing again, adding another drop until finally it was just strong enough to loosen the pigment.

For perhaps a whole hour I worked away on this little square of black, proceeding more and more gently as I came closer to the layer below. Then, a tiny pink spot appeared, and gradually it spread and spread until the whole of my square inch was a clear shining patch of pink. Quickly I neutralized with pure turps.

So far so good. I knew now that the black paint could be removed without disturbing what was underneath. So long as I was patient and industrious I would easily be able to take it all off. Also, I had discovered the right mixture to use and just how hard I could safely rub, so things should go much quicker now.

I must say it was rather an amusing business. I worked first from the middle of her body downward, and as the lower half of her dress came away bit by bit on to my little wads of cotton, a queer pink undergarment began to reveal itself. I didn't for the life of me know what the thing was called, but it was a formidable apparatus constructed of what appeared to be a strong thick elastic material, and its purpose was apparently to contain and to compress the woman's bulging figure into a neat streamlined shape, giving a quite false impression of slimness. As I travelled lower and lower down, I came upon a striking arrangement of suspenders, also pink, which were attached to this elastic armour and hung downwards four or five inches to grip the tops of the stockings.

Quite fantastic the whole thing seemed to me as I stepped back a pace to survey it. It gave me a strong sense of having somehow been cheated; for had I not, during all these past months, been admiring the sylph-like figure of this lady? She was a faker. No question about it. But do many other females practise this sort of deception, I wondered. I knew, of course, that in the days of stays and corsets it was usual for ladies to strap themselves up; yet for some reason I was under the impression that nowadays all they had to do was diet.

When the whole of the lower half of the dress had come away, I immediately turned my attention to the upper portion, working my way slowly upward from the lady's middle. Here, around the midriff, there was an area of naked flesh; then higher up upon the bosom itself and actually containing it, I came upon a contrivance made of some heavy black material edged with frilly lace. This, I knew very well, was the brassière – another formidable appliance upheld by an arrangement of black straps as skilfully and scientifically rigged as the suporting cables of a suspension bridge.

Dear me, I thought. One lives and learns.

But now at last the job was finished, and I stepped back again to take a final look at the picture. It was truly an astonishing sight! This woman, Janet de Pelagia, almost life size, standing there in her underwear – in a sort of drawing-room, I suppose it was – with a great chandelier above her head and a red-plush chair by her side; and she herself – this was the most disturbing part of all – looking so completely unconcerned, with the wide placid blue eyes, the faintly smiling, ugly-beautiful mouth. Also I noticed, with something of a shock, that she was exceedingly bow-legged, like a jockey. I tell you frankly, the whole thing embarrassed me. I felt as though I had no right to be in the room, certainly no right to stare. So after a while I went out and shut the door behind me. It seemed like the only decent thing to do.

Now, for the next and final step! And do not imagine simply because I have not mentioned it lately that my thirst for revenge had in any way diminished during the last few months. On the contrary, it had if anything increased; and with the last act about to be performed, I can tell you I found it hard to contain myself. That night, for example, I didn't even go to bed.

You see, I couldn't wait to get the invitations out. I sat up all night preparing them and addressing the envelopes. There were twenty-two of them in all, and I wanted each to be a personal note. 'I'm having a little dinner on Friday night, the twenty-second, at eight. I do hope you can come along ... I'm so looking forward to seeing you again ...'

The first, the most carefully phrased, was to Janet de Pelagia. In it I regretted not having seen her for so long ... I had been abroad ... It was time we got together again, etc., etc. The next was to Gladys Ponsonby. Then one to Lady Hermione Girdlestone, another to Princess Bicheno, Mrs Cudbird, Sir Hubert Kaul, Mrs Galbally, Peter Euan-Thomas, James Pisker, Sir Eustace Piegrome, Peter van Santen, Elizabeth Moynihan, Lord Mulherrin, Bertram Sturt, Philip Cornelius, Jack Hill, Lady Akeman, Mrs Icely, Himphrey King-Howard, Johnny O'Coffey, Mrs Uvary, and the Dowager Countess of Waxworth.

It was a carefully selected list, containing as it did the most distinguished men, the most brilliant and influential women in the top crust of our society.

I was well aware that a dinner at my house was regarded as quite an occasion; everybody like to come. And now, as I watched the point of my pen moving swiftly over the paper, I could almost see the ladies in their pleasure picking up their bedside telephones the morning the invitations arrived, shrill voices calling to shriller voices over the wires ... 'Lionel's giving a party ... he's asked you too? My dear, how nice ... his food is always *so* good ... and *such* a lovely man, isn't he though, yes ...'

Is that really what they would say? It suddenly occurred to me that it might not be like that at all. More like this perhaps: 'I agree, my dear, yes, not a bad old man ... but a bit of a bore, don't you think? ... What did you say? ... dull? But desperately, my dear. You've hit the nail right on the head ... did you ever hear what Janet de Pelagia once said about him? ... Ah yes, I thought you'd heard that one ... screamingly funny, don't you think? ... poor Janet ... how she stood it as long as she did I don't know ...'

Anyway, I got the invitations off, and within a couple of days everybody with the exception of Mrs Cudbird and Sir Hubert Kaul, who were away, had accepted with pleasure.

At eight-thirty on the evening of the twenty-second, my large drawing-room was filled with people. They stood about the room, admiring the pictures, drinking their Martinis, talking with loud voices. The women smelled strongly of scent, the men were pink-faced and carefully buttoned up in their dinner-jackets. Janet de Pelagia was wearing the same black dress she had used for the portrait, and every time I caught sight of her, a kind of huge bubble-vision – as in those absurd cartoons – would float up above my head, and in it I would see Janet in her underclothes, the black brassière, the pink elastic belt, the suspenders, the jockey's legs.

I moved from group to group, chatting amiably with them all, listening to their talk. Behind me I could hear Mrs Galbally telling Sir Eustace Piegrome and James Pisker how the man at the next table to hers at Claridges the night before had had red lipstick on his white moustache. 'Simply *plastered* with it,' she kept on saying, 'and the old boy was ninety if he was a day ...' On the other side, Lady Girdlestone was telling somebody where one could get truffles cooked in brandy, and I could see Mrs Icely whispering something to Lord Mulherrin while his Lordship kept shaking his head slowly from side to side like an old and dispirited metronome.

Dinner was announced, and we all moved out.

'My goodness!' they cried as they entered the dining-room. 'How dark and sinister!'

'I can hardly see a thing!'

'What divine little candles!'

'But Lionel, how romantic!'

There were six very thin candles set about two feet apart from each other down the centre of the long table. Their small flames made a little glow of light around the table itself, but left the rest of the room in darkness. It was an amusing arrangement and apart from the fact that it suited my purpose well, it made a pleasant change. The guests soon settled themselves in their right places and the meal began.

They all seemed to enjoy the candlelight and things went famously, though for some reason the darkness caused them to speak much louder than usual. Janet de Pelagia's voice struck me as being particularly strident. She was sitting next to Lord Mulherrin, and I could hear her telling him about the boring time she had had at Cap Ferrat the week before. 'Nothing but Frenchmen,' she kept saying. 'Nothing but Frenchmen in the whole place ...'

For my part, I was watching the candles. They were so thin that I knew it would not be long before they burned down to their bases. Also I was mighty nervous – I will admit that – but at the same time intensely exhilarated, almost to the point of drunkenness. Every time I heard Janet's voice or caught sight of her face shadowed in the light of the candles, a little ball of excitement exploded inside me and I felt the fire of it running under my skin.

They were eating their strawberries when at last I decided the time had come. I took a deep breath and in a loud voice I said, 'I'm afraid we'll have to have the lights on now. The candles are nearly finished. Mary,' I called. 'Oh, Mary, switch on the lights, will you please.'

There was a moment of silence after my announcement. I heard the maid walking over to the door, then the gentle click of the switch and the room was flooded with a blaze of light. They all screwed up their eyes, opened them again, gazed about them.

At that point I got up from my chair and slid quietly from the room, but as I went I saw a sight that I shall never forget as long as I live. It was Janet, with both hands in mid-air, stopped, frozen rigid, caught in the act of gesticulating towards someone across the table. Her mouth had dropped open two inches and she wore the surprised, not-quite-understanding look of a person who precisely one second before has been shot dead, right through the heart.

In the hall outside I paused and listened to the beginning of the uproar, the shrill cries of the ladies and the outraged unbelieving exclamations of the men; and soon there was a great hum of noise with everybody talking or shouting at the same time. Then – and this was the sweetest moment of all – I heard Lord Mulherrin's voice, roaring above the rest, 'Here! Someone! Hurry! Give her some water quick!'

Out in the street the chauffeur helped me into my car, and soon we were away from London and bowling merrily along the Great North Road towards this, my other house, which is only ninety-five miles from Town anyway.

The next two days I spent in gloating. I mooned around in a dream of ecstasy, half drowned in my own complacency and filled with a sense of pleasure so great that it constantly gave me pins and needles all along the lower parts of my legs. It wasn't until this morning when Gladys Ponsonby called me on the phone that I suddenly came to my senses and realized I was not a hero at all but an outcast. She informed me – with what I thought was just a trace of relish – that everybody was up in arms, that all of them, all my old and loving friends were saying the most terrible things about me and had sworn never never to speak to me again. Except her, she kept saying. Everybody except her. And didn't I think it would be rather cosy, she asked, if she were to come down and stay with me a few days to cheer me up?

I'm afraid I was too upset by that time even to answer her politely. I put the phone down and went away to weep.

Then at noon today came the final crushing blow. The post arrived, and with it – I can hardly bring myself to write about it, I am so ashamed – came a letter, the sweetest, most tender little note imaginable from none other than Janet de Pelagia herself. She forgave me completely, she wrote, for everything I had done. She knew it was only a joke and I must not listen to the horrid things other people were saying about me. She loved me as she always had and always would to her dying day.

Oh, what a cad, what a brute I felt when I read this! The more so when I found that she had actually sent me by the same post a small present as an added sign of her affection – a half-pound jar of my favourite food of all, fresh caviare.

I can never under any circumstances resist good caviare. It is perhaps my greatest weakness. So although I naturally had no appetite whatsoever for food at dinner-time this evening, I must confess I took a few spoonfuls of the stuff in an effort to console myself in my misery. It is even possible that I took a shade too much, because I haven't been feeling any too chipper this last hour or so. Perhaps I ought to go up right away and get myself some bicarbonate of soda. I can easily come back and finish this later, when I'm in better trim.

You know – now I come to think of it, I really do feel rather ill all of a sudden.

THE GREAT
AUTOMATIC GRAMMATIZATOR

'Well, Knipe, my boy. Now that it's all finished, I just called you in to tell you I think you've done a fine job.'

Adolph Knipe stood still in front of Mr Bohlen's desk. There seemed to be no enthusiasm in him at all.

'Aren't you pleased?'

'Oh yes, Mr Bohlen.'

'Did you see what the papers said this morning?'

'No sir, I didn't.'

The man behind the desk pulled a folded newspaper towards him, and began to read: 'The building of the great automatic computing engine, ordered by the government some time ago, is now complete. It is probably the fastest electronic calculating machine in the world today. Its function is to satisfy the ever-increasing need of science, industry, and administration for rapid mathematical calculation which, in the past, by traditional methods, would have been physically impossible, or would have required more time than the problems justified. The speed with which the new engine works, said Mr John Bohlen, head of the firm of electrical engineers mainly responsible for its construction, may be grasped by the fact that it can provide the correct answer in five seconds to a problem that would occupy a mathematician for a month. In three minutes, it can produce a calculation that by hand (if it were possible) would fill half a million sheets of foolscap paper. The automatic computing engine uses pulses of electricity, generated at the rate of a million a second, to solve all calculations that resolve themselves into addition, subtraction, multiplication, and division. For practical purposes there is no limit to what it can do ...'

Mr Bohlen glanced up at the long, melancholy face of the younger man. 'Aren't you proud, Knipe? Aren't you pleased.'

'Of course, Mr Bohlen.'

'I don't think I have to remind you that your own contribution, especially to the original plans, was an important one. In fact, I might go so far as to say that without you and some of your ideas, this project might still be on the drawing-boards today.'

Adolph Knipe moved his feet on the carpet, and he watched the two small white hands of his chief, the nervous fingers playing with a paper-clip, unbending it, straightening out the hairpin curves. He didn't like the man's hands. He didn't like his face either, with the tiny mouth and the narrow purple-coloured lips. It was unpleasant the way only the lower lip moved when he talked.

'Is anything bothering you, Knipe? Anything on your mind?'

'Oh no, Mr Bohlen. No.'

'How would you like to take a week's holiday? Do you good. You've earned it.'

'Oh, I don't know, sir.'

The older man waited, watching this tall, thin person who stood so sloppily before him. He was a difficult boy. Why couldn't he stand up straight? Always drooping and untidy, with spots on his jacket, and hair falling all over his face.

'I'd like you to take a holiday, Knipe. You need it.'

'All right, sir. If you wish.'

'Take a week. Two weeks if you like. Go somewhere warm. Get some sunshine. Swim. Relax. Sleep. Then come back, and we'll have another talk about the future.'

Adolph Knipe went home by bus to his two-room apartment. He threw his coat on the sofa, poured himself a drink of whisky, and sat down in front of the typewriter that was on the table. Mr Bohlen was right. Of course he was right. Except that he didn't know the half of it. He probably thought it was a woman. Whenever a young man gets depressed, everybody thinks it's a woman.

He leaned forward and began to read through the half-finished sheet of typing still in the machine. It was headed 'A Narrow Escape', and it began *'The night ws dark and stormy, the wind whistled in the trees, the rain poured down like cats and dogs . . .'*

Adolph Knipe took a sip of whisky, tasting the malty-bitter flavour, feeling the trickle of cold liquid as it travelled down his throat and settled in the top of his stomach, cool at first, then spreading and becoming warm, making a little area of warmness in the gut. To hell with Mr John Bohlen anyway. And to hell with the great electrical computing machine. To hell with . . .

At exactly that moment, his eyes and mouth began slowly to open, in a sort of wonder, and slowly he raised his head and became still, absolutely motionless, gazing at the wall opposite with this look that was more perhaps of astonishment than of wonder, but quite fixed now, unmoving, and remaining thus for forty, fifty, sixty seconds. Then gradually (the head still motionless), a subtle change spreading over the face, astonishment becoming pleasure, very slight at first, only around the corners of the mouth, increasing gradually, spreading out until at last the whole face was open wide and shining with extreme delight. It was the first time Adolph Knipe had smiled in many, many months.

'Of course,' he said, speaking aloud, 'it's completely ridiculous.' Again he smiled, raising his upper lip and baring his teeth in a queerly sensual manner.

'It's a delicious idea, but so impracticable it doesn't really bear thinking about at all.'

From then on, Adolph Knipe began to think about nothing else. The idea fascinated him enormously, at first because it gave him a promise – however remote – of revenging himself in a most devilish manner upon his greatest enemies. From this angle alone, he toyed idly with it for perhaps ten or fifteen minutes; then all at once he found himself examining it quite seriously as a practical possibility. He took paper and made some preliminary notes. But he didn't get far. He found himself, almost immediately, up against the old truth that a machine, however ingenious, is incapable of original thought. It can handle no problems except those that resolve themselves into mathematical terms – problems that contain one, and only one, correct answer.

This was a stumper. There didn't seem any way around it. A machine cannot have a brain. On the other hand, it *can* have a memory, can it not? Their own electronic calculator had a marvellous memory. Simply by converting electric pulses, through a column of mercury, into supersonic waves, it could store away at least a thousand numbers at a time, extracting any one of them at the precise moment it was needed. Would it not be possible, therefore, on this principle, to build a memory section of almost unlimited size?

Now what about that?

Then suddenly, he was struck by a powerful but simple little truth, and it was this: *that English grammar is governed by rules that are almost mathematical in their strictness!* Given the words, and given the sense of what is to be said, then there is only one correct order in which those words can be arranged.

No, he thought, that isn't quite accurate. In many sentences there are several alternative positions for words and phrases, all of which may be grammatically correct. But what the hell. The theory itself is basically true. Therefore, it stands to reason that an engine built along the lines of the electric computer could be adjusted to arrange words (instead of numbers) in their right order according to the rules of grammar. Give it the verbs, the nouns, the adjectives, the pronouns, store them in the memory section as a vocabulary, and arrange for them to be extracted as required. Then feed it with plots and leave it to write the sentences.

There was no stopping Knipe now. He went to work immediately, and there followed during the next few days a period of intense labour. The living-room became littered with sheets of paper: formulae and calculations; lists of words, thousands and thousands of words; the plots of stories, curiously broken up and subdivided; huge extracts from *Roget's Thesaurus*; pages filled with the first names of men and women; hundreds of surnames taken from the telephone directory; intricate drawings of wires and circuits and switches and thermionic valves; drawings of machines that could punch holes of different shapes in little cards, and of a strange electric typewriter that could type ten thousand words a minute. Also a kind of control panel with a series of small push-buttons, each one labelled with the name of a famous American magazine.

He was working in a mood of exultation, prowling around the room amidst this littering of paper, rubbing his hands together, talking out loud to himself; and sometimes, with a sly curl of the nose he would mutter a series of murderous imprecations in which the word 'editor' seemed always to be present. On the fifteenth day of continuous work, he collected the papers into two large folders which he carried – almost at a run – to the offices of John Bohlen Inc., electrical engineers.

Mr Bohlen was pleased to see him back.

'Well Knipe, good gracious me, you look a hundred per cent better. You have a good holiday? Where'd you go?'

He's just as ugly and untidy as ever, Mr Bohlen thought. Why doesn't he stand up straight? He looks like a bent stick. 'You look a hundred per cent better, my boy.' I wonder what he's grinning about. Every time I see him, his ears seem to have got larger.

Adolph Knipe placed the folders on the desk. 'Look, Mr Bohlen!' he cried. 'Look at these!'

Then he poured out his story. He opened the folders and pushed the plans in front of the astonished little man. He talked for over an hour, explaining everything, and when he had finished, he stepped back, breathless, flushed, waiting for the verdict.

'You know what I think, Knipe? I think you're nuts.' Careful now, Mr Bohlen told himself. Treat him carefully. He's valuable, this one is. If only he didn't look so awful, with that long horse face and the big teeth. The fellow had ears as big as rhubarb leaves.

'But Mr Bohlen! It'll work! I've proved to you it'll work! You can't deny that!'

'Take it easy now, Knipe. Take it easy, and listen to me.'

Adolph Knipe watched his man, disliking him more every second.

'This idea,' Mr Bohlen's lower lip was saying, 'is very ingenious – I might almost say brilliant – and it only goes to confirm my opinion of your abilities, Knipe. But don't take it too seriously. After all, my boy, what possible use can it be to us? Who on earth wants a machine for writing stories? And where's the money in it, anyway? Just tell me that.'

'May I sit down, sir?'

'Sure, take a seat.'

Adolph Knipe seated himself on the edge of a chair. The older man watched him with alert brown eyes, wondering what was coming now.

'I would like to explain something Mr Bohlen, if I may, about how I came to do all this.'

'Go right ahead, Knipe.' He would have to be humoured a little now, Mr Bohlen told himself. The boy was really valuable – a sort of genius, almost – worth his weight in gold to the firm. Just look at these papers here. Darndest thing you ever saw. Astonishing piece of work. Quite useless, of course. No commercial value. But it proved again the boy's ability.

'It's a sort of confession, I suppose, Mr Bohlen. I think it explains why I've always been so ... so kind of worried.'

'You tell me anything you want, Knipe. I'm here to help you – you know that.'

The young man clasped his hands together tight on his lap, hugging himself with his elbows. It seemed as though suddenly he was feeling very cold.

'You see, Mr Bohlen, to tell the honest truth, I don't really care much for my work here. I know I'm good at it and all that sort of thing, but my heart's not in it. It's not what I want to do most.'

Up went Mr Bohlen's eyebrows, quick like a spring. His whole body became very still.

'You see, sir, all my life I've wanted to be a writer.'

'A writer!'

'Yes, Mr Bohlen. You may not believe it, but every bit of spare time I've had, I've spent writing stories. In the last ten years I've written hundreds, literally hundreds of short stories. Five hundred and sixty-six, to be precise. Approximately one a week.'

'Good heavens, man! What on earth did you do that for?'

'All I know, sir, is I have the urge.'

'What sort of urge?'

'The creative urge, Mr Bohlen.' Every time he looked up he saw Mr Bohlen's lips. They were growing thinner and thinner, more and more purple.

'And may I ask you what you do with these stories, Knipe?'

'Well sir, that's the trouble. No one will buy them. Each time I finish one, I send it out on the rounds. It goes to one magazine after another. That's all that happens, Mr Bohlen, and they simply send them back. It's very depressing.'

Mr Bohlen relaxed. 'I can see quite well how you feel, my boy.' His voice was dripping with sympathy. 'We all go through it one time or another in our lives. But now – now that you've had proof – positive proof – from the experts themselves, from the editors, that your stories are – what shall I say – rather unsuccessful, it's time to leave off. Forget it, my boy. Just forget all about it.'

'No, Mr Bohlen! No! That's not true! I *know* my stories are good. My heavens, when you compare them with the stuff some of those magazines print – oh my word, Mr Bohlen! – the sloppy, boring stuff that you see in the magazines week after week – why, it drives me mad!'

'Now wait a minute, my boy ...'

'Do you ever read the magazines, Mr Bohlen?'

'You'll pardon me, Knipe, but what's all this got to do with your machine?'

'Everything, Mr Bohlen, absolutely everything! What I want to tell you is, I've made a study of magazines, and it seems that each one tends to have its own particular type of story. The writers – the successful ones – know this, and they write accordingly.'

'Just a minute, my boy. Calm yourself down, will you. I don't think all this is getting us anywhere.'

'*Please*, Mr Bohlen, hear me through. It's all terribly important.' He paused to catch his breath. He was properly worked up now, throwing his hands around as he talked. The long, toothy face, with the big ears on either side, simply shone with enthusiasm, and there was an excess of saliva in his mouth which caused him to speak his words wet. 'So you see, on my machine, by having an adjustable co-ordinator between the "plot-memory" section and the "word-memory" section I am able to produce any type of story I desire simply by pressing the required button.'

'Yes, I know, Knipe, I know. This is all very interesting, but what's the point of it?'

'Just this, Mr Bohlen. The market is limited. We've got to be able to produce the right stuff, at the right time, whenever we want it. It's a matter of business, that's all. I'm looking at it from *your* point of view now – as a commercial proposition.'

'My dear boy, it can't possibly be a commercial proposition – ever. You know as well as I do what it costs to build one of these machines.'

'Yes sir, I do. But with due respect, I don't believe you know what the magazines pay writers for stories.'

'What do they pay?'

'Anything up to twenty-five hundred dollars. It probably averages around a thousand.'

Mr Bohlen jumped.

'Yes *sir*, it's true.'

'Absolutely impossible, Knipe! Ridiculous!'

'No sir, it's true.'

'You mean to sit there and tell me that these magazines pay out money like that to a man for ... just for scribbling off a story! Good heavens, Knipe! Whatever next! Writers must all be millionaires!'

'That's exactly it, Mr Bohlen! That's where the machine comes in. Listen a minute, sir, while I tell you some more. I've got it all worked out. The big magazines are carrying approximately three fiction stories in each issue. Now, take the fifteen most important magazines – the ones paying the most money. A few of them are monthlies, but most of them come out every week. All right. That makes, let us say, around forty big stories being bought each week. That's forty thousand dollars. So with our machine – when we get it working properly – we can collar nearly the whole of this market!'

'My dear boy, you're mad!'

'No sir, honestly, it's true what I say. Don't you see that with volume alone we'll completely overwhelm them! This machine can produce a five-thousand word story, all typed and ready for despatch, in thirty seconds. How can the writers compete with that? I ask you, Mr Bohlen, *how?*'

At that point, Adolph Knipe noticed a slight change in the man's expression, an extra brightness in the eyes, the nostrils distending, the whole face becoming still, almost rigid. Quickly, he continued. 'Nowadays, Mr Bohlen, the hand-made article hasn't a hope. It can't possibly compete with mass-production, especially in this country – you know that. Carpets ... chairs ... shoes ... bricks ... crockery ... anything you like to mention – they're all made by machinery now. The quality may be inferior, but that doesn't matter. It's the cost of production that counts. And stories – well – they're just another product, like carpets and chairs, and no one cares how you produce them so long as you deliver the goods. We'll sell them wholesale, Mr Bohlen! We'll undercut every writer in the country! We'll corner the market!'

Mr Bohlen edged up straighter in his chair. He was leaning forward now, both elbows on the desk, the face alert, the small brown eyes resting on the speaker.

'I still think it's impracticable, Knipe.'

'Forty thousand a week!' cried Adolph Knipe. 'And if we halve the price, making it twenty thousand a week, that's still a million a year!' And softly he added, 'You didn't get any million a year for building the old electronic calculator, did you, Mr Bohlen?'

'But seriously now, Knipe. D'you really think they'd buy them?'

'Listen, Mr Bohlen. Who on earth is going to want custom-made stories when they can get the other kind at half the price? It stands to reason, doesn't it?'

'And how will you sell them? Who will you say has written them?'

'We'll set up our own literary agency, and we'll distribute them through that. And we'll invent all the names we want for the writers.'

'I don't like it, Knipe. To me, that smacks of trickery, does it not?'

'And another thing, Mr Bohlen. There's all manner of valuable by-products once you've got started. Take advertising, for example. Beer manufacturers and people like that are willing to pay good money these days if famous writers will lend their names to their products. Why, my heavens, Mr Bohlen! This isn't any children's plaything we're talking about. It's big business.'

'Don't get too ambitious, my boy.'

'And another thing. There isn't any reason why we shouldn't put *your* name, Mr Bohlen, on some of the better stories, if you wished it.'

'My goodness, Knipe. What should I want that for?'

'I don't know, sir, except that some writers get to be very much respected – like Mr Erle Gardner or Kathleen Norris, for example. We've got to have names, and I was certainly thinking of using my own on one or two stories, just to help out.'

'A writer, eh?' Mr Bohlen said, musing. 'Well, it would surely surprise them over at the club when they saw my name in the magazines – the good magazines.'

'That's right, Mr Bohlen!'

For a moment, a dreamy, faraway look came into Mr Bohlen's eyes, and he smiled. Then he stirred himself and began leafing through the plans that lay before him.

'One thing I don't quite understand, Knipe. Where do the plots come from? The machine can't possibly invent plots.'

'We feed those in, sir. That's no problem at all. Everyone has plots. There's three or four hundred of them written down in that folder there on your left. Feed them straight into the "plot-memory" section of the machine.'

'Go on.'

'There are many other little refinements too, Mr Bohlen. You'll see them all when you study the plans carefully. For example, there's a trick that nearly every writer uses, of inserting at least one long, obscure word into each story. This makes the reader think that the man is very wise and clever. So I have the machine do the same thing. There'll be a whole stack of long words stored away just for this purpose.'

'Where?'

'In the "word-memory" section,' he said, epexegetically.

Through most of that day the two men discussed the possibilities of the new engine. In the end, Mr Bohlen said he would have to think about it some more. The next morning, he was quietly enthusiastic. Within a week, he was completely sold on the idea.

'What we'll have to do, Knipe, is to say that we're merely building another mathematical calculator, but of a new type. That'll keep the secret.'

'Exactly, Mr Bohlen.'

And in six months the machine was completed. It was housed in a separate brick building at the back of the premises, and now that it was ready for action, no one was allowed near it excepting Mr Bohlen and Adolph Knipe.

It was an exciting moment when the two men – the one, short, plump, breviped – the other tall, thin and toothy – stood in the corridor before the control panel and got ready to run off the first story. All around them were walls dividing up into many small corridors, and the walls were covered with wiring and plugs and switches and huge glass valves. They were both nervous, Mr Bohlen hopping from one foot to the other, quite unable to keep still.

'Which button?' Adolph Knipe asked, eyeing a row of small white discs that resembled the keys of a typewriter. 'You choose, Mr Bohlen. Lots of magazines to pick from – *Saturday Evening Post, Collier's, Ladies' Home Journal* – any one you like.'

'Goodness me, boy! How do I know?' He was jumping up and down like a man with hives.

'Mr Bohlen,' Adolph Knipe said gravely, 'do you realize that at this moment, with your little finger alone, you have it in your power to become the most versatile writer on this continent?'

'Listen Knipe, just get on with it, will you please – and cut out the preliminaries.'

'Okay, Mr Bohlen. Then we'll make it ... let me see – this one. How's that?' He extended one finger and pressed down a button with the name TODAY'S WOMAN printed across it in diminutive black type. There was a sharp click, and when he took his finger away, the button remained down, below the level of the others.

'So much for the selection,' he said. 'Now – here we go!' He reached up and pulled a switch on the panel. Immediately, the room was filled with a loud humming noise, and a crackling of electric sparks, and the jingle of many, tiny, quickly-moving levers; and almost in the same instant, sheets of quarto paper began sliding out from a slot to the right of the control panel and dropping into a basket below. They came out quick, one sheet a second, and in less than half a minute it was all over. The sheets stopped coming.

'That's it!' Adolph Knipe cried. 'There's your story!'

They grabbed the sheets and began to read. The first one they picked up started as follows: 'Aifkjmbsaoegweztpplnvoqudskigt&,-fuhpekanvbertyuiolkjhgfdsazxcvbnm,peruitrehdjkg mvnb,wmsuy ...' They looked at the others. The style was roughly similar in all of them. Mr Bohlen began to shout. The younger man tried to calm him down.

'It's all right, sir. Really it is. It only needs a little adjustment. We've got a connection wrong somewhere, that's all. You must remember, Mr Bohlen, there's over a million feet of wiring in this room. You can't expect everything to be right first time.'

'It'll never work,' Mr Bohlen said.

'Be patient, sir. Be patient.'

Adolph Knipe set out to discover the fault, and in four days' time he announced that all was ready for the next try.

'It'll never work,' Mr Bohlen said. 'I know it'll never work.'

Knipe smiled and pressed the selector button marked *Reader's Digest*. Then he pulled the switch, and again the strange, exciting, humming sound filled the room. One page of typescript flew out of the slot into the basket.

'Where's the rest?' Mr Bohlen cried. 'It's stopped! It's gone wrong!'

'No, sir, it hasn't. It's exactly right. It's for the *Digest*, don't you see?'

This time it began: 'Fewpeopleyetknowthatarevolutionarynewcure-hasbeendiscoveredwhichmaywellbringpermanentrelieftosufferersofthemostdreadeddiseaseofourtime...' And so on.

'It's gibberish!' Mr Bohlen shouted.

'No sir, it's fine. Can't you see? It's simply that she's not breaking up the words. That's an easy adjustment. But the story's there. Look, Mr Bohlen, look! It's all there except that the words are joined together.'

And indeed it was.

On the next try a few days later, everything was perfect, even the punctuation. The first story they ran off, for a famous women's magazine, was a solid, plotty story of a boy who wanted to better himself with his rich employer. This boy arranged, so that story went, for a friend to hold up the rich man's daughter on a dark night when she was driving home. Then the boy himself, happening by, knocked the gun out of his friend's hand and rescued the girl. The girl was grateful. But the father was suspicious. He questioned the boy sharply. The boy broke down and confessed. Then the father, instead of kicking him out of the house, said that he admired the boy's resourcefulness. The girl admired his honesty – and his looks. The father promised him to be head of the Accounts Department. The girl married him.

'It's tremendous, Mr Bohlen! It's exactly right!'

'Seems a bit sloppy to me, my boy.'

'No sir, it's a seller, a real seller!'

In his excitement, Adolph Knipe promptly ran off six more stories in as many minutes. All of them – except one, which for some reason came out a trifle lewd – seemed entirely satisfactory.

Mr Bohlen was now mollified. He agreed to set up a literary agency in an office downtown, and to put Knipe in charge. In a couple of weeks, this was accomplished. Then Knipe mailed out the first dozen stories. He put his own name to four of them, Mr Bohlen's to one, and for the others he simply invented names.

Five of these stories were promptly accepted. The one with Mr Bohlen's name on it was turned down with a letter from the fiction editor saying, 'This is a skilful job, but in our opinion it doesn't quite come off. We would like to see more of this writer's work ...' Adolph Knipe took a cab out to the factory and ran off another story for the same magazine. He again put Mr Bohlen's name to it, and mailed it immediately. That one they bought.

The money started pouring in. Knipe slowly and carefully stepped up the output, and in six months' time he was delivering thirty stories a week, and selling about half.

He began to make a name for himself in literary circles as a prolific and successful writer. So did Mr Bohlen; but not quite such a good name, although he didn't know it. At the same time, Knipe was building up a dozen or more fictitious persons as promising young authors. Everything was going fine.

At this point it was decided to adapt the machine for writing novels as well as stories. Mr Bohlen, thirsting now for greater honours in the literary world, insisted that Knipe go to work at once on this prodigious task.

'I want to do a novel,' he kept saying. 'I want to do a novel.'

'And so you will, sir. And so you will. But please be patient. This is a very complicated adjustment I have to make.'

'Everyone tells me I ought to do a novel,' Mr Bohlen cried. 'All sorts of publishers are chasing after me day and night begging me to stop fooling around with stories and do something really important instead. A novel's the only thing that counts – that's what they say.'

'We're going to do novels,' Knipe told him. 'Just as many as we want. But please be patient.'

'Now listen to me, Knipe. What I'm going to do is a *serious* novel, something that'll make 'em sit up and take notice. I've been getting rather tired of the sort of stories you've been putting my name to lately. As a matter of fact, I'm none too sure you haven't been trying to make a monkey out of me.'

'A monkey, Mr Bohlen?'

'Keeping all the best ones for yourself, that's what you've been doing.'

'Oh no, Mr Bohlen! No!'

'So this time I'm going to make damn sure I write a high class intelligent book. You understand that.'

'Look, Mr Bohlen. With the sort of switchboard I'm rigging up, you'll be able to write any sort of book you want.'

And this was true, for within another couple of months, the genius of Adolph Knipe had not only adapted the machine for novel writing, but had constructed a marvellous new control system which enabled the author to pre-select literally any type of plot and any style of writing he desired. There were so many dials and levers on the thing, it looked like the instrument panel of some enormous aeroplane.

First, by depressing one of a series of master buttons, the writer made his primary decision: historical, satirical, philosophical, political, romantic, erotic, humorous, or straight. Then, from the second row (the basic buttons), he chose his theme: army life, pioneer days, civil war, world war, racial problem, wild west, country life, childhood memories, seafaring, the sea bottom and many, many more. The third row of buttons gave a choice of literary style: classical, whimsical, racy, Hemingway, Faulkner, Joyce, feminine, etc. The fourth row was for characters, the fifth for wordage – and so on and so on – ten long rows of pre-selector buttons.

But that wasn't all. Control had also to be exercised during the actual writing process (which took about fifteen minutes per novel), and to do this the author had to sit, as it were, in the driver's seat, and pull (or push) a battery of labelled stops, as on an organ. By so doing, he was able continually to modulate or merge fifty different and variable qualities such as tension, surprise, humour, pathos, and mystery. Numerous dials and gauges on the dashboard itself told him throughout exactly how far along he was with his work.

Finally, there was the question of 'passion'. From a careful study of the books at the top of the best-seller lists for the past year, Adolph Knipe had decided that this was the most important ingredient of all – a magical catalyst that somehow or other could transform the dullest novel into a howling success – at any rate financially. But Knipe also knew that passion was powerful, heady stuff, and must be prudently dispensed – the right proportions at the right moments; and to ensure this, he had devised an independent control consisting of two sensitive sliding adjustors operated by foot-pedals, similar to the throttle and brake in a car. One pedal governed the percentage of passion to be injected, the other regulated its intensity. There was no doubt, of course – and this was the only drawback – that the writing of a novel by the Knipe methods was going to be rather like flying a plane and driving a car and playing an organ all at the same time, but this did not trouble the inventor. When all was ready, he proudly escorted Mr Bohlen into the machine house and began to explain the operating procedure for the new wonder.

'Good God, Knipe! I'll never be able to do all that! Dammit, man, it'd be easier to write the thing by hand!'

'You'll soon get used to it, Mr Bohlen, I promise you. In a week or two, you'll be doing it without hardly thinking. It's just like learning to drive.'

Well, it wasn't quite as easy at that, but after many hours of practice, Mr Bohlen began to get the hang of it, and finally, late one evening, he told Knipe to make ready for running off the first novel. It was a tense moment, with the fat little man crouching nervously in the driver's seat, and the tall toothy Knipe fussing excitedly around him.

'I intend to write an important novel, Knipe.'

'I'm sure you will, sir. I'm sure you will.'

With one finger, Mr Bohlen carefully pressed the necessary pre-selector buttons:

Master button – *satirical*
Subject – *racial problem*
Style – *classical*
Characters – *six men, four women, one infant*
Length – *fifteen chapters.*

At the same time he had his eye particularly upon three organ stops marked *power, mystery, profundity.*

'Are you ready, sir?'

'Yes, yes, I'm ready.'

Knipe pulled the switch. The great engine hummed. There was a deep whirring sound from the oiled movement of fifty thousand cogs and rods and levers; then came the drumming of the rapid electrical typewriter, setting up a shrill, almost intolerable clatter. Out into the basket flew the typewritten pages – one every two seconds. But what with the noise and the excitement, and having to play upon the stops, and watch the chapter-counter and the pace-indicator and the passion-gauge, Mr Bohlen began to panic. He reacted in precisely the way a learner driver does in a car – by pressing both feet hard down on the pedals and keeping them there until the thing stopped.

'Congratulations on your first novel,' Knipe said, picking up the great bundle of typed pages from the basket.

Little pearls of sweat were oozing out all over Mr Bohlen's face. 'It sure was hard work, my boy.'

'But you got it done, sir. You got it done.'

'Let me see it, Knipe. How does it read?'

He started to go through the first chapter, passing each finished page to the younger man.

'Good heavens, Knipe! What's this!' Mr Bohlen's thin purple fish-lip was moving slightly as it mouthed the words, his cheeks were beginning slowly to inflate.

'But look here, Knipe! This is outrageous!'

'I must say it's a bit fruity, sir.'

'*Fruity!* It's perfectly revolting! I can't possibly put my name to this!'

'Quite right, sir. Quite right.'

'Knipe! Is this some nasty trick you've been playing on me?'

'Oh no, sir! No!'

'It certainly looks like it.'

'You don't think, Mr Bohlen, that you mightn't have been pressing a little hard on the passion-control pedals, do you?'

'My dear boy, how should *I* know.'

'Why don't you try another?'

So Mr Bohlen ran off a second novel, and this time it went according to plan.

Within a week, the manuscript had been read and accepted by an enthusiastic publisher. Knipe followed with one in his own name, then made a dozen more for good measure. In no time at all, Adolph Knipe's Literary Agency had become famous for its large stable of promising young novelists. And once again the money started rolling in.

It was at this stage that young Knipe began to display a real talent for big business.

'See here, Mr Bohlen,' he said. 'We still got too much competition. Why don't we just absorb all the other writers in the country?'

Mr Bohlen, who now sported a bottle-green velvet jacket and allowed his hair to cover two-thirds of his ears, was quite content with things the way they were. 'Don't know what you mean, my boy. You can't just absorb writers.'

'Of course you can, sir. Exactly like Rockefeller did with his oil companies. Simply buy 'em out, and if they won't sell, squeeze 'em out. It's easy!'

'Careful now, Knipe. Be careful.'

'I've got a list here, sir, of fifty of the most successful writers in the country, and what I intend to do is offer each one of them a lifetime contract with pay. All *they* have to do is undertake never to write another word; and, of course, to let us use their names on our own stuff. How about that.'

'They'll never agree.'

'You don't know writers, Mr Bohlen. You watch and see.'

'What about the creative urge, Knipe?'

'It's bunk! All they're really interested in is the money – just like everybody else.'

In the end, Mr Bohlen reluctantly agreed to give it a try, and Knipe, with his list of writers in his pocket, went off in a large chauffeur-driven Cadillac to make his calls.

He journeyed first to the man at the top of the list, a very great and wonderful writer, and he had no trouble getting into the house. He told his story and produced a suitcase full of sample novels, and a contract for the man to sign which guaranteed him so much a year for life. The man listened politely, decided he was dealing with a lunatic, gave him a drink, then firmly showed him to the door.

The second writer on the list, when he saw Knipe was serious, actually attacked him with a large metal paper-weight, and the inventor had to flee down the garden followed by such a torrent of abuse and obscenity as he had never heard before.

But it took more than this to discourage Adolph Knipe. He was disappointed but not dismayed, and off he went in his big car to seek his next client. This one was a female, famous and popular, whose fat romantic books sold by the million across the country. She received Knipe graciously, gave him tea, and listened attentively to his story.

'It all sounds very fascinating,' she said. 'But of course I find it a little hard to believe.'

'Madam,' Knipe answered. 'Come with me and see it with your own eyes. My car awaits you.'

So off they went, and in due course, the astonished lady was ushered into the machine house where the wonder was kept. Eagerly, Knipe explained its workings, and after a while he even permitted her to sit in the driver's seat and practise with the buttons.

'All right,' he said suddenly 'you want to do a book now?'

'Oh yes!' she cried. 'Please!'

She was very competent and seemed to know exactly what she wanted. She made her own pre-selections, then ran off a long, romantic, passion-filled novel. She read through the first chapter and became so enthusiastic that she signed up on the spot.

'That's one of them out of the way,' Knipe said to Mr Bohlen afterwards. 'A pretty big one too.'

'Nice work, my boy.'

'And you know *why* she signed?'

'Why?'

'It wasn't the money. She's got plenty of that.'

'Then why?'

Knipe grinned, lifting his lip and baring a long pale upper gum. 'Simply because she saw the machine-made stuff was better than her own.'

Thereafter, Knipe wisely decided to concentrate only upon mediocrity. Anything better than that – and there were so few it didn't matter much – was apparently not quite so easy to seduce.

In the end, after several months of work, he had persuaded something like seventy per cent of the writers on his list to sign the contract. He found that the older ones, those who were running out of ideas and had taken to drink, were the easiest to handle. The younger people were more troublesome. They were apt to become abusive, sometimes violent when he approached them; and more than once Knipe was slightly injured on his rounds.

But on the whole, it was a satisfactory beginning. This last year – the first full year of the machine's operation – it was estimated that at least one half of all the novels and stories published in the English language were produced by Adolph Knipe upon the Great Automatic Grammatizator.

Does this surprise you?

I doubt it.

And worse is yet to come. Today, as the secret spreads, many more are hurrying to tie up with Mr Knipe. And all the time the screw turns tighter for those who hesitate to sign their names.

This very moment, as I sit here listening to the howling of my nine starving children in the other room, I can feel my own hand creeping closer and closer to that golden contract that lies over on the other side of the desk.

Give us strength, Oh Lord, to let our children starve.

CLAUD'S DOG

The Ratcatcher

In the afternoon the ratcatcher came to the filling station. He came sidling up the driveway with a stealthy, soft-treading gait, making no noise at all with his feet on the gravel. He had an army knapsack slung over one shoulder and he was wearing an old-fashioned black jacket with large pockets. His brown corduroy trousers were tied around the knees with pieces of white string.

'Yes?' Claud asked, knowing very well who he was.

'Rodent operative.' His small dark eyes moved swiftly over the premises.

'The ratcatcher?'

'That's me.'

The man was lean and brown with a sharp face and two long sulphur-coloured teeth that protruded from the upper jaw, overlapping the lower lip, pressing it inward. The ears were thin and pointed and set far back on the head, near the nape of the neck. The eyes were almost black, but when they looked at you there was a flash of yellow somewhere inside them.

'You've come very quick.'

'Special orders from the Health Office.'

'And now you're going to catch all the rats?'

'Yep.'

The kind of dark furtive eyes he had were those of an animal that lives its life peering out cautiously and forever from a hole in the ground.

'How are you going to catch 'em?'

'Ah-h-h,' the ratman said darkly. 'That's all accordin' to where they is.'

'Trap 'em, I suppose.'

'Trap 'em!' he cried, disgusted. 'You won't catch many rats that way! Rats isn't rabbits, you know.'

He held his face up high, sniffing the air with a nose that twitched perceptibly from side to side.

'No,' he said, scornfully. 'Trappin's no way to catch a rat. Rats is clever, let me tell you that. If you want to catch 'em, you got to know 'em. You got to know rats on this job.'

I could see Claud staring at him with a certain fascination.

'They're more clever'n dogs, rats is.'

'Get away.'

'You know what they do? They watch you! All the time you're goin' round preparin' to catch 'em, they're sittin' quietly in dark places, watchin' you.' The man crouched, stretching his stringy neck far forward.

'So what do you do?' Claud asked, fascinated.

'Ah! That's it, you see. That's where you got to know rats.'

'How d'you catch 'cm?'

'There's ways,' the ratman said, leering. 'There's various ways.'

He paused, nodding his repulsive head sagely up and down. 'It's all dependin',' he said, 'on where they is. This ain't a sewer job, is it?'

'No, it's not a sewer job.'

'Tricky things, sewer jobs. Yes,' he said, delicately sniffing the air to the left of him with his mobile nose-end, 'sewer jobs is very tricky things.'

'Not especially, I shouldn't think.'

'Oh-ho. You shouldn't, shouldn't you! Well, I'd like to see *you* do a sewer job! Just exactly how would *you* set about it, I'd like to know?'

'Nothing to it. I'd just poison 'em, that's all.'

'And where exactly would you put the poison, might I ask?'

'Down the sewer. Where the hell you think I put it!'

'There!' the ratman cried, triumphant. 'I knew it! Down the sewer! And you know what'd happen then? Get washed away, that's all. Sewer's like a river, y'know.'

'That's what *you* say,' Claud answered. 'That's only what *you* say.'

'It's facts.'

'All right, then, all right. So what would *you* do, Mr Know-all?'

'That's exactly where you got to know rats, on a sewer job.'

'Come on then, let's have it.'

'Now listen. I'll tell you.' The ratman advanced a step closer, his voice became secretive and confidential, the voice of a man divulging fabulous professional secrets. 'You works on the understandin' that a rat is a gnawin' animal, see. Rats *gnaws*. Anythin' you give 'em, don't matter what it is, anythin' new they never seen before, and what do they do? They *gnaws* it. So now! There you are! You get a sewer job on your hands. And what d'you do?'

His voice had the soft throaty sound of a croaking frog and he seemed to speak all his words with an immense wet-lipped relish, as though they tasted good on the tongue. The accent was similar to Claud's, the broad soft accent of the Buckinghamshire countryside, but his voice was more throaty, the words more fruity in his mouth.

'All you do is you go down the sewer and you take along some ordinary paper bags, just ordinary brown paper bags, and these bags is filled with plaster of Paris powder. Nothin' else. Then you suspend the bags from the roof of the sewer so they hang down not quite touchin' the water. See? Not quite touchin', and just high enough so a rat can reach 'em.'

Claud was listening, rapt.

'There you are, y'see. Old rat comes swimmin' along the sewer and sees the bag. He stops. He takes a sniff at it and it don't smell so bad anyway. So what's he do then?'

'He *gnaws* it,' Claud cried, delighted.

'There! That's it! That's exactly it! He starts *gnawin'* away at the bag and the bag breaks and the old rat gets a mouthful of powder for his pains.'

'Well?'

'That does him.'

'What? Kills him?'

'Yep. Kills him stony!'

'Plaster of Paris ain't poisonous, you know.'

'Ah! There you are! That's exackly where you're wrong, see. This powder swells. When you wet it, it swells. Gets into the rat's tubes and swells right up and kills him quicker'n anythin' in the world.'

'*No!*'

'That's where you got to know rats.'

The ratman's face glowed with a stealthy pride, and he rubbed his stringy fingers together, holding the hands up close to the face. Claud watched him, fascinated.

'Now – where's them rats?' The word 'rats' came out of his mouth soft and throaty, with a rich fruity relish as though he were gargling with melted butter. 'Let's take a look at them *rraats*.'

'Over there in the hayrick across the road.'

'Not in the house?' he asked, obviously disappointed.

'No. Only around the hayrick. Nowhere else.'

'I'll wager they're in the house too. Like as not gettin' in all your food in the night and spreadin' disease and sickness. You got any disease here?' he asked, looking first at me, then at Claud.

'Everyone fine here.'

'Quite sure?'

'Oh yes.'

'You never know, you see. You could be sickenin' for it weeks and weeks and not feel it. Then all of a sudden – bang! – and it's got you. That's why Dr Arbuthnot's so particular. That's why he sent me out so quick, see. To stop the spreadin' of disease.'

He had now taken upon himself the mantle of the Health Officer.

A most important rat he was now, deeply disappointed that we were not suffering from bubonic plague.

'I feel fine,' Claud said, nervously.

The ratman searched his face again, but said nothing.

'And how are you goin' to catch 'em in the hayrick?'

The ratman grinned, a crafty toothy grin. He reached down into his knapsack and withdrew a large tin which he held up level with his face. He peered around one side of it at Claud.

'Poison!' he whispered. But he pronounced it *pye-zn*, making it into a soft, dark, dangerous word. 'Deadly *pye-zn*, that's what this is!' He was weighing the tin up and down in his hands as he spoke. 'Enough here to kill a million men!'

'Terrifying,' Claud said.

'Exackly it! They'd put you inside for six months if they caught you with even a spoonful of this,' he said, wetting his lips with his tongue. He had a habit of craning his head forward on his neck as he spoke.

'Want to see?' he asked, taking a penny from his pocket, prising open the lid. 'There now! There it is!' He spoke fondly, almost lovingly of the stuff, and he held it forward for Claud to look.

'Corn? Or barley is it?'

'It's oats. Soaked in deadly *pye-zn*. You take just one of them grains in your mouth and you'd be a gonner in five minutes.'

'Honest?'

'Yep. Never out of me sight, this tin.'

He caressed it with his hands and gave it a little shake so that the oat grains rustled softly inside.

'But not today. Your rats don't get this today. They wouldn't have it anyway. That they wouldn't. There's where you got to know rats. Rats is suspicious. Terrible suspicious, rats is. So today they gets some nice clean tasty oats as'll do 'em no harm in the world. Fatten 'em, that's all it'll do. And tomorrow they gets the same again. And it'll taste so good there'll be all the rats in the districk comin' along after a couple of days.'

'Rather clever.'

'You got to be clever on this job. You got to be cleverer'n a rat and that's sayin' something.'

'You've almost got to be a rat yourself,' I said. It slipped out in error, before I had time to stop myself, and I couldn't really help it because I was looking at the man at the time. But the effect upon him was surprising.

'There!' he cried. 'Now you got it! Now you really said something! A good ratter's got to be more like a rat than anythin' else in the world! Cleverer even than a rat, and that's not an easy thing to be, let me tell you!'

'Quite sure it's not.'

'All right, then, let's go. I haven't got all day, you know. There's Lady Leonora Benson asking for me urgent up there at the Manor.'

'She got rats, too?'

'Everybody's got rats,' the ratman said, and he ambled off down the driveway, across the road to the hayrick and we watched him go. The way he walked was so like a rat it made you wonder – that slow, almost delicate ambling walk with a lot of give at the knees and no sound at all from the footsteps on the gravel. He hopped nimbly over the gate into the field, then walked quickly round the hayrick scattering handfuls of oats on to the ground.

The next day he returned and repeated the procedure.

The day after that he came again and this time he put down the poisoned oats. But he didn't scatter these; he placed them carefully in little piles at each corner of the rick.

'You got a dog?' he asked when he came back across the road on the third day after putting down the poison.

'Yes.'

'Now if you want to see your dog die an 'orrible twistin' death, all you got to do is let him in that gate some time.'

'We'll take care,' Claud told him. 'Don't you worry about that.'

The next day he returned once more, this time to collect the dead.

'You got an old sack?' he asked. 'Most likely we goin' to need a sack to put 'em in.'

He was puffed up and important now, the black eyes gleaming with pride. He was about to display the sensational results of his catch to the audience.

Claud fetched a sack and the three of us walked across the road, the ratman leading. Claud and I leaned over the gate, watching. The ratman prowled around the hayrick, bending over to inspect his little piles of poison.

'Somethin' wrong here,' he muttered. His voice was soft and angry.

He ambled over to another pile and got down on his knees to examine it closely.

'Somethin' bloody wrong here.'

'What's the matter?'

He didn't answer, but it was clear that the rats hadn't touched his bait.

'These are very clever rats here,' I said.

'Exactly what I told him, Gordon. These aren't just no ordinary kind of rats you're dealing with here.'

The ratman walked over to the gate. He was very annoyed and showed it on his face and around the nose and by the way the two yellow teeth were pressing down into the skin of his lower lip. 'Don't give me that crap,' he said, looking at me. 'There's nothin' wrong with these rats except somebody's feedin' 'em. They got somethin' juicy to eat somewhere and plenty of it. There's no rats in the world'll turn down oats unless their bellies is full to burstin'.'

'They're clever,' Claud said.

The man turned away, disgusted. He knelt down again and began to scoop up the poisoned oats with a small shovel, tipping them carefully back into the tin. When he had done, all three of us walked back across the road.

The ratman stood near the petrol-pumps, a rather sorry, humble ratman now whose face was beginning to take on a brooding aspect. He had withdrawn into himself and was brooding in silence over his failure, the eyes veiled and wicked, the little tongue darting out to one side of the two yellow teeth, keeping the lips moist. It appeared to be essential that the lips should be kept moist. He looked up at me, a quick surreptitious glance, then over at Claud. His nose-end twitched, sniffing the air. He raised himself up and down a few times on his toes, swaying gently, and in a voice soft and secretive, he said: 'Want to see somethin'?' He was obviously trying to retrieve his reputation.

'What?'

'Want to see somethin' *amazin*'?' As he said this he put his right hand into the deep poacher's pocket of his jacket and brought out a large live rat clasped tight between his fingers.

'Good God!'

'Ah! That's it, y'see!' He was crouching slightly now and craning his neck forward and leering at us and holding this enormous brown rat in his hands, one finger and thumb making a tight circle around the creature's neck, clamping its head rigid so it couldn't turn and bite.

'D'you usually carry rats around in your pockets?'

'Always got a rat or two about me somewhere.'

With that he put his free hand into the other pocket and produced a small white ferret.

'Ferret,' he said, holding it up by the neck.

The ferret seemed to know him and stayed still in his grasp.

'There's nothin'll kill a rat quicker'n a ferret. And there's nothin' a rat's more frightened of either.'

He brought his hands close together in front of him so that the ferret's nose was within six inches of the rat's face. The pink beady eyes of the ferret stared at the rat. The rat struggled, trying to edge away from the killer.

'Now,' he said. 'Watch!'

His khaki shirt was open at the neck and he lifted the rat and slipped it down inside his shirt, next to his skin. As soon as his hand was free, he unbuttoned his jacket at the front so that the audience could see the bulge the body of the rat made under his shirt. His belt prevented it from going down lower than his waist.

Then he slipped the ferret in after the rat.

Immediately there was a great commotion inside the shirt. It appeared that the rat was running around the man's body, being chased by the ferret. Six or seven times they went around, the small bulge chasing the larger one, gaining on it slightly each circuit and drawing closer and closer until at last the two bulges seemed to come together and there was a scuffle and a series of shrill shrieks.

Throughout this performance the ratman had stood absolutely still with legs apart, arms hanging loosely, the dark eyes resting on Claud's face. Now he reached one hand down into his shirt and pulled out the ferret; with the other he took out the dead rat. There were traces of blood around the white muzzle of the ferret.

'Not sure I liked that very much.'

'You never seen anythin' like it before, I'll bet you that.'

'Can't really say I have.'

'Like as not you'll get yourself a nasty little nip in the guts one of these days,' Claud told him. But he was clearly impressed, and the ratman was becoming cocky again.

'Want to see somethin' far more *amazn'n* that?' he asked. 'You want to see somethin' you'd never even *believe* unless you seen it with your own eyes?'

'Well?'

We were standing in the driveway out in front of the pumps and it was one of those pleasant warm November mornings. Two cars pulled in for petrol, one right after the other, and Claud went over and gave them what they wanted.

'You want to see?' the ratman asked.

I glanced at Claud, slightly apprehensive. 'Yes,' Claud said. 'Come on then, let's see.'

The ratman slipped the dead rat back into one pocket, the ferret into the other. Then he reached down into his knapsack and produced – if you please – a second live rat.

'Good Christ!' Claud said.

'Always got one or two rats about me somewhere,' the man announced calmly. 'You got to know rats on this job, and if you want to know 'em you got to have 'em round you. This is a sewer rat, this is. An old sewer rat, clever as buggery. See him watchin' me all the time, wonderin' what I'm goin' to do? See him?'

'Very unpleasant.'

'What are you going to do?' I asked. I had a feeling I was going to like this one even less than the last.

'Fetch me a piece of string.'

Claud fetched him a piece of string.

With his left hand, the man looped the string around one of the rat's hind legs. The rat struggled, trying to turn its head to see what was going on, but he held it tight around the neck with finger and thumb.

'Now!' he said, looking about him. 'You got a table inside?'

'We don't want the rat inside the house,' I said.

'Well – I need a table. Or somethin' flat like a table.'

'What about the bonnet of that car?' Claud said.

We walked over to the car and the man put the old sewer rat on the bonnet. He attached the string to the windshield wiper so that the rat was now tethered.

At first it crouched, unmoving and suspicious, a big-bodied grey rat with bright black eyes and a scaly tail that lay in a long curl upon the car's bonnet. It was looking away from the ratman, but watching him sideways to see what he was going to do. The man stepped back a few paces and immediately the rat relaxed. It sat up on its haunches and began to lick the grey fur on its chest. Then it scratched its muzzle with both front paws. It seemed quite unconcerned about the three men standing near by.

'Now – how about a little bet?' the ratman asked.

'We don't bet,' I said.

'Just for fun. It's more fun if you bet.'

'What d'you want to bet on?'

'I'll bet you I can kill that rat without usin' my hands. I'll put my hands in my pockets and not use 'em.'

'You'll kick it with your feet,' Claud said.

It was apparent that the ratman was out to earn some money. I looked at the rat that was going to be killed and began to feel slightly sick, not so much because it was going to be killed but because it was going to be killed in a special way, with a considerable degree of relish.

'No,' the ratman said. 'No feet.'

'Nor arms?' Claud asked.

'Nor arms. Nor legs, nor hands neither.'

'You'll sit on it.'

'No. No squashin'.'

'Let's see you do it.'

'You bet me first. Bet me a quid.'

'Don't be so bloody daft,' Claud said. 'Why should we give you a quid?'

'What'll you bet?'

'Nothin'.'

'All right. Then it's no go.'

He made as if to untie the string from the windshield wiper.

'I'll bet you a shilling,' Claud told him. The sick gastric sensation in my stomach was increasing, but there was an awful magnetism about this business and I found myself quite unable to walk away or even move.

'You too?'

'No,' I said.

'What's the matter with you?' the ratman asked.

'I just don't want to bet you, that's all.'

'So you want me to do this for a lousy shillin'?'

'I don't want you to do it.'

'Where's the money?' he said to Claud.

Claud put a shilling piece on the bonnet, near the radiator. The ratman produced two sixpences and laid them beside Claud's money. As he stretched out his hand to do this, the rat cringed, drawing its head back and flattening itself against the bonnet.

'Bet's on,' the ratman said.

Claud and I stepped back a few paces. The ratman stepped forward. He put his hands in his pockets and inclined his body from the waist so that his face was on a level with the rat, about three feet away.

His eyes caught the eyes of the rat and held them. The rat was crouching, very tense, sensing extreme danger, but not yet frightened. The way it crouched, it seemed to me it was preparing to spring forward at the man's face; but there must have been some power in the ratman's eyes that prevented it from doing this, and subdued it, and then gradually frightened it so that it began to back away, dragging its body backwards with slow crouching steps until the string tautened on its hind leg. It tried to struggle back further against the string, jerking its leg to free it. The man leaned forward towards the rat, following it with his face, watching it all the time with his eyes, and suddenly the rat panicked and leaped sideways in the air. The string pulled it up with a jerk that must almost have dislocated its leg.

It crouched again, in the middle of the bonnet, as far away as the string would allow, and it was properly frightened now, whiskers quivering, the long grey body tense with fear.

At this point, the ratman again began to move his face closer. Very slowly he did it, so slowly there wasn't really any movement to be seen at all except that the face just happened to be a fraction closer each time you looked. He never took his eyes from the rat. The tension was considerable and I wanted suddenly to cry out and tell him to stop. I wanted him to stop because it was making me feel sick inside, but I couldn't bring myself to say the word. Something extremely unpleasant was about to happen – I was sure of that. Something sinister and cruel and ratlike, and perhaps it really would make me sick. But I had to see it now.

The ratman's face was about eighteen inches from the rat. Twelve inches. Then ten, or perhaps it was eight, and then there was not more than the length of a man's hand separating their faces. The rat was pressing its body flat against the car bonnet, tense and terrified. The ratman was also tense, but with a dangerous active tensity that was like a tight-wound spring. The shadow of a smile flickered around the skin of his mouth.

Then suddenly he struck.

He struck as a snake strikes, darting his head forward with one swift knifelike stroke that originated in the muscles of the lower body, and I had a momentary glimpse of his mouth opening very wide and two yellow teeth and the whole face contorted by the effort of mouth-opening.

More than that I did not care to see. I closed my eyes, and when I opened them again the rat was dead and the ratman was slipping the money into his pocket and spitting to clear his mouth.

'That's what they makes lickerish out of,' he said. 'Rat's blood is what the big factories and the chocolate-people use to make lickerish.'

Again the relish, the wet-lipped, lip-smacking relish as he spoke the words, the throaty richness of his voice and the thick syrupy way he pronounced the word *lickerish*.

'No,' he said, 'there's nothin' wrong with a drop of rat's blood.'

'Don't talk so absolutely disgusting,' Claud told him.

'Ah! But that's it, you see. You eaten it many a time. Penny sticks and lickerish bootlaces is all made from rat's blood.'

'We don't want to hear about it, thank you.'

'Boiled up, it is, in great cauldrons, bubblin' and steamin' and men stirrin' it with long poles. That's one of the big secrets of the chocolate-makin' factories, and no one knows about it – no one except the ratters supplyin' the stuff.'

Suddenly he noticed that his audience was no longer with him, that our faces were hostile and sick-looking and crimson with anger and disgust. He stopped abruptly, and without another word he turned and sloped off down the driveway out on to the road, moving with the slow, that almost delicate ambling walk that was like a rat prowling, making no noise with his footsteps even on the gravel of the driveway.

CLAUD'S DOG

Rummins

The sun was up over the hills now and the mist had cleared and it was wonderful to be striding along the road with the dog in the early morning, especially when it was autumn, with the leaves changing to gold and yellow and sometimes one of them breaking away and falling slowly, turning slowly over in the air, dropping noiselessly right in front of him on to the grass beside the road. There was a small wind up above, and he could hear the beeches rustling and murmuring like a crowd of people.

This was always the best time of the day for Claud Cubbage. He gazed approvingly at the rippling velvety hindquarters of the greyhound trotting in front of him.

'Jackie,' he called softly. 'Hey, Jackson. How you feeling, boy?'

The dog half turned at the sound of its name and gave a quick acknowledging wag of the tail.

There would never be another dog like this Jackie, he told himself. How beautiful the slim streamlining, the small pointed head, the yellow eyes, the black mobile nose. Beautiful the long neck, the way the deep brisket curved back and up out of sight into no stomach at all. See how he walked upon his toes, noiselessly, hardly touching the surface of the road at all.

'Jackson,' he said. 'Good old Jackson.'

In the distance, Claud could see Rummins' farmhouse, small, narrow, and ancient, standing back behind the hedge on the right-hand side.

I'll turn round there, he decided. That'll be enough for today.

Rummins, carrying a pail of milk across the yard, saw him coming down the road. He set the pail down slowly and came forward to the gate, leaning both arms on the topmost bar, waiting.

'Morning, Mr Rummins,' Claud said. It was necessary to be polite to Rummins because of eggs.

Rummins nodded and leaned over the gate, looking critically at the dog.

'Looks well,' he said.

'He is well.'

'When's he running?'

'I don't know, Mr Rummins.'

'Come on. When's he running?'

'He's only ten months yet, Mr Rummins. He's not even schooled properly, honest.'

The small beady eyes of Rummins peered suspiciously over the top of the gate. 'I wouldn't mind betting a couple of quid you're having it off with him somewhere secret soon.'

Claud moved his feet uncomfortably on the black road surface. He disliked very much this man with the wide frog mouth, the broken teeth, the shifty eyes; and most of all he disliked having to be polite to him becaue of eggs.

'That hayrick of yours opposite,' he said, searching desperately for another subject. 'It's full of rats.'

'All hayricks got rats.'

'Not like this one. Matter of fact we've been having a touch of trouble with the authorities about that.'

Rummins glanced up sharply. He didn't like trouble with the authorities. Any man who sells eggs blackmarket and kills pigs without a permit is wise to avoid contact with that sort of people.

'What kind of trouble?'

'They sent the ratcatcher along.'

'You mean just for a few rats?'

'A few! Blimey, it's *swarming*!'

'Never.'

'Honest it is, Mr Rummins. There's hundreds of 'em.'

'Didn't the ratcatcher catch 'em?'

'No.'

'Why?'

'I reckon they're too artful.'

Rummins began thoughtfully to explore the inner rim of one nostril with the end of his thumb, holding the noseflap between thumb and finger as he did so.

'I wouldn't give thank you for no ratcatchers,' he said. 'Ratcatchers is government men working for the soddin' government and I wouldn't give thank you for 'em.'

'Nor me, Mr Rummins. All ratcatchers is slimy cunning creatures.'

'Well,' Rummins said, sliding fingers under his cap to scratch the head, 'I was coming over soon anyway to fetch in that rick. Reckon I might just as well do it today as any other time. I don't want no government men nosing around my stuff thank you very much.'

'Exactly, Mr Rummins.'

'We'll be over later – Bert and me.' With that he turned and ambled off across the yard.

Around three in the afternoon, Rummins and Bert were seen riding slowly up the road in a cart drawn by a ponderous and magnificent black carthorse. Opposite the filling-station the cart turned off into the field and stopped near the hayrick.

'This ought to be worth seeing,' I said. 'Get the gun.'

Claud fetched the rifle and slipped a cartridge into the breech.

I strolled across the road and leaned against the open gate. Rummins was on the top of the rick now and cutting away at the cord that bound the thatching. Bert remained in the cart, fingering the four-foot-long knife.

Bert had something wrong with one eye. It was pale grey all over, like a boiled fish-eye, and although it was motionless in its socket it appeared always to be looking at you and following you round the way the eyes of the people in some of those portraits do, in the museums. Wherever you stood and wherever Bert was looking, there was this faulty eye fixing you sideways with a cold stare, boiled and misty pale with a little black dot in the centre, like a fish-eye on a plate.

In his build he was the opposite of his father who was short and squat like a frog. Bert was a tall, reedy, boneless boy, loose at the joints, even the head loose upon the shoulders, falling sideways as though perhaps it was too heavy for the neck.

'You only made this rick last June,' I said to him. 'Why take it away so soon?'

'Dad wants it.'

'Funny time to cut a new rick, November.'

'Dad wants it,' Bert repeated, and both his eyes, the sound one and the other stared down at me with a look of absolute vacuity.

'Going to all that trouble stacking it and thatching it and then pulling it down five months later.'

'Dad wants it.' Bert's nose was running and he kept wiping it with the back of his hand and wiping the back of the hand on his trousers.

'Come on, Bert,' Rummins called, and the boy climbed up on to the rick and stood in the place where the thatch had been removed. He took the knife and began to cut down into the tight-packed hay with an easy-swinging, sawing movement, holding the handle with both hands and rocking his body like a man sawing wood with a big saw. I could hear the crisp cutting noise of the blade against the dry hay and the noise becoming softer as the knife sank deeper into the rick.

'Claud's going to take a pot at the rats as they come out.'

The man and the boy stopped abruptly and looked across the road at Claud who was leaning against the red pump with rifle in hand.

'Tell him to put that bloody rifle away,' Rummins said.

'He's a good shot. He won't hit you.'

'No one's potting no rats alongside of me, don't matter how good they are.'

'You'll insult him.'

'Tell him to put it away,' Rummins said, slow and hostile, 'I don't mind dogs nor sticks but I'll be buggered if I'll have rifles.'

The two on the hayrick watched while Claud did as he was told, then they resumed their work in silence. Soon Bert came down into the cart, and reaching out with both hands he pulled a slice of solid hay away from the rick so that it dropped neatly into the cart beside him.

A rat, grey-black, with a long tail, came out of the base of the rick and ran into the hedge.

'A rat,' I said.

'Kill it,' Rummins said. 'Why don't you get a stick and kill it?'

The alarm had been given now and the rats were coming out quicker, one or two of them every minute, fat and long-bodied, crouching close to the ground as they ran through the grass into the hedge. Whenever the horse saw one of them it twitched its ears and followed it with uneasy rolling eyes.

Bert had climbed back on top of the rick and was cutting out another bale. Watching him, I saw him suddenly stop, hesitate for perhaps a second, then again begin to cut, but very cautiously this time, and now I could hear a different sound, a muffled rasping noise as the blade of the knife grated against something hard.

Bert pulled out the knife and examined the blade, testing it with his thumb. He put it back, letting it down gingerly into the cut, feeling gently downward until it came again upon the upon the hard object; and once more, when he made another cautious little sawing movement, there came that grating sound.

Rummins turned his head and looked over his shoulder at the boy. He was in the act of lifting an armful of loosened thatch, bending forward with both hands grasping the straw, but he stopped dead in the middle of what he was doing and looked at Bert. Bert remained still, hands holding the handle of the knife, a look of bewilderment on his face. Behind, the sky was a pale clear blue and the two figures up there on the hayrick stood out sharp and black like an etching against the paleness.

Then Rummins' voice, louder than usual, edged with an unmistakable apprehension that the loudness did nothing to conceal: 'Some of them haymakers is too bloody careless what they put on a rick these days.'

He paused, and again the silence, the men motionless, and across the road Claud leaning motionless against the red pump. It was so quiet suddenly we could hear a woman's voice far down the valley on the next farm calling the men to food.

Then Rummins again, shouting where there was no need to shout: 'Go on, then! Go on an' cut through it, Bert! A little stick of wood won't hurt the soddin' knife!'

For some reason, as though perhaps scenting trouble, Claud came strolling across the road and joined me leaning on the gate. He didn't say anything, but both of us seemed to know that there was something disturbing about these two men, about the stillness that surrounded them and especially about Rummins himself. Rummins was frightened. Bert was frightened too. And now as I watched them, I became conscious of a small vague image moving just below the surface of my memory. I tried desperately to reach back and grasp it. Once I almost touched it, but it slipped away and when I went after it I found myself travelling back and back through many weeks, back into the yellow days of summer – the warm wind blowing down the valley from the south, the big beech trees heavy with their foliage, the fields turning to gold, the harvesting, the haymaking, the rick – the building of the rick.

Instantly I felt a fine electricity of fear running over the skin of my stomach.

Yes – the building of the rick. When was it we had built it? June? That was it, of course – a hot muggy day in June with the clouds low overhead and the air thick with the smell of thunder.

And Rummins had said, 'Let's for God's sake get it in quick before the rain comes.'

And Ole Jimmy had said, 'There ain't going to be no rain. And there ain't no hurry either. You know very well when thunder's in the south it don't cross over into the valley.'

Rummins, standing up in the cart handing out the pitch-forks, had not answered him. He was in a furious brooding temper because of his anxiety about getting in the hay before it rained.

'There ain't gin' to be no rain before evening.' Ole Jimmy had repeated, looking at Rummins; and Rummins had stared back at him, the eyes glimmering with a slow anger.

All through the morning we had worked without a pause, loading the hay into the cart, trundling it across the field, pitching it out on to the slowly growing rick that stood over by the gate opposite the filling-station. We could hear the thunder in the south as it came towards us and moved away again. Then it seemed to return and remain stationary somewhere beyond the hills, rumbling intermittently. When we looked up we could see the clouds overhead moving and changing shape in the turbulence of the upper air, but on the ground it was hot and muggy and there was no breath of wind. We worked slowly, listlessly in the heat, shirts wet with sweat, faces shining.

Claud and I had worked beside Rummins on the rick itself, helping to shape it, and I could remember how very hot it had been and the flies around my face and the sweat pouring out everywhere; and especially I could remember the grim scowling presence of Rummins beside me, working with a desperate urgency and watching the sky and shouting at the men to hurry.

At noon, in spite of Rummins, we had knocked off for lunch.

Claud and I had sat down under the hedge with Ole Jimmy and another man called Wilson who was a soldier home on leave, and it was too hot to do much talking. Wilson had some bread and cheese and a canteen of cold tea. Ole Jimmy had a satchel that was an old gas-mask container, and in this, closely packed, standing upright with their necks protruding, were six pint bottles of beer.

'Come on,' he said, offering a bottle to each of us.

'I'd like to buy one from you,' Claud said, knowing very well the old man had little money.

'Take it.'

'I must pay you.'

'Don't be so daft. Drink it.'

He was a very good old man, good and clean, with a clean pink face that he shaved each day. He had used to be a carpenter, but they retired him at the age of seventy and that was some years before. Then the Village Council, seeing him still active, had given him the job of looking after the newly built children's playground, of maintaining the swings and see-saws in good repair and also of acting as a kind of gentle watchdog, seeing that none of the kids hurt themselves or did anything foolish.

That was a fine job for an old man to have and everybody seemed pleased with the way things were going – until a certain Saturday night. That night Ole Jimmy had got drunk and gone reeling and singing down the middle of the High Street with such a howling noise that people got out of their beds to see what was going on below. The next morning they had sacked him saying he was a waster and a drunkard not fit to associate with young children on the playground.

But then an astonishing thing happened. The first day that he stayed away – a Monday it was – not one single child came near the playground.

Nor the next day, nor the one after that.

All week the swings and the see-saws and the high slide with steps going up to it stood deserted. Not a child went near them. Instead they followed Ole Jimmy out into a field behind the Rectory and played their games there with him watching; and the result of all this was that after a while the Council had had no alternative but to give the old man back his job.

He still had it now and he still got drunk and no one said anything about it any more. He left it only for a few days each year, at haymaking time. All his life Old Jimmy had loved to go haymaking and he wasn't going to give it up yet.

'You want one?' he asked now, holding a bottle out to Wilson, the soldier.

'No thanks. I got tea.'

'They say tea's good on a hot day.'

'It is. Beer makes me sleepy.'

'If you like,' I said to Ole Jimmy, 'we could walk across to the filling-station and I'll do you a couple of nice sandwiches? Would you like that?'

'Beer's plenty. There's more food in one bottle of beer, me lad, than twenty sandwiches.'

He smiled at me, showing two rows of pale-pink, toothless gums, but it was a pleasant smile and there was nothing repulsive about the way the gums showed.

We sat for a while in silence. The soldier finished his bread and cheese and lay back on the ground, tilting his hat forward over his face. Ole Jimmy had drunk three bottles of beer, and now he offered the last to Claud and me.

'No thanks.'

'No thanks. One's plenty for me.'

The old man shrugged, unscrewed the stopper, tilted his head back and drank, pouring the beer into his mouth with the lips held open so the liquid ran smoothly without gurgling down his throat. He wore a hat that was of no colour at all and of no shape, and it did not fall off when he tilted back his head.

'Ain't Rummins goin' to give that old horse a drink?' he asked, lowering the bottle, looking across the field at the great carthorse that stood steaming between the shafts of the cart.

'Not Rummins.'

'Horses is thirsty, just the same as us.' Ole Jimmy paused, still looking at the horse. 'You got a bucket of water in that place of yours there?'

'Of course.'

'No reason why we shouldn't give the old horse a drink then, is there?'

'That's a very good idea. We'll give him a drink.'

Claud and I both stood up and began walking towards the gate, and I remember turning and calling to the old man: 'You quite sure you wouldn't like me to bring you a nice sandwich? Won't take a second to make.'

He shook his head and waved the bottle at us and said something about taking himself a little nap. We went on through the gate over the road to the filling station.

I suppose we stayed away for about an hour attending to customers and getting ourselves something to eat, and when at length we returned, Claud carrying the bucket of water, I noticed that the rick was at least six foot high.

'Some water for the old horse,' Claud said, looking hard at Rummins who was up in the cart pitching hay on to the rick.

The horse put its head in the bucket, sucking and blowing gratefully at the water.

'Where's Ole Jimmy?' I asked. We wanted the old man to see the water because it had been his idea.

When I asked the question there was a moment, a brief moment, when Rummins hesitated, pitchfork in mid-air, looking around him.

'I brought him a sandwich,' I added.

'Bloody old fool drunk too much beer and gone off home to sleep,' Rummins said.

I strolled along the hedge back to the place where we had been sitting with Ole Jimmy. The five empty bottles were lying there in the grass. So was the satchel. I picked up the satchel and carried it back to Rummins.

'I don't think Ole Jimmy's gone home, Mr Rummins,' I said, holding up the satchel by the long shoulder-band. Rummins glanced at it but made no reply. He was in a frenzy of haste now because the thunder was closer, the clouds blacker, the heat more oppressive than ever.

Carrying the satchel, I started back to the filling station where I remained for the rest of the afternoon, serving customers. Towards evening, when the rain came, I glanced across the road and noticed that they had got the hay in and were laying a tarpaulin over the rick.

In a few days the thatcher arrived and took the tarpaulin off and made a roof of straw instead. He was a good thatcher and he made a fine roof with long straw, thick and well-packed. The slope was nicely angled, the edges cleanly clipped, and it was a pleasure to look at it from the road or from the door of the filling station.

All this came flooding back to me now as clearly as if it were yesterday – the building of the rick on that hot thundery day in June, the yellow field, the sweet woody smell of the hay; and Wilson the soldier, with tennis shoes on his feet, Bert with the boiled eye, Ole Jimmy with the clean old face, the pink naked gums; and Rummins, the broad dwarf, standing up in the cart scowling at the sky because he was anxious about the rain.

At this very moment, there he was again, this Rummins, crouching on top of the rick with a sheaf of thatch in his arms looking round at the son, the tall Bert, motionless also, both of them black like silhouettes against the sky, and once again I felt the fine electricity of fear as it came and went in little waves over the skin of my stomach.

'Go on and cut through it, Bert,' Rummins said, speaking loudly.

Bert put pressure on the big knife and there was a high grating noise as the edge of the blade sawed across something hard. It was clear from Bert's face that he did not like what he was doing.

It took several minutes before the knife was through – then again at last the softer sound of the blade slicing the tight-packed hay and Bert's face turned sideways to the father, grinning with relief, nodding inanely.

'Go on and cut it out,' Rummins said, and still he did not move.

Bert made a second vertical cut the same depth as the first; then he got down and pulled the bale of hay so it came away cleanly from the rest of the rick like a chunk of cake, dropping into the cart at his feet.

Instantly the boy seemed to freeze, staring stupidly at the newly exposed face of the rick, unable to believe or perhaps refusing to believe what this thing was that he had cut in two.

Rummins, who knew very well what it was, had turned away and was climbing quickly down the other side of the rick. He moved so fast he was through the gate and half-way across the road before Bert started to scream.

CLAUD'S DOG

Mr Hoddy

They got out of the car and went in the front door of Mr Hoddy's house.

'I've an idea Dad's going to question you rather sharp tonight,' Clarice whispered.

'About what, Clarice?'

'The usual stuff. Jobs and things like that. And whether you can support me in a fitting way.'

'Jackie's going to do that,' Claud said. 'When Jackie wins there won't be any need for any jobs ...'

'Don't you ever mention Jackie to my dad, Claud Cubbage, or that'll be the end of it. If there's one thing in the world he can't abide it's greyhounds. Don't you ever forget that.'

'Oh Christ,' Claud said.

'Tell him something else — anything – anything to make him happy, see?' And with that she led Claud into the parlour.

Mr Hoddy was a widower, a man with a prim sour mouth and an expression of eternal disapproval all over his face. He had the small, close-together teeth of his daughter Clarice, the same suspicious, inward look about the eyes, but none of her freshness and vitality, none of her warmth. He was a small sour apple of a man, grey-skinned and shrivelled, with a dozen or so surviving strands of black hair pasted across the dome of his bald head. But a very superior man was Mr Hoddy, a grocer's assistant, one who wore a spotless white gown at his work, who handled large quantities of such precious commodities as butter and sugar, who was deferred to, even smiled at by every housewife in the village.

Claud Cubbage was never quite at his ease in this house and that was precisely as Mr Hoddy intended it. They were sitting round the fire in the parlour with cups of tea in their hands, Mr Hoddy in the best chair to the right of the fireplace, Claud and Clarice on the sofa, decorously separated by a wide space. The younger daughter, Ada, was on a hard upright chair to the left, and they made a little circle round the fire, a stiff, tense little circle, primly tea-sipping.

'Yes, Mr Hoddy,' Claud was saying, 'you can be quite sure both

Gordon and me's got quite a number of nice little ideas up our sleeves this very moment. It's only a question of taking our time and making sure which is going to be the most profitable.'

'What sort of ideas?' Mr Hoddy asked, fixing Claud with his small, disapproving eyes.

'Ah, there you are now. That's it, you see.' Claud shifted uncomfortably on the sofa. His blue lounge suit was tight around his chest, and it was especially tight between his legs, up in the crutch. The tightness in his crutch was actually painful to him and he wanted terribly to hitch it downward.

'This man you call Gordon, I thought he had a profitable business out there as it is,' Mr Hoddy said. 'Why does he want to change?'

'Absolutely right, Mr Hoddy. It's a first-rate business. But it's a good thing to keep expanding, see. New ideas is what we're after. Something I can come in on as well and take a share of the profits.'

'Such as what?'

Mr Hoddy was eating a slice of currant cake, nibbling it round the edges, and his small mouth was like the mouth of a caterpillar biting a tiny curved slice out of the edge of a leaf.

'Such as what?' he asked again.

'There's long conferences, Mr Hoddy, takes place every day between Gordon and me about these different matters of business.'

'Such as what?' he repeated, relentless.

Clarice glanced sideways at Claud, encouraging. Claud turned his large slow eyes upon Mr Hoddy, and he was silent. He wished Mr Hoddy wouldn't push him around like this, always shooting questions at him and glaring at him and acting just exactly like he was the bloody adjutant or something.

'Such as what?' Mr Hoddy said, and this time Claud knew that he was not going to let go. Also, his instinct warned him that the old man was trying to create a crisis.

'Well now,' he said, breathing deep. 'I don't really want to go into details until we got it properly worked out. All we're doing so far is turning our ideas over in our minds, see.'

'All I'm asking,' Mr Hoddy said irritably, 'is what *sort* of business are you contemplating? I presume that it's respectable?'

'Now *please*, Mr Hoddy. You don't for one moment think we'd even so much as *consider* anything that wasn't absolutely and entirely respectable, do you?'

Mr Hoddy grunted, stirring his tea slowly, watching Claud. Clarice sat mute and fearful on the sofa, gazing into the fire.

'I've never been in favour of starting a business,' Mr Hoddy pronounced, defending his own failure in that line. 'A good respectable job is all a man should wish for. A respectable job in respectable surroundings. Too much hokey-pokey in business for my liking.'

'The thing is this,' Claud said, desperate now. 'All I want is to provide my wife with everything she can possibly desire. A house to live in and furniture and a flower garden and a washing-machine and all the best things in the world. That's what I want to do, and you can't do that on an ordinary wage, now can you? It's impossible to get enough money to do that unless you go into business, Mr Hoddy. You'll surely agree with me there?'

Mr Hoddy, who had worked for an ordinary wage all his life, didn't much like this point of view.

'And don't you think *I* provide everything my family wants, might I ask?'

'Oh, yes, and more!' Claud cried fervently. 'But *you've* got a very superior job, Mr Hoddy, and that makes all the difference.'

'But what *sort* of business are you thinking of?' the man persisted.

Claud sipped his tea to give himself a little more time and he couldn't help wondering how the miserable old bastard's face would look if he simply up and told him the truth right there and then, if he'd said what we've got, Mr Hoddy, if you really wants to know, is a couple of greyhounds and one's a perfect ringer for the other and we're going to bring off the biggest goddam gamble in the history of flapping, see. He'd like to watch the old bastard's face if he said that, he really would.

They were all waiting for him to proceed now, sitting there with cups of tea in their hands staring at him and waiting for him to say something good. 'Well,' he said, speaking very slowly because he was thinking deep. 'I've been pondering something a long time now, something as'll make more money even than Gordon's secondhand cars or anything else come to that, and practically no expense involved.' That's better, he told himself. Keep going along like that.

'And what might that be?'

'Something so queer, Mr Hoddy, there isn't one in a million would even believe it.'

'Well, what is it?' Mr Hoddy placed his cup carefully on the little table beside him and leaned forward to listen. And Claud, watching him, knew more than ever that this man and all those like him were his enemies. It was the Mr Hoddys were the trouble. They were all the same. He knew them all, with their clean ugly hands, their grey skin, their acrid mouths, their tendency to develop little round bulging bellies just below the waistcoat; and always the unctuous curl of the nose, the weak chin, the suspicious eyes that were dark and moved too quick. The Mr Hoddys. Oh, Christ.

'Well, what is it?'

'It's an absolute gold-mine, Mr Hoddy, honestly it is.'

'I'll believe that when I hear it.'

'It's a thing so simple and amazing most people wouldn't even bother to do it.' He had it now – something he *had* actually been thinking seriously about for a long time, something he'd always wanted to do. He leaned across and put his teacup carefully on the table beside Mr Hoddy's, then, not knowing what to do with his hands, placed them on his knees, palms downward.

'Well, come on man, what is it?'

'It's maggots,' Claud answered softly.

Mr Hoddy jerked back as though someone had squirted water in his face. 'Maggots!' he said, aghast. '*Maggots?* What on earth do you mean, maggots?' Claud had forgotten that this word was almost unmentionable in any self-respecting grocer's shop. Ada began to giggle, but Clarice glanced at her so malignantly the giggle died on her mouth.

'That's where the money is, starting a maggot factory.'

'Are you trying to be funny?'

'Honestly, Mr Hoddy, it may sound a bit queer, and that's simply because you never heard it before, but it's a little gold-mine.'

'A *maggot-factory*! Really now, Cubbage! Please be sensible!'

Clarice wished her father wouldn't call him Cubbage.

'You never heard speak of a maggot-factory, Mr Hoddy?'

'I certainly have not!'

'There's maggot-factories going now, real big companies with managers and directors and all, and you know what, Mr Hoddy? They're making millions!'

'Nonsense, man.'

'And you know why they're making millions?' Claud paused, but he did not notice now that his listener's face was slowly turning yellow. 'It's because of the enormous demand for maggots, Mr Hoddy.'

At that moment Mr Hoddy was listening also to other voices, the voices of his customers across the counter – Mrs Rabbits, for instance, as he sliced off her ration of butter, Mrs Rabbits with her brown moustache and always talking so loud and saying well, well, well; he could hear her now saying 'Well, well, well Mr Hoddy, so your Clarice got married last week, did she. Very nice too, I must say, and what was it you said her husband does, Mr Hoddy?'

He owns a maggot-factory, Mrs Rabbits.

No, thank you, he told himself, watching Claud with his small, hostile eyes. No thank you very much indeed. I don't want that.

'I can't say,' he announced primly, 'that I myself have ever had occasion to purchase a maggot.'

'Now you come to mention it, Mr Hoddy, nor have I. Nor has many other people we know. But let me ask you something else. How many times you had occasion to purchase ... a crown wheel and pinion, for instance?'

This was a shrewd question and Claud permitted himself a slow mawkish smile.

'What's that got to do with maggots?'

'Exactly this – that certain people buy certain things, see. You never bought a crown wheel and pinion in your life, but that don't say there isn't men getting rich this very moment making them – because there is. It's the same with maggots!'

'Would you mind telling me who these unpleasant people are who buy maggots?'

'Maggots are bought by fishermen, Mr Hoddy. Amateur fishermen. There's thousands and thousands of fishermen all over the country going out every week-end fishing the rivers and all of them wanting maggots. Willing to pay good money for them, too. You go along the river there anywhere you like above Marlow on a Sunday and you'll see them *lining* the banks. Sitting there one beside the other simply *lining* the banks of both sides.'

'Those men don't buy maggots. They go down the bottom of the garden and dig worms.'

'Now that's just where you're wrong, Mr Hoddy, if you'll allow me to say so. That's just where you're absolutely wrong. They want maggots, not worms.'

'In that case they get their own maggots.'

'They don't *want* to get their own maggots. Just imagine Mr Hoddy, it's Saturday afternoon and you're going out fishing and a nice clean tin of maggots arrives by post and all you've got to do is slip it in the fishing bag and away you go. You don't think fellers is going out digging for worms and hunting for maggots when they can have them delivered right to their very doorsteps like that just for a bob or two, do you?'

'And might I ask how you propose to run this maggot-factory of yours?' When he spoke the word maggot, it seemed as if he were spitting out a sour little pip from his mouth.

'Easiest thing in the world to run a maggot-factory.' Claud was gaining confidence now and warming to his subject. 'All you need is a couple of old oil drums and a few lumps of rotten meat or a sheep's head, and you put them in the oil drums and that's all you do. The flies do the rest.'

Had he been watching Mr Hoddy's face he would probably have stopped there.

'Of course, it's not quite as easy as it sounds. What you've got to do next is feed up your maggots with special diet. Bran and milk. And then when they get big and fat you put them in pint tins and post them off to your customers. Five shillings a pint they fetch. *Five shillings a pint!*' he cried, slapping the knee. 'You just imagine that, Mr Hoddy! And they say one bluebottle'll lay twenty pints easy!'

He paused again, but merely to marshal his thoughts, for there was no stopping him now.

'And there's another thing, Mr Hoddy. A good maggot-factory don't just breed ordinary maggots, you know. Every fisherman's got his own tastes. Maggots are commonest, but also there's lug worms. Some fishermen won't have nothing but lug worms. And of course there's coloured maggots. Ordinary maggots are white, but you get them all sorts of different colours by feeding them special foods, see. Red ones and green ones and black ones and you can even get blue ones if you know what to feed them. The most difficult thing of all in a maggot-factory is a blue maggot, Mr Hoddy.'

Claud stopped to catch his breath. He was having a vision now – the same vision that accompanied all his dreams of wealth – of an immense factory building with tall chimneys and hundreds of happy workers streaming in through the wide wrought-iron gates and Claud himself sitting in his luxurious office directing operations with a calm and splendid assurance.

'There's people with brains studying these things this very minute,' he went on. 'So you got to jump in quick unless you want to get left out in the cold. That's the secret of big business, jumping in quick before all the others, Mr Hoddy.'

Clarice, Ada, and the father sat absolutely still looking straight ahead. None of them moved or spoke. Only Claud rushed on.

'Just so long as you make sure your maggots is alive when you post 'em. They've got to be wiggling, see. Maggots is no good unless they're wiggling. And when we really get going, when we've built up a little capital, then we'll put up some glasshouses.'

Another pause, and Claud stroked his chin. 'Now I expect you're all wondering why a person should want glasshouses in a maggot-factory. Well – I'll tell you. It's for the flies in the winter, see. Most important to take care of your flies in the winter.'

'I think that's enough, thank you, Cubbage,' Mr Hoddy said suddenly.

Claud looked up and for the first time he saw the expression on the man's face. It stopped him cold.

'I don't want to hear any more about it,' Mr Hoddy said.

'All I'm trying to do, Mr Hoddy,' Claud cried, 'is give your little girl everything she can possibly desire. That's all I'm thinking of night and day, Mr Hoddy.'

'Then all I hope is you'll be able to do it without the help of maggots.'

'Dad!' Clarice cried, alarmed. 'I simply won't have you talking to Claud like that.'

'I'll talk to him how I wish, thank you Miss.'

'I think it's time I was getting along,' Claud said. 'Good night.'

CLAUD'S DOG

Mr Feasey

We were both up early when the big day came.

I wandered into the kitchen for a shave, but Claud got dressed right away and went outside to arrange about the straw. The kitchen was a front room and through the window I could see the sun just coming up behind the line of trees on top of the ridge the other side of the valley.

Each time Claud came past the window with an armload of straw I noticed over the rim of the mirror the intent, breathless expression on his face, the great round bullet-head thrusting forward and the forehead wrinkled into deep corrugations right up to the hairline. I'd only seen this look on him once before and that was the evening he'd asked Clarice to marry him. Today he was so excited he even walked funny, treading softly as though the concrete around the filling-station were a shade too hot for the soles of his feet; and he kept packing more and more straw into the back of the van to make it comfortable for Jackie.

Then he came into the kitchen to get breakfast, and I watched him put the pot of soup on the stove and begin stirring it. He had a long metal spoon and he kept on stirring and stirring all the time it was coming to the boil, and about every half minute he leaned forward and stuck his nose into that sickly-sweet steam of cooking horseflesh. Then he started putting extras into it – three peeled onions, a few young carrots, a cupful of stinging-nettle tops, a teaspoon of Valentines Meat Juice, twelve drops of cod-liver oil – and everything he touched was handled very gently with the ends of his big fat fingers as though it might have been a little fragment of Venetian glass. He took some minced horsemeat from the icebox, measured one handful into Jackie's bowl, three into the other, and when the soup was ready he shared it out between the two, pouring it over the meat.

It was the same ceremony I'd seen performed each morning for the past five months, but never with such intense and breathless concentration as this. There was no talk, not even a glance my way, and when he turned and went out again to fetch the dogs, even the back of his neck and the shoulders seemed to be whispering, 'Oh,

Jesus, don't let anything go wrong, and especially don't let me *do* anything wrong today.'

I heard him talking softly to the dogs in the pen as he put the leashes on them, and when he brought them around into the kitchen, they came in prancing and pulling to get at the breakfast, treading up and down with their front feet and waving their enormous tails from side to side, like whips.

'All right,' Claud said, speaking at last. 'Which is it?'

Most mornings he'd offer to bet me a pack of cigarettes, but there were bigger things at stake today and I knew all he wanted for the moment was a little extra reassurance.

He watched me as I walked once around the two beautiful, identical, tall, velvety-black dogs, and he moved aside, holding the leashes at arms' length to give me a better view.

'Jackie!' I said, trying the old trick that never worked. 'Hey, Jackie!' Two identical heads with identical expressions flicked around to look at me, four bright, identical, deep-yellow eyes stared into mine. There'd been a time when I fancied the eyes of one were slightly darker yellow than those of the other. There'd also been a time when I thought I could recognize Jackie because of a deeper brisket and a shade more muscle on the hindquarters. But it wasn't so.

'Come on,' Claud said. He was hoping that today of all days I would make a bad guess.

'This one,' I said. 'This is Jackie.'

'Which?'

'This one on the left.'

'There!' he cried, his whole face suddenly beaming. 'You're wrong again!'

'I don't think I'm wrong.'

'You're about as wrong as you could possibly be. And now listen, Gordon, and I'll tell you something. All these last weeks, every morning while you've been trying to pick him out – you know what?'

'What?'

'I've been keeping count. And the result is you haven't been right even *one-half* the time! You'd have done better tossing a coin!'

What he meant was that if I (who saw them every day and side by side) couldn't do it, why the hell should we be frightened of Mr Feasey? Claud knew Mr Feasey was famous for spotting ringers, but he knew also that it could be very difficult to tell the difference between two dogs when there wasn't any.

He put the bowls of food on the floor, giving Jackie the one with the least meat because he was running today. When he stood back to watch them eat, the shadow of deep concern was back again on his face and the large pale eyes were staring at Jackie with the same rapt and melting look of love that up till recently had been reserved only for Clarice.

'You see, Gordon,' he said. 'It's just what I've always told you. For the last hundred years there's been all manner of ringers, some good and some bad, but in the whole history of dog-racing there's never been a ringer like this.'

'I hope you're right,' I said, and my mind began travelling back to that freezing afternoon just before Christmas, four months ago, when Claud had asked to borrow the van and had driven away in the direction of Aylesbury without saying where he was going. I had assumed he was off to see Clarice, but late in the afternoon he had returned bringing with him this dog he said he'd bought off a man for thirty-five shillings.

'Is he fast?' I had said. We were standing out by the pumps and Claud was holding the dog on a leash and looking at him, and a few snowflakes were falling and settling on the dog's back. The motor of the van was still running.

'Fast!' Claud had said. 'He's just about the slowest dog you ever saw in your whole life!'

'Then what you buy him for?'

'Well,' he had said, the big bovine face secret and cunning, 'it occurred to me that maybe he might possibly look a little bit like Jackie. What d'you think?'

'I suppose he does a bit, now you come to mention it.'

He had handed me the leash and I had taken the new dog inside to dry him off while Claud had gone round to the pen to fetch his beloved. And when he returned and we put the two of them together for the first time, I can remember him stepping back and saying, 'Oh, Jesus!' and standing dead still in front of them like he was seeing a phantom. Then he became very quick and quiet. He got down on his knees and began comparing them carefully point by point, and it was almost like the room was getting warmer and warmer the way I could feel his excitement growing every second through this long silent examination in which even the toenails and the dewclaws, eighteen on each dog, were matched alongside one another for colour.

'Look,' he said at last, standing up. 'Walk them up and down the room a few times, will you?' And then he had stayed there for quite five or six minutes leaning against the stove with his eyes half closed and his head on one side, watching them and frowning and chewing his lips. After that, as though he didn't believe what he had seen the first time, he had gone down again on his knees to recheck everything once more; but suddenly, in the middle of it, he had jumped up and looked at me, his face fixed and tense, with a curious whiteness around the nostrils and the eyes. 'All right,' he had said, a little tremor in his voice. 'You know what? We're home. We're rich.'

And then the secret conferences between us in the kitchen, the detailed planning, the selection of the most suitable track, and finally every other Saturday, eight times in all, locking up my filling-station (losing a whole afternoon's custom) and driving the ringer all the way up to Oxford to a scruffy little track out in the fields near Headington where the big money was played but which was actually nothing except a line of old posts and cord to mark the course, an upturned bicycle for pulling the dummy hare, and at the far end, in the distance, six traps and the starter. We had driven this ringer up there eight times over a period of sixteen weeks and entered him with Mr Feasey and stood around on the edge of the crowd in freezing raining cold, waiting for his name to go up on the blackboard in chalk. The Black Panther we called him. And when his time came, Claud would always lead him down to the traps and I would stand at the finish to catch him and keep him clear of the fighters, the gipsy dogs that the gipsies so often slipped in specially to tear another one to pieces at the end of a race.

But you know, there was something rather sad about taking this dog all the way up there so many times and letting him run and watching him and hoping and praying that whatever happened he would always come last. Of course the praying wasn't necessary and we never really had a moment's worry because the old fellow simply couldn't gallop and that's all there was to it. He ran exactly like a crab. The only time he didn't come last was when a big fawn dog by the name of Amber Flash put his boot in a hole and broke a hock and finished on three legs. But even then ours only just beat him. So this way we got him right down to bottom grade with the scrubbers, and the last time we were there all the bookies were laying him twenty or thirty to one and calling his name and begging people to back him.

Now at last, on this sunny April day, it was Jackie's turn to go instead. Claud said we mustn't run the ringer any more or Mr Feasey might begin to get tired of him and throw him out altogether, he was so slow. Claud said this was the exact psychological time to have it off, and that Jackie would win it anything between thirty and fifty lengths.

He had raised Jackie from a pup and the dog was only fifteen months now, but he was a good fast runner. He'd never raced yet; but we knew he was fast from clocking him round the little private schooling track at Uxbridge where Claud had taken him every Sunday since he was seven months old – except once when he was having some inoculations, Claud said he probably wasn't fast enough to win top grade at Mr Feasey's, but where we'd got him now, in bottom grade with the scrubbers, he could fall over and get up again and still win it twenty – well, anyway ten or fifteen lengths, Claud said.

So all I had to do this morning was go to the bank in the village and draw out fifty pounds for myself and fifty for Claud which I would lend him as an advance against wages, and then at twelve o'clock lock up the filling-station and hang the notice on one of the pumps saying GONE FOR THE DAY. Claud would shut the ringer in the pen at the back and put Jackie in the van and off we'd go. I won't say I was as excited as Claud, but there again, I didn't have all sorts of important things depending on it either, like buying a house and being able to get married. Nor was I almost *born* in a kennel with greyhounds like he was, walking about thinking of absolutely nothing else all day – except perhaps Clarice in the evenings. Personally, I had my own career as a filling station owner to keep me busy, not to mention second-hand cars, but if Claud wanted to fool around with dogs that was all right with me, especially a thing like today – if it came off. As a matter of fact, I don't mind admitting that every time I thought about the money we were putting on and the money we might win, my stomach gave a little lurch.

The dogs had finished their breakfast now and Claud took them out for a short walk across the field opposite while I got dressed and fried the eggs. Afterwards, I went to the bank and drew out the money (all in ones), and the rest of the morning seemed to go very quickly serving customers.

At twelve sharp I locked up and hung the notice on the pump. Claud came around from the back leading Jackie and carrying a large suitcase made of reddish-brown cardboard.

'Suitcase?'

'For the money,' Claud answered. 'You said yourself no man can carry two thousand pounds in his pockets.'

It was a lovely yellow spring day with the buds bursting all along the hedges and the sun shining through the new pale green leaves on the big beech tree across the road. Jackie looked wonderful, with two big hard muscles the size of melons bulging on his hindquarters, his coat glistening like black velvet. While Claud was putting the suitcase in the van, the dog did a little prancing jig on his toes to show how fit he was, then he looked up at me and grinned, just like he knew he was off to the races to win two thousand pounds and a heap of glory. This Jackie had the widest most human-smiling grin I ever saw. Not only did he lift his upper lip, but he actually stretched the corners of his mouth so you could see every tooth in his head except perhaps one or two of the molars right at the back; and every time I saw him do it I found myself waiting to hear him start laughing out loud as well.

We got in the van and off we went. I was doing the driving. Claud was beside me and Jackie was standing up on the straw in the rear looking over our shoulders through the windshield. Claud kept turning round and trying to make him lie down so he wouldn't get thrown whenever we went round the sharp corners, but the dog was too

excited to do anything except grin back at him and wave his enormous
tail.

'You got the money, Gordon?' Claud was chain-smoking cigarettes
and quite unable to sit still.

'Yes.'

'Mine as well?'

'I got a hundred and five altogether. Five for the winder like you
said, so he won't stop the hare and make it a no-race.'

'Good,' Claud said, rubbing his hands together hard as though he
were freezing cold. 'Good, good, good.'

We drove through the little narrow High Street of Great Missenden
and caught a glimpse of old Rummins going into The Nag's Head for
his morning pint, then outside the village we turned left and climbed
over the ridge of the Chilterns towards Princes Risborough, and from
there it would only be twenty-odd miles to Oxford.

And now a silence and a kind of tension began to come over us
both. We sat very quiet, not speaking at all, each nursing his own
fears and excitements, containing his anxiety. And Claud kept smoking
his cigarettes and throwing them half finished out the window. Usually,
on these trips, he talked his head off all the way there and back, all
the things he'd done with dogs in his life, the jobs he'd pulled, the
places he'd been, the money he'd won; and all the things other people
had done with dogs, the thievery, the cruelty, the unbelievable trickery
and cunning of owners at the flapping tracks. But today I don't think
he was trusting himself to speak very much. At this point, for that
matter, nor was I. I was sitting there watching the road and trying to
keep my mind off the immediate future by thinking back on all that
stuff Claud had told me about this curious greyhound racing racket.

I swear there wasn't a man alive who knew more about it than
Claud did, and ever since we'd got the ringer and decided to pull this
job, he'd taken it upon himself to give me an education in the business.
By now, in theory at any rate, I suppose I knew nearly as much as
him.

It had started during the very first strategy conference we'd had in
the kitchen. I can remember it was the day after the ringer arrived
and we were sitting there watching for customers through the window,
and Claud was explaining to me all about what we'd have to do, and
I was trying to follow him as best I could until finally there came one
question I had to ask.

'What I don't see,' I had said, 'is why you use the ringer at all.
Wouldn't it be safer if we use Jackie all the time and simply stop him
the first half dozen races so he comes last? Then when we're good and
ready, we can let him go. Same result in the end, wouldn't it be, if
we do it right? And no danger of being caught.'

Well, as I say, that did it. Claud looked up at me quickly and he said, 'Hey! None of that! I'd just like you to know "stopping's" something I never do. What's come over you, Gordon?' He seemed genuinely pained and shocked by what I had said.

'I don't see anything wrong with it.'

'Now, listen to me, Gordon. Stopping a good dog breaks his heart. A good dog knows he's fast, and seeing all the others out there in front and not being able to catch them – it breaks his heart, I tell you. And what's more, you wouldn't be making suggestions like that if you knew some of the tricks them fellers do to stop their dogs at the flapping tracks.'

'Such as what, for example?' I had asked.

'Such as anything in the world almost, so long as it makes the dog go slower. And it takes a lot of stopping, a good greyhound does. Full of guts and so mad keen you can't even let them watch a race they'll tear the leash right out of your hand rearing to go. Many's the time I've seen one with a broken leg insisting on finishing the race.'

He had paused then, looking at me thoughtfully with those large pale eyes, serious as hell and obviously thinking deep. 'Maybe,' he had said, 'if we're going to do this job properly I'd better tell you a thing or two so's you'll know what we're up against.'

'Go ahead and tell me,' I had said. 'I'd like to know.'

For a moment he stared in silence out the window. 'The main thing you got to remember,' he had said darkly, 'is that all these fellers going to the flapping tracks with dogs – they're artful. They're more artful than you could possibly imagine.' Again he paused, marshalling his thoughts.

'Now take for example the different ways of stopping a dog. The first, the commonest, is strapping.'

'Strapping?'

'Yes. Strapping 'em up. That's commonest. Pulling the muzzle-strap tight around their necks so they can't hardly breathe, see. A clever man knows just which hole on the strap to use and just how many lengths it'll take off his dog in a race. Usually a couple of notches is good for five or six lengths. Do it up real tight and he'll come last. I've known plenty of dogs collapse and die from being strapped up tight on a hot day. Strangulated, absolutely strangulated, and a very nasty thing it was too. Then again, some of 'em just tie two of the toes together with black cotton. Dog never runs well like that. Unbalances him.'

'That doesn't sound too bad.'

'Then there's others that put a piece of fresh-chewed gum up under their tails, right up close where the tail joins the body. And there's nothing funny about that,' he had said, indignant. 'The tail of a running dog goes up and down ever so slightly and the gum on the tail keeps sticking to the hairs on the backside, just where it's tenderest.

No dog likes that, you know. Then there's sleeping pills. That's used a lot nowadays. They do it by weight, exactly like a doctor, and they measure the powder according to whether they want to slow him up five or ten or fifteen lengths. Those are just a few of the ordinary ways,' he had said. 'Actually they're nothing. Absolutely nothing, compared with some of the other things that's done to hold a dog back in a race, especially by the gipsies. There's things the gipsies do that are almost too disgusting to mention, such as when they're just putting the dog in the trap, things you wouldn't hardly do to your worst enemies.'

And when he had told me about those – which were, indeed, terrible things because they had to do with physical injury, quickly, painfully inflicted – then he had gone on to tell me what they did when they wanted the dog to win.

'There's just as terrible things done to make 'em go fast as to make 'em go slow,' he had said softly, his face veiled and secret. 'And perhaps the commonest of all is wintergreen. Whenever you see a dog going around with no hair on his back or little bald patches all over him – that's wintergreen. Just before the race they rub it hard into the skin. Sometimes it's Sloan's Liniment, but mostly it's wintergreen. Stings terrible. Stings so bad that all the old dog wants to do is run, run, run as fast as he possibly can to get away from the pain.

'Then there's special drugs they give with the needle. Mind you, that's the modern method and most of the spivs at the track are too ignorant to use it. It's the fellers coming down from London in the big cars with stadium dogs they've borrowed for the day by bribing the trainer – they're the ones who use the needle.'

I could remember him sitting there at the kitchen table with a cigarette dangling from his mouth and dropping his eyelids to keep out the smoke and looking at me through his wrinkled, nearly closed eyes, and saying, 'What you've got to remember, Gordon, is this. There's nothing they won't do to make a dog win if they want him to. On the other hand, no dog can run faster than he's built, no matter what they do to him. So if we can get Jackie down into bottom grade, then we're home. No dog in bottom grade can get near him, not even with wintergreen and needles. Not even with ginger.'

'Ginger?'

'Certainly. That's a common one, ginger is. What they do, they take a piece of raw ginger about the size of a walnut, and about five minutes before the off they slip it into the dog.'

'You mean in his mouth? He eats it?'

'No,' he had said. 'Not in his mouth.'

And so it had gone on. During each of the eight long trips we had subsequently made to the track with the ringer I had heard more and more about this charming sport – more, especially, about the methods of stopping them and making them go (even the names of the drugs and the quantities to use). I heard about 'The rat treatment' (for non-chasers, to make them chase the dummy hare), where a rat is placed in a can which is then tied around the dog's neck. There's a small hole in the lid of the can just large enough for the rat to poke its head out and nip the dog. But the dog can't get at the rat, and so naturally he goes half crazy running around and being bitten in the neck, and the more he shakes the can the more the rat bites him. Finally, someone releases the rat, and the dog, who up to then was a nice docile tail-wagging animal who wouldn't hurt a mouse, pounces on it in a rage and tears it to pieces. Do this a few times, Claud had said – 'mind you, I don't hold with it myself' – and the dog becomes a real killer who will chase anything, even the dummy hare.

We were over the Chilterns now and running down out of the beechwoods into the flat elm- and oak-tree country south of Oxford. Claud sat quietly beside me, nursing his nervousness and smoking cigarettes, and every two or three minutes he would turn round to see if Jackie was all right. The dog was at last lying down, and each time Claud turned round, he whispered something to him softly, and the dog acknowledged his words with a faint movement of the tail that made the straw rustle.

Soon we would be coming into Thame, the broad High Street where they penned the pigs and cows and sheep on market day, and where the Fair came once a year with the swings and roundabouts and bumping cars and gipsy caravans right there in the street in the middle of the town. Claud was born in Thame, and we'd never driven though it yet without him mentioning the fact.

'Well,' he said as the first houses came into sight, 'here's Thame. I was born and bred in Thame, you know, Gordon.'

'You told me.'

'Lots of funny things we used to do around here when we was nippers,' he said, slightly nostalgic.

'I'm sure.'

He paused, and I think more to relieve the tension building up inside him than anything else, he began talking about the years of his youth.

'There was a boy next door,' he said. 'Gilbert Gomm his name was. Little sharp ferrety face and one leg a bit shorter'n the other. Shocking things him and me used to do together. You know one thing we done, Gordon?'

'What?'

'We'd go into the kitchen Saturday nights when mum and dad were at the pub, and we'd disconnect the pipe from the gas-ring and bubble the gas into a milk bottle full of water. Then we'd sit down and drink it out of teacups.'

'Was that so good?'

'Good! It was absolutely disgusting! But we'd put lashings of sugar in and then it didn't taste so bad.'

'Why did you drink it?'

Claud turned and looked at me, incredulous. 'You mean you never drunk "Snakes Water"!'

'Can't say I have.'

'I thought everyone done that when they was kids! It intoxicates you, just like wine only worse, depending on how long you let the gas bubble through. We used to get reeling drunk together there in the kitchen Saturday nights and it was marvellous. Until one night Dad comes home early and catches us. I'll never forget that night as long as I live. There was me holding the milk bottle, and the gas bubbling through it lovely, and Gilbert kneeling on the floor ready to turn off the tap the moment I give the word, and in walks Dad.'

'What did he say?'

'Oh, Christ, Gordon, that was terrible. He didn't say one word, but he stands there by the door and he starts feeling for his belt, undoing the buckle very slow and pulling the belt slow out of his trousers, looking at me all the time. Great big feller he was, with great big hands like coal hammers and a black moustache and them little purple veins running all over his cheeks. Then he comes over quick and grabs me by the coat and lets me have it, hard as he can, using the end with the buckle on it and honest to God, Gordon, I thought he was going to kill me. But in the end he stops and then he puts on the belt again, slow and careful, buckling it up and tucking in the flap and belching with the beer he'd drunk. And then he walks out again back to the pub, still without saying a word. Worst hiding I ever had in my life.'

'How old were you then?'

'Round about eight, I should think,' Claud said.

As we drew closer to Oxford, he became silent again. He kept twisting his neck to see if Jackie was all right, to touch him, to stroke his head, and once he turned around and knelt on the seat to gather more straw around the dog, murmuring something about a draught. We drove around the fringe of Oxford and into a network of narrow open country roads, and after a while we turned into a small bumpy lane and along this we began to overtake a thin stream of men and women all walking and cycling in the same direction. Some of the men were leading greyhounds. There was a large saloon car in front of us and through the rear window we could see a dog sitting on the back seat between two men.

'They come from all over,' Claud said darkly. 'That one there's probably come up special from London. Probably slipped him out from one of the big stadium kennels just for the afternoon. That could be a Derby dog probably, for all we know.'

'Hope he's not running against Jackie.'

'Don't worry,' Claud said. 'All new dogs automatically go in top grade. That's one rule Mr Feasey's very particular about.'

There was an open gate leading into a field, and Mr Feasey's wife came forward to take our admission money before we drove in.

'He'd have her winding the bloody pedals too if she had the strength,' Claud said. 'Old Feasey don't employ more people than he has to.'

I drove across the field and parked at the end of a line of cars along the top hedge. We both got out and Claud went quickly round the back to fetch Jackie. I stood beside the car, waiting. It was a very large field with a steepish slope on it and we were at the top of the slope, looking down. In the distance I could see the six starting traps and the wooden posts marking the track which ran along the bottom of the field and turned sharp at right angles and came on up the hill towards the crowd, to the finish. Thirty yards beyond the finishing line stood the upturned bicycle for driving the hare. Because it is portable, this is the standard machine for hare-driving used at all flapping tracks. It comprises a flimsy wooden platform about eight feet high, supported on four poles knocked into the ground. On top of the platform there is fixed, upside down with wheels in the air, an ordinary old bicycle. The rear wheel is to the front, facing down the track, and from it the tyre has been removed, leaving a concave metal rim. One end of the cord that pulls the hare is attached to this rim, and the winder (or hare driver), by straddling the bicycle at the back and turning the pedals with his hands, revolves the wheel and winds in the cord around the rim. This pulls the dummy hare towards him at any speed he likes up to forty miles an hour. After each race someone takes the dummy hare (with cord attached) all the way down to the starting traps again, thus unwinding the cord on the wheel, ready for a fresh start. From his high platform, the winder can watch the race and regulate the speed of the hare to keep it just ahead of the leading dog. He can also stop the hare any time he wants and make it a 'no race' (if the wrong dog looks like winning) by suddenly turning the pedals backwards and getting the cord tangled up in the hub of the wheel. The other way of doing it is to slow down the hare suddenly, for perhaps one second, and that makes the lead dog automatically check a little so that the others catch up with him. He is an important man, the winder.

I could see Mr Feasey's winder already standing atop his platform, a powerful-looking man in a blue sweater, leaning on the bicycle and looking down at the crowd through the smoke of his cigarette.

There is a curious law in England which permits race meetings of this kind to be held only seven times a year over one piece of ground.

That is why all Mr Feasey's equipment was movable, and after the seventh meeting he would simply transfer to the next field. The law didn't bother him at all.

There was already a good crowd and the bookmakers were erecting their stands in a line over to the right. Claud had Jackie out of the van now and was leading him over to a group of people clustered around a small stocky man dressed in riding-breeches – Mr Feasey himself. Each person in the group had a dog on a leash and Mr Feasey kept writing names in a notebook that he held folded in his left hand. I sauntered over to watch.

'Which you got there?' Mr Feasey said, pencil poised above the notebook.

'Midnight,' a man said who was holding a black dog.

Mr Feasey stepped back a pace and looked most carefully at the dog.

'Midnight. Right. I got him down.'

'Jane,' the next man said.

'Let me look. Jane ... Jane ... yes, all right.'

'Soldier.' This dog was led by a tall man with long teeth who wore a dark-blue, double-breasted lounge suit, shiny with wear, and when he said 'Soldier' he began slowly to scratch the seat of his trousers with the hand that wasn't holding the leash.

Mr Feasey bent down to examine the dog. The other man looked up at the sky.

'Take him away,' Mr Feasey said.

The man looked down quick and stopped scratching.

'Go on, take him away.'

'Listen, Mr Feasey,' the man said, lisping slightly through his long teeth. 'Now don't talk so bloody silly, *please*.'

'Go on and beat it, Larry, and stop wasting my time. You know as well as I do the Soldier's got two white toes on his off fore.'

'Now look, Mr Feasey,' the man said. 'You ain't even seen Soldier for six months at least.'

'Come on now, Larry, and beat it. I haven't got time arguing with you.' Mr Feasey didn't appear the least angry. 'Next,' he said.

I saw Claud step forward leading Jackie. The large bovine face was fixed and wooden, the eyes staring at something about a yard above Mr Feasey's head, and he was holding the leash so tight his knuckles were like a row of little white onions. I knew just how he was feeling. I felt the same way myself at that moment, and it was even worse when Mr Feasey suddenly started laughing.

'Hey!' he cried. 'Here's the Black Panther. Here's the champion.'

'That's right, Mr Feasey,' Claud said.

'Well, I'll tell you,' Mr Feasey said, still grinning. 'You can take him right back home where he come from. I don't want him.'

'But look here, Mr Feasey . . .'

'Six or eight times at least I've run him for you now and that's enough. Look – why don't you shoot him and have done with it?'

'Now, listen, Mr Feasey, *please*. Just once more and I'll never ask you again.'

'Not even once! I got more dogs than I can handle here today. There's no room for crabs like that.'

I thought Claud was going to cry.

'Now honest, Mr Feasey,' he said. 'I been up at six every morning this past two weeks giving him roadwork and massage and buying him beefsteaks, and believe me he's a different dog absolutely than what he was last time he run.'

The words 'different dog' caused Mr Feasey to jump like he'd been pricked with a hatpin. 'What's that!' he cried. 'Different dog!'

I'll say this for Claud, he kept his head. 'See here, Mr Feasey,' he said. 'I'll thank you not to go implying things to me. You know very well I didn't mean that.'

'All right, all right. But just the same, you can take him away. There's no sense running dogs as slow as him. Take him home now, will you please, and don't hold up the whole meeting.'

I was watching Claud. Claud was watching Mr Feasey. Mr Feasey was looking round for the next dog to enter up. Under his brown tweedy jacket he wore a yellow pullover, and this streak of yellow on his breast and his thin gaitered legs and the way he jerked his head from side to side made him seem like some sort of a little perky bird – a goldfinch, perhaps.

Claud took a step forward. His face was beginning to purple slightly with the outrage of it all and I could see his Adam's apple moving up and down as he swallowed.

'I'll tell you what I'll do, Mr Feasey. I'm so absolutely sure this dog's improved I'll bet you a quid he don't finish last. There you are.'

Mr Feasey turned slowly around and looked at Claud. 'You crackers?' he asked.

'I'll bet you a quid, there you are, just to prove what I'm saying.'

It was a dangerous move, certain to cause suspicion, but Claud knew it was the only thing left to do. There was silence while Mr Feasey bent down and examined the dog. I could see the way his eyes were moving slowly over the animal's whole body, part by part. There was something to admire in the man's thoroughness, and in his memory; something to fear also in this self-confident little rogue who held in his head the shape and colour and markings of perhaps several hundred different but very similar dogs. He never needed more than one little clue – a small scar, a splay toe, a trifle in at the hocks, a less pronounced wheelback, a slightly darker brindle – Mr Feasey always remembered.

So I watched him now as he bent down over Jackie. His face was pink and fleshy, the mouth small and tight as though it couldn't stretch enough to make a smile, and the eyes were like two little cameras focused sharply on the dog.

'Well,' he said, straightening up. 'It's the same dog, anyway.'

'I should hope so too!' Claud cried. 'Just what sort of a fellow you think I am, Mr Feasey?'

'I think you're crackers, that's what I think. But it's a nice easy way to make a quid. I suppose you forgot how Amber Flash nearly beat him on three legs last meeting?'

'This one wasn't fit then,' Claud said. 'He hadn't had beefsteak and massage and roadwork like I've been giving him lately. But look, Mr Feasey, you're not to go sticking him in top grade just to win the bet. This is a bottom grade dog, Mr Feasey. You know that.'

Mr Feasey laughed. The small button mouth opened into a tiny circle and he laughed and looked at the crowd who laughed with him. 'Listen,' he said, laying a hairy hand on Claud's shoulder. 'I know my dogs. I don't have to do any fiddling around to win *this* quid. He goes in bottom.'

'Right,' Claud said. 'That's a bet.' He walked away with Jackie and I joined him.

'Jesus, Gordon, that was a near one!'

'Shook me.'

'But we're in now,' Claud said. He had that breathless look on his face again and he was walking about quick and funny, like the ground was burning his feet.

People were still coming through the gate into the field and there were easily three hundred of them now. Not a very nice crowd. Sharp-nosed men and women with dirty faces and bad teeth and quick shifty eyes. The dregs of the big town. Oozing out like sewage from a cracked pipe and trickling along the road through the gate and making a smelly little pond of sewage at the top end of the field. They were all there, all the spivs, and the gipsies and the touts and the dregs and the sewage and the scraping and the scum from the cracked drainpipes of the big town. Some with dogs, some without. Dogs led about on pieces of string, miserable dogs with hanging heads, thin mangy dogs with sores on their quarters (from sleeping on board), sad old dogs with grey muzzles, doped dogs, dogs stuffed with porridge to stop them winning, dogs walking stiff-legged – one especially, a white one. 'Claud, why is that white one walking so stiff-legged?'

'Which one?'

'That one over there.'

'Ah. Yes, I see. Very probably because he's been hung.'

'Hung?'

'Yes, hung. Suspended in a harness for twenty-four hours with his legs dangling.'

'Good God, but why?'

'To make him run slow, of course. Some people don't hold with dope or stuffing or strapping up. So they hang 'em.'

'I see.'

'Either that,' Claud said, 'or they sandpaper them. Rub their pads with rough sandpaper and take the skin off so it hurts when they run.'

'Yes, I see.'

And then the fitter, brighter-looking dogs, the better-fed ones who get horsemeat every day, not pig-swill or rusk and cabbage water, their coats shinier, their tails moving, pulling at their leads, undoped, unstuffed, awaiting perhaps a more unpleasant fate, the muzzle-strap to be tightened an extra four notches. *But make sure he can breathe now, Jock. Don't choke him completely. Don't let's have him collapse in the middle of the race. Just so he wheezes a bit, see. Go on tightening it up an extra notch at a time until you can hear him wheezing. You'll see his mouth open and he'll start breathing heavy. Then it's just right, but not if his eyeballs is bulging. Watch out for that, will you? Okay?*

Okay.

'Let's get away from the crowd, Gordon. It don't do Jackie no good getting excited by all these other dogs.'

We walked up the slope to where the cars were parked, then back and forth in front of the line of cars, keeping the dog on the move. Inside some of the cars I could see men sitting with their dogs, and the men scowled at us through the windows as we went by.

'Watch out now, Gordon. We don't want any trouble.'

'No, all right.'

These were the best dogs of all, the secret ones kept in the cars and taken out quick just to be entered up (under some invented name) and put back again quick and held there till the last minute, then straight down to the traps and back again into the cars after the race so no nosy bastard gets too close a look. The trainer at the big stadium said so. *All right, he said. You can have him, but for Christsake don't let anybody recognize him. There's thousands of people know this dog, so you've got to be careful, see. And it'll cost you fifty pound.*

Very fast dogs these, but it doesn't much matter how fast they are they probably get the needle anyway, just to make sure. One and a half c.c.s. of ether, subcutaneous, done in the car, injected very slow. That'll put ten lengths on any dog. Or sometimes it's caffein in oil, or camphor. That makes them go too. The men in the big cars know all about that. And some of them know about whisky. But that's intravenous. Not so easy when it's intravenous. Might miss the vein. All you got to do is miss the vein and it don't work and where are you then? So it's ether, or it's caffein, or it's camphor. *Don't give her too much of that stuff now, Jock. What does she weigh? Fifty-eight pounds. All right then, you know what the man told us. Wait a minute now. I got it written down on a piece of paper. Here it is. Point 1 of a c.c. per 10 pounds bodyweight equals 5 lengths over 300 yards. Wait a minute now while I work it out. Oh Christ, you better guess it. Just guess it, Jock. It'll be all right you'll find. Shouldn't be any trouble anyway because I picked the others in the race myself. Cost me a tenner to old Feasey. A bloody tenner I gave him, and dear Mr Feasey, I says, that's for your birthday and because I love you.*

Thank you ever so much, Mr Feasey says. Thank you, my good and trusted friend.

And for stopping them, for the men in the big cars, it's chlorbutal. That's beauty, chlorbutal, because you can give it the night before, especially to someone else's dog. Or Pethidine. Pethidine and Hyoscine mixed, whatever that may be.

'Lot of fine old English sporting gentry here,' Claud said.

'Certainly are.'

'Watch your pockets, Gordon. You got that money hidden away?'

We walked around the back of the line of cars – between the cars and the hedge – and I saw Jackie stiffen and begin to pull forward on the leash, advancing with a stiff crouching tread. About thirty yards away there were two men. One was holding a large fawn greyhound, the dog stiff and tense like Jackie. The other was holding a sack in his hands.

'Watch,' Claud whispered, 'they're giving him a kill.'

Out of the sack on to the grass tumbled a small white rabbit, fluffy white, young, tame. It righted itself and sat still, crouching in the hunched up way rabbits crouch, its nose close to the ground. A frightened rabbit. Out of the sack so suddenly on to the grass with such a bump. Into the bright light. The dog was going mad with excitement now, jumping up against the leash, pawing the ground, throwing himself forward, whining. The rabbit saw the dog. It drew in its head and stayed still, paralysed with fear. The man transferred his hold to the dog's collar, and the dog twisted and jumped and tried to get free. The other man pushed the rabbit with his foot but it was too terrified to move. He pushed it again, flicking it forward with his toe like a football, and the rabbit rolled over several times, righted itself and began to hop over the grass away from the dog. The other man released the dog which pounced with one huge pounce upon the rabbit, and then came the squeals, not very loud but shrill and anguished and lasting rather a long time.

'There you are,' Claud said. 'That's a kill.'

'Not sure I liked it very much.'

'I told you before, Gordon. Most of 'em does it. Keens the dog up before a race.'

'I still don't like it.'

'Nor me. But they all do it. Even in the big stadiums the trainers do it. Proper barbary I call it.'

We strolled away and below us on the slope of the hill the crowd was thickening and the bookies' stands with the names written on them in red and gold and blue were all erected now in a long line back of the crowd, each bookie already stationed on an upturned box beside his stand, a pack of numbered cards in one hand, a piece of chalk in the other, his clerk behind him with book and pencil. Then we saw Mr Feasey walking over to a blackboard that was nailed to a post stuck in the ground.

'He's chalking up the first race,' Claud said. 'Come on, quick!'

We walked rapidly down the hill and joined the crowd. Mr Feasey was writing the runners on the blackboard, copying names from his soft-covered notebook, and a little hush of suspense fell upon the crowd as they watched.

1. Sally
2. Three Quid
3. Snailbox Lady
4. Black Panther
5. Whisky
6. Rockit

'He's in it!' Claud whispered. 'First race! Trap four! Now, listen, Gordon! Give me a fiver quick to show the winder.' Claud could hardly speak from excitement. That patch of whiteness had returned around his nose and eyes, and when I handed him a five pound note, his whole arm was shaking as he took it. The man who was going to wind the bicycle pedals was still standing on top of the wooden platform in his blue jersey, smoking. Claud went over and stood below him, looking up.

'See this fiver,' he said, talking softly, holding it folded small in the palm of his hand.

The man glanced at it without moving his head.

'Just so long as you wind her true this race, see. No stopping and no slowing down and run her fast. Right?'

The man didn't move but there was a slight, almost imperceptible lifting of the eyebrows. Claud turned away.

'Now, look, Gordon. Get the money on gradual, all in little bits like I told you. Just keep going down the line putting on little bits so you don't kill the price, see. And I'll be walking Jackie down very slow, as slow as I dare, to give you plenty of time. Right?'

'Right.'

'And don't forget to be standing ready to catch him at the end of the race. Get him clear away from all them others when they start

fighting for the hare. Grab a hold of him tight and don't let go till I
come running up with the collar and lead. That Whisky's a gipsy dog
and he'll tear the leg off anything as gets in his way.'

'Right,' I said. 'Here we go.'

I saw Claud lead Jackie over to the finishing post and collect a
yellow jacket with 4 written on it large. Also a muzzle. The other five
runners were there too, the owners fussing around them, putting on
their numbered jackets, adjusting their muzzles. Mr Feasey was
officiating, hopping about in his tight riding-breeches like an anxious
perky bird, and once I saw him say something to Claud and laugh.
Claud ignored him. Soon they would all start to lead the dogs down
the track, the long walk down the hill and across to the far corner of
the field to the starting-traps. It would take them ten minutes to walk
it. I've got at least ten minutes, I told myself, and then I began to
push my way through the crowd standing six or seven deep in front
of the line of bookies.

'Even money Whisky! Even money Whisky! Five to two Sally! Even
money Whisky! Four to one Snailbox! Come on now! Hurry up, hurry
up! Which is it?'

On every board all down the line the Black Panther was chalked
up at twenty-five to one. I edged forward to the nearest book.

'Three pounds Black Panther,' I said, holding out the money.

The man on the box had an inflamed magenta face and traces of
some white substance around the corners of his mouth. He snatched
the money and dropped it in his satchel. 'Seventy-five pounds to three
Black Panther,' he said. 'Number forty-two.' He handed me a ticket
and his clerk recorded the bet.

I stepped back and wrote rapidly on the back of the ticket 75 to 3,
then slipped it into the inside pocket of my jacket with the money.

So long as I continued to spread the cash out thin like this, it ought
to be all right. And anyway, on Claud's instructions, I'd made a point
of betting a few pounds on the ringer every time he'd run so as not
to arouse any suspicion when the real day arrived. Therefore, with
some confidence, I went all the way down the line staking three pounds
with each book. I didn't hurry, but I didn't waste any time either,
and after each bet I wrote the amount on the back of the card before
slipping it into my pocket. There were seventeen bookies. I had
seventeen tickets and had laid out fifty-one pounds without disturbing
the price one point. Forty-nine pounds left to get on. I glanced quickly
down the hill. One owner and his dog had already reached the traps.
The others were only twenty or thirty yards away. Except for Claud.
Claud and Jackie were only half way there. I could see Claud in his
old khaki greatcoat sauntering slowly along with Jackie pulling ahead
keenly on the leash, and once I saw him stop completely and bend
down pretending to pick something up. When he went on again he

seemed to have developed a limp so as to go slower still. I hurried back to the other end of the line to start again.

'Three pounds Black Panther.'

The bookmaker, the one with the magenta face and the white substance around the mouth, glanced up sharply, remembering the last time, and in one swift almost graceful movement of the arm he licked his fingers and wiped the figure twenty-five neatly off the board. His wet fingers left a small dark patch opposite Black Panther's name.

'All right, you got one more seventy-five to three,' he said. 'But that's the lot.' Then he raised his voice and shouted, 'Fifteen to one Black Panther! Fifteens the Panther!'

All down the line the twenty-fives were wiped out and it was fifteen to one the Panther now. I took it quick, but by the time I was through the bookies had had enough and they weren't quoting him any more. They'd only taken six pounds each, but they stood to lose a hundred and fifty, and for them – small-time bookies at a little country flapping-track – that was quite enough for one race, thank you very much. I felt pleased the way I'd managed it. Lots of tickets now. I took them out of my pockets and counted them and they were like a thin pack of cards in my hand. Thirty-three tickets in all. And what did we stand to win? Let me see ... something over two thousand pounds. Claud had said he'd win it thirty lengths. Where was Claud now?

Far away down the hill I could see the khaki greatcoat standing by the traps and the big black dog alongside. All the other dogs were already in and the owners were beginning to walk away. Claud was bending down now, coaxing Jackie into number four, and then he was closing the door and turning away and beginning to run up the hill towards the crowd, the greatcoat flapping around him. He kept looking back over his shoulder as he ran.

Beside the traps the starter stood, and his hand was up waving a handkerchief. At the other end of the track, beyond the winning-post, quite close to where I stood, the man in the blue jersey was straddling the upturned bicycle on top of the wooden platform and he saw the signal and waved back and began to turn the pedals with his hands. Then a tiny white dot in the distance – the artificial hare that was in reality a football with a piece of white rabbit-skin tacked on to it – began to move away from the traps, accelerating fast. The traps went up and the dogs flew out. They flew out in a single dark lump, all together, as though it were one wide dog instead of six, and almost at once I saw Jackie drawing away from the field. I knew it was Jackie because of the colour. There weren't any other black dogs in the race. It was Jackie, all right. Don't move, I told myself. Don't move a muscle or an eyelid or a toe or a finger-tip. Stand quite still and don't move. Watch him going. Come on Jackson, boy! No, don't shout. It's unlucky to shout. And don't move. Be all over in twenty seconds.

Round the sharp bend now and coming up the hill and he must be fifteen or twenty lengths clear. Easy twenty lengths. Don't count the lengths, it's unlucky. And don't move. Don't move your head. Watch him out of your eye-corners. Watch that Jackson go! He's really laying down to it now up that hill. He's won it now! He can't lose it now ...

When I got over to him he was fighting the rabbit-skin and trying to pick it up in his mouth, but his muzzle wouldn't allow it, and the other dogs were pounding up behind him and suddenly they were all on top of him grabbing for the rabbit and I got hold of him round the neck and dragged him clear like Claud had said and knelt down on the grass and held him tight with both arms round his body. The other catchers were having a time all trying to grab their own dogs.

Then Claud was beside me, blowing heavily, unable to speak from blowing and excitement, removing Jackie's muzzle, putting on the collar and lead, and Mr Feasey was there too standing with hands on hips, the button mouth pursed up tight like a mushroom, the two little cameras staring at Jackie all over again.

'So that's the game, is it?' he said.

Claud was bending over the dog and acting like he hadn't heard.

'I don't want you here no more after this, you understand that?'

Claud went on fiddling with Jackie's collar.

I heard someone behind us saying, 'That flat-faced bastard swung it properly on old Feasey this time.' Someone else laughed. Mr Feasey walked away, Claud straightened up and went over with Jackie to the hare driver in the blue jersey who had dismounted from his platform.

'Cigarette,' Claud said, offering the pack.

The man took one, also the five pound note that was folded up small in Claud's fingers.

'Thanks,' Claud said. 'Thanks very much.'

'Don't mention,' the man said.

Then Claud turned to me. 'You get it all on, Gordon?' He was jumping up and down and rubbing his hands and patting Jackie, and his lips trembled as he spoke.

'Yes. Half at twenty-fives, half at fifteens.'

'Oh Christ, Gordon, that's marvellous. Wait here till I get the suitcase.'

'You take Jackie,' I said, 'and go and sit in the car. I'll see you later.'

There was nobody around the bookies now. I was the only one with anything to collect, and I walked slowly with a sort of dancing stride and a wonderful bursting feeling in my chest, towards the first one in the line, the man with the magenta face and the white substance on his mouth. I stood in front of him and I took all the time I wanted going through my pack of tickets to find the two that were his. The name was Syd Pratchett. It was written up large across his board in gold letters on a scarlet field – 'SYD PRATCHETT. THE BEST ODDS IN THE MIDLANDS. PROMPT SETTLEMENT.'

I handed him the first ticket and said, 'Seventy-eight pounds to come.' It sounded so good I said it again, making a delicious little song of it. 'Seventy-eight pounds to come on this one.' I didn't mean to gloat over Mr Pratchett. As a matter of fact, I was beginning to like him quite a lot. I even felt sorry for him having to fork out so much money. I hoped his wife and kids wouldn't suffer.

'Number forty-two,' Mr Pratchett said, turning to his clerk who held the big book. 'Forty-two wants seventy-eight pounds.'

There was a pause while the clerk ran his finger down the column of recorded bets. He did this twice, then he looked up at the boss and began to shake his head.

'No,' he said. 'Don't pay. That ticket backed Snailbox Lady.'

Mr Pratchett, standing on his box, leaned over and peered down at the book. He seemed to be disturbed by what the clerk had said, and there was a look of genuine concern on the huge magenta face.

The clerk is a fool, I thought, and any moment now Mr Pratchett's going to tell him so.

But when Mr Pratchett turned back to me, the eyes had become narrow and hostile. 'Now, look Charley,' he said softly. 'Don't let's have any of that. You know very well you bet Snailbox. What's the idea?'

'I bet Black Panther,' I said. 'Two separate bets of three pounds each at twenty-five to one. Here's the second ticket.'

This time he didn't even bother to check it with the book. 'You bet Snailbox, Charley,' he said. 'I remember you coming round.' With that, he turned away from me and started wiping the names of the last race runners off his board with a wet rag. Behind him, the clerk had closed the book and was lighting himself a cigarette. I stood watching them, and I could feel the sweat beginning to break through the skin all over my body.

'Let me see the book.'

Mr Pratchett blew his nose in the wet rag and dropped it to the ground. 'Look,' he said, 'why don't you go away and stop annoying me?'

The point was this: a bookmaker's ticket, unlike a totalisator ticket, never has anything written on it regarding the nature of your bet. This is normal practice, the same at every race-track in the country, whether it's the Silver Ring at Newmarket, the Royal Enclosure at Ascot, or a tiny country flapping-track near Oxford. All you receive is a card bearing the bookie's name and a serial number. The wager is (or should be) recorded by the bookie's clerk in his book alongside the number of the ticket, but apart from that there is no evidence at all of how you betted.

'Go on,' Mr Pratchett was saying. 'Hop it.'

I stepped back a pace and glanced down the long line of bookmakers. None of them was looking my way. Each was standing motionless on his little wooden box beside his wooden placard, staring straight ahead into the crowd. I went up to the next one and presented a ticket.

'I had three pounds on Black Panther at twenty-five to one,' I said firmly. 'Seventy-eight pounds to come.'

This man, who had a soft inflamed face, went through exactly the same routine as Mr Pratchett, questioning his clerk, peering at the book, and giving me the same answers.

'Whatever's the matter with you?' he said quietly, speaking to me as though I were eight years old. 'Trying such a silly thing as that.'

This time I stepped well back. 'You dirty thieving bastards!' I cried. 'The whole lot of you!'

Automatically, as though they were puppets, all the heads down the line flicked round and looked at me. The expressions didn't alter. It was just the heads that moved, all seventeen of them, and seventeen pairs of cold glassy eyes looked down at me. There was not the faintest flicker of interest in any of them.

'Somebody spoke,' they seemed to be saying. 'We didn't hear it. It's a nice day today.'

The crowd, sensing excitement, was beginning to move in around me. I ran back to Mr Pratchett, right up close to him and poked him in the stomach with my finger. 'You're a thief! A lousy little thief!' I shouted.

The extraordinary thing was, Mr Pratchett didn't seem to resent this at all.

'Well, I never,' he said. '*Look* who's talking.'

Then suddenly the big face broke into a wide, frog-like grin, and he looked over at the crowd and shouted. '*Look* who's talking!'

All at once everybody started to laugh. Down the line the bookies were coming to life and turning to each other and laughing and pointing at me and shouting, '*Look* who's talking! *Look* who's talking!' The crowd began to take up the cry as well, and I stood there on the grass alongside Mr Pratchett with his wad of tickets as thick as a pack of cards in my hand, listening to them and feeling slightly hysterical. Over the heads of the people I could see Mr Feasey beside his blackboard, already chalking up the runners for the next race; and then beyond him, far away up the top of the field, I caught sight of Claud standing by the van, waiting for me with the suitcase in his hand.

It was time to go home.

FOUR TALES
OF THE
UNEXPECTED

THE UMBRELLA MAN

I'm going to tell you about a funny thing that happened to my mother and me yesterday evening. I am twelve years old and I'm a girl. My mother is thirty-four but I am nearly as tall as her already.

Yesterday afternoon, my mother took me up to London to see the dentist. He found one hole. It was in a back tooth and he filled it without hurting me too much. After that, we went to a café. I had a banana split and my mother had a cup of coffee. By the time we got up to leave, it was about six o'clock.

When we came out of the café it had started to rain. 'We must get a taxi,' my mother said. We were wearing ordinary hats and coats, and it was raining quite hard.

'Why don't we go back into the café and wait for it to stop?' I said. I wanted another of those banana splits. They were gorgeous.

'It isn't going to stop,' my mother said. 'We must get home.'

We stood on the pavement in the rain, looking for a taxi. Lots of them came by but they all had passengers inside them 'I wish we had a car with a chauffeur,' my mother said.

Just then, a man came up to us. He was a small man and he was pretty old, probably seventy or more. He raised his hat politely and said to my mother, 'Excuse me, I do hope you will excuse me ...' He had a fine white moustache and bushy white eyebrows and a wrinkly pink face. He was sheltering under an umbrella which he held high over his head.

'Yes?' my mother said, very cool and distant.

'I wonder if I could ask a small favour of you,' he said. 'It is only a very small favour.'

I saw my mother looking at him suspiciously. She is a suspicious person, my mother. She is especially suspicious of two things – strange men and boiled eggs. When she cuts the top off a boiled egg, she pokes around inside it with her spoon as though expecting to find a mouse or something. With strange men, she has a golden rule which says, 'The nicer the man seems to be, the more suspicious you must become.' This little old man was particularly nice. He was polite. He was well-spoken. He was well-dressed. He was a real gentleman. The reason I knew he was a gentleman was because of his shoes. 'You can always spot a gentleman by the shoes he wears,' was another of my mother's favourite sayings. This man had beautiful brown shoes.

'The truth of the matter is,' the little man was saying, 'I've got myself into a bit of a scrape. I need some help. Not much, I assure you. It's almost nothing, in fact, but I do need it. You see, madam, old people like me often become terribly forgetful ...'

My mother's chin was up and she was staring down at him along the full length of her nose. It is a fearsome thing, this frosty-nosed stare of my mother's. Most people go to pieces completely when she gives it to them. I once saw my own headmistress begin to stammer and simper like an idiot when my mother gave her a really foul frosty-noser. But the little man on the pavement with the umbrella over his head didn't bat an eyelid. He gave a gentle smile and said, 'I beg you to believe, madam, that I am not in the habit of stopping ladies in the street and telling them my troubles.'

'I should hope not,' my mother said.

I felt quite embarrassed by my mother's sharpness. I wanted to say to her, 'Oh, mummy, for heaven's sake, he's a very very old man, and he's sweet and polite, and he's in some sort of trouble, so don't be so beastly to him.' But I didn't say anything.

The little man shifted his umbrella from one hand to the other. 'I've never forgotten it before,' he said.

'You've never forgotten what?' my mother asked sternly.

'My wallet,' he said. 'I must have left it in my other jacket. Isn't that the silliest thing to do?'

'Are you asking me to give you money?' my mother said.

'Oh, good gracious me, no!' he cried. 'Heaven forbid I should ever do that!'

'Then what *are* you asking?' my mother said. 'Do hurry up. We're getting soaked to the skin standing here.'

'I know you are,' he said. 'And that is why I'm offering you this umbrella of mine to protect you, and to keep forever, if ... if only ...'

'If only what?' my mother said.

'If only you would give me in return a pound for my taxi-fare just to get me home.'

My mother was still suspicious. 'If you had no money in the first place,' she said, 'then how did you get here?'

'I walked,' he answered. 'Every day I go for a lovely long walk and then I summon a taxi to take me home. I do it every day of the year.'

'Why don't you walk home now?' my mother asked.

'Oh, I wish I could,' he said. 'I do wish I could. But I don't think I could manage it on these silly old legs of mine. I've gone too far already.'

My mother stood there chewing her lower lip. She was beginning to melt a bit, I could see that. And the idea of getting an umbrella to shelter under must have tempted her a good deal.

'It's a lovely umbrella,' the little man said.

'So I've noticed,' my mother said.

'It's silk,' he said.

'I can see that.'

'Then why don't you take it, madam,' he said. 'It cost me over twenty pounds, I promise you. But that's of no importance so long as I can get home and rest these old legs of mine.'

I saw my mother's hand feeling for the clasp on her purse. She saw me watching her. I was giving her one of my *own* frosty-nosed looks this time and she knew exactly what I was telling her. Now listen, mummy, I was telling her, you simply *mustn't* take advantage of a tired old man in this way. It's a rotten thing to do. My mother paused and looked back at me. Then she said to the little man, 'I don't think it's quite right that I should take a silk umbrella from you worth twenty pounds. I think I'd just better *give* you the taxi-fare and be done with it.'

'No, no, no!' he cried. 'It's out of the question! I wouldn't dream of it! Not in a million years! I would never accept money from you like that! Take the umbrella, dear lady, and keep the rain off your shoulders!'

My mother gave me a triumphant sideways look. There you are, she was telling me. You're wrong. He *wants* me to have it.

She fished into her purse and took out a pound note. She held it out to the little man. He took it and handed her the umbrella. He pocketed the pound, raised his hat, gave a quick bow from the waist, and said, 'Thank you, madam, thank you.' Then he was gone.

'Come under here and keep dry, darling,' my mother said. 'Aren't we lucky. I've never had a silk umbrella before. I couldn't afford it.'

'Why were you so horrid to him in the beginning?' I asked.

'I wanted to satisfy myself he wasn't a trickster,' she said. 'And I did. He was a gentleman. I'm very pleased I was able to help him.'

'Yes, mummy,' I said.

'A *real* gentleman,' she went on. 'Wealthy, too, otherwise he wouldn't have had a silk umbrella. I shouldn't be surprised if he isn't a titled person. Sir Harry Goldsworthy or something like that.'

'Yes, mummy.'

'This will be a good lesson to you,' she went on. 'Never rush things. Always take your time when you are summing someone up. Then you'll never make mistakes.'

'There he goes,' I said. 'Look.'

'Where?'

'Over there. He's crossing the street. Goodness, mummy, what a hurry he's in.'

We watched the little man as he dodged nimbly in and out of the traffic. When he reached the other side of the street, he turned left, walking very fast.

'He doesn't look very tired to me, does he to you, mummy?'

My mother didn't answer.

'He doesn't look as though he's trying to get a taxi, either,' I said.

My mother was standing very still and stiff, staring across the street at the little man. We could see him clearly. He was in a terrific hurry. He was bustling along the pavement, sidestepping the other pedestrians and swinging his arms like a soldier on the march.

'He's up to something,' my mother said, stony-faced.

'But what?'

'I don't know,' my mother snapped. 'But I'm going to find out. Come with me.' She took my arm and we crossed the street together. Then we turned left.

'Can you see him?' my mother asked.

'Yes. There he is. He's turning right down the next street.'

We came to the corner and turned right. The little man was about twenty yards ahead of us. He was scuttling along like a rabbit and we had to walk fast to keep up with him. The rain was pelting down harder than ever now and I could see it dripping from the brim of his hat on to his shoulders. But we were snug and dry under our lovely big silk umbrella.

'What *is* he up to?' my mother said.

'What if he turns round and sees us?' I asked.

'I don't care if he does,' my mother said. 'He lied to us. He said he was too tired to walk any further and he's practically running us off our feet! He's a barefaced liar! He's a crook!'

'You mean he's *not* a titled gentleman?' I asked.

'Be quiet,' she said.

At the next crossing, the little man turned right again.

Then he turned left.

Then right.

'I'm not giving up now,' my mother said.

'He's disappeared!' I cried. 'Where's he gone?'

'He went in that door!' my mother said. 'I saw him! Into that house! Great heavens, it's a pub!'

It was a pub. In big letters right across the front it said THE RED LION.

'You're not going in, are you, mummy?'

'No,' she said. 'We'll watch from outside.'

There was a big plate-glass window along the front of the pub, and although it was a bit steamy on the inside, we could see through it very well if we went close.

We stood huddled together outside the pub window. I was clutching my mother's arm. The big raindrops were making a loud noise on our umbrella. 'There he is,' I said. 'Over there.'

The room we were looking into was full of people and cigarette smoke, and our little man was in the middle of it all. He was now without his hat or coat, and he was edging his way through the crowd towards the bar. When he reached it, he placed both hands on the bar itself and spoke to the barman. I saw his lips moving as he gave his order. The barman turned away from him for a few seconds and came back with a smallish tumbler filled to the brim with light brown liquid. The little man placed a pound note on the counter.

'That's my pound!' my mother hissed. 'By golly, he's got a nerve!'

'What's in the glass?' I asked.

'Whisky,' my mother said. 'Neat whisky.'

The barman didn't give him any change from the pound.

'That must be a treble whisky,' my mummy said.

'What's a treble?' I asked.

'Three times the normal measure,' she answered.

The little man picked up the glass and put it to his lips. He tilted it gently. Then he tilted it higher ... and higher ... and higher ... and very soon all the whisky had disappeared down his throat in one long pour.

'That was a jolly expensive drink,' I said.

'It's ridiculous!' my mummy said. 'Fancy paying a pound for something you swallow in one go!'

'It cost him more than a pound,' I said. 'It cost him a twenty-pound silk umbrella.'

'So it did,' my mother said. 'He must be mad.'

The little man was standing by the bar with the empty glass in his hand. He was smiling now, and a sort of golden glow of pleasure was spreading over his round pink face. I saw his tongue come out to lick the white moustache, as though searching for the last drop of that precious whisky.

Slowly, he turned away from the bar and edged back through the crowd to where his hat and coat were hanging. He put on his hat. He put on his coat. Then, in a manner so superbly cool and casual that you hardly noticed anything at all, he lifted from the coat-rack one of the many wet umbrellas hanging there, and off he went.

'Did you see that!' my mother shrieked. 'Did you see what he did!'

'Ssshh!' I whispered. 'He's coming out!'

We lowered the umbrella to hide our faces, and peeped out from under it.

Out he came. But he never looked in our direction. He opened his new umbrella over his head and scurried off down the road the way he had come.

'So that's his little game!' my mother said.

'Neat,' I said. 'Super.'

We followed him back to the main street where we had first met him, and we watched him as he proceeded, with no trouble at all, to exchange his new umbrella for another pound note. This time it was with a tall thin fellow who didn't even have a coat or hat. And as soon as the transaction was completed, our little man trotted off down the street and was lost in the crowd. But this time he went in the opposite direction.

'You see how clever he is!' my mother said. 'He never goes to the same pub twice!'

'He could go on doing this all night,' I said.

'Yes,' my mother said. 'Of course. But I'll bet he prays like mad for rainy days.'

MR BOTIBOL

Mr Botibol pushed his way through the revolving doors and emerged into the large foyer of the hotel. He took off his hat, and holding it in front of him with both hands, he advanced nervously a few paces, paused and stood looking around him, searching the faces of the lunchtime crowd. Several people turned and stared at him in mild astonishment, and he heard – or he thought he heard – at least one woman's voice saying, 'My dear, *do* look what's just come in!'

At last he spotted Mr Clements sitting at a small table in the far corner, and he hurried over to him. Clements had seen him coming, and now, as he watched Mr Botibol threading his way cautiously between the tables and the people, walking on his toes in such a meek and self-effacing manner and clutching his hat before him with both hands, he thought how wretched it must be for any man to look as conspicuous and as odd as this Botibol. He resembled, to an extraordinary degree, an asparagus. His long narrow stalk did not appear to have any shoulders at all; it merely tapered upwards, growing gradually narrower and narrower until it came to a kind of point at the top of the small bald head. He was tightly encased in a shiny blue double-breasted suit, and this, for some curious reason, accentuated the illusion of a vegetable to a preposterous degree.

Clements stood up, they shook hands, and then at once, even before they had sat down again, Mr Botibol said, 'I have decided, yes I have decided to accept the offer which you made to me before you left my office last night.'

For some days Clements had been negotiating, on behalf of clients, for the purchase of the firm known as Botibol & Co., of which Mr Botibol was sole owner, and the night before, Clements had made his first offer. This was merely an exploratory, much-too-low bid, a kind of signal to the seller that the buyers were seriously interested. And by God, thought Clements, the poor fool has gone and accepted it. He nodded gravely many times in an effort to hide his astonishment, and he said, 'Good, good. I'm so glad to hear that, Mr Botibol.' Then he signalled a waiter and said, 'Two large martinis.'

'No, please!' Mr Botibol lifted both hands in horrified protest.

'Come on,' Clements said. 'This is an occasion.'

'I drink very little, and never, no never during the middle of the day.'

But Clements was in a gay mood now and he took no notice. He ordered the martinis and when they came along Mr Botibol was forced, by the banter and good-humour of the other, to drink to the deal which had just been concluded. Clements then spoke briefly about the drawing up and signing of documents, and when all that had been arranged, he called for two more cocktails. Again Mr Botibol protested, but not quite so vigorously this time, and Clements ordered the drinks and then he turned and smiled at the other man in a friendly way. 'Well, Mr Botibol,' he said, 'now that it's all over, I suggest we have a pleasant non-business lunch together. What d'you say to that? And it's on me.'

'As you wish, as you wish,' Mr Botibol answered without any enthusiasm. He had a small melancholy voice and a way of pronouncing each word separately and slowly, as though he was explaining something to a child.

When they went into the dining-room Clements ordered a bottle of Lafite 1912 and a couple of plump roast partridges to go with it. He had already calculated in his head the amount of his commission and he was feeling fine. He began to make bright conversation, switching smoothly from one subject to another in the hope of touching on something that might interest his guest. But it was no good. Mr Botibol appeared to be only half listening. Every now and then he inclined his small bald head a little to one side or the other and said, 'Indeed.' When the wine came along Clements tried to have a talk about that.

'I am sure it is excellent,' Mr Botibol said, 'but please give me only a drop.'

Clements told a funny story. When it was over, Mr Botibol regarded him solemnly for a few moments, then he said, 'How amusing.' After that Clements kept his mouth shut and they ate in silence. Mr Botibol was drinking his wine and he didn't seem to object when his host reached over and refilled his glass. By the time they had finished eating, Clements estimated privately that his guest had consumed at least three-quarters of the bottle.

'A cigar, Mr Botibol?'

'Oh no, thank you.'

'A little brandy?'

'No really. I am not accustomed ...' Clements noticed that the man's cheeks were slightly flushed and that this eyes had become bright and watery. Might as well get the old boy properly drunk while I'm about it, he thought, and to the waiter he said, 'Two brandies.'

When the brandies arrived, Mr Botibol looked at his large glass suspiciously for a while, then he picked it up, took one quick birdlike sip and put it down again. 'Mr Clements,' he said suddenly, 'how I envy you.'

'Me? But why?'

'I will tell you, Mr Clements, I will tell you, if I may make so bold.' There was a nervous, mouselike quality in his voice which made it seem he was apologizing for everything he said.

'Please tell me,' Clements said.

'It is because to me you appear to have made such a success of your life.'

He's going to get melancholy drunk, Clements thought. He's one of the ones that gets melancholy and I can't stand it. 'Success,' he said, 'I don't see anything especially successful about me.'

'Oh yes, indeed. Your whole life, if I may say so, Mr Clements, appears to be such a pleasant and successful thing.'

'I'm a very ordinary person,' Clements said. He was trying to figure just how drunk the other really was.

'I believe,' said Mr Botibol, speaking slowly, separating each word carefully from the other, 'I believe that the wine has gone a little to my head, but ...' He paused, searching for words. '... But I do want to ask you just one question.' He had poured some salt on to the tablecloth and he was shaping it into a little mountain with the tip of one finger.

'Mr Clements,' he said without looking up, 'do you think that it is possible for a man to live to the age of fifty-two without ever during his whole life having experienced one single small success in anything that he has done?'

'My dear Mr Botibol,' Clements laughed, 'everyone has his little successes from time to time, however small they may be.'

'Oh no,' Mr Botibol said gently. 'You are wrong. I, for example, cannot remember having had a single success of any sort during my whole life.'

'Now come!' Clements said, smiling. 'That can't be true. Why only this morning you sold your business for a hundred thousand. I call that one hell of a success.'

'The business was left me by my father. When he died nine years ago, it was worth four times as much. Under my direction it has lost three-quarters of its value. You can hardly call that a success.'

Clements knew this was true. 'Yes yes, all right,' he said. 'That may be so, but all the same you know as well as I do that every man alive has his quota of little successes. Not big ones maybe. But lots of little ones. I mean, after all, goddammit, even scoring goal at school was a little success, a little triumph, at the time; or making some runs or learning to swim. One forgets about them, that's all. One just forgets.'

'I never scored a goal,' Mr Botibol said. 'And I never learned to swim.'

Clements threw up his hands and made exasperated noises. 'Yes yes, I know, but don't you see, don't you see there are thousands, literally thousands of other things, things like ... well ... like catching a good fish, or fixing the motor of the car, or pleasing someone with a present, or growing a decent row of French beans, or winning a little bet or ... or ... why hell, one can go on listing them for ever!'

'Perhaps *you* can, Mr Clements, but to the best of my knowledge, I have never done any of those things. That is what I am trying to tell you.'

Clements put down his brandy glass and stared with new interest at the remarkable shoulderless person who sat facing him. He was annoyed and he didn't feel in the least sympathetic. The man didn't inspire sympathy. He was a fool. He must be a fool. A tremendous and absolute fool. Clements had a sudden desire to embarrass the man as much as he could. 'What about women, Mr Botibol?' There was no apology for the question in the tone of his voice.

'Women?'

'Yes women! Every man under the sun, even the most wretched filthy down-and-out tramp has some time or other had some sort of silly little success with ...'

'Never!' cried Mr Botibol with sudden vigour. 'No sir, never!'

I'm going to hit him, Clements told himself. I can't stand this any longer and if I'm not careful I'm going to jump right up and hit him. 'You mean you don't like them?' he said.

'Oh dear me yes, of course I like them. As a matter of fact I admire them very much, very much indeed. But I'm afraid ... oh dear me ... I do not know quite how to say it ... I am afraid that I do not seem to get along with them very well. I never have. Never. You see, Mr Clements, I *look* queer. I know I do. They stare at me, and often I see them laughing at me. I have never been able to get within ... well, within striking distance of them, as you might say.' The trace of a smile, weak and infinitely sad, flickered around the corners of his mouth.

Clements had had enough. He mumbled something about how he was sure Mr Botibol was exaggerating the situation, then he glanced at his watch, called for the bill, and said he was sorry but he would have to get back to the office.

They parted in the street outside the hotel and Mr Botibol took a cab back to his house. He opened the front door, went into the living-room and switched on the radio; then he sat down in a large leather chair, leaned back and closed his eyes. He didn't feel exactly giddy, but there was a singing in his ears and his thoughts were coming and going more quickly than usual. That solicitor gave me too much wine, he told himself. I'll stay here for a while and listen to some music and I expect I'll go to sleep and after that I'll feel better.

They were playing a symphony on the radio. Mr Botibol had always been a casual listener to symphony concerts and he knew enough to identify this as one of Beethoven's. But now, as he lay back in his chair listening to the marvellous music, a new thought began to expand slowly within his tipsy mind. It wasn't a dream because he was not asleep. It was a clear conscious thought and it was this: I am the composer of this music. I am a great composer. This is my latest symphony and this is the first performance. The huge hall is packed with people – critics, musicians and music-lovers from all over the country – and I am up there in front of the orchestra, conducting.

Mr Botibol could see the whole thing. He could see himself up on the rostrum dressed in a white tie and tails, and before him was the orchestra, the massed violins on his left, the violas in front, the cellos on his right, and back of them were all the woodwinds and bassoons and drums and cymbals, the players watching every movement of his baton with an intense, almost a fanatical reverence. Behind him, in the half-darkness of the huge hall, was row upon row of white enraptured faces, looking up towards him, listening with growing excitement as yet another new symphony by the greatest composer the world had ever seen unfolded itself majestically before them. Some of the audience were clenching their fists and digging their nails into the palms of their hands because the music was so beautiful that they could hardly stand it. Mr Botibol became so carried away by this exciting vision that he began to swing his arms in time with the music in the manner of a conductor. He found it was such fun doing this that he decided to stand up, facing the radio, in order to give himself more freedom of movement.

He stood there in the middle of the room, tall, thin and shoulderless, dressed in his tight blue double-breasted suit, his small bald head jerking from side to side as he waved his arms in the air. He knew the symphony well enough to be able occasionally to anticipate changes in tempo or volume, and when the music became loud and fast he beat the air so vigorously that he nearly knocked himself over, when it was soft and hushed, he leaned forward to quieten the players with gentle movements of his outstretched hands, and all the time he could feel the presence of the huge audience behind him, tense, immobile, listening. When at last the symphony swelled to its tremendous conclusion, Mr Botibol became more frenzied than ever and his face seemed to thrust itself round to one side in an agony of effort as he tried to force more and still more power from his orchestra during those final mighty chords.

Then it was over. The announcer was saying something, but Mr Botibol quickly switched off the radio and collapsed into his chair, blowing heavily.

'Phew!' he said aloud. 'My goodness gracious me, what *have* I been doing!' Small globules of sweat were oozing out all over his face and forehead, trickling down his neck inside his collar. He pulled out a handkerchief and wiped them away, and he lay there for a while, panting, exhausted, but exceedingly exhilarated.

'Well, I must say,' he gasped, still speaking aloud, 'that *was* fun. I don't know that I have ever had such fun before in all my life. My goodness, it *was* fun, it really *was!*' Almost at once he began to play with the idea of doing it again. But should he? Should he allow himself to do it again? There was no denying that now, in retrospect, he felt a little guilty about the whole business, and soon he began to wonder whether there wasn't something downright immoral about it all. Letting himself go like that! And imagining he was a genius! It was wrong. He was sure other people didn't do it. And what if Mason had come in in the middle and seen him at it! That would have been terrible!

He reached for the paper and pretended to read it, but soon he was searching furtively among the radio programmes for the evening. He put his finger under a line which said '8.30 Symphony Concert. Brahms Symphony No. 2'. He stared at it for a long time. The letters in the word 'Brahms' began to blur and recede, and gradually they disappeared altogether and were replaced by letters which spelt 'Botibol'. Botibol's Symphony No. 2. It was printed quite clearly. He was reading it now, this moment. 'Yes, yes,' he whispered. 'First performance. The world is waiting to hear it. Will it be as great, they are asking, will it perhaps be greater than his earlier work? And the composer himself has been persuaded to conduct. He is shy and retiring, hardly ever appears in public, but on this occasion he has been persuaded ...'

Mr Botibol leaned forward in his chair and pressed the bell beside the fireplace. Mason, the butler, the only other person in the house, ancient, small and grave, appeared at the door.

'Er ... Mason, have we any wine in the house?'

'Wine, sir?'

'Yes, wine.'

'Oh no, sir. We haven't had any wine this fifteen or sixteen years. Your father, sir ...'

'I know, Mason, I know, but will you get some please. I want a bottle with my dinner.'

The butler was shaken. 'Very well, sir, and what shall it be?'

'Claret, Mason. The best you can obtain. Get a case. Tell them to send it round at once.'

When he was alone again, he was momentarily appalled by the simple manner in which he had made this decision. Wine for dinner! Just like that! Well, yes, why not? Why ever not now he came to think of it? He was his own master. And anyway it was essential that he have wine. It seemed to have a good effect, a very good effect indeed. He wanted it and he was going to have it and to hell with Mason.

He rested for the remainder of the afternoon, and at seven-thirty Mason announced dinner. The bottle of wine was on the table and he began to drink it. He didn't give a damn about the way Mason watched him as he refilled his glass. Three times he refilled it; then he left the table saying that he was not to be disturbed and returned to the living-room. There was quarter of an hour to wait. He could think of nothing now except the coming concert. He lay back in the chair and allowed his thoughts to wander deliciously towards eight-thirty. He was the great composer waiting impatiently in his dressing-room in the concert-hall. He could hear in the distance the murmur of excitement from the crowd as they settled themselves in their seats. He knew what they were saying to each other. Same sort of thing the newspapers had been saying for months. Botibol is a genius, greater, far greater than Beethoven or Bach or Brahms or Mozart or any of them. Each new work of his is more magnificent than the last. What will the next one be like? We can hardly wait to hear it! Oh yes, he knew what they were saying. He stood up and began to pace the room. It was nearly time now. He seized a pencil from the table to use as a baton, then he switched on the radio. The announcer had just finished the preliminaries and suddenly there was a burst of applause which meant that the conductor was coming on to the platform. The previous concert in the afternoon had been from gramophone records, but this one was the real thing. Mr Botibol turned around, faced the fireplace and bowed graciously from the waist. Then he turned back to the radio and lifted his baton. The clapping stopped. There was a moment's silence. Someone in the audience coughed. Mr Botibol waited. The symphony began.

Once again, as he began to conduct, he could see clearly before him the whole orchestra and the faces of the players and even the expressions on their faces. Three of the violinists had grey hair. One of the cellists was very fat, another wore heavy brown-rimmed glasses, and there was a man in the second row playing a horn who had a twitch on one side of his face. But they were all magnificent. And so was the music. During certain impressive passages Mr Botibol experienced a feeling of exultation so powerful that it made him cry out for joy, and once during the Third Movement, a little shiver of ecstasy radiated spontaneously from his solar plexus and moved downward over the skin of his stomach like needles. But the thunderous applause and the cheering which came at the end of the symphony was the most splendid thing of all. He turned slowly towards the fireplace and bowed. The clapping continued and he went on bowing until at last the noise died away and the announcer's voice jerked him suddenly back into the living-room. He switched off the radio and collapsed into his chair, exhausted but very happy.

As he lay there, smiling with pleasure, wiping his wet face, panting for breath, he was already making plans for his next performance. But why not do it properly? Why not convert one of the rooms into a sort of concert-hall and have a stage and row of chairs and do the thing properly? And have a gramophone so that one could perform at any time without having to rely on the radio programme. Yes by heavens, he would do it!

The next morning Mr Botibol arranged with a firm of decorators that the largest room in the house be converted into a miniature concert-hall. There was to be a raised stage at one end and the rest of the floor-space was to be filled with rows of red plush seats. 'I'm going to have some little concerts here,' he told the man from the firm, and the man nodded and said that would be very nice. At the same time he ordered a radio shop to instal an expensive self-changing gramophone with two powerful amplifiers, one on the stage, the other at the back of the auditorium. When he had done this, he went off and bought all of Beethoven's nine symphonies on gramophone records, and from a place which specialized in recorded sound effects he ordered several records of clapping and applauding by enthusiastic audiences. Finally he bought himself a conductor's baton, a slim ivory stick which lay in a case lined with blue silk.

In eight days the room was ready. Everything was perfect; the red chairs, the aisle down the centre and even a little dais on the platform with a brass rail running round it for the conductor. Mr Botibol decided to give the first concert that evening after dinner.

At seven o'clock he went up to his bedroom and changed into white tie and tails. He felt marvellous. When he looked at himself in the mirror, the sight of his own grotesque shoulderless figure didn't worry him in the least. A great composer, he thought, smiling, can look as he damn well pleases. People *expect* him to look peculiar. All the same he wished he had some hair on his head. He would have liked to let it grow rather long. He went downstairs to dinner, ate his food rapidly, drank half a bottle of wine and felt better still. 'Don't worry about me, Mason,' he said. 'I'm not mad. I'm just enjoying myself.'

'Yes, sir.'

'I shan't want you any more. Please see that I'm not disturbed.' Mr Botibol went from the dining-room into the miniature concert-hall. He took out the records of Beethoven's First Symphony, but before putting them on the gramophone, he placed two other records with them. The one, which was to be played first of all, before the music began, was labelled 'prolonged enthusiastic applause'. The other, which would come at the end of the symphony, was labelled 'Sustained applause, clapping, cheering, shouts of encore'. By a simple mechanical device on the record changer, the gramophone people had arranged that the sound from the first and the last records – the applause – would come only from the loudspeaker in the auditorium. The sound from all the others – the music – would come from the speaker hidden among the chairs of the orchestra. When he had arranged the records in the correct order, he placed them on the machine but he didn't switch on at once. Instead he turned out all the lights in the room except one small one which lit up the conductor's dais and he sat down in a chair up on the stage, closed his eyes and allowed his thoughts to wander into the usual delicious regions; the great composer, nervous, impatient, waiting to present his latest masterpiece, the audience assembling, the murmur of their excited talk, and so on. Having dreamed himself right into the part, he stood up, picked up his baton and switched on the gramophone.

A tremendous wave of clapping filled the room. Mr Botibol walked across the stage, mounted the dais, faced the audience and bowed. In the darkness he could just make out the faint outline of the seats on either side of the centre aisle, but he couldn't see the faces of the people. They were making enough noise. What an ovation! Mr Botibol turned and faced the orchestra. The applause behind him died down. The next record dropped. The symphony began.

This time it was more thrilling than ever, and during the performance he registered any number of prickly sensations around his solar plexus. Once, when it suddenly occurred to him that this music was being broadcast all over the world, a sort of shiver ran right down the length of his spine. But by far the most exciting part was the applause which came at the end. They cheered and clapped and stamped and shouted encore! encore! encore! and he turned towards the darkened auditorium and bowed gravely to the left and right. Then he went off the stage, but they called him back. He bowed several more times and went off again, and again they called him back. The audience had gone mad. They simply wouldn't let him go. It was terrific. It was truly a terrific ovation.

Later, when he was resting in his chair in the other room, he was still enjoying it. He closed his eyes because he didn't want anything to break the spell. He lay there and he felt like he was floating. It was really a most marvellous floating feeling, and when he went upstairs and undressed and got into bed, it was still with him.

The following evening he conducted Beethoven's – or rather Botibol's – Second Symphony, and they were just as mad about that one as the first. The next few nights he played one symphony a night, and at the end of nine evenings he had worked through all nine of Beethoven's symphonies. It got more exciting every time because before each concert the audience kept saying 'He can't do it again, not another masterpiece. It's not humanly possible.' But he did. They were all of them equally magnificent. The last symphony, the Ninth, was especially exciting because here the composer surprised and delighted everyone by suddenly providing a choral masterpiece. He had to conduct a huge choir as well as the orchestra itself, and Benjamino Gigli had flown over from Italy to take the tenor part. Enrico Pinza sang bass. At the end of it the audience shouted themselves hoarse. The whole musical world was on its feet cheering, and on all sides they were saying how you never could tell what wonderful things to expect next from this amazing person.

The composing, presenting and conducting of nine great symphonies in as many days is a fair achievement for any man, and it was not astonishing that it went a little to Mr Botibol's head. He decided now that he would once again surprise his public. He would compose a mass of marvellous piano music and he himself would give the recitals. So early the next morning he set out for the show room of the people who sold Bechsteins and Steinways. He felt so brisk and fit that he walked all the way, and as he walked he hummed little snatches of new and lovely tunes for the piano. His head was full of them. All the time they kept coming to him and once, suddenly, he had the feeling that thousands of small notes, some white, some black, were cascading down a chute into his head through a hole in his head, and that his brain, his amazing musical brain, was receiving them as fast as they could come and unscrambling them and arranging them neatly in a certain order so that they made wondrous melodies. There were Nocturnes, there were Études and there were Waltzes, and soon, he told himself, soon he would give them all to a grateful and admiring world.

When he arrived at the piano-shop, he pushed the door open and walked in with an air almost of confidence. He had changed much in the last few days. Some of his nervousness had left him and he was no longer wholly preoccupied with what others thought of his appearance. 'I want,' he said to the salesman, 'a concert grand, but you must arrange it so that when the notes are struck, no sound is produced.'

The salesman leaned forward and raised his eyebrows.

'Could that be arranged?' Mr Botibol asked.

'Yes, sir, I think so, if you desire it. But might I inquire what you intend to use the instrument for?'

'If you want to know, I'm going to pretend I'm Chopin. I'm going to sit and play while a gramophone makes the music. It gives me a kick.' It came out, just like that, and Mr Botibol didn't know what had made him say it. But it was done now and he had said it and that was that. In a way he felt relieved, because he had proved he didn't mind telling people what he was doing. The man would probably answer what a jolly good idea. Or he might not. He might say well you ought to be locked up.

'So now you know,' Mr Botibol said.

The salesman laughed out loud. 'Ha ha! Ha ha ha! That's very good, sir. Very good indeed. Serves me right for asking silly questions.' He stopped suddenly in the middle of the laugh and looked hard at Mr Botibol. 'Of course, sir, you probably know that we sell a simple noiseless keyboard specially for silent practising.'

'I want a concert grand,' Mr Botibol said. The salesman looked at him again.

Mr Botibol chose his piano and got out of the shop as quickly as possible. He went on to the store that sold gramophone records and there he ordered a quantity of albums containing recordings of all Chopin's Nocturnes, Études and Waltzes, played by Arthur Rubinstein.

'My goodness, you *are* going to have a lovely time!'

Mr Botibol turned and saw standing beside him at the counter a squat, short-legged girl with a face as plain as a pudding.

'Yes,' he answered. 'Oh yes, I am.' Normally he was strict about not speaking to females in public places, but this one had taken him by surprise.

'I love Chopin,' the girl said. She was holding a slim brown paper bag with string handles containing a single record she had just bought. 'I like him better than any of the others.'

It was comforting to hear the voice of this girl after the way the piano salesman had laughed. Mr Botibol wanted to talk to her but he didn't know what to say.

The girl said, 'I like the Nocturnes best, they're so soothing. Which are your favourites?'

Mr Botibol said, 'Well ...' The girl looked up at him and she smiled pleasantly, trying to assist him with his embarrassment. It was the smile that did it. He suddenly found himself saying, 'Well now, perhaps, would you, I wonder ... I mean I was wondering ...' She smiled again; she couldn't help it this time. 'What I mean is I would be glad if you would care to come along some time and listen to these records.'

'Why how nice of you.' She paused, wondering whether it was all right. 'You really mean it?'

'Yes, I should be glad.'

She had lived long enough in the city to discover that old men, if they are dirty old men, do not bother about trying to pick up a girl as unattractive as herself. Only twice in her life had she been accosted in public and each time the man had been drunk. But this one wasn't drunk. He was nervous and he was peculiar-looking, but he wasn't drunk. Come to think of it, it was she who had started the conversation in the first place. 'It would be lovely,' she said. 'It really would. When could I come?'

Oh dear, Mr Botibol thought. Oh dear, oh dear, oh dear, oh dear.

'I could come tomorrow,' she went on. 'It's my afternoon off.'

'Well, yes, certainly,' he answered slowly. 'Yes, of course. I'll give you my card. Here it is.'

'A. W. Botibol,' she read aloud. 'What a funny name. Mine's Darlington. Miss L. Darlington. How d'you do, Mr Botibol.' She put out her hand for him to shake. 'Oh I *am* looking forward to this! What time shall I come?'

'Any time,' he said. 'Please come any time.'

'Three o'clock?'

'Yes. Three o'clock.'

'Lovely! I'll be there.'

He watched her walk out of the shop, a squat, stumpy, thick-legged little person and my word, he thought, what have I done! He was amazed at himself. But he was not displeased. Then at once he started to worry about whether or not he should let her see his concert-hall. He worried still more when he realized that it was the only place in the house where there was a gramophone.

That evening he had no concert. Instead he sat in his chair brooding about Miss Darlington and what he should do when she arrived. The next morning they brought the piano, a fine Bechstein in dark mahogany which was carried in minus its legs and later assembled on the platform in the concert hall. It was an imposing instrument and when Mr Botibol opened it and pressed a note with his finger, it made no sound at all. He had originally intended to astonish the world with a recital of his first piano compositions – a set of Études – as soon as the piano arrived, but it was no good now. He was too worried about Miss Darlington and three o'clock. At lunch-time his trepidation had increased and he couldn't eat. 'Mason,' he said, 'I'm, I'm expecting a young lady to call at three o'clock.'

'A what, sir?' the butler said.

'A young lady, Mason.'

'Very good, sir.'

'Show her into the sitting-room.'

'Yes, sir.'

Precisely at three he heard the bell ring. A few moments later Mason was showing her into the room. She came in, smiling, and Mr Botibol stood up and shook her hand. 'My!' she exclaimed. 'What a lovely house! I didn't know I was calling on a millionaire!'

She settled her small plump body into a large armchair and Mr Botibol sat opposite. He didn't know what to say. He felt terrible. But almost at once she began to talk and she chattered away gaily about this and that for a long time without stopping. Mostly it was about his house and the furniture and the carpets and about how nice it was of him to invite her because she didn't have such an awful lot of excitement in her life. She worked hard all day and she shared a room with two other girls in a boarding-house and he could have no idea how thrilling it was for her to be here. Gradually Mr Botibol began to feel better. He sat there listening to the girl, rather liking her, nodding his bald head slowly up and down, and the more she talked, the more he liked her. She was gay and chatty, but underneath all that any fool could see that she was a lonely tired little thing. Even Mr Botibol could see that. He could see it very clearly indeed. It was at this point that he began to play with a daring and risky idea.

'Miss Darlington,' he said. 'I'd like to show you something.' He led her out of the room straight to the little concert-hall. 'Look,' he said.

She stopped just inside the door. 'My goodness! Just look at that! A theatre! A real little theatre!' Then she saw the piano on the platform and the conductor's dais with the brass rail running round it. 'It's for concerts!' she cried. 'Do you really have concerts here! Oh, Mr Botibol, how exciting!'

'Do you like it?'

'Oh yes!'

'Come back into the other room and I'll tell you about it.' Her enthusiasm had given him confidence and he wanted to get going. 'Come back and listen while I tell you something funny.' And when they were seated in the sitting-room again, he began at once to tell her his story. He told the whole thing, right from the beginning, how one day, listening to a symphony, he had imagined himself to be the composer, how he had stood up and started to conduct, how he had got an immense pleasure out of it, how he had done it again with similar results and how finally he had built himself the concert-hall where already he had conducted nine symphonics. But he cheated a little bit in the telling. He said that the only real reason he did it was in order to obtain the maximum appreciation from the music. There was only one way to listen to music, he told her, only one way to make yourself listen to every single note and chord. You had to do two things at once. You had to imagine that you had composed it, and at the same time you had to imagine that the public were hearing it for the first time. 'Do you think,' he said, 'do you really think that any outsider has ever got half as great a thrill from a symphony as the composer himself when he first heard his work played by a full orchestra?'

'No,' she answered timidly. 'Of course not.'

'Then become the composer! Steal his music! Take it away from him and give it to yourself!' He leaned back in his chair and for the first time she saw him smile. He had only just thought of this new complex explanation of his conduct, but to him it seemed a very good one and he smiled. 'Well, what do you think, Miss Darlington?'

'I must say it's very very interesting.' She was polite and puzzled but she was a long way away from him now.

'Would you like to try?'

'Oh no. Please.'

'I wish you would.'

'I'm afraid I don't think I should be able to feel the same way as you do about it, Mr Botibol. I don't think I have a strong enough imagination.'

She could see from his eyes he was disappointed. 'But I'd love to sit in the audience and listen while you do it,' she added.

Then he leapt up from his chair. 'I've got it!' he cried. 'A piano concerto! You play the piano, I conduct. You the greatest pianist, the greatest in the world. First performance of my Piano Concerto No. 1. You playing, me conducting. The greatest pianist and the greatest composer together for the first time. A tremendous occasion! The audience will go mad! There'll be queueing all night outside the hall to get in. It'll be broadcast around the world. It'll, it'll ...' Mr Botibol stopped. He stood behind the chair with both hands resting on the back of the chair and suddenly he looked embarrassed and a trifle sheepish. 'I'm sorry,' he said, 'I get worked up. You see how it is. Even the thought of another performance gets me worked up.' And then plaintively, 'Would you, Miss Darlington, would you play a piano concerto with me?'

'It's like children,' she said, but she smiled.

'No one will know. No one but us will know anything about it.'

'All right,' she said at last. 'I'll do it. I think I'm daft but just the same I'll do it. It'll be a bit of a lark.'

'Good!' Mr Botibol cried. 'When? Tonight?'

'Oh well, I don't ...'

'Yes,' he said eagerly. 'Please. Make it tonight. Come back and have dinner here with me and we'll give the concert afterwards.' Mr Botibol was excited again now. 'We must make a few plans. Which is your favourite piano concerto, Miss Darlington?'

'Oh well, I should say Beethoven's Emperor.'

'The Emperor it shall be. You will play it tonight. Come to dinner at seven. Evening dress. You must have evening dress for the concert.'

'I've got a dancing dress but I haven't worn it for years.'

'You shall wear it tonight.' He paused and looked at her in silence for a moment, then quite gently, he said, 'You're not worried, Miss Darlington? Perhaps you would rather not do it. I'm afraid, I'm afraid I've let myself get rather carried away. I seem to have pushed you into this. And I know how stupid it must seem to you.'

That's better, she thought. That's much better. Now I know it's all right. 'Oh no,' she said. 'I'm really looking forward to it. But you frightened me a bit, taking it all so seriously.'

When she had gone, he waited for five minutes, then went out into the town to the gramophone shop and bought the records of the Emperor Concerto, conductor, Toscanini – soloist, Horowitz. He turned at once, told his astonished butler that there would be a guest for dinner, then went upstairs and changed into his tails.

She arrived at seven. She was wearing a long sleeveless dress made of some shiny green material and to Mr Botibol she did not look quite so plump or quite so plain as before. He took her straight in to dinner and in spite of the silent disapproving manner in which Mason prowled around the table, the meal went well. She protested gaily when Mr Botibol gave her a second glass of wine, but she didn't refuse it. She chattered away almost without a stop throughout the three courses and Mr Botibol listened and nodded and kept refilling her glass as soon as it was half empty.

Afterwards, when they were seated in the living-room, Mr Botibol said, 'Now Miss Darlington, now we begin to fall into our parts.' The wine, as usual, had made him happy, and the girl, who was even less used to it than the man, was not feeling so bad either. 'You, Miss Darlington, are the great pianist. What is your first name, Miss Darlington?'

'Lucille,' she said.

'The great pianist Lucille Darlington. I am the composer Botibol. We must talk and act and think as though we are pianist and composer.'

'What is *your* first name, Mr Botibol? What does the A stand for?'

'Angel,' he answered.

'Not Angcl.'

'Yes,' he said irritably.

'Angel Botibol,' she murmured and she began to giggle. But she checked herself and said, 'I think it's a most unusual and distinguished name.'

'Are you ready, Miss Darlington?'

'Yes.'

Mr Botibol stood up and began pacing nervously up and down the room. He looked at his watch. 'It's nearly time to go on,' he said. 'They tell me the place is packed. Not an empty seat anywhere. I always get nervous before a concert. Do you get nervous, Miss Darlington?'

'Oh yes, I do, always. Especially playing with you.'

'I think they'll like it. I put everything I've got into this concerto, Miss Darlington. It nearly killed me composing it. I was ill for weeks afterwards.'

'Poor you,' she said.

'It's time now,' he said. 'The orchestra are all in their places. Come on.' He led her out and down the passage, then he made her wait outside the door of the concert-hall while he nipped in, arranged the lighting and switched on the gramophone. He came back and fetched her and as they walked on to the stage, the applause broke out. They both stood and bowed towards the darkened auditorium and the applause was vigorous and it went on for a long time. Then Mr Botibol mounted the dais and Miss Darlington took her seat at the piano. The applause died down. Mr Botibol held up his baton. The next record dropped and the Emperor Concerto began.

It was an astonishing affair. The thin stalk-like Mr Botibol, who had no shoulders, standing on the dais in his evening clothes waving his arms about in approximate time to the music; and the plump Miss Darlington in her shiny green dress seated at the keyboard of the enormous piano thumping the silent keys with both hands for all she was worth. She recognized the passages where the piano was meant to be silent, and on these occasions she folded her hands primly on her lap and stared straight ahead with a dreamy and enraptured expression on her face. Watching her, Mr Botibol thought that she was particularly wonderful in the slow solo passages of the Second Movement. She allowed her hands to drift smoothly and gently up and down the keys and she inclined her head first to one side, then to the other, and once she closed her eyes for a long time while she played. During the exciting last movement, Mr Botibol himself lost his balance and would have fallen off the platform had he not saved himself by clutching the brass rail. But in spite of everything, the concerto moved on majestically to its mighty conclusion. Then the real clapping came. Mr Botibol walked over and took Miss Darlington by the hand and led her to the edge of the platform, and there they stood, the two of them, bowing, and bowing, and bowing again as the clapping and the shouting of 'encore' continued. Four times they left the stage and came back, and then, the fifth time, Mr Botibol whispered, 'It's you they want. You take this one alone.' 'No,' she said. 'It's you. Please.' But he pushed her forward and she took her call, and came back and said, 'Now you. They want you. Can't you hear them shouting for you?' So Mr Botibol walked alone on to the stage, bowed gravely to right, left and centre and came off just as the clapping stopped altogether.

He led her straight back to the living-room. He was breathing fast and the sweat was pouring down all over his face. She too was a little breathless, and her cheeks were shining red.

'A tremendous performance, Miss Darlington. Allow me to congratulate you.'

'But what a concerto, Mr Botibol! What a superb concerto!'

'You played it perfectly, Miss Darlington. You have a real feeling for my music.' He was wiping the sweat from his face with a handkerchief. 'And tomorrow we perform my Second Concerto.'

'Tomorrow?'

'Of course. Had you forgotten, Miss Darlington? We are booked to appear together for a whole week.'

'Oh ... oh yes ... I'm afraid I had forgotten that.'

'But it's all right, isn't it?' he asked anxiously. 'After hearing you tonight I could not bear to have anyone else play my music.'

'I think it's all right,' she said. 'Yes, I think that'll be all right.' She looked at the clock on the mantelpiece. 'My heavens, it's late! I must go! I'll never get up in the morning to get to work!'

'To work?' Mr Botibol said. 'To work?' Then slowly, reluctantly, he forced himself back to reality. 'Ah yes, to work. Of course, you have to get to work.'

'I certainly do.'

'Where do you work, Miss Darlington?'

'Me? Well,' and now she hesitated a moment, looking at Mr Botibol. 'As a matter of fact I work at the old Academy.'

'I hope it is pleasant work,' he said. 'What Academy is that?'

'I teach the piano.'

Mr Botibol jumped as though someone had stuck him from behind with a hatpin. His mouth opened very wide.

'It's quite all right,' she said, smiling. 'I've always wanted to be Horowitz. And could I, do you think could I please be Schnabel tomorrow?'

VENGEANCE IS MINE INC.

It was snowing when I woke up.

I could tell that it was snowing because there was a kind of brightness in the room and it was quiet outside with no footstep-noises coming up from the street and no tyre-noises but only the engines of the cars. I looked up and I saw George over by the window in his green dressing-gown, bending over the paraffin-stove, making the coffee.

'Snowing,' I said.

'It's cold,' George answered. 'It's really cold.'

I got out of bed and fetched the morning paper from outside the door. It was cold all right and I ran back quickly and jumped into bed and lay still for a while under the bedclothes, holding my hands tight between my legs for warmth.

'No letters?' George said.

'No. No letters.'

'Doesn't look as if the old man's going to cough up.'

'Maybe he thinks four hundred and fifty is enough for one month,' I said.

'He's never been to New York. He doesn't know the cost of living here.'

'You shouldn't have spent it all in one week.'

George stood up and looked at me. '*We* shouldn't have spent it, you mean.'

'That's right,' I said. 'We.' I began reading the paper.

The coffee was ready now and George brought the pot over and put it on the table between our beds. 'A person can't live without money,' he said. 'The old man ought to know that.' He got back into his bed without taking off his green dressing-gown. I went on reading. I finished the racing page and the football page and then I started on Lionel Pantaloon, the great political and society columnist. I always read Pantaloon – same as the other twenty or thirty million people in the country. He's a habit with me; he's more than a habit; he's a part of my morning, like three cups of coffee, or shaving.

'This fellow's got a nerve,' I said.

'Who?'

'This Lionel Pantaloon.'

'What's he saying now?'

'Same sort of thing he's always saying. Same sort of scandal. Always about the rich. Listen to this: "... seen at the Penguin Club ... banker William S. Womberg with beauteous starlet Theresa Williams ... three nights running ... Mrs Womberg at home with a headache ... which is something anyone's wife would have if hubby was out squiring Miss Williams of an evening ..."'

'That fixes Womberg.' George said.

'I think it's a shame,' I said. 'That sort of thing could cause a divorce. How can this Pantaloon get away with stuff like that?'

'He always does, they're all scared of him. But if I was William S. Womberg,' George said, 'you know what I'd do? I'd go right out and punch this Lionel Pantaloon right on the nose. Why, that's the only way to handle those guys.'

'Mr Womberg couldn't do that.'

'Why not?'

'Because he's an old man,' I said. 'Mr Womberg is a dignified and respectable old man. He's a very prominent banker in the town. He couldn't possibly ...'

And then it happened. Suddenly, from nowhere, the idea came. It came to me right in the middle of what I was saying to George and I stopped short and I could feel the idea itself kind of flowing into my brain and I kept very quiet and let it come and it kept on coming and almost before I knew what had happened I had it all, the whole plan, the whole brilliant magnificent plan worked out clearly in my head; and right then I knew it was a beauty.

I turned and I saw George staring at me with a look of wonder on his face. 'What's wrong?' he said. 'What's the matter?'

I kept quite calm. I reached out and got some more coffee before I allowed myself to speak.

'George,' I said, and I still kept calm. 'I have an idea. Now listen very carefully because I have an idea which will make us both very rich. We are broke, are we not?'

'We are.'

'And this William S. Womberg,' I said, 'would you consider that he is angry with Lionel Pantaloon this morning?'

'Angry!' George shouted. 'Angry! Why, he'll be madder than hell!'

'Quite so. And do you think that he would like to see Lionel Pantaloon receive a good hard punch on the nose?'

'Damn right he would!'

'And now tell me, is it not possible that Mr Womberg would be prepared to pay a sum of money to someone who would undertake to perform this nose-punching operation efficiently and discreetly on his behalf?'

George turned and looked at me, and gently, carefully, he put down his coffee-cup on the table. A slowly widening smile began to spread across his face. 'I get you,' he said. 'I get the idea.'

'That's just a little part of the idea. If you read Pantaloon's column here you will see that there is another person who has been insulted today.' I picked up the paper. 'There is a Mrs Ella Gimple, a prominent socialite who has perhaps a million dollars in the bank ...'

'What does Pantaloon say about her?'

I looked at the paper again. 'He hints,' I answered, 'at how she makes a stack of money out of her own friends by throwing roulette parties and acting as the bank.'

'That fixes Gimple,' George said. 'And Womberg. Gimple and Womberg.' He was sitting up straight in bed waiting for me to go on.

'Now,' I said, 'we have two different people both loathing Lionel Pantaloon's guts this morning, both wanting desperately to go out and punch him on the nose, and neither of them daring to do it. You understand that?'

'Absolutely.'

'So much then,' I said, 'for Lionel Pantaloon. But don't forget that there are others like him. There are dozens of other columnists who spend their time insulting wealthy and important people. There's Harry Weyman, Claude Taylor, Jacob Swinski, Walter Kennedy, and all the rest of them.'

'That's right,' George said. 'That's absolutely right.'

'I'm telling you, there's nothing that makes the rich so furious as being mocked and insulted in the newspapers.'

'Go on,' George said. 'Go on.'

'All right. Now this is the plan.' I was getting rather excited myself. I was leaning over the side of the bed, resting one hand on the little table, waving the other about in the air as I spoke. 'We will set up immediately an organization and we will call it ... what shall we call it ... we will call it ... let me see ... we will call it "Vengeance Is Mine Inc." ... How about that?'

'Peculiar name.'

'It's biblical. It's good. I like it. "Vengeance Is Mine Inc." It sounds fine. And we will have little cards printed which we will send to all our clients reminding them that they have been insulted and mortified in public and offering to punish the offender in consideration of a sum of money. We will buy all the newspapers and read all the columnists and every day we will send out a dozen or more of our cards to prospective clients.'

'It's marvellous!' George shouted. 'It's terrific!'

'We shall be rich,' I told him. 'We shall be exceedingly wealthy in no time at all.'

'We must start at once!'

I jumped out of bed, fetched a writing-pad and a pencil and ran back to bed again. 'Now,' I said, pulling my knees under the blankets and propping the writing-pad against them, 'the first thing is to decide what we're going to say on the printed cards which we'll be sending to our clients,' and I wrote, 'VENGEANCE IS MINE INC.' as a heading on top of the sheet of paper. Then, with much care, I composed a finely phrased letter explaining the functions of the organization. It finished up with the following sentence: '*Therefore VENGEANCE IS MINE INC. will undertake, on your behalf and in absolute confidence, to administer suitable punishment to columnist .... and in this regard we respectfully submit to you a choice of methods (together with prices) for your consideration.*'

'What do you mean, "a choice of methods"?' George said.

'We must give them a choice. We must think up a number of things ... a number of different punishments. Number one will be ...' and I wrote down, '*1. Punch him on the nose, once, hard.*' 'What shall we charge for that?'

'Five hundred dollars,' George said instantly.

I wrote it down. 'What's the next one?'

'Black his eye,' George said.

I wrote it down, '*2. Black his eye ... $500.*'

'No!' George said. 'I disagree with the price. It definitely requires more skill and timing to black an eye nicely than to punch a nose. It is a skilled job. It should be six hundred.'

'OK,' I said. 'Six hundred. And what's the next one?'

'Both together, of course. The old one two.' We were in George's territory now. This was right up his street.

'Both together?'

'Absolutely. Punch his nose *and* black his eye. Eleven hundred dollars.'

'There should be a reduction for taking the two,' I said. 'We'll make it a thousand.'

'It's dirt cheap,' George said. 'They'll snap it up.'

'What's next?'

We were both silent now, concentrating fiercely. Three deep parallel grooves of wrinkled skin appeared upon George's rather low sloping forehead. He began to scratch his scalp, slowly but very strongly. I looked away and tried to think of all the terrible things which people had done to other people. Finally I got one, and with George watching the point of my pencil moving over the paper, I wrote: '*4. Put a rattlesnake (with venom extracted) on the floor of his car, by the pedals, when he parks it.*'

'Jesus Christ!' George whispered. 'You want to kill him with fright!'

'Sure,' I said.

'And where'd you get a rattlesnake, anyway?'

'Buy it. You can always buy them. How much shall we charge for that one?'

'Fifteen hundred dollars,' George said firmly. I wrote it down. 'Now we need one more.'

'Here it is,' George said. 'Kidnap him in a car, take all his clothes away except his underpants and his shoes and socks, then dump him out on Fifth Avenue in the rush hour.' He smiled, a broad triumphant smile.

'We can't do that.'

'Write it down. And charge two thousand five hundred bucks. You'd do it all right if old Womberg were to offer you that much.'

'Yes,' I said. 'I suppose I would.' And I wrote it down. 'That's enough now,' I added. 'That gives them a wide choice.'

'And where will we get the card printed?' George asked.

'George Karnoffsky,' I said. 'Another George. He's a friend of mine. Runs a small printing shop down on Third Avenue. Does wedding invitations and things like that for the big stores. He'll do it. I know he will.'

'Then what are we waiting for?'

We both leapt out of bed and began to dress. 'It's twelve o'clock,' I said. 'If we hurry we'll catch him before he goes to lunch.'

It was still snowing when we went out into the street and the snow was four or five inches thick on the sidewalk, but we covered the fourteen blocks to Karnoffsky's shop at a tremendous pace and we arrived there just as he was putting on his coat to go out.

'Claude!' he shouted. 'Hi boy! How you been keeping,' and he pumped my hand. He had a fat friendly face and a terrible nose with great wide-open nose-wings which overlapped his cheeks by at least an inch on either side. I greeted him and told him that we had come to discuss some most urgent business. He took off his coat and led us back into the office, then I began to tell him about our plans and what we wanted him to do.

When I'd got about quarter way through my story, he started to roar with laughter and it was impossible for me to continue; so I cut it short and handed him the piece of paper with the stuff on it that we wanted him to print. And now, as he read it, his whole body began to shake with laughter and he kept slapping the desk with his hand and coughing and choking and roaring like someone crazy. We sat watching him. We didn't see anything particular to laugh about.

Finally he quietened down and he took out a handkerchief and made a great business about wiping his eyes. 'Never laughed so much,' he said weakly. 'That's a great joke, that is. Its worth a lunch. Come on out and I'll give you lunch.'

'Look,' I said severely, 'this isn't any joke. There is nothing to laugh at. You are witnessing the birth of a new and powerful organization ...'

'Come on,' he said and he began to laugh again. 'Come on and have lunch.'

'When can you get those cards printed?' I said. My voice was stern and businesslike.

He paused and stared at us. 'You mean ... you really mean ... you're serious about this thing?'

'Absolutely. You are witnessing the birth ...'

'All right,' he said, 'all right,' he stood up. 'I think you're crazy and you'll get in trouble. Sure as hell you'll get in trouble. Those boys like messing other people about, but they don't much fancy being messed about themselves.'

'When can you get them printed, and without any of your workers reading them?'

'For this,' he answered gravely, 'I will give up my lunch. I will set the type myself. It is the least I can do.' He laughed again and the rims of his huge nostrils twitched with pleasure. 'How many do you want?'

'A thousand – to start with, and envelopes.'

'Come back at two o'clock,' he said and I thanked him very much and as we went out we could hear his laughter rumbling down the passage into the back of the shop.

At exactly two o'clock we were back. George Karnoffsky was in his office and the first thing I saw as we went in was the high stack of printed cards on his desk in front of him. They were large cards, about twice the size of ordinary wedding or cocktail invitation-cards. 'There you are,' he said. 'All ready for you.' The fool was still laughing.

He handed us each a card and I examined mine carefully. It was a beautiful thing. He had obviously taken much trouble over it. The card itself was thick and stiff with narrow gold edging all the way around, and the letters of the heading were exceedingly elegant. I cannot reproduce it here in all its splendour, but I can at least show you how it read:

VENGEANCE IS MINE INC.

Dear.......................

You have probably seen columnist ....'s slanderous and unprovoked attack upon your character in today's paper. It is an outrageous insinuation, a deliberate distortion of the truth.

Are you yourself prepared to allow this miserable malice-monger to insult you in this manner without doing anything about it?

The whole world knows that it is foreign to the nature of the American people to permit themselves to be insulted either in public or in private without rising up in righteous indignation and demanding – nay, exacting – a just measure of retribution.

On the other hand, it is only natural that a citizen of your standing and reputation will not wish *personally* to become further involved in this sordid petty affair, or indeed to have any *direct* contact whatsoever with this vile person.

How then are you to obtain satisfaction?

The answer is simple, VENGEANCE IS MINE INC. will obtain it for you. We will undertake, on your behalf and in absolute confidence, to administer individual punishment to columnist ...., and in this regard we respectfully submit to you a choice of methods (together with prices) for your consideration:

1. Punch him on the nose, once, hard $500
2. Black his eye $600
3. Punch him on the nose and black his eye $1000
4. Introduce a rattlesnake (with venom extracted) into
   his car, on the floor by the pedals, when he parks it $1500
5. Kidnap him, take all his clothes away except his
   underpants, his shoes and socks, then dump him out
   on Fifth Ave. in the rush hour $2500

This work executed by a professional.

If you desire to avail yourself of any of these offers, kindly reply to VENGEANCE IS MINE INC. at the address indicated upon the enclosed slip of paper. If it is practicable, you will be notified in advance of the place where the action will occur and of the time, so that you may, if you wish, watch the proceedings in person from a safe and anonymous distance.

No payment need be made until after your order has been satisfactorily executed, when an account will be rendered in the usual manner.

George Karnoffsky had done a beautiful job of printing.

'Claude,' he said, 'you like?'

'It's marvellous.'

'It's the best I could do for you. It's like in the war when I would see soldiers going off perhaps to get killed and all the time I would want to be giving them things and doing things for them.' He was beginning to laugh again, so I said, 'We'd better be going now. Have you got large envelopes for these cards?'

'Everything is here. And you can pay me when the money starts coming in.' That seemed to set him off worse than ever and he collapsed into his chair, giggling like a fool. George and I hurried out of the shop into the street, into the cold snow-falling afternoon.

We almost ran the distance back to our room and on the way up I borrowed a Manhattan telephone directory from the public telephone in the hall. We found 'Womberg, William S,' without any trouble and while I read out the address – somewhere up in the East Nineties – George wrote it on one of the envelopes.

'Gimple, Mrs Ella H,' was also in the book and we addressed an envelope to her as well. 'We'll just send to Womberg and Gimple today,' I said. 'We haven't really got started yet. Tomorrow we'll send a dozen.'

'We'd better catch the next post,' George said.

'We'll deliver them by hand,' I told him. 'Now, at once. The sooner they get them the better. Tomorrow might be too late. They won't be half so angry tomorrow as they are today. People are apt to cool off through the night. See here,' I said, 'you go ahead and deliver those two cards right away. While you're doing that I'm going to snoop around the town and try to find out something about the habits of Lionel Pantaloon. See you back here later in the evening ...'

At about nine o'clock that evening I returned and found George lying on his bed smoking cigarettes and drinking coffee.

'I delivered them both,' he said. 'Just slipped them through the letter-boxes and rang the bells and beat it up the street. Womberg had a huge house, a huge white house. How did you get on?'

'I went to see a man I know who works in the sports section of the *Daily Mirror*. He told me all.'

'What did he tell you?'

'He said Pantaloon's movements are more or less routine. He operates at night, but wherever he goes earlier in the evening, he *always* – and this is the important point – he *always* finishes up at the Penguin Club. He gets there round about midnight and stays until two or two-thirty. That's when his legmen bring him all the dope.'

'That's all we want to know,' George said happily.

'It's too easy.'

'Money for old rope.'

There was a full bottle of blended whisky in the cupboard and George fetched it out. For the next two hours we sat upon our beds drinking the whisky and making wonderful and complicated plans for the development of our organization. By eleven o'clock we were employing a staff of fifty, including twelve famous pugilists, and our offices were in Rockefeller Center. Towards midnight we had obtained control over all columnists and were dictating their daily columns to them by telephone from our headquarters, taking care to insult and infuriate at least twenty rich persons in one part of the country or another every day. We were immensely wealthy and George had a British Bentley, I had five Cadillacs. George kept practising telephone talks with Lionel Pantaloon. 'That you, Pantaloon?' 'Yes, sir.' 'Well, listen here. I think your column stinks today. It's lousy.' 'I'm very sorry, sir. I'll try to do better tomorrow.' 'Damn right you'll do better, Pantaloon. Matter of fact we've been thinking about getting someone else to take over.' 'But please, please sir, just give me another chance.' 'OK, Pantaloon, but this is the last. And by the way, the boys are putting a rattlesnake in your car tonight, on behalf of Mr Hiram C. King, the soap manufacturer. Mr King will be watching from across the street so don't forget to act scared when you see it.' 'Yes, sir, of course, sir. I won't forget, sir ...'

When we finally went to bed and the light was out, I could still hear George giving hell to Pantaloon on the telephone.

The next morning we were both woken up by the church clock on the corner striking nine. George got up and went to the door to get the papers and when he came back he was holding a letter in his hand.

'Open it!' I said.

He opened it and carefully he unfolded a single sheet of thin notepaper.

'Read it!' I shouted.

He began to read it aloud, his voice low and serious at first but rising gradually to a high, almost hysterical shout of triumph as the full meaning of the letter was revealed to him. It said:

'*Your methods appear curiously unorthodox. At the same time anything you do to that scoundrel has my approval. So go ahead. Start with Item 1, and if you are successful I'll be only too glad to give you an order to work right on through the list. Send the bill to me. William S. Womberg.*'

I recollect that in the excitement of the moment we did a kind of dance around the room in our pyjamas, praising Mr Womberg in loud voices and singing that we were rich. George turned somersaults on his bed and it is possible that I did the same.

'When shall we do it?' he said. 'Tonight?'

I paused before replying. I refused to be rushed. The pages of history are filled with the names of great men who have come to grief by permitting themselves to make hasty decisions in the excitement of a moment. I put on my dressing-gown, lit a cigarette and began to pace up and down the room. 'There is no hurry,' I said. 'Womberg's order can be dealt with in due course. But first of all we must send out today's cards.'

I dressed quickly, went out to the newsstand across the street, bought one copy of every daily paper there was and returned to our room. The next two hours was spent in reading the columnists' columns, and in the end we had a list of eleven people – eight men and three women – all of whom had been insulted in one way or another by one of the columnists that morning. Things were going well. We were working smoothly. It took us only another half hour to look up the addresses of the insulted ones – two we couldn't find – and to address the envelopes.

In the afternoon we delivered them, and at about six in the evening we got back to our room, tired but triumphant. We made coffee and we fried hamburgers and we had supper in bed. Then we re-read Womberg's letter aloud to each other many many times.

'What he's doing he's giving us an order for six thousand one hundred dollars,' George said. 'Items 1 to 5 inclusive.'

'It's not a bad beginning. Not bad for the first day. Six thousand a day works out at ... let me see ... it's nearly two million dollars a year, not counting Sundays. A million each. It's more than Betty Grable.'

'We are very wealthy people,' George said. He smiled, a slow and wondrous smile of pure contentment.

'In a day or two we will move to a suite of rooms at the St Regis.'

'I think the Waldorf,' George said.

'All right, the Waldorf. And later on we might as well take a house.'

'One like Womberg's?'

'All right. One like Womberg's. But first,' I said, 'we have work to do. Tomorrow we shall deal with Pantaloon. We will catch him as he comes out of the Penguin Club. At two-thirty a.m. we will be waiting for him, and when he comes out into the street you will step forward and you will punch him once, hard, right upon the point of the nose as per contract.'

'It will be a pleasure,' George said. 'It will be a real pleasure. But how do we get away? Do we run?'

'We shall hire a car for an hour. We have just enough money left for that, and I shall be sitting at the wheel with the engine running, not ten yards away, and the door will be open and when you've punched him you'll just jump back into the car and we'll be gone.'

'It is perfect. I shall punch him very hard.' George paused. He clenched his right fist and examined his knuckles. Then he smiled again and he said slowly, 'This nose of his, is it not possible that it will afterwards be so much blunted that it will no longer poke well into other peoples' business?'

'It is quite possible,' I answered, and with that happy thought in our minds we switched out the light and went early to sleep.

The next morning I was woken by a shout and I sat up and saw George standing at the foot of my bed in his pyjamas, waving his arms. 'Look!' he shouted, 'there are four! There are four!' I looked, and indeed there were four letters in his hand.

'Open them. Quickly, open them.'

The first one he read aloud: '"*Dear Vengeance Is Mine Inc., That's the best proposition I've had in years. Go right ahead and give Mr Jacob Swinski the rattlesnake treatment (Item 4). But I'll be glad to pay double if you'll forget to extract the poison from its fangs. Yours Gertrude Porter-Vandervelt. PS You'd better insure the snake. That guy's bite carries more poison than any rattler's."'*

George read the second one aloud: *"'My cheque for $500 is made out and lies before me on my desk. The moment I receive proof that you have punched Lionel Pantaloon hard on the nose, it will be posted to you, I should prefer a fracture, if possible. Yours etc. Wilbur H. Gollogly."'*

George read the third one aloud: *"'In my present frame of mind and against my better judgement, I am tempted to reply to your card and to request that you deposit that scoundrel Walter Kennedy upon Fifth Avenue dressed only in his underwear. I make the proviso that there shall be snow upon the ground at the time and that the temperature shall be sub-zero. H. Gresham."'*

The fourth one also he read aloud: *"'A good hard sock on the nose for Pantaloon is worth five hundred of mine or anyone else's money. I should like to watch. Yours sincerely, Claudia Calthorpe Hines."'*

George laid the letters down gently, carefully upon the bed. For a while there was silence. We stared at each other, too astonished, too happy to speak. I began to calculate the value of those four orders in terms of money.

'That's five thousand dollars worth,' I said softly.

Upon George's face there was a huge bright grin. 'Claude,' he said, 'should we not move now to the Waldorf?'

'Soon,' I answered, 'but at the moment we have no time for moving. We have not even time to send out any fresh cards today. We must start to execute the orders we have in hand. We are overwhelmed with work.'

'Should we not engage extra staff and enlarge our organization?'

'Later,' I said. 'Even for that there is no time today. Just think what we have to do. We have to put a rattlesnake in Jacob Swinski's car ... we have to dump Walter Kennedy on Fifth Avenue in his underpants ... we have to punch Pantaloon on the nose ... let me see ... yes, for three different people we have to punch Pantaloon ...'

I stopped. I closed my eyes. I sat still. Again I became conscious of a small clear stream of inspiration flowing into the tissues of my brain. 'I have it!' I shouted. 'I have it! I have it! Three birds with one stone! Three customers with one punch!'

'How?'

'Don't you see? We only need to punch Pantaloon once and each of the three customers ... Womberg, Gollogly and Claudia Hines ... will think it's being done specially for him or her.'

'Say it again.' I said it again.

'It's brilliant.'

'It's common-sense. And the same principle will apply to the others. The rattlesnake treatment and the other one can wait until we have more orders. Perhaps in a few days we shall have ten orders for rattlesnakes in Swinski's car. Then we will do them all in one go.'

'It's wonderful.'

'This evening then,' I said, 'we will handle Pantaloon. But first we must hire a car. Also we must send telegrams, one to Womberg, one to Gollogly and one to Claudia Hines, telling them where and when the punching will take place.'

We dressed rapidly and went out.

In a dirty silent little garage down on East 9th Street we managed to hire a car, a 1934 Chevrolet, eight dollars for the evening. We then sent three telegrams, each one identical and cunningly worded to conceal its true meaning from inquisitive people: *'Hope to see you outside Penguin Club two-thirty a.m. Regards V.I.Mine.'*

'There is one thing more,' I said. 'It is essential that you should be disguised. Pantaloon, or the doorman, for example, must not be able to identify you afterwards. You must wear a false moustache.'

'What about you?'

'Not necessary. I'll be sitting in the car. They won't see me.'

We went to a children's toy-shop and we bought for George a magnificent black moustache, a thing with long pointed ends, waxed and stiff and shining, and when he held it up against his face he looked exactly like the Kaiser of Germany. The man in the shop also sold us a tube of glue and he showed us how the moustache should be attached to the upper lip. 'Going to have fun with the kids?' he asked, and George said, 'Absolutely.'

All was now ready, but there was a long time to wait. We had three dollars left between us and with this we bought a sandwich each and then went to a movie. Then, at eleven o'clock that evening, we collected our car and in it we began to cruise slowly through the streets of New York waiting for the time to pass.

'You'd better put on your moustache so as you get used to it.'

We pulled up under a street lamp and I squeezed some glue on to George's upper lip and fixed on the huge black hairy thing with its pointed ends. Then we drove on. It was cold in the car and outside it was beginning to snow again. I could see a few small snowflakes falling through the beams of the car-lights. George kept saying, 'How hard shall I hit him?' and I kept answering, 'Hit him as hard as you can, and on the nose. It must be on the nose because that is a part of the contract. Everything must be done right. Our clients may be watching.'

At two in the morning we drove slowly past the entrance to the Penguin Club in order to survey the situation. 'I will park there,' I said, 'just past the entrance in that patch of dark. But I will leave the door open for you.'

We drove on. Then George said, 'What does he look like? How do I know it's him?'

'Don't worry,' I answered. 'I've thought of that,' and I took from my pocket a piece of paper and handed it to him. 'You take this and fold it up small and give it to the doorman and tell him to see it gets to Pantaloon quickly. Act as though you are scared to death and in an awful hurry. It's a hundred to one Pantaloon will come out. No columnist could resist that message.'

On the paper I had written: '*I am a worker in Soviet Consulate. Come to the door very quickly please I have something to tell but come quickly as I am in danger. I cannot come in to you.*'

'You see,' I said, 'your moustache will make you look like a Russian. All Russians have big moustaches.'

George took the paper and folded it up very small and held it in his fingers. It was nearly half past two in the morning now and we began to drive towards the Penguin Club.

'You all set?' I said.

'Yes.'

'We're going in now. Here we come. I'll park just past the entrance ... here. Hit him hard,' I said, and George opened the door and got out of the car. I closed the door behind him but I leant over and kept my hand on the handle so I could open it again quick, and I let down the window so I could watch. I kept the engine ticking over.

I saw George walk swiftly up to the doorman who stood under the red and white canopy which stretched out over the sidewalk. I saw the doorman turn and look down at George and I didn't like the way he did it. He was a tall proud man dressed in a fine magenta-coloured uniform with gold buttons and gold shoulders and a broad white stripe down each magenta trouser-leg. Also he wore white gloves and he stood there looking proudly down at George, frowning, pressing his lips together hard. He was looking at George's moustache and I thought Oh my God we have overdone it. We have over-disguised him. He's going to know it's false and he's going to take one of the long pointed ends in his fingers and then he'll give it a tweak and it'll come off. But he didn't. He was distracted by George's acting, for George was acting well. I could see him hopping about, clasping and unclasping his hands, swaying his body and shaking his head, and I could hear him saying, 'Plees plees plees you must hurry. It is life and teth. Plees plees take it kvick to Mr Pantaloon.' His Russian accent was not like any accent I had heard before, but all the same there was a quality of real despair in his voice.

Finally, gravely, proudly, the doorman said, 'Give me the note.' George gave it to him and said, 'Tank you, tank you, but say it is urgent,' and the doorman disappeared inside. In a few moments he returned and said, 'It's being delivered now.' George paced nervously up and down. I waited, watching the door. Three or four minutes elapsed. George wrung his hands and said, 'Vere is he? Vere is he? Plees to go see if he is not coming!'

'What's the matter with you?' the doorman said. Now he was looking at George's moustache again.

'It is life and teth! Mr Pantaloon can help! He must come!'

'Why don't you shut up,' the doorman said, but he opened the door again and he poked his head inside and I heard him saying something to someone.

To George he said, 'They say he's coming now.'

A moment later the door opened and Pantaloon himself, small and dapper, stepped out. He paused by the door, looking quickly from side to side like a nervous inquisitive ferret. The doorman touched his cap and pointed at George. I heard Pantaloon say, 'Yes, what did you want?'

George said, 'Plees, dis vay a leetle so as novone can hear,' and he led Pantaloon along the pavement, away from the doorman and towards the car.

'Come on, now,' Pantaloon said. 'What is it you want?'

Suddenly George shouted 'Look!' and he pointed up the street. Pantaloon turned his head and as he did so George swung his right arm and he hit Pantaloon plumb on the point of the nose. I saw George leaning forward on the punch, all his weight behind it, and the whole of Pantaloon appeared somehow to lift slightly off the ground and to float backwards for two or three feet until the façade of the Penguin Club stopped him. All this happened very quickly, and then George was in the car beside me and we were off and I could hear the doorman blowing a whistle behind us.

'We've done it!' George gasped. He was excited and out of breath. 'I hit him good! Did you see how good I hit him!'

It was snowing hard now and I drove fast and made many sudden turnings and I knew no one would catch us in this snowstorm.

'Son of a bitch almost went through the wall I hit him so hard.'

'Well done, George,' I said. 'Nice work, George.'

'And did you see him lift? Did you see him lift right up off the ground?'

'Womberg will be pleased,' I said.

'And Gollogly, and the Hines woman.'

'They'll all be pleased,' I said. 'Watch the money coming in.'

'There's a car behind us!' George shouted. 'It's following us! It's right on our tail! Drive like mad!'

'Impossible!' I said. 'They couldn't have picked us up already. It's just another car going somewhere.' I turned sharply to the right.

'He's still with us,' George said. 'Keep turning. We'll lose him soon.'

'How the hell can we lose a police-car in a nineteen thirty-four Chev,' I said. 'I'm going to stop.'

'Keep going!' George shouted. 'You're doing fine.'

'I'm going to stop,' I said. 'It'll only make them mad if we go on.'

George protested fiercely but I knew it was no good and I pulled in to the side of the road. The other car swerved out and went past us and skidded to a standstill in front of us.

'Quick,' George said. 'Let's beat it.' He had the door open and he was ready to run.

'Don't be a fool,' I said. 'Stay where you are. You can't get away now.'

A voice from outside said, 'All right boys, what's the hurry?'

'No hurry,' I answered. 'We're just going home.'

'Yea?'

'Oh yes, we're just on our way home now.'

The man poked his head in through the window on my side, and he looked at me, then at George, then at me again.

'It's a nasty night,' George said. 'We're just trying to reach home before the streets get all snowed up.'

'Well,' the man said, 'you can take it easy. I just thought I'd like to give you this right away.' He dropped a wad of banknotes on to my lap. 'I'm Gollogly,' he added, 'Wilbur H. Gollogly,' and he stood out there in the snow grinning at us, stamping his feet and rubbing his hands to keep them warm. 'I got your wire and I watched the whole thing from across the street. You did a fine job. I'm paying you double. It was worth it. Funniest thing I ever seen. Goodbye boys. Watch your steps. They'll be after you now. Get out of town if I were you. Goodbye.' And before we could say anything, he was gone.

When finally we got back to our room I started packing at once.

'You crazy?' George said. 'We've only got to wait a few hours and we receive five hundred dollars each from Womberg and the Hines woman. Then we'll have two thousand altogether and we can go anywhere we want.'

So we spent the next day waiting in our room and reading the papers, one of which had a whole column on the front page headed, 'Brutal assault on famous columnist'. But sure enough the late afternoon post brought us two letters and there was five hundred dollars in each.

And right now, at this moment, we are sitting in a Pullman car, drinking Scotch whisky and heading south for a place where there is always sunshine and where the horses are running every day. We are immensely wealthy and George keeps saying that if we put the whole of our two thousand dollars on a horse at ten to one we shall make another twenty thousand and we will be able to retire. 'We will have a house at Palm Beach,' he says, 'and we will entertain upon a lavish scale. Beautiful socialites will loll around the edge of our swimming pool sipping cool drinks, and after a while we will perhaps put another large sum of money upon another horse and we shall become wealthier still. Possibly we will become tired of Palm Beach and then we will move around in a leisurely manner among the playgrounds of the rich.

Monte Carlo and places like that. Like the Ali Khan and the Duke of Windsor. We will become prominent members of the international set and film stars will smile at us and head-waiters will bow to us and perhaps, in time to come, perhaps we might even get ourselves mentioned in Lionel Pantaloon's column.'

'That would be something,' I said.

'Wouldn't it just,' he answered happily. 'Wouldn't that just be something.'

THE BUTLER

As soon as George Cleaver had made his first million, he and Mrs Cleaver moved out of their small suburban villa into an elegant London house. They acquired a French chef called Monsieur Estragon and an English butler called Tibbs, both wildly expensive. With the help of these two experts, the Cleavers set out to climb the social ladder and began to give dinner parties several times a week on a lavish scale.

But these dinners never seemed quite to come off. There was no animation, no spark to set the conversation alight, no style at all. Yet the food was superb and the service faultless.

'What the heck's wrong with our parties, Tibbs?' Mr Cleaver said to the butler. 'Why don't nobody never loosen up and let themselves go?'

Tibbs inclined his head to one side and looked at the ceiling. 'I hope, sir, you will not be offended if I offer a small suggestion.'

'What is it?'

'It's the wine, sir.'

'What about the wine?'

'Well, sir, Monsieur Estragon serves superb food. Superb food should be accompanied by superb wine. But you serve them a cheap and very odious Spanish red.'

'They why in heaven's name didn't you say so before, you twit?' cried Mr Cleaver. 'I'm not short of money. I'll give them the best flipping wine in the world if that's what they want! What *is* the best wine in the world?'

'Claret, sir,' the butler replied, 'from the greatest *châteaux* in Bordeaux – Lafite, Latour, Haut-Brion, Margaux, Mouton-Rothschild and Cheval Blanc. And from only the very greatest vintage years, which are, in my opinion, 1906, 1914, 1929 and 1945. Cheval Blanc was also magnificent in 1895 and 1921, and Haut-Brion in 1906.'

'Buy them all!' said Mr Cleaver. 'Fill the flipping cellar from top to bottom!'

'I can try, sir,' the butler said. 'But wines like these are extremely rare and cost a fortune.'

'I don't give a hoot what they cost!' said Mr Cleaver. 'Just go out and get them!'

That was easier said than done. Nowhere in England or in France could Tibbs find any wine from 1895, 1906, 1914 or 1921. But he did manage to get hold of some twenty-nines and forty-fives. The bills for these wines were astronomical. They were in fact so huge that even Mr Cleaver began to sit up and take notice. And his interest quickly turned into outright enthusiasm when the butler suggested to him that a knowledge of wine was a very considerable social asset. Mr Cleaver bought books on the subject and read them from cover to cover. He also learned a great deal from Tibbs himself, who taught him, among other things, just how wine should properly be tasted. 'First, sir, you sniff it long and deep, with your nose right inside the top of the glass, like this. Then you take a mouthful and you open your lips a tiny bit and suck in air, letting the air bubble through the wine. Watch me do it. Then you roll it vigorously around your mouth. And finally you swallow it.'

In due course, Mr Cleaver came to regard himself as an expert on wine, and inevitably he turned into a colossal bore. 'Ladies and gentlemen,' he would announce at dinner, holding up his glass, 'this is a Margaux '29! The greatest year of the century! Fantastic bouquet! Smells of cowslips! And notice especially the after taste and how the tiny trace of tannin gives it that glorious astringent quality! Terrific, ain't it?'

The guests would nod and sip and mumble a few praises, but that was all.

'What's the matter with the silly twerps?' Mr Cleaver said to Tibbs after this had gone on for some time. 'Don't none of them appreciate a great wine?'

The butler laid his head to one side and gazed upward. 'I think they *would* appreciate it, sir,' he said, 'if they were able to taste it. But they can't.'

'What the heck d'you mean, they can't taste it?'

'I believe, sir, that you have instructed Monsieur Estragon to put liberal quantities of vinegar in the salad-dressing.'

'What's wrong with that? I like vinegar.'

'Vinegar,' the butler said, 'is the enemy of wine. It destroys the palate. The dressing should be made of pure olive oil and a little lemon juice. Nothing else.'

'Hogwash!' said Mr Cleaver.

'As you wish, sir.'

'I'll say it again, Tibbs. You're talking hogwash. The vinegar don't spoil my palate one bit.'

'You are very fortunate, sir,' the butler murmured, backing out of the room.

That night at dinner, the host began to mock his butler in front of the guests. 'Mister Tibbs,' he said, 'has been trying to tell me I can't taste my wine if I put vinegar in the salad-dressing. Right, Tibbs?'

'Yes, sir,' Tibbs replied gravely.

'And I told him hogwash. Didn't I, Tibbs?'

'Yes, sir.'

'This wine,' Mr Cleaver went on, raising his glass, 'tastes to me exactly like a Château Lafite '45, and what's more it is a Château Lafite '45.'

Tibbs, the butler, stood very still and erect near the sideboard, his face pale. 'If you'll forgive me, sir,' he said, 'that is not a Lafite '45.'

Mr Cleaver swung round in his chair and stared at the butler. 'What the heck d'you mean,' he said. 'There's the empty bottles beside you to prove it!'

These great clarets, being old and full of sediment, were always decanted by Tibbs before dinner. They were served in cut-glass decanters, while the empty bottles, as is the custom, were placed on the sideboard. Right now, two empty bottles of Lafite '45 were standing on the sideboard for all to see.

'The wine you are drinking, sir,' the butler said quietly, 'happens to be that cheap and rather odious Spanish red.'

Mr Cleaver looked at the wine in his glass, then at the butler. The blood was coming to his face now, his skin was turning scarlet. 'You're lying, Tibbs!' he said.

'No sir, I'm not lying,' the butler said. 'As a matter of fact, I have never served you any other wine but Spanish red since I've been here. It seemed to suit you very well.'

'I don't believe him!' Mr Cleaver cried out to his guests. 'The man's gone mad.'

'Great wines,' the butler said, 'should be treated with reverence. It is bad enough to destroy the palate with three or four cocktails before dinner, as you people do, but when you slosh vinegar over your food into the bargain, then you might just as well be drinking dishwater.'

Ten outraged faces around the table stared at the butler. He had caught them off balance. They were speechless.

'This,' the butler said, reaching out and touching one of the empty bottles lovingly with his fingers, 'this is the last of the forty-fives. The twenty-nines have already been finished. But they were glorious wines. Monsieur Estragon and I enjoyed them immensely.'

The butler bowed and walked quite slowly from the room. He crossed the hall and went out of the front door of the house into the street where Monsieur Estragon was already loading their suitcases into the boot of the small car which they owned together.

MY
UNCLE
OSWALD

I

I am beginning, once again, to have an urge to salute my Uncle Oswald. I mean, of course, Oswald Hendryks Cornelius deceased, the connoisseur, the bon vivant, the collector of spiders, scorpions and walking-sticks, the lover of opera, the expert on Chinese porcelain, the seducer of women, and without much doubt the greatest fornicator of all time. Every other celebrated contender for that title is diminished to a point of ridicule when his record is compared with that of my Uncle Oswald. Especially poor old Casanova. He comes out of the contest looking like a man who was suffering from a severe malfunction of his sexual organ.

Fifteen years have passed since I released for publication in 1964 the first small excerpt from Oswald's diaries. I took trouble at the time to select something unlikely to give offence, and that particular episode concerned, if you remember, a harmless and rather frivolous description of coitus between my uncle and a certain female leper in the Sinai Desert.

So far so good. But I waited a full ten years more (1974) before risking the release of a second piece. And once again I was careful to choose something that was, at any rate by Oswald's standards, as nearly as possible suitable for reading by the vicar to Sunday School in the village church. That one dealt with the discovery of a perfume so potent that any man who sniffed it upon a woman was unable to prevent himself from ravishing her on the spot.

No serious litigation resulted from the publication of this little bit of trivia. But there were plenty of repercussions of another kind. I found my mailbox suddenly clogged with letters from hundreds of female readers, all clamouring for a drop of Oswald's magic perfume. Innumerable men also wrote to me with the same request, including a singularly unpleasant African dictator, a British left-wing Cabinet Minister and a Cardinal from the Holy See. A Saudi-Arabian prince offered me an enormous sum in Swiss currency, and a man in a dark suit from the American Central Intelligence Agency called on me one afternoon with a briefcase full of hundred-dollar bills. Oswald's perfume, he told me, could be used to compromise just about every senior Russian statesman and diplomat in the world, and his people wanted to buy the formula.

Unfortunately, I had not one drop of the magic liquid to sell, so there the matter ended.

Today, five years after publication of that perfume story, I have decided to permit the public yet another glimpse into my uncle's life. The section I have chosen comes from Volume XX, written in 1938, when Oswald was forty-three years old and in the prime of life. Many famous names are mentioned in this one, and there is obviously a grave risk that families and friends are going to take offence at some of the things Oswald has to say. I can only pray that those concerned will grant me indulgence and will understand that my motives are pure. For this is a document of considerable scientific and historical importance. It would be a tragedy if it never saw the light of day.

Here then is the extract from Volume XX of the Diaries of Oswald Hendryks Cornelius, word for word as he wrote it:

London, July 1938

Have just returned from a satisfactory visit to the Lagonda works at Staines. W. O. Bentley gave me lunch (salmon from the Usk and a bottle of Montrachet) and we discussed the extras for my new V12. He has promised me a set of horns that will play Mozart's *Son gia mille e Tre* in perfect pitch. Some of you may think this to be a rather childish conceit, but it will serve as a nice incentive to be reminded, every time I press the button, that good old Don Giovanni had by then deflowered 1003 buxom Spanish damsels. I told Bentley that the seats are to be upholstered in fine-grain alligator, and the panelling to be veneered in yew. Why yew? Simply because I prefer the colour and grain of English yew to that of any other wood.

But what a remarkable fellow this W. O. Bentley is. And what a triumph it was for Lagonda when he went over to them. It is somehow sad that this man, having designed and given his name to one of the finest cars in the world, should be forced out of his own company and into the arms of a rival. It means, however, that the new Lagondas are now peerless, and I for one would have no other machine. But this one isn't going to be cheap. It is costing me more thousands than I ever thought it possible to pay for an automobile.

Yet who cares about money? Not me, because I've always had plenty of it. I made my first hundred thousand pounds when I was seventeen and later I was to make a lot more. Having said that, it occurs to me that I have never once throughout these journals made any mention of the manner in which I became a wealthy man.

Perhaps the time has come when I should do this. I think it has. For although these diaries are designed to be a history of the art of seduction and the pleasures of copulation, they would be incomplete without some reference also to the art of money-making and the pleasures attendant thereon.

Very well, then. I have talked myself into it. I shall proceed at once to tell you something about how I set about making money. But just in case some of you may be tempted to skip this particular section and go on to juicier things, let me assure you that there will be juice in plenty dripping from these pages. I wouldn't have it otherwise.

Great wealth, when uninherited, is usually acquired in one of four ways – by chicanery, by talent, by inspired judgement or by luck. Mine was a combination of all four. Listen carefully and you shall see what I mean.

In the year 1912, when I was barely seventeen, I won a scholarship in natural sciences to Trinity College, Cambridge. I was a precocious youth and had taken the exam a year earlier than usual. This meant that I had a twelve-month wait doing nothing because Cambridge would not receive me until I was eighteen. My father therefore decided that I should fill in the time by going to France to learn the language. I myself hoped that I should learn a fair bit more than just the language in that splendid country. Already, you see, I had begun to acquire a taste for rakery and wenching among the London debutantes. Already, also, I was beginning to get a bit bored with these young English girls. They were, I decided, a pretty pithless lot, and I was impatient to sow a few bushels of wild oats in foreign fields. Especially. in France. I had been reliably informed that Parisian females knew a thing or two about the act of lovemaking that their London cousins had never even dreamed of. Copulation, so rumour had it, was in its infancy in England.

On the evening before I was due to depart for France, I gave a small party at our family house in Cheyne Walk. My father and mother had purposely gone out to dinner at seven o'clock so that I might have the place to myself. I had invited a dozen or so friends of both sexes, all of them about my own age, and by nine o'clock we were sitting around making pleasant talk, drinking wine and consuming some excellent boiled mutton and dumplings. The front doorbell rang. I went to answer it, and on the doorstep there stood a middle-aged man with a huge moustache, a magenta complexion and a pigskin suitcase. He introduced himself as Major Grout and asked for my father. I said he was out to dinner. 'Good gracious me,' said Major Grout. 'He has invited me to stay. I'm an old friend.'

'Father must have forgotten,' I said. 'I'm awfully sorry. You had better come in.'

Now I couldn't very well leave the Major alone in the study reading *Punch* while we were having a party in the next room, so I asked him if he'd care to come in and join us. He would indeed. He'd love to join us. So in he came, moustache and all, a beaming jovial old boy who settled down among us quite comfortably despite the fact that he was three times the age of anyone else present. He tucked into the mutton and polished off a whole bottle of claret in the first fifteen minutes.

'Excellent vittles,' he said. 'Is there any more wine?'

I opened another bottle for him, and we all watched with a certain admiration as he proceeded to empty that one as well. His cheeks were swiftly turning from magenta to a very deep purple and his nose seemed to be catching on fire. Halfway through the third bottle, he began to loosen up. He worked, he told us, in the Anglo-Egyptian Sudan and was home on leave. His job had to do with the Sudan Irrigation Service and a very hot and arduous business it was. But fascinating. Lots of fun, y'know. And the wogs weren't too much trouble so long as one kept the old shambok handy all the time.

We sat round him, listening and not a little intrigued by this purple-faced creature from distant lands.

'A great country, the Sudan,' he said. 'It is enormous. It is remote. It is full of mysteries and secrets. Would you like me to tell you about one of the great secrets of the Sudan?'

'Very much, sir,' we said. 'Yes please.'

'One of its great secrets,' he said, tipping another glass of wine down his throat, 'a secret that is known only to a few old timers out there like myself and to the natives, is a little creature called the Sudanese Blister Beetle or to give him his right name, *cantharis vesicatoria sudanii*.'

'You mean a scarab?' I said.

'Certainly not,' he said. 'The Sudanese Blister Beetle is a winged insect, as much a fly as a beetle and is about three-quarters of an inch long. It's very pretty to look at, with a brilliant iridescent shell of golden green.'

'Why is it so secret?' we asked.

'These little beetles,' the Major said, 'are found only in one part of the Sudan. It's an area of about twenty square miles, north of Khartoum, and that's where a tree called the hashab grows. The leaves of the hashab tree are what the beetles feed on. Men spend their whole lives searching for these beetles. Beetle hunters, they are called. They are very sharp-eyed natives who know all there is to know about the haunts and habits of the tiny brutes. And when they catch them, they kill them and dry them in the sun and crunch them up into a fine powder. This powder is greatly prized among the natives who usually keep it in small elaborately carved Beetle Boxes. A tribal chief will have his Beetle Box made of silver.'

'But this powder,' we said, 'what do they do with it?'

'It's not what *they* do with *it*,' the Major said. 'It's what *it* does to *you*. One tiny pinch of that powder is the most powerful aphrodisiac in the world.'

'The Spanish Fly!' someone shouted. 'It's the Spanish Fly!'

'Well not quite,' the Major said, 'but you're on the right track. The common Spanish Fly is found in Spain and Southern Italy. The one I'm talking about is the *Sudanese Fly* and although it's of the same family, it's a different kettle of fish altogether. It is approximately ten times as powerful as the ordinary Spanish Fly. The reaction produced by the little *Sudanese* fellow is so incredibly vicious it is dangerous to use even in small doses.'

'But they do use it?'

'Oh God, yes. Every wog in Khartoum and northwards uses the old Beetle. White men, the ones who know about it, are inclined to leave it alone because it's so damn dangerous.'

'Have *you* used it?' someone asked.

The Major looked up at the questioner and gave a little smile under his enormous moustache. 'We'll come to that in a moment or two, shall we?' he said.

'What does it actually do to you?' one of the girls asked.

'My God,' the Major said, 'what doesn't it do to you? It builds a fire under your genitals. It is both a violent aphrodisiac and a powerful irritant. It not only makes you uncontrollably randy but it also guarantees you an enormous and long-lasting erection at the same time. Could you give me another glass of wine, dear boy?'

I leaped up to fetch more wine. My guests had suddenly become very still. The girls were all staring at the Major, rapt and motionless, their eyes shining like stars. The boys were staring at the girls, watching to see how they would react to these sudden indiscretions. I refilled the Major's glass.

'Your father always kept a decent cellar,' he said. 'And good cigars, too.' He looked up at me, waiting.

'Would you like a cigar, sir?'

'That's very civil of you,' he said.

I went to the dining-room and fetched my father's box of Montecristos. The Major put one in his breast pocket and another in his mouth. 'I will tell you a true story if you like,' he said, 'about myself and the Blister Beetle.'

'Tell us,' we said. 'Go on, sir.'

'You'll like this story,' he said, removing the cigar from his mouth and snapping off the end of it with a thumbnail. 'Who has a match?'

I lit the cigar for him. Clouds of smoke enveloped his head, and through the smoke we could see his face dimly, but dark and soft like some huge over-ripe purple fruit.

'One evening,' he began, 'I was sitting on the verandah of my bungalow way upcountry about fifty miles north of Khartoum. It was hot as hell and I'd had a hard day. I was drinking a strong whiskey and soda. It was my first that evening and I was lying back in the deckchair with my feet resting on the little balustrade that ran round the verandah. I could feel the whiskey hitting the lining of my stomach and I can promise you there is no greater sensation at the end of a long day in a fierce climate than when you feel that first whiskey hitting your stomach and going through into the bloodstream. A few minutes later, I went indoors and got myself a second drink, then I returned to the verandah. I lay back again in the deckchair. My shirt was soaked with sweat but I was too tired to take a shower. Then all of a sudden I went rigid. I was just about to put the glass of whiskey to my lips and my hand froze, it literally froze in mid-air and there it stayed with my fingers clenched around the glass. I couldn't move. I couldn't even speak. I tried to call out to my boy for help but I couldn't. Rigor mortis. Paralysis. My entire body had turned to stone.'

'Were you frightened?' someone asked.

'Of course I was frightened,' the Major said. 'I was bloody terrified, especially out there in the Sudan desert miles from anywhere. But the paralysis didn't last very long. Maybe a minute, maybe two. I don't really know. But when I came to, as it were, the first thing I noticed was a burning sensation in the region of my groin. "Hullo," I said, "what the hell's going on now?" But it was pretty obvious what was going on. The activity inside my trousers was becoming very violent indeed and within another few seconds my member was as stiff and erect as the mainmast of a topsail schooner.'

'What do you mean, your *member*?' asked a girl whose name was Gwendoline.

'I expect you will catch on as we go along, my dear,' the Major said.

'Carry on, Major,' we said. 'What happened next?'

'Then it started to throb,' he said.

'What started to throb?' Gwendoline asked him.

'My member,' the Major said. 'I could feel every beat of my heart all the way along it. Pulsing and throbbing most terribly it was, and as tight as a balloon. You know those long sausage-shaped balloons children have at parties? I kept thinking about one of those, and with every beat of my heart it felt as if someone was pumping in more air and it was going to burst.'

The Major drank some wine. Then he studied the ash on his cigar. We sat still, waiting.

'So of course I began trying to puzzle out what might have happened,' he went on. 'I looked at my glass of whiskey. It was where I always put it, on top of the little white-painted balustrade surrounding the verandah. Then my eye travelled upward to the roof of the bungalow and to the edge of the roof and suddenly, presto! I'd got it! I knew for certain what must have happened.'

'What?' we said, all speaking at once.

'A large Blister Beetle, taking an evening stroll on the roof, had ventured too close to the edge and had fallen off.'

'Right into your glass of whiskey!' we cried.

'Precisely,' the Major said. 'And I, thirsting like mad in the heat, had gulped him down without looking.'

The girl called Gwendoline was staring at the Major with huge eyes. 'Quite honestly I don't see what all the fuss was about,' she said. 'One teeny weeny little beetle isn't going to hurt anyone.'

'My dear child,' the Major said, 'when the Blister Beetle is dried and crushed the resulting powder is called cantharidin. That's its pharmaceutical name. The Sudanese variety is called *cantharidin sudanii*. And this *cantharidin sudanii* is absolutely deadly. The maximum safe dose for a human, if there is such a thing as a safe dose, is one minim. A minim is *one-sixtieth* of a fluid ounce. Assuming I had just swallowed one whole fully grown Blister Beetle, that meant I'd received God knows how many hundreds of times the maximum dose.'

'Jesus,' we said. 'Jesus Christ.'

'The throbbing was so tremendous now, it was shaking my whole body,' the Major said.

'A headache, you mean?' Gwendoline said.

'No,' the Major said.

'What happened next?' we asked him.

'My member,' the Major said, 'was now like a white-hot rod of iron burning into my body. I leapt from my chair and rushed to my car and drove like a madman for the nearest hospital, which was in Khartoum. I got there in forty minutes flat. I was scared fartless.'

'Now wait just a minute,' the Gwendoline creature said. 'I'm still not quite following you. Exactly why were you so frightened?'

What a dreadful girl. I should never have invited her. The Major, to his great credit, ignored her completely this time.

'I dashed into the hospital,' he went on, 'and found the casualty room where an English doctor was stitching up somebody's knife wound. "Look at this!" I cried, taking it out and waving it at him.'

'Waving *what* at him, for heaven's sake?' the awful Gwendoline asked.

'Shut up, Gwendoline,' I said.

'Thank you,' the Major said. 'The doctor stopped stitching and regarded the object I was holding out to him with some alarm. I quickly told him my story. He looked glum. There was no antidote for Blister Beetle, he informed me. I was in grave trouble. But he would do his best. So they stomach-pumped me and put me to bed and packed ice all around my poor throbbing member.'

'Who did?' someone asked. 'Who's they?'

'A nurse,' the Major answered. 'A young Scottish nurse with dark hair. She brought the ice in small rubber bags and packed it round and kept the bags in place with a bandage.'

'Didn't you get frostbite?'

'You can't get frostbite on something that's practically red-hot,' the Major said.

'What happened next?'

'They kept changing the ice every three hours day and night.'

'Who, the Scottish nurse?'

'They took it in turns. Several nurses.'

'Good God.'

'It took two weeks to subside.'

'Two weeks!' I said. 'Were you all right afterwards, sir? Are you all right now?'

The Major smiled and took another sip of wine. 'I am deeply touched,' he said, 'by your concern. You are obviously a young man who knows what comes first in this world, and what comes second. I think you will go far.'

'Thank you, sir,' I said. 'But what happened in the end?'

'I was out of action for six months,' the Major said, smiling wanly, 'but that is no hardship in the Sudan. Yes, if you want to know, I'm all right now. I made a miraculous recovery.'

That was the story Major Grout had told us at my little party on the eve of my departure for France. And it set me thinking. It set me thinking very deeply indeed. In fact, that night, as I lay in bed with my bags all packed on the floor, a tremendously daring plan began rapidly to evolve in my head. I say 'daring' because, by God, it damn well was daring when you consider I was only seventeen years old at the time. Looking back on it now, I take my hat off to myself for even contemplating that sort of action. But the following morning my mind was made up.

2

I bade farewell to my parents on the platform at Victoria Station and boarded the boat train for Paris. I arrived that afternoon and checked in at the house where my father had arranged for me to board. It was on the Avenue Marceau, and the family, who were called Boisvain, took paying guests. Monsieur Boisvain was a civil servant of sorts and as unremarkable as the rest of his breed. His wife, a pale woman with short fingers and a flaccid rump, was in much the same mould as her husband, and I guessed that neither of them would give me any trouble. They had two daughters: Jeanette, aged fifteen, and Nicole who was nineteen. Mademoiselle Nicole was some kind of a freak, for while the rest of the family were typically small and neat and French, this girl was of Amazonian proportions. She looked to me like a sort of female gladiator. She could not possibly have stood less than six foot three in her bare feet, but she was none the less a well-made young gladiator with long nicely-turned legs and a pair of dark eyes that seemed to hold a number of secrets. It was the first time since puberty that I had encountered a woman who was not only tremendously tall but also attractive, and I was much impressed by what I saw. Since then, over the years, I have naturally sampled many a lofty wench and I must say that I rate them higher, on the whole, than their more diminutive sisters. When a woman is very tall, there is greater power and greater traction in her limbs for one thing, and of course there is also a good deal more substance to tangle with.

In other words, I do enjoy a tall woman. And why shouldn't I? There's nothing freakish about that. But what *is* pretty freakish, in my opinion, is the extraordinary fact that women in general, and by that I mean all women everywhere, go absolutely dotty about tiny men. Let me explain at once that by 'tiny men' I don't mean ordinary tiny men like horse-jockeys and chimney-sweeps. I mean genuine dwarfs, those minuscule bowlegged characters you see running around in circus arenas wearing pantaloons. Believe it or not, any one of these little fellows can, if he puts his mind to it, drive the most frigid woman to distraction. Protest all you like, you lady readers. Tell me I'm crazy, misguided, ill-informed. But before you do that, I suggest you go away and talk to a female who has actually been worked over by one of these little men. She will confirm my findings. She will say yes yes yes, it's true, I'm afraid it's true. She will tell you they are repulsive but irresistible. An exceedingly ugly middle-aged circus-dwarf who stood no more than three feet six inches tall once told me that he could always have his pick of any woman in any room at any time. Very odd I find that.

But to go back to Mademoiselle Nicole, the Amazonian daughter. She interested me at once, and as we shook hands, I applied a touch of extra pressure to her knuckles and watched her face. Her lips parted and I saw the tip of her tongue push out suddenly between her teeth. Very well, young lady, I told myself. You shall be number one in Paris.

In case this sounds a bit brash coming from a seventeen-year-old stripling like me, I think you should know that even at that tender age, fortune had endowed me with far more than my share of good looks. Going back now over the family photographs of the time, I can see that I was a youth of quite piercing beauty. This is no more than a simple fact and it would be silly to pretend it wasn't true. Certainly,

it had made things easy for me in London and I could honestly say
that up to then I had not received a single snub. But I had not, of
course, been playing the game for very long and no more than fifty
or sixty young birds had come into my sights.

In order to carry out the plan which the good Major Grout had
put into my head, I straight away announced to Madame Boisvain
that I would be leaving first thing in the morning to stay with friends
in the country. We were still standing in the hall and we had just
completed the handshakes. 'But Monsieur Oswald, you have only this
minute arrived!' the good lady cried.

'I believe my father has paid you six months in advance,' I said. 'If
I am not here, you will save money on food.'

Arithmetic like that will mollify the heart of any landlady in France,
and Madame Boisvain made no further protest. At seven pm we sat
down to the evening meal. It was boiled tripe with onions. This I
consider to be the second most repulsive dish in the entire world. The
most repulsive dish is something that is eaten with gusto by jackaroos
on sheep-stations in Australia.

These jackaroos – and I might as well tell you about it so that you
can avoid it if ever you should go that way – these jackaroos or sheep
cowboys invariably castrate their male lambs in the following barbaric
manner: two of them hold the creature upside down by its fore and
hind legs. A third fellow slits the scrotum and squeezes the testicles
outside the sac. He then bends forward and takes the testicles in his
mouth. He closes his teeth on them and jerks them free from the
unfortunate animal and spits this nauseating mouthful into a basin.
It's no good you telling me these things don't happen because they
do. I saw it all last year with my own eyes on a station near Cowra
in New South Wales. And these idiots went on to inform me with
pride that three competent jackaroos could castrate sixty lambs in
sixty minutes and go on doing it all day long. A little jaw-ache was
all one got, they said, but it was well worth it because the rewards
were great.

'What rewards?'

'Ah ha,' they said, 'you just wait!' And in the evening I had to
stand and watch while they fried the spoils in a pan with mutton fat
over a wood fire. This gastronomic miracle is, I can assure you, the
most revolting, the toughest, the most nauseating dish it is possible to
imagine. Boiled tripe comes second.

I keep digressing. I must get on. We are still in the Boisvain
household having boiled tripe for supper. Monsieur B went into
ecstasies over the stuff, making loud sucking noises and smacking his
lips and shouting 'Délicieux! Ravissant! Formidable! Merveilleux!'
with every mouthful. And then, when he had finished – would horrors

never cease? – he calmly removed his entire set of false teeth and rinsed them in his fingerbowl.

At midnight, when Monsieur and Madame B were well asleep, I slipped along the corridor and entered the bedroom of Mademoiselle Nicole. She was tucked up in an enormous bed and there was a candle burning on the table beside her. She received me, oddly enough, with a formal French handshake, but I can assure you there was nothing formal about what followed after that. I do not intend to dwell upon this little episode. It has nothing at all to do with the main part of my story. Let me just say that every rumour I had ever heard about the girls of Paris was substantiated during those few hours I spent with Mademoiselle Nicole. She made the glacial London debutantes seem like so many slabs of petrified wood. She went for me like a mongoose for a cobra. She suddenly had ten pairs of hands and half a dozen mouths. She was a contortionist to boot, and more than once amidst the whirring of limbs, I caught a glimpse of her ankles locked around the back of her neck. The girl was putting me through the wringer. She was stretching me beyond the point of endurance. I was not really ready at my age for such a severe examination as this, and after an hour or so of unremitting activity, I began to hallucinate. I remember imagining that my entire body was one long well-lubricated piston sliding smoothly back and forth within a cylinder whose walls were made of the smoothest steel. God only knows how long it went on, but at the end of it all I was suddenly brought back to my senses, by the sound of a deep calm voice saying, 'Very well, monsieur, that will do for the first lesson. I think, though, that it will be a long time before you get out of the kindergarten.'

I staggered back to my room, bruised and chastened, and fell asleep.

The next morning, in order to carry out my plan, I said farewell to the Boisvains and took a train for Marseilles. I had on me the six months expense money my father had provided before I left London, two hundred pounds in French francs. That was a lot of money in the year 1912.

At Marseilles, I booked passage for Alexandria on a French steamship of nine thousand tons called *L'Impératrice Josephine*, a pleasant little passenger boat that ran regularly between Marseilles, Naples, Palermo and Alexandria.

The trip was without incident except that I encountered on the first day out yet another tall female. This time she was a Turk, a tall dark-skinned Turkish lady who was so smothered in jewellery of all sorts that she tinkled as she walked. My first thought was that she would have worked wonders on top of a cherry tree to keep the birds away. My second thought, which followed very soon after the first, was that she had an exceptional shape to her body. The undulations in the region of her chest were so magnificent that I felt, as I gazed at them across the boat-deck, like a traveller in Tibet who was seeing for the first time the highest peaks in the Himalayas. The woman returned my gaze, her chin high and arrogant, her eyes travelling slowly down my body from head to toe, then up again. A minute later, she calmly strolled across and invited me to her cabin for a glass of absinthe. I'd never heard of the stuff in my life, but I went willingly, and stayed willingly and I did not emerge again from that cabin until we docked at Naples three days later. I may well, as Mademoiselle Nicole had said, have been in the kindergarten and Mademoiselle Nicole herself was perhaps in the sixth form, but if that was so then the tall Turkish lady was a university professor.

Things were made more difficult for me during this encounter by the fact that all the way between Marseilles and Naples, the ship was battling against a terrible storm. It pitched and rolled in the most alarming manner and more than once I thought we were going to capsize. When at last we were safely anchored in the Bay of Naples, and I was leaving the cabin, I said, 'Well, by gosh, I'm glad we made it. That was some storm we went through.'

'My dear boy,' she said, hanging another cluster of jewellery round her neck, 'the sea has been as calm as glass all the way.'

'Oh no, madame,' I said. 'It was a tremendous storm.'

'That was no storm,' she said. 'It was me.'

I was learning fast. I had learned above all – and I have confirmed this many times since – that to tangle with a Turk is like running fifty miles before breakfast. You have to be fit.

I spent the rest of the voyage getting my wind back and by the time we docked at Alexandria four days later, I was feeling quite bouncy again. From Alexandria I took a train to Cairo. There I changed trains and went on to Khartoum.

By God, it was hot in the Sudan. I was not dressed for the tropics but I refused to waste money on clothes that I would only be wearing for a day or two. In Khartoum, I got a room at a large hotel where the foyer was filled with Englishmen wearing khaki shorts and topees. They all had moustaches and magenta cheeks like Major Grout, and every one of them had a drink in his hand. There was a Sudanese hall-porter of sorts lounging by the entrance. He was a splendid handsome fellow in a white robe with a red tarbouche on his head, and I went up to him.

'I wonder if you could help me?' I said, taking some French banknotes from my pocket and riffling them casually.

He looked at the money and grinned.

'Blister Beetles,' I said. 'You know about Blister Beetles?'

Here it was, then. This was *le moment critique*. I had come all the way from Paris to Khartoum to ask that one question, and now I watched the man's face anxiously. It was certainly possible that Major Grout's story had been nothing more than an entertaining hoax.

The Sudanese hall-porter's grin became wider still. 'Everyone knows about Blister Beetles, sahib,' he said. 'What you want?'

'I want you to tell me where I can go out and catch one thousand of them.'

He stopped grinning and stared at me as though I'd gone barmy. 'You mean *live* beetles?' he exclaimed. 'You want to go out and catch yourself one thousand *live* Blister Beetles?'

'I do, yes.'

'What you want live beetles for, sahib? They no good to you at all, those old live beetles.'

Oh my God, I thought. The Major *has* been pulling our legs.

The hall-porter moved closer to me and placed an almost jet black hand on my arm. 'You want jig-a-jig, right? You want stuff to make you go jig-a-jig?'

'That's about it,' I said. 'More or less.'

'Then you don't want to bother with them *live* beetles, sahib. All you want is *powdered* beetles.'

'I had an idea I might take the beetles home and breed them,' I said. 'That way I'd have a permanent supply.'

'In England?' he said.

'England or France. Somewhere like that.'

'No good,' he said, shaking his head. 'This little Blister Beetle he live only here in the Sudan. He needs very hot sun. Beetles will all die in your country. Why you not take the powder?'

I could see I was going to have to make a slight adjustment in my plans. 'How much does the powder cost?' I asked him.

'How much you want?'

'A lot.'

'You have to be very very careful with that powder, sahib. All you take is the littlest pinch otherwise you get into *very serious trouble*.'

'I know that.'

'Over here, we Sudanese men measure up one dose by pouring the powder over the head of a pin and what stays on the pinhead is one dose exactly. And that is not very much. So you better be careful, young sahib.'

'I know all about that,' I said. 'Just tell me how I go about getting hold of a large quantity.'

'What you mean by large quantity?'

'Well, say about ten pounds in weight.'

'Ten pounds!' he cried. 'That would take care of all the people in the whole of Africa put together!'

'Five pounds then.'

'What in the world you going to do with *five pounds* of Blister Beetle powder, sahib? Just a few *ounces* is a lifetime supply even for a big strong man like me.'

'Never mind what I'm going to do with it,' I said. 'How much would it cost?'

He laid his head on one side and considered this question carefully. 'We buy it in tiny packets,' he said. 'Quarter ounce each. Very expensive stuff.'

'I want five pounds,' I said. 'In bulk.'

'Are you staying here in the hotel?' he asked me.

'Yes.'

'Then I see you tomorrow with the answer. I must go around asking some questions.'

I left it at that for the time being.

The next morning the tall black hall-porter was in his usual place by the hotel entrance. 'What news of the powder?' I asked him.

'I fix,' he said. 'I find a place where I can get you five pounds in weight of pure powder.'

'How much will it cost?' I asked him.

'You have English money?'

'I can get it.'

'It will cost you one thousand English pounds, sahib. Very cheap.'

'Then forget it,' I said, turning away.

'Five hundred,' he said.

'Fifty,' I said. 'I'll give you fifty pounds.'

'One hundred.'

'No. Fifty. That's all I can afford.'

He shrugged and spread his palms upward. 'You find the money,' he said. 'I find the powder. Six o'clock tonight.'

'How will I know you won't be giving me sawdust or something?'

'Sahib!' he cried. 'I never cheat anyone.'

'I'm not so sure.'

'In that case,' he said, 'we will test the powder on *you* by giving you a little dose before you pay me. How's that?'

'Good idea,' I said. 'See you at six.'

One of the London banks had an overseas branch in Khartoum. I went there and changed some of my French francs for pounds. At six pm I sought out the hall-porter. He was now in the foyer of the hotel.

'You got it?' I asked him.

He pointed to a large brown-paper parcel standing on the floor behind a pillar. 'You want to test it first, sahib? You are very welcome because this is the absolute top class quality beetle powder in the Sudan. One pinhead of this and you go jig-a-jig all night long and half the next day.'

I didn't think he would have offered me a trial run if the stuff hadn't been right, so I gave him the money and took the parcel.

An hour later, I was on the night train to Cairo. Within ten days, I was back in Paris and knocking on the door of Madame Boisvain's house in the Avenue Marceau. I had my precious parcel with me. There had been no trouble with the French customs as I disembarked at Marseilles. In those days, they searched for knives and guns but nothing else.

3

I announced to Madame B that I was now going to stay for quite a while but that I had one request to make. I was a science student, I told her. She said she knew that. It was my wish, I went on, not only to learn French during my stay in France, but also to pursue my scientific studies. I would therefore be conducting certain experiments in my room which involved the use of apparatus and chemicals that could be dangerous or poisonous to the inexperienced. Because of this, I wished to have a key to my room, and nobody should enter it.

'You are going to blow us all up!' she cried, clutching her cheeks.

'Have no fear, madame,' I said. 'I am merely taking the normal precautions. My professors have taught me always to do this.'

'And who will clean your room and make your bed?'

'I will,' I said. 'This will save you much trouble.'

She muttered and grumbled a fair bit, but gave way to me in the end.

Supper with the Boisvains that evening was pigs' trotters in white sauce, another repellent dish. Monsieur B tucked into it with all the usual sucking noises and exclamations of ecstasy, and the glutinous white sauce was smeared over his entire face by the time he had finished. I excused myself from the table just as he was preparing to transfer his false teeth from mouth to fingerbowl. I went upstairs to my room and locked the door.

For the first time, I opened my big brown-paper parcel. The powder had been packed, thank goodness, in two large biscuit tins. I opened one up. The stuff was pale grey and almost as fine as flour. Here before me, I told myself, lay what was probably the biggest crock of gold a man could ever find. I say 'probably' because as yet I had no proof of anything. I had only the Major's word that the stuff worked and the hall-porter's word that it was the genuine article.

I lay on my bed and read a book until midnight. I then undressed and got into my pyjamas. I took a pin and held it upright over the open tin of powder. I sprinkled a pinch of powder over the upright pinhead. A tiny cluster of grey powder grains remained clinging to the top of the pin. Very carefully, I raised this to my mouth and licked off the powder. It tasted of nothing. I noted the time by my watch, then I sat on the edge of the bed to await results.

They weren't long coming. Precisely nine minutes later, my whole body went rigid. I began to gasp and gurgle. I froze where I was sitting, just as Major Grout had frozen on his verandah with the glass of whiskey in his hand. But because I'd had a much weaker dose than him, this period of paralysis lasted only for a few seconds. Then I felt, as the good Major had so aptly put it, a burning sensation in the region of my groin. Within another minute, my member – and again the Major had said it better than I can – my member had become as stiff and erect as the mainmast of a topsail schooner.

Now for the final test. I stood up and crossed to the door. I opened it quietly and slipped along the passage. I entered the bedroom of Mademoiselle Nicole, and surely enough, there she was tucked up in bed with the candle already lit, waiting for me. 'Bonsoir, monsieur,' she whispered, giving me another of those formal handshakes. 'You have come along for your lesson number two, yes?'

I didn't say anything. Already, as I got into bed beside her, I was beginning to slide off into another of those weird fantasies that seem to engulf me whenever I come to close quarters with a female. This time I was back in the Middle Ages and Richard Coeur de Lion was King of England. I was the champion jouster of the country, the noble knight who was once more about to display his prowess and strength before the King and all his courtiers in the Field of the Cloth of Gold.

My opponent was a gigantic and fearsome female from France who had butchered seventy-eight valiant Englishmen in tournaments of jousting. But my steed was brave and my lance was of tremendous length and thickness, sharp-pointed, vibrant and made of the strongest steel. And the King shouted out 'Bravo, Sir Oswald, the man with the mighty lance! No one but he has the strength to wield so huge a weapon! Run her through, my lad! Run her through!' So I went into battle with my giant lance pointed straight and true at the Frenchy's most vital region, and I thrust at her with mighty thrusts, all swift and sure, and in a trice I had pierced her armour and had her screaming for mercy. But I was in no mood to be merciful. Spurred on by the cheers of the King and his courtiers, I drove my steely lance ten thousand times into that writhing body and then ten thousand times more, and I heard the courtiers shouting, 'Thrust away, Sir Oswald! Thrust away and keep on thrusting!' And then the King's voice was saying, 'Begad, methinks the brave fellow is going to shatter that great lance of his if he doesn't stop soon!' But my lance did not shatter, and in a glorious finale, I impaled the giant Frenchy female upon the spiked end of my trusty weapon and went galloping around the arena, waving the body high above my head to shouts of 'Bravo!' and 'Gadzooks!' and 'Victor ludorum!'

All this, as you can imagine, took some time. How long, I had not the faintest idea, but when I finally surfaced again, I jumped out of the bed and stood there triumphant, looking down upon my prostrate victim. The girl was panting like a stag at bay and I began to wonder whether I might not have done her an injury. Not that I cared much about that.

'Well, mademoiselle,' I said, 'am I still in the kindergarten?'

'Oh no!' she cried, twitching her long limbs. 'Oh no, monsieur! No, no, no! You are ferocious and you are marvellous and I feel like my boiler has exploded!'

That made me feel pretty good. I left without another word and sneaked back along the corridor to my own room. What a triumph! The powder was fantastic! The Major had been right! And the hall-porter in Khartoum had not let me down! I was on my way now to the Crock of Gold and nothing could stop me. With these happy thoughts, I fell asleep.

The next morning, I immediately began to set matters in train. You will remember that I had a science scholarship. I was, therefore, well-versed in physics and chemistry and several other things besides, but chemistry had always been my strongest subject.

I therefore knew already all about the process of making a simple pill. In the year 1912, which is where we are now, it was customary for pharmacists to make many of their own pills on the premises, and for this they always used something called a pill-machine. So I went shopping in Paris that morning, and in the end I found, in a back street on the Left Bank, a supplier of secondhand pharmaceutical apparatus. From him I bought an excellent little pill-machine that turned out good professional pills in groups of twenty-four at a time. I bought also a pair of highly sensitive chemists' scales.

Next, I found a pharmacy that sold me a large quantity of calcium carbonate and a smaller amount of tragacanth. I also bought a bottle of cochineal. I carried all this back to my room and then I cleared the dressing-table and laid out my supplies and my apparatus in good order.

Pill-making is a simple matter if you know how. The calcium carbonate, which is neutral and harmless, comprises the bulk of the pill. You then add the precise quantity by weight of the active ingredient, in my case cantharadin powder. And finally, as an excipient, you put in a little tragacanth. An excipient is simply the cement that makes everything stick together and harden into an attractive pill. I weighed out sufficient of each substance to make twenty-four fairly large and impressive pills. I added a few drops of cochineal which is a tasteless scarlet colouring matter. I mixed everything together well and truly in a bowl and fed the mixture into my pill-machine. In a trice, I had before me twenty-four large red pills of perfect shape and hardness. And each one, if I had done my weighing and mixing properly, contained exactly the amount of cantharadin powder that would lie on top of a pinhead. Each one, in other words, was a potent and explosive aphrodisiac.

I was still not ready to make my move.

I went out again into the streets of Paris and found a commercial box-maker. From him, I bought one thousand small round cardboard boxes, one inch in diameter. I also bought cotton wool.

Next, I went to a printer and ordered one thousand tiny round labels. On each label the following legend was to be printed in English:

PROFESSOR
YOUSOUPOFF'S
POTENCY PILLS

These pills are exceedingly powerful. Use them sparingly otherwise you may drive both yourself and your partner beyond the point of exhaustion. Recommended dose, one per week.
Sole European agent,
O. Cornelius, 192
Avenue Marceau,
Paris.

The labels were designed to fit exactly upon the lids of my little cardboard boxes.

Two days later, I collected the labels. I bought a pot of glue. I returned to my room and stuck labels on to twenty-four box-lids. Inside each box, I made a nest of white cotton-wool. Upon this I placed a single scarlet pill and closed the lid.

I was ready to go.

As you will have guessed long ago, I was about to enter the commercial world. I was going to sell my Potency Pills to a clientele that would soon be screaming for more and still more. I would sell them individually, one only in each box, and I would charge an exorbitant price.

And the clientele? Where would they come from? How would a seventeen-year-old boy in a foreign city set about finding customers for this wonder-pill of his? Well, I had no qualms about that. I had only to find one single person of the right type and let him try one single pill and the ecstatic recipient would immediately come galloping back for a second helping. He would also whisper the news to his friends and the glad tidings would spread like a forest fire.

I already knew who my first victim was going to be.

I have not yet told you that my father, William Cornelius, was in the Diplomatic Service. He had no money of his own, but he was a skilful diplomat and he managed to live very comfortably on his pay. His last post had been Ambassador to Denmark, and he was presently marking time with some job in the Foreign Office in London before getting a new and more senior appointment. The current British Ambassador to France was someone by the name of Sir Charles Makepiece. He was an old friend of my father's and before I left England my father had written a letter to Sir Charles asking him to keep an eye on me.

I knew what I had to do now, and I set about doing it straight away. I put on my best suit of clothes and made my way to the British Embassy. I did not, of course, go in by the Chancery Entrance. I knocked on the door of the Ambassador's Private Residence, which was in the same imposing building as the Chancery, but at the rear. The time was four in the afternoon. A flunkey in white knee-breeches and a scarlet coat with gold buttons opened the door and glared at me. I had no visiting card, but I managed to convey the news that my father and mother were close friends of Sir Charles and Lady Makepiece and would he kindly inform her Ladyship that Oswald Cornelius Esquire had come to pay his respects.

I was put into a sort of vestibule where I sat down and waited. Five minutes later, Lady Makepiece swept into the room in a flurry of silk and chiffon. 'Well, well!' she cried, taking both my hands in hers. 'So *you* are William's son! He always had good taste, the old rascal! We got his letter and we've been waiting for you to call.'

She was an imposing wench. Not young, of course, but not exactly fossilized either. I put her around forty. She had one of those dazzling ageless faces that seemed to be carved out of marble, and lower down there was a torso that tapered to a waist I could have circled with my two hands. She sized me up with one swift penetrating glance, and she seemed to be satisfied with what she saw because the next thing she said was, 'Come in, William's son, and we shall have a dish of tea together and a chat.'

She led me by the hand through a number of vast and superbly appointed rooms until we arrived at a smallish, rather cosy place furnished with a sofa and armchairs. There was a Boucher pastel on one wall and a Fragonard watercolour on another. 'This,' she said, 'is my own private little study. From here I organize the social life of the Embassy.' I smiled and blinked and sat down on the sofa. One of those fancy-dress flunkeys brought tea and sandwiches on a silver tray. The tiny triangular sandwiches were filled with Gentleman's Relish. Lady Makepiece sat beside me and poured the tea. 'Now tell me all about yourself,' she said.

There followed a whole lot of questions and answers about my family and about me. It was all pretty banal but I knew I must stick it out for the sake of my great plan. So we went on talking for maybe

forty minutes, with her Ladyship frequently patting my thigh with a
jewelled hand to emphasize a point. In the end, the hand remained
resting on my thigh and I felt a slight finger pressure. Ho-ho, I thought.
What's the old bird up to now? Then suddenly she sprang to her feet
and began pacing nervously up and down the room. I sat watching
her. Back and forth she paced, hands clasped together across her front,
head twitching, bosom heaving. She was like a tightly coiled spring.
I didn't know what to make of it. 'I'd better be going,' I said, standing
up.

'No, no! Don't go!'

I sat down again.

'Have you met my husband?' she blurted out. 'Obviously you
haven't. You've just arrived. He's a lovely man. A brilliant person.
But he's getting on in years, poor lamb, and he can't take as much
exercise as he used to.'

'Bad luck,' I said. 'No more polo and tennis.'

'Not even ping-pong,' she said.

'Everyone gets old,' I said.

'I'm afraid so. But the point is this.' She stopped and waited.

I waited, too.

We both waited. There was a very long silence.

I didn't know what to do with the silence. It made me fidget. 'The
point is what, madame?' I said.

'Can't you see I'm trying to ask you something?' she said at last.

I couldn't think of an answer to that one, so I helped myself to
another of those little sandwiches and chewed it slowly.

'I want to ask you a favour, mon petit garçon,' she said. 'I imagine
you are quite good at games?'

'I am rather,' I said, resigning myself to a game of tennis with her,
or ping-pong.

'And you wouldn't mind?'

'Not at all. It would be a pleasure.' It was necessary to humour
her. All I wanted was to meet the Ambassador. The Ambassador was
my target. He was the chosen one who would receive the first pill and
thus start the whole ball rolling. But I could only reach him through
her.

'It's not much I'm asking,' she said.

'I am at your service, madame.'

'You really mean it.'

'Of course.'

'You did say you were good at games?'

'I played rugger for my school,' I said. 'And cricket. I'm a pretty
decent fast bowler.'

She stopped pacing and gave me a long look.

At that point a tiny little warning-bell began tinkling somewhere inside my head. I ignored it. Whatever happened, I must not antagonize this woman.

'I'm afraid I don't play rugger,' she said. 'Or cricket.'

'My tennis is all right, too,' I said. 'But I haven't brought my racquet.' I took another sandwich. I loved the taste of anchovies. 'My father says anchovies destroy the palate,' I said, chewing away. 'He won't have Gentleman's Relish in the house. But I adore it.'

She took a great big deep breath and her breasts blew up like two gigantic balloons. 'I'll tell you what I want,' she whispered softly. 'I want you to ravish me and ravish me and ravish me! I want you to ravish me to death! I want you to do it now! Now! Quickly!'

By golly, I thought. Here we go again.

'Don't be shocked, dear boy.'

'I'm not shocked.'

'Oh yes you are. I can see it on your face. I should never have asked you. You are so young. You are far too young. How old are you? No, don't tell me. I don't want to know. You are very delicious, but schoolboys are forbidden fruit. What a pity. It's quite obvious you have not yet entered the fiery world of women. I don't suppose you've ever even touched one.'

That nettled me. 'You are mistaken, Lady Makepiece,' I said. 'I have frolicked with females on both sides of the Channel. Also on ships at sea.'

'Why, you naughty boy! I don't believe it!'

I was still on the sofa. She was standing above me. Her big red mouth was open and she was beginning to pant. 'You do understand I would never have mentioned it if Charles hadn't been ... sort of past it, don't you?'

'Of course I understand,' I said, wriggling a bit. 'I understand very well. I am full of sympathy. I don't blame you in the least.'

'You really mean that?'

'Of course.'

'Oh, you gorgeous boy!' she cried and she came at me like a tigress.

There is nothing particularly illuminating to report about the barney that followed, except perhaps to mention that her Ladyship astounded me with her sofa-work. Up until then, I had always regarded the sofa as a rotten romping-ground, though heavens knows I had been forced to use it often enough with the London debutantes while the parents were snoring away upstairs. The sofa to me was a beastly uncomfortable thing surrounded on three sides by padded walls and with a horizontal area that was so narrow one was continually rolling off it onto the floor. But Lady Makepiece was a sofa-wizard. For her, the sofa was a kind of gymnastic horse upon which one vaulted and bounced and flipped and rolled and achieved the most remarkable contortions.

'Were you ever a gym teacher?' I asked her.

'Shut up and concentrate,' she said, rolling me around like a lump of puff-pastry.

It was lucky for me I was young and pliable otherwise I'm quite sure I would have suffered a fracture. And that got me thinking about poor old Sir Charles and what he must have gone through in his time. Small wonder he had chosen to go into mothballs. But just wait, I thought, until he swallows the old Blister Beetle! Then it'll be *her* that starts blowing the whistle for time out, not him.

Lady Makepiece was a quick-change artist. A couple of minutes after our little caper had ended, there she was, seated at her small Louis Quinze desk looking as well-groomed and as unruffled as when I had first met her. The steam had gone out of her now, and she had the sleepy contented expression of a boa constrictor that has just swallowed a live rat.

'Look here,' she said, studying a piece of paper. 'Tomorrow we're giving a rather grand dinner-party because it's Mafeking Day.'

'But Mafeking was relieved twelve years ago,' I said.

'We still celebrate it,' she said. 'What I'm saying is that Admiral Joubert has dropped out. He's reviewing his fleet in the Mediterranean. How would you like to take his place?'

I only just stopped myself from shouting hooray. It was exactly what I wanted. 'I would be honoured,' I said.

'Most of the Government Ministers will be there,' she said. 'And all the senior Ambassadors. Do you have a white tie?'

'I do,' I said. In those days, one never travelled anywhere without taking full evening-dress, even at my age.

'Good,' she said, writing my name on the guest-list. 'Eight o'clock tomorrow evening then. Good afternoon, my little man. It was nice meeting you.' Already she had gone back to studying the guest-list, so I found my own way out.

4

The next evening, sharp at eight o'clock, I presented myself at the Embassy. I was fully rigged-up in white tie and tails. A tailcoat, in those days, had a deep pocket on the inside of each tail, and in these pockets I had secreted a total of twelve small boxes, each with a single pill inside. The Embassy was a blaze of lights, and carriages were rolling up at the gates from all directions. Uniformed flunkeys were everywhere. I marched in and joined the receiving line.

'Dear boy,' said Lady Makepiece, 'I'm so glad you could come. Charles, this is Oswald Cornelius, William's son.'

Sir Charles Makepiece was a tiny little fellow with a full head of elegant white hair. His skin was the colour of biscuits, and there was an unhealthy powdery look about it, as though it had been lightly dusted over with brown sugar. The entire face, from forehead to chin, was criss-crossed with deep hairline cracks, and this, together with the powdery, biscuity skin, made him look like a terracotta bust that was beginning to crumble.

'So you arc William's boy, are you?' he said, shaking my hand. 'How are you making out in Paris? Anything I can do for you, just let me know.'

I moved on into the glittering crowd. I seemed to be the only male present who was not smothered in decorations and ribbons. We stood around drinking champagne. Then we went in to dinner. It was quite a sight, that dining-room. About one hundred guests were seated on either side of a table as long as two cricket pitches. Small place cards told us where to sit. I was between two incredibly ugly old females. One was the wife of the Bulgarian Ambassador and the other was an aunt of the King of Spain. I concentrated on the food, which was superb. I still remember the large truffle, as big as a golf ball, baked in white wine in a little earthenware pot with the lid on. And the way in which the poached turbot was so superlatively undercooked, with the centre almost raw but still very hot. (The English and the Americans invariably overcook their fish.) And then the wines! They were something to remember, those wines!

But what, pray, did seventeen-year-old Oswald Cornelius know about wines? A fair question. And yet the answer is that he knew rather a lot. Because what I have not yet told you is that my own father loved wine above all other things in life, including women. He was, I think, a genuine expert. His passion was for burgundy. He adored claret, too, but he always considered even the greatest of the clarets to be just a touch on the feminine side. 'Claret,' he used to say, 'may have a prettier face and a better figure, but it's the burgundies that have the muscles and the sinews.'

By the time I was fourteen, he had begun to communicate some of this wine passion to me, and only a year ago, he had taken me on a ten-day walking tour through Burgundy during the vendange in September. We had started out at Chagny and from there we had strolled in our own time northward to Dijon, so that in the week that followed we traversed the entire length of the Côte de Nuits. It was a thrilling experience. We walked not on the main road but on the narrow rutted tracks that led us past practically every great vineyard on that famous golden slope, first Montrachet, then Meursault, then Pommard and a night in a wonderful small hotel in Beaune where we ate *écrevisses* swimming in white wine, and thick slices of *foie gras* on buttered toast.

I can remember the two of us the next day eating lunch while sitting on the low white wall along the boundary of Romanée Conti – cold chicken, French bread, a *fromage dur* and a bottle of Romanée Conti itself. We spread our food on the top of the wall and stood the bottle alongside, together with two good wine-glasses. My father drew the cork and poured the wine while I did my best to carve the chicken, and there we sat in the warm autumn sun, watching the grape-pickers combing the rows of vines, filling their baskets, bringing them to the heads of the rows, dumping the grapes into larger baskets which in turn were emptied into carts drawn by pale creamy-brown horses. I can remember my father sitting on the wall and waving a half-eaten drumstick in the direction of this splendid scene and saying, 'You are sitting, my boy, on the edge of the most famous piece of land in the whole world! Just look at it! Four and a half acres of flinty red clay! That's all it is! But those grapes you can see them picking at this very moment will produce a wine that is a glory among wines. It is also almost unobtainable because so little of it is made. This bottle we are drinking now came from here eleven years ago. Smell it! Inhale the bouquet! Taste it! Drink it! But never try to describe it! It is impossible to put such a flavour into words! To drink a Romanée Conti is like having an orgasm in the mouth and the nose both at the same time.'

I loved it when my father got himself worked up like this. Listening to him during those early years, I began to realize how important it was to be an enthusiast in life. He taught me that if you are interested in something, no matter what it is, go at it full speed ahead. Embrace it with both arms, hug it, love it and above all become passionate about it. Lukewarm is no good. Hot is no good, either. White hot and passionate is the only thing to be.

We visited Clos de Vougeot and Bonnes-Mares and Clos de la Roche and Chambertin and many other marvellous places. We went down into the cellars of the châteaux and tasted last year's wine from the barrels. We watched the grapes being pressed in gigantic wooden screw-presses that required six men to turn the screw. We saw the juice being run off from the presses into the great wooden vats, and at Chambolle-Musigny, where they had started picking a week earlier than most of the others, we saw the grape juice coming alive in the colossal twelve-foot-high wooden vats, boiling and bubbling as it began its own magic process of converting sugar into alcohol. And while we actually stood there watching, the wine became so fiercely active and the boiling and bubbling reached such a pitch of frenzy that several men had to climb up and sit upon the cover of each vat to hold it down.

I have wandered again. I must get back to my story. But I did want to demonstrate to you very quickly that despite my tender years, I was quite capable of appreciating the quality of the wines I drank that evening at the British Embassy in Paris. They were indeed something to remember.

We started with a Chablis Grand Cru 'Grenouilles'. Then a Latour. Then a Richebourg. And with the dessert, an Yquem of great age. I cannot remember the vintage of any one of them, but they were all pre-phylloxera.

When dinner was over, the women, led by Lady Makepiece, left the room. Sir Charles shepherded the men into a vast adjoining sitting-room to drink port and brandy and coffee.

In the sitting-room, as the men began to split up into groups, I quickly manoeuvred myself alongside the host himself. 'Ah, there you are, my boy,' he said. 'Come and sit here with me.'

Perfect.

There were eleven of us, including me, in this particular group, and Sir Charles courteously introduced me to each one of them in turn. 'This is young Oswald Cornelius,' he said. 'His father was our man in Copenhagen. Meet the German Ambassador, Oswald.' I met the German Ambassador. Then I met the Italian Ambassador and the Hungarian Ambassador and the Russian Ambassador and the Peruvian Ambassador and the Mexican Ambassador. Then I met the French Minister for Foreign Affairs and a French Army General and lastly a funny little dark man from Japan who was introduced simply as Mr Mitsouko. Every one of them spoke English, and it seemed that out of courtesy to their host they were making it the language of the evening.

'Have a glass of port, young man,' Sir Charles Makepiece said to me, 'and pass it round.' I poured myself some port and carefully passed the decanter to my left. 'This is a good bottle. Fonseca '87. Your father tells me you've got a scholarship to Trinity. Is that right?'

'Yes, sir,' I said. My moment was coming any second now. I must not miss it. I must plunge in.

'What's your subject?' Sir Charles asked me.

'Science, sir,' I answered. Then I plunged. 'As a matter of fact,' I said, lifting my voice just enough for them all to hear me, 'there's some absolutely amazing work being done in one of the laboratories up there at this moment. Highly secret. You simply wouldn't believe what they've just discovered.'

Ten heads came up and ten pairs of eyes rose from port glasses and coffee cups and regarded me with mild interest.

'I didn't know you'd already gone up,' Sir Charles said. 'I thought you had a year to wait and that's why you're over here.'

'Quite right,' I said, 'but my future tutor invited me to spend most of last term working in the Natural Sciences Lab. That's my favourite subject, natural science.'

'And what, may I ask, have they just discovered that is so secret and so remarkable?' There was a touch of banter in Sir Charles's voice now and who could blame him?

'Well, sir,' I murmured, and then purposely, I stopped.

Silence for a few seconds. The nine foreigners and the British Ambassador sat still, waiting politely for me to go on. They were regarding me with a mixture of tolerance and amusement. This young lad, they seemed to be saying, has a bit of a nerve to be holding forth like this in front of us. But let's hear him out. It's better than talking politics.

'Don't tell me they are letting a fellow of your age handle secrets,' Sir Charles said, smiling a little with his crumbling terracotta face.

'These aren't *war* secrets, sir,' I said. 'They couldn't help an enemy. These are secrets that are going to help all of mankind.'

'Then tell us about them,' Sir Charles said, lighting a huge cigar. 'You have a distinguished audience here and they are all waiting to hear from you.'

'I think it's the greatest scientific breakthrough since Pasteur,' I said. 'It's going to change the world.'

The Foreign Minister of France made a sharp whistling sound by sucking air up through his hairy nostrils. 'You have another Pasteur in England at this moment?' he said. 'If so, I would very much like to hear about him.' He was a sleek oily Frenchman, this Foreign Minister, and sharp as a knife. I would have to watch him.

'If the world is about to be changed,' Sir Charles said, 'I'm a little surprised that this information hasn't yet found its way to my desk.'

Steady on, Oswald, I told myself. You've hardly begun and already you've been laying it on too thick.

'Forgive me, sir, but the point is he hasn't published yet.'

'Who hasn't? Who's *he*?'

'Professor Yousoupoff, sir.'

The Russian Ambassador put down his glass of port and said, 'Yousoupoff? Is he a Russian?'

'Yes, sir, he's a Russian.'

'Then why haven't *I* heard of him?'

I wasn't about to get into a tangle with this black-eyed black-beared Cossack, so I kept silent.

'Come on, then, young man,' Sir Charles said. 'Tell us about the greatest scientific breakthrough of our time. You mustn't keep us in suspense, you know.'

I took a few deep breaths and a gulp of port. This was the great moment. Pray heaven I wouldn't mess it up.

'For years,' I said, 'Professor Yousoupoff has been working on the theory that the seeds of a ripe pomegranate contain an ingredient that has powerful rejuvenative properties.'

'We have millions and millions of pomegranates in my country!' the Italian Ambassador exclaimed, looking proud.

'Be quiet, Emilio,' Sir Charles said. 'Let the boy go on.'

'For twenty-seven years,' I said, 'Professor Yousoupoff has been studying the seed of the pomegranate. It became an obsession with him. He used to sleep in the laboratory. He never went out socially. He never married. The whole place was littered with pomegranates and their seeds.'

'Excuse me, please,' said the little Japanese man. 'But why the pomegranate? Why not the grape or the blackcurrant?'

'I cannot answer that question, sir,' I said. 'I suppose it was simply what you might call a hunch.'

'Hell of a long time to spend on a hunch,' Sir Charles said. 'But go on, my boy. We mustn't interrupt you.'

'Last January,' I said, 'the Professor's patience was at last rewarded. What he did was this. He dissected the seed of a pomegranate and examined the contents bit by bit under a powerful microscope. And it was only then that he observed in the very centre of the seed a minuscule speck of red vegetable tissue that he'd never seen before. He proceeded to isolate this tiny speck of tissue. But it was obviously too small to be of any use on its own. So the Professor set out to dissect one hundred seeds and to obtain from them one hundred of these tiny red particles. This is where he allowed me to assist him. I mean by dissecting out these particles under a microscope. This alone occupied us for a whole week.'

I took another sip of port. My audience waited for me to go on.

'So we now had one hundred red particles, but even when we put them all together on a glass slide, the result could still not be seen by the naked eye.'

'And you say they were red, these little things?' said the Hungarian Ambassador.

'Under the microscope they were a brilliant scarlet,' I said.

'And what did this famous professor do with them?'

'He fed them to a rat,' I said.

'A rat!'

'Yes,' I said. 'A big white rat.'

'Vy vould anybody vish to feed deese little red bomegranate tings to a rat?' the German Ambassador asked.

'Give him a chance, Wolfgang,' Sir Charles said to the German.

'Let him finish. I want to know what happened.' He nodded for me to go on.

'You see, sir,' I said, 'Professor Yousoupoff had in the laboratory a lot of white rats. He took the one hundred tiny red particles and fed every one of them to a single large healthy male rat. He did this by inserting them, under a microscope, into a piece of meat. He then put the rat in a cage together with ten female rats. I remember very clearly how the Professor and I stood beside the cage watching the male rat. It was late afternoon and we were so excited we had forgotten all about lunch.'

'Excuse me one moment, please,' the clever French Foreign Minister said. 'But why were you so excited? What made you think that *anything* was going to happen with this rat?'

Here we go, I thought. I knew I'd have to watch this wily Frenchman. 'I was excited, sir, simply because the Professor was excited,' I said. 'He seemed to *know* something was going to happen. I can't tell you how. Don't forget, gentlemen, I was only a very young junior assistant. The Professor did not tell me all his secrets.'

'I see,' the Foreign Minister said. 'Then let us proceed.'

'Yes, sir,' I said. 'Well, we were watching the rat. At first, nothing happened. Then suddenly, after exactly nine minutes, the rat became very still. He crouched down, quivering all over. He was looking at the females. He crept toward the nearest one and grabbed her by the skin of her neck with his teeth and mounted her. It did not take long. He was very fierce with her and very swift. But here's the extraordinary thing. The moment the rat had finished copulating with the first female, he grabbed a second one and set about her in just the same way. Then he took a third female rat, and a fourth and a fifth. He was absolutely tireless. He went from one female to another, fornicating with each in turn until he had covered all ten of them. Even then, gentlemen, he hadn't had enough!'

'Good gracious me!' Sir Charles murmured. 'What a curious experiment.'

'I should add,' I went on, 'that rats are not normally promiscuous creatures. They are in fact rather moderate in their sexual habits.'

'Are you sure of that?' the French Foreign Minister said. 'I thought rats were extraordinarily lascivious.'

'No, sir,' I answered firmly. 'Rats are actually very intelligent and gentle creatures. They are easy to domesticate.'

'Go on, then,' Sir Charles said. 'What did all this tell you?'

'Professor Yousoupoff got very excited. "Oswaldsky!" he shouted – that's what he called me. "Oswaldsky, my boy, I think I have discovered the absolutely greatest most powerful sexual stimulant in the whole history of mankind!"

' "I think you have, too," I said. We were still standing by the cage of rats and the male rat was still leaping on the wretched females, one after the other. Within an hour, he had collapsed from exhaustion. "We give him too big a dose," the Professor said.'

'This rat,' the Mexican Ambassador said, 'what came of him in the end?'

'He died,' I said.

'From too much women, yes?'

'Yes,' I said.

The little Mexican clapped his hands together hard and cried out, 'That is exactly how I wish to go when I die! From too much women!'

'From too much goats and donkeys iss more like it in Mexico,' the German Ambassador snorted.

'That's enough of that, Wolfgang,' Sir Charles said. 'Let's not start any wars. We are listening to a most interesting story. Carry on, my boy.'

'So the next time,' I said, 'we only isolated twenty of these tiny red microscopic nuclei. We inserted them in a pellet of bread and then went out looking for a very old man. With the help of the local newspaper, we found our old man in Newmarket – that's a town not far from Cambridge. His name was Mr Sawkins and he was one hundred and two years old. He was suffering from advanced senility. His mind was wandering and he had to be fed by spoon. He had not been out of bed for seven years. The Professor and I knocked on the door of his house and his daughter, aged eighty, opened it. "I am Professor Yousoupoff," the Professor announced. "I have discovered a great medicine to help old people. Will you allow us to give some to your poor old father?"

' "You can give 'im anything you damn well please," the daughter said. "The old fool doesn't know what's goin' on from one day to the next. 'Ee's a flamin' nuisance."

'We went upstairs and the Professor somehow managed to poke the bread pellet down the old man's throat. I noted the time by my watch. "Let us retire to the street outside and observe," the Professor said.

'We went out and stood in the street. I was counting each minute aloud as it went by. And then – you won't believe this, gentlemen, but I swear it's exactly what happened – precisely on the dot of nine minutes, there was a thunderous bellow from inside the Sawkins's house. The front door burst open and the old man himself rushed out into the street. He was in bare feet, wearing dirty blue and grey striped pyjamas and his long white hair was all over his shoulders. "I want me a woman!" he bellowed. "I want me a woman and by God I'm goin' to get me a woman!" The Professor clutched my arm. "Don't move!" he ordered. "Just observe!"

'The eighty-year-old daughter came rushing out after the father.

"Come back, you old fool!" she yelled. "What the 'ell d'you think you're up to?"

'We were, by the way, in a little street with a row of identical connected houses on either side. Mr Sawkins ignored his daughter and ran, he actually ran, to the next-door house. He started banging on the door with his fists. "Open up, Mrs Twitchell!" he bellowed. "Come on, my beauty, open up and let's 'ave a bit of fun!"

'I caught a glimpse of the terrified face of Mrs Twitchell at the window. Then it went away. Mr Sawkins, still bellowing, put his shoulder to the flimsy door and smashed the lock. He dived inside. We stayed out on the street, waiting for the next development. The Professor was very excited. He was jumping up and down in his funny black boots and shouting, "We have a breakthrough! We've done it! We shall rejuvenate the world!"

'Suddenly, piercing screams and yells came issuing from Mrs Twitchell's house. Neighbours were beginning to gather on the street. "Go in and get 'im!" shouted the old daughter. " 'Ee's' gone stark starin' mad!" Two men ran into the Twitchell house. There were sounds of a scuffle. Soon, out came the two men, frog-marching old Mr Sawkins between them. "I 'ad 'er!" he was yelling. "I 'ad the old bitch good and proper! I near rattled 'er to death!" At that point, the Professor and I moved quietly away from the scene.'

I paused in my story. Seven Ambassadors, the Foreign Minister of France, the French Army General and the little Japanese man were all now leaning forward in their seats, their eyes upon me.

'Is this *exactly* what happened?' Sir Charles asked me.

'Every word of it, sir, is the gospel truth,' I lied. 'When Professor Yousoupoff publishes his findings, the whole world will be reading what I have just told you.'

'So what happened next?' the Peruvian Ambassador asked.

'From then on, it was comparatively simple,' I said. 'The Professor conducted a series of experiments designed to discover what the proper absolutely safe dose should be for a normal adult male. For this, he used undergraduate volunteers. And you can be quite sure, gentlemen, that he had no trouble getting young men to come forward. As soon as the news spread around the University, there was a waiting list of over eight hundred. But to cut the story short, the Professor finally demonstrated that the safe dose was no more than five of those tiny microscopic nuclei from the pomegranate seed. So, using calcium carbonate as a base, he manufactured a pill containing exactly this quantity of the magic substance. And he proved beyond any doubt that just one of these pills would, in precisely nine minutes, turn any man, even a very old man, into a marvellously powerful sex-machine that was capable of pleasuring his partner for six hours nonstop, *without exception*.'

'Gott in Himmel!' shouted the German Ambassador. 'Ver can I get hold of ziss stuff?'

'Me, too!' cried the Russian Ambassador. 'I haff priority claim because it voss invented by my countryman! I muss inform zee Tsar at vonce!'

Suddenly, they were all speaking at the same time. Where could they get it? They wanted it now! How much did it cost? They were willing to pay handsomely! And the little Japanese fellow sitting on my left leaned over and hissed, 'You get me big supply of pills, yes. I give you very much money.'

'Now just a moment, gentlemen,' Sir Charles said, raising a wrinkled hand for silence. 'Our young friend here has told us a fascinating story, but as he correctly pointed out, he was only a junior assistant to Professor whatever-his-name-is. I am quite sure, therefore, that he is not in a position to supply us with this remarkable new pill. Perhaps though, my dear Oswald,' and here Sir Charles leaned toward me and placed a withered hand gently on my forearm, 'perhaps, my dear Oswald, you could put me in touch with the great Professor. One of my duties here at the Embassy is to keep the Foreign Office informed of all new scientific discoveries.'

'I quite understand,' I said.

'If I could obtain a bottle of these pills, preferably a *large* bottle, I would send it straight to London.'

'And I vould sent it to Petrograd,' said the Russian Ambassador.

'And me to Budapest.'

'And me to Mexico City.'

'And me to Lima.'

'And me to Rome.'

'Rubbish!' cried the German Ambassador. 'You vont dem for yourselves, you dirty olt men!'

'Now then, Wolfgang,' Sir Charles said, squirming a bit.

'Vy not, my dear Sharles? I too vont dem for myself. For zee Kaiser as well, of course, but me first.'

I decided I rather liked the German Ambassador. He was anyway honest.

'I think it best, gentlemen,' Sir Charles said, 'if I myself make all the arrangements. I shall write personally to the Professor.'

'The Japanese people,' Mr Mitsouko said, 'are very interested in all massage techniques and hot baths and in all similar technological advances, especially the Emperor himself.'

I allowed them to finish. I was in control now and that gave me a good feeling. I helped myself to another glass of port but refused the huge cigar Sir Charles offered me. 'Would you prefer a smaller one, dear boy?' he asked me eagerly. 'Or a Turkish cigarette? I have some Balkan Sobranies.'

'No, thank you, sir,' I said, 'but the port is delicious.'

'Help yourself, dear boy! Fill your glass!'

'I have some interesting news,' I said, and suddenly everyone became silent. The German Ambassador cupped a hand behind his ear. The Russian leaned forward in his seat. So did all the rest of them.

'What I am about to tell you is extremely confidential,' I said. 'May I rely upon all of you to keep it to yourselves?'

There was a chorus of 'Yes, yes! Of course! Absolutely! Carry on, young fellow!'

'Thank you,' I said. 'Now the point is this. As soon as I knew that I was going to Paris I decided I simply must take with me a supply of these pills, especially for my father's great friend, Sir Charles Makepiece.'

'My dear boy!' Sir Charles cried out. 'What a generous thought!'

'I could not, of course, ask the Professor to give any of them to me,' I said. 'He would never have agreed to that. After all, they are still on the secret list.'

'So what did you do?' asked Sir Charles. He was dribbling with excitement. 'Did you purloin them?'

'Certainly not, sir,' I said. 'Stealing is a criminal act.'

'Never mind about us, dear boy. We won't tell a soul.'

'So vott did you do?' the German Ambassador asked. 'You say you haff dem and you didn't steal them?'

'I made them myself,' I said.

'Brilliant!' they cried. 'Magnifique!'

'Having assisted the Professor at every stage,' I said, 'I naturally knew exactly how to manufacture these pills. So I ... well ... simply made them in his laboratory each day when he was out to lunch.' Slowly, I reached behind me and took one small round box from my tail-coat pocket. I placed it on the low table. I opened the lid. And there, lying in its little nest of cotton-wool, was a single scarlet pill.

Everyone leaned forward to look. Then I saw the plump white hand of the German Ambassador sliding across the surface of the table towards the box like a weasel stalking a mouse. Sir Charles saw it, too. He smacked the palm of his own hand on top of the German's, pinning it down. 'Now, Wolfgang,' he said, 'don't be impatient.'

'I vont zee pill!' Ambassador Wolfgang shouted.

Sir Charles put his other hand over the pill-box and kept it there. 'Do you have more?' he asked me.

I fished in my tail-coat pockets and brought out nine more boxes. 'There is one for each of you,' I said.

Eager hands reached across, grabbing the little boxes. 'I pay,' said Mr Mitsouko. 'How much you want?'

'No,' I said. 'These are presents. Try them out, gentlemen. See what you think.'

Sir Charles was studying the label on the box. 'Ah-ha,' he said. 'I see you have your address printed here.'

'That's just in case,' I said.

'In case of what?'

'In case anyone wishes to get a second pill,' I said.

I noticed that the German Ambassador had taken out a little book and was making notes. 'Sir,' I said to him, 'I expect you are thinking of telling your scientists to investigate the seed of the pomegranate. Am I not right?'

'Zatt iss exactly vot I am thinking,' he said.

'No good,' I said. 'Waste of time.'

'May I ask vy?'

'Because it's not the pomegranate,' I said. 'It's something else.'

'So you lie to us!'

'It is the only untruth I have told you in the entire story,' I said. 'Forgive me, but I had to do it. I had to protect Professor Yousoupoff's secret. It was a point of honour. All the rest is true. Believe me it's true. It is especially true that each of you has in his possession the most powerful rejuvenator the world has ever known.'

At that point, the ladies returned and each man in our group quickly and rather surreptitiously pocketed his pill-box. They stood up. They greeted their wives. I noticed that Sir Charles had suddenly become absurdly jaunty. He hopped across the room and splashed a silly sort of kiss smack on Lady Makepiece's scarlet lips. She gave him one of those cool what-on-earth-was that for looks. Unabashed, he took her arm and led her across the room into a throng of people. I last saw Mr Mitsouko prowling around the floor inspecting the womenflesh at very close quarters, like a horse-coper examining a bunch of mares on the market-place. I slipped quietly away.

Half an hour later, I was back at my boarding-house in the Avenue Marceau. The family had retired and all the lamps were out, but as I passed the bedroom of Mademoiselle Nicole in the upstairs corridor, I could see in the crack between the door and the floor a flicker of candlelight. The little trollop was waiting for me again. I decided not to go in. There was nothing new for me in there. Even at this early stage in my career, I had already decided that the only women who interested me were new women. Second time round was no good. It was like reading a detective novel twice over. You knew exactly what was going to happen next. The fact that I had recently broken this rule by visiting Mademoiselle Nicole a second time was beside the point. That was done simply to test my Blister Beetle powder. And by the way, this principle of no-woman-more-than-once is one that I have stuck to rigorously all my life and I commend it to all men of action who enjoy variety.

5

That night I slept well. I was still fast asleep at eleven o'clock the next morning when the sound of Madame Boisvain's fists hammering at my door jerked me awake. 'Get up, Monsieur Cornelius!' she was shouting. 'You must come down at once! People have been ringing my bell and demanding to see you since before breakfast!'

I was dressed and downstairs in two minutes flat. I went to the front door and there, standing on the cobblestones of the sidewalk, were no less than seven men, none of whom I had ever seen before. They made a picturesque little group in their many-coloured fancy uniforms with all manner of gilt and silver buttons on their jackets.

They turned out to be Embassy Messengers, and they came from the British, the German, the Russian, the Hungarian, the Italian, the Mexican and the Peruvian Embassies. Each man carried a letter addressed to me. I accepted the letters and opened them on the spot. All of them said roughly the same thing: *They wanted more pills.* They begged for more pills. They instructed me to give the pills to the bearer of the letter, etc. etc.

I told the messengers to wait on the street and I went back up to my room. Then, I wrote the following message on each of the letters: *Honoured Sir, these pills are extremely expensive to manufacture. I regret that in future the cost of each pill will be one thousand francs.* In those days there were twenty francs to the pound, which meant that I was asking exactly fifty pounds sterling per pill. And fifty pounds in 1912 was worth maybe ten times as much as it is today. By today's standards, I was probably asking about five hundred pounds per pill. It was a ridiculous price, but these were wealthy men. They were also sex-crazy men, and as any sensible woman will tell you, a man who is very wealthy and grossly sex-crazy both at the same time is the easiest touch in the world.

I trotted downstairs again and handed the letters back to their respective carriers and told them to deliver them to their masters. As I was doing this, two more messengers arrived, one from the Quai d'Orsay (the Foreign Minister) and one from the General at the Ministry of War or whatever it is called. And while I was scribbling the same statement about price on these last two letters, who should turn up in a very fine hansom cab but Mr Mitsouko himself. His appearance shocked me. The previous night he had been a bouncy, dapper, bright-eyed little Jap. This morning he hardly had the strength to get out of his cab, and as he came tottering toward me, his legs began to buckle. I grabbed hold of him just in time.

'My dear sir!' he gasped, putting both hands on my shoulders for support. 'My dear, dear sir! It's a miracle! It's a wonder-pill! It's ... it's the greatest invention of all time!'

'Hang on,' I said. 'Are you feeling all right?'

'Of course I am all right,' he gasped. 'I am a little bit jiggered, that's all.' He started to giggle, and there he stood, this tiny oriental person dressed in a top hat and tails, clinging to my shoulders and giggling quite uncontrollably now. He was so small that the top of his top hat came no higher than my lowest rib. 'I am a little bit jiggered and a little bit pokered,' he said, 'but who would not be, my dear boy, who would not be?'

'What happened, sir?' I asked him.

'I molested *seven women!*' he cried. 'And these were not our dinky-tinky little Japanese women! No, no, no! They were enormous strong French wenchies! I took them in rotation, *bang bang bang!* And every one of them was screaming out *camarade camarade camarade!* I was a giant among these women, do you understand that, my dear young sir? I was a giant and I swung my giant club and I sent them all squiggling in every direction!'

I led him inside and sat him down in Madame Boisvain's parlour. I found him a glass of brandy. He gulped it down and a faint yellowish colour began returning to his white cheeks. I noticed that there was a leather satchel suspended by a cord around his right wrist, and when he took it off and dumped it on the table, there was the clinking of coins inside it.

'You must be careful, sir,' I said to him. 'You are a small man and these are large pills. I think it would be safer if you took only half the normal dose each time. Just half a pill instead of one.'

'Bunkum, sir!' he cried. 'Bunkum and horseradish sauce as we say in Japan! Tonight I propose to take not one pill but three!'

'Have you read what it says on the label?' I asked him anxiously. The last thing I wanted was a dead Jap around the place. Think of the outcry, the autopsy, the inquiries, and the pill-boxes with my name on them in this house.

'I examine the label,' he said, holding his glass out for more of Madame Boisvain's brandy, 'and I ignore it. We Japanese, we may be small in body but our organs are of gigantic size. That is why we walk bowlegged.'

I decided I would try to discourage him by doubling the price. 'I'm afraid they are terrifically expensive, these pills,' I said.

'Money no object,' he said, pointing to the leather satchel on the table. 'I pay in gold coins.'

'But Mr Mitsouko,' I said, 'each pill is going to cost you *two thousand* francs! They are very difficult to manufacture. That's an awful lot of money for one pill.'

'I take twenty,' he said without even blinking.

My God, I thought, he *is* going to kill himself. 'I cannot allow you to have them,' I told him, 'unless you give me your word you will never take more than one at a time.'

'Do not lecture me, young buckeroo,' he said. 'Just get me the pills.'

I went upstairs and counted out twenty pills and put them in a plain bottle. I wasn't going to risk having my name and address on this lot.

'Ten I shall send to the Emperor in Tokyo,' Mr Mitsouko said when I handed them to him. 'It will put me in a very hot position with His Royal Highness.'

'It'll put the Empress in some pretty hot positions, too,' I said.

He grinned and took up the leather satchel and emptied a vast pile of gold coins on to the table. They were all one hundred franc pieces. 'Twenty coins for each pill,' he said, starting to count them out. 'That is four hundred coins altogether. And well worth it, my young magician.'

When he had gone, I scooped up the coins and carried them up to my room.

My God, I thought. I am rich already.

But before the day was done, I was a lot richer. One by one, the messengers started trickling back from their respective Embassies and Ministries. They all carried precise orders and exact amounts of money, most of it in gold twenty-franc pieces. This is how it went:

Sir Charles Makepiece, 4 pills	=	4,000 francs
The German Ambassador, 8 pills	=	8,000 francs
The Russian Ambassador, 10 pills	=	10,000 francs
The Hungarian Ambassador, 3 pills	=	3,000 francs
The Peruvian Ambassador, 2 pills	=	2,000 francs
The Mexican Ambassador, 6 pills	=	6,000 francs
The Italian Ambassador, 4 pills	=	4,000 francs
The French Foreign Minister, 6 pills	=	6,000 francs
The Army General, 3 pills	=	3,000 francs
		46,000 francs
Mr Mitsouko, 20 pills (double price)	=	40,000 francs
GRAND TOTAL		86,000 francs

Eighty-six thousand francs! At the exchange rate of one hundred francs to five pounds, I was all of a sudden worth four thousand, three hundred English pounds! It was incredible. One could buy a good house for money like that, with a carriage and a pair of horses thrown in, as well as one of those dashing new-fangled automobiles!

For supper that night, Madame Boisvain served oxtail stew and it wasn't at all bad except that the sloshiness of it all encouraged Monsieur B to suck and swig and gulp in the most disgusting fashion. At one point, he picked up his plate and tipped the gravy straight into his mouth together with a couple of carrots and a large onion. 'My wife tells me that you had a lot of peculiar visitors today,' he said. His face was plastered with brown fluid and strands of meat were hanging from his moustache. 'Who were these men?'

'They were friends of the British Ambassador,' I answered. 'I am doing a little business for Sir Charles Makepiece.'

'I cannot have my house turned into a marketplace,' Monsieur B said, speaking with his mouth full of fat. 'These activities must cease.'

'Don't worry,' I said. 'Tomorrow I am finding alternative accommodation.'

'You mean you're leaving?' he cried.

'I'm afraid I must. But you may keep the advance rent my father has paid you.'

There was a bit of an uproar around the table about all this, much of it from Mademoiselle Nicole, but I stuck to my guns. And the next morning I went out and found myself a quite grand ground-floor apartment with three large rooms and a kitchen. It was on the Avenue Jena. I packed all my possessions and loaded them into a hackney coach. Madame Boisvain was at the front door to see me off. 'Madame,' I said, 'I have a small favour to ask of you.'

'Yes?'

'And in return I want you to take this,' I held out five gold twenty-franc pieces. She nearly fell over. 'From time to time,' I said, 'people will call at your house asking for me. All you have to do is tell them I have moved and redirect them to this address.' I gave her a piece of paper with my new address written on it.

'But that is too much money, Monsieur Oswald!'

'Take it,' I said, pushing the coins into her hand. 'Keep it for yourself. Don't tell your husband. But it is very important that you inform everyone who calls where I am living.'

She promised to do this, and I drove away to my new quarters.

6

My business flourished. My ten original clients all whispered the great news to their own friends and those friends whispered it to other friends and in a month or so a large snowball had been created. I spent half of each day making pills. I thanked heaven I had had the foresight to bring such a large quantity of powder from the Sudan in the first place. But I did have to reduce my price. Not everyone was an Ambassador or a Foreign Minister, and I found early on that a lot of people simply couldn't afford to pay my absurd original fee of one thousand francs per pill. So I made it two hundred and fifty instead.

The money gushed in.

I started buying fine clothes and going out into Paris society.

I purchased a motor car and learned to drive it. It was De Dion-Bouton's brand new model, the Sports DK, a marvellous little monobloc four with a three-speed gearbox and a pull-on handbrake. Top speed, believe it or not, was as much as 50 mph, and more than once I took her to the limit up the Champs-Elysées.

But above all, I rollocked and frolicked with women to my heart's content. Paris in those days was an exceptionally cosmopolitan city. It was filled with ladies of quality from practically every country in the world, and it was during this period that a curious truth began to dawn upon me. We all know that people of different nations have different national characteristics and different temperaments. What is not quite so well recognized is the fact that these different national characteristics become even more marked during sexual, as opposed to merely social, intercourse. I became an expert on national sexual characteristics. It was extraordinary how the women of one nation or another ran true to form. You could take, for example, half a dozen Serbian ladies (and don't think I didn't) and you would find, if you were paying close attention, that every one of them possessed a number of very definite common eccentricities, common skills and common preferences. Polish women also, because of certain habits they all had in common, were easily recognizable. So were the Basques, the Moroccans, the Equadorians, the Norwegians, the Dutch, the Guatemalians, the Belgians, the Russians, the Chinese and all the rest of them. Toward the end of my stay in Paris, you could have put me on a couch blindfold with any lady from any country, and within five minutes, though she never uttered a word, I would have told you her nationality.

Now for the obvious question. Which country produced the most exhilarating females?

I myself became rather partial to Bulgarian ladies of aristocratic stamp. They had, amongst other things, the most unusual tongues. Not only were these tongues of theirs exceptionally muscular and vibrant, but they had a roughness about them, a kind of abrasive quality that one normally finds only in cats' tongues. Get a cat to lick your finger some time and you will see exactly what I mean.

Turkish ladies (I think I've mentioned them before) were also high on my list. They were like water-wheels. They never stopped turning until the river dried up. But by gad, you had to be fit before you challenged a Turkish lady, and I personally never allowed one into my house until after I'd had a good breakfast.

Hawaiian women interested me because they had prehensile toes, and in almost any situation you cared to mention, they used their feet rather than their hands.

As far as Chinese women went, I learned by experience to tamper only with those that came from Peking and the neighbouring province of Shan-Tung. And even then, it was essential that they were from noble families. In those days, it was the custom among the nobility of Peking and Shan-Tung to put their girls into the hands of wise old women as soon as they reached the age of fifteen. For two years thereafter, these girls were subjected to a rigorous course of instruction designed to teach them only one thing – the art of giving physical pleasure to their future husbands. And at the end of it all, after a severe practical examination, certificates were issued indicating a pass or a failure. If the girl was exceptionally dexterous and inventive, she might get what was called a 'Pass with Distinction', and most prized of all was the 'Diploma of Merit'. A young lady with a Diploma could virtually pick her own husband. Unfortunately though, at least half the Diploma girls were whisked away at once into the Emperor's Palace.

I discovered only one Chinese lady in Paris who had earned a Diploma of Merit. She was the wife of an opium millionaire and she had come over to select a wardrobe. She selected me as well, and I must admit it was a memorable experience. She had developed into a sublime art the practice of what she called *so-far-and-no-further*. Nothing ever quite finished. She didn't allow it to. She took one to the brink. Two hundred times she took me to the brink of the golden threshold, and for three and a half hours, which was the duration of my suffering, it felt as though a long live nerve was being drawn very very slowly and with exquisite patience out of my burning body. I hung on to the edge of the cliff with my fingertips, screaming for succour or release, but the blissful torture went on and on and on. It was an amazing demonstration of skill and I have never forgotten it.

I could describe if I wished the curious feminine habits of at least fifty other nationalities, but I am not going to do so. Not here anyway, because I really must proceed with the main theme of this story, which is how I made money.

During my seventh month in Paris, a lucky incident took place that doubled my income. This is what happened. One afternoon, I had a Russian lady in my apartment who was some sort of relation to the Tsar. She was a slim white-skinned little herring, rather cool and casual, almost offhand she was, and I had to stroke her up pretty vigorously before I succeeded in raising a good head of steam in her boilers. That sort of blasé attitude only makes me more determined than ever, and I can promise you that by the time I'd finished with her, she'd had a fair old roasting.

When it was over, I lay back on the couch sipping a glass of champagne as a cooler. The Russian was languidly dressing herself and wandering round my room looking at this and that.

'What are all these red pills in this bottle?' she asked me.

'They're none of your business,' I said.

'When am I going to see you again?'

'Never,' I said. 'I told you my rules.'

'You are being very disagreeable,' she said pouting. 'Tell me what these pills are for or I also will become disagreeable. I will throw them all out the window.' She picked up the bottle that contained five hundred of my precious Blister Beetle pills just made that morning and she opened the window.

'Don't,' I said.

'Then tell me.'

'They are tonic pills for men,' I said. 'Pick-me-ups, that's all.'

'Why not for women also?'

'They're only for men.'

'I shall try one,' she said, unscrewing the bottle-top and tipping out a pill. She popped it into her mouth and washed it down with champagne. Then she continued putting on her clothes.

She was fully dressed and was adjusting her hat in front of the looking-glass when suddenly she froze. She turned and faced me. I lay where I was, sipping my drink, but I was now watching her closely and with some trepidation.

She remained frozen for maybe thirty seconds, staring at me with a cold hard dangerous stare. Then all at once, she reached both hands up to her neckline and ripped her silk dress clean off her body. She tore off her underclothes. She flung her hat across the room. She crouched. She began to move forward. She came softly across the room toward me with the slow deliberate tread of a tigress stalking an antelope.

'What's up?' I said. But by now I knew very well what was up. Nine minutes had gone by and the pill had hit her.

'Steady on,' I said.

She kept coming.

'Go away,' I said.

Still she kept coming.

Then she sprang, and all I could see in those first few moments was a blurred flurry of legs and arms and mouth and hands and fingers. She went quite mad. She was wild with lust. I hauled in my canvas and lay there trying to ride out the storm. That wasn't good enough for her. She began to throw me around all over the place, snorting and grunting as she did so. I didn't like it. I'd had my fill. This must stop, I decided. But I still had a terrific job pinning her down. In the end, I got her wrists locked behind her back and I carried her kicking and screaming into my bathroom and held her under the cold shower. She tried to bite me but I gave her an uppercut to the chin with my elbow. I held her under that freezing shower for at least twenty minutes while she went on yelling and swearing in Russian all the time.

'Had enough?' I said at last. She was half drowned and pretty cold.

'I want you!' she spluttered.

'No,' I said. 'I'm going to keep you here until you cool down.'

Finally she gave in. I let her go. Poor girl, she was shivering terribly and she looked a sight. I got a towel and gave her a good rub down. Then a glass of brandy.

'It was that red pill,' she said.

'I know it was.'

'I want some of them to take home.'

'Those are too strong for ladies,' I said. 'I will make you some that are just right.'

'Now?'

'No. Come back tomorrow and they'll be ready.'

Because her dress was ruined, I wrapped her in my overcoat and drove her home in the De Dion. Actually, she had done me a good turn. She had demonstrated that my pill worked just as well on the female as it did on the male. Probably better. I immediately set about making some Ladies' Pills. I made them half the strength of the Men's Pills, and I turned out one hundred of them, anticipating a ready market. But the market was even more ready than I had anticipated. When the Russian woman came back the next afternoon, she demanded five hundred of them on the spot!

'But they cost two hundred and fifty francs each.'

'I don't care about that. All my girl friends want them. I told them what happened to me yesterday and now they all want them.'

'I can give you a hundred, that's all. The rest later. Do you have money?'

'Of course I have money.'

'May I make a suggestion, madame?'

'What is it?'

'If a lady takes one of these pills on her own, I fear she may appear unduly aggressive. Men don't like that. I didn't like it yesterday.'

'What is your suggestion?'

'I suggest that any lady who intends taking one of these pills should persuade her partner also to take one. And at exactly the same time. Then they'll be all square.'

'That makes good sense,' she said.

It not only made good sense, it would also double the sales.

'The partner,' I said, 'could take a larger pill. It's called the Men's Pill. That's simply because men are bigger than women and need a bigger dose.'

'Always assuming,' she said, smiling a little, 'that the partner is a male.'

'Whatever you like,' I said.

She shrugged her shoulders and said, 'Very well, then, give me also one hundred of these Men's Pills.'

By gum, I thought, there's going to be some fun and frolics around the boudoirs of Paris tonight. Things were hot enough with just one man getting himself all pilled-up but I shuddered to think what was going to happen when both parties took the medicine.

It was a howling success. Sales doubled. They trebled. By the time my twelve months in Paris were up, I had around two million francs in the bank! That was one hundred thousand pounds! I was now nearly eighteen. I was rich. But I was not rich enough. My year in France had shown me very clearly the path I wanted to follow in my life. I was a sybarite. I wished to lead a life of luxury and leisure. I would never get bored. That was not my style. But I would never be completely satisfied unless the luxury was intensely luxurious and the leisure was unlimited. One hundred thousand pounds was not enough for that. I needed more. I needed a million pounds at least. I felt sure I would find a way to earn it. Meanwhile, I had not made a bad start.

I had enough sense to realize that first of all I must continue my education. Education is everything. I have a horror of uneducated people. And so in the summer of 1913, I transferred my money to a London bank and returned to the land of my fathers. In September, I went up to Cambridge to begin my undergraduate studies. I was a scholar remember, a scholar of Trinity College, and as such I had a number of privileges and was well-treated by those in authority.

It was here at Cambridge that the second and final phase of my fortune-making began. Bear with me a little longer and you shall hear all about it in the pages to come.

7

My chemistry tutor at Cambridge was called A. R. Woresley. He was a middle-aged, shortish man, paunchy, untidily dressed and with a grey moustache whose edges were stained yellow ochre by the nicotine from his pipe. In appearance, therefore, a typical university don. But he struck me as being exceptionally able. His lectures were never routine. His mind was always darting about in search of the unusual. Once he said to us:

'And now we need as it were a tompion to protect the contents of this flask from invading bacteria. I presume you know what a tompion is, Cornelius?'

'I can't say I do, sir,' I said.

'Can anyone give me a definition of that common English noun?' A. R. Woresley said.

Nobody could.

'Then you'd better look it up,' he said. 'It's not my business to teach you elementary English.'

'Oh, come on, sir,' someone said. 'Tell us what it means.'

'A tompion,' A. R. Woresley said, 'is a small pellet made out of mud and saliva which a bear inserts into his anus before hibernating for the winter, to stop the ants getting in.'

A strange fellow, A. R. Woresley, a mixture of many attitudes, occasionally witty, more often pompous and sombre, but underneath everything there was a curiously complex mind. I began to like him very much after that little tompion episode. We struck up a pleasant student-tutor relationship. I was invited to his house for sherry. He was a bachelor. He lived with his sister who was called Emmaline of all names. She was dumpy and frowsy and seemed to have something greenish on her teeth that looked like verdigris. She had a kind of surgery in the house where she did things to people's feet. A pedicurist, I think she called herself.

Then the Great War broke out. It was 1914 and I was nineteen years old. I joined the Army. I had to, and for the next four years I concentrated all my efforts on trying to survive. I am not going to talk about my wartime experiences. Trenches, mud, mutilation and death have no place in these journals. I did my bit. Actually, I did well, and by November 1918, when it all came to an end, I was a twenty-three-year-old captain in the infantry with a Military Cross. I had survived.

At once, I returned to Cambridge to resume my education. The survivors were allowed to do that, though heaven knows there weren't many of us. A. R. Woresley had also survived. He had remained in

Cambridge doing some sort of wartime scientific work and had had a
fairly quiet war. Now he was back at his old job of teaching chemistry
to undergraduates, and we were pleased to see one another again. Our
friendship picked up where it had left off four years before.

One evening in February 1919, in the middle of the Lent term, A.
R. Woresley invited me to supper at his house. The meal was not
good. We had cheap food and cheap wine, and we had his pedicurist
sister with verdigris on her teeth. I would have thought they could
have lived in slightly better style than they did, but when I broached
this delicate subject rather cautiously to my host, he told me that they
were still struggling to pay off the mortgage on the house. After supper,
A. R. Woresley and I retired to his study to drink a good bottle of
port that I had brought him as a present. It was a Croft 1890, if I
remember rightly.

'Don't often taste stuff like this,' he said. He was very comfortable
in an old armchair with his pipe lit and a glass of port in his hand.
What a thoroughly decent man he was, I thought. And what a terribly
dull life he leads.

I decided to liven things up a bit by telling him about my time in
Paris six years before in 1913 when I had made one hundred thousand
pounds out of Blister Beetle pills. I started at the beginning. Very
quickly I got caught up in the fun of story-telling. I remembered
everything, but in deference to my tutor, I left out the more salacious
details. It took me nearly an hour to tell.

A. R. Woresley was enraptured by the whole escapade. 'By gad,
Cornelius!' he cried. 'What a nerve you've got! What a splendid nerve!
And now you are a very wealthy young man!'

'Not wealthy enough,' I said. 'I want to make a million pounds
before I'm thirty.'

'And I believe you will,' he said. 'I believe you will. You have a
flair for the outrageous. You have a nose for the successful stunt. You
have the courage to act swiftly. And what's more, you are totally
unscrupulous. In other words, you have all the qualities of the nouveau
riche millionaire.'

'Thank you,' I said.

'Yes, but how many boys of seventeen would have gone all the way
out to Khartoum on their own to look for a powder that might not
have existed? Precious few.'

'I wasn't going to miss a chance like that,' I said.

'You have a great flair, Cornelius. A very great flair. I am a little
envious of you.'

We sat there drinking our port. I was enjoying a small Havana
cigar. I had offered one to my host but he preferred his stinking pipe.
That pipe of his made more smoke than any other pipe I had ever
seen. It was like a miniature warship laying a smokescreen in front of

his face. And behind the smokescreen, A. R. Woresley was brooding on my Paris story. He kept snorting and grunting and mumbling things like 'Remarkable exploit! ... What a nerve! ... What panache! ... Good chemistry, too, making those pills.'

Then there was silence. The smoke billowed around his head. The glass of port disappeared through the smokescreen as he put it to his lips. Then it reappeared, empty. I had talked enough, so I kept my peace.

'Well, Cornelius,' A. R. Woresley said at last. 'You have just given me your confidence. Perhaps I had better give you mine in return.'

He paused. I waited. What's coming, I wondered.

'You see,' he said, 'I myself have also had a little bit of a coup in the last few years.'

'You have?'

'I'm going to write a paper on it when I get the time. And I might even be successful in getting it published.'

'Chemistry?' I asked.

'A bit of chemistry,' he said. 'And a good deal of bio-chemistry. It's a mixture.'

'I'd love to hear about it.'

'Would you really?' He was longing to tell it.

'Of course,' I poured him another glass of port. 'You've got plenty of time,' I said, 'because we're going to finish this bottle tonight.'

'Good,' he said. Then he began his story.

'Exactly fourteen years ago,' he said, 'in the winter of 1905, I observed a goldfish frozen solid in the ice in my garden pond. Nine days later there was a thaw. The ice melted and the goldfish swam away, apparently none the worse. That set me thinking. A fish is cold-blooded. So what other forms of cold-blooded life could be preserved at low temperatures? Quite a few, I guessed. And from there, I began speculating about preserving *bloodless* life at low temperatures. By bloodless I mean bacteria, etcetera. Then I said to myself, "Who wants to preserve bacteria? Not me." So then I asked myself another question. "What living organism above all others would you like to see kept alive for very long periods?" And the answer came back, spermatozoa!'

'Why spermatozoa?' I asked.

'I'm not quite sure why,' he said, 'especially as I'm a chemist, not a bio man. But I had a feeling that somehow it would be a valuable contribution. So I started my experiments.'

'What with?' I asked.

'With sperm, of course. Living sperm.'

'Whose?'

'My own.'

In the silence that followed, I felt a twinge of embarrassment. Whenever someone tells me he has done something, no matter what it is, I simply cannot help conjuring up a vivid picture of the scene. It's only a flash, but it always happens and I was doing it now. I was looking at scruffy old A. R. Woresley in his lab, as he did what he had to do for the sake of his experiments, and I felt embarrassed.

'In the cause of science everything is permissible,' he said, sensing my discomfort.

'Oh, I agree. I absolutely agree.'

'I worked alone,' he said, 'and mostly late at night. Nobody knew what I was up to.'

His face disappeared again behind the smokescreen, then swam back into view.

'I won't recite the hundreds of failed experiments I did,' he said. 'I shall speak instead of my successes. I think you may find them interesting. For example, the first important thing I discovered was that exceedingly low temperatures were required to keep spermatozoa alive for any length of time. I kept freezing the semen to lower and still lower temperatures, and with each lowering of the temp. I got a longer and longer life span. By using solid carbon dioxide, I was able to freeze my semen down to $-97°$ Centigrade. But even that wasn't enough. At minus ninety-seven the sperm lived for about a month but no more. "I must go lower," I told myself. But how could I do that? Then I hit upon a way to freeze the stuff all the way down to $-197°$ Centigrade.'

'Impossible,' I said.

'What do you think I used?'

'I haven't the foggiest.'

'I used liquid nitrogen. That did it.'

'But liquid nitrogen is tremendously volatile,' I said. 'How could you prevent it from vaporizing? What did you store it in?'

'I devised special containers,' he said. 'Very strong and rather elaborate vacuum flasks. In these, the nitrogen remained liquid at minus one-nine-seven degrees virtually for ever. A little topping up was required now and again, but that was all.'

'Not for ever, surely.'

'Oh, yes,' he said. 'You are forgetting that nitrogen is a gas. If you liquefy a gas, it will stay liquid for a thousand years if you don't allow it to vaporize. And you do this simply by making sure that the flask is completely sealed and efficiently insulated.'

'I see. And the sperm stayed alive?'

'Yes and no,' he said. 'They stayed alive long enough to tell me I'd got the right temperature. But they did not stay alive indefinitely. There was still something wrong. I pondered this and in the end I decided that what the sperm needed was some sort of buffer, an overcoat if you like, to cushion them from the intense cold. And after

experimenting with about eighty different substances, I at last hit on
the perfect one.'

'What was it?'

'Glycerol.'

'Just plain glycerol?'

'Yes. But even that didn't work at first. It didn't work properly
until I also discovered that the cooling process must be done very
gradually. Spermatozoa are delicate little fellows. They don't like
shocks. You cause them distress if you subject them straight away to
minus one-nine-seven degrees.'

'So you cooled them gradually?'

'Exactly. Here is what you must do. You mix the sperm with the
glycerol and put it in a small rubber container. A test tube is no good.
It would crack at low temperatures. And by the way, you must do all
this as soon as the sperm has been obtained. You must hurry. You
cannot hang about or it will die. So first you put your precious package
on ordinary ice to reduce the temperature to freezing point. Next, you
put it into nitrogen vapour to freeze it deeper. Finally you pop it into
the deepest freeze of all, liquid nitrogen. It's a step by step process.
You acclimatize the sperm gradually to coldness.'

'And it works?'

'Oh, it works all right. I am quite certain that sperm which has
been protected with glycerol and then frozen slowly will stay alive at
minus one-nine-seven for as long as you like.'

'For a hundred years?'

'Absolutely, provided you keep it at minus one-nine-seven degrees.'

'And you could thaw it out after that time and it would fertilize a
woman?'

'I'm quite sure of it. But having got that far I began to lose interest
in the human aspect. I wanted to go a lot further. I had many more
experiments to do. But one cannot experiment with men and women,
not in the way I wanted to.'

'How did you want to experiment?'

'I wanted to find out how much sperm wastage there was in a single
ejaculation.'

'I'm not with you. What d'you mean by sperm wastage?'

'The average ejaculation from a large animal such as a bull or a
horse produces five ccs of semen. Each cc contains one thousand million
separate spermatozoa. This means five thousand million sperm
altogether.'

'Not five thousand *million*! Not in one go!'

'That's what I said.'

'It's unbelievable.'

'It's true.'

'How much does a human produce?'

'About half that. About two ccs and two thousand million.'

'You mean to tell me,' I said, 'that every time I pleasure a young lady, I shoot into her two thousand million spermatozoa?'

'Absolutely.'

'All squiggling and squirming and thrashing about?'

'Of course.'

'No wonder it gives her a charge,' I said.

A. R. Woresley was not interested in that aspect. 'The point is this,' he said. 'A bull, for example, definitely does *not* need five thousand million spermatozoa in order to achieve fertilization with a cow. Ultimately, he needs only a single sperm. But in order to make sure of hitting the target, he has to use a few million at least. But how many million? That was my next question.'

'Why?' I asked.

'Because, my dear fellow, I wanted to find out just how many females, whether they were cows, mares, humans or whatever, could ultimately be fertilized by a single ejaculation. I was assuming, of course, that all those millions of sperm could be divided up and shared among them. Do you see what I'm driving at?'

'Perfectly. What animals did you use for these experiments?'

'Bulls and cows,' A. R. Woresley said. 'I have a brother who owns a small dairy farm over at Steeple Bumpstead not far from here. He had a bull and about eighty cows. We had always been good friends, my brother and I. So I confided in him, and he agreed to let me use his animals. After all, I wasn't going to hurt them. I might even do him a favour.'

'How could you do him a favour?'

'My brother has never been well-off. His own bull, the only one he could afford, was of moderate quality. He would dearly love to have had his whole herd of cows bear calves by a splendid prize bull from very high milk-yielding stock.'

'You mean someone else's bull?'

'Yes, I do.'

'How would you go about obtaining semen from someone else's valuable prize bull?'

'I would steal it.'

'Ah-ha.'

'I would steal one ejaculation, and then, provided of course that I was successful with my experiments, I would share out that single ejaculation, those five thousand million sperm, among all of my brother's eighty cows.'

'How would you share it out?' I asked.

'By what I call hypodermic insemination. By injecting the sperm into the cow with a syringe.'

'I suppose that's possible.'

'Of course it's possible,' he said. 'After all, the male sexual organ is itself really nothing more than a syringe for injecting semen.'

'Steady on,' I said. 'Mine's a bit more than that.'

'I don't doubt it, Cornelius, I don't doubt it,' he answered dryly. 'But shall we stick to the point?'

'Sorry.'

'So I started experimenting with bulls' semen.'

I picked up the bottle of port and refilled his glass. I had the feeling now that old Woresley was on to something pretty interesting and I wanted to keep him going.

'I've told you,' he said, 'that the average bull produces about five ccs of fluid each time. That's not much. Even when mixed with glycerol there wouldn't be enough there for me to start dividing it up into a great many parts and then expect to be able to inject each of those tiny parts into separate cows. So I had to find a dilutant, something to increase the volume.'

'Why not add more glycerol?'

'I tried it. It didn't work. Altogether too viscous. I won't bore you with a list of all the curious substances I experimented with. I will simply tell you the one that works. Skimmed milk works. Eighty per cent skimmed milk, ten per cent egg yolk and ten per cent glycerol. That's the magic mixture. The sperm love it. You simply mix the whole cocktail thoroughly, and that, as you can see, gave me a practical volume of fluid to experiment with. So for several years, I worked with my brother's cows, and finally I arrived at the optimum dose.'

'What was it?'

'The optimum dose was no more than twenty million spermatozoa per cow. When I injected that into a cow at the right time, I got eighty per cent pregnancies. And don't forget, Cornelius,' he went on excitedly, 'that each bull's ejaculation contains five thousand million sperm. Divided up into doses of twenty million, that gives two hundred and fifty separate doses! It was amazing! I was flabbergasted!'

'Does that mean,' I said, 'that with just one of my own ejaculations I could make two hundred and fifty women pregnant?'

'You are not a bull, Cornelius, much as you may like to think you are.'

'How many females could one of my ejaculations do?'

'About a hundred. But I am not about to help you.'

By God, I thought, I could knock up about seven hundred women a week at that rate! 'Have you actually proved this with your brother's bull?' I asked.

'Many times,' A. R. Woresley said. 'It works. I collect one ejaculation, then I quickly mix it up with skimmed milk, egg yolk and glycerol, then I measure it into single doses before freezing.'

'What volume of fluid in each dose?' I asked.

'Very small. Just half a cc.'

'Is that all you inject into the cow, just half a cc of fluid?'

'That's all. But don't forget there's twenty million living spermatozoa in that half cc.'

'Ah, yes.'

'I put these little doses separately into small rubber tubes,' he said. 'I call them straws. I seal both ends, then I freeze. Just think of it, Cornelius! Two hundred and fifty highly potent straws of spermatozoa from a single ejaculation!'

'I *am* thinking about it,' I said. 'It's a bloody miracle.'

'And I can store them for as long as I like, deep frozen. All I have to do when a cow starts bulling is take out one straw from the liquid nitrogen flask, thaw it, which doesn't take a minute, transfer the contents to a syringe and shoot it into the cow.'

The bottle of port was three-quarters empty now and A. R. Woresley was getting a bit tipsy. I refilled his glass again.

'What about this prize bull you were talking about?' I said.

'I'm coming to that, my boy. That's the lovely part of the whole thing. That's the dividend.'

'Tell me.'

'Of course I'll tell you. So I said to my brother ... this was three years ago, right in the middle of the war ... my brother was exempt from the army, you see, because he was a farmer ... so I said to Ernest, "Ernest," I said, "if you had the choice of any bull in England to service your entire herd, which one would you choose?"

' "I don't know about in England," Ernest said, "but the finest bull in these parts is Champion Glory of Friesland, owned by Lord Somerton. He's a pure-bred Friesian, and those Friesians are the best milk producers in the world. My God, Arthur," he says, "you should see that bull! He's a giant! He cost ten thousand pounds and every calf he gets turns out to be a tremendous milker!"

' "Where is this bull kept?" I asked my brother.

' "On Lord Somerton's estate. That's over in Birdbrook."

' "Birdbrook? That's quite close, isn't it?"

' "Three miles away," my brother said. "They've got around two hundred pedigree Friesian dairy cattle and the bull runs with the herd. He's beautiful, Arthur, he really is."

' "Right," I said. "In the next twelve months, eighty per cent of your cows are going to have calves by that bull. Would you like that?"

' "Like it!" my brother said. "It would double my milk-yield." Could I trouble you, my dear Cornelius for one last glass of your excellent port?'

I gave him what there was. I even gave him the lees in the bottom of the bottle. 'Tell me what you did,' I said.

'We waited until one of my brother's cows was bulling good and proper. Then, in the dead of night ... this took courage, Cornelius, it took a lot of courage ...'

'I'm sure it did.'

'In the dead of night, Ernest put a halter on the cow and he led her along the country lanes to Lord Somerton's place three miles away.'

'Didn't you go with them?'

'I went beside them on a bicycle.'

'Why the bicycle?'

'You'll see in a moment. It was the month of May, nice and warm, and the time was around one in the morning. There was a bit of a moon shining which made it more dangerous, but we had to have some light to do what we were going to do. The journey took us an hour.

' "There you are," my brother said. "Over there. Can you see them?"

'We were by a gate leading into a twenty-acre field and in the moonlight I could see the great herd of Friesians grazing all over the field. To one side, not far away, was the big house itself, Somerton Hall. There was a single light in one of the upstairs windows. "Where's the bull?" I said.

' "He'll be in there somewhere," my brother said. "He's with the herd."

'Our cow,' A. R. Woresley said to me, 'was mooing away like mad. They always do when they're bulling. They're calling the bull, you see. The gate into the field was padlocked with a chain, but my brother was ready for that. He pulled out a hacksaw and sawed through the chain. He opened the gate. I leaned my bike against the hedge and we went into the field, leading the cow. The field was milky white in the moonlight. Our cow, sensing the presence of other animals, began mooing louder than ever.'

'Were you frightened?' I asked.

'Terrified,' A. R. Woresley said. 'I am a quiet man, Cornelius. I lead a quiet life. I am not cut out for escapades like this. Every second I expected to see his Lordship's bailiff coming running towards us with a shotgun in his hands. But I forced myself to keep going because this thing we were doing was in the cause of science. Also, I had an obligation to my brother. He had helped me greatly. Now I must help him.'

The pipe had gone out. A. R. Woresley began to refill it from a tin of cheap tobacco.

'Go on,' I said.

'The bull must have heard our cow calling to him. "There he is!" my brother cried. "Here he comes!"

'A massive white and black creature had detached himself from the herd and was trotting our way. He had a pair of short sharp horns on his head. Lethal, they looked. "Get ready!" my brother snapped. "He won't wait! He'll go right at her! Give me the rubber bag! Quick!"'

'What rubber bag?' I said to Woresley.

'The semen collector, my dear boy. My own invention, an elongated bag with thick rubber lips, a kind of false vagina. Very effective too. But let me go on.'

'Go on,' I said.

'"Where's the bag?" my brother shouted. "Hurry up, man!" I was carrying the thing in a knapsack. I got it out and handed it to my brother. He took up his station near the cow's rear and to one side. I stood on the other, ready to do my bit. I was so frightened, Cornelius, I was sweating all over and I kept wanting to urinate. I was frightened of the bull and I was frightened of that light in the window of Somerton Hall behind me, but I stood my ground.

'The bull came trotting up, snorting and dribbling. I could see a brass ring in his nose, and by God, Cornelius, he was a dangerous-looking brute. He didn't hesitate. He knew his business. He took one sniff at our cow, then he reared up and thrust his front legs onto the cow's back. I crouched alongside him. His pizzle was coming out now. He had a gigantic scrotum and just above it this incredible pizzle was getting longer and longer. It was like a telescope. It started quite short and very quickly it got longer and longer until it was as long as my arm. But not very thick. About as thick as a walking-stick, I'd say. I made a grab for it but in my excitement I missed it. "Quick!" my brother said. "Where is it? Get hold of it quick!" But it was too late. The old bull was an expert marksman. He'd hit the target first time and the end of his pizzle was already inside the cow. It was halfway in. "Get it!" my brother shouted. I grabbed for it again. There was still quite a bit of it showing. I got both hands on it and pulled. It was alive and throbbing and slightly slimy. It was like pulling on a snake. The bull was thrusting it in and I was pulling it out. I pulled so hard on it I felt it bend. But I kept my head and started synchronizing my pulls with the animal's backward movements. Do you see what I mean? He would thrust forward, then he would have to arch his back before going forward again. Each time he arched his back, I gave a pull and gained a few inches. Then the bull thrust forward and in it went once more. But I was gaining on him and in the end, using both hands, I managed to bend it almost double and flip it out. The end of it whacked me across the cheek. That hurt. But quickly I jammed it into the bag my brother was holding. The bull was still bashing away. He was totally absorbed in his work. Thank God he was. He didn't even seem to be aware of our presence. But the pizzle was in the bag now and my brother was holding it and in less than a minute it was all over. The bull lurched backwards off the cow. And then suddenly he saw us. He stood there staring at us. He seemed a bit perplexed and who could blame him. He gave a deep bellow and started pawing the ground with his front legs. He was going to charge. But my brother, who knew about bulls, walked straight up to him and slapped him across the nose. "Git away!" he said. The bull turned and ambled back toward the herd. We hurried out through the gate, closing it behind us. I took the rubber bag from my brother and jumped on the bicycle and rode hell for leather back to the farm. I made it in fifteen minutes.

'At the farm I had everything ready. I scooped out the bull's semen from the bag and mixed it with my special solution of milk, egg yolk and glycerol. I filled two hundred and fifty of my little rubber straws with half a cc each. This was not as difficult as it sounds. I always have the straws lined up in rows on a metal rack and I use an eye-dropper. I transferred the rack of filled straws onto ice for half an hour. Then I lifted it into a container of nitrogen vapour for ten minutes. Finally, I lowered it into a second vacuum container of liquid nitrogen. The whole process was finished before my brother arrived back with the cow. I now had enough semen from a prize Friesian bull to fertilize two hundred and fifty cows. At least I hoped I had.'

'Did it work?' I asked.

'It worked fantastically,' A. R. Woresley said. 'The following year my brother's Hereford cattle began producing calves that were one-half Friesian. I had taught him how to do the hypodermic insemination himself, and I left the canister of frozen "straws" with him on the farm. Today, my dear Cornelius, three years later, nearly every cow in his herd is a cross between a Hereford and a prize Friesian. His milk yield is up by something like sixty per cent and he has sold his bull. The only trouble is that he's running out of straws. He wants me to go with him on another of those dangerous journeys to Lord Somerton's bull. Quite frankly, I dread it.'

'I'll go,' I said. 'I'll take your place.'

'You wouldn't know what to do.'

'Just grab the old pizzle and bung it in the bag,' I said. 'You can be waiting back at the farm all ready to freeze the semen.'

'Can you manage a bicycle?'

'I'll take my car,' I said. 'Twice as quick.'

I had just bought a brand new Continental Morris Cowley, a machine superior in every way to the 1912 De Dion of my Paris days. The body was chocolate brown. The upholstery was leather. It had nickel fittings, mahogany cappings and a driver's door. I was very proud of it. 'I'll get the semen back to you in no time,' I said.

'What a splendid idea,' he said. 'Would you really do that for me, Cornelius?'

'I'd love to,' I said.

I left him soon after that and drove back back to Trinity. My brain was humming with all the things A. R. Woresley had told me. There was little doubt he had made a tremendous discovery, and when he published his findings he would be hailed all over the world as a great man. He was probably a genius.

But that didn't bother me one way or the other. What did concern me was this: how could I myself make a million pounds out of it all? I had no objection to A. R. Woresley getting rich at the same time. He deserved it. But yours truly came first. The more I thought about it, the more convinced I became that there was a fortune waiting for me just around the corner. But I doubted it was from bulls and cows.

I lay awake in bed that night and applied my mind assiduously to this problem. I may seem, to a reader of these diaries, like a pretty casual sort of fellow where most things are concerned, but I promise you that when my own most important interests are at stake I am capable of some very concentrated thinking. Somewhere around midnight an idea came to me and began whizzing around in my head. It appealed to me at once, this idea, for the simple reason that it involved the two things in life that I found most entertaining – seduction and copulation. It appealed to me even more when I realized that it involved a *tremendous amount* of seduction and copulation.

I got out of bed and put on my dressing-gown. I began making notes. I examined the problems that would arise. I thought up ways of overcoming them. And at the end of it all I came to the very definite conclusion that the scheme would work. It was bound to work.

There was only one snag. A. R. Woresley had to be persuaded to go along with it.

8

The next day, I sought him out in college and invited him to dine with me that evening.

'I never dine out,' he said. 'My sister expects me home for dinner.'

'It's business,' I said. 'It's your whole future. Tell her it's vital, which it is. I am about to make you a rich man.' Eventually he agreed to come.

At seven pm, I took him to the Blue Boar in Trinity Street and I ordered for both of us. A dozen oysters each and a bottle of Clos

Vougeot Blanc, a very rare wine. Then a dish of roast beef and a good
Volnay.

'I must say you do yourself well, Cornelius,' he said.

'I wouldn't do myself any other way,' I told him. 'You do like
oysters, don't you?'

'Very much.'

A man opened the oysters at the bar of the restaurant and we
watched him doing it. They were Colchesters, medium sized, plump.
A waiter brought them to us. The wine-waiter opened the Clos Vougeot
Blanc. We began the meal.

'I see you are chewing your oysters,' I said.

'What do you expect me to do?'

'Swallow them whole.'

'That's ridiculous.'

'On the contrary,' I said. 'When eating oysters, the primary pleasure
comes from the sensation you get as they slide down your throat.'

'I can't believe that.'

'And then again, the knowledge that they are actually alive as you
swallow them adds enormously to that pleasure.'

'I prefer not to think about it.'

'Oh, but you must. If you concentrate hard enough, you can
sometimes feel the living oyster wriggling in your stomach.'

A. R. Woresley's nicotine moustache began twitching about. It
looked like a bristly nervous little animal clinging to his upper lip.

'If you examine very closely a certain part of the oyster,' I said,
'just here ... you can see a tiny pulse beating. There it is. D'you see
it? And when you stick your fork in ... like this ... the flesh moves.
It makes a shrinking movement. It does the same if you squeeze lemon
juice on to it. Oysters don't like lemon juice. They don't like forks
being stuck into them either. They shrink away. The flesh quivers.
I shall now swallow this one ... isn't he a beauty? ... There, down
he goes ... and now I shall sit very still for a few seconds so as
to experience the sensation of him moving about gently in my
stomach ...'

The little bristly brown animal on A. R. Woresley's upper lip began
jumping around more than ever and his cheeks had become visibly
paler. Slowly, he pushed his plate of oysters to one side.

'I'll get you some smoked salmon.'

'Thank you.'

I ordered the salmon and took the rest of his oysters on to my plate.
He watched me eating them as he waited for the waiter to bring the
salmon. He was silent now, subdued, and this was how I wanted him
to be. Dash it, the man was twice my age, and all I was trying to do
was to soften him up a trifle before dumping my big proposition in
his lap. I simply had to soften him up first and try to dominate him

if I was to have the slightest chance of getting him to go along with my plan. I decided to soften him up a bit more. 'Did I ever tell you about my old nanny?' I asked.

'I thought we came here to talk about my discovery,' he said. The waiter put a plate of smoked salmon in front of him. 'Ah,' he said. 'That looks good.'

'When I went away to boarding-school at the age of nine,' I said, 'my dear old nanny was pensioned off by my parents. They bought her a small cottage in the country and there she lived. She was about eighty-five and a marvellously tough old bird. She never complained about anything. But one day, when my mother went down to see her, she found her looking very ill. She questioned her closely and nanny at last admitted that she had the most awful pains in her stomach. Had she had them for long, my mother asked her. Well, as a matter of fact, yes, she had had pains in her stomach, she finally admitted, for many years. But never as bad as they were now. My mother got a doctor. The doctor sent her to hospital. They X-rayed her and the X-ray showed something quite unusual. There were two smallish opaque objects about three inches apart in the middle of her stomach. They looked like transparent marbles. Nobody at the hospital had any idea what these two objects might be, so it was decided to perform an exploratory operation.'

'I hope this is not another of your unpleasant anecdotes,' A. R. Woresley said, chewing his salmon.

'It's fascinating,' I said. 'It'll interest you enormously.'

'Go on, then.'

'When the surgeon opened her up,' I said, 'what do you think he found these two round objects to be?'

'I haven't the faintest idea.'

'They were eyes.'

'What do you mean, eyes?'

'The surgeon found himself staring straight into a pair of alert unblinking round eyes. And the eyes were staring back at him.'

'Ridiculous.'

'Not at all,' I said. 'And who did they belong to, those eyes?'

'Who?'

'They belonged to a *rather large octopus*.'

'You're being facetious.'

'It's the gospel truth. This enormous octopus was actually living in dear old nanny's stomach as a parasite. It was sharing her food, eating well . . .'

'I think that'll do, Cornelius.'

'And all of its eight beastly tentacles were twined inextricably around her liver and lights. They couldn't untangle them. She died on the table.'

A. R. Woresley had stopped chewing his salmon.

'Now what's so interesting about all this is how the octopus got there in the first place. I mean after all, how *does* an old lady come to find herself with a fully grown octopus in her stomach? It was far too big to have gone down her throat. It was like the problem of the ship in the bottle. How on earth did it get in?'

'I prefer not to know,' A. R. Woresley said.

'I'll tell you how,' I said. 'Every summer, my parents used to take nanny and me to Beaulieu, in the South of France. And twice a day we used to go swimming in the sea. So obviously what happened was that nanny, many years before, must have swallowed a tiny new-born octopus, and this little creature had somehow managed to fasten itself on to the wall of her stomach with its suckers. Nanny ate well, so the little octopus ate well. Nanny always ate with the family. Sometimes it would be liver and bacon for dinner, sometimes roast lamb or pork. And believe it or not, she was particularly fond of smoked salmon.'

A. R. Woresley put down his fork. There was one thin slice of salmon left on his plate. He let it stay there.

'So the little octopus grew and grew. It became a gourmet octopus. I can just see it, can't you, down there in the dark caverns of the tummy, saying to itself, "Now I wonder what we're going to have for supper tonight. I do hope it's coq au vin. I feel like a bit of coq au vin tonight. And some crusty bread to go with it."'

'You have an unsavoury predilection for the obscene, Cornelius.'

'That case made medical history,' I said.

'I find it repugnant,' A. R. Woresley said.

'I'm sorry about that. I'm only trying to make conversation.'

'I didn't come here just to make conversation.'

'I'm going to turn you into a rich man,' I said.

'Then get on with it and tell me how.'

'I thought I'd leave that until the port is on the table. No good plans are ever made without a bottle of port.'

'Have you had enough, sir,' the waiter asked him, eyeing the rest of the smoked salmon.

'Take it away,' A. R. Woresley said.

We sat in silence for a while. The waiter brought the roast beef. The Volnay was opened. This was the month of March so we had roast parsnips with our beef as well as roast potatoes and Yorkshire pudding. A. R. Woresley perked up a bit when he saw the beef. He drew his chair closer to the table and began to tuck in.

'Did you know my father was a keen student of naval history?' I asked.

'No, I didn't.'

'He told me a stirring story once,' I said, 'about the English captain who was mortally wounded on the deck of his ship in the American

War of Independence. Would you like some horse-radish with your beef?'

'Yes, I would.'

'Waiter,' I called, 'bring us a little fresh shredded horse-radish. Now, as he lay dying, the captain . . .'

'Cornelius,' A. R. Woresley said, 'I have had enough of your stories.'

'This isn't *my* story. It's my father's. It's not like the others. You'll love it.'

He was attacking his roast beef and didn't answer.

'So as he lay dying,' I said, 'the captain extracted from his second-in-command a promise that his body would be taken home and buried in English soil. This created a bit of a problem because the ship was somewhere off the coast of Virginia at the time. It would take at least five weeks to sail back to Britain. So it was decided that the only way to get the body home in fair condition was to pickle it in a barrel of rum, and this was done. The barrel was lashed to the foremast and the ship set sail for England. Five weeks later, she dropped anchor in Plymouth Hoe, and the entire ship's company was lined up to pay a last tribute to their captain as his body was lifted from the barrel into a coffin. But when the lid of the barrel was prised off, there came out a stench so appalling that strong men were seen rushing to the ship's rail. Others fainted.

'Now this was a puzzler, for one can normally pickle anything in navy rum. So why, oh why the appalling stench? You may well ask that question.'

'I don't ask it,' A. R. Woresley snapped. His moustache was jumping about more than ever now.

'Let me tell you what had happened.'

'Don't.'

'I must,' I said. 'During the long voyage, some of the sailors had surreptitiously drilled a hole in the bottom of the barrel and had put a bung in it. Then over the weeks, they had drunk up all the rum.'

A. R. Woresley said nothing. He was not looking at all well.

' "Finest rum I ever tasted," one of the sailors was heard to remark afterwards. Now what shall we have for dessert?'

'No dessert,' A. R. Woresley said.

I ordered the best bottle of port in the house and some Stilton cheese. There was absolute silence between us as we waited for the port to be decanted. It was a Cockburn and a good one, though I've forgotten the year.

The port was served and the splendid crumbly green Stilton was on our plates. 'Now,' I said, 'let me tell you how I am going to make you a million pounds.'

He was watchful and a shade truculent now, but he was not aggressive. He was definitely softened up.

9

'You are virtually broke,' I said. 'You have crippling mortgage interest to pay. You have a meagre salary from the university. You have no savings. You live, if you'll forgive me for saying so, on slops.'

'We live very well.'

'No, you don't. And you never will, unless you let me help you.'

'So what is your plan?'

'You, sir,' I said, 'have made a great scientific discovery. There's no doubt about that.'

'You agree it's important?' he said, perking up.

'Very important. But if you publish your findings, just look what will happen. Every Tom, Dick and Harry all over the world will steal your process for their own use. You won't be able to stop them. It's been the same all through the history of science. Look at pasteurization. Pasteur published. Everyone stole his process. And where did that leave old Pasteur?'

'He became a famous man,' A. R. Woresley said.

'If that's all you want to be, then by all means go ahead and publish. I shall retire gracefully from the scene.'

'With your scheme,' A. R. Woresley said, 'would I ever be able to publish?'

'Of course. As soon as you've got the million in your pocket.'

'How long would that be?'

'I don't know. I'd say five or ten years at the most. After that, you would be free to become famous.'

'Come on, then,' he said. 'Let's hear about this brilliant scheme.'

The port was very good. The Stilton was good, too, but I only nibbled it to clear my palate. I called for an apple. A hard apple, thinly sliced, is the best partner for port.

'I propose that we deal only with *human* spermatozoa,' I said. 'I propose that we select only the truly great and famous men alive in the world today and that we establish a sperm vault for these men. We will store two hundred and fifty straws of sperm from each man.'

'What is the point of that?' A. R. Woresley said.

'Go back just sixty years,' I said, 'to around 1860, and pretend that you and I were living then and that we had the knowledge and the ability to store sperm indefinitely. So which living geniuses, in 1860, would you have chosen as donors?'

'Dickens,' he said.

'Go on.'

'And Ruskin ... and Mark Twain.'

'And Brahms,' I said, 'and Wagner and Tchaikovsky and Dvorak.

The list is very long. Authentic geniuses every one of them. Go back further in the century, if you like, to Balzac, to Beethoven, to Napoleon, to Goya, to Chopin. Wouldn't it be exciting if we had in our liquid nitrogen bank a couple of hundred straws of the living sperm of Beethoven?'

'What would you do with them?'

'Sell them, of course.'

'To whom?'

'To women. To very rich women who wanted babies by one of the greatest geniuses of all time.'

'Now wait a minute, Cornelius. Women, rich or not, aren't going to allow themselves to be inseminated with the sperm of some long-dead stranger just because he was a genius.'

'That's what you think. Listen, I could take you to any Beethoven concert you like and I'd guarantee to find half a dozen females there who'd give almost anything to have a baby today by the great man.'

'You mean spinsters?'

'No. Married women.'

'What would their husbands say?'

'Their husbands wouldn't know. Only the mother would know that she was pregnant by Beethoven.'

'That's knavery, Cornelius.'

'Can't you see her,' I said, 'this rich unhappy woman who is married to some incredibly ugly, coarse, ignorant, unpleasant industrialist from Birmingham, and all at once she has something to live for. As she goes strolling through the beautifully kept garden of her husband's enormous country house, she is humming the slow movement of Beethoven's Eroica and thinking to herself, "My God, isn't it wonderful! I am pregnant by the man who wrote that music a hundred years ago!"'

'We don't have Beethoven's sperm.'

'There are plenty of others,' I said. 'There are great men in every century, in every decade. It's our job to get them. And listen,' I went on, 'there's one tremendous thing in our favour. You will find that very rich men are nearly always ugly, coarse, ignorant and unpleasant. They are robber bandits, monsters. Just think of the mentality of men who spend their lives amassing million after million – Rockefeller, Carnegie, Mellon, Krupp. Those are the old-timers. Today's batch are just as unattractive. Industrialists, war profiteers. All horrible fellows. Invariably, they marry women for their beauty and the women marry them for their money. The beauties have ugly useless children by their ugly grasping husbands. They get to hate their husbands. They get bored. They take up culture. They buy paintings by the Impressionists and go to Wagner concerts. And at that stage, my dear sir, these women are ripe for the picking. So in steps Oswald Cornelius offering to impregnate them with guaranteed genuine Wagner sperm.'

'Wagner's dead, too.'

'I am simply trying to show you what our sperm vault will look like in forty years' time if we start it now, in 1919.'

'Who would we put in it?' A. R. Woresley said.

'Who would you suggest? Who are the geniuses of today?'

'Albert Einstein.'

'Good,' I said. 'Who else?'

'Sibelius.'

'Splendid. And what about Rachmaninov?'

'And Debussy,' he said.

'Who else?'

'Sigmund Freud in Vienna.'

'Is he great?'

'He's going to be,' A. R. Woresley said. 'He is already world famous in medical circles.'

'I'll take your word for it. Go on.'

'Igor Stravinsky,' he said.

'I didn't know you knew music.'

'Of course.'

'I'd like to propose the painter Picasso in Paris,' I said.

'Is he a genius?'

'Yes,' I said.

'Would you accept Henry Ford in America?'

'Oh, yes,' I said. 'That's a good one. And our own King George the Fifth.'

'*King George the Fifth!*' he cried. 'What's he got to do with it?'

'He's royal blood. Just imagine what some women would pay for a child by the King of England!'

'You're being ridiculous, Cornelius. You can't go crashing into Buckingham Palace and start asking His Majesty the King if he would be good enough to provide you with an ejaculation of semen.'

'You wait,' I said. 'You haven't heard the half of it yet. And we won't stop at George the Fifth. We must have a very comprehensive stock indeed of royal sperm. All the Kings in Europe. Let's see. There's Haakon of Norway. There's Gustav of Sweden. Christian of Denmark. Albert of Belgium. Alfonso of Spain. Carol of Romania. Boris of Bulgaria. Victor Emmanuel of Italy.'

'You're being silly.'

'No, I'm not. Wealthy Spanish ladies of aristocratic blood would crave for a baby by Alfonso. It'll be the same in every country. The aristocracy worships the monarchy. It is essential that we have a good stock of royal sperm in our vault. And I'll get it. Don't you worry. I'll get it.'

'It's a hare-brained and impracticable stunt,' A. R. Woresley said.

He put a lump of Stilton in his mouth and swilled it round with port. Thus he ruined both the cheese and the wine.

'I am prepared,' I said slowly, 'to invest every penny of my one hundred thousand pounds into our partnership. That's how hare-brained I think it is.'

'You're mad.'

'You'd have told me I was mad if you'd seen me setting off for the Sudan at the age of seventeen in search of Blister Beetle powder. You would, wouldn't you?'

That pulled him up a little. 'What would you charge for this sperm?' he said.

'A fortune,' I said. 'Nobody is going to get a baby Einstein cheap. Or a baby Sibelius. Or a baby King Albert of the Belgians. Hey! I've just had a thought. Would a king's baby be in line for the throne?'

'He'd be a bastard.'

'He'd be in line for something. Royal bastards always are. We must charge a packet for a king's sperm.'

'How much would you charge?'

'I think about twenty thousand pounds a shot. Commoners would be slightly cheaper. We would have a price list and a range of prices. But kings would be the most expensive.'

'H. G. Wells!' he said suddenly. 'He's around.'

'Yes. We might put him on the list.'

A. R. Woresley leaned back in his chair and sipped his port. 'Assuming,' he said, 'just assuming we did have this remarkable sperm vault, who would go out and find the rich women buyers?'

'I would.'

'And who would inseminate them?'

'I would.'

'You don't know how to do it.'

'I could soon learn. It might be rather fun.'

'There is a flaw in this scheme of yours,' A. R. Woresley said. 'A serious flaw.'

'What is it?'

'The really valuable sperm is not Einstein's or Stravinsky's. It's Einstein's father's. Or Stravinsky's father's. Those are the men who actually sired the geniuses.'

'Agreed,' I said. 'But by the time a man becomes a recognized genius, his father is dead.'

'So your scheme is fraudulent.'

'We're out to make money,' I said, 'not to breed geniuses. These women aren't going to want Sibelius's father's sperm anyway. What they'll be after is a nice hot inject of twenty million living spermatozoa from the great man himself.'

A. R. Woresley had his awful pipe going now and clouds of smoke enveloped his head. 'I will admit,' he said, 'yes, I am prepared to grant you that you could find wealthy female buyers for the sperm of geniuses and royalty. But your entire bizarre scheme is unfortunately doomed to failure for the simple reason that you will be unable to obtain your supplies of sperm. You don't seriously believe that great men and kings will be prepared to go through the ... the extremely embarrassing motions of producing an ejaculation of sperm for some totally unknown young man ...'

'That's not the way I'll do it.'

'How will you do it?'

'The way I'll do it, not a single one of them will be able to resist becoming a donor.'

'Rubbish. I'd resist it.'

'No, you wouldn't.'

I put a thin slice of apple in my mouth and ate it. I raised the glass of port to my nose. It had a bouquet of mushrooms. I took a sip and rolled it on my tongue. The flavour filled my mouth. It reminded me of potpourri. For a few moments I was captivated by the loveliness of the wine I was tasting. And what a remarkable follow-through it had after the swallow. The flavour lingered in the back of the nose for a long time. 'Give me three days,' I said, 'and I guarantee that I'll have in my possession one complete and genuine ejaculation of your own sperm together with a statement signed by you certifying that it is yours.'

'Don't be so foolish, Cornelius. You can't make me do something I don't want to do.'

'That's all I'm prepared to say.'

He squinted at me through the pipe smoke. 'You wouldn't threaten me in some way, would you?' he said. 'Or torture me?'

'Of course not. The act would be of your own free will. Would you like to bet me that I won't succeed?'

'Of my own free will, you say?'

'Yes.'

'Then I'll bet anything you like.'

'Right,' I said. 'The bet is that if you lose, you promise the following: firstly, to withhold publication until we've each made a million. Secondly, to become a full and enthusiastic partner. Thirdly, to supply all the technical knowledge necessary for me to set up the sperm vault.'

'I don't mind making a promise I'll never have to keep,' he said.

'Then you promise?'

'I promise,' he said.

I paid the bill and offered to drive A. R. Woresley home in my motor car. 'Thank you,' he said, 'but I have my bicycle. We poor dons are not as affluent as some.'

'You soon will be,' I said.

I stood on Trinity Street and watched him pedalling away into the night. It was still only about nine-thirty p.m. I decided to make my next move immediately. I got into the motor car and headed straight for Girton.

I O

Girton, in case you don't know it, was and still is a ladies' college and a part of the University. Within those sombre walls there dwelt in 1919 a cluster of young ladies so physically repulsive, so thick-necked and long-snouted I could hardly bring myself to look at them. They reminded me of crocodiles. They sent shivers down the back of my neck as I passed them in the street. They seldom washed and the lenses of their spectacles were smudged with greasy fingermarks. Brainy they certainly were. Many were brilliant. To my mind, that was small conpensation.

But wait.

Only one week before, I had discovered among these zoological specimens a creature of such dazzling loveliness that I refused to believe she was a Girton girl. Yet she was. I had discovered her in a bunshop at lunchtime. She was eating a doughnut. I asked if I might sit at her table. She nodded and went on eating. And there I sat, gaping and goggling at her as though she were Cleopatra herself reincarnated. Never in my short life had I seen a girl or a woman with such a stench of salacity about her. She was absolutely soaked in sex. It made no difference that there was sugar and doughnut all over her face. She was wearing a mackintosh and a woolly scarf but she might just as well have been stark naked. Only once or twice in a lifetime docs one mect a girl like that. The face was beautiful beyond words, but there was a flare to the nostrils and a curious little twist of the upper lip that had me wriggling all over my chair. Not even in Paris had I met a female who inspired such instant lust. She went on eating her doughnut. I went on goggling at her. Once, but only once, her eyes rose slowly to my face and there they rested, cool and shrewd, as if calculating something, then they fell again. She finished her doughnut and pushed back her chair.

'Hang on,' I said.

She paused, and for a second time those calculating brown eyes came up and rested on my face.

'What did you say?'

'I said, hang on. Don't go. Have another doughnut ... or a Bath bun or something.'

'If you want to talk to me, why don't you say so.'

'I want to talk to you.'

She folded her hands in her lap and waited. I began to talk. Soon she joined in. She was a biology student at Girton and, like me, she had a scholarship. Her father was English, her mother Persian. Her name was Yasmin Howcomely. What we said to one another is irrelevant. We went straight from the bunshop up to my rooms and stayed there until the next morning. Eighteen hours we stayed together and at the end of it all I felt like a piece of pemmican, a strip of desiccated dehydrated meat. She was electric, that girl, and wicked beyond belief. Had she been Chinese and living in Peking, she could have gotten her Diploma of Merit with her hands tied behind her back and iron shackles on her feet.

I went so dotty about her that I broke the golden rule and saw her a second time.

And now it was twenty to ten in the evening and A. R. Woresley was bicycling home and I myself was in the Porter's Lodge at Girton asking the old porter kindly to inform Miss Yasmin Howcomely that Mr Oswald Cornelius wished to see her on a matter of the most urgent nature.

She came down at once. 'Hop in the car,' I said. 'We have things to talk about.' She hopped in and I drove her back to Trinity where I gave the Trinity porter half a sovereign to look the other way as she slid past him to my rooms.

'Keep your clothes on,' I said to her. 'This is business. How would you like to get rich?'

'I'd like it very much,' she said.

'Can I trust you completely?'

'Yes,' she said.

'You won't tell a soul?'

'Go on,' she said. 'It sounds like fun already.'

I then proceeded to tell her the entire story of A. R. Woresley's discovery.

'My God!' she said when I had finished. 'This is a great scientific discovery! Who the hell is A. R. Woresley? He's going to be world famous! I'd like to meet him!'

'You soon will,' I said.

'When?' Being herself a bright young scientist, she was genuinely excited.

'Wait,' I said. 'Here's the next instalment.' I then told her about my plans for exploiting the discovery and making a fortune by starting a sperm vault for the great geniuses of the world and all the kings.

When I had finished, she asked me if I had any wine. I opened a bottle of claret and poured a glass for each of us. I found some good dry biscuits to go with it.

'It's sort of a funny idea, this sperm vault of yours,' she said, 'but I'm afraid it's not going to work.' She proceeded to put forward all the same old reasons that A. R. Woresley had given me earlier in the evening. I allowed her to spout on. Then I placed my ace of spades.

'Last time we met I told you the story of my Parisian caper,' I said. 'You remember that?'

'The splendid Blister Beetle,' she said. 'I keep wishing you'd brought some back with you.'

'I did.'

'You're not serious!'

'When you use only a pinhead at a time, five pounds of powder goes an awful long way. I've got about a pound left.'

'Then that's the answer!' she cried, clapping her hands.

'I know.'

'Slip them a powder and they'll give us a thousand million of their little squigglers every time!'

'Using you as the teaser.'

'Oh, I'll be the teaser all right,' she said. 'I'll tease them to death. Even the ancient ones will be able to deliver! Show me this magic stuff.'

I fetched the famous biscuit tin and opened it. The powder lay an inch deep in the tin. Yasmin dipped a finger in it and started to put it to her mouth. I grabbed her wrist. 'Are you mad?' I shouted. 'You've got about six full doses sticking to the skin of that finger!' I hung onto her wrist and dragged her to the bathroom and held her finger under the tap.

'I want to try it,' she said. 'Come on, darling. Just give me a tiny bit.'

'My God, woman,' I said, 'have you any idea what it does to you!'

'You already told me.'

'If you want to see it working, just watch what it does to A. R. Woresley when you give it to him tomorrow.'

'Tomorrow?'

'Absolutely,' I said.

'Whoopee! When tomorrow?'

'You get old Woresley to deliver and I win my bet,' I said. 'That means he's got to join us. Woresley, you and me. We'll make a great team.'

'I like it,' she said. 'We'll rock the world.'

'We'll rock more than that,' I said. 'We'll rock all the crowned heads of Europe. But we must rock Woresley first.'

'He has to be alone.'

'No problem,' I said. 'He's alone in the lab every evening between five-thirty and six-thirty. Then he goes home to his supper.'

'How am I going to feed it to him?' she asked. 'The powder?'

'In a chocolate,' I said. 'In a delicious little chocolate. It has to be small so that he'll pop the whole thing into his mouth in one go.'

'And where pray do we get delicious little chocolates these days?' she asked. 'You forget there's been a war on.'

'That's the whole point,' I said. 'A. R. Woresley won't have had a decent bit of chocolate since 1914. He'll gobble it up.'

'But do you have any?'

'Right here,' I said. 'Money can buy anything.' I opened a drawer and produced a box of chocolate truffles. Each was identical. Each was the size of a small marble. They were supplied to me by Prestat, the great chocolateers of Oxford Street, London. I took one of them and made a hole in it with a pin. I enlarged the hole a bit. I then used the head of the same pin to measure out one dose of Blister Beetle powder. I tipped this into the hole. I measured a second dose and tipped that in also.

'Hey!' Yasmin cried. 'That's two doses!'

'I know. I want to make absolutely sure Mr Woresley delivers.'

'It'll drive him round the twist.'

'He'll get over it.'

'What about me?'

'I think you can take care of yourself,' I said. I pressed the soft chocolate together to seal up the hole. I then stuck a matchstick into the chocolate. 'I'm giving you two chocolates,' I said. 'One for you and one for him. His is the one with the match in it.' I put the chocolates in a paper bag and passed them over. We discussed at some length the plan of battle.

'Will he become violent?' she asked.

'Just a tiny bit.'

'And where do I get that thing you were talking about?'

I produced the thing in question. She examined it to make sure it was in good condition, then put it in her handbag.

'All set?'

'Yes,' she said.

'Don't forget this one will be a dress rehearsal for all the others you'll be doing later on. So learn all you can.'

'I wish I knew judo,' she said.

'You'll be all right.'

I drove her back to Girton and saw her safely in through the gates of the college.

11

We now move forward to five-thirty in the afternoon of the following day. I myself was lying comfortably on the floor behind a row of wooden filing-cabinets in A. R. Woresley's laboratory. I had spent much of the day wandering casually in and out of the lab, reconnoitring the terrain and gradually easing the cabinets twenty inches away from the wall so that I could squeeze in behind them. I had also left a one inch gap between two of the cabinets so that by looking through it I was able to get an excellent view along the whole length of the lab. A. R. Woresley always worked at the far end of the room, about twenty feet from where I was stationed. He was there now. He was fooling about with a rack of test tubes and a pipette and some blue liquid. He was not wearing his usual white coat today. He was in shirtsleeves and a pair of grey flannels. There was a knock on the door.

'Come in!' he called out, not looking up.

Yasmin entered. I had not told her I was going to be watching. Why should I? But a general must always keep an eye on his troops during battle. My girl looked ravishing in a cotton print dress that fitted tightly around her superstructure, and as she came into the room there came with her that elusive aura of lust and lechery that followed her like a shadow wherever she went.

'Mr Woresley?'

'Yes, I'm Woresley,' he said, still not looking up. 'What do you want?'

'Please forgive me for barging in on you like this, Mr Woresley,' she said. 'I'm not a chemist. I'm actually a biology student. But I've run up against a rather difficult problem which is more chemical than biological. I've asked around all over the place but no one seems able to give me the answer. They all referred me to you.'

'They did, did they,' A. R. Woresley said, sounding pleased. He went on carefully measuring out blue liquid from a beaker into the test tubes with his pipette. 'Just let me finish this,' he added. Yasmin stood still, waiting, sizing up the victim.

. 'Now, my dear,' A. R. Woresley said, laying down the pipette and turning round for the first time. 'What was it you ...' He stopped dead in mid-sentence. His mouth dropped open and his eyes became as large and round as half-crowns. Then the tip of his red tongue appeared underneath the bristle of his nicotined moustache and began sliding wetly over his lips. For a man who had seen little else but Girton girls and his own diabolic sister for years on end, Yasmin must have appeared before him like the creation, the first morning, the spirit moving over the waters. But he recovered quickly.

'You had something to ask me, my dear?'

Yasmin had prepared her question brilliantly. I have forgotten precisely how it went, but it dealt with a situation where chemistry (his subject) and biology (her subject) became intertwined in a most complex manner, and where a deep knowledge of chemistry was required in order to unravel the problem. The answer, as she had so shrewdly calculated, would take at least nine minutes to deliver, probably more.

'A fascinating question,' A. R. Woresley said. 'Let me see how best to answer it for you.' He crossed to a long blackboard fixed to the wall of the lab. He picked up a piece of chalk.

'Would you like a chocolate?' Yasmin said. She had the paper bag in her hand and when A. R. Woresley turned round, she popped one into her own mouth. She took the second chocolate from the bag and held it towards him in her fingertips.

'My goodness gracious me!' he burbled. 'What a treat!'

'Delicious,' she said. 'Try it.'

A. R. Woresley took it and sucked it and rolled it round in his mouth and chewed it and finally swallowed it. 'Glorious,' he said. 'How very kind of you.'

At the moment when the chocolate went down his gullet, I noted the time on my watch. I saw Yasmin doing exactly the same thing. Such a sensible girl. A. R. Woresley was standing at the blackboard giving a long exposition with many splendid chemical formulae written in chalk. I didn't listen to it. I was counting the minutes passing by. So was Yasmin. She hardly took her eyes from the watch on her wrist.

Seven minutes gone by . . .

Eight minutes . . .

Eight minutes and fifty seconds . . .

Nine minutes! And dead on time, the hand that held the chalk against the blackboard suddenly stopped writing. A. R. Woresley went rigid.

'Mr Woresley,' Yasmin said brightly, timing it to perfection. 'I wonder if you'd mind giving me your autograph. You are the only science lecturer whose autograph I still don't have for my collection.' She was holding out a pen and a sheet of Chemistry Department notepaper.

'What's that?' he stammered, putting one hand into his trouser pocket before turning round to face her.

'Just there,' Yasmin said, placing a finger halfway down the sheet as I had instructed her. 'Your autograph. I collect them. I shall treasure yours more than any of the others.'

In order to take the pen, A. R. Woresley had to remove his hand from the pocket. It was a comical sight. The poor man looked as though he had a live snake in his trousers. And now he was beginning to bounce up and down on his toes.

'Just there,' Yasmin said, keeping her finger on the notepaper. 'Then I shall paste it in my autograph book along with all the others.'

With his mind fogged by gathering passions, A. R. Woresley signed. Yasmin folded the paper and put it in her purse. A. R. Woresley clutched the edge of the wooden lab bench with both hands. He started rocking about all over the place as if the whole building were in a storm at sea. His forehead was damp with sweat. I reminded myself that he had had a double dose. I think Yasmin was reminding herself of the same thing. She took a couple of paces backwards and braced herself for the coming onslaught.

Slowly, A. R. Woresley turned his head and stared at her. The powder was hitting him hard and there was a glimmer of madness in his eyes.

'I ... er ... I ... I ...'

'Is something wrong, Mr Woresley?' Yasmin said sweetly. 'Are you feeling all right?'

He went on clutching the bench and staring at her. The sweat was all over his face now and running on to his moustache.

'Can I do something to help?' Yasmin said.

A funny gurgling noise came out of his throat.

'Can I get you a glass of water?' she asked. 'Or some smelling salts perhaps?'

And still he stood there, clutching the bench and waggling his head and making those queer gurgling noises. He reminded me of a man who'd got a fishbone stuck in his throat.

Suddenly he let out a great bellow and made a rush at the girl. He grasped her by the shoulders with both hands and tried to push her to the floor but she skipped back out of his reach.

'Ah-ha!' she said, 'so that's what's bothering you, is it? Well, it's nothing to be ashamed about, my darling man.' Her voice as she spoke to him was as cool as a thousand cucumbers.

He came at her again with hands outstretched, pawing at her, but she was too nimble for him. 'Hold on a sec,' she said, flipping open her purse and taking out the rubbery thing I had given her the night before. 'I'm perfectly willing to have a bit of fun with you, Mr W, but we don't want anyone around here to get preggers now, do we? So be a good boy and stand still for a moment while I put your little mackintosh on.'

But A. R. Woresley didn't care about the little mackintosh. He had no intention of standing still. I don't think he *could* have stood still if he'd wanted to. From my own point of view, it was instructive to observe the curious effect a double dose had upon the subject. Above all, it made him hop. He kept hopping up and down as though he were doing calisthenics. And he kept making these absurd bellowing noises. And he kept waving his arms round and round windmill fashion. And the sweat kept trickling down his face. And there was Yasmin, dancing around him and holding out the ridiculous rubbery thing with both hands and shouting, 'Oh, do keep *still*, Mr Woresley! I'm not letting you come *near* me till I get this on!'

I don't think he even heard her. And although he was clearly going mad with lust, he also gave the impression of a man who was in great discomfort. He was hopping, it appeared, because excessive irritation was taking place. Something was *stinging* him. It was stinging him so much he couldn't stand still. In greyhound racing, to make a dog run faster, they frequently insert a piece of ginger up its rectum and the dog runs flat out in an effort to get away from the terrible sting in its backside. With A. R. Woresley, the sting was in a rather different part of his body, and the pain of it was making him hop, skip and jump all over the lab, and at the same time he was telling himself, or so it seemed, that only a woman could help him to get rid of that terrible sting. But the wretched woman was being too quick for him. He couldn't catch her. And the stinging feeling kept getting worse all the time.

Suddenly, using both hands, he ripped open the front of his trousers and half a dozen buttons scattered across the room with little tinkling sounds. He dropped the trousers. They fell around his ankles. He tried to kick them off, but couldn't do so because he still had his shoes on.

With the trousers now around his ankles, A. R. Woresley was temporarily but effectively hobbled. He couldn't run. He couldn't even walk. He could only hop. Yasmin saw her chance and took it. She made a dive for the erect and quivering rod that was sticking out through the slit in his underpants. She grabbed it in her right hand and held on to it as tightly as if it were the handle of a tennis racquet. She had him now. He began to bellow even louder.

'For God's sake shut up!' she said, 'or you'll have the whole university in here! And keep *still* so I can get this damn thing on you!'

But A. R. Woresley was deaf to everything except his fierce and fundamental desires. He simply could *not* stand still. Hobbled as he was by the trousers round his ankles, he went on hopping about and waving his arms and bellowing like a bull. For Yasmin, it must have been like trying to thread a needle on a sewing-machine while the machine was still in motion.

Finally, she lost patience and I saw her right hand, the one which was grasping, as it were, the handle of the tennis racquet, I saw it give a wicked little flick. It was as though she were making a sharp backhand return to a half volley with a quick roll of the wrist at the end of the shot to impart topspin. A vicious wristy little flick it was, and it was certainly a winner, because the victim let out a howl that rattled every test tube in the lab. It stopped him cold for five seconds, which gave her just enough time to get the rubbery thing on and then to jump back out of reach.

'Couldn't we calm down just a teeny weeny little bit?' she said. 'This isn't a bullfight.'

He was tearing off his shoes now and throwing them across the room, and when he kicked off his trousers and became fully mobile again, Yasmin must have known that the moment of truth had arrived at last.

It had indeed. But there is no profit in describing the coarse rough and tumble that followed. There were no intermissions, no pauses, no halftime. The vigour that my double dose of Blister Beetle had imparted to that man was astounding. He went at her as though she were an uneven road surface and he was trying to flatten out the bumps. He raked her from stem to stern. He raked her fore and aft, and still he kept reloading and firing away although his cannon must by then have been scorching hot. They say that the Ancient Britons used to make fire by rotating the point of a wooden stick very fast and for a long time on a wooden block. Well, if that made fire then A. R. Woresley was about to start a raging conflagration any moment, wood or no wood. It wouldn't have surprised me in the least to see a puff of smoke come up from the wrestlers on the floor.

While all this was going on, I took the opportunity of making a few notes with pad and pencil for future reference.

Note one: Endeavour always to arrange for Yasmin to confront the subject in a room where there is a couch or an armchair or at the very least a carpet on the floor. She is undoubtedly a strong and resilient girl, but having to work on a hard wooden surface in exceptionally severe circumstances as she is doing now is asking rather a lot. The way things are going, she could easily suffer damage to her lumbar region or even a pelvic fracture. And where would our clever little scheme be then, tra-la-la?

Note two: Never again prescribe a double dose for any man. Too much powder causes excessive irritation in the vital regions and gives the victim a sort of St Vitus's Dance. This makes it almost impossible for Yasmin to roll on the sperm-collector without resorting to foul play. An overdose also makes the victim bellow, which could be embarrassing if the wife of the victim, the Queen of Denmark, for example, or Mrs Bernard Shaw, happened to be sitting quietly in the next room doing needlepoint.

Note three: Try to think of a way of helping Yasmin to get out from under and to do a bunk with the precious sperm as soon as possible after the stuff is in the bag. The devilish powder, even when sparingly administered, might easily keep a ninety-year-old genius bashing away for a couple of hours or more. And quite apart from any discomfort Yasmin might be suffering, it is vital to get the little squigglers into the freezer quickly, while they are still fresh. Look, for example at old Woresley right now and how he's still grinding away although he's obviously delivered the goods at least six times in succession. Perhaps a sharp jab in the buttocks with a hatpin would do the trick in the future.

Out there on the floor of the lab Yasmin had no hatpin to help her, and to this day I do not know precisely what it was she did to A. R. Woresley that caused him to let out yet another of those horrendous howls and to freeze so suddenly in his tracks. Nor do I wish to know, because it's none of my business. But whatever it was, I was quite certain a nice girl like her would never have done it to a nice man like him if it had not been absolutely necessary. The next thing I knew, Yasmin was up and away and dashing for the door with the spoils of victory in her hand. I nearly stood up and clapped her as she left the stage. What a performance! What a splendid exit! The door slammed shut and she was gone.

All at once, the laboratory became silent. I saw A. R. Woresley picking himself up slowly off the floor. He stood there dazed and wobbly. He looked like a man who had been struck on the head with a cricket bat. He staggered over to the sink and began splashing water on to his face, and while he was doing this, I myself crept from my hiding place and tip-toed out of the room, closing the door softly behind me.

There was no sign of Yasmin in the corridor. I had told her I would be sitting in my rooms at Trinity throughout the operation, so she was probably making her way there now. I hurried outside and jumped into my motor car and drove from the Science Building to the College by a roundabout route so as not to pass her on the way. I parked the car and went up to my rooms and waited.

A few minutes later, in she came.

'Give me a drink,' she said, crossing to an armchair. I noticed she was walking sort of bowlegged and treating herself tenderly.

'You look as though you've brought the good news from Ghent to Aix riding bareback,' I said.

She didn't answer me. I poured her two inches of gin and added a cubic centimetre of lime juice. She took a good gulp of the splendid stuff and said, 'Ah-h-h, that's better.'

'How did it go?'

'We gave him a little bit too much.'

'I thought we might have done,' I said.

She opened her purse and took out the repulsive rubbery thing which she had very sensibly knotted at the open end. Also the sheet of notepaper with A. R. Woresley's signature on it.

'Tremendous!' I cried. 'You did it! It all worked! Did you enjoy it?'

Her answer astonished me. 'As a matter of fact I rather did,' she said.

'You *did*? You mean he wasn't too rough?'

'He made every other man I've ever met look like a eunuch,' she said.

I laughed at that.

'Including you,' she said.

I stopped laughing.

'That,' she said softly, taking another gulp of gin, 'is exactly how I want my men to be from now on.'

'But you said we gave him too much.'

'Just a teensy bit,' she said. 'I couldn't stop him. He was absolutely tireless.'

'How *did* you stop him?'

'Never you mind.'

'Would a hatpin be helpful next time?'

'That's a good idea,' she said. 'I shall carry a hatpin. But I'd much rather get the dose exactly right so I don't have to use it.'

'We'll get it right.'

'I really would prefer not to go sticking hatpins into the King of Spain's bum, if you see what I mean.'

'Oh, I do, I do.'

'I like to part company on friendly terms.'

'And didn't you?'

'Not exactly, no,' she said, smiling slightly.

'Well done, anyway,' I said. 'You pulled it off.'

'He was so funny,' she said. 'I wish you could have seen him. He kept hopping up and down.'

I took the sheet of notepaper with A. R. Woresley's signature on it and placed it in my typewriter. I sat down and typed the following legend directly above the signature:

I hereby certify that I have on this day, the 27th of March 1919, delivered personally a quantity of my own semen to Oswald Cornelius Esquire, President of the International Semen's Home of Cambridge, England. It is my wish that this semen shall be stored indefinitely, using the revolutionary and recently discovered Woresley Technique, and I further agree that the aforementioned Oswald Cornelius may at any time use portions of that semen to fertilize selected females of high quality in order to disseminate my own bloodline throughout the world for the benefit of future generations.

Signed, A. R. Woresley
Lecturer in Chemistry,
Cambridge University

I showed it to Yasmin. 'Obviously it doesn't apply to Woresley,' I said, 'because his stuff isn't going into the freezer. But what do you think of it otherwise? Will it look all right over the signature of kings and geniuses?'

She read it through carefully. 'It's good,' she said. 'It'll do nicely.'

'I've won my bet,' I said. 'Woresley will have to capitulate now.'

She sat sipping her gin. She was relaxed and amazingly cool. 'I have a strange feeling,' she said, 'that this whole thing's actually going to work. At first it sounded ridiculous. But now I can't see what's to stop us.'

'Nothing can stop us,' I said. 'You'll win every time so long as you can always reach your man and feed him the powder.'

'It really is fantastic stuff.'

'I found that out in Paris.'

'You don't think it might give some of the very old ones a heart attack, do you?'

'Of course not,' I said, although I had been wondering the same thing myself.

'I don't want to leave a trail of corpses around the world,' she said. 'Especially the corpses of great and famous men.'

'You won't,' I said. 'Don't worry about it.'

'Take for example Alexander Graham Bell,' she said. 'According to you, he is now seventy-two years old. Do you think *he* could stand up to it?'

'Tough as nuts,' I said. 'All the great men are. But I'll tell you what we might do if it'll make you feel a bit easier. We'll regulate the dose according to age. The older they are, the less they'll get.'

'I'll buy that,' she said. 'It's a good idea.'

I took Yasmin out and treated her to a superb dinner at the Blue Boar. She deserved it. Then I delivered her safely back to Girton.

12

The next morning, carrying the rubbery thing and the signed letter in my pocket, I went looking for A. R. Woresley. They told me in the Science Building that he had not shown up that morning. So I drove out to his house and rang the bell. The diabolic sister came to the door.

'Arthur's a bit under the weather,' she said.

'What happened?'

'He fell off his bike.'

'Oh dear.'

'He was cycling home in the dark and he collided with a pillar-box.'

'I *am* sorry. Is he much hurt?'

'He's bruised all over,' she said.

'Nothing broken, I hope?'

'Well,' she said, and there was an edge of bitterness to her voice, 'not *bones*.'

Oh God, I thought. Oh Yasmin. What have you done to him?

'Please offer him my sincere condolences,' I said. Then I left.

The following day, a very fragile A. R. Woresley reported for duty. I waited until I had him alone in the lab, then I placed before him the sheet of Chemistry Department notepaper containing the legend I had typed out over his own signature. I also dumped about a thousand million of his very own spermatozoa (by now dead) on the bench and said, 'I've won my bet.'

He stared at the obscene rubbery thing. He read the letter and recognized the signature.

'You bounder!' he cried. 'You tricked me!'

'You assaulted a lady.'

'Who typed this?'

'I did.'

He stood there taking it all in.

'All right,' he said. 'But what *happened* to me? I went absolutely crazy. What in God's name did you do?'

'You had a double dose of *cantharis vesicatoria sudanii*,' I said. 'The old Blister Beetle. Powerful stuff that.'

He stared at me, comprehension dawning on his face. 'So *that's* what it was,' he said. 'Inside the bloody chocolate, I suppose.'

'Naturally. And if *you* swallowed it, then so will the King of the Belgians and the Prince of Wales and Mr Joseph Conrad and all the rest of them.'

He started pacing up and down the lab, albeit a trifle gingerly.

'I told you once before, Cornelius,' he said, 'that you are a totally unscrupulous fellow.'

'Absolutely,' I said, grinning.

'Do you *know* what that woman did to me?'

'I can make a pretty good guess.'

'She's a witch! She's a ... a vampire! She's disgusting!'

'*You* seemed to like her well enough,' I said, pointing to the thing on the bench.

'I was drugged!'

'You raped her. You raped her like an animal. *You* were the disgusting one.'

'That was the Blister Beetle.'

'Of course it was,' I said. 'But when M. Marcel Proust rapes her like an animal, or King Alfonso of Spain, will *they* know they've had the Blister Beetle?'

He didn't answer me.

'They most certainly will not,' I said. 'They may well wonder what the hell came over them, just as you did. But they'll never know the answer and in the end they'll simply have to put it down to the incredible attractiveness of the girl. That's all they *can* put it down to. Right?'

'Well ... yes.'

'They will be embarrassed at having raped her, just as you are. They will be very contrite, just as you are. They will want to hush the whole thing up, just as you do. In other words, they will give us no more trouble. We skedaddle with the signed notepaper and the precious sperm and that will be the end of it.'

'You are a rapscallion of the first water, Cornelius. You are an unmitigated scoundrel.'

'I know,' I said, grinning again. But the logic of my argument was irrefutable. The plan was watertight. A. R. Woresley, who was certainly no fool, was beginning to realize this. I could see him weakening.

'What about the girl?' he said. 'Who was she?'

'She's the third member of our organization. She's our official teaser.'

'Some teaser,' he said.

'That's why I chose her.'

'I shall be embarrassed, Cornelius, if I have to meet her again.'

'No, you won't,' I said. 'She's a great girl. You'll like her very much. She happens to like you, too.'

'Rubbish. What makes you think that?'

'She said you were absolutely and positively the greatest. She said that from now on she wants all her men to be like you.'

'She said that? Did she actually say that, Cornelius?'

'Word for word.'

A. R. Woresley beamed.

'She said you make all other men look like eunuchs,' I said, ramming it home.

A. R. Woresley's whole face began to glow with pleasure. 'You're not pulling my leg, are you, Cornelius?'

'Ask her youself when you see her.'

'Well, well, well,' he said, beaming away and preening his horrible moustache lightly with the back of his fingers. 'Well, well, well,' he said again. 'And may I ask what her name is, this remarkable young lady?'

'Yasmin Howcomely. She's half Persian.'

'How interesting.'

'You must have been terrific,' I said.

'I have my moments, Cornelius,' he said, 'Ah yes indeed, I certainly have my moments.' He seemed to have forgotten about the Blister Beetle. He wanted all the credit himself now and I let him have it.

'She can't wait to meet you again.'

'Splendid,' he said, rubbing his hands. 'And she's going to be a part of our little organization, you say?'

'Absolutely. You'll be seeing a lot of her from now on.'

'Good,' he said. 'Goody good.'

And thus A. R. Woresley joined the firm. It was as easy as that. What's more, he was a man of his word.

He agreed to withhold publication of his discovery.

He agreed to assist Yasmin and me in every possible way.

He agreed to construct for us a portable container for liquid nitrogen which we could take with us on our travels.

He agreed to instruct me in the exact procedure for diluting the collected semen and measuring it out into straws for freezing.

Yasmin and I would be the travellers and the collectors.

A. R. Woresley would remain at his post in Cambridge but would establish at the same time in a convenient and secret place a large central freezer, the Semen's Home.

From time to time, the travellers, Yasmin and I, would return with our spoils and transfer them from the portable suitcase freezer to the Semen's Home.

I would provide ample funds for everything. I would pay all travelling expenses, hotels, etc. while Yasmin and I were on the road. I would give Yasmin a generous dress allowance so that she might buy herself a superb wardrobe.

It was all straightforward and simple.

I resigned from the University and so did Yasmin.

I found and bought a house not far from where A. R. Woresley lived. It was a plain red brick affair with four bedrooms and two fairly large living-rooms. Some retired Empire-builder in years gone by had christened it, of all things, 'Dunroamin'. 'Dunroamin' would be the headquarters of the Home. It would be where Yasmin and I lived during the preparatory period, and it would also be a secret laboratory for A. R. Woresley. I spent a lot of money equipping that lab with apparatus for making liquid nitrogen, with mixers, microscopes and everything else we needed. I furnished the house. Yasmin and I moved in. But from now on, ours was a business relationship only.

Within a month, A. R. Woresley had constructed our portable liquid nitrogen container. It had double vacuum walls of aluminium and all manner of neat little trays and other contraptions to hold the tiny straws of sperm. It was the size of a large suitcase, and what's more it looked like a suitcase because the outside was sheathed in leather.

A second, smaller, travelling case contained compartments for ice, a hand-mixer and bottles for carrying glycerol, egg yolk and skimmed milk. Also a microscope for testing the potency of newly collected sperm in the field. Everything was got ready with meticulous care.

Finally, A. R. Woresley set about building the Semen's Home in the cellar of the house.

13

By early June, 1919, we were almost ready to go. I say almost because we still had not agreed upon the list of names. Who would be the great men in the world to be honoured by a visit from Yasmin – and lurking in the background, me? The three of us had many meetings in 'Dunroamin' to discuss this knotty problem. The kings were easy. We wanted all the kings. We wrote them down first:

KING ALBERT OF THE BELGIANS	present age		45
KING BORIS OF BULGARIA	,,	,,	25
KING CHRISTIAN OF DENMARK	,,	,,	49
KING ALEXANDER OF GREECE	,,	,,	23
KING VITTORIO EMMANUELE OF ITALY	,,	,,	50
KING HAAKON OF NORWAY	,,	,,	47
KING FERDINAND OF ROMANIA	,,	,,	54
KING ALFONSO OF SPAIN	,,	,,	33
KING GUSTAV OF SWEDEN	,,	,,	61
KING PETER OF YUGOSLAVIA	,,	,,	75

The Netherlands was out because it had only a queen. Portugal was out because the monarchy had been overthrown in the Revolution of 1910. And Monaco was not worth fooling with. There remained only our own King George V. After much debate, we decided to leave the old boy alone. It was all just a little bit too much on our own doorstep for comfort and in any event I had plans for using this particular gentleman in quite another way, as you will see in a moment. We decided, though, to put EDWARD, PRINCE OF WALES on the list as a possible extra. Yasmin plus Blister Beetle would roll him over any time she wished. What's more, she could hardly wait.

The list of great men and geniuses were more difficult to compile. A few of them, like Puccini and Joseph Conrad and Richard Strauss, were obvious. So were Renoir and Monet, two rather ancient candidates who must clearly be visited pretty soon. But there was more to it than that. We had to decide which of the present-day (1919) great and famous men would still be great and famous ten, twenty and even fifty years hence.

There was also a more difficult group, the younger ones who were at present only moderately famous but who looked as though they might well become great and famous later on. This part of it was a bit of a gamble. It was also a matter of flair and judgement. Would the young James Joyce, for example, who was only thirty-seven years old, come to be regarded as a genius by later generations? I voted yes. So did A. R. Woresley. Yasmin had never heard of him. By a vote of two to one we put him on the list.

In the end, we decided to make two separate lists. The first would be top priority. The second would contain the possibles. We would get round to the possibles only after we had polished off the top-priority boys. We would also pay attention to age. The older ones should, whenever possible, be attended to first in case they expired before we got to them.

We agreed that lists should be updated each year to include any new possibles who might suddenly have shot into prominence.

Our priority list, compiled in June 1919, was as follows, in alphabetical order:

BELL, Alexander Graham	present age	72
BONNARD, Pierre	,, ,,	52
CHURCHILL, Winston	,, ,,	45
CONRAD, Joseph	,, ,,	62
DOYLE, Arthur Conan	,, ,,	60
EINSTEIN, Albert	,, ,,	40
FORD, Henry	,, ,,	56
FREUD, Sigmund	,, ,,	63
KIPLING, Rudyard	,, ,,	54
LAWRENCE, David Herbert	,, ,,	34

Lawrence, Thomas Edward	,,	,,	31
Lenin, Vladimir Ilyich	,,	,,	49
Mann, Thomas	,,	,,	45
Marconi, Guglielmo	,,	,,	45
Matisse, Henri	,,	,,	50
Monet, Claude	,,	,,	79
Munch, Edvard	,,	,,	56
Proust, Marcel	,,	,,	48
Puccini, Giacomo	,,	,,	61
Rachmaninov, Sergei	,,	,,	46
Renoir, Auguste	,,	,,	78
Shaw, George Bernard	,,	,,	63
Sibelius, Jean	,,	,,	54
Strauss, Richard	,,	,,	55
Stravinsky, Igor	,,	,,	37
Yeats, William Butler	,,	,,	54

And here was our second list comprising some fairly speculative younger men as well as a few borderline cases:

Amundsen, Roald	present age		47
Braque, Georges	,,	,,	37
Caruso Enrico	,,	,,	46
Casals, Pablo	,,	,,	43
Clemenceau, Georges	,,	,,	79
Delius, Frederick	,,	,,	57
Foch, Maréchal Ferdinand	,,	,,	68
Gandhi, Mohandas	,,	,,	50
Haig, General Sir Douglas	,,	,,	58
Joyce, James	,,	,,	37
Kandinsky, Wassily	,,	,,	53
Lloyd George, David	,,	,,	56
Nijinski, Vaslav	,,	,,	27
Pershing, General John J.	,,	,,	59
Picasso, Pablo	,,	,,	38
Ravel, Maurice	,,	,,	44
Russell, Bertrand	,,	,,	47
Schoenberg, Arnold	,,	,,	45
Tagore, Rabindranath	,,	,,	58
Trotsky, Lev Davidovich	,,	,,	40
Valentino, Rudolph	,,	,,	24
Wilson, Woodrow	,,	,,	63

Of course there were errors and omissions in these lists. There is no more difficult game than to try spotting an authentic and enduring genius during his lifetime. Fifty years after he's dead it becomes easier. But dead men were no use to us. One more point. Rudolph Valentino was included not because we thought he was a genius. It was a commercial decision. We were guessing that the semen of a man who had such an immense and fanatical band of followers might well be a good seller in days to come. Nor did we think Woodrow Wilson was a genius, or Caruso. But they were world-famous figures, and we had to take that into consideration.

Europe, of course, must be covered first. The long trip to America would have to wait. So on to one wall of the living-room we fixed an enormous map of Europe and covered it with little flags. Each flag pinpointed the precise whereabouts of a candidate: red flags for the priorities, yellow for the second group, with a name and address on each flag. Thus, Yasmin and I would be able to plan our visits geographically, area by area, instead of rushing from one end of the continent to the other, and back again. France had the most flags of all, and the Paris region was literally cluttered with them.

'What a pity both Degas and Rodin died two years ago,' I said.

'I want to do the kings first,' Yasmin said. The three of us were sitting in the living-room of 'Dunroamin' discussing the next move.

'Why the kings?'

'Because I have a terrific urge to be ravished by royalty,' she said.

'You are being flippant,' A. R. Woresley said.

'Why shouldn't I choose,' she said. 'I'm the one at the receiving end, not you. I'd like to do the King of Spain first. Then we can nip over to Italy and do old Vittorio Emmanuele, then Yugoslavia, then Greece, and so on. We'll polish off the whole lot of them in a couple of weeks.'

'May I ask how you intend to gain access to all these royal palaces?' A. R. Woresley said to me. 'Yasmin can't just go knocking on the front door and expect to be received in private by the King. And don't forget it's got to be in private or it's no good.'

'That part shouldn't be too difficult,' I said.

'It's going to be impossible,' Woresley said. 'We shall probably have to forget about the kings.'

I had been working on this problem for several weeks and I had my answer ready. 'Easy as pie,' I said. 'We shall use King George the Fifth as a decoy. He'll get her in.'

'Don't be ridiculous, Cornelius.'

I went to a drawer and took out some sheets of notepaper. 'Let's assume you want to do the King of Spain first,' I said, riffling through the sheets. 'Ah yes, here we are. My dear Alfonso ...' I handed the notepaper to Woresley. Yasmin got up from her chair to look at it over his shoulder.

'What in God's name is this?' he cried.

'It's an extremely personal letter from King George the Fifth to King Alfonso,' I said. And indeed it was.

The notepaper had a heavily embossed royal coat of arms in red at the top centre, and on the top right, also embossed in red, it said simply BUCKINGHAM PALACE, LONDON. Below, in a reasonable imitation of the King's hand-writing, I had written the following:

My Dear Alfonso
This will introduce to you a dear friend of mine, Lady Victoria Nottingham. She is travelling alone to Madrid to clear up a small matter that has to do with an estate that has come to her through her Spanish maternal grandmother.

My request is that you see Lady Victoria briefly and in absolute privacy. She is having some trouble with the local authorities over title deeds and I am sure that if you yourself, after she has explained her problem, will drop a hint with the right people, then everything will go smoothly for her.

I am taking you, my dear Alfonso, very deeply into my confidence when I tell you that Lady Victoria is an especially close personal friend of mine. Let us leave it at that and say no more. But I know I can rely upon you to keep this intelligence entirely to yourself.

When you receive this note, the lady in question will be at the Ritz Hotel, Madrid. Do please send her a message as soon as possible granting her a private audience.

Burn this letter when read, and make no reply to me.
I am at your service at all times.

> *With warmest personal regards,*
> *George RI*

Both A. R. Woresley and Yasmin looked up at me with eyes popping.
'Where did you get this notepaper?' Woresley said.
'I had it printed.'
'Did you write this yourself?'
'I did and I'm rather proud of it. It's a very fair imitation of the King's handwriting. And the signature is almost perfect. I practised it for days.'
'You'll be had up for forgery! You'll be sent to prison!'
'No, I won't,' I said. 'Alfonso won't dare tell a soul. Don't you see the beauty of it. Our great and noble King is hinting that he is having a backstairs affair with Yasmin. That, my dear sir, is very, very confidential and dangerous material. And don't forget, European royalty is the most tight-knit and exclusive club in the world. They work together. Every ruddy one of them is related to the other in some crazy way. They're tangled up like spaghetti. No – there is not the slightest chance of Alfonso letting the King of England down. He'll see Yasmin at once. He'll be dying to see her. He'll want to take a good look at this woman who is the secret mistress of old George Five.

Remember also that right now our King is the most respected of all the royals. He's just won the war.'

'Cornelius,' A. R. Woresley said, 'you frighten me to death. You'll have us all behind bars.'

'I think it's terrific,' Yasmin said. 'It's brilliant. It's bound to work.'

'What if a secretary opens the envelope?' Woresley said.

'That won't happen,' I said. I took a bunch of envelopes from the drawer and found the right one and gave it to Woresley. It was a long high-quality white envelope with the red royal coat of arms top left, and BUCKINGHAM PALACE top right. In the King's handwriting, I had written on it:

His Royal Highness, King Alfonso XIII
Personal and Confidential. To be
opened only by HRH himself.

'That should do it,' I said. 'The envelope will be delivered to the Oriente Palace in Madrid by my own hand.'

A. R. Woresley opened his mouth to say something, then closed it again.

'I have a roughly similar letter for each of the other nine kings,' I said. 'Obviously there are small changes. Each message is tailored to the individual. Haakon of Norway, for instance, is married to King George's sister, Maud – I'll bet you didn't know that – and so there we finish up with "Give my love to Maud, but I trust you absolutely to make no mention to her of this private little piece of business." And so on and so on. It's foolproof, my dear Arthur.' I was calling him by his first name now.

'You appear to have done your homework, Cornelius.' He himself, in the manner of all dons and schoolmasters, refused to use my given name. 'But how do you propose to get in to see all the others, the non-kings?'

'There will be no problem,' I said. 'Not many men will refuse to see a girl like Yasmin when she knocks on the door. *You* certainly didn't. I'll bet you began dribbling with excitement as soon as she came into the lab.'

That shut him up.

'So can we do the King of Spain first?' Yasmin asked. 'He's only thirty-three and from his photograph he's rather dishy.'

'Very well,' I said. 'Madrid first stop. But then we must move into France. Renoir and Monet are top priority. One's seventy-eight and the other seventy-nine. I want to nobble them both before it's too late.'

'With Blister Beetle it'll be heart attack time for those old boys,' Yasmin said.

'We'll reduce the dose,' I said.

'Now see here, Cornelius,' A. R. Woresley said. 'I won't be a party to the murder of Mr Renoir or Mr Monet. I don't want blood on my hands.'

'You'll have a lot of valuable sperm on your hands and that's all,' I said. 'Leave it to us.'

14

The stage was set. Yasmin and I packed our bags and left for Madrid. We had with us the vital liquid nitrogen suitcase, the smaller case containing glycerol, etc., a supply of Prestat's best chocolate truffles and four ounces of Blister Beetle powder. I must again mention that in those days the examination of luggage by customs was virtually non-existent. There would be no trouble with our curious suitcases. We crossed the Channel and travelled to Madrid via Paris by Wagon-Lits. The trip took only nineteen hours altogether. In Madrid, we registered at the Ritz where we had booked separate rooms by telegram, one for Oswald Cornelius Esquire and one for Lady Victoria Nottingham.

The next morning I went to the Oriente Palace, where I was stopped at the gates by a couple of soldiers on guard duty. Waving my envelope and shouting, 'This is for the King!' in Spanish, I reached the big main entrance. I pulled the bell-knob. A flunkey opened one of the doors. I then spoke a Spanish sentence that I had committed to memory, which said, 'This is for His Majesty Alfonso from King George of Great Britain. It is most urgent.' I walked away.

Back at the hotel, I settled down with a book in Yasmin's room to await developments.

'What if he's out of town?' she said.

'He isn't,' I said. 'The flag was flying over the Palace.'

'What if he doesn't answer?'

'He'll answer. He wouldn't dare not to, after reading that letter on that notepaper.'

'But can he read English?'

'All kings can read English,' I said. 'It's a part of their education. Alfonso speaks perfect English.'

Just before lunchtime, there was a knock on the door. Yasmin opened it and there stood the manager of the hotel himself with a look of importance on his face. He had a silver tray in his hand on which lay a white envelope. 'An urgent message, my lady,' he said bowing. Yasmin took the envelope, thanked him and closed the door.

'Rip it open!' I said.

She ripped it open and took out a letter handwritten on magnificent Palace notepaper.

My Dear Lady Victoria, it said. *We shall be pleased to see you at four o'clock this afternoon. If you will give your name at the gates you will be admitted immediately.*
Alfonso R

'Simple, isn't it?' I said.

'What does he mean *we*?'

'All monarchs refer to themselves as we. You have three hours to get ready and be at the Palace gates,' I said. 'Let's fix the chocolate.'

I had obtained from Prestat a number of very small and elegant boxes, each holding no more than six truffles. Yasmin was to give one box to the King as a small present. She was to say to him, 'I have brought you, sir, a little present of chocolates. They're delicious. George has them specially made for me.' She was then to open the box and say with a most disarming smile, 'Do you mind if I steal one? I simply can't resist them.' She pops one into her mouth, then picks up the marked chocolate and holds it out to the King delicately between forefinger and thumb, saying, 'Try one.' The poor man will be charmed. He will eat the choc just as A. R. Woresley did in the lab. And that will be that. Thereafter, Yasmin will simply have to carry on nine minutes of flirtatious small talk without getting entangled in any complicated reason for her visit.

I got out the Blister Beetle powder and we prepared the fatal truffle. 'No double doses this time,' Yasmin said. 'I don't want to have to use the hatpin.' I agreed. She herself marked the truffle with small scratches on the surface of the chocolate.

It was June and very hot in Madrid. Yasmin dressed with great care but wore the lightest possible clothes. I gave her a rubbery thing from my large stock and she put it in her purse.

'For God's sake don't fail to get it on him,' I said. 'That's what it's all about. And hurry back here with it quickly afterwards. Come straight to my room next door.' I wished her good luck and off she went.

In my own room I made careful preparations for dealing with the sperm as soon as it arrived. This was my very first time under actual field conditions and I wanted to get everything just right. I will admit I felt nervous. Yasmin was at the Palace. She was giving Blister Beetle to the King of Spain and after that there would be a good old wrestling match and I only hoped she would handle things properly.

The time went slowly. I finished my preparations. I leaned out of the window and watched the carriages in the street below. Once or twice a motor car came by, but there were not so many here as in London. I looked at my watch. It was after six o'clock. I made myself a whiskey and soda. I carried it to the open window and sipped it there. I was hoping to see Yasmin stepping out of the carriage at the hotel entrance. I didn't see her. I got myself a second whiskey. I sat down and tried to read a book. It was now six-thirty. She had been gone two and a half hours. Suddenly there was a loud knocking on my door. I got up and opened it. Yasmin, with cheeks afire, swept into the room.

'I did it!' she cried, waving her handbag at me like a flag. 'I've got it! It's in here!'

'Give it to me quick,' I said.

There was at least three ccs of royal semen in the knotted rubbery thing Yasmin handed to me. I put a drop under the microscope to test it for potency. The tiny royal squigglers were squiggling madly all over the place, supremely active. 'First rate stuff,' I said. 'Let me get this into the straws and frozen up before you say a word. After that, I want to hear exactly what happened.'

Yasmin went to her room to bathe and change. I set about the business in hand. A. R. Woresley and I had agreed that we would make exactly fifty straws of semen for each person. More than that would take up too much room in our travelling sperm-freezer. I set about diluting the semen with egg yolk, skimmed milk and glycerol. I mixed it. I measured it out with a graduated eye-dropper into the little rubber straws. I sealed the straws. I put them on ice for half an hour. I exposed them to nitrogen vapour for a few minutes. Then finally I lowered them gently into the liquid nitrogen and closed the container. It was done. We now had fifty doses of the King of Spain's semen, and strong doses at that. The equation was simple. He gave us three ccs originally. Three ccs would contain approximately three thousand million sperm and those three thousand million, when divided up into fifty doses, would produce a potency of sixty million sperm per dose. This was exactly three times A. R. Woresley's optimum figure of twenty million per dose. In other words, the Spanish Royal straws were of prime potency. I was elated. I rang the bell for service and ordered a bottle of Krug on ice.

Yasmin came in looking cool and clean. The champagne arrived at the same time. We waited until the servant had opened the bottle and filled the glasses and left the room. 'Now,' I said, 'tell me all.'

'It was amazing,' she said. 'The preliminaries went exactly as you said they would. I was ushered into an enormous room with Goyas and El Grecos all over the walls. The King was at the far end sitting behind a huge desk. He was dressed in a plain suit. He stood up and came forward to greet me. He had a moustache and was not a bad looking little fellow. He kissed my hand. And my God, Oswald, you should have seen the way he fawned all over me because he thought I was the King of England's mistress. "Madame," he said, "I am enchanted to meet you. And how is our mutual friend?"

' "He has a slight touch of gout," I said, "but otherwise he's in splendid condition." Then I went through the chocolate routine and he ate his little truffle like a lamb and with a good deal of relish. "These are magnificent," he said, chewing away. "I must have my ambassador send me a few pounds." As he swallowed the last bit of chocolate, I noted the time on my watch. "Pray be seated," he said.

'There were four big sofa things in the room and before sitting down I examined them carefully. I wanted to choose the softest and most practical of the four. I knew that in nine minutes' time the one I selected would become a battlefield.'

'Good thinking,' I said.

'I chose an enormous sort of chaise longue covered in plum-coloured velvet. The King remained standing and as we talked he strolled about the room with his hands clasped behind his back, trying to look regal.

'I said, "Our mutual friend has asked me to tell you, sire, that if you yourself should ever require any confidential assistance in his country, you could rely upon him absolutely."

' "I shall bear it in mind," he said.

' "He sent you another message as well, Your Majesty."

' "What was that?"

' "You promise you won't be cross if I tell you?"

' "Certainly not, madame. Tell me what else he said."

' "He said, you tell that good-looking Alfonso to keep his hands off my girl. That's word for word what he said, your Majesty." Little Alfonso laughed and clapped his hands and said, "Dear lady, I shall respect his wishes but only with the greatest difficulty." '

'Yasmin,' I said, 'you're a clever little bitch.'

'Oh, it was such fun,' she said. 'I loved twisting him around. He was madly curious about my so-called affair but he didn't quite dare to mention it. He kept putting leading questions to me. He said, "I presume you have a house in London?"

' "Of course," I said. "I have my own London house where I entertain in the normal fashion. Then I have a small very private place in Windsor Great Park where a certain person can call on me when he is out riding. And I have a cottage on the Sandringham Estate where again that certain person can pop in for a cup of tea when he is out shooting pheasants. As you probably know, he adores shooting."

' "I know that," Alfonso said. "And I hear he is the best shot in England."

' "Yes,' I said, "and in more ways than one, Your Majesty."

' "Ha!" he said. "I see you are a funny lady." '

'Were you watching the time?' I said to Yasmin.

'You bet I was. I've forgotten exactly what he was saying when the moment arrived, but the interesting thing is that he froze right in the middle of a sentence just as old Woresley had done in the lab. Here it comes, I told myself. Put on the boxing gloves.'

'Did he jump you?'

'No, he didn't. Don't forget Woresley had had a double dose.'

'Ah yes.'

'Anyway, he was standing in front of me when he froze and he was wearing tight trousers so I could see very clearly what was going on around there. At precisely that moment, I told him I collected the autographs of great men and asked him if he would give me his signature on Palace notepaper. I got up and went to his desk myself and found the paper and told him where to sign. It was too easy. The wretched man hardly knew what he was doing. He signed and I put the paper in my purse and sat down again. You know, Oswald, you can make them do just about anything you want if you catch them right at the very moment when the powder first hits them. They're so astonished and embarrassed by the suddenness of it all they'll do absolutely anything. We're never going to have any trouble getting their signatures. Anyway, I was back again on the sofa now and Alfonso was standing there goggling at me and he kept swallowing which made his Adam's apple jump up and down. Red in the face he was, too, and then he started taking deep breaths. "Come and sit down, Your Majesty," I said, patting a place beside me. He came and sat down. The swallowing and the goggling and the fidgeting went on for about a minute and I could see this absolutely terrific lech building up inside him as the powder got to work. It was like steam building up in a boiler with nowhere to escape except through the safety valve. And the safety valve was little me. If he didn't get little me he was going to explode. Suddenly he said in a chokey and rather prim sort of voice, "I wish you to remove your clothes, madame."

' "Oh sire!" I cried, putting both hands on my breast. "What are you saying!"

' "Take them off," he said, gulping.

' "But then you will ravish me, Your Majesty!" I cried.

' "Please don't keep me waiting," he said, gulping some more.

' "If you ravish me, sire, I will become pregnant and our mutual friend will know something has happened between us. He will be so angry he will send warships to bombard your cities."

' "You must tell him it was he who got you pregnant. Come along now, I cannot wait!"

' "He'll know it wasn't him, Your Majesty, because he and I always take precautions."

' "Then take precautions now!" he snapped. "And please do not argue with me, madame!" '

'You handled it beautifully,' I said to Yasmin. 'So you put the thing on him.'

'No problem,' she said. 'It was easy. With Woresley I had had the most awful fight, but this time it was as easy as putting a tea-cosy on a teapot.'

'Then what?'

'They're pretty odd, these royals,' Yasmin said. 'They know a few tricks us ordinary mortals have never heard of.'

'Such as what?'

'Well,' she said, 'for one thing he doesn't move. I suppose the theory is that kings don't do any manual labour.'

'So he made you do all the work.'

'I wasn't allowed to move either.'

'Now don't be silly, Yasmin. You can't have static copulation.'

'Kings can,' she said. 'Wait till you hear this. You won't believe it. You simply won't believe this sort of thing could happen.'

'What sort of thing?' I said.

'I told you I had chosen a chaise longue covered in purple velvet,' Yasmin said.

'Yes.'

'Well, it turned out I'd picked exactly the right one. This damn sofa was some sort of a specially constructed royal romping ground. It was the most fantastic experience I've ever had. It had something underneath it, God knows what, but it was some sort of engine and when the King pulled a lever the whole sofa began to joggle up and down.'

'You're having me on.'

'I am *not* having you on!' she cried. 'I couldn't make that up even if I wanted to and you jolly well know it.'

'You really mean there was an *engine* under the sofa? Did you see it?'

'Of course not. But I heard it all right. It made the most godawful grinding noise.'

'You mean a *petrol* engine?'

'No, it wasn't a petrol engine.'

'What was it then?'

'Clockwork,' she said.

'*Clockwork*! It's not possible! How did you know it was clockwork?'

'Because when it started to run down, he had to roll off and wind the thing up again with a handle.'

'I don't believe a word of this,' I said. 'What sort of a handle?'

'A big handle,' she said, 'like the starting handle of a motor-car and when he was winding it up it went *clickety-click*. That's how I knew it was clockwork. You always get that clicking noise when you wind up clockwork.'

'Jesus,' I said. 'I still don't believe it.'

'You don't know much about kings,' Yasmin said. 'Kings are different. They get very bored, therefore they are always trying to think up ways of amusing themselves. Look at that mad King of Bavaria who had a hole drilled in the middle of the seat of each chair around his dining-room table. And halfway through dinner, when all the guests were sitting there in their wonderful expensive clothes, he would turn on a secret tap and jets of water would squirt up through the holes. Very powerful jets of cold water right up their backsides. Kings are crazy.'

'Go on with the clockwork sofa,' I said. 'Was it amazing and terrific?'

Yasmin sipped her champagne and didn't answer me at once.

'Did it have the maker's name on it?' I said. 'Where can I get one?'

'I wouldn't get one,' she said.

'Why not?'

'It's not worth it. It's only a toy. It's a toy for silly kings. It has a kind of shock value that's all. When it first started up I got the shock of my life. "Hey!" I shouted. "What the hell's going on?"'

'"Silence!" the King said. "Talking is forbidden!"'

'There was a loud whirring noise coming from underneath the damn sofa and the thing was vibrating most terribly. And at the same time it was jogging up and down. Honestly Oswald, it was like riding a horse on the deck of a boat in a rough sea. Oh God, I thought, I'm going to be seasick. But I wasn't and after he'd wound it up a second time I began to get the hang of it. You see, it *was* rather like riding a horse. You had to go along with it. You had to get the rhythm.'

'So you began to enjoy it?'

'I wouldn't say that. But it does have its advantages. For one thing, you never get tired. It would be great for old people.'

'Alfonso's only thirty-three.'

'Alfonso's crazy,' Yasmin said. 'Once when he was winding up the motor, he said, "I usually have a servant doing this." Christ, I thought, the silly sod really is crazy.'

'How did you get away?'

'It wasn't easy,' Yasmin said. 'You see, with him not having to do any work except winding the thing up now and again, he never got puffed. After about an hour, I'd had enough. "Switch off," I said. "I've had enough."'

' "We go on till I give the order," he said.
' "Don't be like that," I, said. "Come on, pack it in."
' "Nobody gives orders here except me," he said.
'Oh well, I thought. I suppose it'll have to be the hatpin.'
'Did you use it? Did you actually stick him?' I asked.
'You're damn right I did,' she said. 'It went in about two inches!'
'What happened?'
'He nearly hit the ceiling. He gave a piercing yell and bounced off on to the floor. "You stuck me!" he shrieked, clutching his backside. I was up in a flash and starting to put my clothes on and he was jumping up and down stark naked and shrieking, "You stuck me! You stuck me! How dare you do that to me!" '
'Terrific,' I said to Yasmin. 'Marvellous. Wonderful. I wish I'd seen it. Did he bleed?'
'I don't know and I don't care, but I was really fed up with him by then and I got a bit ratty and I said, "Listen to me, you, and listen carefully. Our mutual friend would have you by the balls if he ever heard about this. You raped me, you do realize that, don't you?" That shut him up. "What on earth came over you?" I said. I was getting dressed as fast as I could and stalling for time. "Whatever made you do a thing like that to me?" I shouted. I had to shout because the damn sofa was still rattling away behind me.
' "I don't know," he said. Suddenly he had become all meek and mild. When I was ready to go, I went up to him and kissed him on the cheek and said, "Let's just forget it ever happened, shall we?" At the same time, I quickly removed the sticky rubbery thing from his royal knob and marched grandly out of the room.'
'Did anyone try to stop you?' I asked.
'Not a soul.'
'Full marks,' I said. 'You did a great job. You'd better give me that notepaper.' She gave me the sheet of Palace notepaper with the signature on it and I filed it carefully away. 'Now go and pack your bags,' I said. 'We're leaving town on the next train.'

15

Within half an hour we had packed our bags and checked out of the hotel and were heading for the railway station. Paris next stop.

And so it was. We went to Paris on the night sleeper and arrived there on a sparkling June morning. We took rooms at the Ritz. 'Wherever you are,' my father used to say, 'when in doubt, stay at the Ritz.' Wise words. Yasmin came into my room to discuss strategy over an early lunch – a cold lobster for each of us and a bottle of Chablis. I had the list of priority candidates in front of me on the table.

'Whatever happens, Renoir and Monet come first,' I said. 'In that order.'

'Where do we find them?' Yasmin asked.

It is never difficult to discover the whereabouts of famous men. 'Renoir is at Essoyes,' I said. 'That's a small town about 120 miles south-west of Paris, between Champagne and Burgundy. He is now seventy-eight and I'm told he's in a wheelchair.'

'Jesus Christ, Oswald, I'm not going to feed Blister Beetle to some poor old bastard in a wheelchair!' Yasmin said.

'He'll love it,' I told her. 'There's nothing wrong with him except a bit of arthritis. He's still painting. He is easily the most celebrated painter alive today and I'll tell you another thing. No living painter in the history of art has ever received such high prices for his pictures during his lifetime as Renoir. He's a giant. In ten years' time we'll be selling his straws for a fortune.'

'Where's his wife?'

'Dead. He's a lonely old man. You'll cheer him up no end. When he sees you, he'll probably want to paint you in the nude on the spot.'

'I'd like that.'

'On the other hand, he has a model called Dédée he's absolutely mad about.'

'I'll soon fix her,' Yasmin said.

'Play your cards right and he might even give you a picture.'

'Hey, I'd like that, too.'

'Work on it,' I said.

'What about Monet?' she asked.

'He is also a lonely old man. He's seventy-nine, a year older than Renoir, and he's living the life of a recluse at Giverny. That's not far from here. Just outside Paris. Very few people visit him now. Clemenceau drops in occasionally, so I'm told, but almost no one else. You'll be a little sunbeam in his life. And another canvas perhaps? A Monet landscape? Those things are going to be worth hundreds of thousands later on. They're worth thousands already.'

The possibility of getting a picture from one or both of these great artists excited Yasmin a good deal. 'You'll be visiting lots of other painters before we're finished,' I said. 'You could form a collection.'

'That's a pretty good idea,' she said. 'Renoir, Monet, Matisse,

Bonnard, Munch, Braque and all the rest of them. Yes, it's a *very* good idea. I must remember that.'

The lobsters were huge and delicious, with enormous claws. The Chablis was good, too – a Grand Cru Bougros. I have a passion for fine Chablis, not only for the steely-dry Grands Crus but also for some of the Premiers Crus where the fruit is a little closer to the surface. This particular Bougros was as steely as any I had ever tasted. Yasmin and I discussed strategy while we ate and drank. It was my contention that no man was going to turn away a young lady who possessed the charm and the devastating beauty of Yasmin. No male, however ancient, was capable of treating her with indifference. Wherever we went I kept seeing evidence of this. Even the suave marble-faced receptionist downstairs had gone all over queer when he caught sight of Yasmin standing before him. I had been watching him closely and I had seen that famous old spark flashing in the very centre of the pupil of each of his jet-black eyes, and then his tongue had poked out and had begun sliding over his upper lip, and his fingers had fumbled inanely with our registration forms, and at the end of it all he had given us the wrong keys. A scintillating and sex-soaked creature our Yasmin was, a kind of human Blister Beetle all on her own, and as I say, no man on earth was going to send her packing.

But none of this sexual chemistry was going to help us one bit unless the girl was able actually to present herself to the customer. Formidable housekeepers and equally formidable wives could well be a problem. My optimism, however, was based on the fact that the fellows we were after were nearly all painters or musicians or writers. They were artists. And artists are probably the most approachable people you can find. Even the very great ones are never guarded, as businessmen are, by iron-mouthed secretaries and amateur gangsters in black suits. Big businessmen and their like live in caves that can be reached only by passing through long tunnels and many rooms, with a Cerberus around every corner. Artists are loners, and more often than not they open the front door themselves when you ring the bell.

But why would Yasmin be ringing the bell in the first place?

Ah well, she was a young English girl, a student of art (or music or literature, whichever was applicable) who had such a massive admiration for the work of Monsieur Renoir or Monet or Stravinsky or whoever that she had come all the way from England to pay homage to the great man, to say hello to him, to give him a little present and then to go away again. Nunc dimittis.

'That,' I said to Yasmin as I polished off the last succulent lobster claw – and by the way, don't you love it when you are able to draw the flesh of the claw out of the shell whole and pinky-red in one piece? There is some kind of tiny personal triumph in that. I may be childish, but I experience a similar triumph when I succeed in getting a walnut out of its shell without breaking it in two. As a matter of fact, I never approach a walnut without this particular ambition in mind. Life is more fun if you play games. But back to Yasmin. 'That,' I said to her, 'will get you invited right into the house or the studio ninety-nine times out of a hundred. With your smile and your lascivious looks, I cannot see any of these lads turning you away.'

'What about their watchdogs or their wives?'

'I think you'll get past them, too. Occasionally they may tell you the man's busy painting or writing and to come back at six o'clock. But you're always going to win in the end. Don't forget, you've travelled a long way just to pay homage. And make a point of saying you won't stay more than a few minutes.'

'Nine,' Yasmin said, grinning. 'Just nine minutes. When do we start?'

'Tomorrow,' I said. 'I shall buy a motor car this afternoon. We're going to need it for our French and European operations. And tomorrow we will drive to Essoyes and you will meet Monsieur Renoir.'

'You never waste time, do you, Oswald?'

'My darling,' I said, 'as soon as I have made a fortune I propose to spend the rest of my life wasting time. But until the money is in the bank, I shall work very hard indeed. And so must you.'

'How long do you think it will take?'

'To make our fortunes? About seven or eight years. No more. That's not such a long stretch when it means you can laze about doing nothing for ever after.'

'No,' she said, 'it isn't. And anyway, I'm rather enjoying this.'

'I know you are.'

'What I'm enjoying,' she said, 'is the thought of being ravished by all the greatest men in the world. And all the kings. It tickles my fancy.'

'Let's go out and buy a French motor car,' I said. So out we went and this time I bought a splendid little 10 hp Citroën *Torpedo*, a four-seater, a brand new model only just out. It cost me the equivalent of £350 in French money and it was exactly what I wanted. Although it had no luggage compartment, there was plenty of room on the back seats for all my equipment and suitcases. It was an open tourer and had a canvas roof that could be put up in less than a minute if it started to rain. The body was dark blue, the colour of royal blood, and its top speed was an exhilarating 55 mph.

The next morning we set off for Essoyes with my travelling laboratory packed away in the back of the Citroën. We stopped at Troyes for lunch, where we ate trout from the Seine (I had two, they were so good) and drank a bottle of white *vin du pays*. We got to Essoyes at four in the afternoon and booked into a small hotel whose name I have forgotten. My bedroom again became my laboratory and as soon as everything had been laid out in readiness for the immediate testing and mixing and freezing of semen, Yasmin and I went out to find Monsieur Renoir. This was not difficult. The woman at the desk gave us precise instructions. A large white house, she said, on the right-hand side, three hundred metres beyond the church or some such thing.

I spoke fluent French after my year in Paris. Yasmin spoke just enough of it to get along. She had had a French governess sometime or other during her childhood and that had been a help.

We found the house without any trouble. It was a medium-sized white wooden building standing on its own in a pleasant garden. It was not, I knew, the great man's main residence. That was down south in Cagnes, but he probably found it cooler up here in the summer months.

'Good luck,' I said to Yasmin. 'I'll be waiting about a hundred yards down the road.'

She got out of the car and went towards the gates. I watched her going. She wore flat-heeled shoes and a creamy-coloured linen dress, no hat. Cool and demure, she passed through the gates and moved on up the drive swinging her arms as she went. There was a lilt in her walk, a little shadow attending her, and she looked more like a young postulant going in to see the Mother Superior than someone who was about to cause a saucy explosion within the mind and body of one of the great painters of the world.

It was a warm sunshiny evening. Sitting there in the open motor car I dozed off and did not wake up until two hours later when I found Yasmin getting into the seat beside me.

'What happened?' I said. 'Tell me quick! Was everything all right? Did you see him? Have you got the stuff?'

She had a small brown paper parcel in one hand, her purse in the other. She opened the purse, and took out the signed notepaper and the all-important rubbery thing. She handed them to me without speaking. She had a funny look on her face, a mixture of ecstasy and awe, and when I spoke to her she didn't appear to hear me. Miles away she seemed, miles and miles away.

'What's the matter?' I said. 'Why the great silence?'

She gazed straight ahead through the windscreen, not hearing me. Her eyes were very bright, her face serene, beatific almost, with a queer radiance.

'Christ, Yasmin,' I said. 'What the hell's the matter with you? You look like you've seen a vision.'

'Just get going,' she said, 'and leave me alone.'

We drove back to the hotel without talking and each went to our separate rooms. I made an immediate microscopic examination of the semen. The sperm were alive but the count was low, very low. I was able to make no more than ten straws. But they were ten sound straws with a count of about twenty million sperm in each. By God, I thought, these are going to cost somebody a lot of money in years to come. They'll be as rare as the First Folio of Shakespeare. I ordered champagne and a plate of *foie gras* and toast, and I sent the message to Yasmin's room telling her I hoped she would come in and join me.

She arrived half an hour later and she had with her the little brown paper parcel. I poured her a glass of champagne and put a slice of *foie gras* on toast for her. She accepted the champagne, ignored the *foie gras* and remained silent.

'Come on,' I said, 'what's bothering you?'

She emptied her glass in one long swallow and held it out for more. I refilled the glass. She drank half of it, then put it down. 'For God's sake, Yasmin!' I cried. 'What happened?'

She looked at me very straight and said simply, 'He smote me.'

'You mean he *hit* you? Good God, I am sorry! You mean he actually struck you?'

'Don't be an ass, Oswald.'

'What *do* you mean then?'

'I mean I was smitten by him. He's the first man who's ever bowled me completely over.'

'Oh, I *see* what you mean! Good heavens!'

'He is a wonder, that man,' she said. 'He is a genius.'

'Of course he's a genius. That's why we chose him.'

'Yes, but he's a beautiful genius. He is so beautiful, Oswald, and so gentle and wonderful, I've never met anyone like him.'

'He smote you all right.'

'He certainly did.'

'So what's your problem?' I said. 'Are you feeling guilty about it?'

'Oh no,' she said. 'I don't feel in the least guilty. I'm just overwhelmed.'

'You're going to be a hell of a lot more overwhelmed before we've finished,' I said. 'He's not the only genius you're going to call on.'

'I know that.'

'You're not running out, are you?'

'Certainly not. Give me some more drink.'

I filled her glass for the third time in as many minutes. She sat sipping it. Then she said, 'Listen, Oswald ...'

'I'm listening.'

'We've been pretty jokey about this whole thing up to now, haven't we? It's all been a bit of a lark, right?'

'Rubbish! I take it very seriously.'

'What about Alfonso?'

'You were the one who joked about him,' I said.

'I know that,' she said, 'but he deserved it. He's a joker.'

'I can't quite see what you're getting at,' I said.

'Renoir was different,' she said. 'That's what I'm getting at. He's a giant. His work is going to live through the ages.'

'So will his sperm.'

'Stop it and hear me out,' she said. 'What I'm saying is this. Some people are jokers. Some are not. Alfonso is a joker. All the kings are jokers. We have a few other jokers on our list, too.'

'Who?'

'Henry Ford's a joker,' she said. 'I think that fellow Freud in Vienna is a joker. And the wireless boy, Marconi. He's a joker.'

'What's the point of all this?'

'The point is,' Yasmin said, 'I don't in the least mind being jokey about jokers. I don't mind treating them a little rough either if I have to. But I'll be damned if I'm going to start sticking hatpins into men like Renoir and Conrad and Stravinsky. Not after what I saw today.'

'What did you see today?'

'I told you, I saw a really great and wonderful old man.'

'And he smote you.'

'You're damn right he did.'

'Let me ask you this, did *he* have a good time?'

'Amazing,' she said. 'He had an amazing time.'

'Tell me what happened.'

'No,' she said. 'I don't mind telling you about the jokers. But the non-jokers are private.'

'Was he in a wheelchair?'

'Yes. And now he has to strap the paintbrush to his wrist because he can't hold it in his fingers.'

'Because of arthritis?'

'Yes.'

'And you gave him the Blister Beetle?'

'Of course.'

'It wasn't too much for him?'

'No,' she said. 'When you're that age you have to have it.'

'And he gave you a picture,' I said, pointing to the brown paper parcel.

She unwrapped it now and held it up for me to see. It was a small unframed canvas of a young rosy-cheeked girl with long golden hair and blue eyes, a wondrous little picture, a magic thing, a marvel to look at. A warm glow came out of it and filled the entire room. 'I didn't ask him for it,' Yasmin said. 'He made me take it. Isn't it beautiful?'

'Yes,' I said. 'It is beautiful.'

16

The effect that Renoir had upon Yasmin during that dramatic visit to Essoyes did not, thank heaven, take all the fun out of our future operations. I myself have always found it difficult to treat anything too seriously and I believe the world would be a better place if everyone followed my example. I am completely without ambition. My motto – 'It is better to incur a mild rebuke than to perform an onerous task' – should be well known to you by now. All I want out of life is to enjoy myself. But before one can achieve this happy end one must obviously get hold of a lot of money. Money is essential to a sybarite. It is the key of the kingdom. To which the carping reader will almost certainly reply, 'You say you are without ambition, but do you not realize that the desire for wealth is in itself one of the most obnoxious ambitions of them all?'

This is not necessarily true. It is the *manner* in which one acquires wealth that determines whether or not it is obnoxious. I myself am scrupulous about the methods I employ. I refuse to have anything to do with moneymaking unless the process obeys two golden rules. First, it must amuse me tremendously. Second, it must give a great deal of pleasure to those from whom I extract the loot. This is a simple philosophy and I recommend it wholeheartedly to all business tycoons, casino operators, Chancellors of the Exchequer and Budget Directors everywhere.

Two things stood out vividly during this period. First, the unusual sense of fulfilment Yasmin was getting from each artist she visited. She would emerge from house or studio with eyes shining like stars and a bright red rose on each cheek. All of which caused me to ruminate many times upon the sexual dexterity of men of outstanding creative genius. Did this prodigious creativity of theirs spill over into other fields? And if so, did they know deep secrets and magic methods of exciting a lady that were beyond the reach of ordinary mortals like me? The red roses upon Yasmin's cheeks and the shine in her eyes made me suspect, a trifle reluctantly let me say, that this was so.

The second surprising facet of the whole operation was its extraordinary simplicity. Yasmin never seemed to have the slightest trouble in getting her man to deliver the goods. Mind you, the more one thinks about this, the more obvious it becomes that she never *was* going to have any trouble in the first place. Men are by nature polygamous creatures. Add to that the well-substantiated fact that supreme creative artists tend to be more viripotent than their fellows (just as they also tend to be heavier drinkers) and you can begin to see why no one was going to give Yasmin much of an argument. So what do you have?

You have a bunch of supremely gifted and therefore hyperactive artists loaded with the very finest Sudanese Blister Beetle who find themselves staring goggle-eyed at a young female of indescribable beauty. They were jiggered. They were scrambled and dished up on buttered toast from the moment they swallowed the fatal chocolate. I am positive that the Pope of Rome himself, in the same situation, would have had his cassock off in nine minutes flat just like the rest of them.

But I must go back for a moment to where we left off.

After Renoir, we returned to our headquarters at the Ritz in Paris. From there we went after old Monet. We drove out to his splendid house at Giverny and I dropped Yasmin off at the gates in the approved fashion. She was inside for over three hours, but I didn't mind that. Knowing there would be lots of other long waits like this coming along, I had installed a small library in the back of the car – a complete Shakespeare, some Jane Austen, some Dickens, some Balzac and the latest Kipling.

Yasmin emerged at last and I saw she had a large canvas under one arm. She was walking slowly, just sauntering along the sidewalk in a dreamy sort of way, but when she came closer, the first thing I noticed was the old glint of ecstasy in her eyes and the brilliant roses on her cheeks. She looked like a nice tame tigress who had just swallowed the Emperor of India and had liked the taste.

'Everything all right?'

'Fine,' she murmured.

'Let's see the picture.'

It was a shimmering study of waterlilies on the lake in Monet's Giverny garden, a real beauty.

'He said I was a miracle worker.'

'He's right.'

'He said I was the most beautiful woman he'd ever seen in his life. He asked me to stay.'

Monet's semen, as it turned out, had a better count than Renoir's in spite of him being a year older, and I was fortunate in being able to make twenty-five straws. Admittedly, each straw had the minimum count of only twenty million sperm, but they would do. They would do very well. They would be worth hundreds of thousands, I reckoned, those Monet straws, in the years to come.

Then we had a stroke of luck. In Paris at this time there was a dynamic and extraordinary producer of ballets called Diaghilev. Diaghilev had a talent for spotting great artists, and in 1919 he was regrouping his company after the war and preparing a new repertory of ballets. He had gathered around him for this purpose a group of remarkably gifted men. For example, at that very moment:

Igor Stravinsky had come up from Switzerland to write the music for Diaghilev's *Pulcinella*. Pablo Picasso was designing the sets.

Picasso was also doing the sets for *Three-Cornered Hat*.

Henri Matisse had been hired to design the costumes and the decor for *Le Chant de Rossignol*.

And another painter we had not heard of called André Derain was busy preparing the sets for *La Boutique Fantasque*.

Stravinsky, Picasso and Matisse were all on our list. On the theory that Monsieur Diaghilev's judgement was probably sounder than ours, we decided to put Derain's name on as well. All of these men were in Paris.

We took Stravinsky first. Yasmin walked right in on him while he was working at the piano on *Pulcinella*. He was more surprised than angry. 'Hello,' he said. 'Who are you?'

'I have come all the way from England to offer you a chocolate,' she said.

This absurd remark, which Yasmin was to use on many other occasions, disarmed completely this kind and friendly man. The rest was simple, and although I longed for salacious details, Yasmin remained mute.

'You might at least tell me what he was like as a person.'

'Sparkling bright,' she said. 'Oh, he was so sparkling bright and so quick and clever. He had a huge head and a nose like a boiled egg.'

'Is he a genius?'

'Yes,' she said, 'he's a genius. He's got the spark, the same as Monet and Renoir.'

'What is this spark?' I said. 'Where is it? Is it in the eyes?'

'No,' she said. 'It isn't anywhere special. It's just *there*. You know it's there. It's like an invisible halo.'

I made fifty straws from Stravinsky.

Next it was Picasso's turn. He had a studio at that time in the Rue de la Boétie and I dropped Yasmin off in front of a rickety-looking door with brown paint peeling off it. There was no bell or knocker so Yasmin simply pushed it open and went in. Outside in the car I settled down with *La Cousine Bette* which I still think is the best thing the old French master ever wrote.

I don't believe I had read more than four pages when the car door was flung open and Yasmin tumbled in and flopped on to the seat beside me. Her hair was all over the place and she was blowing like a sperm whale.

'Christ, Yasmin! What happened?'

'My God!' she gasped. 'Oh, my God!'

'Did he throw you out?' I cried. 'Did he hurt you?'

She was too out of breath to answer me at once. A trickle of sweat was running down the side of her forehead. She looked as though she'd been chased around the block four times by a maniac with a carving knife. I waited for her to simmer down.

'Don't worry,' I said. 'We're bound to have one or two washouts.'

'He's a demon!' she said.

'What did he do to you?'

'He's a bull! He's like a little brown bull!'

'Go on.'

'He was painting on a huge canvassy thing when I went in and he turned round and his eyes opened so wide they became circles and they were black and he shouted "Olé" or something like that and then he came towards me very slowly and sort of crouching as though he was going to spring . . .'

'And did he spring?'

'Yes,' she said. 'He sprang.'

'Good Lord.'

'He didn't even put his paintbrush down.'

'So you had no chance to get the mackintosh on?'

'Afraid not. Didn't even have time to open my purse.'

'Hell.'

'I was hit by a hurricane, Oswald.'

'Couldn't you have slowed him down a bit? You remember what you did to old Woresley to make him keep still?'

'Nothing would have stopped this one.'

'Were you on the floor?'

'No. He threw me on to a filthy sofa thing. There were tubes of paint everywhere.'

'It's all over you now. Look at your dress.'

'I know.'

One couldn't blame Yasmin for the failure, I knew that. But I felt pretty ratty all the same. It was our first miss. I only hoped there wouldn't be many more.

'Do you know what he did afterwards?' Yasmin said. 'He just buttoned up his trousers and said, "Thank you, mademoiselle. That was very refreshing. Now I must get back to my work." And he turned away, Oswald! He just turned away and started painting again!'

'He's Spanish,' I said, 'like Alfonso.' I stepped out of the car and cranked the starting-handle and when I got back in again Yasmin was tidying her hair in the car mirror. 'I hate to say it,' she said, 'but I rather enjoyed that one.'

'I know you did.'

'Phenomenal vitality.'

'Tell me,' I said, 'is Monsieur Picasso a genius?'

'Yes,' she said. 'It was very strong. He will be wildly famous one day.'

'Damn.'

'We can't win them all, Oswald.'

'I suppose not.'

Matisse was next.

Yasmin was with Monsieur Matisse for about two hours and blow me if the little thief didn't come out with yet another painting. It was sheer magic, that canvas, a Fauve landscape with trees that were blue and green and scarlet, signed and dated 1905.

'Terrific picture,' I said.

'Terrific man,' she said. And that was all she would say about Henri Matisse. Not a word more.

Fifty straws.

17

My travelling container of liquid nitrogen was beginning to fill up with straws. We now had King Alfonso, Renoir, Monet, Stravinsky and Matisse. But there was room for a few more. Each straw held only ¼cc of fluid and the straw itself was only slightly thicker than a matchstick and about half as long. Fifty straws stacked neatly in a metal rack took up very little room. I decided we could accommodate three more batches on this trip and I told Yasmin we would be visiting Marcel Proust, Maurice Ravel and James Joyce. All of them were living in the Paris area.

If I have given the impression that Yasmin and I were paying our visits more or less on consecutive days, that is wrong. We were, in fact, moving slowly and carefully. Usually about a week went by between each visit. This gave me time to investigate thoroughly the next victim before we moved in on him. We never drove up to a house and rang the bell and hoped for the best. Before we made a call, I knew all about the man's habits and his working hours, about his family and his servants if he had any, and we would choose our time with care. But even then Yasmin would occasionally have to wait outside in the motor car until a wife or a servant came out to go shopping.

Monsieur Proust was our next choice. He was forty-eight years old, and six years back, in 1913, he had published *Du Côté de chez Swann*. Now he had just brought out *A l'Ombre de Jeunes Filles en Fleurs*. This book had been received with much enthusiasm by the reviewers and had won him the Goncourt Prize. But I was a bit nervous about Monsieur Proust. My inquiries showed him to be a very queer duck indeed. He was independently wealthy. He was a snob. He was anti-semitic. He was vain. He was a hypochondriac who suffered from asthma. He slept until four in the afternoon and stayed awake all night. He lived with a faithful watchdog servant called Céleste and his present address was an apartment at No. 8 bis Rue Laurent-Pichet. The house belonged to the celebrated actress Réjane, and Réjane's son lived in the flat immediately below Proust, while Réjane herself occupied the rest of the place.

I learned that Monsieur Proust was, from a literary point of view, totally unscrupulous and would use both persuasion and money to inspire rave articles about his books in newspapers and magazines. And on top of all this, he was completely homosexual. No woman, other than the faithful Céleste, was ever permitted into his bedroom. In order to study the man more closely, I got myself invited to a dinner at the house of his close friend, Princess Soutzo. And there I discovered that Monsieur Proust was nothing to look at. With his black moustache, his round bulging eyes and his baggy little figure, he bore an astonishing resemblance to an actor on the cinematograph screen called Charlie Chaplin. At Princess Soutzo's, he complained a lot about draughts in the dining-room and he held court among the guests and expected everyone to be silent when he spoke. I can remember two incredible pronouncements he made that evening. Of a man who preferred women, he said, 'I can answer for him. He is completely abnormal.' And another time, I heard him say, 'Fondness for men leads to virility.' In short, he was a tricky fellow.

'Now wait just a minute,' Yasmin had said to me when I told her all this. 'I'll be damned if I'm going to take on a bugger.'

'Why not?'

'Don't be so stupid, Oswald. If he's a raging hundred per cent fairy . . .'

'He calls it an invert.'

'I don't care what he calls it.'

'It's a very Proustian word,' I said. 'Look up "to invert" in the dictionary and you'll find the definition is "to turn upside down".'

'He's not turning me upside down thank you very much,' Yasmin said.

'Now don't get excited.'

'Anyway, it's a waste of time,' she said. 'He wouldn't even look at me.'

'I think he would.'

'What d'you want me to do, dress up as a choirboy?'

'We'll give him a double dose of Blister Beetle.'

'That's not going to change his habits.'

'No,' I said, 'but it'll make him so bloody horny he won't care what sex you are.'

'He'll invert me.'

'No, he won't.'

'He'll invert me like a comma.'

'Take a hatpin with you.'

'It's still not going to work,' she said. 'If he's a genuine twenty-four carat queer, then all women are physically repulsive to him.'

'It's essential we get him,' I said. 'Our collection won't be complete without fifty Proust straws.'

'Is he really so important?'

'He's going to be,' I said. 'I'm sure of it. There'll be a strong demand for Proust children in the years to come.'

Yasmin gazed out of the Ritz windows at the cloudy-grey summer sky over Paris. 'If that's the case, then there's only one thing for it,' she said.

'What's that?'

'You do it yourself.'

I was so shocked I jumped.

'Steady on,' I said.

'He wants a man,' she said. 'Well, you're a man. You're perfect. You're young, you're beautiful and you're lecherous.'

'Yes, but I am not a catamite.'

'You don't have the guts?'

'Of course I've got the guts. But field work is your province, not mine.'

'Who said so?'

'I can't cope with a man, Yasmin, you know that.'

'This isn't a man. It's a fairy.'

'For God's sake!' I cried. 'I'll be damned if I'll let that little sod come near me! I'll have you know that even an enema gives me the shakes for a week!'

Yasmin burst into shrieks of laughter. 'I suppose you're going to tell me next,' she said, 'that you have a small sphincter.'

'Yes and I'm not having Mr Proust enlarge it, thanks very much,' I said.

'You're a coward, Oswald,' she said.

It was an impasse. I sulked. Yasmin got up and poured herself a drink. I did the same. We sat there drinking in silence. It was early evening.

'Where shall we have dinner tonight?' I said.

'I don't care,' she said. 'I think we ought to try to solve this Proust thing first. I'd hate to see this little bugger get away.'

'Do you have any ideas?'

'I'm thinking,' she said.

I finished my drink and got myself another. 'You want one?' I said to her.

'No,' she said. I left her to go on thinking. After a while she said, 'Well now, I wonder if that will work.'

'What?'

'I've just had a tiny little idea.'

'Tell me.'

Yasmin didn't answer. She stood up and walked over to the window and leaned out. She stayed leaning out of that window for fully five minutes, immobile, deep in thought, and I watched her but kept my mouth shut. Then all of a sudden I saw her reach behind her with her right hand, and the hand started snatching at the air as though she were catching flies. She didn't look round as she did this. She just went on hanging out of the window and snatching away at those invisible non-existent flies behind her.

'What the hell's going on?' I said.

She turned round and faced me, and now there was a big smile on her face. 'It's great!' she cried. 'I love it! I *am* a clever little girl!'

'Out with it then.'

'It's going to be tricky,' she said, 'and I'm going to have to be very quick, but I'm good at catching. Come to think of it, I was always better than my brother at catching cricket balls.'

'What the hell are you talking about?' I said.

'It would mean disguising me as a man.'

'Easy,' I said. 'No problem.'

'A beautiful young man.'

'Will you give him the Beetle?'

'A double dose,' she said.

'Isn't that a bit risky? Don't forget what it did to old Woresley.'

'That's just how I want him,' she said. 'I want him out of his mind.'

'Would you please tell me exactly what you propose to do?' I asked her.

'Don't ask so many questions, Oswald. Just leave that side of it to me. I regard Monsieur Proust as fair game. He's in the joker class and I shall treat him as a joker.'

'Actually he's not,' I said. 'He's another genius. But take the hatpin by all means. The royal hatpin. The one that's been two inches into the King of Spain's bum.'

'I'd feel happier with a carving-knife,' she said.

We spent the next few days dressing Yasmin up as a boy. We told the couturier and the wigmaker and the shoe people that we were rigging her up for a very grand fancy-dress party, and they rallied round with enthusiasm. It is amazing what a good wig can do to a face. From the moment the wig was on and the make-up was off, Yasmin became a male. We chose slightly effeminate pale grey trousers, a blue shirt, a silk stock tie, a flowered silk waistcoat and a fawn jacket. The shoes were brogues, white and brown. The hat was a soft felt trilby the colour of snuff, with a large brim. We took the curves out of her noble bosom by strapping it with a wide crêpe bandage. I taught her to speak in a soft whispering voice to disguise the pitch, and I rehearsed her diligently in what she was to say, first to Céleste when the door was opened, and then to Monsieur Proust when she was shown into his presence.

Within a week, we were ready to go. Yasmin had still not told me how she intended to save herself from being inverted in true Proustian fashion and I did not press her any further about this. I was happy enough that she had agreed to take the man on.

We decided that she should arrive at his house at seven p.m. By then our victim would have been up and about for a good three hours. In her bedroom at the Ritz, I helped Yasmin to dress. The wig was a beauty. It gave her a head of hair that was golden-bronze in colour, slightly curly and a bit on the long side. The grey trousers, the flowered waistcoat and the fawn jacket turned her into an effeminate but ravishingly beautiful young man.

'No bugger could resist buggering you,' I said.

She smiled but made no comment.

'Hang on,' I said. 'There's something missing. Your trousers look distinctly empty. It's a dead giveaway.' There was a bowl of fruit on the sideboard, a present from the hotel management. I selected a small banana. Yasmin lowered her trousers and we strapped the banana to the inside of her upper thigh with sticking plaster. When she pulled up her trousers again, the effect was electric – a tell-tale and tantalizing bulge in exactly the right place.

'He'll see it,' I said. 'It'll drive him dotty.'

18

We went downstairs and got into the motor car. I drove to the Rue Laurent-Pichet and stopped the car about twenty yards short of number eight, on the other side of the street. We examined the house. It was a large stone building with a black front door. 'Off you go,' I said, 'and good luck. He's on the second floor.'

Yasmin got out of the car. 'This banana's a bit uncomfortable,' she said.

'Now you know what it's like to be a man,' I said.

She turned away and strode toward the house with her hands in her trouser pockets. I saw her try the door. It was unlocked, presumably because the place was divided into separate apartments. She went in.

I settled down in the motor car to await the outcome. I, the general, had done all I could to prepare for the battle. The rest was up to Yasmin, the soldier. She was well armed. She carried a double dose (we had finally decided) of Blister Beetle and a long hatpin whose sharp end still bore the crusted traces of Spanish royal blood which Yasmin had refused to wipe off.

It was a warm cloudy August evening in Paris. The canvas hood of my blue Citroën *Torpedo* was folded back. My seat was comfortable but I was too fidgety to concentrate on a book. I had a good view of the house and I fixed my eyes upon it with a certain fascination. I could see the large windows on the second floor where Monsieur Proust lived, and the green velvet curtains that were drawn back on either side, but I couldn't see in. Yasmin was up there now, probably in that very room, and she would be saying, as I had so carefully instructed her to say, 'Pray forgive me, monsieur, but I am in love with your work. I have come all the way from England simply to pay homage to your greatness. Please accept this little box of chocolates ... they are delicious ... do you mind if I have one ... and here's one for you ...'

I waited twenty minutes. I waited thirty minutes. I was watching the clock. The way Yasmin felt about 'that little bugger' as she called him, I reckoned there would be no tête-à-tête and pleasant conversation afterwards, as there had been with Renoir and Monet. This, I reflected, would be a brief sharp visit and possibly a rather painful one for the great writer.

I was correct about it being brief. Thirty-three minutes after Yasmin had gone in, I saw the big black front door opening and out she came.

As she walked toward me, I looked for traces of dishevelment in her clothes. There were none. The snuff-coloured trilby was at the same saucy angle as before and altogether she looked as trim and crisp coming out as she had going in.

Or did she? Was there not a slight lack of bounce in her walk? There was indeed. And was there not a tendency to move those splendid long limbs of hers rather carefully? Unquestionably yes. She was walking, in fact, like a person who had just dismounted from a bicycle after a long ride upon an uncomfortable saddle.

These small observations comforted me. They were evidence, surely, that my gallant soldier had been engaged in fierce combat.

'Well done,' I said as she got into the car.

'What makes you think it was so successful?'

She was a cool one, our Yasmin.

'Don't tell me it went wrong.'

She didn't answer me. She settled herself in the seat and closed the car door.

'I have to know, Yasmin, because if you do have the loot I must rush it back quickly and freeze it up.'

She had it. Of course she had it. I rushed it back to the hotel and made fifty exceptional straws. Each straw, according to my microscopic density count, contained no less than seventy-five million sperm. I know they were potent straws because at this very moment, as I write these words nineteen years after the event, I am able to state positively that there are fourteen children running around in France who have Marcel Proust as their father. Only I know who they are. Such matters are great secrets. They are secrets between me and the mothers. The husbands don't know. It's a mother's secret. But my goodness me, you should see those fourteen silly rich ambitious literary-minded mothers. Each one of them, as she gazes proudly upon her Proustian offspring, is telling herself that she has almost certainly given birth to a great writer. Well, she is wrong. All of them are wrong. There is no evidence whatsoever that great writers beget great writers. Occasionally they beget minor writers, but that's as far as it goes.

There is, I think, slightly more evidence that great painters sometimes beget great painters. Look at Teniers and Breughel and Tiepolo, and even Pissarro. And in music, the wonderful Johann Sebastian had such an overwhelming genius that it was impossible for him not to pass some of it on to his children. But writers, no. Great writers seem to spring more often than not from stony soil – the sons of coal-miners or pork butchers or impoverished teachers. But that simple truth was never going to prevent a small number of wealthy literary-snob ladies from wishing to have a baby by the brilliant Monsieur Proust or the extraordinary Mr James Joyce. My job, anyway, was not to propagate geniuses but to make money.

By the time I had filled those fifty Proust straws and had immersed them safely in liquid nitrogen, it was nearly nine o'clock at night. Yasmin was now bathed and changed into fine feminine clothes and I took her out to Maxims for supper to celebrate our success. She had not yet told me anything of what went on.

My diary from that date informs me that we both started the meal with a dozen *escargots*. It was mid-August and the grouse were just beginning to come in from Yorkshire and Scotland, so we ordered one each and I told the head-waiter we wanted them blood-rare. The wine was to be a bottle of Volnay, one of my favourite burgundies.

'Now,' I said when we had given our order. 'Tell me all.'

'You want a blow by blow account?'

'Every tiny detail.'

There was a bowl of radishes on the table and Yasmin popped one into her mouth and crunched it up. 'He had a bell on his door,' she said, 'so I rang it. Céleste opened the door and glared at me. You should see that Céleste, Oswald. She's skinny and sharp-nosed with a mouth like a knife and two small brown eyes that looked me up and down with utter distaste. "What is it you wish?" she said sharply, and I gave her the bit about having travelled from England to bring a present to the famous writer whom I worshipped. "Monsieur Proust is working," Céleste said and tried to shut the door. I put my foot in it and pushed it open and marched in. "I have not travelled all this distance to have a door slammed in my face," I said. "Kindly inform your master that I am here to see him." '

'Well done, you,' I said.

'I had to bluff it out,' she said. 'Céleste glared at me. "What name?" she snapped. "Mister Bottomley," I said, "of London." I was rather pleased with that name.'

'Apt,' I said. 'Did the maid announce you?'

'Oh yes. And out he came into the hall, this funny little pop-eyed bugger, still holding a pen in his hand.'

'What happened next?'

'I immediately launched into the long speech you taught me, starting with, "Pray forgive me, monsieur . . ." but I'd hardly got half a dozen words out when he raised his hand and cried, "Stop! I have already forgiven you!" He was goggling at me as though I were the most beautiful and desirable and spicy little lad he'd ever seen in his life, which I'll bet I was.'

'Was he speaking in English or French?'

'A bit of each. His English was pretty good, about like my French, so it didn't matter.'

'And he fell for you right away?'

'He couldn't take his eyes off me. "That will be all, thank you, Céleste," he said, licking his lips. But Céleste didn't like it. She stayed put. She scented trouble.

' "You may *go*, Céleste," Monsieur Proust said, raising his voice.

'But she still refused to go. "You do not wish anything more, Monsieur Proust?"

' "I wish to be left alone," he snapped, and the woman stalked out of the room in a huff.

' "Pray sit down, Monsieur Bottomley," he said. "May I take your hat? I do apologize for my servant. She's a trifle over-protective."

' "What is she protecting you from, monsieur?"

'He smiled at me, showing horrid teeth with wide gaps. "From you," he said softly.

'By golly, I thought, I'm going to be inverted any moment. At this point, Oswald, I seriously considered skipping the Blister Beetle altogether. The man was drooling with lust. If I'd so much as bent down to do up a shoelace, he'd have been on me.'

'But you didn't skip it?'

'No,' she said. 'I gave him the chocolate.'

'Why?'

'Because in some ways they're easier to handle when they're under the influence. They don't quite know what they're doing.'

'Did the chocolate work well?'

'It always works well,' she said. 'But this was a double dose so it worked better.'

'How much better?'

'Buggers are different,' she said.

'I believe you.'

'You see,' she said, 'when an ordinary man is driven crazy by the Beetle, all he wants to do is to rape the woman on the spot. But when a bugger is driven crazy by the powder, his first thought is not to start buggering right away. He begins by making violent grabs for the other fellow's pizzle.'

'A bit awkward, that.'

'Very,' Yasmin said. 'I know that if I let him come near enough to grab me, all he'd get in his hand would be a squashed banana.'

'So what did you do?'

'I kept jumping out of the way,' she said. 'And in the end, of course, it became a chase with him chasing me all round the room and knocking things over right and left.'

'Rather strenuous.'

'Yes, and in the middle of it all the door opened and there stood that dreadful little maid again. "Monsieur Proust," she said, "all this exercise is bad for your asthma."'

'"Get out!" he yelled. "Get out, you witch!"'

'I imagine she's fairly used to that sort of thing.'

'I'm sure she is,' Yasmin said. 'Anyway, there was a round table in the middle of the room and so long as I stayed close to it I knew he couldn't catch me. Many a girl has been saved from a dirty old man by a round table. The trouble was he seemed to be enjoying this part of it, and soon I got to thinking that a good old chase around the room was probably an essential preliminary for those chaps.'

'A sort of pipe-opener.'

'Right,' she said. 'And he kept saying things to me as we circled round and round the table.'

'What sort of things?'

'Dirty stuff,' she said. 'Not worth repeating. By the way, putting that banana in was a mistake.'

'Why?'

'Too big a bulge,' she said. 'He noticed it at once. And all the time he was chasing me round the table, he kept pointing at it and singing its praises. I was longing to tell him it was just a silly old banana from the Ritz Hotel, but that wasn't on. It was driving him up the wall that banana, and the Blister Beetle was hitting him harder every second, and suddenly I had another problem on my hands. How in God's name, I thought, am I going to get the rubbery thing on him before he jumps me? I couldn't exactly say it was a necessary precaution, could I?'

'Not really.'

'I mean after all, what earthly reason had I even to be carrying the bloody thing?'

'Tricky,' I said. 'Very tricky. How did you get out of it?'

'In the end I said to him, "Do you want me, Monsieur Proust?"

' "Yes!" he screamed. "I want you more than anyone in my life! Stop running!"

' "Not yet," I said. "First you must put this funny little thing on him to keep him warm." I took it from my pocket and slung it across the table. He stopped chasing me and stared at it. I doubt he'd ever set eyes on one before. "What is this?" he cried.

' "It's called a tickler," I said. "It's one of our famous English ticklers invented by Mr Oscar Wilde."

' "Oscar Wilde!" he cried. "Ha, ha! A great fellow!"

' "He invented the tickler," I said. "And Lord Alfred Douglas helped him."

' "Lord Alfred was another fine fellow!" he cried.

' "King Edward the Seventh," I said, laying it on, "carried a tickler on his person wherever he went."

' "King Edward the Seventh!" he cried. "My God!" He picked up the little thing lying on the table. "It is good, yes?"

' "It doubles the rapture," I said. "Put it on quickly like a good boy. I'm getting impatient."

' "You help me."

' "No," I said. "Do it yourself." And while he was fiddling around with it, I ... well ... I absolutely had to make sure he didn't see the banana and all the rest of it, didn't I? ... and yet I knew the dreaded time had come when I was going to have to take my trousers down ...'

'A bit risky, that.'

'It couldn't be helped, Oswald. So while he was fiddling around with Oscar Wilde's great invention, I turned my back on him and whipped down my trousers and assumed what I imagined was the correct position by bending over the back of the sofa ...'

'My God, Yasmin, you don't mean you were going to allow him ...'

'Of course not,' she said, 'but I had to hide my banana and keep it out of his reach.'

'Yes, but didn't he jump you?'

'He came at me like a battering-ram.'

'How did you dodge it?'

'I didn't,' she said, smiling. 'That's the whole point.'

'I'm not with you,' I said. 'If he came at you like a battering-ram and you didn't dodge it, then he must have rammed you.'

'He didn't ram me the way you're *thinking* he rammed me,' she said. 'You see, Oswald, I had remembered something. I had remembered the story about A. R. Woresley and his brother's bull and how the bull was fooled into thinking his pizzle was in one place while actually it was in another. A. R. Woresley had grabbed hold of it and directed it somewhere else.'

'Is that what you did?'

'Yes.'

'But surely not into a bag like Woresley did?'

'Don't be an ass, Oswald. I don't need a bag.'

'Of course not ... no ... I see what you mean now ... but wasn't it a bit tricky? ... What I mean is ... you facing the other way and all that ... and him coming at you like a battering-ram ... you had to be pretty quick, didn't you?'

'I was quick. I caught it in mid-air.'

'But didn't he twig?'

'No more than the bull did,' she said. 'Less so, in fact, and I'll tell you why.'

'Why?'

'First of all, he was going mad with the Beetle, right?'

'Right.'

'He was grunting and snorting and flapping his arms, right?'

'Right.'

'And his head was in the air just like the bull's, right?'

'Probably, yes.'

'But most important of all, he was assuming I was a *man*. He thought he was doing it to a *man*, right?'

'Of course.'

'And his pizzle was in a good place. It was having a good time, right?'

'Right.'

'So in his own mind there was only one place it could be. A man doesn't *have* any other place.'

I stared at her in admiration.

'Bound to fool him,' she said. She twisted a snail out of its shell and popped it into her mouth.

'Brilliant,' I said. 'Absolutely brilliant.'

'I was rather pleased with it myself.'

'It's the ultimate deception.'

'Thank you, Oswald.'

'There's just one thing I can't fathom,' I said.

'What's that?'

'When he came at you like a battering-ram, didn't he take aim?'

'Only after a fashion.'

'But he's a very experienced marksman.'

'My dear old frump,' she said, 'you can't seem to get it into your head what a man's like when he's had a double dose.'

I jolly well can, I told myself. I was behind the filing-cabinets when A. R. Woresley got his.

'No,' I said. 'I can't. What is a man like when he's had a double dose?'

'Berserk,' she said. 'He literally doesn't know what the other end of him's doing. I could have shoved it in a jar of pickled onions and he wouldn't have known the difference.'

Over the years I have discovered a surprising but simple truth about young ladies and it is this: *the more beautiful their faces, the less delicate their thoughts*. Yasmin was no exception. There she sat now across the table from me in Maxims wearing a gorgeous Fortuny dress and looking for all the world like Queen Semiramis on the throne of Egypt, but she was talking vulgar. 'You're talking vulgar,' I said.

'I'm a vulgar girl,' she said, grinning.

The Volnay arrived and I tasted it. Wonderful wine. My father used to say never pass up a Volnay by a good shipper if you see one on the wine card. 'How did you get away so soon?' I asked her.

'He was very rough,' she said. 'Rough and sort of spiky. It felt as though I had a gigantic lobster on my back.'

'Beastly.'

'It was horrid,' she said. 'He had a heavy gold watchchain across his waistcoat which kept grinding into my spine. And a big watch in the waistcoat pocket.'

'Not good for the watch.'

'No,' she said. 'It went crunch. I heard it.'

'Yes, well . . .'

'Terrific wine this, Oswald.'

'I know. But how *did* you get away so quickly?'

'That's bound to be a problem with the younger ones after they've had the Beetle,' she said. 'How old is this fellow?'

'Forty-eight.'

'In the prime of life,' she said. 'It's different when they're seventy-six. At that age, even with the Beetle, they soon grind to a halt.'

'But not this chap?

'God no,' she said. 'Perpetual motion. A mechanical lobster.'

'So what did you do?'

'What could I do? It's either me or him I said. So as soon as he'd had his explosion and delivered the goods, I reached into my jacket pocket and got out the trusty hatpin.'

'And you let him have it?'

'Yes, but don't forget it had to be a backhander this time and that wasn't so easy. It's hard to get a good swing.'

'I can see that.'

'Luckily my backhand's always been my strongest point.'

'At tennis you mean?'

'Yes,' she said.

'And you got him first time?'

'Deep to the baseline,' she said. 'Deeper than the King of Spain. A winner.'

'Did he protest?'

'Oh my God,' she said, 'he squealed like a pig. And he danced round the room clutching himself and yelling, "Céleste! Céleste! Fetch a doctor! I have been stabbed!" The woman must have been looking through the key hole because she came bursting in at once and rushed up to him crying. "Where? Where? Let me see!" And while she was examining his backside, I ripped the all-important rubbery thing off him and dashed out of the room pulling up my trousers as I went.'

'Bravo,' I said. 'What a triumph.'

'Bit of a lark actually,' she said. 'I enjoyed it.'

'You always do.'

'Lovely snails,' she said. 'Great big juicy ones.'

'The snail farms put them on sawdust for two days before they sell them for eating,' I said.

'Why?'

'So the snails can purge themselves. When did you get the signed notepaper? Right at the beginning?'

'At the beginning, yes. I always do.'

'But why did it say Boulevard Haussmann on it, instead of Rue Laurent-Pichet?'

'I asked him that myself,' she said. 'He told me that's where he used to live. He's only just moved.'

'That's all right, then,' I said.

They took the empty snail-shells away and soon afterwards they brought on the grouse. By grouse I mean red grouse. I do not mean black grouse (black cock and grey hen) or wood grouse (capercailzie) or white grouse (ptarmigan). These others are good, especially the ptarmigan, but the red grouse is the king. And provided of course they are this year's birds, there is no meat more tender or more tasty in the entire world. Shooting starts on the twelfth of August, and every year I look forward to that date with even greater impatience than I do to the first of September when the oysters come in from Colchester and Whitstable. Like a fine sirloin, red grouse should be eaten rare with the blood just a shade darker than scarlet, and at Maxims they would not like you to order it any other way.

We ate our grouse slowly, slicing off one thin sliver of breast at a time, allowing it to melt on the tongue and following each mouthful with a sip of fragrant Volnay.

'Who's next on the list?' Yasmin asked me.

I had been thinking about that myself, and now I said to her, 'It was going to be Mr James Joyce, but perhaps it would be nice if we took a short trip down to Switzerland for a change of scenery.'

'I'd like that,' she said. 'Who's in Switzerland?'

'Nijinski.'

'I thought he was up here with that Diaghilev chap.'

'I wish he was,' I said, 'but it seems he's gone a bit dotty. He thinks he's married to God, and he walks about with a big gold cross around his neck.'

'What rotten luck,' Yasmin said. 'Does that mean his dancing days are over?'

'Nobody knows,' I said. 'They say he was dancing at an hotel in St Moritz only a few weeks ago. But that was just for fun, to amuse the guests.'

'Does he live in an hotel?'

'No, he's got a villa above St Moritz.'

'Alone?'

'Unfortunately not,' I said. 'There's a wife and a child and a whole bunch of servants. He's a rich man. Fabulous sums he used to get. I know Diaghilev paid him twenty-five thousand francs for each performance.'

'Good Lord. Did you ever see him dance?'

'Only once,' I said. 'The year the war broke out, nineteen fourteen, at the old Palace Theatre in London. He did *Les Sylphides*. Stunning it was. He danced like a god.'

'I'm crazy to meet him,' Yasmin said. 'When do we leave?'

'Tomorrow,' I said. 'We have to keep moving.'

19

At this point in my narrative, just as I was about to describe our trip to Switzerland to find Nijinski, my pen suddenly came away from the paper and I found myself hesitating. Was I not perhaps getting into a rut? Becoming repetitious? Yasmin was going to be meeting an awful lot of fascinating people over the next twelve months, no doubt about that. But in nearly every case (there would of course be one or two exceptions) the action was going to be very much the same. There would be the giving of the Beetle powder, the ensuing cataclysm, the escape with the spoils, and all the rest of it, and that, however interesting the men themselves might be, was going to become pretty boring for the reader. Nothing would have been easier than for me to describe in great detail how the two of us met Nijinski on a path through the pinewoods below his villa, as indeed we did, and how we gave him a chocolate, and how we held him in conversation for nine minutes until the powder hit him, and how he chased Yasmin into the dark wood, leaping from boulder to boulder and rising so high in the air with each leap he seemed to be flying. But if I did that, then it would be fitting also to describe the James Joyce encounter, Joyce in Paris, Joyce in a dark blue serge suit, a black felt hat, old tennis shoes on his feet, twirling an ashplant and talking obscenities. And after Joyce, it would be Mr Bonnard and Mr Braque and then a quick trip back to Cambridge to unload our precious spoils in the Semen's Home. A very quick trip that was because Yasmin and I were in the rhythm of it now and we wanted to push on until it was finished.

A. R. Woresley was wildly excited when I showed him our haul. We now had King Alfonso, Renoir, Monet, Matisse, Proust, Stravinsky, Nijinski, Joyce, Bonnard and Braque. 'And you've done a fine job with the freezing,' he said to me as he carefully transferred the racks of straws with their labels on them from my suitcase freezer to the big freezer in 'Dunroamin', our headquarters house. 'Keep going, children,' he said, rubbing his hands together like a grocer. 'Keep going.'

We kept going. It was the beginning of October now, and we went down south into Italy, looking for D. H. Lawrence. We found him living at the Palazzo Ferraro in Capri with Frieda, and on this occasion I had to distract fat Frieda for two hours out on the rocks while Yasmin went to work on Lawrence. We got a bit of a shock with Lawrence though. When I rushed his semen back to our Capri hotel and examined it under the microscope, I found that the spermatozoa were all stone dead. There was no movement there at all.

'Jesus,' I said to Yasmin. 'The man's sterile.'

'He didn't act like it,' she said. 'He was like a goat. Like a randy goat.'

'We'll have to cross him off the list.'

'Who's next?' she asked.

'Giacomo Puccini.'

20

'Puccini is a big one,' I said. 'A giant. We mustn't fail.'

'Where does he live?' Yasmin asked.

'Near Lucca, about forty miles west of Florence.'

'Tell me about him.'

'Puccini is an enormously rich and famous man,' I said. 'He has built himself a huge house, the Villa Puccini, on the edge of a lake beside the tiny village where he was born, which is called Torre del Lago. Now this is the man, Yasmin, who has written *Manon*, *La Bohème*, *Tosca*, *Madame Butterfly* and *The Girl of the Golden West*. Classics every one of them. He is probably not a Mozart or a Wagner or even a Verdi, but he's still a genius and a giant. He's a bit of a lad, too.'

'In what way?'

'Terrific womanizer.'

'Super.'

'He is now sixty-one but that hasn't stopped him,' I said. 'He's a roustabout, a drinker, a crazy car-driver, a mad-keen fisherman and an even keener duck shooter. But above all, he's a lecher. Someone once said of him that he hunts women, wildfowl and libretti in that order.'

'Sounds like a good chap.'

'Splendid fellow,' I said. 'He's got a wife, an old bag called Elvira, and believe it or not, this Elvira was once sentenced to five months in prison for causing the death of one of Puccini's girlfriends. The girl was a servant in the house, and the beastly Elvira caught Puccini out in the garden with her late one night. There was a tremendous scene, the girl was sacked and thereafter Elvira hounded her to such an extent that the poor thing took poison and killed herself. Her family went to court and Elvira was given five months in the clink.'

'Did she go?'

'No,' I said. 'Puccini got her off by paying twelve thousand lire to the girl's family.'

'So what's the plan?' Yasmin asked me. 'Do I just knock on the door and walk in?'

'That won't work,' I said. 'He's surrounded by faithful watchdogs and his bloody wife. You'd never get near him.'

'What do you suggest then?'

'Can you sing?' I asked her.

'I'm not Melba,' Yasmin said, 'but I have quite a decent little voice.'

'Great,' I said. 'Then that's it. That's what we'll do.'

'What?'

'I'll tell you on the way up,' I said.

We had just returned to the mainland from Capri and we were in Sorrento now. It was warm October weather in this part of Italy and the sky was blue as we loaded up the trusty Citroën *Torpedo* and headed north for Lucca. We had the hood down and it was a great pleasure to be driving along the lovely coastal road from Sorrento to Naples.

'First of all, let me tell you how Puccini met Caruso,' I said, 'because this has a bearing on what you're going to be doing. Puccini was world-famous. Caruso was virtually unknown, but he desperately wanted to get the part of Rodolfo in a forthcoming production of *La Bohème* at Livorno. So one day he turned up at the Villa Puccini and asked to see the great man. Almost every day second-rate singers were trying to get in to see Puccini, and it was necessary that he be protected from these people or he would get no peace. "Tell him I'm busy," Puccini said. The servant told Puccini that the man absolutely refused to go. "He says he'll camp in your garden for a year if necessary." "What does he look like?" Puccini asked. "He's a small stubby little chap with a moustache and a bowler hat on his head. He says he's a Neapolitan." "What kind of a singer?" Puccini asked. "He says he's the best tenor in the world," the servant reported. "They all say that," Puccini said, but something prompted him, and to this day he doesn't know what it was, to put down the book he was reading and to go into the hallway. The front door was open and little Caruso was standing just outside in the garden. "Who the hell are you?" Puccini shouted. Caruso lifted up his full-throated magnificent voice and answered with the words of Rodolfo in *La Bohème*, "*Chi son? Sono un poeta*" ... "Who am I? I am a poet." Puccini was absolutely bowled over by the quality of the voice. He'd never heard a tenor like it before. He rushed up to Caruso and embraced him and cried out "Rodolfo is yours!" That's a true story, Yasmin. Puccini himself loves to tell it. And now of course Caruso *is* the greatest tenor in the world and he and Puccini are the closest of friends. Rather marvellous, don't you agree?'

'What's this got to do with me singing?' Yasmin asked. 'My voice is hardly going to bowl Puccini over.'

'Of course not. But the general idea is the same. Caruso wanted a part. You want three cubic centimetres of semen. The latter is easier for Puccini to give than the former, especially to someone as gorgeous as you. The singing is simply a way to attract the man's attention.'

'Go on, then.'

'Puccini works only at night,' I said, 'from about ten-thirty pm to three or four in the morning. At that time the rest of the household will be asleep. At midnight, you and I will creep into the garden of the Villa Puccini and locate his studio, which I believe is on the ground floor. A window will certainly be open because the nights are still warm. So while I hide in the bushes, you will stand outside the open window and sing softly the gentle aria *"Un bel di vedremo"* from *Madame Butterfly*. If everything goes right, Puccini will rush to the window and will see standing there a girl of surpassing beauty – you. The rest should be easy.'

'I rather like that,' Yasmin said. 'Italians are always singing outside each other's windows.'

When we got to Lucca, we holed up in a small hotel, and there, beside an ancient piano in the hotel sitting-room, I taught Yasmin to sing the aria. She had almost no Italian but she soon learnt the words by heart, and in the end she was able to sing the complete aria very nicely indeed. Her voice was small but she had perfect pitch. I then taught her to say in Italian, 'Maestro, I adore your work. I have travelled all the way from England ...' etc., etc., and a few other useful phrases, including of course, 'All I ask is to have your signature on your own notepaper.'

'I don't think you're going to need the Beetle with this chap,' I said.

'I don't think I am either,' Yasmin said. 'Let's skip it for once.'

'And no hatpin,' I told her. 'This man is a hero of mine. I won't have him stuck.'

'I won't need the hatpin if we don't use the Beetle,' she said. 'I'm really looking forward to this one, Oswald.'

'Ought to be fun,' I said.

When all was ready, we drove out one afternoon to the Villa Puccini to scout the premises. It was a massive mansion set on the edge of a large lake and completely surrounded by an eight-foot-high spiked iron fence. Not so good, that. 'We'll need a small ladder,' I said. So back we drove to Lucca and bought a wooden ladder which we placed in the open car.

Just before midnight we were once again outside the Villa Puccini. We were ready to go. The night was dark and warm and silent. I placed the ladder up against the railings. I climbed up it and dropped down into the garden. Yasmin followed. I lifted the ladder over on to our side and left it there, ready for the escape.

We saw at once the one room in the entire place that was lit up. It was facing towards the lake. I took Yasmin's hand in mine and we crept closer. Although there was no moon, the light from the two big ground floor windows reflected on to the water of the lake and cast a pale illumination over the house and garden. The garden was full of trees and bushes and shrubs and flowerbeds. I was enjoying this. It was what Yasmin called 'a bit of a lark'. As we came closer to the window, we heard the piano. One window was open. We tiptoed right up to it and peeped in. And there he was, the man himself, sitting in his shirtsleeves at an upright piano with a cigar in his mouth, tap-

tapping away, pausing to write something down and then tapping away again. He was thickset, a bit paunchy and he had a black moustache. There was a pair of candlesticks in elaborate brass holders screwed on to either side of the piano but the candles were not lit. There was a tall stuffed white bird, a crane of some sort, standing on a shelf alongside the piano. And around the walls of the room there were oil paintings of Puccini's celebrated ancestors – his great-great-grandfather, his great-grandfather, his grandfather and his own father. All these men had been famous musicians. For over two hundred years, the Puccini males had been passing on musical gifts of a high order to their children. Puccini straws, if only I could get them, were going to be immensely valuable. I resolved to make one hundred of them instead of the usual fifty.

And now there we stood, Yasmin and I, peering through the open window at the great man. I noticed that he had a fine head of thick black hair brushed straight back from the forehead.

'I'm going out of sight,' I whispered to Yasmin. 'Wait until he's not playing, then start to sing.'

She nodded.

'I'll meet you by the ladder.'

She nodded again.

'Good luck,' I said and I tiptoed away and stood behind a bush only five yards from the window. Through the foliage of the bush I could still see not only Yasmin but I could also see into the room where the composer was sitting because the big window was low to the ground.

The piano tinkled. There was a pause. It tinkled again. He was working out the melody with one finger only, and it was wonderful to be standing out there somewhere in Italy on the edge of a lake at midnight listening to Giacomo Puccini composing what was almost certainly a graceful aria for a new opera. There was another pause. He had got the phrase right this time and he was writing it down. He was leaning forward with a pen in his hand and writing on the manuscript paper in front of him. He was jotting his musical notes above the words of the librettist.

Then suddenly, in the absolute stillness that prevailed, Yasmin's small sweet voice began to sing '*Un bel di vedremo*'. The effect was stunning. In that place, in that atmosphere, in the dark night beside the lake outside Puccini's window, I was moved beyond words. I saw the composer freeze. The pen was in his hand against the paper and the hand froze and his whole body became motionless as he sat listening to the voice outside the window. He didn't look round. I don't think he dared to look round for fear of breaking the spell. Outside his window a young maiden was singing one of his favourite arias in a small clear voice in absolutely perfect pitch. His face didn't change expression. His mouth didn't move. Nothing about him moved while the aria was in progress. It was a magic moment. Then Yasmin stopped singing. For a few seconds longer Puccini remained sitting at the piano. He seemed to be waiting for more, or for a sign of some sort from outside. But Yasmin didn't move or speak either. She simply stood there with her face upturned to the window, waiting for the man to come to her.

And come to her he did. I saw him put down his pen and rise slowly from the piano stool. He walked to the window. Then he saw Yasmin. I have spoken many times of her scintillating beauty, and the sight of her standing out there so still and serene must have come as a glorious shock to Puccini. He stared. He gaped. Was this a dream? Then Yasmin smiled at him and that broke the spell. I saw him come suddenly out of his trance and I heard him say, 'Dio mio come bello!' Then he jumped clear out of the window and clasped Yasmin in a powerful embrace.

That was more like it, I thought. That was the real Puccini. Yasmin was not slow to respond. Then I heard him say softly to her in Italian, which I'm sure Yasmin didn't understand, 'We must go back inside. If the piano stops playing for too long a time, my wife wakes up and becomes suspicious.' I saw him smile at this, showing fine white teeth. Then he picked Yasmin up and hoisted her through the window and climbed in after her.

I am not a voyeur. I watched A. R. Woresley's antics with Yasmin for purely professional reasons, but I had no intention of peeping through the window at Yasmin and Puccini. The act of copulation is like that of picking the nose. It's all right to be doing it yourself but it is a singularly unattractive spectacle for the onlooker. I walked away. I climbed the ladder and dropped over the fence and went for a stroll along the edge of the lake. I was away about an hour. When I returned to the ladder there was no sign of Yasmin. When three hours had gone by, I climbed back into the garden to investigate.

I was creeping cautiously between the bushes when suddenly I heard footsteps on the gravel path and Puccini himself with Yasmin on his arm walked past me not ten feet away. I heard him saying to her in Italian, 'No gentleman is going to permit a lady to walk back to Lucca all alone at this time of night.'

Was he going to walk her back to the hotel? I followed them to see where they were going. Puccini's motor car was standing in the drive in the front of the house. I saw him help Yasmin into the passenger seat. Then, with a great deal of fuss and match-striking, he got the acetylene headlamps alight. He cranked the starting-handle. The engine fired and ticked over. He unlocked the gates, jumped into the driver's seat and off they went with the motor roaring and revving.

I ran out to my own car and got the thing started. I drove fast towards Lucca but I never caught up with Puccini. In fact, I was only halfway there when he passsed me on his way home again, alone this time.

I found Yasmin at the hotel.

'Did you get the stuff?'

'Of course,' she said.

'Give it to me quickly.'

She handed it over and by dawn I had made one hundred Puccini straws of good quality. While I was working on them, Yasmin sat in an armchair in my room drinking red Chianti and giving her report.

'Great time,' she said. 'Really marvellous. I wish they were all like him.'

'Good.'

'He was so *jolly*,' she said. 'Lots of laughs. And he sang me a bit from the new opera he's doing.'

'Did he say what he's calling it?'

'Turio,' she said. 'Turidot. Something like that.'

'No trouble from the wife upstairs?'

'Not a peep,' she said. 'But it was so funny because even when we were plunged in passion on the sofa, he had to keep reaching out every now and again to bang the piano. Just to let her know he was working hard and not banging some woman.'

'A great man, you think?'

'Terrific,' Yasmin said. 'Stupendous. Find me another like him.'

From Lucca we headed north for Vienna, and on the way we called on Sergei Rachmaninov in his lovely house on Lake Lucerne.

'It's a funny thing,' Yasmin said to me when she came back to the car after what had obviously been a fairly energetic session with the great musician, 'it's a funny thing, but there's an amazing resemblance between Mr Rachmaninov and Mr Stravinsky.'

'You mean facially?'

'I mean everything,' she said. 'They've both got small bodies and great big lumpy faces. Enormous strawberry noses. Beautiful hands. Tiny feet. Thin legs. And gigantic pizzles.'

'Is it your experience so far,' I asked her, 'that geniuses have larger pizzles than ordinary men.'

'Definitely,' she said. 'Much larger.'

'I was afraid you'd say that.'

'And they make better use of them,' she said, rubbing it in. 'Their swordsmanship is superb.'

'Rubbish.'

'It's not rubbish, Oswald. I ought to know.'

'Aren't you forgetting they've all had the Beetle.'

'The Beetle helps,' she said. 'Of course it helps. But there's no comparison between the way a great creative genius handles his sword and the way an ordinary fellow does it. That's why I'm having such a nice time.'

'Am I an ordinary fellow?'

'Don't get grumpy,' she said. 'We can't all be Rachmaninov or Puccini.'

I was deeply wounded. Yasmin had pricked me in my most sensitive area. I sulked all the way to Vienna, but the sight of that noble city soon restored my humour.

In Vienna, Yasmin had an hilarious encounter with Dr Sigmund Freud in his consulting room at Berggasse 19, and I think this visit merits a brief description.

First of all, she made a proper application for an appointment with the famous man, stating that she was in urgent need of psychiatric treatment. She was told there would be four days to wait. So I arranged for her to fill in the time by calling first upon the august Mr Richard Strauss. Mr Strauss had just been appointed co-director of the Vienna State Opera and he was, according to Yasmin, rather pompous. But he was easy meat and I got fifty excellent straws from him.

Then it was Dr Freud's turn. I regarded the celebrated psychiatrist as being in the semi-joker class and saw no reason why we shouldn't have a bit of fun with him. Yasmin agreed. So the two of us cooked up an interesting psychiatric malady for her to be suffering from, and in she went to the big greystone house on Berggasse at two-thirty on a cool sunny October afternoon. Here is her own description of the encounter as she told it to me later that day over a bottle of Krug after I had frozen the straws.

'He's a goosey old bird,' she said. 'Very severe looking and correctly dressed, like a banker or something.'

'Did he speak English?'

'Quite good English but with that dreadful German accent. He sat me down on the other side of his desk and right away I offered him a chocolate. He took it like a lamb. Isn't it odd, Oswald, how every one of them takes the chocolate without any argument?'

'I don't think it's odd,' I said. 'It's the natural thing to do. If a pretty girl offered me a chocolate, I'd take it.'

'He was a hairy sort of fellow,' Yasmin said. 'He had a moustache and a thick pointed beard which looked as though it had been trimmed very carefully in front of a mirror with scissors. Whitish-grey it was. But the hair had been cut well back from his mouth above and below so that the bristles made a sort of frame for his lips. That's what I noticed above everything else, his lips. Very striking, those lips of his, and very thick. They looked like a pair of false lips made out of rubber which had been stuck on over the real ones.

'"So now fräulein," he said, munching away at his chocolate, "tell me about this so urgent problem of yours."

'"Oh, Dr Freud, I do hope you can help me!" I cried, working myself up at once. "Can I speak to you frankly?"

'"That's vot you are here for," he said. "Lie down on that couch over there, please, and just let yourself go."

'So I lay down on the goddamn couch, Oswald, and as I did so I thought well anyway I'm going to be in a reasonably comfy place for once when the fireworks start.'

'I see your point.'

'So I said to him, "Something terrible is wrong with me, Dr Freud! Something terrible and shocking!"

'"And vot is that?" he asked, perking up. He obviously enjoyed hearing about terrible and shocking things.

'"You won't believe it," I said, "but it is impossible for me to be in the presence of a man for more than a few minutes before he tries to rape me! He becomes a wild animal! He rips off my clothes! He exposes his organ ... is that the right word?"

'"It is as good a word as any," he said. "Continue, fräulein."

'"He jumps on top of me!" I cried. "He pins me down! He takes his pleasure of me! Every man I meet does this to me, Mr Freud! You must help me! I am being raped to death!"

'"Dear lady," he said, "this is a very common fantasy among certain types of hysterical vimmen. These vimmen are all frightened of having physical relations with men. Actually, they long to indulge in fornication and copulation and all other sexy frolics but they are terrified of the consequences. So they fantasize. They imagine they are being raped. But it never happens. They are all firgins."

'"No, no!" I cried. "You are wrong, Dr Freud! I'm not a virgin! I'm the most over-raped girl in the world!"

'"You are hallucinating," he said. "Nobody has ever raped you. Vy you do not admit it and you will feel better instamatically?"

'"How can I admit it when it isn't true?" I cried. "Every man I've ever met has had his way with me! And it'll be just the same with you if I stay here much longer, you see if it isn't!"

'"Do not be ridiculous, fräulein," he snapped.

'"It will, it will!" I cried. "You'll be as bad as all the rest of them before this session's over!"

'When I said that, Oswald, the old buzzard rolled his eyes up at the ceiling and smiled a thin supercilious smile. "Fantasy, fantasy," he said, "all fantasy."

'"What makes you think you're so right and I'm so wrong?" I asked him.

'"Allow me to explain a little further," he said, leaning back in his chair and clasping his hands across his tummy. "In your subconscious mind, my dear fräulein, you believe that the masculine organ is a machine-gun ..."

' "That's just about what it is so far as I'm concerned!" I cried. "It's a lethal weapon!"

' "Exactly," he said. "Now vee are getting somewhere. And you also believe that any man who points it at you is going to pull the trigger and riddle you with bullets."

' "Not bullets," I said. "Something else."

' "So you run away," he said. "You reject all men. You hide from them. You sit alone through the nights ...'

' "I do not sit alone,' I said. "I sit with my lovely old Doberman Pincher, Fritzy."

' "Male or female?" he snapped.

' "Fritzy's a male."

' "Vorse than ever," he said. "Do you with this Doberman Pincher indulge in sexual relations?"

' "Don't be so daft, Dr Freud. Who do you think I am?"

' "You run avay from men," he said. "You run avay from dogs. You run away from anything that an organ has ..."

' "I've never heard such codswallop in all my life!" I cried. "I am not frightened of anyone's organ! I do not think it's a machine-gun! I think it's a bloody nuisance, that's all! I'm fed up with it! I've had enough!"

' "Do you like carrots, fräulein?" he asked me suddenly.

' "Carrots?" I said. "Good God. Not particularly, no. If I do have them I usually dice them. I chop them up."

' "Vot about cucumbers, fräulein?"

' "Pretty tasteless," I said. "I prefer them pickled."

' "Ja ja," he said, writing all this down on my record sheet. "It may interest you to know, fräulein, that the carrot and the cucumber are both very powerful sexuality symbols. They represent the masculine phallic member. And you are vishing either to chop it up or to pickle it!"

'I tell you, Oswald,' Yasmin said to me, 'it was as much as I could do to stop myself screaming with laughter. And to think people actually believe this horseshit.'

'He believes it himself,' I said.

'I know he does. He sat there writing it all down on a large sheet of paper. Then he said, "And vot also have you got to tell me, fräulein?"

' "I can tell you what *I* think is wrong with me," I said.

' "Proceed, please."

' "I believe I have a little dynamo inside me," I said, "and this dynamo goes whizzing round and round and gives off a terrific charge of sexual electricity."

' "Very interesting," he said, scribbling away. "Continue please."

' "This sexual electricity is of such high voltage," I said, "that as soon as a man comes close to me, it jumps across the gap from me to him and it jiggers him up."

' "Vot is meaning, please, jiggers him up?"

' "It means it excites him," I said. "It electrifies his private parts. It makes them red hot. And that's when he starts to go crazy and he jumps on me. Don't you believe me, Dr Freud?"

' "This is a serious case," the old geezer said. "It is going to take many psychoanalytical sessions on the couch to make you normal."

'Now all this time, Oswald,' Yasmin said to me, 'I was keeping an eye on my watch. And when eight minutes had gone by, I said to him, "Please don't rape me, Dr Freud. You ought to be above that sort of thing."

' "Do not be ridiculous, fräulein," he said. "You are hallucinating again."

' "But my electricity!" I cried. "It's going to jigger you up! I know it is! It's going to jump across from me to you and electrify your private parts! Your pizzle will become red hot! You will rip my clothes off! You will have your way with me!"

' "Stop this hysterical shoutings at once," he snapped and he got up from his desk and came and stood near where I was lying on the couch. "Here I am," he said, spreading out his arms. "I am not harming you, am I? I am not trying to jump upon you, yes?"

'And at that very moment, Oswald,' Yasmin said to me, 'the Beetle suddenly hit him and his doodly came alive and stuck out as though he had a walking-stick in his trousers.'

'You timed it lovely,' I said.

'Not bad, was it? So I thrust out my arm and pointed an accusing finger and shouted, "There! It's happening to you, you old goat! My electricity has jolted you! Will you believe me now, Dr Freud? Will you believe what I am saying?"

'You should have seen his face, Oswald. You really should have seen it. The Beetle was hitting him and the sex-crazy glint was coming into his eyes and he was beginning to flap his arms like an old crow. But I'll say this for him. He didn't jump me right away. He held off for at least a minute or so while he tried to analyse what the hell was happening. He looked down at his trousers. Then he looked up at me. Then he started muttering. "This is incredible! ... amazing! ... unbelievable! ... I must make notes ... I must record every moment. Vere is my pen, for God's sake? Vere is the ink? Vere is some paper? Oh, to hell with the paper! Please to remove your clothes, fräulein! I cannot vait any longer!" '

'Must have shaken him,' I said.

'Shook him rigid,' Yasmin said. 'It was undermining one of his most famous theories.'

'You didn't hatpin him, did you?'

'Of course not. He was really very decent about it all. As soon as he'd had his first explosion, and although the Beetle was still hitting him hard, he jumped away and ran back to his desk stark naked and began writing notes. He must be terrifically strong-minded. Great intellectual curiosity. But he was completely foxed and bewildered by what had happened to him.'

'"Do you believe me now, Dr Freud?" I asked him.

'"I have to believe you!" he cried. "You have opened up a whole new field with this sexual electricity of yours! This case will make history! I must see you again, fräulein."

'"You'll jump me," I said. "You won't be able to stop yourself."

'"I know," he said, smiling for the first time. "I know that, fräulein, I know."'

I got fifty first-class straws from Dr Freud.

21

From Vienna we drove north in the pale autumn sunshine to Berlin. The war had been over for only eleven months and the city was bleak and dreary, but we had two important persons to visit here and I was determined to collar them. The first was Mr Albert Einstein, and at his house in Haberlandstrasse 9, Yasmin had a pleasant and successful encounter with this amazing fellow.

'How was it?' I said, asking her the usual question in the car.

'He had a great time,' she said.

'Didn't you?'

'Not really,' she said. 'He's all brains and no body. Give me Puccini any day.'

'Will you please try to forget that Italian Romeo.'

'Yes, Oswald, I will. But I'll tell you what's odd. The brainy ones, the great intellects behave quite differently to the artistic ones when the Beetle hits them.'

'How?'

'The brainy ones stop and think. They try to figure out what on earth has happened to them and why it's happened. The artists just take it for granted and plunge right in.'

'What was Einstein's reaction?'

'He couldn't believe it,' she said. 'In fact he smelled a rat. He's the very first one who has ever suspected us of jiggery-pokery. Shows how bright he is.'

'What did he say?'

'He stood there and looked at me from under those bushy eyebrows and he said, "There is something extremely fishy here, fräulein. This is not my normal reaction to a pretty visitor."

' "Doesn't that depend on how pretty she is?" I said.

' "No, fräulein, it does not," he said. "Was that an ordinary chocolate you gave me?"

' "Perfectly ordinary," I said, quaking a bit. "I had one myself."

'The little chap was strongly hotted-up by the Beetle, Oswald, but like old Freud, he managed to hold off in the beginning. He paced up and down the room muttering "What is happening to me? This is not natural ... There is something wrong ... I would never allow this ..."

'I was draped all over the sofa in a seductive attitude waiting for him to get on with it, but no, Oswald, absolutely not. For about five whole minutes his thinking process completely blocked out his carnal desires or whatever you call them. I could almost hear the old brain whizzing round as he tried to puzzle it out.'

' "Mr Einstein," I said, "relax." '

'You were dealing with the greatest intellect in the world,' I said. 'The man has supernatural powers of reasoning. Try to understand what he says about relativity and you'll see what I mean.'

'We'd be finished if someone twigged what we were doing.'

'No one will,' I said. 'There's only one Einstein.'

Our second important donor in Berlin was Mr Thomas Mann. Yasmin reported that he was pleasant but uninspiring.

'Like his books,' I said.

'Then why did you choose him?'

'He's done some fine work. I think his name is going to live.'

My travelling liquid nitrogen suitcase now contained Puccini, Rachmaninov, Strauss, Freud, Einstein and Mann. So once again we went back to Cambridge with our precious cargo.

A. R. Woresley was ecstatic. He knew damn well we were on to something big now. All three of us were ecstatic, but I was in no mood to waste time yet with celebrations. 'While we're here,' I said, 'we'll polish off some of the English lads. We'll start tomorrow.'

Joseph Conrad was possibly the most important of these, so we took him first. Capel House, Orlestone, Kent was his address and we drove down there in mid-November. To be precise, it was November 16th, 1919. I have already said that I am not keen to give a detailed description of too many of our visits for fear of becoming repetitious. I will not break this rule again unless something juicy or amusing comes along. Our visit to Mr Conrad was neither juicy nor amusing.

It was routine, although Yasmin did comment afterwards that he was one of the nicest men she had met so far.

From Kent we drove to Crowborough in Sussex where we nobbled Mr H. G. Wells. 'Not a bad sort of egg,' Yasmin said when she came out. 'Rather portly and pontificating but quite pleasant. It's an odd thing about great writers,' she added. 'They look so ordinary. There's nothing about them that gives you the slightest clue to their greatness, as there is with painters. A great painter somehow *looks* like a great painter. But the great writer usually looks like the wages clerk in a cheese factory.'

From Crowborough we drove on to Rottingdean, also in Sussex, to call on Mr Rudyard Kipling. 'Bristly little bugger,' was Yasmin's only comment on that one. Fifty straws from Kipling.

We were very much in the rhythm now and the next day in the same country of Sussex we picked off Sir Arthur Conan Doyle as easily as picking a cherry. Yasmin simply rang the doorbell and told the maid who answered it that she was from his publishers and had important papers to deliver to him. She was at once shown into his study.

'What did you think of Mr Sherlock Holmes?' I asked her.

'Nothing special,' she said. 'Just another writer with a thin pencil.'

'Wait,' I said. 'The next on the list is also a writer, but I doubt you'll find this one boring.'

'Who is he?'

'Mr Bernard Shaw.'

We had to drive through London to get to Ayot St Lawrence in Hertfordshire where Shaw lived, and on the way I told Yasmin something about this smug literary clown. 'First of all,' I said, 'he's a rabid vegetarian. He eats only raw vegetables and fruit and cereal. So I doubt he'll accept the chocolate.'

'What do we do, give it to him in a carrot?'

'What about a radish?' I suggested.

'Will he eat it?'

'Probably not,' I said. 'So it had better be a grape. We'll get a good bunch of grapes in London and doctor one of them with the powder.'

'That'll work,' Yasmin said.

'It's got to work,' I said. 'This lad won't do it without the Beetle.'

'What's wrong with him?'

'Nobody quite knows.'

'Doesn't he practise the noble art?'

'No,' I said. 'He's not interested in sex. He appears to be a sort of capon.'

'Oh hell.'

'He's a lanky garrulous old capon with an overwhelming conceit.'

'Are you suggesting his machinery is out of order?' Yasmin asked.

'I'm not sure. He's sixty-three. He married at forty-two, a marriage of companionship and convenience. No sex.'

'How do you know that?'

'I don't. But that's the general opinion. He himself has stated that "I had no adventures of a sexual kind until I was twenty-nine ..."'

'A bit retarded.'

'I doubt he's had any at all,' I said. 'Many famous women have pursued him, but without success. Mrs Pat Campbell, gorgeous actress, said "He's all hen and no cock."'

'I like that.'

'His diet,' I said, 'is deliberately aimed at mental efficiency. "I flatly declare," he once wrote, "that a man fed on whiskey and dead bodies cannot possibly do good work."'

'As opposed to whiskey and live bodies, I suppose.'

Pretty quick our Yasmin was. 'He's a Marxist Socialist,' I added. 'He thinks the State should run everything.'

'Then he's an even bigger ass than I thought,' Yasmin said. 'I can't wait to see his face when the old Beetle strikes.'

On the way through London, we bought a bunch of superb hothouse Muscatel grapes from Jackson's in Piccadilly. They were very costly, very pale yellowish-green and very large. North of London, we stopped on the side of the road and got out the tin of Blister Beetle powder.

'Shall we give him a double shot?' I asked.

'Triple,' Yasmin said.

'D'you think that's safe?'

'If what you say about him is true he's going to need half the tin.'

'Very well, then,' I said. 'Triple it is.'

We chose the grape that was hanging at the lowest point of the bunch and carefully made a tiny nick in its skin with a knife. I scooped out a little of the inside and then inserted a triple dose of powder, pushing the stuff well into the grape with a pin. Then we continued on to Ayot St Lawrence.

'You do realize,' I said, 'that this will be the first time anyone's had a triple dose?'

'I'm not worried,' Yasmin said. 'The man's obviously wildly undersexed. I wonder if he's a eunuch. Does he have a high voice?'

'I don't know.'

'Bloody writers,' Yasmin said. She settled herself deeper into the seat and kept a grumpy silence for the rest of the trip.

The house, known as Shaw's Corner, was a large unremarkable brick pile with a good garden. The time, as I pulled up outside, was four-twenty in the afternoon.

'What do I do?' Yasmin asked.

'You walk round to the back of the house and all the way down to the bottom of the garden,' I said. 'There, you will find a small wooden

shed with a sloping roof. That's where he works. He's certain to be in
it now. Just barge in and give him the usual patter.'

'What if the wife sees me?'

'That's a chance you'll have to take,' I said. 'You'll probably make
it. And tell him that you're a vegetarian. He'll like that.'

'What are the names of his plays?'

'*Man and Superman*,' I said. '*The Doctor's Dilemma, Major Barbara,
Caesar and Cleopatra, Androcles and the Lion* and *Pygmalion*.'

'He'll ask me which I like best.'

'Say *Pygmalion*.'

'All right, I'll say *Pygmalion*.'

'Flatter him. Tell him he is not only the greatest playwright but
also the greatest music critic that ever lived. You don't have to worry.
He'll do the talking.'

Yasmin stepped out of the car and walked with a firm step through
the gate into Shaw's garden. I watched her until she had disappeared
around the back of the house, then I drove up the road and booked
a room in a pub called The Waggon and Horses. Up in the room, I
laid out my equipment and got everything ready for the rapid
conversion of Shaw's semen into frozen straws. An hour later, I
returned to Shaw's Corner to wait for Yasmin. I didn't wait long, but
I am not going to tell you what happened next until you have heard
what happened first. Such things are better in their right order.

'I walked down the garden,' Yasmin told me afterwards in the pub
over an excellent steak and kidney pudding and a bottle of reasonable
Beaune, 'I walked down the garden and I saw the hut. I walked
quickly towards it. I was expecting any moment to hear Mrs Shaw's
voice behind me shouting "Halt!" But no one saw me. I opened the
door of the hut and looked in. It was empty. There was a cane
armchair, a plain table covered with sheets of paper and a spartan
atmosphere. But no Shaw. Well, that's it, I thought. Better get out.
Back to Oswald. Total failure. I banged the door shut.

' "Who is there?" shouted a voice from behind the hut. It was a
male voice but high-pitched and almost squeaky. Oh, my God, I
thought, the man *is* a eunuch after all.

' "Is that you Charlotte?" the squeaky voice demanded.

'What effect, I wondered, would the Beetle have upon a one hundred
per cent eunuch?'

' "Charlotte!" he called. "What are you doing?"

'Then a tall bony creature with an enormous beard came round the
corner of the hut holding a pair of garden clippers in one hand. "Who,
may I inquire, are *you*?" he demanded. "This is private property."

'I'm looking for the public lavatory,' I said.

' "What is your business, young lady?" he demanded, pointing the clippers at me like a pistol. "You went into my hut. What have you stolen?"

' "I haven't stolen a damn thing," I said. "I came, if you want to know, to bring you a present."

' "A present, eh?" he said, softening a little.

'I lifted the fine bunch of grapes out of the bag and held it up by the stem.

' "And what have I done to deserve such munificence?" he said.

' "You have given me a terrific amount of pleasure at the theatre," I said. "So I thought it would be nice if I gave you something in return. That's all there is to it. Here, try one." I picked off the bottom grape and offered it to him. "They're really awfully good."

'He stepped forward and took the grape and pushed it through all those whiskers into his mouth.

' "Excellent," he said, chewing away. "A Muscatel." He glared at me under those beetly brows. "It is fortunate for you, young lady, that I wasn't working or I'd have kicked you out, grapes or no grapes. As it happens, I was pruning my roses."

' "I apologize for barging in," I said. "Will you forgive me?"

' "I will forgive you when I am convinced that your motives are pure," he said.

' "As pure as the Virgin Mary," I said.

' "I doubt it," he said. "A woman never pays a visit to a man unless she is seeking some advantage. I have made that point many times in my plays. The female, madam, is a predatory animal. She preys upon men."

' "What a damn stupid thing to say," I told him. "*Man* is the hunter."

' "I have never hunted a woman in my life," he said. "Women hunt me. And I flee like a fox with a pack of hounds at his heels. Rapacious creatures," he added, spitting out a seed from the grape. "Rapacious, predatory, all-devouring animals."

' "Oh, come on," I said. "Everyone hunts a bit now and again. Women hunt men for marriage and what's wrong with that? But men hunt women because they want to get into bed with them. Where shall I put these grapes?"

' "We'll put them in the hut," he said, taking them from me. He went into the hut and I followed. I was praying for the nine minutes to pass quickly. He sat down in his cane armchair and stared at me under great bushy eyebrows. I quickly sat myself on the only other chair in the place.

' "You are a spirited young lady," he said. "I admire spirit."

' "And you talk a lot of bosh about women," I said. "I don't believe you know the first thing about them. Have you ever fallen passionately in love?"

' "A typical woman's question," he said. "For me, there is only one kind of passion. Intelligence is passion. The activity of the intellect is the keenest passion I can experience."

' "What about physical passion?" I asked. "Isn't that in the running?"

' "No madam, it is not. Descartes got far more passion and pleasure out of life than Casanova."

' "What about Romeo and Juliet?"

' "Puppy love," he said. "Superficial tosh."

' "Are you saying that your *Caesar and Cleopatra* is a greater play than *Romeo and Juliet*?"

' "Without a doubt," he said.

' "Boy, you've got a nerve, Mr Shaw."

' "So have you, young lady." He picked up a sheet of paper from the table. "Listen to this," he said and he started to read aloud in that squeaky voice of his "... the body always ends by being a bore. Nothing remains beautiful and interesting except thought, because thought is life ..."

' "Of course it *ends* by being a bore," I said. "That's a pretty obvious remark. But it isn't a bore at my age. It's a juicy fruit. What's the play?"

' "It's about Methuselah," he said. "And now I must ask you to leave me in peace. You are pert and pretty but that does not entitle you to take up my time. I thank you for the grapes."

'I glanced at my watch. Just over a minute to go. I had to keep talking. "I'll be off then," I said, "but in exchange for my grapes I'd love it if you gave me your autograph on one of your famous postcards."

'He reached for a postcard and signed it. "Now be off with you," he said. "You have wasted enough of my time."

' "I'm going," I said, fumbling about and trying to string out the seconds. The nine minutes were up now. Oh Beetle, lovely Beetle, kind Beetle, where are you? Why have you deserted me?'

'A bit dicy, that,' I said.

'I was desperate, Oswald. It had never happened before. "Mr Shaw," I said, pausing by the door, searching for a time-killer, "I promised my dear old mother who thinks you are God the Father himself to be sure to ask you one question ..."

' "You are a pest, madam!" he barked.

' "I know I am, I know, I know, but please answer it for her. Here's the question. Is it really true that you disapprove of all artists who create works of art for purely aesthetic reasons?"

' "I do, madam."

' "You mean pure beauty is not enough?"

' "It is not," he said. "Art should always be didactic, serving a social purpose."

' "Did Beethoven serve a social purpose, or Van Gogh?"

' "Get out of here!" he roared. "I have no wish to bandy words ..."
He stopped in mid-sentence. For at that moment, Oswald, heaven be
praised, the Beetle struck.'

'Hooray. Did it hit him hard?'

'This was a triple dose, remember.'

'I know. So what happened?'

'I don't think it's safe to give triples, Oswald. I'm not going to do
it again.'

'Rocked him a bit, did it?'

'Phase one was devastating,' Yasmin said. 'It was as if he were
sitting in an electric chair and someone had pulled the switch and
jolted him with a million volts.'

'Bad as that?'

'Listen, his whole body rose up off the chair and there it hung, in
mid-air, rigid, quivering, the eyes popping, the face all twisted.'

'Oh dear.'

'Rattled me.'

'I'll bet.'

'What do we do now, I thought. Artificial respiration, oxygen,
what?'

'You're not exaggerating, are you, Yasmin?'

'God no. The man was contorted. He was paralysed. He was
garotted. He couldn't speak.'

'Was he conscious?'

'Who knows?'

'Did you think he might kick the bucket?'

'I reckoned it was about even money.'

'You really thought that?'

'You only had to look at him.'

'Christ, Yasmin.'

'I stood there by the door and I remember thinking well whatever
happens, this old buzzard's written his last play. "Hello there, Mr
Shaw," I said. "Wakey wakey." '

'Could he hear you?'

'I doubt it. And through his whiskers I could see white stuff, like
brine, forming on his lips.'

'How long did all this last?'

'A couple of minutes. And on top of everything else I began worrying
about his heart.'

'Why his heart, for God's sake?'

'He was going purple in the face. I could see his skin going purple.'

'Asphyxia?'

'Something like that,' Yasmin said. 'Isn't this steak and kidney
delicious?'

'It's very good.'

'Then all of a sudden he came back to earth. He blinked his eyes, took one look at me, gave a sort of Indian whoop, leaped out of his chair and started tearing off his clothes. "The Irish are coming!" he yelled. "Gird up your loins, madam! Gird up your loins and prepare for battle!"'

'Not exactly a eunuch then.'

'It didn't look like it.'

'How did you manage to roll the old rubbery thing on him?'

'There's only one way when they get violent,' Yasmin said. 'I grabbed hold of his snozzberry and hung on to it like grim death and gave it a twist or two to make him hold still.'

'Ow.'

'Very effective.'

'I'll bet it is.'

'You can lead them around anywhere you want like that.'

'I'm sure.'

'It's like putting a twitch on a horse.'

I took a mouthful of Beaune, tasting it with care. It had been shipped by Louis Latour and it was really very fair. One was fortunate to find something like that in a country pub. 'So then what?' I said.

'Chaos. Wooden floor. Horrible bruises. The lot. But I'll tell you what's interesting, Oswald. He didn't know quite what to do. I had to show him.'

'So he *was* a virgin?'

'Must've been. But a damn quick learner. I've never seen such energy in a man of sixty-three.'

'That's the vegetarian diet.'

'It could be,' Yasmin said, spearing a piece of kidney with her fork and popping it into her mouth. 'But don't forget he had a brand new engine.'

'A what?'

'A new engine. Most men of that age are more or less worn out by then. Their equipment I mean. It's done so much mileage things are beginning to rattle.'

'You mean the fact that he was a virgin ...'

'Precisely, Oswald. The engine was brand new, completely unused. Therefore no wear and tear.'

'Had to run it in a bit though, didn't he?'

'No,' she said. 'He just let her rip. Flat out all the time. Full throttle. And when he'd got the hang of it he shouted, "*Now* I see what Mrs Pat Campbell was on about!"'

'I suppose in the end you had to get out the old hatpin?'

'Of course. But you know something, Oswald. With a triple dose they're so far gone they don't feel a thing. I might've been tickling his arse with a feather for all the good it did.'

'How many jabs?'

'Till my arm got tired.'

'So what then?'

'There are other ways,' Yasmin said darkly.

'Ow again,' I said. I was remembering what Yasmin had once done to A. R. Woresley in the lab to get away from him. 'Did he jump?'

'About a yard straight up,' she said. 'And that gave me just enough time to grab the spoils and dash for the door.'

'Lucky you kept your clothes on.'

'I had to,' she said. 'Whenever we give an extra dose it's always a sprint to get away.'

So that was Yasmin's story. But let me now take it up from there myself and go back to where I was sitting quietly in my motor car outside 'Shaw's Corner' in the gathering dusk while all this was going on. Suddenly out came Yasmin at the gallop, flying down the garden path with her hair streaming out behind her and I quickly opened the passenger door for her to jump in. But she didn't jump in. She ran to the front of the car and grabbed the starting-handle. No self-starters in those days, remember. 'Switch on, Oswald!' she shouted. 'Switch on! He's coming after me!' I switched on the ignition. Yasmin cranked the handle. The motor started first kick. Yasmin dashed back and jumped into the seat next to me, yelling 'Go man, go! Full speed ahead!' But before I could get the gear lever properly engaged, I heard a yell from the garden and in the half-darkness I saw this tall, ghostlike, white-bearded figure charging down upon us stark naked and yelling, 'Come back, you strumpet! I haven't finished with you yet!'

'Go!' Yasmin shouted. I got the car into gear and let out the clutch and off we went.

There was a street-lamp outside the Shaw house and when I glanced back I saw Mr Shaw capering about on the sidewalk under the gaslight, white-skinned all over save for a pair of socks on his feet, bearded above and bearded below as well, with his massive pink member protruding like a sawn-off shotgun from the lower beard. It was a sight I shall not readily forget, this mighty and supercilious playwright who had always mocked the passions of the flesh, himself impaled now upon the sword of lust and screaming for Yasmin to come back. *Cantharis vesicatoria sudanii*, I reflected, could make a monkey out of the Messiah.

22

By now Christmas was nearly on us and Yasmin said she wanted a holiday. I wanted to keep going. 'Come on,' I said, 'let's do a Royal Tour first, kings only. We'll nobble all the nine remaining monarchs of Europe. Then we'll both take a good long rest.'

Romping with the royals, as Yasmin called it, was an irresistible prospect and she agreed to delay her holiday and spend Christmas in wintry Europe. Together we worked out a sensible itinerary which would take us, in the following order, to Belgium, Italy, Yugoslavia, Greece, Bulgaria, Romania, Denmark, Sweden and Norway. I checked over all nine of my carefully prepared letters from George V. A. F. Woresley refilled my travelling liquid nitrogen container and supplied me with a new stock of straws, and off we went in the trusty Citroën, heading for Dover and the cross-channel steamer, with the Royal Palace in Brussels our first stop.

The effect that the King of England's letter had upon the first eight monarchs on our list was virtually identical. They jumped on it. They couldn't wait to please King George and they couldn't wait to get a peek at his secret mistress. For them it was a fruity business. On every single occasion Yasmin was invited to the Palace only a few hours after I had delivered the letter. We had success after success. Sometimes the hatpin had to be used, sometimes not. There were some funny scenes and one or two tricky moments, but Yasmin always got her man in the end. She even got seventy-six-year-old King Peter of Yugoslavia, although he passed out at the end of it all and my girl had to revive him by throwing a chamberpot of cold water over his face. By the time we reached Christiania (now Oslo) at the beginning of April, we had eight kings in the bag and there was only Haakon of Norway left. He was forty-eight years old.

In Christiania we booked into the Grand Hotel on Carl Johan's Gate and from the balcony of my room I could look straight up that splendid street to the Royal Palace on the hill. I delivered my letter at ten o'clock on a Tuesday morning. By lunchtime Yasmin had a reply in the King's own handwriting. She was invited to present herself at the palace at two-thirty that afternoon.

'This is going to be my very last king,' she said. 'I shall miss popping into palaces and wrestling with royals.'

'What's your general opinion of them,' I said, 'now that it's nearly over? How do they measure up?'

'They vary,' she said. 'That fellow Boris of Bulgaria was terrifying the way he rolled me up in chicken wire.'

'Bulgarians are not easy.'

'Ferdinand of Romania was pretty crazy, too.'

'The one who had distorting mirrors all around the room?'

'That's him. Let us now see what revolting habits this Norwegian chap has got.'

'I hear he's a very decent fellow.'

'Nobody's decent when he's had the Beetle, Oswald.'

'I'll bet he's nervous,' I said.

'Why?'

'I told you why. His wife, Queen Maud, is King George V's sister. So our fake letter was supposedly written to Haakon by his brother-in-law. It's all a bit close to the bone.'

'Spicy,' Yasmin said. 'I like it.' And off she bounced to the palace with her little box of chocolates and her hatpin and other necessary items. I stayed behind and laid out my equipment in readiness for her return.

In less than one hour she was back. She came flying into my room like a hurricane.

'I blew it!' she cried. 'Oh, Oswald, I did something frightful awful terrible! I blew the whole thing!'

'What happened?' I said, starting to quake.

'Give me a drink,' she said. 'Brandy.'

I got her a stiff brandy. 'Come on then,' I said. 'Let's have it. Tell me the worst.'

Yasmin took a huge gulp of brandy, then she leaned back and closed her eyes and said, 'Ah, that's better.'

'For God's sake,' I cried, 'tell me what happened!'

She drank the rest of the brandy and asked for another. I gave it to her quickly.

'Lovely big room,' she said. 'Lovely tall king. Black moustache, courtly, kind and handsome. Took the chocolate like a lamb and I started counting the minutes. Spoke almost perfect English. "I am not very happy about this business, Lady Victoria," he said, tapping King George's letter with one finger. "This is not like my brother-in-law at all. King George is the most upright and honourable man I've ever met."

' "He's only human, Your Majesty."

' "He's the perfect husband," he said.

' "The trouble is he's married," I said.

' "Of course he's married. What are you implying?"

' "Married men make rotten husbands, Your Majesty."

' "You're talking rubbish, madam!" he snapped.'

'Why didn't you shut up right then and there, Yasmin?' I cried.

'Oh, I couldn't, Oswald. Once I get going like that I can't ever seem to stop. Do you know what I said next?'

'I can't wait,' I said. I was beginning to sweat.

'I said, "Look, Your Majesty, I mean after all when a strong good-looking fellow like George has been having rice pudding every night for years and years, it's only natural he's going to start wanting a dish of caviar." '

'Oh, my God!'

'It was a silly thing to say, I know that.'

'What did he answer?'

'He went green in the face. I thought he was going to strike me but he just stood there spluttering and fizzing like one of those fireworks, those bangers, the ones that go on spluttering for a long time before the big explosion comes.'

'And did it come?'

'Not then. He was very dignified. He said, "I will thank you, madam, not to refer to the Queen of England as a rice pudding." '

' "I'm sorry, Your Majesty," I said. "I didn't mean it." I was still standing in the middle of the room because he hadn't asked me to sit down. To hell with it, I thought, and I chose a large green sofa and draped myself along it, all ready for the Beetle to strike.

' "I simply cannot understand George going off the rails like this," he said.

' "Oh come on, Your Majesty," I said. "He's only following in his dad's footsteps."

' "Pray what do you mean by that, madam?"

' "Old Edward VII," I said. "Dash it all, he was dipping the royal wick all over the country."

' "How dare you!" he cried, exploding for the first time. "It's all lies!"

' "What about Lily Langtry?"

' "King Edward was my wife's father," he said in an icy voice. "I will not have him insulted in my house." '

'What in God's name, Yasmin, made you go on like that for?' I cried. 'You get a really nice king for once and all you do is insult the hell out of him.'

'He was a lovely man.'

'Then why did you *do* it?'

'I had the devil in me, Oswald. And I was enjoying it, I suppose.'

'You simply cannot *talk* like that to kings.'

'Oh yes I can,' Yasmin said. 'I have discovered, you see Oswald, that it doesn't really matter what you say to them in the beginning or how angry you make them because the good old Beetle always rescues you in the end. It's always them that finish up looking silly.'

'But you said you'd blown it?'

'Let me go on and you'll see what happened. The tall King kept pacing up and down the room and muttering to himself and of course I kept watching the clock all the time. For some reason the nine minutes seemed to be going rather slowly. Then the King said, "How could you *do* this to your own queen? How could you *lower* yourself to seducing her dear husband? Queen Mary is the purest lady in the land."

' "You really think so?" I said.

' "I know it," he said. "She's as pure as the driven snow."

' "Now just you hang on one second there, Your Majesty," I said. "Haven't you heard all the naughty rumours?"

'When I said that, Oswald, he whipped round as though he'd been bitten by a scorpion.'

'Jesus, Yasmin, you've got a bloody nerve!'

'It was fun,' she said. 'I only meant it as a joke.'

'Some joke.'

' "Rumours!" the king shouted. "What sort of rumours?"

' "Very naughty rumours," I said.

' "How dare you!" he roared. "How dare you come in here and talk like that about the Queen of England. You are a strumpet and a liar, madam!"

' "I may be a strumpet," I said, "but I'm not a liar. There is, you see, Your Majesty, a certain equerry at Buckingham Palace, a colonel in the Grenadiers, a fine good-looking fellow he is, too, with his big black bristly moustache, and every morning he meets the Queen in the gymnasium and gives her keep-fit lessons."

' "And why shouldn't he?" snapped the King. "What's wrong with keep-fit exercises? I do them myself."

'I looked at my watch. The nine minutes were just coming up. Any moment now this tall proud King would be transformed into a randy old lecher. "Your Majesty," I said, "many's the time George and I have peeped through the window at the end of the gym and seen ..." I stopped. I lost my voice, Oswald. I just couldn't go on.'

'What happened, for God's sake?'

'I thought I was having a heart-attack. I began to gasp. I couldn't breathe properly and a sort of goose-pimply feeling was spreading over my whole body. I really thought, honestly I did, I really thought I might be going to kick the bucket.'

'What was it, for God's sake?'

'That's what the King asked me. He's truly a decent man, Oswald. Half a minute before I'd been saying beastly insulting things about his in-laws in England and all of a sudden he was deeply concerned for my welfare. "Do you wish me to call a doctor?" he said. I couldn't even answer him. I just gurgled at him. Then all of a sudden this terrific tingling sensation started in the soles of my feet and it spread quickly all the way up my legs. I'm getting paralysed, I thought. I can't talk. I can't move. I can hardly think. I'm going to die any moment. Then *wham!* It hit me!'

'What hit you?'

'*The Beetle* of course.'

'Now wait a minute ...'

'I'd eaten the wrong goddamn chocolate, Oswald! I'd mixed them up! I'd given him the plain one and eaten the Beetle myself!'

'Jesus Christ, Yasmin!'

'I know. But by then I'd guessed what had happened and my first thought was I'd better get the hell out of the Palace before I make an even bigger ass out of myself than I already have.'

'And did you?'

'Well, that was a bit easier said than done. For the first time in my life I was finding out what it felt like to get the Beetle.'

'Strong stuff.'

'Terrifying. It freezes your mind. You can't think straight. All you've got is this fierce throbbing sexy sensation pouring all over you. Sex is the only thing you can think about. It was all *I* could think about anyway, and I'm very much afraid, Oswald ... I couldn't stop myself, you understand ... I simply couldn't stop myself ... so I ... well, I leaped off the sofa and made a dive for the king's trousers ...'

'Oh, my God.'

'There's more to come,' Yasmin said, taking another gulp of brandy.

'Don't tell me. I can't bear it.'

'All right, then, I won't.'

'Yes,' I said. 'Go on.'

'I was like a mad woman. I was all over him. I caught him off balance and pushed him down on to the sofa. But he's an athletic kind of bird, that old King. He was very quick. He was up in a flash. He got behind his desk. I climbed over the desk. He kept shouting, "Stop woman! What's the matter with you! Get away from me!" And then he really started yelling, yelling out loud I mean. "Help!" he yelled. "Someone get this woman out of here!" And then, my dear Oswald, the door opened and the Queen herself, little Queen Maud in all her glory, came sailing into the room holding a piece of needlework in her hand.'

'Bound to happen.'

'I know.'

'Where were you when she came in?'

'I was leaping over his big Chippendale desk to get at him. Chairs were flying all over the place and in she came, this tiny quite pretty woman ...'

'What did she say?'

'She said, "What *are* you doing, Haakon?"'

'"Get her out!" yelled the King.'

'"I want him!" I shouted. "And I'm going to have him!"'

'"Haakon!" she said. "Stop this at once!"'

' "It's not me, it's her!" he cried, running for his life round the room. But I had him cornered now and I was just about to fling myself at him good and proper when I was grabbed from behind by two guards. Soldiers they were. Lovely-looking Norwegian boys.

' "Take her away," gasped the king.

' "Where to, sire?"

' "Just get her out of here quick! Dump her in the street!"

' "So I was frog-marched out of the Palace and all I remember is I kept saying awful dirty things to the young soldiers and making all sorts of sexy suggestions and they were hooting with laughter ...'

'So they dumped you?'

'In the street,' Yasmin said. 'Outside the Palace gates.'

'You're damned lucky it wasn't the King of Bulgaria or somewhere like that,' I said. 'You'd have been thrown into a dungeon.'

'I know.'

'So they dumped you in the street outside the Palace?'

'Yes. I was dazed. I sat on a bench under some trees trying to pull myself together. I had one great advantage, you see Oswald, over all my victims. *I knew* what was wrong with me. *I knew* it was the Beetle that was doing it to me. It must be simply awful feeling the way I felt and not knowing why. I think that would scare me to death. So I was able to fight it. I remember sitting there and saying to myself what you need Yasmin old girl, what you need to straighten you out is a few good digs in the backside with the hatpin. That made me giggle. And after that, but very slowly, this ghastly sexy feeling began to go away and I got a hold of myself and I stood up and walked along the street to the hotel and here I am. I'm sorry I messed it up, Oswald, I really am. It's the first time ever.'

'We'd better get out of here,' I said. 'I don't think these people would ever do anything nasty to us but the king is bound to start asking a few questions.'

'I'm sure he is.'

'I think he's going to guess my letter was a forgery,' I said. 'I bet anything you like he's checking it out with George V right this very minute.'

'I'll bet he is, too,' Yasmin said.

'Hurry up and pack then,' I said. 'We'll slide out of here at once and drive back across the border into Sweden. We're going to get lost.'

23

We got back home via Sweden and Denmark around the middle of April and we had with us the sperm of eight kings – fifty straws each from seven of them and twenty from old Peter of Yugoslavia. It was a pity about Norway. It spoiled our record although I didn't feel it was going to make much difference in the long run.

'Now I want my holiday,' Yasmin said. 'A good one. Aren't we about finished anyway?'

'America's next,' I said.

'There aren't many there.'

'No, but we have to get them. We'll go over in style on the *Mauretania*.'

'I want a holiday first,' Yasmin said. 'You promised me. I'm not going anywhere until I've had nice long rest.'

'How long?'

'A month.'

We had driven straight to Cambridge after disembarking from the Danish boat at Harwich and we were having a drink in the living-room at 'Dunroamin'. A. R. Woresley came in rubbing his hands.

'Congratulations,' he said. 'You've done a great job with those kings.'

'Yasmin wants a month's holiday,' I said. 'But personally I think we ought to bash on and get America done first.'

A. R. Woresley, puffing his disgusting pipe, looked at Yasmin through the smoke and said, 'I agree with Cornelius. Get the job done first, take a holiday later.'

'No,' Yasmin said.

'Why not?' Woresley said.

'Because I don't want to, that's why.'

'Well, I suppose it's up to you,' Woresley said.

'You bet your life it's up to me,' Yasmin said.

'Aren't you having a good time?' I said.

'The fun's wearing off,' she said. 'In the beginning it was a lark. Terrific joke. But now all of a sudden I seem to have had enough.'

'Don't say that.'

'I've said it.'

'Hell.'

'What both of you seem to be forgetting,' she said, 'is that every time we want the sperm of some bloody genius, *I'm* the one who has to go in and do the fighting. I'm the one who gets it in the neck.'

'Not in the neck,' I said.

'Stop trying to be funny, Oswald.' She sat there looking glum. A. R. Woresley said nothing.

'If you have a month's holiday now,' I said, 'will you come to America with me immediately after that?'

'Yes, all right.'

'You're going to enjoy Rudolph Valentino.'

'I doubt it,' she said. 'I think my romping days are over.'

'Never!' I cried. 'You might as well be dead!'

'Romping isn't everything.'

'Jesus, Yasmin. You're talking like Bernard Shaw!'

'Maybe I'll become a nun.'

'But you will come to America first?'

'I've already told you I would,' she said.

A. R. Woresley took his pipe out of his mouth and said, 'We've got a remarkable collection, Cornelius, truly remarkable. When do we start selling?'

'We mustn't hurry it,' I said. 'My feeling is that we should not put any man's sperm up for sale until after he's dead.'

'Why do you say that?'

'Great men are more interesting dead than alive. They become legends when they're dead.'

'Maybe you're right,' Woresley said.

'We've got plenty of ancient ones on the list,' I said. 'Most of them aren't going to last very long. I'll bet you fifty per cent of the whole lot will be gone in five or ten years.'

'Who's going to do the selling when the time comes?' Woresley asked.

'I am,' I said.

'You think you can manage it?'

'Look,' I said. 'At the tender age of seventeen I had no trouble whatsoever in selling red pills to the French Foreign Minister, to a dozen Ambassadors and to just about every big shot in Paris. And just recently I have successfully sold Lady Victoria Nottingham to all the crowned heads of Europe bar one.'

'I did that,' Yasmin said. 'Not you.'

'Oh no you didn't,' I said. 'King George's letter did the selling and that was my idea. So you don't seriously think I'm going to have any trouble selling the seeds of genius to a bunch of rich females, do you?'

'Perhaps not,' Woresley said.

'And by the way,' I said, 'if I'm the one who does all the selling, I think I ought to be entitled to a bigger cut of the profits.'

'Hey!' Yasmin cried. 'Now you just stop that, Oswald!'

'The agreement was equal shares all round,' Woresley said, looking hostile.

'Calm down,' I said. 'I was only joking.'

'I should damn well hope so,' Yasmin said.

'As a matter of fact, I think Arthur should have the major share because he invented the whole process,' I said.

'Well, I must say that's very generous of you, Cornelius,' Woresley said, beaming.

'Forty per cent to the inventor and thirty per cent each to Yasmin and me,' I said. 'Would you agree to that, Yasmin?'

'I'm not sure I would,' she said. 'I've worked damn hard on this. I want my one-third.'

What neither of them knew was that I had long since decided that I myself was the one who would take the major share in the end. Yasmin, after all, would never need very much. She liked to dress well and to eat good food but that was about as far as it went. As for old Woresley, I doubted whether he'd know what to do with a large sum of money even if he had it. Pipe tobacco was about the only luxury he ever permitted himself. But I was different. The style of living to which I aspired made it absolutely necessary that I have a fortune at my fingertips. It was impossible for me to tolerate indifferent champagne or mild discomfort of any sort. The way I looked at it, the best, and by that I mean only the very best, was not nearly good enough for me.

I figured that if I gave them ten per cent each and took eighty for myself, then they ought to be happy. They would scream blue murder at first, but when they realized there was nothing they could do about it, they would soon settle down and be grateful for small mercies. Now there was of course only one way in which I could put myself in the position of being able to dictate terms to the other two. I must get possession of The Semen's Home and all the treasures it contained. Then I must move it to a safe and secret place where neither of them could reach it. That would not be difficult. As soon as Yasmin and I had returned from America, I would hire a removal van and drive up to 'Dunroamin' when the place was empty and make off with the precious treasure chest.

No problem.

But a bit of a dirty trick, some of you may be thinking? A bit caddish?

Rubbish, I say. You'll never get anywhere in this world unless you grab your opportunities. Charity has never begun at home. Not in my home anyway.

'So when will you two be going to America?' A. R. Woresley asked us.

I got my diary. 'One month from now will be Saturday the fifteenth of May,' I said. 'How's that with you, Yasmin?'

'The fifteenth day of May,' she said, taking her own diary from her purse. 'That seems all right. I'll meet you here on the fifteenth. In four weeks' time.'

'And I'll book cabins on the *Mauretania* for as soon as possible after that.'

'Fine,' she said, writing the date in her diary.

'Then we'll collar old Henry Ford and Mr Marconi and Rudolph Valentino and all the other Yanks.'

'Don't forget Alexander Graham Bell,' Woresley said.

'We'll get the lot,' I said. 'After a month's rest, the old girl will be roaring to go again, you see if she isn't.'

'Hope so,' Yasmin said. 'But I do need a rest, honestly I do.'

'Where will you go?'

'Up to Scotland to stay with an uncle.'

'Nice uncle?'

'Very,' she said. 'My father's brother. He fishes for salmon.'

'When are you leaving?'

'Right now,' she said. 'My train goes in about an hour. Will you take me to the station?'

'Of course I will,' I said. 'I myself am off to London.'

I drove Yasmin to the station and helped her into the waiting-room with her bags. 'See you in exactly a month,' I said. 'At "Dumroamin".'

'I'll be there,' she said.

'Have good hols.'

'Same to you, Oswald.'

I kissed her farewell and drove down to London. I went straight to my house in Kensington Square. I was feeling good. The great scheme was actually coming to pass. I could see myself in about five years' time sitting with some silly rich female and her saying to me, 'I rather fancy Renoir, Mr Cornelius. I do so adore his pictures. How much does he cost?'

'Renoir is seventy-five thousand, madam.'

'And how much is a king?'

'That depends which one.'

'This one here. The dark good-looking one – King Alfonso of Spain.'

'King Alfonso is forty thousand dollars, madam.'

'You mean he's less than Renoir?'

'Renoir was a greater man, madam. His sperm is exceedingly rare.'

'What happens if it doesn't work, Mr Cornelius? I mean if I don't become pregnant.'

'You get a free go.'

'And who would actually perform the insemination?'

'A senior gynaecologist, madam. It would all be most carefully planned.'

'And my husband would never find out?'

'How could he? He'd think he'd done it himself.'

'I suppose he would, wouldn't he?' She giggles.

'Bound to, madam.'

'It *would* be rather nice to have a child by the King of Spain, wouldn't it?'

'Have you considered Bulgaria, madam. Bulgaria is a bargain at twenty thousand.'

'I don't want a Bulgar brat, Mr Cornelius, even if he is royal.'

'I quite understand, madam.'

'And then of course there's Mr Puccini. *La Bohème* is absolutely my favourite opera. How much is Mr Puccini?'

'Giacomo Puccini is sixty-seven thousand five hundred, madam. He is strongly recommended. The child would almost certainly be a musical genius.'

'I play the piano a bit myself.'

'That would help the baby's chances enormously.'

'I expect it would, wouldn't it?'

'Confidentially, madam, I can tell you that a certain lady in Dallas, Texas had a Puccini boy three weeks ago and the child has already composed his first opera.'

'You don't say.'

'Thrilling, isn't it?'

I was going to have a lot of fun once the selling started. But right now I had before me one whole month in which to do nothing except enjoy myself. I decided to remain in London. I'd have a real fling. I deserved it. Throughout most of the winter I'd been chasing after kings all over Europe and the time had come for some serious wenching.

And what wenching it was. I went on a proper bender. For three weeks out of the four I had a glorious time (see Vol. III). Then suddenly, at the beginning of the fourth and final week of my vacation when I was really in full flood and churning the ladies of London to such purpose you could hear the bones rattling all over Mayfair, a devilish incident occurred that put an immediate stopper on all my activities. Terrible it was. Diabolical. Even to *think* about it at this distance causes me sharp physical pain. None the less, I feel I ought to describe this sordid episode in the hope that it may save a few other sportsmen from a similar catastrophe.

I do not usually sit in the bathtub at the wrong end with my back to the taps. Few people do. But on this particular afternoon, the other end, the comfortable slopy end, was occupied by a saucy little imp who possessed hyperactive carnal proclivities. That's why she was there. The fact that she happened also to be an English duchess is not entirely beside the point either. Had I been a few years older I would have known what to expect from a female of high rank, and I'd have been a good deal less careless. Most of these women have acquired their titles by ensnaring some poor benighted. peer or duke, and it takes a very special kind of mendacity and guile to succeed at that game. To become a duchess you must be a prime manipulator of men. I have tangled with a fair number of them in my time and they're all alike. Marchionesses and countesses are not quite so ghoulish but they run the duchesses a close second. Dally with them by all means. It is a piquant experience. But for heaven's sake keep your wits about you while you're at it. You never know, you positively never can tell when they're going to turn and bite the hand that strokes them. Watch out, I say, for the female with a grand title.

Anyway, this duchess and I had been jouncing for an hour or so in the bathtub, and now that she had had enough she threw the soap at my face and stepped out of the water. The large slimy missile caught me on the mouth, but as none of my teeth were dislodged or even loosened I ignored the incident. In point of fact, she had done it simply to quieten me down and to give her a chance to get away, which it did.

'Come back in,' I said, wanting a second helping.

'I've got to go,' she answered. She was keeping her distance as she dried her trim little body with one of my huge towels.

'It's only half-time,' I pleaded.

'The trouble with you, Oswald, is you don't know when to stop,' she said. 'One day someone's going to lose patience with you.'

'Frigid bitch,' I said. It was a silly thing to say and quite untrue, but I said it.

She went into the next room to get dressed. I remained sitting in the bath, silent and feeling thwarted. I didn't like it when others called the tune.

'Goodbye, darling,' she said coming back into the bathroom. She was wearing a short-sleeved silk dress, dark green.

'Go home, then,' I said. 'Go back to your ridiculous duke.'

'Don't be so grumpy,' she said. She walked over to me and bent down and began to massage my back under the water. Then her hand slid around to other areas, caressing and teasing gently. I sat still, enjoying it all and wondering whether she wasn't perhaps gong to start melting all over again.

Now you won't believe this, but all the time the little vixen was pretending to play around with me, what she was actually doing was surreptitiously and with consummate stealth removing the plug from the plughole in the bottom of the bathtub. As you know, when the plug is withdrawn from a bath that is brimful of water, the suction down the plughole is immensely powerful. And when a man is sitting astride that plughole as I was at that moment, then it is inevitable that the two most tender and valuable objects in his possession are going to be sucked very suddenly into that dreadful hole. There was a dull *plop* as my scrotum took the full force of the suction and flew into the neck of the hole. I let out a scream that must have been heard clear across Kensington Square.

'Goodbye, darling,' said the duchess, sweeping out of the bathroom.

In the excruciating moments that followed I learned exactly what it must feel like to fall into the hands of those Bedouin women who delight in depriving a traveller of his masculinity with blunt knives. 'Help!' I screamed. 'Save me!' I was impaled. I was glued to the tub. I was clutched in the claws of a mighty crab.

It seemed like hours but I don't suppose I was actually stuck in that position for more than ten or fifteen minutes. It was quite long enough though. I don't even know how I eventually managed to prise myself free all in one piece. But the damage was done. Powerful suction is a terrible thing and those two precious jewels of mine which were normally no bigger than a couple of greengages had suddenly assumed the size of cantaloupe melons. I think it was old Geoffrey Chaucer way back in the fourteenth century who wrote:

> *Ladies with titles*
> *Will go for your vitals*

and those immortal words, believe me, are now engraved upon my heart. For three days I was on crutches and for God knows how long after that I walked about like a man who was harbouring a porcupine between his thighs.

It was in this crippled condition that I made my way up to Cambridge on May 15th to keep my appointment with Yasmin at 'Dunroamin'. As I got out of the car and hobbled towards the front-door, my marbles were still on fire and throbbing like the devil's drum. Yasmin, of course, would be wanting to know what had happened to me. So would Woresley. Should I tell them the truth? If I did, Yasmin would fall all over the room laughing, and I could already hear Woresley in his silly pompous way saying, 'You are altogether too carnal, my dear Cornelius. No man can debauch himself the way you do without paying a heavy price.'

I didn't think I could stand that sort of thing right then so I decided to tell them I had strained a ligament in my thigh. I had done it while helping an old lady after she had stumbled and taken a heavy fall on the pavement outside my house. I had carried her indoors and looked after her until the ambulance came, but it had all been a bit too much for me, etc., etc. That would do it.

I stood under the little porch outside the front door of 'Dunroamin' and fished for my key. As I was doing this, I noticed there was an envelope pinned to the door. Someone had fixed it on firmly with a drawing-pin. Damn silly thing to do. I couldn't get the pin out so I ripped the envelope away. There was no name on it so I opened it. Foolish not to put a name on the envelope. Was it for me? Yes, it was.

Dear Oswald,
Arthur and I got married last week ...

Arthur? Who the hell was Arthur?

We have gone far away and I hope you won't mind too much but we've taken the Semen's Home with us, at least all of it except Proust ...

Jesus Christ! Arthur must be Woresley! Arthur Woresley!

Yes, we have left you Proust. I never did like the little bugger anyway. All fifty of his straws are safely stored in the travelling container in the basement and the Proust letter is in the desk. We have all the other letters with us safe and sound ...

I was reeling. I couldn't read on. I unlocked the door and staggered inside and found a bottle of whiskey. I sloshed some into a glass and gulped it down.

If you stop and think about it, Oswald, I'm sure you'll agree we're not really doing the dirty on you and I'll tell you why. Arthur says ...

I didn't give a damn what Arthur said. They'd stolen the precious sperm. It was worth millions. I was willing to bet it was that little sod Woresley who'd put Yasmin up to it.

Arthur says that after all it was him who invented the process, wasn't it? And it was me who did all the hard work of collecting it. Arthur sends you his best wishes.

Toodle-oo
Yasmin Woresley

A real snorter, that. Right below the belt. It had me gasping.

I roared round the house in a wild fury. My stomach was boiling and I'm sure steam was spurting out of my nostrils. Had there been a dog in the place I'd have kicked it to death. I kicked the furniture instead. I smashed a lot of nice big things and then I set about picking up all the smaller objects, including a Baccarat paperweight and an Etruscan bowl, and flinging them through the windows, yelling bloody murder and watching the window-panes shatter.

But after an hour or so, I began to simmer down, and finally I collapsed into an armchair with a large glass of malt whiskey in my hand.

I am, as you may have gathered, a fairly resilient fellow. I explode when provoked, but I never brood about it afterwards. I scrub it out. There's always another day. What's more, nothing stimulates my mind so much as a whopping disaster. In the aftermath, in that period of deadly calm and absolute silence that follows the tempest, my brain becomes exceedingly active. As I sat drinking my whiskey during that terrible evening amidst the ruins of 'Dunroamin', I was already beginning to ponder and plan my future all over again.

So that's that, I told myself. I've been diddled. It's all over. Need a new start. I still have Proust and in years to come I shall do well with those fifty straws (and don't think I didn't), but that isn't going to make me a millionaire. So what next?

It was at this point that the great and wonderful answer began trickling into my head. I sat quite still, allowing the idea to take root and grow. It was inspired. It was beautiful in its simplicity. It couldn't fail. It would make me millions. Why hadn't I thought of it before?

I promised at the beginning of this diary to tell you how I became a wealthy man. I have taken a long time so far in telling you how I did not succeed. Let me therefore make up for lost time and describe to you in no more than a few paragraphs how I did in the end become a real multi-millionaire. The great idea that came to me so suddenly in 'Dunroamin' was as follows:

I would go back at once to the Sudan. I would negotiate with a corrupt government official for a lease of that precious tract of land where the hashab tree grows and the Blister Beetle flourishes. I would obtain sole rights to all beetle-hunting. I would gather the native beetle-hunters together and form them into an organized unit. I would pay them generously, far more than they were getting at present by flogging their Beetles in the open market. They would work exclusively for me. Poachers would be ruthlessly eliminated. I would, in fact, corner the market in Sudanese Blister Beetles. When all this was arranged and I was assured of a large and regular supply of Beetles, I would build a little factory in Khartoum and there I would process my Beetles and manufacture in quantity Professor Yousoupoff's famous Potency Pills. I would package the pills in the factory. I would then set up a small secret underground sales unit with offices in Paris, London, New York, Amsterdam and other cities throughout the world. I told myself that if a callow seventeen-year-old youth had been able to earn himself a hundred thousand pounds in one year in Paris all by himself, just think what I could do now on a world-wide basis.

And that, my friends, is almost exactly what happened. I went back to the Sudan. I stayed there for a little over two years, and I don't mind telling you that although I learned a great deal about the Blister

Beetle, I also learned a thing or two about the ladies who inhabit those regions. The tribes were sharply divided and they seldom mixed. But I mixed with them all right, with the Nubians, the Hassarians, the Beggaras, the Shilluks, the Shukrias and the curiously light-coloured Niam-Niams who live west of the Blue Nile. I found the Nubians especially to my taste and I wouldn't be surprised if that was where the word *nubile* originated.

By the end of 1923, my little factory was going full blast and turning out a thousand pills a day.

By 1925, I had agents in eight cities. I had chosen them carefully. All, without exception, were retired army generals. Unemployed generals are common in every country, and these men, I discovered, were cut out for this particular type of job. They were efficient. They were unscrupulous. They were brave. They had little regard for human life. And they lacked sufficient intelligence to cheat me without being caught.

It was an immensely lucrative operation. The profits were astronomical. But after a few years I grew bored with running such a big operation and I turned the whole thing over to a Greek syndicate in exchange for one-half of the profits. The Greeks were happy, I was happy and hundreds of thousands of customers have been happy ever since.

I am unashamedly proud of my contribution to the happiness of the human race. Not many men of business and certainly very few millionaires can tell themselves with a clear conscience that the accumulation of their wealth has spread such a high degree of ecstasy and joy among their clients. And it pleases me very much to have discovered that the dangers to human health of *cantharis vesicatoria sudanii* have been grossly exaggerated. My records show that not more than four or five dozen a year at the most suffer any serious or crippling effects from the magic substance. Very few die.

Just one more thing. In 1935, some fifteen years later, I was having breakfast in my Paris house and reading the morning paper when my eye was caught and held by the following item in one of the gossip columns (translated from the French):

'*La Maison d'Or*' at Cap Ferrat, the largest and most luxurious private property on the entire Côte d'Azur, has recently changed hands. It has been bought by an English couple, Professor Arthur Woresley and his beautiful wife Yasmin. The Woresleys have come to France from Buenos Aires where they have been living for many years, and very welcome they are. They will add great lustre to the glittering Riviera scene. As well as buying the magnificent '*La Maison d'Or*', they have just taken delivery of a superb ocean-going yacht which is the envy of every millionaire on the Mediterranean. It has a crew of eighteen and cabin accommodation for ten people. The

Woresleys have named the yacht SPERM. When I asked Mrs Woresley why they had chosen that rather curious name, she laughed and said, 'Oh, I don't know. I suppose because it's such a whale of a ship.'

Quite a girl, that Yasmin. I have to admit it. Though what she ever saw in old Woresley with his donnish airs and his nicotine-stained moustache I cannot imagine. They say a good man is hard to find. Maybe Woresley was one of those. But who on earth wants a good man? Who for that matter wants a good woman?

Not me.